W9-BYJ-682

The Collected Stories of
Robert Silverberg

VOLUME NINE

The Millennium Express
1995-2009

The Collected Stories of
Robert Silverberg

VOLUME NINE

The Millennium Express
1995-2009

ROBERT SILVERBERG

SUBTERRANEAN PRESS 2014

The Millennium Express Copyright © 2014 by Agberg, Ltd. All rights reserved.

Interior design Copyright © 2014 by Desert Isle Design, LLC. All rights reserved.

First Edition

ISBN
978-1-59606-668-7

Subterranean Press
PO Box 190106
Burton, MI 48519

subterraneanpress.com

COPYRIGHT ACKNOWLEDGMENTS:

"Diana of the Hundred Breasts" and "The Church at Monte Saturno" first appeared in *Realms of Fantasy*.

"Beauty in the Night" and "The Tree that Grew from the Sky" first appeared in *Science Fiction Age*.

"Call Me Titan" first appeared in *Asimov's Science Fiction*.

"Hanosz Prime Goes to Old Earth" first appeared in *Asimov's Science Fiction*.

"The Millennium Express" first appeared in *Playboy*.

"Travelers" first appeared in *Amazing Stories*.

"The Colonel Returns to the Stars" first appeared in *Between Worlds*, edited by Robert Silverberg.

"The Eater of Dreams" first appeared in *Asimov's Science Fiction*.

"A Piece of the Great World" first appeared in *One Million A.D.*, edited by Gardner Dozois.

"Against the Current" first appeared in *Fantasy & Science Fiction*.

"The True Vintage of Erzuine Thale" first appeared in *Songs of the Dying Earth*, edited by George R.R. Martin and Gardner Dozois.

"Defenders of the Frontier" first appeared in *Warriors*, edited by George R.R. Martin and Gardner Dozois.

"The Prisoner" first appeared in *The Book of Dreams*, edited by Nick Gevers.

"Smithers and the Ghosts of the Thar" first appeared in *Ghosts by Gaslight*, edited by Nick Gevers and Jack Dann.

Copyright © 1996, 1997, 1999, 2004, 2005, 2006, 2007, 2009, 2010, 2011 by Agberg, Ltd.

Introductory matter copyright © 2014 by Agberg, Ltd.

For
Scott Edelman
Shawna McCarthy
Martin H. Greenberg
Luis Ortiz
John R. Fultz
Alice K. Turner
Gardner Dozois
George R.R. Martin
Kim Mohan
Dave Gross
Sheila Williams
Gordon van Gelder
Nick Gevers
Jack Dann

TABLE OF CONTENTS

INTRODUCTION

S o we come now to the ninth and, I suspect, the last of these volumes, covering the sixth decade of my writing career. I'm still here,
and I'm still reasonably healthy, but my eightieth birthday is not very
far in the future as I write this, and I've become less and less active as a
writer. I've done only a couple of stories since I wrote the ones collected
here, and they were Majipoor stories that I have included in my book
Tales of Majipoor. I've learned over the course of my long career that it's
a good idea never to say never, but I suspect that in the time remaining
to me I'm not going to write enough new material to fill another volume
of the size of these nine, so this is—probably—the final book of this
nine-volume Subterranean Press series.

The stories in this book represent the short-story work I did
between July of 1995 and December of 2009. Not a great quantity of fiction to show for the work of a decade and a half, I suppose, not by the
Silverberg standards of an earlier day, but, as I note in the introduction
to one of the stories here, every writer tends to slow down a bit with
age, even one as prolific as I have been. A certain drying-up of inspiration sets in, I suppose, or, perhaps, a certain unwillingness to seize on a
bit of inspiration and see where it will take one. There have been plenty
of occasions in recent years when the edge of a story idea seemed to
present itself to me, and I simply shrugged and let it go fading back into
invisibility, because I didn't feel much like writing anything just then.
That wouldn't have happened fifty or forty or even thirty years ago.

The inroads of age can't be given all the blame, though. There's also—and perhaps this is a side effect of aging, too—the dwindling of the drive to excel that propels one through the early years of one's career. When I was twenty or so, I felt the need to sell as many stories as possible—to write as fast as I could, to fill every science-fiction magazine with my work. It was a gloriously sweaty time for me, when I banged away at the typewriter keys all day long, shipped two or three stories a week to my editors, and sold them all. A decade later, when I had proven whatever point I had set out to make with that lunatic prolificity, I wanted now to show that I was not only a greatly productive writer but that I was one who had something of his own to add to the body of literature that is science fiction; and then there came flying from me a host of novels—*Thorns, The Masks of Time, The Man in the Maze, Downward to the Earth,* and on and on to *The Book of Skulls* and *Dying Inside,* along with the dozens of short stories that fill the middle volumes of this series—that won me my reputation in the field and brought me the awards that sit on a shelf before me as I write this. But, having won that reputation and those awards, I began to feel, as the years went along, that I had no need of defending it by continuing to publish three or four novels and ten short stories a year, and so I slowed down, even stopped writing entirely for one four-year period in the 1970s. By the time the Science Fiction Writers of America, to my great delight, bestowed its Grand Master award on me in 2004, putting me in an exclusive club almost entirely made up of the writers (Robert A. Heinlein, Isaac Asimov, Jack Williamson, Alfred Bester, A.E. van Vogt, Ray Bradbury, Poul Anderson, Fritz Leiber, Jack Vance, Clifford Simak, L. Sprague de Camp, etc.) whose work I had read and admired when I was a youngster just starting out, I felt I had no worlds left to conquer.

Then, too, as a writer moving through his seventies, and getting rapidly toward the end of them, I feel a certain sense that I am no longer really a part of the contemporary world, from which all extrapolation must flow. My own success has isolated me from everyday mundane reality. I don't have a day job and write after hours; writing has always been my day job, a full-time one, and I've spent my whole life as a self-employed man working at home. I'm not out there in the fast-moving flow of daily toil. Thus I have only a superficial acquaintance with the sort of life that most people accept as routine. Like everyone else, I use a computer, and I know enough about it to make it do the things I need it to do, but I have made no attempt to keep up with changes in computer technology, nor am I a master of computer jargon. You will not see me walking through the streets peering at the screen of my smartphone, either, because I don't have one, and I have had no interest in entering what I have come to think of as the iPod/iPhone/YouTube/Facebook culture. I don't scorn those things—far from it. They have reshaped our world into the fantastic glittering high-tech future that I used to write about. But, having lived on into that future myself, I find that at my age such things don't fill any need for me, and so I can't claim to be familiar with them, and thus I have put myself at some distance from the people who read science fiction today. I don't know enough about their world to be able to write convincingly about the transformations of it that lie ahead. If you don't participate in today's world to any significant extent, you can't write convincingly about the world of tomorrow. And if I can't do that convincingly, I'd rather not do it at all.

Wider cultural changes than the coming of new gadgetry have affected me as a writer, too. I had a classical education, nearly sixty years ago. It seems almost Victorian now. Hardly anyone studies the things I studied. Who would understand the buried references in my stories to Jacobean playwrights, Virgil, Dante, Monteverdi, Bach, even Mann and Kafka and Joyce? Nor are the cultural issues that seem to concern the modern-day academic world anything like the ones that concerned us in my college days; and the whole world of popular culture is a mystery to me. What do I know of the current pop-music stars and graphic-novel artists and television shows? My world is as alien to modern readers as theirs is to me. Even the language has changed radically in my lifetime. Most science-fiction readers are relatively young. My grammar is not their grammar. My vocabulary is not their vocabulary. If I'm not able to speak to them in an understandable way, how can I tell them stories?

There have been changes in the publishing of science fiction in the United States, also, that put a premium on repetitious sequels, formulaic themes, and lengthy, overstuffed plots full of ferocious melodramatic conflict. I thought we had outgrown all that fifty years ago. I was wrong. It has all come back, and come back with a vengeance, in shiny modern guise. Not that all science fiction published today is like that, of course; but I have the ineradicable conviction that the bang-bang multi-volume stuff is what the publishers really want, and that the quieter sort of fiction that I preferred to read and write is merely tolerated at best. At my age it's easier not to go to the effort of writing than to try to fight against that kind of gentle toleration.

But, for all that, I went on writing short fiction all through the seventh and eighth decades of my life, and though I'm not very active these days, I would still pay attention if someone were to approach me with an interesting and challenging short-story project, or if some absolutely irresistible story idea were to come into my mind. I will not, at this point, try to claim that the stories that are collected here are the last short stories I will ever write. Surely some editor, in the years ahead, will tickle my imagination with a proposal I can't resist. But I doubt that thaat will be happening very often; and, meanwhile, here's the harvest of the fourteen years that began in 1995—not an enormous number of stories, no, but stories nevertheless that I think are worth reading and reprinting.

—Robert Silverberg

DIANA OF THE HUNDRED BREASTS

We visited Turkey in April, 1994—Turkey is a country that has exerted continued fascination on me since my first trip there in 1967, which produced my Byzantine time-travel novel Up the Line—and this time we went down the Aegean coast, which is rich in the ruins of the ancient Greek culture that formerly flourished there. Among our stops was Ephesus, once the site of the Temple of Artemis, one of the Seven Wonders of the Ancient World. There's nothing left of that glorious temple today—it was burned down by a disgruntled parishioner in 356 B.C., rebuilt by Alexander the Great, sacked by the Goths, and later stripped of its masonry to build the Byzantine cathedral of Hagia Sophia in Constantinople, so all that remains is an open field with a single column rising above a scattering of stonework. But in the small museum in the adjacent Turkish town of Seljuk are the two mysterious statues of Artemis that once were worshipped there: huge stone figures of a woman whose midsection is festooned with what seem to be dozens of breasts, though perhaps they are eggs. Breasts or eggs, no one is sure, but either way they are symbols of fertility, and it is apparent that the Artemis of Ephesus was a fertility goddess rather than the virginal huntress of classical Greek myth.

Artemis passed into Roman mythology as the goddess Diana, and continued to be worshipped there into the Christian era. We read in the Book of Acts, 19, that the Apostle Paul turned up there in the first century A.D. and denounced the cult of Diana and the famed statues thereof, saying, "They

15

be no gods, which are made by hands." He called for the destruction of her shrine. The citizens of Ephesus, full of wrath at this, gathered and cried out with one voice, the Bible tells us, "Great is Diana of the Ephesians!" Eventually things quieted down, though, and Paul got out of town with his skin intact, and ultimately neither Diana nor Jesus emerged victorious from the fray, because today Ephesus is a very picturesque ruin and Allah is the god of the region where it was located.

Avram Davidson wrote a clever, charming, complex little story (did he ever write any other kind?) in 1958 called "Great is Diana," which makes oblique reference to the famed many-breasted statues of Ephesus. The Davidson story is mostly about breasts, rather than the cult of Diana/ Artemis, but in any case I had long forgotten it in July of 1995, when, brimming with images from the previous year's Turkish trip, I set about to write a fantasy story that would explain what those strange statues were doing in Ephesus.

The immediate precipitating factor was a plaintive phone-call from Alice K. Turner, the fiction editor of Playboy, for whom I had written a great many stories over many years and with whom I had a remarkable editor-writer relationship that was for two decades a fascinating creative challenge for me. Alice called up to complain that her inventory of science-fiction stories had dwindled to zero, and wondered if I would mind writing one for her. I have attempted, since 1970 or so, to do no writing at all in the summer months, and here we were in the splendid California June of unending sunshine, and yet, and yet, how could I ignore such a request from Alice Turner? So I wrote her, on June 30, 1995, that I was halfway through the six-month holiday from writing that I had bestowed upon myself after a particularly grueling winter of work, but I was getting a bit restless with a daily life of swimming, gardening, and sitting on the porch reading, so perhaps I might just interrupt my dolce far niente and do a story for her.

And so I did, although things didn't work out quite as planned. Within ten days I had written "Diana of the Hundred Breasts," which I sent to her with a note saying, "Herewith is a report for you on What I Did On My Summer Vacation In Turkey Last Year. The scenery is rendered reliably; I did make up a few of the details of the events, I have to confess."

But Alice didn't like the story. It was what she called an "IRS Story", she said—stories that I would set in exotic places merely to prove, so she said, that my travel expenses were legitimately tax-deductible. Alice had rejected two or three of my foreign-based stories over the years, always with that same reason and always to my bewilderment, because I couldn't understand her objection to foreign-based stories, whether they were IRS-connected or not. Also she didn't care much for the plot and she didn't think one of the characters was realistically rendered. And I think she was bothered by the fact that I had given her a fantasy story rather than the pure science-fiction tale that she had asked me for. (Though something in my excessively rational mind seems to recoil at the irrationality that lies at the heart of most fantasy themes, so that when I set out to write fantasy it usually turns out to have a science-fictional explanation, as can be seen here.)

Well, rejections happen. Playboy under Alice Turner was not only the highest-paying fiction market around, but also one of the toughest, and though I sold her plenty of stories over the years, I had to expect that once in a while she would turn one down. I replied to her rejection note on July 31: "Well, of course I disagree, but what the hell. I'll sell it somewhere else and sell you something else next year."

Which I did. I shipped the story off to the new fantasy magazine Realms of Fantasy, edited by Shawna McCarthy, for whom I had written one of my favorite stories, "Sailing to Byzantium," when she had been editor of Isaac Asimov's Science Fiction Magazine ten years before. Shawna bought it instantly and published it in her February, 1996 issue. I don't like having stories rejected any more than any other writer would, but in a long career it's bound to happen now and then to anybody, and I am quick on the rebound when it does.

The two famous marble statues stand facing each other in a front room of the little museum in the scruffy Turkish town of Seljuk, which lies just north of the ruins of the once-great Greek and Roman city of Ephesus. There was a photograph of the bigger one in my guidebook, of course. But it hadn't prepared me—photos never really do—for the full bizarre impact of the actuality.

The larger of the statues is about nine feet tall, the other one about six. Archaeologists found both of them in the courtyard of a building of this ancient city where the goddess Diana was revered. They show—you must have seen a picture of one, some time or other—a serene, slender woman wearing an ornamental headdress that is all that remains of an huge, intricate crown. Her arms are outstretched and the lower half of her body is swathed in a tight cylindrical gown. From waist to ankles, that gown is decorated with rows of vividly carved images of bees and of cattle. But that's not where your eyes travel first, because the entire midsection of Diana of Ephesus is festooned with a grotesque triple ring of bulging pendulous breasts. Dozens of them, or several dozens. A great many.

"Perhaps they're actually eggs," said my brother Charlie the professor, standing just behind me. For the past eighteen months Charlie had been one of the leaders of the team of University of Pennsylvania archaeologists that has been digging lately at Ephesus. "Or fruits of some kind, apples, pears. Nobody's really sure. Globular fertility symbols, that's all we can say. But I think they're tits, myself. The tits of the Great Mother, with an abundance of milk for all. Enough tits to satisfy anybody's oral cravings, and then some."

"An abomination before the Lord," murmured our new companion Mr. Gladstone, the diligent Christian tourist, just about when I was expecting him to say something like that.

"Tits?" Charlie asked.

"These statues. They should be smashed in a thousand pieces and buried in the earth whence they came." He said it mildly, but he meant it.

"What a great loss to art that would be," said Charlie in his most pious way. "Anyway, the original statue from which these were copied fell from heaven. That's what the Bible says, right? Book of Acts. The image that Jupiter tossed down from the sky. It could be argued that Jupiter is simply one manifestation of Jehovah. Therefore this is a holy image. Wouldn't you say so, Mr. Gladstone?"

There was a cruel edge on Charlie's voice; but, then, Charlie is cruel. Charming, of course, and ferociously bright, but above all else a smart-ass. He's three years older than I am, and three times as intelligent. You can imagine what my childhood was like. If I had ever taken his cruelties seriously, I suspect I would hate him; but the best defense against Charlie is never to take him seriously. I never have, nor anything much else, either. In that way Charlie and I are similar, I suppose. But only in that way.

Mr. Gladstone refused to be drawn into Charlie's bantering defense of idolatry. Maybe he too had figured out how to handle Charlie, a lot quicker than I ever did.

"You are a cynic and a sophist, Dr. Walker," is all that he said. "There is no profit in disputing these matters with cynics. Or with sophists. Especially with sophists." And to me, five minutes later, as we rambled through a room full of mosaics and frescoes and little bronze statuettes: "Your brother is a sly and very clever man. But there's a hollowness about him that saddens me. I wish I could help him. I feel a great deal of pity for him, you know."

❈

That anyone would want to feel pity for Charlie was a new concept to me. Envy, yes. Resentment, disapproval, animosity, even fear, perhaps. But *pity*? For the six-foot-three genius with the blond hair and blue eyes, the movie-star face, the seven-figure trust fund, the four-digit I.Q.? I am tall too, and when I reached 21 I came into money also, and I am neither stupid nor ugly; but it was always Charlie who got the archery trophy, the prom queen, the honor-roll scroll, the Phi Beta Kappa key. It was Charlie who always got anything and everything he wanted, effortlessly, sometimes bestowing his leftovers on me, but always in a patronizing way that thoroughly tainted them. I have sensed people pitying me, sometimes, because they look upon me as Charlie-minus, an inadequate simulacrum of the genuine article, a pallid secondary version of the extraordinary Charlie. In truth I think their compassion for me, if that's what it is, is misplaced: I don't see myself as all that goddamned pitiful. But Charlie? Pitying *Charlie*?

I was touring Greece and Turkey that spring, mostly the usual Aegean resorts, Mykonos and Corfu and Crete, Rhodes and Bodrum and Marmaris. I wander up and down the Mediterranean about half the year, generally, and, though I'm scarcely a scholar, I do of course look in on the various famous classical sites along my way. By now, I suppose, I've seen every ruined Roman and Greek temple and triumphal arch and ancient theater there is, from Volubilis and Thuburbo Majus in North Africa up through Sicily and Pompeii, and out to Spain and France on one side and Syria and Lebanon on the other. They all blur and run together in my mind, becoming a single generic site—fallen marble columns, weatherbeaten foundations, sand, little skittering lizards, blazing sun, swarthy men selling picture-postcards—but I keep on prowling them anyway. I don't quite know why.

There are no hotels remotely worthy of the name in or around the Ephesus ruins. But Charlie had tipped me off that I would find, about six miles down the road, a lavish new deluxe place high up on a lonely point overlooking the serene Aegean that catered mostly to groups of sun-worshipping Germans. It had an immense lobby with marble floors and panoramic windows, an enormous swimming pool, and an assortment of dining rooms that resounded day and night with the whoops and hollers of the beefy Deutschers, who never seemed to leave the hotel. Charlie drove out there to have dinner with me the night I arrived, and that was when we met Mr. Gladstone.

"Excuse me," he said, hovering beside our table, "but I couldn't help hearing you speaking in English. I don't speak German at all and, well, frankly, among all these foreigners I've been getting a little lonely for the mother tongue. Do you mind if I join you?"

"Well—" I said, not really eager for his company, because tonight was the first time I had seen my brother in a couple of years. But Charlie grandly waved him to a seat.

He was a grayish, cheerful man of about sixty, a small-town pastor from Ohio or Indiana or maybe Iowa, and he had been saving for something like twenty years to take an extensive tour of the Christian holy places of the Middle East. For the past three months he had been traveling with a little group of—pilgrims, I guess one could call them, six weeks bussing through Israel from Jerusalem to Beersheba, down to Mount Sinai, back up through the Galilee to Lebanon to see Sidon and Tyre, then out to Damascus, and so on and and so on, the full Two-Testament Special. His traveling companions all had flown home by now, but Mr. Gladstone had bravely arranged a special side trip just for himself to Turkey—to poky little Seljuk in particular—because his late wife had had a special interest in an important Christian site here. He had never traveled anywhere by himself before, not even in the States, and going it alone in Turkey was a bit of a stretch for him. But he felt he owed it to his wife's memory to make the trip, and so he was resolutely plugging along on his own here, having flown from Beirut to Izmir and then hired a car and driver to bring him down to Seljuk. He had arrived earlier this day.

"I didn't realize there was anything of special Christian interest around here," I said.

"The Cave of the Seven Sleepers of Ephesus," Mr. Gladstone explained. "My wife once wrote a little book for children about the Seven Sleepers. It was always her great hope to see their actual cave."

"The Seven Sleepers?"

He sketched the story for me quickly: the seven devout Christian boys who took refuge in a cave rather than offer sacrifices in the temple of the Roman gods, and who fell into a deep sleep and came forth two hundred years later to discover that Christianity had miraculously become the official religion of Rome while they were doing their Rip van Winkle act. What was supposedly their cave may still be seen just beyond the Roman stadium of Ephesus.

"There's also the Meryemana," Charlie said.

Mr. Gladstone gave him a polite blank smile. "Beg your pardon?"

"The house where the Virgin Mary lived in the last years of her life. Jesus told St. John the Apostle to look after her, and he brought her to Ephesus, so it's said. About a hundred years ago some Eastern Orthodox priests went looking for her house and found it, sure enough, about three miles outside town."

"Indeed."

"More likely it's sixth century Byzantine," said Charlie. "But the foundations are much older. The Orthodox Christians go there on pilgrimage there every summer. You really ought to see it." He smiled his warmest, most savage smile. "Ephesus has always been a center of mother-goddess worship, you know, and apparently it has continued to be one even in post-pagan times."

Mr. Gladstone's lips quirked ever so slightly. Though I assumed—correctly—that he was Protestant, even a Presbyterian was bound to be annoyed at hearing someone call the Virgin Mary a mother-goddess. But all he said was, "It would be interesting to see, yes."

Charlie wouldn't let up. "You will, of course, look in at the Seljuk Museum to see the predecessor goddess's statue, won't you? Diana, I mean. Diana of the Hundred Breasts. It's best to visit the museum before you begin your tour of the ruins, anyway. And the statues—there are two, actually—sum up the whole concept of the sacred female principle in a really spectacular way. The primordial mother, the great archetype. The celestial cow that nourishes the world. You need to see it, if you want truly to understand the bipolar sexual nature of the divine, eh, Mr. G?" He glanced toward me. "You too, Tim. The two of you, meet me in front of the museum at nine tomorrow, okay? Basic orientation lecture by Dr. Walker. Followed by a visit to ancient Ephesus, including the Cave of the Seven Sleepers. Perhaps the Meryemana afterward." Charlie flashed a dazzling grin. "Will you have some wine, Mr. Gladstone?"

"No, thank you," Mr. Gladstone said, quickly putting his hand over the empty glass in front of him.

✸

After the museum, the next morning, we doubled back to the ruins of Ephesus proper. Mobs of tour groups were already there, milling around befuddledly as tour groups will do, but Charlie zipped right around them to the best stuff. The ruins are in a marvelous state of preservation—a nearly intact Roman city of the first century A.D., the usual forum and temples and stadium and gymnasium and such, and of course the famous two-story library that the Turks feature on all those tourist posters.

We had the best of all possible guides. Charlie has a genuine passion for archaeology—it's the only thing, I suspect, that he really cares for, other than himself—and he pointed out a million details that we would otherwise have missed. With special relish he dwelled on the grotesqueries of the cult of Diana, telling us not only about the metaphorical significance of the goddess's multiplicity of breasts, but about the high priest who was always a eunuch—"His title," said Charlie, "meant 'He who has been set free by God'"—and the staff of virgins who assisted him, and the special priests known as the Acrobatae, or "walkers on tip-toe," et cetera, et cetera. Mr. Gladstone showed signs of definite distaste as Charlie went on to speculate on some of the more flamboyant erotic aspects of pagan worship hereabouts, but he wouldn't stop. He never does, when he has a chance to display his erudition and simultaneously offend and unsettle someone.

Eventually it was mid-afternoon and the day had become really hot and we were only halfway through our tour of the ancient city, with the Cave of the Seven Sleepers still a mile or two in the distance. And clearly Mr. Gladstone was wilting. We decided to call it a day, and had a late lunch of kebabs and stewed eggplant at one of the innumerable and interchangeable little bistros in town. "We can go to the cave first thing tomorrow morning, when it's still cool," Charlie offered.

"Thank you. But I think I would prefer to visit it alone, if you don't mind. A private pilgrimage—for my late wife's sake, do you see? Something of a ceremonial observance."

"Certainly," Charlie intoned reverently. "I quite understand."

I asked him if he would be coming out to the hotel again that evening for dinner with me. No, he said, he would be busy at the dig—the cool of the evening was a good time to work, without the distraction of gawking tourists—but we arranged to meet in the morning for breakfast and a little brotherly catching up on family news. I left him in town and drove back to the hotel with Mr. Gladstone.

"Your brother isn't a religious man, is he?" he said.

"I'm afraid that neither of us is, especially. It's the way we were raised."

"But he *really* isn't. You're merely indifferent; he is hostile."

"How can you tell?"

"Because," he said, "he was trying so hard to provoke me with those things he was saying about Diana of Ephesus. He makes no distinction between Christianity and paganism. All religions must be the same to him, mere silly cults. And so he thinks he can get at my beliefs somehow by portraying pagan worship as absurd and bizarre."

"He looks upon them all as cults, yes. But silly, no. In fact Charlie takes religion very seriously, though not exactly in the same way you do. He regards it as a conspiracy by the power elite to remain on top at the expense of the masses. And holy scriptures are just works of fiction dreamed up to perpetuate the authority of the priests and their bosses."

"He sees all religions that way, does he, without making distinctions?"

"Every one of them, yes. Always the same thing, throughout the whole of human history."

"The poor man," said Mr. Gladstone. "The poor empty-souled man. If only I could set him straight, somehow!"

There it was again: the compassion, the pity. For Charlie, of all people! Fascinating. Fascinating.

"I doubt that you'd succeed," I told him. "He's inherently a skeptical person. He's never been anything else. And he's a scientist, remember, a man who lives or dies by rational explanations. If it can't be explained, then it probably isn't real. He doesn't have a smidgeon of belief in anything he can't see and touch and measure."

"He is incapable of giving credence to the evidence of things not seen?"

"Excuse me?"

"'The substance of things hoped for, the evidence of things not seen.' Book of Hebrews, 11:1. It's St. Paul's definition of faith."

"Ah."

"St. Paul was here, you know. In this town, in Ephesus, on a missionary journey. Gods that are fashioned by human hands are no gods at all, he told the populace. Whereupon a certain Demetrius, a silversmith who earned his living making statuettes of the many-breasted goddess whose images we saw today in the museum, called his colleagues

together and said, If this man has his way, the temple of the great goddess Diana will be destroyed and we will lose our livelihoods. 'And
when they heard these sayings, they were full of wrath, and cried out,
saying, "Great is Diana of the Ephesians." And the whole city was filled
with confusion.' That's the Book of Acts, 19:28. And there was such a
huge uproar in town over the things that Paul was preaching that he
found it prudent to depart very quickly for Macedonia."

"I see."

"But the temple of the goddess was destroyed anyway, eventually.
And her statues were cast down and buried in the earth, and now are
seen only in museums."

"And the people of Ephesus became Christians," I said. "And
Moslems after that, it would seem."

He looked startled. My gratuitous little dig had clearly stung him.
But then he smiled.

"I see that you are your brother's brother," he said.

I was up late reading, and thinking about Charlie, and staring at
the moonlight shimmering on the bay. About half past eleven I hit the
sack. Almost immediately my phone rang.

Charlie. "Are you alone, bro?"

"No," I said. "As a matter of fact, Mr. Gladstone and I are hunkering
down getting ready to commit abominations before the Lord."

"I thought maybe one of those horny Kraut ladies—"

"Cut it out. I'm alone, Charlie. And pretty sleepy. What is it?"

"Can you come down to the ruins? There's something I want to
show you."

"Right now?"

"Now is a good time for this."

"I told you I was sleepy."

"It's something big, Tim. I need to show it to somebody, and you're
the only person on this planet I even halfway trust."

"Something you discovered tonight?"

"Get in your car and come on down. I'll meet you by the Magnesian
Gate. That's the back entrance. Go past the museum and turn right at
the crossroads in town."

"Charlie—"

"Move your ass, bro. *Please*."

That "please," from Charlie, was something very unusual. In twenty minutes I was at the gate. He was waiting there, swinging a huge flashlight. A tool-sack was slung over one shoulder. He looked wound up tight, as tense as I had ever seen him.

Selecting a key from a chain that held at least thirty of them, he unlocked the gate and led me down a long straight avenue paved with worn blocks of stone. The moon was practically full and the ancient city was bathed in cool silvery light. He pointed out the buildings as we went by them: "The baths of Varius. The basilica. The necropolis. The temple of Isis." He droned the names in a singsong tone as though this were just one more guided tour. We turned to the right, onto another street that I recognized as the main one, where earlier that day I had seen the gate of Hercules, the temple of Hadrian, the library. "Here we are. Back of the brothel and the latrine."

We scrambled uphill perhaps fifty yards through gnarled scrubby underbrush until we came to a padlocked metal grate set in the ground in an otherwise empty area. Charlie produced the proper key and pulled back the grate. His flashlight beam revealed a rough earthen-walled tunnel, maybe five feet high, leading into the hillside. The air inside was hot and stale, with a sweet heavy odor of dry soil. After about twenty feet the tunnel forked. Crouching, we followed the right-hand fork, pushing our way through some bundles of dried leaves that seemed to have been put there to block its entrance.

"Look there," he said.

He shot the beam off to the left and I found myself staring at a place where the tunnel wall had been very carefully smoothed. An upright circular slab of rough-hewn marble perhaps a yard across was set into it there.

"What is it?" I asked him. "A gravestone? A commemorative plaque?"

"Some sort of door, more likely. Covering a funeral chamber, I would suspect. You see these?" He indicated three smaller circles of what looked like baked clay, mounted in a symmetrical way over the marble slab, arranged to form the angles of an equilateral triangle. They overlapped the edges of the slab as though sealing it into the wall. I went closer and saw inscriptions carved into the clay circles, an array of mysterious symbols and letters.

"What language is this? Not Greek. Hebrew, maybe?"

"No. I don't actually know what it is. Some unknown Anatolian script, or some peculiar form of Aramaic or Phoenician—I just can't say, Timmo. Maybe it's a nonsense script, even. Purely decorative sacred scribbles conveying spells to keep intruders away, maybe. You know, some kind of magical mumbo-jumbo. It might be anything."

"You found this tonight?"

"Three weeks ago. We've known this tunnel was here for a long time, but it was thought to be empty. I happened to be doing some sonar scanning overhead and I got an echo back from a previously uncharted branch, so I came down and took a look around. Nobody knows about it but me. And you."

Gingerly I ran my hand over the face of the marble slab. It was extraordinarily smooth, cool to the touch. I had the peculiar illusion that my fingertips were tingling, as though from a mild electrical charge.

"What are you going to do?" I asked.

"Open it."

"Now?"

"Now, bro. You and me."

"You can't do that!"

"I can't?"

"You're part of an expedition, Charlie. You can't just bust into a tomb, or whatever this is, on your own. It isn't proper procedure, is it? You need to have the other scientists here. And the Turkish antiquities officials— they'll string you up by the balls if they find out you've done a bit of secret free-lance excavating without notifying any local authorities."

"We break the seals. We look inside. If there's anything important in there, we check it out just to gratify our own curiosity and then we go away, and in the morning I discover it all over again and raise a big hullaballoo and we go through all the proper procedure then. Listen, bro, there could be something big in there, don't you see? The grave of a high priest. The grave of some prehistoric king. The lost treasure of the Temple of Diana. The Ark of the Covenant. Anything. Anything. Whatever it is, I want to know. And I want to see it before anybody else does."

He was lit up with a passion so great that I could scarcely recognize him as my cool brother Charlie.

"How are you going to explain the broken seals?"

"Broken by some tomb-robber in antiquity," he said. "Who got frightened away before he could finish the job."

He had always been a law unto himself, my brother Charlie. I argued with him a little more, but I knew it would do no good. He had never been much of a team player. He wasn't going to have five or six wimpy colleagues and a bunch of Turkish antiquities officials staring over his shoulder while that sealed chamber was opened for the first time in two thousand years.

He drew a small battery-powered lamp from his sack and set it on the ground. Then he began to pull the implements of his trade out of the sack, the little chisels, the camel's-hair brushes, the diamond-bladed hacksaw.

"Why did you wait until I got here before you opened it?" I asked.

"Because I thought I might need help pulling that slab out of the wall, and who could I trust except you? Besides, I wanted an audience for the grand event."

"Of course."

"You know me, Timmo."

"So I do, bro. So I do."

He began very carefully to chisel off one of the clay seals. It came away in two chunks. Setting it to one side, he went to work on the second one, and then the third. Then he dug his fingertips into the earthen wall at the edge of the slab and gave it an experimental tug.

"I do need you," he said. "Put your shoulder against the slab and steady it as I pry it with this crowbar. I don't want it just toppling out."

Bit by bit he wiggled it free. As it started to pivot and fall forward I leaned all my weight into it, and Charlie reached across me and caught it too, and together we were able to brace it as it left its aperture and guide it down carefully to the ground.

We stared into the blackest of black holes. Ancient musty air came roaring forth in a long dry whoosh. Charlie leaned forward and started to poke the flashlight into the opening.

But then he pulled back sharply and turned away, gasping as though he had inhaled a wisp of something noxious.

"Charlie?"

"Just a second." He waved his hand near his head a couple of times, the way you might do when brushing away a cobweb. "Just—a—goddamn—second, Tim!" A convulsive shiver ran through him. Automatically I moved toward him to see what the matter was and as I came up beside him in front of that dark opening I felt a sudden weird sensation, a jolt, a jab, and my head began to spin. And for a moment—just a moment—I seemed to hear a strange music, an eerie high-pitched wailing sound like the keening of elevator cables far, far away. In that crazy incomprehensible moment I imagined that I was standing at the rim of a deep ancient well, the oldest well of all, the well from which all creation flows, with strange shadowy things churning and throbbing down below, and from its depths rose a wild rush of perfumed air that dizzied and intoxicated me.

Then the moment passed and I was in my right mind again and I looked at Charlie and he looked at me.

"You felt it too, didn't you?" I said.

"Felt what?" he demanded fiercely. He seemed almost angry.

I searched for the words. But it was all fading, fading fast, and there was only Charlie with his face jammed into mine, angry Charlie, terrifying Charlie, practically daring me to claim that anything peculiar had happened.

"It was very odd, bro," I said finally. "Like a drug thing, almost."

"Oxygen deprivation, is all. A blast of old stale air."

"You think?"

"I know."

But he seemed uncharacteristically hesitant, even a little befuddled. He stood at an angle to the opening, head turned away, shoulders slumping, the flashlight dangling from his hand.

"Aren't you going to look inside?" I asked, after a bit.

"Give me a moment, Timmo."

"Charlie, are you all right?"

"Christ, yes! I breathed in a little dust, that's all." He knelt, rummaged in the tool sack, pulled out a canteen, took a deep drink. "Better," he said hoarsely. "Want some?" I took the canteen from him and he leaned into the opening again, flashing the beam around.

"What do you see?"

"Nothing. Not a fucking thing."

"They put up a marble slab and plaster it with inscribed seals and there's nothing at all behind it?"

"A hole," he said. "Maybe five feet deep, five feet high. A storage chamber of some kind, I would guess. Nothing in it. Absolutely fucking nothing, bro."

"Let me see."

"Don't you trust me?"

In fact I didn't, not very much. But I just shrugged; and he handed me the flashlight, and I peered into the hole. Charlie was right. The interior of the chamber was smooth and regular, but it was empty, not the slightest trace of anything.

"Shit," Charlie said. He shook his head somberly. "My very own Tut-ankh-amen tomb, only nothing's in it. Let's get the hell out of here."

"Are you going to report this?"

"What for? I come in after hours, conduct illicit explorations, and all I have to show for my sins is an empty hole? What's the good of telling anybody that? Just for the sake of making myself look like an unethical son of a bitch? No, bro. None of this ever happened."

"But the seals—the inscriptions in an unknown script—"

"Not important. Let's go, Tim."

He still sounded angry, and not, I think, just because the little chamber behind the marble slab had been empty. Something had gotten to him just now, and gotten to him deeply. Had he heard the weird music too? Had he looked into that fathomless well? He hated all mystery, everything inexplicable. I think that was why he had become an archaeologist. Mysteries had a way of unhinging him. When I was maybe ten and he was thirteen, we had spent a rainy evening telling each other ghost stories, and finally we made one up together, something about spooks from another world who were haunting our attic, and our own story scared me so much that I began to cry. I imagined I heard strange creaks overhead. Charlie mocked me mercilessly, but it seemed to me that for a time he had looked a little nervous too, and when I said so he got very annoyed indeed; and then, bluffing all the way, I invited him to come up to the attic with me right then and there to see that it was safe, and he punched me in the chest and knocked me down. Later he denied the whole episode.

"I'm sorry I wasted your time tonight, keed," he said, as we hiked back up to our cars.

"That's okay. It just might have been something special."

"Just might have been, yeah." He grinned and winked. He was himself again, old devil-may-care Charlie. "Sleep tight, bro. See you in the morning."

But I didn't sleep tight at all. I kept waking and hearing the wailing sound of far-off elevator cables, and my dreams were full of blurry strangenesses.

* * *

The next day I hung out at the hotel all day, breakfasting with Charlie—he didn't refer to the events of the night before at all—and lounging by the pool the rest of the time. I had some vague thought of hooking up with one of the German tourist ladies, I suppose, but no openings presented themselves, and I contented myself with watching the show. Even in puritanical Turkey, where the conservative politicians are trying to put women back into veils and ankle-length skirts, European women of all ages go casually topless at coastal resorts like this, and it was remarkable to see how much savoir-faire the Turkish poolside waiters displayed while taking bar orders from *saftig* bare-breasted grandmothers from Hamburg or Munich and their stunning topless granddaughters.

Mr. Gladstone, who hadn't been around in the morning, turned up in late afternoon. I was in the lobby bar by then, working on my third or fourth post-lunch *raki*. He looked sweaty and tired and sunburned. I ordered a Coke for him.

"Busy day?"

"Very. The Cave of the Seven Sleepers was my first stop. A highly emotional experience, I have to say, not because of the cave itself, you understand, although the ancient ruined church there is quite interesting, but because—the associations—the memories of my dear wife that it summoned—"

"Of course."

"After that my driver took me out to the so-called House of the Virgin. Perhaps it's genuine, perhaps not, but either way it's a moving thing to see. The invisible presence of thousands of pilgrims hovers over it, the aura of centuries of faith." He smiled gently. "Do you know what I mean, Mr. Walker?"

"I think I do, yes."

"And in the afternoon I saw the Basilica of St. John, on Ayasuluk Hill."

I didn't know anything about that. He explained that it was the acropolis of the old Byzantine city—the steep hill just across the main highway from the center of the town of Seljuk. Legend had it that St. John the Apostle had been buried up there, and centuries later the Emperor Justinian built an enormous church on the site, which was, of course, a ruin now, but an impressive one.

"And you?" he said. "You visited with your brother?"

"In the morning, yes."

"A brilliant man, your brother. If only he could be happier, eh?"

"Oh, I think Charlie's happy, all right. He's had his own way every step of his life."

"Is that your definition of happiness? Having your own way?"

"It can be very helpful."

"And you haven't had *your* own way, is that it, Mr. Walker?"

"My life has been reasonably easy by most people's standards, I have to admit. I was smart enough to pick a wealthy great-grandfather. But compared with Charlie—he has an extraordinary mind, he's had a splendid scientific career, he's admired by all the members of his profession. I don't even have a profession, Mr. Gladstone. I just float around."

"You're young, Mr. Walker. You'll find something to do and someone to share your life with, and you'll settle down. But your brother—I wonder, Mr. Walker. Something vital is missing from his life. But he will never find it, because he is not willing to admit that it's missing."

"Religion, do you mean?"

"Not specifically, no. Belief, perhaps. Not religion, but belief. Do you follow me, Mr. Walker? One must believe in *something*, do you see? And your brother will not permit himself to do that." He gave me the gentle smile again. "Would you excuse me, now? I've had a rather strenuous day. I think a little nap, before supper—"

Since we were the only two Americans in the place, I invited him to join me again for dinner that night. He did most of the talking, reminiscing about his wife, telling me about his children—he had three, in their thirties—and describing some of the things he had seen in his tour of the Biblical places. I had never spent much time with anyone of his sort. A kindly man, an earnest man; and, I suspect, not quite as simple a man as a casual observer might think.

He went upstairs about half past eight. I returned to the bar and had a couple of raw Turkish brandies and thought hopeful thoughts about the stunning German granddaughters. Somewhere about ten, as I was considering going to bed, a waiter appeared and said, "You are Mr. Timothy Walker?"

"Yes."

"Your brother Charles is at the security gate and asks that you come out to meet him."

Mystified, I went rushing out into the courtyard. The hotel grounds are locked down every night and nobody is admitted except guests and the guests of guests. I saw the glare of headlights just beyond the gate. Charlie's car.

"What's up, bro?"

His eyes were wild. He gestured at me with furious impatience. "In. In!" Almost before I closed the door he spun the car around and was zooming down the narrow, winding road back to Seljuk. He was hunched over the wheel in the most peculiar rigid way.

"Charlie?"

"Exactly what did you experience," he said tightly, "when we pulled that marble slab out of the wall?"

My reply was carefully vague.

"Tell me," he said. "Be very precise."

"I don't want you to laugh at me, Charlie."

"Just tell me."

I took a deep breath. "Well, then. I imagined that I heard far-off music. I had a kind of vision of—well, someplace weird and mysterious. I thought I smelled perfume. The whole thing lasted maybe half a second and then it was over."

He was silent a moment.

Then he said, in a strange little quiet way, "It was the same for me, bro."

"You denied it. I asked you, and you said no, Charlie."

"Well, I lied. It was the same for me." His voice had become very odd—thin, tight, quavering. Everything about him right now was tight. Something had to pop. The car was traveling at maybe eighty miles an hour on that little road and I feared for my life. After a very long time he said, "Do you think there's any possibility, Tim, that we might have let something out of that hole in the ground when we broke those seals and pulled that slab out?"

I stared at him. "That's crazy, Charlie."

"I know it is. Just answer me: do you think we felt something moving past us as we opened that chamber?"

"Hey, we're too old to be telling each other spook stories, bro."

"I'm being serious."

"Bullshit you are," I said. "I hate it when you play with me like this."

"I'm not playing," Charlie said, and he turned around so that he was practically facing me for a moment. His face was twisted with strain. "Timmo, some goddamned thing that looks awfully much like Diana of Ephesus has been walking around in the ruins since sundown. Three people I know of have seen her. Three very reliable people."

I couldn't believe that he was saying stuff like this. Not Charlie.

"Keep your eyes on the road, will you?" I told him. "You'll get us killed driving like that."

"Do you know how much it costs me to say these things? Do you know how lunatic it sounds to me? But she's real. She's there. She was sealed up in that hole, and we let her out. The foreman of the excavations has seen her, and Judy, the staff artist, and Mike Dornan, the ceramics guy."

"They're fucking with your head, Charlie. Or you're fucking with mine."

"No. No. No. No."

"Where are we going?" I asked.

"To look for her. To find out what the hell it is that those people think they saw. I've got to know, Tim. This time, I've absolutely got to know."

The desperation in Charlie's voice was something new in my experience of him. *I've absolutely got to know.* Why? Why? It was all too crazy. And dragging me out like this: why? To bear witness? To help him prove to himself that he actually was seeing the thing that he was seeing, if indeed he saw it? Or, maybe, to help him convince himself that there was nothing there to see?

But he wasn't going to see anything. I was sure of that.

"Charlie," I said. "Oh, Charlie, Charlie, Charlie, this isn't happening, is it? Not really."

We pulled up outside the main gate of the ruins. A watchman was posted there, a Turk. He stepped quickly aside as Charlie went storming through into the site. I saw flashlights glowing in the distance, and then four or five American-looking people. Charlie's colleagues, the archaeologists.

"Well?" Charlie yelled. He sounded out of control.

A frizzy-haired woman of about forty came up from somewhere to our left. She looked as wild-eyed and agitated as Charlie. For the first time I began to think this might not be just some goofy practical joke.

"Heading east," the woman blurted. "Toward the stadium or maybe all the way out to the goddess sanctuary. Dick saw it too. And Edward thinks he did."

"Anybody get a photo?"

"Not that I know of," the woman said.

"Come on," Charlie said to me, and went running off at an angle to the direction we had just come. Frantically I chased after him. He was chugging uphill, into the thorny scrub covering the unexcavated areas of the city. By moonlight I saw isolated shattered pillars rising from the ground like broken teeth, and tumbledown columns that had been tossed around like so many toothpicks. As I came alongside him he said, "There's a little sanctuary of the Mother Goddess back there. Wouldn't that be the logical place that she'd want to go to?"

"For shit's sake, Charlie! What are you saying?"

He kept on running, giving me no answer. I fought my way up the hill through a tangle of brambles and canes that slashed at me like daggers, all the while wondering what the hell we were going to find on top. We were halfway up when shouts came to us from down the hill, people behind us waving and pointing. Charlie halted and listened, frowning. Then he swung around and started sprinting back down the hill. "She's gone outside the ruins," he called to me over his shoulder. "Through the fence, heading into town! Come on, Tim!"

I went running after him, scrambling downhill, then onward along the main entrance road and onto the main highway. I'm in good running shape, but Charlie was moving with a maniacal zeal that left me hard pressed to keep up with him. Twenty feet apart, we came pounding down the road past the museum and into town. All the dinky restaurants were open, even this late, and little knots of Turks had emerged from them to gather in the crossroads. Some were kneeling in prayer, hammering their heads against the pavement, and others were wildly gesticulating at one other in obvious shock and bewilderment. Charlie, without breaking stride, called out to them in guttural Turkish and got a whole babble of replies.

"Ayasuluk Hill," he said to me. "That's the direction she's going in."

We crossed the broad boulevard that divides the town in half. As we passed the bus station half a dozen men came running out of a side street in front of us, screaming as though they had just been disemboweled. You don't expect to hear adult male Turks screaming. They are a nation of tough people, by and large. These fellows went flying past us without halting, big men with thick black mustachios. Their eyes were wide and gleaming like beacons, their faces rigid and distended with shock and horror, as though twenty devils were coming after them.

"Charlie—"

"Look there," he said, in an utterly flat voice, and pointed into the darkness.

Something—*something*—was moving away from us down that side street, something very tall and very strange. I saw a tapering conical body, a hint of weird appendages, a crackling blue-white aura. It seemed to be floating rather than walking, carried along by a serene but inexorable drifting motion almost as if its feet were several inches off the ground. Maybe they were.

As we watched, the thing halted and peered into the open window of a house. There was a flash of blinding light, intense but short-lived. Then the front door popped open and a bunch of frantic Turks came boiling out like a pack of Keystone Cops, running in sixty directions at once, yelling and flinging their arms about as though trying to surrender.

One of them tripped and went sprawling down right at the creature's feet. He seemed unable to get up; he knelt there all bunched up, moaning and babbling, shielding his face with outspread hands. The thing paused and looked down, and seemed to reach its arms out in fluid gestures, and the blue-white glow spread for a moment like a mantle over the man. Then the light withdrew from him and the creature, gliding smoothly past the trembling fallen man, continued on its serene silent way toward the dark hill that loomed above the town.

"Come," Charlie said to me.

We went forward. The creature had disappeared up ahead, though we caught occasional glimpses of the blue-white light as it passed between the low little buildings of the town. We reached the man who had tripped; he had not arisen, but lay face down, shivering, covering his head with his hands. A low rumbling moan of fear came steadily from him. From in front of us, hoarse cries of terror drifted to us from here and there as this villager or that encountered the thing that was passing through their town, and now and again we could see that cool bright light, rising steadily above us until finally it was shining down from the upper levels of Ayasuluk Hill.

"You really want to go up there?" I asked him.

He didn't offer me an answer, nor did he stop moving forward. I wasn't about to turn back either, I realized. Willy-nilly I followed him to the end of the street, around a half-ruined mosque at the base of the hill, and up to a lofty metal gate tipped with spikes. Stoned on our own adrenaline, we swarmed up that gate like Crusaders attacking a Saracen fortress, went over the top, dropped down in the bushes on the far side. I was able to see, by the brilliant gleam of the full moon, the low walls of the destroyed Basilica of St. John just beyond, and, behind it, the massive Byzantine fortification that crowned the hill. Together we scrambled toward the summit.

"You go this way, Tim. I'll go the other and we'll meet on the far side."

"Right."

I didn't know what I was looking for. I just ran, leftward around the hill. Along the ramparts, into the church, down the empty aisles, out the gaping window-frames.

Suddenly I caught a glimpse of something up ahead. Light, cool white light, an unearthly light very much like moonlight, only concentrated into a fiercely gleaming point hovering a couple of yards above the ground, thirty or forty feet in front of me.

"Charlie?" I called. My voice was no more than a hoarse gasp.

I edged forward. The light was so intense now that I was afraid it might damage my eyes. But I continued to stare, as if the thing would disappear if I were to blink for even a millionth of a second.

I heard the wailing music again.

Soft, distant, eerie. Cables rubbing together in a dark shaft. This time it seemed to be turned outward, rising far beyond me, reaching into distant space or perhaps some even more distant dimension. Something calling, announcing its regained freedom, summoning—whom? *What?*

"Charlie?" I said. It was a barely audible croak. "Charlie?"

I noticed him now, edging up from the other side. I pointed at the source of the light. He nodded.

I moved closer. The light seemed to change, to grow momentarily less fierce. And then I was able to see her.

She wasn't exactly identical to the statues in the museum. Her face wasn't really a face, at least not a human one. She had beady eyes, faceted the way an insect's are. She had an extra set of arms, little dangling ones, coming out at her hips. And, though the famous breasts were there, at least fifty of them and maybe the hundred of legend, I don't think they were actual breasts because I don't think this creature was a mammal. More of a reptile, I would guess: leathery skin, more or less scaly the way a snake's is, and tiny dots of nostrils, and a black slithery tongue, jagged like a lightning bolt, that came shooting quickly out between her slitted lips again and again and again, as though checking on the humidity or the ambient temperature or some such thing.

I saw, and Charlie saw. For a fraction of a second I wanted to drop down on my knees and rub my forehead in the ground and give worship. And then I just wanted to run.

I said, "Charlie, I definitely think we ought to get the hell out of—"

"Cool it, bro," he said. He stepped forward. Walked right up to her, stared her in the face. I was terrified for him, seeing him get that close. She dwarfed him. He was like a doll in front of her. How had a thing this big managed to fit in that opening in the tunnel wall? How had those ancient Greeks ever managed to get her in there in the first place?

That dazzling light crackled and hissed around her like some sort of electrical discharge. And yet Charlie stood his ground, unflinching, rock-solid. The expression on my brother's face was a nearly incomprehensible mixture of anger and fear.

He jabbed his forefinger through the air at her.

"You," he said to her. It was almost a snarl. "Tell me what the hell you are."

They were maybe ten feet apart, the man and the—what? The goddess? The monster?

Charlie had to know.

"You speak English?" he demanded. "Turkish? Tell me. I'm the one who let you out of that hole. Tell me what you are. I want to know." Eye to eye, face to face. "Something from another planet, are you, maybe? Another dimension? An ancient race that used to live on the Earth before humans did?"

"Charlie," I whispered.

But he wouldn't let up. "Or maybe you're an actual and literal goddess," he said. His tone had turned softer, a mocking croon now. "Diana of Ephesus, is that who you are? Stepping right out of the pages of mythology in all your fantastic beauty? Well, do me some magic, goddess, if that's who you are. Do a miracle for me, just a little one." The angry edge was back in his voice. "Turn that tree into an elephant. Turn me into a sheep, if you can. What's the matter, Diana, you no spikka da English? All right. Why the hell should you? But how about Greek, then? Surely you can understand Greek."

"For Christ's sake, Charlie—"

He ignored me. It was as if I wasn't there. He was talking to her in Greek, now. I suppose it was Greek. It was harsh, thick-sounding, jaggedly rhythmic. His eyes were wild and his face was flushed with fury. I was afraid that she would hurl a thunderbolt of blue-white light at him, but no, no, she just stood there through all his whole harangue, as motionless as those statues of her in the little museum, listening patiently as my furious brother went on and on and on at her in the language of Homer and Sophocles.

He stopped, finally. Waited as if expecting her to respond.

No response came. I could hear the whistling sound of her slow steady breathing; occasionally there was some slight movement of her body; but that was all.

"Well, Diana?" Charlie said. "What do you have to say for yourself, Diana?"

Silence.

"You fraud!" Charlie cried, in a great and terrible voice. "You fake! Some goddess you are! You aren't real at all, and that's God's own truth. You aren't even here. You're nothing but a fucking hallucination. A projection of some kind. I bet I could walk up to you and put my hand right through you."

Still no reaction. Nothing. She just stood there, those faceted eyes glittering, that little tongue flickering. Saying nothing, offering him no help.

That was when he flipped out. Charlie seemed to puff up as if about to explode with rage, and went rushing toward her, arms upraised, fists clenched in a wild gesture of attack. I wanted desperately to stop him, but my feet were frozen in place. I was certain that he was going to die. We both were.

"Damn you!" he roared, with something like a sob behind the fury. "Damn you, damn you, damn you!"

But before he could strike her, her aura flared up around her like a sheath, and for a moment the air was full of brilliant flares of cold flame that went whirling and whirling around her in a way that was too painful to watch. I caught a glimpse of Charlie staggering back from her, and I backed away myself, covering my face with my forearm, but even so the whirling lights came stabbing into my brain, forcing me to the ground. It seemed then that they all coalesced into a single searing point of white light, which rose like a dagger into the sky, climbing, climbing, becoming something almost like a comet, and—then—

Vanishing.

And then I blanked out.

It was just before dawn when I awakened. My eyes fluttered open almost hesitantly. The moon was gone, the first pink streaks of light beginning to appear. Charlie sat beside me. He was already awake.

"Where is it?" I asked immediately.

"Gone, bro."

"Gone?"

He nodded. "Without a trace. If it ever was up here with us at all."

"What do you mean, *if*?"

"*If*, that's what I mean. Who the hell knows what was going on up here last night? Do you?"

"No."

"Well, neither do I. All I know is that it isn't going on any more. There's nobody around but me and thee."

He was trying to sound like the old casual Charlie I knew, the man who had been everywhere and done everything and took it all in his stride. But there was a quality in his voice that I had never heard in it before, something entirely new.

"Gone?" I said, stupidly. "Really gone?"

"Really gone, yes. Vanished. You hear how quiet everything is?" Indeed the town, spread out below us, was silent except for the crowing of the first roosters and the far-off sound of a farm tractor starting up somewhere.

"Are you all right?" I asked him.

"Fine," he said. "Absolutely fine."

But he said it through clenched teeth. I couldn't bear to look at him. A thing had happened here that badly needed explanation, and no explanations were available, and I knew what that must be doing to him. I kept staring at the place where that eerie being had been, and I remembered that single shaft of light that had taken its place, and I felt a crushing sense of profound and terrible loss. Something strange and weirdly beautiful and utterly fantastic and inexplicable had been loose in the world for a little while, after centuries of— what? Imprisonment? Hibernation?—and now it was gone, and it would never return. It had known at once, I was sure, that this was no era for goddesses. Or whatever it was.

We sat side by side in silence for a minute or two.

"I think we ought to go back down now," I said finally.

"Right. Let's go back down," Charlie said.

And without saying another word as we descended, we made our way down the hill of Ayasuluk, the hill of St. John the Apostle, who was the man who wrote the Book of Revelations.

Mr. Gladstone was having breakfast in the hotel coffee shop when Charlie and I came in. He saw at once that something was wrong and asked if he could help in any way, and after some hesitation we told him something of what had happened, and then we told him more, and then we told him the whole story right to the end.

He didn't laugh and he didn't make any sarcastic skeptical comments. He took it all quite seriously.

"Perhaps the Seal of Solomon was what was on that marble slab," he suggested. "The Turks would say some such thing, at any rate. King Solomon had power over the evil jinn, and locked them away in flasks and caves and tombs, and put his seal on them to keep them locked up. It's in the Koran."

"You've read the Koran?" I asked, surprised.

"I've read a lot of things," said Mr. Gladstone.

"The Seal of Solomon," Charlie said, scowling. He was trying hard to be his old self again, and almost succeeding. Almost. "Evil spirits. Magic. Oh, Jesus Christ!"

"Perhaps," said Mr. Gladstone.

"What?" Charlie said.

The little man from Ohio or Indiana or Iowa put his hand over Charlie's. "If only I could help you," he said. "But you've been undone, haven't you, by the evidence of things seen."

"You have the quote wrong," said Charlie. "'The substance of things hoped for, the evidence of things *not* seen.' Book of Hebrews, 11:1."

Mr. Gladstone was impressed. So was I.

"But this is different," he said to Charlie. "This time, you actually *saw*. You were, I think, a man who prided himself on believing in nothing at all. But now you can no longer even believe in your own disbelief."

Charlie reddened. "Saw *what*? A goddess? Jesus! You think I believe that that was a goddess? A genuine immortal supernatural being of a higher order of existence? Or—what?—some kind of actual alien creature? You want me to believe it was an alien that had been locked up in there all that time? An alien from where? Mars? And who locked it up? Or was it one of King Solomon's jinn, maybe?"

"Does it really matter which it was?" Mr. Gladstone asked softly.

Charlie started to say something; but he choked it back. After a moment he stood. "Listen, I need to go now," he said. "Mr. Gladstone—Timmo—I'll catch up with you later, is that all right?"

40

And then he turned and stalked away. But before he left, I saw the look in his eyes.

His eyes. Oh, Charlie. Oh. Those eyes. Those frightened, empty eyes.

BEAUTY IN THE NIGHT

The Alien Years, which I look upon as one of the most successful novels I wrote in what I call my post-"retirement" period (I had, I thought, given up writing science fiction forever in 1975, but I didn't stick to my resolve), had a curious composite history. Between 1983 and 1986 I had written a number of stories in which the Earth is invaded by virtually omnipotent alien beings. The first of these was "Against Babylon," done late in 1983 for Omni *(which took two years to publish it). Then came 1985's "Hannibal's Elephants," also for* Omni *(published in 1988), and 1986's "The Pardoner's Tale," written for* Playboy *and published in 1987. These stories were in no way intended as a series, and in fact were contradictory and incompatible in most details beyond the basic concept of an invaded Earth. But over time it dawned on me that the seeds of a major novel lay in these relatively light-hearted tales of interplanetary conquest.*

In 1995 I offered the book to HarperCollins, my publisher at that time, and wrote it in the winter of 1996-97. "Against Babylon," virtually in its entirety, became the opening chapter. A small piece of "Hannibal's Elephants" was incorporated into one of the early sequences. Then I used nearly all of "The Pardoner's Tale" in the latter part of the book. In each case I altered the names of characters to make them fit the overall story I had devised for the novel.

It was all done so smoothly that very few people—not even my own bibliographer—noticed that I had tucked two and a half decade-old short stories into the lengthy new novel. And to make life even more difficult for bibliographers, I then proceeded to carve three new stories out of the recently written part of the book and sell them as individual items to the glossy, high-paying new science-fiction magazine Science Fiction Age, *which Scott Edelman was editing.*

They needed a little bending and polishing around the edges to turn into properly rounded short stories, of course. But the process of extraction and revision turned out to be a success. Especially the first of the three, "Beauty in the Night." Scott used it in his September, 1997 issue, and it was chosen the following year not only for Gardner Dozois's annual Year's Best Science Fiction *anthology but also for David Hartwell's similar collection,* Year's Best SF. *It has gone on to various other sorts of publication, both in the United States and abroad, since then.*

*The other two—"On the Inside" (*Science Fiction Age, *November, 1997) and the novella "The Colonel in Autumn" (*Science Fiction Age, *March, 1998)—have had successful independent afterlives as well. But "Beauty in the Night" strikes me as the strongest of the extracted segments of* The Alien Years, *and a fitting representative of my work in the second half of the 1990s.*

ONE: NINE YEARS FROM NOW

He was a Christmas child, was Khalid—Khalid the Entity-Killer, the first to raise his hand against the alien invaders who had conquered Earth in a single day, sweeping aside all resistance as though we were no more than ants to them. Khalid Haleem Burke, that was his name, English on his father's side, Pakistani on his mother's, born on Christmas Day amidst his mother's pain and shame and his family's grief. Christmas child though he was, nevertheless he was not going to be the new Savior of mankind, however neat a coincidence that might have been. But he would live, though his mother had not, and in the fullness of time he would do his little part, strike his little blow, against the awesome beings who had with such contemptuous ease taken possession of the world into which he had been born.

✹

To be born at Christmastime can be an awkward thing for mother and child, who even at the best of times must contend with the risks inherent in the general overcrowding and understaffing of hospitals at that time of year. But prevailing hospital conditions were not an issue for the mother of the child of uncertain parentage and dim prospects who was about to come into the world in unhappy and disagreeable circumstances in an unheated upstairs storeroom of a modest Pakistani restaurant grandly named Khan's Mogul Palace in Salisbury, England, very early in the morning of this third Christmas since the advent of the conquering Entities from the stars.

Salisbury is a pleasant little city that lies to the south and west of London and is the principal town of the county of Wiltshire. It is noted particularly for its relatively unspoiled medieval charm, for its graceful and imposing thirteenth-century cathedral, and for the presence, eight miles away, of the celebrated prehistoric megalithic monument known as Stonehenge.

Which, in the darkness before the dawn of that Christmas day, was undergoing one of the most remarkable events in its long history; and, despite the earliness (or lateness) of the hour, a goodly number of Salisbury's inhabitants had turned out to witness the spectacular goings-on.

But not Haleem Khan, the owner of Khan's Mogul Palace, nor his wife Aissha, both of them asleep in their beds. Neither of them had any interest in the pagan monument that was Stonehenge, let alone the strange thing that was happening to it now. And certainly not Haleem's daughter Yasmeena Khan, who was seventeen years old and cold and frightened, and who was lying half naked on the bare floor of the upstairs storeroom of her father's restaurant, hidden between a huge sack of raw lentils and an even larger sack of flour, writhing in terrible pain as shame and illicit motherhood came sweeping down on her like the avenging sword of angry Allah.

She had sinned. She knew that. Her father, her plump, reticent, overworked, mortally weary, and in fact already dying father, had several times in the past year warned her of sin and its consequences, speaking with as much force as she had ever seen him muster; and yet she had chosen to take the risk. Just three times, three different boys, only one time each, all three of them English and white.

Andy. Eddie. Richie.

Names that blazed like bonfires in the neural pathways of her soul.

Her mother—no, not really her mother; her true mother had died when Yasmeena was three; this was Aissha, her father's second wife, the robust and stolid woman who had raised her, had held the family and the restaurant together all these years—had given her warnings too, but they had been couched in entirely different terms. "You are a woman now, Yasmeena, and a woman is permitted to allow herself some pleasure in life," Aissha had told her. "But you must be careful." Not a word about sin, just taking care not to get into trouble.

Well, Yasmeena had been careful, or thought she had, but evidently not careful enough. Therefore she had failed Aissha. And failed her sad quiet father too, because she had certainly sinned despite all his warnings to remain virtuous, and Allah now would punish her for that. Was punishing her already. Punishing her terribly.

She had been very late discovering she was pregnant. She had not expected to be. Yasmeena wanted to believe that she was still too young for bearing babies, because her breasts were so small and her hips were so narrow, almost like a boy's. And each of those three times when she had done It with a boy—impulsively, furtively, half reluctantly, once in a musty cellar and once in a ruined omnibus and once right here in this very storeroom—she had taken precautions afterward, diligently swallowing the pills she had secretly bought from the smirking Hindu woman at the shop in Winchester, two tiny green pills in the morning and the big yellow one at night, five days in a row.

The pills were so nauseating that they *had* to work. But they hadn't. She should never have trusted pills provided by a Hindu, Yasmeena would tell herself a thousand times over; but by then it was too late.

The first sign had come only about four months before. Her breasts suddenly began to fill out. That had pleased her, at first. She had always been so scrawny; but now it seemed that her body was developing at last. Boys liked breasts. You could see their eyes quickly flicking down to check out your chest, though they seemed to think you didn't notice it when they did. All three of her lovers had put their hands into her blouse to feel hers, such as they were; and at least one—Eddie, the second—had actually been disappointed at what he found there. He had said so, just like that: "Is that *all*?"

But now her breasts were growing fuller and heavier every week, and they started to ache a little, and the dark nipples began to stand out oddly from the smooth little circles in which they were set. So Yasmeena began to feel fear; and when her bleeding did not come on time, she feared even more. But her bleeding had *never* come on time. Once last year it had been almost a whole month late, and she an absolute pure virgin then.

Still, there were the breasts; and then her hips seemed to be getting wider. Yasmeena said nothing, went about her business, chatted pleasantly with the customers, who liked her because she was slender and pretty and polite, and pretended all was well. Again and again at night her hand would slide down her flat boyish belly, anxiously searching for hidden life lurking beneath the taut skin. She felt nothing.

But something was there, all right, and by early October it was making the faintest of bulges, only a tiny knot pushing upward below her navel, but a little bigger every day. Yasmeena began wearing her blouses untucked, to hide the new fullness of her breasts and the burgeoning rondure of her belly. She opened the seams of her trousers and punched two new holes in her belt. It became harder for her to do her work, to carry the heavy trays of food all evening long and to put in the hours afterward washing the dishes, but she forced herself to be strong. There was no one else to do the job. Her father took the orders and Aissha did the cooking and Yasmeena served the meals and cleaned up after the restaurant closed. Her brother Khalid was gone, killed defending Aissha from a mob of white men during the riots that had broken out after the Entities came, and her sister Leila was too small, only five, no use in the restaurant.

No one at home commented on the new way Yasmeena was dressing. Perhaps they thought it was the current fashion. Life was very strange, in these early years of the Conquest.

Her father scarcely glanced at anyone these days; preoccupied with his failing restaurant and his failing health, he went about bowed over, coughing all the time, murmuring prayers endlessly under his breath. He was forty years old and looked sixty. Khan's Mogul Palace was nearly empty, night after night, even on the weekends. People did not travel any more, now that the Entities were here. No rich foreigners came from distant parts of the world to spend the night at Salisbury before going on to visit Stonehenge. The inns and hotels closed; so did most of the restaurants, though a few, like Khan's, struggled on because their proprietors had no other way of earning a living. But the last thing on Haleem Khan's mind was his daughter's changing figure.

As for her stepmother, Yasmeena imagined that she saw her giving her sidewise looks now and again, and worried over that. But Aissha said nothing. So there was probably no suspicion. Aissha was not the sort to keep silent, if she suspected something.

The Christmas season drew near. Now Yasmeena's swollen legs were as heavy as dead logs and her breasts were hard as boulders and she felt sick all the time. It was not going to be long, now. She could no longer hide from the truth. But she had no plan. If her brother Khalid were here, he would know what to do. Khalid was gone, though. She would simply have to let things happen and trust that Allah, when He was through punishing her, would forgive her and be merciful.

Christmas Eve, there were four tables of customers. That was a surprise, to be so busy on a night when most English people had dinner at home. Midway through the evening Yasmeena thought she would fall down in the middle of the room and send her tray, laden with chicken biriani and mutton vindaloo and boti kebabs and schooners of lager, spewing across the floor. She steadied herself then; but an hour later she did fall; or, rather, sagged to her knees, in the hallway between the kitchen and the garbage bin where no one could see her. She crouched there, dizzy, sweating, gasping, nauseated, feeling her bowels quaking and strange spasms running down the front of her body and into her thighs; and after a time she rose and continued on with her tray toward the bin.

It will be this very night, she thought.

And for the thousandth time that week she ran through the little calculation in her mind: *December 24 minus nine months is March 24. Therefore it is Richie Burke, the father. At least he was the one who gave me pleasure also.*

Andy, he had been the first. Yasmeena couldn't remember his last name. Pale and freckled and very thin, with a beguiling smile, and on a humid summer night just after her sixteenth birthday when the restaurant was closed because her father was in hospital for a few days with the beginning of his trouble, Andy invited her dancing and treated her to a couple of pints of brown ale and then, late in the evening, told her of a special party at a friend's house that he was invited to, only there turned out to be no party, just a shabby stale-smelling cellar room and an old spavined couch, and Andy's busy hands roaming the front of her blouse and then going between her legs and her trousers coming off and then, quick, *quick!*, the long hard narrow reddened thing emerging from him and sliding into her, done and done and done in just a couple of moments, a gasp from him and a shudder and his head buried against her cheek and that was that, all over and done with. She had thought it was supposed to hurt, the first time, but she had felt almost nothing at all, neither pain nor anything that might have been delight. The next time Yasmeena saw him in the street Andy grinned and turned crimson and winked at her, but said nothing to her, and they had never exchanged a word since.

Then Eddie Glossop, in the autumn, the one who had found her breasts insufficient and told her so. Big broad-shouldered Eddie, who worked for the meat merchant and who had an air of great worldliness about him. He was old, almost twenty-five. Yasmeena went with him because she knew there was supposed to be pleasure in it and she had not had it from Andy. But there was none from Eddie either, just a lot of huffing and puffing as he lay sprawled on top of her in the aisle of that burned-out omnibus by the side of the road that went toward Shaftesbury. He was much bigger down there than Andy, and it hurt when he went in, and she was glad that this had not been her first time. But she wished she had not done it at all.

And then Richie Burke, in this very storeroom on an oddly warm night in March, with everyone asleep in the family apartments downstairs at the back of the restaurant. She tiptoeing up the stairs, and Richie clambering up the drainpipe and through the window, tall, lithe, graceful Richie who played the guitar so well and sang and told everyone that some day he was going to be a general in the war against the Entities and wipe them from the face of the Earth. A wonderful lover, Richie. Yasmeena kept her blouse on because Eddie had made her uneasy about her breasts. Richie caressed her and stroked her for what seemed like hours, though she was terrified that they would be discovered and wanted him to get on with it; and when he entered her, it was like an oiled shaft of smooth metal gliding into her, moving so easily, easily, easily, one gentle thrust after another, on and on and on until marvelous palpitations began to happen inside her and then she erupted with pleasure, moaning so loud that Richie had to put his hand over her mouth to keep her from waking everyone up.

That was the time the baby had been made. There could be no doubt of that. All the next day she dreamed of marrying Richie and spending the rest of the nights of her life in his arms. But at the end of that week Richie disappeared from Salisbury—some said he had gone off to join a secret underground army that was going to launch guerrilla warfare against the Entities—and no one had heard from him again.

Andy. Eddie. Richie.

✴

And here she was on the floor of the storeroom again, with her trousers off and the shiny swollen hump of her belly sending messages of agony and shame through her body. Her only covering was a threadbare blanket that reeked of spilled cooking oil. Her water had burst about midnight. That was when she had crept up the stairs to wait in terror for the great disaster of her life to finish happening. The contractions were coming closer and closer together, like little earthquakes within her. Now the time had to be two, three, maybe four in the morning. How long would it be? Another hour? Six? Twelve?

Relent and call Aissha to help her?

No. No. She didn't dare.

Earlier in the night voices had drifted up from the streets to her. The sound of footsteps. That was strange, shouting and running in the street, this late. The Christmas revelry didn't usually go on through the night like this. It was hard to understand what they were saying; but then out of the confusion there came, with sudden clarity:

"The aliens! They're pulling down Stonehenge, taking it apart!"

"Get your wagon, Charlie, we'll go and see!"

Pulling down Stonehenge. Strange. Strange. Why would they do that? Yasmeena wondered. But the pain was becoming too great for her to be able to give much thought to Stonehenge just now, or to the Entities who had somehow overthrown the invincible white men in the twinkling of an eye and now ruled the world, or to anything else except what was happening within her, the flames dancing through her brain, the ripplings of her belly, the implacable downward movement of—of—

Something.

"Praise be to Allah, Lord of the Universe, the Compassionate, the Merciful," she murmured timidly. "There is no god but Allah, and Mohammed is His prophet."

And again: "Praise be to Allah, Lord of the Universe."

And again.

And again.

The pain was terrible. She was splitting wide open.

"Abraham, Isaac, Ishmael!" That *something* had begun to move in a spiral through her now, like a corkscrew driving a hot track in her flesh. "Mohammed! Mohammed! Mohammed! There is no god but Allah!"

The words burst from her with no timidity at all, now. Let Mohammed and Allah save her, if they really existed. What good were they, if they would not save her, she so innocent and ignorant, her life barely begun? And then, as a spear of fire gutted her and her pelvic bones seemed to crack apart, she let loose a torrent of other names, Moses, Solomon, Jesus, Mary, and even the forbidden Hindu names, Shiva, Krishna, Shakti, Kali, anyone at all who would help her through this, anyone, anyone, anyone, anyone—

She screamed three times, short, sharp, piercing screams.

She felt a terrible inner wrenching and the baby came spurting out of her with astonishing swiftness. A gushing Ganges of blood followed it, a red river that spilled out over her thighs and would not stop flowing.

Yasmeena knew at once that she was going to die.

Something wrong had happened. Everything would come out of her insides and she would die. That was absolutely clear to her. Already, just moments after the birth, an eerie new calmness was enfolding her. She had no energy left now for further screaming, or even to look after the baby. It was somewhere down between her spread thighs, that was all she knew. She lay back, drowning in a rising pool of blood and sweat. She raised her arms toward the ceiling and brought them down again to clutch her throbbing breasts, stiff now with milk. She called now upon no more holy names. She could hardly remember her own.

She sobbed quietly. She trembled. She tried not to move, because that would surely make the bleeding even worse.

An hour went by, or a week, or a year.

Then an anguished voice high above her in the dark:

"What? Yasmeena? Oh, my god, my god, my god! Your father will perish!"

Aissha, it was. Bending to her, engulfing her. The strong arm raising her head, lifting it against the warm motherly bosom, holding her tight.

"Can you hear me, Yasmeena? Oh, Yasmeena! My god, my god!" And then an ululation of grief rising from her stepmother's throat like some hot volcanic geyser bursting from the ground. "Yasmeena! Yasmeena!"

"The baby?" Yasmeena said, in the tiniest of voices.

"Yes! Here! Here! Can you see?"

Yasmeena saw nothing but a red haze.

"A boy?" she asked, very faintly.

"A boy, yes."

In the blur of her dimming vision she thought she saw something small and pinkish-brown, smeared with scarlet, resting in her stepmother's hands. Thought she could hear him crying, even.

"Do you want to hold him?"

"No. No." Yasmeena understood clearly that she was going. The last of her strength had left her. She was moored now to the world by a mere thread.

"He is strong and beautiful," said Aissha. "A splendid boy."

"Then I am very happy." Yasmeena fought for one last fragment of energy. "His name—is—Khalid. Khalid Haleem Burke."

"Burke?"

"Yes. Khalid Haleem Burke."

"Is that the father's name, Yasmeena? Burke?"

"Burke. Richie Burke." With her final sliver of strength she spelled the name.

"Tell me where he lives, this Richie Burke. I will get him. This is shameful, giving birth by yourself, alone in the dark, in this awful room! Why did you never say anything? Why did you hide it from me? I would have helped. I would—"

But Yasmeena Khan was already dead. The first shaft of morning light now came through the grimy window of the upstairs storeroom. Christmas Day had begun.

Eight miles away, at Stonehenge, the Entities had finished their night's work. Three of the towering alien creatures had supervised while a human work crew, using hand-held pistol-like devices that emitted a bright violet glow, had uprooted every single one of the ancient stone slabs of the celebrated megalithic monument on windswept Salisbury Plain as though they were so many jackstraws. And had rearranged them so that what had been the outer circle of immense sandstone blocks now had become two parallel rows running from north to south; the lesser inner ring of blue slabs had been moved about to form an equilateral triangle; and the sixteen-foot-long block of sandstone at the center of the formation that people called the Altar Stone had been raised to an upright position at the center.

A crowd of perhaps two thousand people from the adjacent towns had watched through the night from a judicious distance as this inexplicable project was being carried out. Some were infuriated; some were saddened; some were indifferent; some were fascinated. Many had theories about what was going on, and one theory was as good as another, no better, no worse.

TWO: SIXTEEN YEARS FROM NOW

You could still see the ghostly lettering over the front door of the former restaurant, if you knew what to look for, the pale greenish outlines of the words that once had been painted there in bright gold: KHAN'S MOGUL PALACE. The old swinging sign that had dangled above the door was still lying out back, too, in a clutter of cracked basins and discarded stewpots and broken crockery.

But the restaurant itself was gone, long gone, a victim of the Great Plague that the Entities had casually loosed upon the world as a warning to its conquered people, after an attempt had been made at an attack on an Entity encampment. Half the population of Earth had died so that the Entities could teach the other half not to harbor further rebellious thoughts. Poor sad Haleem Khan himself was gone too, the ever-weary little brown-skinned man who in ten years had somehow saved five thousand pounds from his salary as a dishwasher at the Lion and Unicorn Hotel and had used that, back when England had a queen and Elizabeth was her name, as the seed money for the unpretentious little restaurant that was going to rescue him and his family from utter hopeless poverty. Four days after the Plague had hit Salisbury, Haleem was dead. But if the Plague hadn't killed him, the tuberculosis that he was already harboring probably would have done the job soon enough. Or else simply the shock and disgrace and grief of his daughter Yasmeena's ghastly death in childbirth two weeks earlier, at Christmastime, in an upstairs room of the restaurant, while bringing into the world the bastard child of the long-legged English boy, Richie Burke, the future traitor, the future quisling.

Haleem's other daughter, the little girl Leila, had died in the Plague also, three months after her father and two days before what would have been her sixth birthday. As for Yasmeena's older brother, Khalid, he was already two years gone by then. That was during the time that now was known as the Troubles. A gang of long-haired yobs had set forth late one Saturday afternoon in fine English wrath, determined to vent their resentment over the conquest of the Earth by doing a lively spot of Paki-bashing in the town streets, and they had encountered Khalid escorting Aissha home from the market. They had made remarks; he had replied hotly; and they beat him to death.

Which left, of all the family, only Aissha, Haleem's hardy and tireless second wife. She came down with the Plague, too, but she was one of the lucky ones, one of those who managed to fend the affliction off and survive—for whatever that was worth—into the new and transformed and diminished world. But she could hardly run the restaurant alone, and in any case, with three quarters of the population of Salisbury dead in the Plague, there was no longer much need for a Pakistani restaurant there.

Aissha found other things to do. She went on living in a couple of rooms of the now gradually decaying building that had housed the restaurant, and supported herself, in this era when national currencies had ceased to mean much and strange new sorts of money circulated in the land, by a variety of improvised means. She did housecleaning and laundry for those people who still had need of such services. She cooked meals for elderly folks too feeble to cook for themselves. Now and then, when her number came up in the labor lottery, she put in time at a factory that the Entities had established just outside town, weaving little strands of colored wire together to make incomprehensibly complex mechanisms whose nature and purpose were never disclosed to her.

And when there was no such work of any of those kinds available, Aissha would make herself available to the lorry-drivers who passed through Salisbury, spreading her powerful muscular thighs in return for meal certificates or corporate scrip or barter units or whichever other of the new versions of money they would pay her in. That was not something she would have chosen to do, if she had had her choices. But she would not have chosen to have the invasion of the Entities, for that matter, nor her husband's early death and Leila's and Khalid's, nor Yasmeena's miserable lonely ordeal in the upstairs room, but she had not been consulted about any of those things, either. Aissha needed to eat in order to survive; and so she sold herself, when she had to, to the lorry-drivers, and that was that.

As for why survival mattered, why she bothered at all to care about surviving in a world that had lost all meaning and just about all hope, it was in part because survival for the sake of survival was in her genes, and—mostly—because she wasn't alone in the world. Out of the wreckage of her family she had been left with a child to look after—her grandchild, her dead stepdaughter's baby, Khalid Haleem Burke, the child of shame. Khalid Haleem Burke had survived the Plague too. It was one of the ugly little ironies of the epidemic that the Entities had released upon the world that children who were less than six months old generally did not contract it. Which created a huge population of healthy but parentless babes.

He was healthy, all right, was Khalid Haleem Burke. Through every deprivation of those dreary years, the food shortages and the fuel shortages and the little outbreaks of diseases that once had been thought to be nearly extinct, he grew taller and straighter and stronger all the time. He had his mother's wiry strength and his father's long legs and dancer's grace. And he was lovely to behold. His skin was tawny golden-brown, his eyes were a glittering blue-green, and his hair, glossy and thick and curly, was a wonderful bronze color, a magnificent Eurasian hue. Amidst all the sadness and loss of Aissha's life, he was the one glorious beacon that lit the darkness for her.

There were no real schools, not any more. Aissha taught little Khalid herself, as best she could. She hadn't had much schooling herself, but she could read and write, and showed him how, and begged or borrowed books for him wherever she might. She found a woman who understood arithmetic, and scrubbed her floors for her in return for Khalid's lessons. There was an old man at the south end of town who had the Koran by heart, and Aissha, though she was not a strongly religious woman herself, sent Khalid to him once a week for instruction in Islam. The boy was, after all, half Moslem. Aissha felt no responsibility for the Christian part of him, but she did not want to let him go into the world unaware that there was—somewhere, *somewhere!*—a god known as Allah, a god of justice and compassion and mercy, to whom obedience was owed, and that he would, like all people, ultimately come to stand before that god upon the Day of Judgment.

"And the Entities?" Khalid asked her. He was six, then. "Will they be judged by Allah too?"

"The Entities are not people. They are jinn."

"Did Allah make them?"

"Allah made all things in heaven and on Earth. He made us out of potter's clay and the jinn out of smokeless fire."

"But the Entities have brought evil upon us. Why would Allah make evil things, if He is a merciful god?"

"The Entities," Aissha said uncomfortably, aware that wiser heads than hers had grappled in vain with that question, "*do* evil. But they are not evil themselves. They are merely the instruments of Allah."

"Who has sent them to us to do evil," said Khalid. "What kind of god is that, who sends evil among His own people, Aissha?"

She was getting beyond her depth in this conversation, but she was patient with him. "No one understands Allah's ways, Khalid. He is the One God and we are nothing before him. If He had reason to send the Entities to us, they were good reasons, and we have no right to question them." *And also to send sickness, she thought, and hunger, and death, and the English boys who killed your uncle Khalid in the street, and even the English boy who put you into your mother's belly and then ran away. Allah sent all of those into the world, too.* But then she reminded herself that if Richie Burke had not crept secretly into this house to sleep with Yasmeena, this beautiful child would not be standing here before her at this moment. And so good sometimes could come forth from evil. Who were we to demand reasons from Allah? Perhaps even the Entities had been sent here, ultimately, for our own good.

Perhaps.

Of Khalid's father, there was no news all this while. He was supposed to have run off to join the army that was fighting the Entities; but Aissha had never heard that there was any such army, anywhere in the world.

Then, not long after Khalid's seventh birthday, when he returned in mid-afternoon from his Thursday Koran lesson at the house of old Iskander Mustafa Ali, he found an unknown white man sitting in the room with his grandmother, a man with a great untidy mass of light-colored curling hair and a lean, angular, almost fleshless face with two cold, harsh blue-green eyes looking out from it as though out of a mask. His skin was so white that Khalid wondered whether he had any blood in his body. It was almost like chalk. The strange white man was sitting in his grandmother's own armchair, and his grandmother was looking very edgy and strange, a way Khalid had never seen her look before, with glistening beads of sweat along her forehead and her lips clamped together in a tight thin line.

The white man said, leaning back in the chair and crossing his legs, which were the longest legs Khalid had ever seen, "Do you know who I am, boy?"

"How would he know?" his grandmother said.

The white man looked toward Aissha and said, "Let me do this, if you don't mind." And then, to Khalid: "Come over here, boy. Stand in front of me. Well, now, aren't we the little beauty? What's your name, boy?"

"Khalid."

"Khalid. Who named you that?"

"My mother. She's dead now. It was my uncle's name. He's dead too."

"Devil of a lot of people are dead who used to be alive, all right. Well, Khalid, my name is Richie."

"Richie," Khalid said, in a very small voice, because he had already begun to understand this conversation.

"Richie, yes. Have you ever heard of a person named Richie? Richie *Burke*."

"My—father." In an even smaller voice.

"Right you are! The grand prize for that lad! Not only handsome but smart, too! Well, what would one expect, eh?—Here I be, boy, your long-lost father! Come here and give your long-lost father a kiss."

Khalid glanced uncertainly toward Aissha. Her face was still shiny with sweat, and very pale. She looked sick. After a moment she nodded, a tiny nod.

He took half a step forward and the man who was his father caught him by the wrist and gathered him roughly in, pulling him inward and pressing him up against him, not for an actual kiss but for what was only a rubbing of cheeks. The grinding contact with that hard, stubbly cheek was painful for Khalid.

"There, boy. I've come back, do you see? I've been away seven worm-eaten miserable years, but now I'm back, and I'm going to live with you and be your father. You can call me 'dad'."

Khalid stared, stunned.

"Go on. Do it. Say, 'I'm so very glad that you've come back, dad.'"

"Dad," Khalid said uneasily.

"The rest of it too, if you please."

"I'm so very glad—" He halted.

"That I've come back."

"That you've come back—"

"*Dad.*"

Khalid hesitated. "Dad," he said.

"There's a good boy! It'll come easier to you after a while. Tell me, did you ever think about me while you were growing up, boy?"

Khalid glanced toward Aissha again. She nodded surreptitiously.

Huskily he said, "Now and then, yes."

"Only now and then? That's all?"

"Well, hardly anybody has a father. But sometimes I met someone who did, and then I thought of you. I wondered where you were. Aissha said you were off fighting the Entities. Is that where you were, dad? Did you fight them? Did you kill any of them?"

"Don't ask stupid questions. Tell me, boy: do you go by the name of Burke or Khan?"

"Burke. Khalid Haleem Burke."

"Call me '*sir*' when you're not calling me '*dad*'. Say, 'Khalid Haleem Burke, sir.'"

"Khalid Haleem Burke, sir. Dad."

"One or the other. Not both." Richie Burke rose from the chair, unfolding himself as though in sections, up and up and up. He was enormously tall, very thin. His slenderness accentuated his great height. Khalid, though tall for his age, felt dwarfed beside him. The thought came to him that this man was not his father at all, not even a man, but some sort of demon, rather, a jinni, a jinni that had been let out of its bottle, as in the story that Iskander Mustafa Ali had told him. He kept that thought to himself. "Good," Richie Burke said. "Khalid Haleem Burke. I like that. Son should have his father's name. But not the Khalid Haleem part. From now on your name is—ah—Kendall. Ken for short."

"Khalid was my—"

"—uncle's name, yes. Well, your uncle is dead. Practically everybody is dead, Kenny. Kendall Burke, good English name. Kendall *Hamilton* Burke, same initials, even, only English. Is that all right, boy? What a pretty one you are, Kenny! I'll teach you a thing or two, I will. I'll make a man out of you."

❋

Here I be, boy, your long-lost father!

Khalid had never known what it meant to have a father, nor ever given the idea much examination. He had never known hatred before, either, because Aissha was a fundamentally calm, stable, accepting person, too steady in her soul to waste time or valuable energy hating anything, and Khalid had taken after her in that. But Richie Burke, who taught Khalid what it meant to have a father, made him aware of what it was like to hate, also.

Richie moved into the bedroom that had been Aissha's, sending Aissha off to sleep in what had once had been Yasmeena's room. It had long since gone to rack and ruin, but they cleaned it up, some, chasing the spiders out and taping oilcloth over the missing window-panes and nailing down a couple of floor-boards that had popped up out of their proper places. She carried her clothes-cabinet in there by herself, and set up on it the framed photographs of her dead family that she had kept in her former bedroom, and draped two of her old saris that she never wore any more over the bleak places on the wall where the paint had flaked away.

It was stranger than strange, having Richie living with them. It was a total upheaval, a dismaying invasion by an alien life-form, in some ways as shocking in its impact as the arrival of the Entities had been.

He was gone most of the day. He worked in the nearby town of Winchester, driving back and forth in a small brown pre-Conquest automobile. Winchester was a place where Khalid had never been, though his mother had, to purchase the pills that were meant to abort him. Khalid had never been far from Salisbury, not even to Stonehenge, which now was a center of Entity activity anyway, and not a tourist sight. Few people in Salisbury traveled anywhere these days. Not many had automobiles, because of the difficulty of obtaining petrol, but Richie never seemed to have any problem about that.

Sometimes Khalid wondered what sort of work his father did in Winchester; but he asked about it only once. The words were barely out of his mouth when his father's long arm came snaking around and struck him across the face, splitting his lower lip and sending a dribble of blood down his chin.

Khalid staggered back, astounded. No one had ever hit him before. It had not occurred to him that anyone would.

"You must never ask that again!" his father said, looming mountain-high above him. His cold eyes were even colder, now, in his fury. "What

I do in Winchester is no business of yours, nor anyone else's, do you hear me, boy? It is my own private affair. My own—private—affair."

Khalid rubbed his cut lip and peered at his father in bewilderment. The pain of the slap had not been so great; but the surprise of it, the shock—that was still reverberating through his consciousness. And went on reverberating for a long while thereafter.

He never asked about his father's work again, no. But he was hit again, more than once, indeed with fair regularity. Hitting was Richie's way of expressing irritation. And it was difficult to predict what sort of thing might irritate him. Any sort of intrusion on his father's privacy, though, seemed to do it. Once, while talking with his father in his bedroom, telling him about a bloody fight between two boys that he had witnessed in town, Khalid unthinkingly put his hand on the guitar that Richie always kept leaning against his wall beside his bed, giving it only a single strum, something that he had occasionally wanted to do for months; and instantly, hardly before the twanging note had died away, Richie unleashed his arm and knocked Khalid back against the wall. "You keep your filthy fingers off that instrument, boy!" Richie said; and after that Khalid did. Another time Richie struck him for leafing through a book he had left on the kitchen table, that had pictures of naked women in it; and another time, it was for staring too long at Richie as he stood before the mirror in the morning, shaving. So Khalid learned to keep his distance from his father; but still he found himself getting slapped for this reason and that, and sometimes for no reason at all. The blows were rarely as hard as the first one had been, and never ever created in him that same sense of shock. But they were blows, all the same. He stored them all up in some secret receptacle of his soul.

Occasionally Richie hit Aissha, too—when dinner was late, or when she put mutton curry on the table too often, or when it seemed to him that she had contradicted him about something. That was more of a shock to Khalid than getting slapped himself, that anyone should dare to lift his hand to Aissha.

The first time it happened, which occurred while they were eating dinner, a big carving knife was lying on the table near Khalid, and he might well have reached for it had Aissha not, in the midst of her own fury and humiliation and pain, sent Khalid a message with her furious blazing eyes that he absolutely was not to do any such thing. And so he controlled himself, then and any time afterward when Richie hit her. It was a skill that Khalid had, controlling himself—one that in some circuitous way he must have inherited from the ever-patient, all-enduring grandparents whom he had never known and the long line of oppressed Asian peasants from whom they descended. Living with Richie in the house gave Khalid daily opportunity to develop that skill to a fine art.

Richie did not seem to have many friends, at least not friends who visited the house. Khalid knew of only three.

There was a man named Arch who sometimes came, an older man with greasy ringlets of hair that fell from a big bald spot on the top of his head. He always brought a bottle of whiskey, and he and Richie would sit in Richie's room with the door closed, talking in low tones or singing raucous songs. Khalid would find the empty whiskey bottle the following morning, lying on the hallway floor. He kept them, setting them up in a row amidst the restaurant debris behind the house, though he did not know why.

The only other man who came was Syd, who had a flat nose and amazingly thick fingers, and gave off such a bad smell that Khalid was able to detect it in the house the next day. Once, when Syd was there, Richie emerged from his room and called to Aissha, and she went in there and shut the door behind her and was still in there when Khalid went to sleep. He never asked her about that, what had gone on while she was in Richie's room. Some instinct told him that he would rather not know.

There was also a woman: Wendy, her name was, tall and gaunt and very plain, with a long face like a horse's and very bad skin, and stringy tangles of reddish hair. She came once in a while for dinner, and Richie always specified that Aissha was to prepare an English dinner that night, lamb or roast beef, none of your spicy Paki curries tonight, if you please. After they ate, Richie and Wendy would go into Richie's room and not emerge again that evening, and the sounds of the guitar would be heard, and laughter, and then low cries and moans and grunts.

One time in the middle of the night when Wendy was there, Khalid got up to go to the bathroom just at the time she did, and encountered her in the hallway, stark naked in the moonlight, a long white ghostly figure. He had never seen a woman naked until this moment, not a real one, only the pictures in Richie's magazine; but he looked up at her calmly, with that deep abiding steadiness in the face of any sort of surprise that he had mastered so well since the advent of Richie. Coolly he surveyed her, his eyes rising from the long thin legs that went up and up and up from the floor and halting for a moment at the curious triangular thatch of woolly hair at the base of her flat belly, and from there his gaze mounted to the round little breasts set high and far apart on her chest, and at last came to her face, which, in the moonlight had unexpectedly taken on a sort of handsomeness if not actual comeliness, though before this Wendy had always seemed to him to be tremendously ugly. She didn't seem displeased at being seen like this. She smiled and winked at him, and ran her hand almost coquettishly through her straggly hair, and blew him a kiss as she drifted on past him toward the bathroom. It was the only time that anyone associated with Richie had ever been nice to him: had even appeared to notice him at all.

But life with Richie was not entirely horrid. There were some good aspects.

One of them was simply being close to so much strength and energy: what Khalid might have called *virility*, if he had known there was any such word. He had spent all his short life thus far among people who kept their heads down and went soldiering along obediently, people like patient plodding Aissha, who took what came to her and never complained, and shriveled old Iskander Mustafa Ali, who understood that Allah determined all things and one had no choice but to comply, and the quiet, tight-lipped English people of Salisbury, who had lived through the Conquest, and the Great Silence when the aliens had turned off all the electrical power in the world, and the Troubles, and the Plague, and who were prepared to be very, very English about whatever horror was coming next.

Richie was different, though. Richie hadn't a shred of passivity in him. "We shape our lives the way we want them to be, boy," Richie would say again and again. "We write our own scripts. It's all nothing but a bloody television show, don't you see that, Kenny-boy?"

That was a startling novelty to Khalid: that you might actually have any control over your own destiny, that you could say "no" to this and "yes" to that and "not right now" to this other thing, and that if there was something you wanted, you could simply reach out and take it. There was nothing Khalid wanted. But the *idea* that he might even have it, if only he could figure out what it was, was fascinating to him.

Then, too, for all of Richie's roughness of manner, his quickness to curse you or kick out at you or slap you when he had had a little too much to drink, he did have an affectionate side, even a charming one. He often sat with them and played his guitar, and taught them the words of songs, and encouraged them to sing along with them, though Khalid had no idea what the songs were about and Aissha did not seem to know either. It was fun, all the same, the singing; and Khalid had known very little fun. Richie was immensely proud of Khalid's good looks and agile, athletic grace, also, and would praise him for them, something which no one had ever done before, not even Aissha. Even though Khalid understood in some way that Richie was only praising himself, really, he was grateful even so.

Richie took him out behind the building and showed him how to throw and catch a ball. How to kick one, too, a different kind of ball. And sometimes there were cricket matches in a field at the edge of town; and when Richie played in these, which he occasionally did, he brought Khalid along to watch. Later, at home, he showed Richie how to hold the bat, how to guard a wicket.

Then there were the drives in the car. These were rare, a great privilege. But sometimes, of a sunny Sunday, Richie would say, "Let's take the old flivver for a spin, eh, Kenny, lad?" And off they would go into the green countryside, usually no special destination in mind, only driving up and down the quiet lanes, Khalid gawking in wonder at this new world beyond the town. It made his head whirl in a good way, as he came to understand that the world actually did go on and on past the boundaries of Salisbury, and was full of marvels and splendors.

So, though at no point did he stop hating Richie, he could see at least some mitigating benefits that had come from his presence in their home. Not many. Some.

THREE: NINETEEN YEARS FROM NOW

Once Richie took him to Stonehenge. Or as near to it as it was possible now for humans to go. It was the year Khalid turned ten: a special birthday treat.

"Do you see it out there in the plain, boy? Those big stones? Built by a bunch of ignorant prehistoric buggers who painted themselves blue and danced widdershins in the night. Do you know what 'widdershins' means, boy? No, neither do I. But they did it, whatever it was. Danced around naked with their thingummies jiggling around, and then at midnight they'd sacrifice a virgin on the big altar stone. Long, long ago. Thousands of years.—Come on, let's get out and have a look."

Khalid stared. Huge gray slabs, set out in two facing rows flanking smaller slabs of blue stone set in a three-cornered pattern, and a big stone standing upright in the middle. And some other stones lying sideways on top of a few of the gray ones. A transparent curtain of flickering reddish-green light surrounded the whole thing, rising from hidden vents in the ground to nearly twice the height of a man. Why would anyone have wanted to build such a thing? It all seemed like a tremendous waste of time.

"Of course, you understand this isn't what it looked like back then. When the Entities came, they changed the whole business around from what it always was, buggered it all up. Got laborers out here to move every single stone. And they put in the gaudy lighting effects, too. Never used to be lights, certainly not that kind. You walk through those lights, you die, just like a mosquito flying through a candle flame. Those stones there, they were set in a circle originally, and those blue ones there—hey, now, lad, look what we have! You ever see an Entity before, Ken?"

Actually, Khalid had: twice. But never this close. The first one had been right in the middle of the town at noontime. It had been standing outside the entrance of the cathedral cool as you please, as though it happened to be in the mood to go to church: a giant purple thing with orange spots and big yellow eyes. But Aissha had put her hand over his face before he could get a good look, and had pulled him quickly down the street that led away from the cathedral, dragging him along as fast as he was able to could go. Khalid had been about five then. He dreamed of the Entity for months thereafter.

The second time, a year later, he had been with friends, playing within sight of the main highway, when a strange vehicle came down the road, an Entity car that floated on air instead of riding on wheels, and two Entities were standing in it, looking right out at them for a moment as they went floating by. Khalid saw only the tops of their heads that time: their great eyes again, and a sort of a curving beak below, and a great V-shaped slash of a mouth, like a frog's. He was fascinated by them. Repelled, too, because they were so bizarre, these strange alien beings, these enemies of mankind, and he knew he was supposed to loathe and disdain them. But fascinated. Fascinated. He wished he had been able to see them better.

Now, though, he had a clear view of the creatures, three of them. They had emerged from what looked like a door that was set right in the ground, out on the far side of the ancient monument, and were strolling casually among the great stones like lords or ladies inspecting their estate, paying no heed whatever to the tall man and the small boy standing beside the car parked just outside the fiery barrier. It amazed Khalid, watching them teeter around on the little ropy legs that supported their immense tubular bodies, that they were able to keep their balance, that they didn't simply topple forward and fall with a crash.

It amazed him, too, how beautiful they were. He had suspected that from his earlier glances, but now their glory fell upon him with full impact.

The luminous golden-orange spots on the glassy, gleaming purple skin—like fire, those spots were. And the huge eyes, so bright, so keen: you could read the strength of their minds in them, the power of their souls. Their gaze engulfed you in a flood of light. Even the air about the Entities partook of their beauty, glowing with a liquid turquoise radiance.

"There they be, boy. Our lords and masters. You ever see anything so bloody hideous?"

"Hideous?"

"They ain't pretty, isn't that right?"

Khalid made a noncommittal noise. Richie was in a good mood; he always was, on these Sunday excursions. But Khalid knew only too well the penalty for contradicting him in anything. So he looked upon the Entities in silence, lost in wonder, awed by the glory of these strange gigantic creatures, never voicing a syllable of his admiration for their elegance and majesty.

Expansively Richie said, "You heard correctly, you know, when they told you that when I left Salisbury just before you were born, it was to go off and join an army that meant to fight them. There was nothing I wanted more than to kill Entities, nothing. Christ Eternal, boy, did I ever hate those creepy bastards! Coming in like they did, taking our world away quick as you please. But I got to my senses pretty fast, let me tell you. I listened to the plans the underground army people had for throwing off the Entity yoke, and I had to laugh. I had to *laugh*! I could see right away that there wasn't a hope in hell of it. This was even before they put the Great Plague upon us, you understand. I knew. I damn well knew, I did. They're as powerful as gods.

You want to fight against a bunch of gods, lots of luck to you. So I quit the underground then and there. I still hate the bastards, mind you, make no mistake about that, but I know it's foolish even to dream about overthrowing them. You just have to fashion your accommodation with them, that's all there is. You just have to make your peace within yourself and let them have their way. Because anything else is a fool's own folly."

Khalid listened. What Richie was saying made sense. Khalid understood about not wanting to fight against gods. He understood also how it was possible to hate someone and yet go on unprotestingly living with him.

"Is it all right, letting them see us like this?" he asked. "Aissha says that sometimes when they see you, they reach out from their chests with the tongues that they have there and snatch you up, and they take you inside their buildings and do horrible things to you there."

Richie laughed harshly. "It's been known to happen. But they won't touch Richie Burke, lad, and they won't touch the son of Richie Burke at Richie Burke's side. I guarantee you that. We're absolutely safe."

Khalid did not ask why that should be. He hoped it was true, that was all.

Two days afterward, while he was coming back from the market with a packet of lamb for dinner, he was set upon by two boys and a girl, all of them about his age or a year or two older, whom he knew only in the vaguest way. They formed themselves into a loose ring just beyond his reach and began to chant in a high-pitched, nasal way: *"Quisling, quisling, your father is a quisling!"*

"What's that you call him?"

"Quisling."

"He is not."

"He is! He is! *Quisling, quisling, your father is a quisling!"*

Khalid had no idea what a quisling was. But no one was going to call his father names. Much as he hated Richie, he knew he could not allow that. It was something Richie had taught him: *Defend yourself against scorn, boy, at all times.* He meant against those who might be rude to Khalid because he was part Pakistani; but Khalid had experienced very little of that. Was a quisling someone who was English but had had a child with a Pakistani woman? Perhaps that was it. Why would these children care, though? Why would anyone?

"Quisling, quisling—"

Khalid threw down his package and lunged at the closest boy, who darted away. He caught the girl by the arm, but he would not hit a girl, and so he simply shoved her into the other boy, who went spinning up against the side of the market building. Khalid pounced on him there, holding him close to the wall with one hand and furiously hitting him with the other.

His two companions seemed unwilling to intervene. But they went on chanting, from a safe distance, more nasally than ever.

"Quis-ling, quis-ling, your fa-ther is a quis-ling!"

"Stop that!" Khalid cried. "You have no right!" He punctuated his words with blows. The boy he was holding was bleeding, now, his nose, the side of his mouth. He looked terrified.

"Quis-ling, quis-ling—"

They would not stop, and neither would Khalid. But then he felt a hand seizing him by the back of his neck, a big adult hand, and he was yanked backward and thrust against the market wall himself. A vast meaty man, a navvy, from the looks of him, loomed over Khalid. "What do you think you're doing, you dirty Paki garbage? You'll kill the boy!"

"He said my father was a quisling!"

"Well, then, he probably is. Get on with you, now, boy! Get on with you!"

He gave Khalid one last hard shove, and spat and walked away. Khalid looked sullenly around for his three tormentors, but they had run off already. They had taken the packet of lamb with them, too.

That night, while Aissha was improvising something for dinner out of yesterday's rice and some elderly chicken, Khalid asked her what a quisling was. She spun around on him as though he had cursed Allah to her ears. Her face all ablaze with a ferocity he had not seen in it before, she said, "Never use that word in this house, Khalid. Never! Never!" And that was all the explanation she would give. Khalid had to learn, on his own, what a quisling was; and when he did, which was soon thereafter, he understood why his father had been unafraid, that day at Stonehenge when they stood outside that curtain of light and looked upon the Entities who were strolling among the giant stones. And also why those three children had mocked him in the street. *You just have to fashion your accommodation with them, that's all there is. Yes. Yes. Yes. To fashion your accommodation.*

FOUR: TWENTY YEARS FROM NOW

It was after the time that Richie beat Aissha so severely, and then did worse than that—violated her, raped her—that Khalid definitely decided that he was going to kill an Entity.

Not kill Richie. Kill an Entity.

It was a turning point in Khalid's relationship with his father, and indeed in Khalid's whole life, and in the life of any number of other citizens of Salisbury, Wiltshire, England, that time when Richie hurt Aissha so. Richie had been treating Aissha badly all along, of course. He treated *everyone* badly. He had moved into her house and had taken possession of it as though it were his own. He regarded her as a servant, there purely to do his bidding, and woe betide her if she failed to meet his expectations. She cooked; she cleaned the house; Khalid understood now that sometimes, at his whim, Richie would make her come into his bedroom to amuse him or his friend Syd or both of them together. And there was never a word of complaint out of her. She did as he wished; she showed no sign of anger or even resentment; she had given herself over entirely to the will of Allah. Khalid, who had not yet managed to find any convincing evidence of Allah's existence, had not. But he had learned the art of accepting the unacceptable from Aissha. He knew better than to try to change what was unchangeable. So he lived with his hatred of Richie, and that was merely a fact of daily existence, like the fact that rain did not fall upward.

Now, though, Richie had gone too far.

Coming home plainly drunk, red-faced, enraged over something, muttering to himself. Greeting Aissha with a growling curse, Khalid with a stinging slap. No apparent reason for either. Demanding his dinner early. Getting it, not liking what he got. Aissha offering mild explanations of why beef had not been available today. Richie shouting that beef bloody well *should* have been available to the household of Richie Burke.

So far, just normal Richie behavior when Richie was having a bad day. Even sweeping the serving-bowl of curried mutton off the table, sending it shattering, thick oily brown sauce splattering everywhere, fell within the normal Richie range.

But then, Aissha saying softly, despondently, looking down at what had been her prettiest remaining sari now spotted in twenty places, "You have stained my clothing." And Richie going over the top. Erupting. Berserk. Wrath out of all measure to the offense, if offense there had been.

Leaping at her, bellowing, shaking her, slapping her. Punching her, even. In the face. In the chest. Seizing the sari at her midriff, ripping it away, tearing it in shreds, crumpling them and hurling them at her. Aissha backing away from him, trembling, eyes bright with fear, dabbing at the blood that seeped from her cut lower lip with one hand, spreading the other one out to cover herself at the thighs.

Khalid staring, not knowing what to do, horrified, furious.

Richie yelling. "I'll stain you, I will! I'll give you a sodding stain!" Grabbing her by the wrist, pulling away what remained of her clothing, stripping her all but naked right there in the dining room. Khalid covering his face. His own grandmother, forty years old, decent, respectable, naked before him: how could he look? And yet how could he tolerate what was happening? Richie dragging her out of the room, now, toward his bedroom, not troubling even to close the door. Hurling her down on his bed, falling on top of her. Grunting like a pig, a pig, a pig, a pig.

I must not permit this.

Khalid's breast surged with hatred: a cold hatred, almost dispassionate. The man was inhuman, a jinni. Some jinn were harmless, some were evil; but Richie was surely of the evil kind, a demon.

His father. An evil jinni.

But what did that make him? What? What? What? What?

Khalid found himself going into the room after them, against all prohibitions, despite all risks. Seeing Richie plunked between Aissha's legs, his shirt pulled up, his trousers pulled down, his bare buttocks pumping in the air. And Aissha staring upward past Richie's shoulder at the frozen Khalid in the doorway, her face a rigid mask of horror and shame: gesturing to him, making a repeated brushing movement of her hand through the air, wordlessly telling him to go away, to get out of the room, not to watch, not to intervene in any way.

He ran from the house and crouched cowering amid the rubble in the rear yard, the old stewpots and broken jugs and his own collection of Arch's empty whiskey bottles. When he returned, an hour later, Richie was in his room, chopping malevolently at the strings of his guitar, singing some droning tune in a low, boozy voice. Aissha was dressed again, moving about in a slow, downcast way, cleaning up the mess in the dining room. Sobbing softly. Saying nothing, not even looking at Khalid as he entered. A sticking-plaster on her lip. Her cheeks looked puffy and bruised. There seemed to be a wall around her. She was sealed away inside herself, sealed from all the world, even from him.

"I will kill him," Khalid said quietly to her.

"No. That you will not do." Aissha's voice was deep and remote, a voice from the bottom of the sea.

She gave him a little to eat, a cold chapati and some of yesterday's rice, and sent him to his room. He lay awake for hours, listening to the sounds of the house, Richie's endless drunken droning song, Aissha's barely audible sobs. In the morning nobody said anything about anything.

Khalid understood that it was impossible for him to kill his own father, however much he hated him. But Richie had to be punished for what he had done. And so, to punish him, Khalid was going to kill an Entity.

The Entities were a different matter. They were fair game.

For some time now, on his better days, Richie had been taking Khalid along with him as he drove through the countryside, doing his quisling tasks, gathering information that the Entities wanted to know and turning it over to them by some process that Khalid could not even begin to understand, and by this time Khalid had seen Entities on so many different occasions that he had grown quite accustomed to being in their presence.

And had no fear of them. To most people, apparently, Entities were scary things, ghastly alien monsters, evil, strange; but to Khalid they still were, as they always had been, creatures of enormous beauty. Beautiful the way a god would be beautiful. How could you be frightened by anything so beautiful? How could you be frightened of a god?

They didn't ever appear to notice him at all. Richie would go up to one of them and stand before it, and some kind of transaction would take place. While that was going on, Khalid simply stood to one side, looking at the Entity, studying it, lost in admiration of its beauty. Richie offered no explanations of these meetings and Khalid never asked.

The Entities grew more beautiful in his eyes every time he saw one. They were beautiful beyond belief. He could almost have worshipped them. It seemed to him that Richie felt the same way about them: that he was caught in their spell, that he would gladly fall down before them and bow his forehead to the ground.

And so.

I will kill one of them, Khalid thought.

Because they are so beautiful. Because my father, who works for them, must love them almost as much as he loves himself, and I will kill the thing he loves. He says he hates them, but I think it is not so: I think he loves them, and that is why he works for them. Or else he loves them and hates them both. He may feel the same way about himself. But I see the light that comes into his eyes when he looks upon them.

So I will kill one, yes. Because by killing one of them I will be killing some part of *him*. And maybe there will be some other value in my doing it, besides.

FIVE: TWENTY-TWO YEARS FROM NOW

Richie Burke said, "Look at this goddamned thing, will you, Ken? Isn't it the goddamnedest fantastic piece of shit anyone ever imagined?"

They were in what had once been the main dining room of the old defunct restaurant. It was early afternoon. Aissha was elsewhere, Khalid had no idea where. His father was holding something that seemed something like a rifle, or perhaps a highly streamlined shotgun, but it was like no rifle or shotgun he had ever seen. It was a long, slender tube of greenish-blue metal with a broad flaring muzzle and what might have been some type of gunsight mounted midway down the barrel and a curious sort of computerized trigger arrangement on the stock. A one-of-a-kind sort of thing, custom made, a home inventor's pride and joy.

"Is it a weapon, would you say?"

"A weapon? A weapon? What the bloody hell do you *think* it is, boy? It's a fucking Entity-killing gun! Which I confiscated this very day from a nest of conspirators over Warminster way. The whole batch of them are under lock and key this very minute, thank you very much, and I've brought Exhibit A home for safe keeping. Have a good look, lad. Ever seen anything so diabolical?"

Khalid realized that Richie was actually going to let him handle it. He took it with enormous care, letting it rest on both his outstretched palms. The barrel was cool and very smooth, the gun lighter than he had expected it to be.

"How does it work, then?"

"Pick it up. Sight along it. You know how it's done. Just like an ordinary gunsight."

Khalid put it to his shoulder, right there in the room. Aimed at the fireplace. Peered along the barrel.

A few inches of the fireplace were visible in the crosshairs, in the most minute detail. Keen magnification, wonderful optics. Touch the right stud, now, and the whole side of the house would be blown out, was that it? Khalid ran his hand along the butt.

"There's a safety on it," Richie said. "The little red button. There. That. Mind you don't hit it by accident. What we have here, boy, is nothing less than a rocket-powered grenade gun. A bomb-throwing machine, virtually. You wouldn't believe it, because it's so skinny, but what it hurls is a very graceful little projectile that will explode with almost incredible force and cause an extraordinary amount of damage, altogether extraordinary. I know because I tried it. It was amazing, seeing what that thing could do."

"Is it loaded now?"

"Oh, yes, yes, you bet your little brown rump it is! Loaded and ready! An absolutely diabolical Entity-killing machine, the product of months and months of loving work by a little band of desperados with marvelous mechanical skills. As stupid as they come, though, for all their skills.—Here, boy, let me have that thing before you set it off somehow."

Khalid handed it over.

"Why stupid?" he asked. "It seems very well made."

"I *said* they were skillful. This is a goddamned triumph of miniaturization, this little cannon. But what makes them think they could kill an Entity at all? Don't they imagine anyone's ever tried? Can't be done, Ken, boy. Nobody ever has, nobody ever will."

Unable to take his eyes from the gun, Khalid said obligingly, "And why is that, sir?"

"Because they're bloody unkillable!"

"Even with something like this? Almost incredible force, you said, sir. An extraordinary amount of damage."

"It would fucking well blow an Entity to smithereens, it would, if you could ever hit one with it. Ah, but the trick is to succeed in firing your shot, boy! Which cannot be done. Even as you're taking your aim, they're reading your bloody mind, that's what they do. They know exactly what you're up to, because they look into our minds

the way we would look into a book. They pick up all your nasty little unfriendly thoughts about them. And then—bam!—they give
you the bloody Push, the thing they do to people with their minds,
you know, and you're done for, piff paff poof. We've heard of four
cases, at least. Attempted Entity assassination. Trying to take a shot
as an Entity went by. Found the bodies, the weapons, just so much
trash by the roadside." Richie ran his hands up and down the gun,
fondling it almost lovingly. "—This gun here, it's got an unusually
great range, terrific sight, will fire upon the target from an enormous distance. Still wouldn't work, I wager you. They can do their
telepathy on you from three hundred yards away. Maybe five hundred. Who knows, maybe a thousand. Still, a damned good thing that
we broke this ring up in time. Just in case they could have pulled it
off somehow."

"It would be bad if an Entity was killed, is that it?" Khalid asked.

Richie guffawed. "Bad? Bad? It would be a bloody catastrophe. You
know what they did, the one time anybody managed to damage them
in any way? No, how in hell would you know? It was right around
the moment you were getting born. Some buggerly American idiots
launched a laser attack from space on an Entity building. Maybe killed
a few, maybe didn't, but the Entities paid us back by letting loose a
plague on us that wiped out damn near every other person there was
in the world. Right here in Salisbury they were keeling over like flies.
Had it myself. Thought I'd die. Damned well hoped I *would*, I felt so
bad. Then I arose from my bed of pain and threw it off. But we don't
want to risk bringing down another plague, do we, now? Or any other
sort of miserable punishment that they might choose to inflict. Because
they certainly will inflict one. One thing that has been clear from the
beginning is that our masters will take no shit from us, no, lad, not one
solitary molecule of shit."

He crossed the room and unfastened the door of the cabinet that
had held Khan's Mogul Palace's meager stock of wine in the long-gone
era when this building had been a licensed restaurant. Thrusting the
weapon inside, Richie said, "This is where it's going to spend the night.
You will make no reference to its presence when Aissha gets back. I'm
expecting Arch to come here tonight, and you will make no reference
to it to him, either. It is a top secret item, do you hear me? I show it to
you because I love you, boy, and because I want you to know that your
father has saved the world this day from a terrible disaster, but I don't

want a shred of what I have shared with you just now to reach the ears of another human being. Or another inhuman being for that matter. Is that clear, boy? Is it?"

"I will not say a word," said Khalid.

✹

And said none. But thought quite a few.

All during the evening, as Arch and Richie made their methodical way through Arch's latest bottle of rare pre-Conquest whiskey, salvaged from some vast horde found by the greatest of good luck in a Southampton storehouse, Khalid clutched to his own bosom the knowledge that there was, right there in that cabinet, a device that was capable of blowing the head off an Entity, if only one could manage to get within firing range without announcing one's lethal intentions.

Was there a way of achieving that? Khalid had no idea.

But perhaps the range of this device was greater than the range of the Entities' mind-reading capacities. Or perhaps not. Was it worth the gamble? Perhaps it was. Or perhaps not.

Aissha went to her room soon after dinner, once she and Khalid had cleared away the dinner dishes. She said little these days, kept mainly to herself, drifted through her life like a sleepwalker. Richie had not laid a violent hand on her again, since that savage evening several years back, but Khalid understood that she still harbored the pain of his humiliation of her, that in some ways she had never really recovered from what Richie had done to her that night. Nor had Khalid.

He hovered in the hall, listening to the sounds from his father's room until he felt certain that Arch and Richie had succeeded in drinking themselves into their customary stupor. Ear to the door: silence. A faint snore or two, maybe.

He forced himself to wait another ten minutes. Still quiet in there. Delicately he pushed the door, already slightly ajar, another few inches open. Peered cautiously within.

Richie slumped head down at the table, clutching in one hand a glass that still had a little whiskey in it, cradling his guitar between his chest and knee with the other. Arch on the floor opposite him, head dangling to one side, eyes closed, limbs sprawled every which way. Snoring, both of them. Snoring. Snoring. Snoring.

Good. Let them sleep very soundly.

Khalid took the Entity-killing gun now from the cabinet. Caressed its satiny barrel. It was an elegant thing, this weapon. He admired its design. He had an artist's eye for form and texture and color, did Khalid: some fugitive gene out of forgotten antiquity miraculously surfacing in him after a dormancy of centuries, the eye of a Gandharan sculptor, of a Rajput architect, a Gujerati miniaturist coming to the fore in him after passing through all those generations of the peasantry. Lately he had begun doing little sketches, making some carvings. Hiding everything away so that Richie would not find it. That was the sort of thing that might offend Richie, his taking up such piffling pastimes. Sports, drinking, driving around: those were proper amusements for a man.

On one of his good days last year Richie had brought a bicycle home for him: a startling gift, for bicycles were rarities nowadays, none having been available, let alone manufactured, in England in ages. Where Richie had obtained it, from whom, with what brutality, Khalid did not like to think. But he loved his bike. Rode long hours through the countryside on it, every chance he had. It was his freedom; it was his wings. He went outside now, carrying the grenade gun, and carefully strapped it to the bicycle's basket.

He had waited nearly three years for this moment to make itself possible.

Nearly every night nowadays, Khalid knew, one could usually see Entities traveling about on the road between Salisbury and Stonehenge, one or two of them at a time, riding in those cars of theirs that floated a little way above the ground on cushions of air. Stonehenge was a major center of Entity activities nowadays and there were more and more of them in the vicinity all the time. Perhaps there would be one out there this night, he thought. It was worth the chance: he would not get a second opportunity with this captured gun that his father had brought home.

About halfway out to Stonehenge there was a place on the plain where he could have a good view of the road from a little copse several hundred yards away. Khalid had no illusion that hiding in the copse would protect him from the mind-searching capacities the Entities were said to have. If they could detect him at all, the fact that he was standing in the shadow of a leafy tree would not make the slightest difference. But it was a place to wait, on this bright moonlit night. It was a place where he could feel alone, unwatched.

He went to it. He waited there.

He listened to night-noises. An owl; the rustling of the breeze through the trees; some small nocturnal animal scrabbling in the underbrush.

He was utterly calm.

Khalid had studied calmness all his life, with his grandmother Aissha as his tutor. From his earliest days he had watched her stolid acceptance of poverty, of shame, of hunger, of loss, of all kinds of pain. He had seen her handling the intrusion of Richie Burke into her household and her life with philosophical detachment, with stoic patience. To her it was all the will of Allah, not to be questioned. Allah was less real to Khalid than He was to Aissha, but Khalid had drawn from her her infinite patience and tranquility, at least, if not her faith in God. Perhaps he might find his way to God later on. At any rate, he had long ago learned from Aissha that yielding to anguish was useless, that inner peace was the only key to endurance, that everything must be done calmly, unemotionally, because the alternative was a life of unending chaos and suffering. And so he had come to understand from her that it was possible even to hate someone in a calm, unemotional way. And had contrived thus to live calmly, day by day, with the father whom he loathed.

For the Entities he felt no loathing at all. Far from it. He had never known a world without them, the vanished world where humans had been masters of their own destinies. The Entities, for him, were an innate aspect of life, simply *there*, as were hills and trees, the moon, or the owl who roved the night above him now, cruising for squirrels or rabbits. And they were very beautiful to behold, like the moon, like an owl moving silently overhead, like a massive chestnut tree.

He waited, and the hours passed, and in his calm way he began to realize that he might not get his chance tonight, for he knew he needed to be home and in his bed before Richie awakened and could find him and the weapon gone. Another hour, two at most, that was all he could risk out here.

Then he saw turquoise light on the highway, and knew that an Entity vehicle was approaching, coming from the direction of Salisbury. It pulled into view a moment later, carrying two of the creatures standing serenely upright, side by side, in their strange wagon that floated on a cushion of air.

Khalid beheld it in wonder and awe. And once again marveled, as ever, at their elegance of these Entities, their grace, their luminescent splendor.

How beautiful you are! Oh, yes. Yes.

They moved past him on their curious cart as though traveling on a river of light, and it seemed to him, dispassionately studying the one on the side closer to him, that what he beheld here was surely a jinni of the jinn: Allah's creature, a thing made of smokeless fire, a separate creation. Which none the less must in the end stand before Allah in judgment, even as we.

How beautiful. How beautiful.

I love you.

He loved it, yes. For its crystalline beauty. A jinni? No, it was a higher sort of being than that; it was an angel. It was a being of pure light—of cool clear fire, without smoke. He was lost in rapt admiration of its angelic perfection.

Loving it, admiring it, even worshipping it, Khalid calmly lifted the grenade gun to his shoulder, calmly aimed, calmly stared through the gun-sight. Saw the Entity, distant as it was, transfixed perfectly in the crosshairs. Calmly he released the safety, as Richie had inadvertently showed him how to do. Calmly put his finger to the firing stud.

His soul was filled all the while with love for the beautiful creature before him as—calmly, calmly, calmly—he pressed the stud. He heard a whooshing sound and felt the weapon kicking back against his shoulder with astonishing force, sending him thudding into a tree behind him and for a moment knocking the breath from him; and an instant later the left side of the beautiful creature's head exploded into a cascading fountain of flame, a shower of radiant fragments. A greenish-red mist of what must be alien blood appeared and went spreading outward into the air.

The stricken Entity swayed and fell backward, dropping out of sight on the floor of the wagon.

In that same moment the second Entity, the one that was riding on the far side, underwent so tremendous a convulsion that Khalid wondered if he had managed to kill it, too, with that single shot. It stumbled forward, then back, and crashed against the railing of the wagon with such violence that Khalid imagined he could hear the thump. Its great tubular body writhed and shook, and seemed even to change color, the purple hue deepening almost to black for an instant and the orange spots becoming a fiery red. At so great a distance it was hard to be sure, but Khalid thought, also, that its leathery hide was rippling and puckering as if in a demonstration of almost unendurable pain.

It must be feeling the agony of its companion's death, he realized. Watching the Entity lurch around blindly on the platform of the wagon in what had to be terrible pain, Khalid's soul flooded with compassion for the creature, and sorrow, and love. It was unthinkable to fire again. He had never had any intention of killing more than one; but in any case he knew that he was no more capable of firing a shot at this stricken survivor now than he would be of firing at Aissha.

During all this time the wagon had been moving silently onward as though nothing had happened; and in a moment more it turned the bend in the road and was gone from Khalid's sight, down the road that led toward Stonehenge.

He stood for a while watching the place where the vehicle had been when he had fired the fatal shot. There was nothing there now, no sign that anything had occurred. *Had* anything occurred? Khalid felt neither satisfaction nor grief nor fear nor, really, any emotion of any other sort. His mind was all but blank. He made a point of keeping it that way, knowing he was as good as dead if he relaxed his control even for a fraction of a second.

Strapping the gun to the bicycle basket again, he pedaled quietly back toward home. It was well past midnight; there was no one at all on the road. At the house, all was as it had been; Arch's car parked in front, the front lights still on, Richie and Arch snoring away in Richie's room.

Only now, safely home, did Khalid at last allow himself the luxury of letting the jubilant thought cross his mind, just for a moment, that had been flickering at the threshold of his consciousness for an hour:

Got you, Richie! Got you, you bastard!

He returned the grenade gun to the cabinet and went to bed, and was asleep almost instantly, and slept soundly until the first bird-song of dawn.

In the tremendous uproar that swept Salisbury the next day, with Entity vehicles everywhere and platoons of the glossy balloon-like aliens that everybody called Spooks going from house to house, it was Khalid himself who provided the key clue to the mystery of the assassination that had occurred in the night.

"You know, I think it might have been my father who did it," he said almost casually, in town, outside the market, to a boy named Thomas whom he knew in a glancing sort of way. "He came home yesterday with a strange sort of big gun. Said it was for killing Entities with, and put it away in a cabinet in our front room."

Thomas would not believe that Khalid's father was capable of such a gigantic act of heroism as assassinating an Entity. No, no, no, Khalid argued eagerly, in a tone of utter and sublime disingenuousness: he did it, I know he did it, he's always talked of wanting to kill one of them one of these days, and now he has.

He has?

Always his greatest dream, yes, indeed.

Well, then—

Yes. Khalid moved along. So did Thomas. Khalid took care to go nowhere near the house all that morning. The last person he wanted to see was Richie. But he was safe in that regard. By noon Thomas evidently had spread the tale of Khalid Burke's wild boast about the town with great effectiveness, because word came traveling through the streets around that time that a detachment of Spooks had gone to Khalid's house and had taken Richie Burke away.

"What about my grandmother?" Khalid asked. "She wasn't arrested too, was she?"

"No, it was just him," he was told. "Billy Cavendish saw them taking him, and he was all by himself. Yelling and screaming, he was, the whole time, like a man being hauled away to be hanged."

Khalid never saw his father again.

During the course of the general reprisals that followed the killing, the entire population of Salisbury and five adjacent towns was rounded up and transported to walled detention camps near Portsmouth. A good many of the deportees were executed within the next few days, seemingly by random selection, no pattern being evident in the choosing of those who were put to death. At the beginning of the following week the survivors were sent on from Portsmouth to other places, some of them quite remote, in various parts of the world.

Khalid was not among those executed. He was merely sent very far away.

He felt no guilt over having survived the death-lottery while others around him were being slain for his murderous act. He had trained himself since childhood to feel very little indeed, even while aiming a rifle at one of Earth's beautiful and magnificent masters. Besides, what affair was it of his, that some of these people were dying and he was allowed to live? Everyone died, some sooner, some later. Aissha would have said that what was happening was the will of Allah. Khalid more simply put it that the Entities did as they pleased, always, and knew that it was folly to ponder their motives.

Aissha was not available to discuss these matters with. He was separated from her before reaching Portsmouth and Khalid never saw her again, either. From that day on it was necessary for him to make his way in the world on his own.

He was not quite thirteen years old. Often, in the years ahead, he would look back at the time when he had slain the Entity; but he would think of it only as the time when he had rid himself of Richie Burke, for whom he had had such hatred. For the Entities he had no hatred at all, and when his mind returned to that event by the roadside on the way to Stonehenge, to the alien being centered in the crosshairs of his weapon, he would think only of the marvelous color and form of the two starborn creatures in the floating wagon, of that passing moment of beauty in the night.

CALL ME TITAN

Roger Zelazny jumped into the science-fiction arena midway through the 1960s, scattering masterpieces right and left with joyous abandon: "A Rose for Ecclesiastes", This Immortal, "The Doors of His Face, the Lamps of His Mouth," The Dream Master, Lord of Light, and many, many more, all appearing within a few years of each other and gathering him wide acclaim and a shelf full of Hugo and Nebula awards.

Something else that Roger gathered during those years was an assortment of friends who loved him greatly—for, though he was a shy man, he was a sweet and gracious one, and everyone who came in contact with him liked him on first meeting and liked him more and more as acquaintance deepened. I met Roger somewhere around 1966 and, like everybody else, I found him immediately congenial: we became close friends, visited each other frequently, exchanged bits of professional helpfulness. I found him a man of high good humor, warm good will, and great patience, as I learned when the inordinately punctual Robert Silverberg showed up an hour late for dinner with him two times running in consecutive years, for a different silly reason each time. (Both had something to do with the time-zone difference separating California and New Mexico.) It was a somber moment when I discovered in the autumn of 1994 that Roger was seriously ill, and a stunning one when I learned of his death from cancer the following June at the age of 58.

A memorial anthology soon was in the works, under the aegis of that master anthologist, Martin H. Greenberg. Marty called it Lord of the Fantastic: Stories in Honor of Roger Zelazny *and rounded up a group of Roger's friends*

81

to contribute stories. Mine was "Call Me Titan," and in it I attempted to mimic not only Roger's inimitable style but also some of his thematic concerns (the Mediterranean world, the ancient gods, the comic possibilities of the survival of those gods into our own day.) For the few days in January, 1996 that it took me to do it I was able to masquerade in my own mind as Roger Zelazny, and for that reason it was an easy and enjoyable story to write—except for the ugly realization that would surface from time to time that the only reason I was writing it was as a memorial to my dead friend.

The stories in Lord of the Fantastic *were supposed to be previously unpublished ones. Through an error somewhat akin to the time-zone slip-up that had made me late for dinner with Roger (and George R.R. Martin also) twice running, I sold the story to editor Gardner Dozois of* Asimov's Science Fiction, *where it made its first appearance in the world in the February, 1997 issue, many months ahead of the Greenberg anthology. I could do nothing but apologize. Luckily, Marty Greenberg, like Roger Zelazny, was a sweet, lovable, and patient man, and he forgave me for my malfeasance. Would that all my sins were so readily forgiven.*

<hr />

In Memoriam: RZ

How did *you* get loose?" the woman who was Aphrodite asked me.

"It happened. Here I am."

"Yes," she said. "You. Of all of them, you. In this lovely place." She waved at the shining sun-bright sea, the glittering white stripe of the beach, the whitewashed houses, the bare brown hills. A lovely place, yes, this isle of Mykonos. "And what are you going to do now?"

"What I was created to do," I told her. "*You* know."

She considered that. We were drinking ouzo on the rocks, on the hotel patio, beneath a hanging array of fishermen's nets. After a moment she laughed, that irresistible tinkling laugh of hers, and clinked her glass against mine.

"Lots of luck," she said.

That was Greece. Before that was Sicily, and the mountain, and the eruption....

The mountain had trembled and shaken and belched, and the red streams of molten fire began to flow downward from the ashen top, and in the first ten minutes of the eruption six little towns around the slopes were wiped out. It happened just that fast. They shouldn't have been there, but they were, and then they weren't. Too bad for them. But it's always a mistake to buy real estate on Mount Etna.

The lava was really rolling. It would reach the city of Catania in a couple of hours and take out its whole northeastern quarter, and all of Sicily would be in mourning the next day. Some eruption. The biggest of all time, on this island where big eruptions have been making the news since the dinosaur days.

As for me, I couldn't be sure what was happening up there at the summit, not yet. I was still down deep, way down, three miles from sunlight.

But in my jail cell down there beneath the roots of the giant volcano that is called Mount Etna I could tell from the shaking and the noise and the heat that this one was something special. That the prophesied Hour of Liberation had come round at last for me, after five hundred centuries as the prisoner of Zeus.

I stretched and turned and rolled over, and sat up for the first time in fifty thousand years.

Nothing was pressing down on me.

Ugly limping Hephaestus, my jailer, had set up his forge right on top of me long ago, his heavy anvils on my back. And had merrily hammered bronze and iron all day and all night for all he was worth, that clomp-legged old master craftsman. Where was Hephaestus now? Where were his anvils?

Not on me. Not any longer.

That was *good*, that feeling of nothing pressing down.

I wriggled my shoulders. That took time. You have a lot of shoulders to wriggle, when you have a hundred heads, give or take three or four.

"Hephaestus?" I yelled, yelling it out of a hundred mouths at once. I felt the mountain shivering and convulsing above me, and I knew that my voice alone was enough to make great slabs of it fall off and go tumbling down, down, down.

No answer from Hephaestus. No clangor of his forge, either. He just wasn't there any more.

I tried again, a different, greater name.

"Zeus?"

Silence.

"You hear me, Zeus?"

No reply.

"Where the hell are you? Where is everybody?"

All was silence, except for the hellish roaring of the volcano.

Well, okay, *don't* answer me. Slowly I got to my feet, extending myself to my full considerable height. The fabric of the mountain gave way for me. I have that little trick.

Another good feeling, that was, rising to an upright position. Do you know what it's like, not being allowed to stand, not even once, for fifty thousand years? But of course you don't, little ones. How could you?

One more try. *"ZEUS???"*

All my hundred voices crying his name at once, fortissimo fortissimo. A chorus of booming echoes. Every one of my heads had grown back, over the years. I was healed of all that Zeus had done to me. That was especially good, knowing that I was healed. Things had looked really bad, for a while.

Well, no sense just standing there and caterwauling, if nobody was going to answer me back. This was the Hour of Liberation, after all. I was free—my chains fallen magically away, my heads all sprouted again. Time to get out of here. I started to move.

Upward. Outward.

I moved up through the mountain's bulk as though it was so much air. The rock was nothing to me. Unimpeded I rose past the coiling internal chambers through which the lava was racing up toward the summit vent, and came out into the sunlight, and clambered up the snow-kissed slopes of the mountain to the ash-choked summit itself, and stood there right in the very center of the eruption as the volcano puked its blazing guts out. I grinned a hundred big grins on my hundred faces, with hot fierce winds swirling like swords around my head and torrents of lava flowing down all around me. The view from up there was terrific. And what a fine feeling that was, just looking around at the world again after all that time underground.

There below me off to the east was the fish-swarming sea. Over there behind me, the serried tree-thickened hills. Above me, the fire-hearted sun.

What beautiful sights they all were!

CALL ME TITAN

"Hoo-*ha!*" I cried.

My jubilant roar went forth from that lofty mountaintop in Sicily like a hundred hurricanes at once. The noise of it broke windows in Rome and flattened farmhouses in Sardinia and knocked over ten mosques deep in the Tunisian Sahara. But the real blast was aimed eastward across the water, over toward Greece, and it went across that peninsula like a scythe, taking out half the treetops from Agios Nikolaus on the Ionian side to Athens over on the Aegean, and kept on going clear into Turkey.

It was a little signal, so to speak. I was heading that way myself, with some very ancient scores to settle.

I started down the mountainside, fast. The lava surging all around my thudding feet meant nothing to me.

Call me Typhoeus. Call me Titan.

I suppose I might have attracted a bit of attention as I made my way down those fiery slopes and past all the elegant seaside resorts that now were going crazy with hysteria over the eruption, and went striding into the sea midway between Fiumefreddo and Taormina. I am, after all, something of a monster, by your standards: four hundred feet high, let us say, with all those heads, dragon heads at that, and eyes that spurt flame, and thick black bristles everywhere on my body and swarms of coiling vipers sprouting from my thighs. The gods themselves have been known to turn and run at the mere sight of me. Some of them, once upon a time, fled all the way to Egypt when I yelled "Boo!"

But perhaps the eruption and the associated earthquakes kept the people of eastern Sicily so very preoccupied just then that they didn't take time to notice what sort of being it was that was walking down the side of Mount Etna and perambulating off toward the sea. Or maybe they didn't believe their eyes. Or it could be that they simply nodded and said, "Sure. Why not?"

I hit the water running and put my heads down and swam swiftly Greeceward across the cool blue sea without even bothering to come up for breath. What would have been the point? The air behind me smelled of fire and brimstone. And I was in a hurry.

Zeus, I thought. *I'm coming to get you, you bastard!*

As I said, I'm a Titan. It's the family name, not a description. We Titans were the race of Elder Gods—the first drafts, so to speak, for the deities that you people would eventually worship—the ones that Zeus walloped into oblivion long before Bill Gates came down from

Mount Sinai with MS-DOS. Long before Homer sang. Long before the Flood. Long before, as a matter of fact, anything that might mean anything to you.

Gaea was our mother. The Earth, in other words. The mother of us all, really.

In the early days of the world broad-bosomed Gaea brought forth all sorts of gods and giants and monsters. Out of her came far-seeing Uranus, the sky, and then he and Gaea created the first dozen Titans, Oceanus and Cronus and Rhea and that bunch.

The original twelve Titans spawned a lot of others: Atlas, who now holds up the world, and tricky Prometheus, who taught humans how to use fire and got himself the world's worst case of cirrhosis for his trouble, and silly scatterbrained Epimetheus, who had that thing with Pandora, and so on. There were snake-limbed giants like Porphyrion and Alcyoneus, and hundred-armed fifteen-headed beauties like Briareus and Cottus and Gyes, and other oversized folk like the three one-eyed Cyclopes, Arges of the storms and Brontes of the thunder and Steropes of the lightning, and so on. Oh, what a crowd we were!

The universe was our oyster, so I'm told. It must have been good times for all and sundry. I hadn't been born yet, in that era when Uranus was king.

But very early on there was that nasty business between Uranus and his son Cronus, which ended very badly for Uranus, the bloody little deal with the sharp sickle, and Cronus became the top god for a while, until he made the mistake of letting Zeus get born. That was it, for Cronus. In this business you have to watch out for overambitious sons. Cronus tried—he swallowed each of his children as they were born, to keep them from doing to him what he had done to Uranus—but Zeus, the last-born, eluded him. Very unfortunate for Cronus.

Family history. Dirty linen.

As for Zeus, who as you can see showed up on the scene quite late but eventually came to be in charge of things, he's my half-sister Rhea's son, so I suppose you'd call him my nephew. I call him my nemesis.

After Zeus had finished off Cronus he mopped up the rest of the Titans in a series of wild wars, thunderbolts ricocheting all over the place, the seas boiling, whole continents going up in flame. Some of us stayed neutral and some of us, I understand, actually allied themselves with him, but none of that made any difference. When all the shouting was over the whole pack of Titans were all prisoners in various disagreeable places, such as, for example, deep down underneath Mount Etna with the forge of Hephaestus sitting on your back; and Zeus and his outfit, Hades and Poseidon and Apollo and Aphrodite and the rest, ruled the roost.

I was Gaea's final experiment in maternity, the youngest of the Titans, born very late in the war with Zeus. Her final monster, some would say, because of my unusual looks and size. Tartarus was my father: the Underworld, he is. I was born restless. Dangerous, too. My job was to avenge the family against the outrages Zeus had perpetrated on the rest of us. I came pretty close, too.

And now I was looking for my second chance.

Greece had changed a lot since I last had seen it. Something called civilization had happened in the meanwhile. Highways, gas stations, telephone poles, billboards, high-rise hotels, all those nice things.

Still and all, it didn't look so very bad. That killer blue sky with the golden blink in it, the bright sparkle of the low rolling surf, the white-walled cubes of houses climbing up the brown knifeblade hillsides: a handsome land, all things considered.

I came ashore at the island of Zakynthos on the Peloponnesian coast. There was a pleasant waterfront town there with an old fortress on a hilltop and groves of olives and cypresses all around. The geological disturbances connected with my escape from my prison cell beneath Mount Etna did not appear to have done much damage here.

I decided that it was probably not a great idea to let myself be seen in my actual form, considering how monstrous I would look to mortal eyes and the complications that that would create for me. And so, as I approached the land, I acquired a human body that I found swimming a short way off shore at one of the beachfront hotels.

It was a serviceable, athletic he-body, a lean, trim one, not young but full of energy, craggy-faced, a long jaw and a long sharp nose and a high forehead. I checked out his mind. Bright, sharp, observant. And packed with data, both standard and quirkily esoteric. All that stuff about Bill Gates and Homer and high-rises and telephone poles: I got that from him. And how to behave like a human being. And a whole lot more, all of which I suspected would be useful to acquire.

A questing, creative mind. A good person. I liked him. I decided to use him.

In half a wink I transformed myself into a simulacrum of him and went on up the beach into town, leaving him behind just as he had been, all unknowing. The duplication wouldn't matter. Nobody was likely to care that there were two of him wandering around Greece at the same time, unless they saw both of us at the same moment, which wasn't going to happen.

I did a little further prowling behind his forehead and learned that he was a foreigner in Greece, a tourist. Married, three children, a house on a hillside in a dry country that looked a little like Greece, but was far away. Spoke a language called English, knew a smattering of other tongues. Not much Greek. That would be okay: I have my ways of communicating.

To get around the countryside properly, I discovered, I was going to need land-clothing, money, and a passport. I took care of these matters. Details like those don't pose problems for such as we.

Then I went rummaging in his mind to see whether he had any information in there about the present whereabouts of Zeus.

It was a very orderly mind. He had Zeus filed under "Greek Mythology." *Mythology?*

Yes. Yes! He knew about Gaea, and Uranus, and the overthrow of Uranus by Cronus. He knew about the other Titans, at any rate some of them—Prometheus, Rhea, Hyperion, Iapetus. He knew some details about a few of the giants and miscellaneous hundred-armed monsters, and about the war between Zeus and the Titans and the Titans' total downfall, and the takeover by the big guy and his associates, Poseidon and Apollo and Ares & Company. But these were all stories to him. Fables. *Mythology.*

I confess I looked in his well-stocked mental archives for myself, Typhoeus—even a Titan has some vanity, you know—but all I found was a reference that said, "Typhon, child of Hera, is often confused with the earlier Titan Typhoeus, son of Gaea and Tartarus."

Well, yes. The names are similar; but Typhon was the bloated she-dragon that Apollo slew at Delphi, and what does that have to do with me?

That was bad, very bad, to show up in this copiously furnished mind only as a correction of an erroneous reference to someone else. Humiliating, you might actually say. I am not as important as Cronus or Uranus in the scheme of things, I suppose, but I did have my hour of glory, that time I went up against Zeus single-handed and came very close to defeating him. But what was even worse than such neglect, far worse, was to have the whole splendid swaggering tribe of us, from the great mother Gaea and her heavenly consort down to the merest satyr and wood-nymph, tucked away in there as so much mythology.

What had happened to the world, and to its gods, while I lay writhing under Etna?

Mount Olympus seemed a reasonable first place for me to go to look for some answers.

I was at the absolute wrong end of Greece for that: down in the southwestern corner, whereas Olympus is far up in the northeast. All decked out in my new human body and its new human clothes, I caught a hydrofoil ferry to Patra, on the mainland, and another ferry across the Gulf of Corinth to Nafpaktos, and then, by train and bus, made my way up toward Thessaly, where Olympus is. None of these places except Olympus itself had been there last time I was in Greece, nor were there such things as trains or ferries or buses then. But I'm adaptable. I am, after all, an immortal god. A sort of a god, anyway.

It was interesting, sitting among you mortals in those buses and trains. I had never paid much attention to you in the old days, any more than I would give close attention to ants or bumblebees or cockroaches. Back there in the early ages of the world, humans were few and far between, inconsequential experimental wildlife. Prometheus made you, you know, for some obscure reason of his own: made you out of assorted dirt and slime, and breathed life into you, and turned you loose to decorate the landscape. You certainly did a job of decorating it, didn't you?

Sitting there among you in those crowded garlicky trains, breathing your exhalations and smelling your sweat, I couldn't help admiring the persistence and zeal with which you people had covered so much of the world with your houses, your highways, your shopping malls, your amusement parks, your stadiums, your power-transmission lines, and your garbage. Especially your garbage. Very few of these things could be considered any sort of an improvement over the basic virgin terrain, but I had to give you credit for effort, anyway. Prometheus, wherever he might be now, would surely be proud of you.

But where *was* Prometheus? Still chained up on that mountaintop, with Zeus's eagle gnawing away on his liver?

I roamed the minds of my traveling companions, but they weren't educated people like the one I had chanced upon at that beach, and they knew zero about Prometheus. Or anybody else of my own era, for that matter, with the exception of Zeus and Apollo and Athena and a few of the other latecomer gods. Who also were mere mythology to them. Greece had different gods these days, it seemed. Someone called Christos had taken over here. Along with his father and his mother, and assorted lesser deities whose relation to the top ones was hard to figure out.

Who were these new gods? Where had they come from? I was pleased by the thought that Zeus had been pushed aside by this Christos the way he had nudged old Cronus off the throne, but how had it happened? When?

Would I find Christos living on top of Mount Olympus in Zeus's old palace?

Well, no. I very shortly discovered that nobody was living on top of Olympus at all.

The place had lost none of its beauty, infested though modern-day Greece is by you and your kind. The enormous plateau on which the mountain stands is still unspoiled; and Olympus itself rises as ever in that great soaring sweep above the wild, desolate valley, the various summits forming a spectacular natural amphitheater and the upper tiers of rock splendidly shrouded by veils of cloud.

There are some roads going up, now. In the foothills I hired a car and a driver to take me through the forests of chestnut and fir to a refuge hut two thirds of the way up that is used by climbers, and there I left my driver, telling him I would go the rest of the way myself. He gave me a peculiar look, I suppose because I was wearing the wrong kind of clothing for climbing, and had no mountaineering equipment with me.

When he was gone, I shed my borrowed human form and rose up once again taller than the tallest tree in the world, and gave myself a set of gorgeous black-feathered wings as well, and went wafting up into that region of clean, pure air where Zeus had once had his throne.

No throne. No Zeus.

My cousins the giants Otus and Ephialtes had piled Mount Pelion on top of Mount Ossa to get up here during the war of the gods, and were flung right back down again. But I had the place to myself, unchallenged. I hovered over the jagged fleece-kissed peaks of the ultimate summit, spiraling down through the puffs of white cloud, ready for battle, but no battle was offered me.

"Zeus? Zeus?"

Once I had stood against him hissing terror from my grim jaws, and my eyes flaring gorgon lightning that had sent his fellow gods packing in piss-pants terror. But Zeus had withstood me, then. He blasted me with sizzling thunderbolts and seared me to an ash, and hurled me to rack and ruin; and jammed what was left of me down under Mount Etna amid rivers of fire, with the craftsman god Hephaestus piling the tools of his workshop all over me to hold me down, and there I lay for those fifty thousand years, muttering to myself, until I had healed enough to come forth.

I was forth now, all right, and looking for a rematch. Etna had vomited rivers of fire all over the fair plains of Sicily, and I was loose upon the world; but where was my adversary?

"Zeus!" I cried, into the emptiness.

I tried the name of Christos, too, just to see if the new god would answer. No go. He wasn't there either. Olympus was as stunning as ever, but nobody godly seemed to have any use for it these days.

I flew back down to the Alpine Club shelter and turned myself back into the lean-shanked American tourist with the high forehead and the long nose. I think three hikers may have seen me make the transformation, for as I started down the slope I came upon them standing slackjawed and goggle-eyed, as motionless as though Medusa had smitten them into stone.

"Hi, there, fellas," I called to them. "Have a nice day!"

They just gaped. I descended the fir-darkened mountainside to the deep-breasted valley, and just like any hungry mortal I ate dolmades and keftedes and moussaka in a little taverna I found down there, washing it down with a few kilos of retsina. And then, not so much like any mortal, I walked halfway across the country to Athens. It took me a goodly number of days, resting only a few hours every night. The body I had copied was a fundamentally sturdy one, and of course I had bolstered it a little.

A long walk, yes. But I was beginning to comprehend that there was no need for me to hurry, and I wanted to see the sights.

✹

Athens was a horror. It was the kingdom of Hades risen up to the surface of the world. Noise, congestion, all-around general grittiness, indescribable ugliness, everything in a miserable state of disrepair, and the air so thick with foul vapor that you could scratch your initials in it with your fingernails, if you had initials, if you had fingernails.

I knew right away I wasn't going to find any members of the old pantheon in this town. No deity in his right mind would want to spend ten minutes here. But Athens is the city of Athena, and Athena is the goddess of knowledge, and I thought there might be a possibility that somewhere here in her city that I would be able to learn how and why and when the assorted divinities of Greece had made the transition from omnipotence to mythology, and where I might find them (or at least the one I was looking for) now.

I prowled the nightmare streets. Dust and sand and random blocks of concrete everywhere, rusting metal girders standing piled for no particular reason by the side of the road, crumbling buildings. Traffic, frantic and fierce: what a mistake giving up the ox-cart had been! Cheap, tacky shops. Skinny long-legged cats hissed at me. They knew what I was. I hissed right back. We understood each other, at least.

Up on a hilltop in the middle of everything, a bunch of ruined marble temples. The Acropolis, that hilltop is, the highest and holiest place in town. The temples aren't bad, as mortal buildings go, but in terrible shape, fallen columns scattered hither and yon, caryatids eroded to blurs by the air pollution. Why are you people such dreadful custodians of your own best works?

I went up there to look around, thinking I might find some lurking god or demigod in town on a visit. I stood by the best of the tumble-down temples, the one called the Parthenon, and listened to a little man with big eyeglasses who was telling a group of people who looked exactly like him how the building had looked when it was new and Athena was still in town. He spoke a language that my host body didn't understand at all, but I made a few adjustments and comprehended. So many languages, you mortals! *We* all spoke the same language, and that was good enough for us; but we were only gods, I suppose.

When he was through lecturing them about the Parthenon, the tour guide said, "Now we will visit the Sanctuary of Zeus. This way, please."

The Sanctuary of Zeus was just back of the Parthenon, but there really wasn't very much left of it. The tour guide did a little routine about Zeus as father of the gods, getting six facts out of every five wrong.

"Let me tell you a few things about Zeus," I wanted to say, but I didn't. "How he used to cheat at cards, for instance. And the way he couldn't keep his hands off young girls. Or, maybe, the way he bellowed and moaned the first time he and I fought, when I tangled him in the coils of my snakes and laid him low, and cut the tendons of his hands and feet to keep him from getting rambunctious, and locked him up in that cave in Cilicia."

I kept all that to myself. These people didn't look like they'd care to hear any commentary from a stranger. Anyway, if I told that story I'd feel honor bound to go on and explain how that miserable sneak Hermes crept into the cave when I wasn't looking and patched Zeus up—and then how, once Zeus was on his feet again, he came after me and let me have it with such a blast of lightning-bolts that I was fried halfway to a crisp and wound up spending the next few epochs as a prisoner down there under Etna.

A dispiriting place, the Acropolis.

I went slinking down and over to the Plaka, which is the neighborhood in back of it, for some lunch. Human bodies need to be fed again and again, all day long. Swordfish grilled on skewers with onions and tomatoes; more retsina; fruit and cheese. All right. Not bad. Then to the National Museum, a two-hour walk, sweat-sticky and dusty. Where I looked at broken statues and bought a guidebook that told me about the gods whose statues these were. Not even close to the actualities, any of them. Did they seriously think that brawny guy with the beard was Poseidon? And the woman with the tin hat, Athena? And that blowhard—Zeus? Don't make me laugh. Please. My laughter destroys whole cities.

Nowhere in the whole museum were there any representations of Titans. Just Zeus, Apollo, Aphrodite, Poseidon, and the rest of them, the junior varsity, the whole mob of supplanters, over and over and over. It was as if we didn't count at all in the historical record.

That hurt. I was in one hell of a sour mood when I left the museum.

There was a Temple of Olympian Zeus in town, the guidebook said, somewhere back in the vicinity of the Acropolis. I kept hoping that I would find some clue to Zeus's present place of residence at one of the sites that once had been sacred to him. A vestige, a lingering whiff of divinity.

But the Temple of Olympian Zeus was nothing but an incomplete set of ruined columns, and the only whiff I picked up there was the whiff of mortality and decay. And now it was getting dark and the body I was inhabiting was hungry again. Back to the Plaka; grilled meat, wine, a sweet pudding.

Afterwards, as I roamed the winding streets leading down to the newer part of the city with no special purpose in mind, a feeble voice out of a narrow alley said, in the native language of my host body, "Help! Oh, please, help!"

I was not put into this world for the purpose of helping anyone. But the body that I had duplicated in order to get around in modern Greece was evidently the body of a kindly and responsible person, because his reflexes took over instantly, and I found myself heading into that alleyway to see what aid I could render the person who was so piteously crying out.

Deep in the shadows I saw someone—a woman, I realized—lying on the ground in what looked like a pool of blood. I went to her side and knelt by her, and she began to mutter something in a bleary way about being attacked and robbed.

"Can you sit up?" I said, slipping my arm around her back. "It'll be easier for me to carry you if—"

Then I felt a pair of hands grasping me by the shoulders, not gently, and something hard and sharp pressing against the middle of my back, and the supposedly bloodied and battered woman I was trying to help rolled deftly out of my grasp and stepped back without any trouble at all, and a disagreeable rasping voice at my left ear said quietly, "Just give us your wristwatch and your wallet and you won't get hurt at all."

I was puzzled for a moment. I was still far from accustomed to human ways, and it was often necessary to peer into my host-mind to find out what was going on.

Quickly, though, I came to understand that there was such a thing as crime in your world, and that some of it was being tried on me at this very moment. The woman in the alley was bait; I was the prey; two accomplices had been lurking in the shadows.

I suppose I could have given them my wristwatch and wallet without protest, and let them make their escape. What did a wristwatch mean to me? And I could create a thousand new wallets just like the one I had, which I had created also, after all. As for harm, they could do me none with their little knife. I had survived even the lightnings of Zeus. Perhaps I should have reacted with godlike indifference to their little attempt at mugging me.

But it had been a long dreary discouraging day, and a hot one, too. The air was close and vile-smelling. Maybe I had allowed my host body to drink a little too much retsina with dinner. In any event, godlike indifference was not what I displayed just then. Mortal petulance was more like the appropriate term.

"Behold me, fools," I said.

I let them see my true form.

There I was before them, sky-high, mountainous, a horrendous gigantic figure of many heads and fiery eyes and thick black bristles and writhing viperish excrescences, a sight to make even gods quail.

Of course, inasmuch as I'm taller than the tallest tree and appropriately wide, manifesting myself in such a narrow alleyway might have posed certain operational problems. But I have access to dimensions unavailable to you, and I made room for myself there with the proper interpenetrational configurations. Not that it mattered to the three muggers, because they were dead of shock the moment they saw me towering before them.

I raised my foot and ground them into the pavement like noxious vermin.

Then, in the twinkling of an eye, I was once more a slender, lithe middle-aged American tourist with thinning hair and a kindly smile, and there were three dark spots on the pavement of the alley, and that was that.

It was, I admit, overkill.

But I had had a trying day. In fact, I had had a trying fifty thousand years.

Athens had been so hellish that it put me in mind of the authentic kingdom of Hades, and so that was my next destination, for I thought I might get some answers down there among the dead. It wasn't much of a trip, not for me. I opened a vortex for myself and slipped downward and there right in front of me were the black poplars and willows of the Grove of Persephone, with Hades' Gate just behind it.

"Cerberus?" I called. "Here, doggy doggy doggy! Good Cerberus! Come say hello to Daddy!"

Where was he, my lovely dog, my own sweet child? For I myself was the progenitor of the three-headed guardian of the gate of Hell, by virtue of my mating with my sister, Tartarus and Gaea's scaly-tailed daughter Echidna. We made the Harpies too, did Echidna and I, and the Chimera, and Scylla, and also the Hydra, a whole gaudy gorgeous brood of monsters. But of all my children I was always most fond of Cerberus, for his loyalty. How I loved to see him come running toward me when I called! What pleasure I took in his serpent-bristled body, his voice like clanging bronze, his slavering jaws that dripped black venom!

This day, though, I wandered dogless through the Underworld. There was no sign of Cerberus anywhere, no trace even of his glittering turds. Hell's Gate stood open and the place was deserted. I saw nothing of Charon the boatman of the Styx, nor Hades and Queen Persephone, nor any members of their court, nor the spirits of the dead who should have been in residence here. An abandoned warehouse, dusty and empty. Quickly I fled toward the sunshine.

The island of Delos was where I went next, looking for Apollo. Delos is, or was, his special island, and Apollo had always struck me as the coolest, most level-headed member of the Zeus bunch. Perhaps he had survived whatever astounding debacle it was that had swept the Olympian gods away. And, if so, maybe he could give me a clue to Zeus's current location.

Big surprise! I went to Delos, but no Apollo.

It was yet another dismal disillusioning journey through the tumbledown sadness that is Greece. This time I flew; not on handsome black-feathered wings, but on a clever machine, a metal tube called an airplane, full of travelers looking more or less like me in my present form. It rose up out of Athens in a welter of sound and fury and took up a course high above the good old wine-dark sea, speckled with tawny archipelagos, and in very short order came down on a small dry island to the south. This island was called Mykonos, and there I could buy myself passage in one of the boats that made outings several times a day to nearby Delos.

Delos was a dry rubble-field, strewn with fragments of temples, their columns mostly broken off close to the ground. Some marble lions were still intact, lean and vigilant, crouching on their hind legs. They looked hungry. But there wasn't much else to see. The place had the parched gloom of death about it, the bleak aura of extinction.

I returned to Mykonos on the lunchtime boat, and found myself lodgings in a hillside hotel a short distance outside the pretty little narrow-streeted shorefront town. I ordered me some more mortal food and drank mortal drink. My borrowed body needed such things.

It was on Mykonos that I met Aphrodite.

Or, rather, she met me.

I was sitting by myself, minding my own business, in the hotel's outdoor bar, which was situated on a cobblestoned patio bedecked with mosaics and hung with nets and oars and other purported fishing artifacts. I was on my third ouzo of the hour, which possibly was a bit much for the capacities of the body I was using, and I was staring down the hillside pensively at, well, what I have to call the wine-dark sea. (Greece brings out the cliches in anyone. Why should I resist?)

A magnificent long-legged full-bodied blonde woman came over to me and said, in a wonderfully throaty, husky voice, "New in town, sailor?"

I stared at her, astounded.

There was the unmistakable radiance of divinity about her. My Geiger counter of godliness was going clickity-clack, full blast. How could I have failed to pick up her emanations the moment I arrived on Mykonos? But I hadn't, not until she was standing right next to me. She had picked up mine, though.

"Who are you?" I blurted.

"Won't you ask a lady to sit down, even?"

I jumped to my feet like a nervous schoolboy, hauled a deck chair scrapingly across and positioned it next to mine, and bowed her into it. Then I wigwagged for a waiter. "What do you want to drink?" I rasped. My throat was dry. Nervous schoolboy, yes, indeed.

"I'll have what you're having."

"*Parakalo*, ouzo on the rocks," I told the waiter.

She had showers of golden hair tumbling to shoulder length, and catlike yellow eyes, and full ripe lips that broke naturally into the warmest of smiles. The aroma that came from her was one of young wine and green fields at sunrise and swift-coursing streams, but also of lavender and summer heat, of night rain, of surging waves, of midnight winds.

I knew I was consorting with the enemy. I didn't care.

"Which one are you?" I said again.

"Guess."

"Aphrodite would be too obvious. You're probably Ares, or Hephaestus, or Poseidon."

She laughed, a melodic cadenza of merriment that ran right through the scale and into the infra-voluptuous. "You give me too much credit for deviousness. But I like your way of thinking. Ares in drag, really? Poseidon with a close shave? Hephaestus with a blonde wig?" She leaned close. The fragrance of her took on hurricane intensity. "You were right the first time."

"Aphrodite."

"None other. I live in Los Angeles now. Taking a little holiday in the mother country. And you? You're one of the old ones, aren't you?"

"How can you tell?"

"The archaic emanation you give off. Something out of the pre-Olympian past." She clinked the ice-cubes thoughtfully in her glass, took a long pull of the ouzo, stared me straight in the eyes. "Prometheus? Tethys?" I shook my head. "Someone of that clan, though. I thought all of you old ones were done for a long time ago. But there's definitely a Titan vibe about you. Which one, I wonder? Most likely one of the really strange ones. Thaumas? Phorcys?"

"Stranger than those," I said.

She took a few more guesses. Not even close.

"Typhoeus," I told her finally.

We walked into town for dinner. People turned to look at us in the narrow streets. At her, I mean. She was wearing a filmy orange sun-dress with nothing under it and when you were east of her on a westbound street you got quite a show.

"You really don't think that I'm going to find Zeus?" I asked her.

"Let's say you have your work cut out for you."

"Well, so be it. I *have* to find him."

"Why is that?"

"It's my job," I said. "There's nothing personal about it. I'm the designated avenger. It's my sole purpose in existence: to punish Zeus for his war against the children of Gaea. You know that."

"The war's been over a long time, Typhoeus. You might as well let bygones be bygones. Anyway, it's not as though Zeus got to enjoy his victory for long." We were in the middle of the maze of narrow winding streets that is Mykonos Town. She pointed to a cheerful little restaurant called Catherine's. "Let's go in here. I ate here last night and it was pretty good."

We ordered a bottle of white wine. "I like the body you found for yourself," she said. "Not particularly handsome, no, but *pleasing*.

The eyes are especially nice. Warm and trustworthy, but also keen, penetrating."

I would not be drawn away from the main theme. "What happened to the Olympians?" I asked.

"Died off, most of them. One by one. Of neglect. Starvation."

"Immortal gods don't die."

"Some do, some don't. You know that. Didn't Argus of the Hundred Eyes kill your very own Echidna? And did she come back to life?"

"But the major gods—"

"Even if they don't die, they can be forgotten, and the effect's pretty much the same. While you were locked up under Etna, new gods came in. There wasn't even a battle. They just moved in, and we had to move along. We disappeared entirely."

"So I've noticed."

"Yes. Totally out of business. You've seen the shape our temples are in? Have you seen anybody putting out burnt offerings to us? No, no, it's all over for us, the worship, the sacrifices. Has been for a long time. We went into exile, the whole kit and kaboodle of us, scattered across the world. I'm sure a lot of us simply died, despite that theoretical immortality of ours. Some hung on, I suppose. But it's a thousand years since the last time I saw any of them."

"Which ones did you see then?"

"Apollo—he was getting gray and paunchy. And I caught sight of Hermes, once—I think it was Hermes—slow and short-winded, and limping like Hephaestus."

"And Zeus?" I asked. "You never ran into him anywhere, after you all left Olympus?"

"No. Never even once."

I pondered that. "So how did *you* manage to stay so healthy?"

"I'm Aphrodite. The life-force. Beauty. Passion. Those things don't go out of fashion for long. I've done all right for myself, over the years."

"Ah. Yes. Obviously you have."

The waitress fluttered around us. I was boiling with questions to ask Aphrodite, but it was time to order, and that was what we did. The usual Greek things, stuffed grape leaves, grilled fish, over-cooked vegetables. Another bottle of wine. My head was pulsating. The restaurant was small, crowded, a whirlpool of noise. The near-ness of Aphrodite was overwhelming. I felt dizzy. It was a surprisingly pleasant sensation.

I said, after a time, "I'm convinced that Zeus is still around somewhere. I'm going to find him and this time I'm going to whip his ass and put *him* under Mount Etna."

"It's amazing how much like a small boy an immortal being can be. Even one as huge and frightful as you."

My face turned hot. I said nothing.

"Forget Zeus," she urged. "Forget Typhoeus, too. Stay human. Eat, drink, be merry." Her eyes were glistening. I felt as if I were falling forward, tumbling into the sweet chasm between her breasts. "We could take a trip together. I'd teach you how to enjoy yourself. How to enjoy me, too. Tell me: have you ever been in love?"

"Echidna and I—"

"Echidna! Yes! You and she got together and made a bunch of hideous monsters like yourselves, with too many heads and drooling fangs. I don't mean Echidna. This is Earth, here and now. I'm a woman now and you're a man."

"But Zeus—"

"*Zeus*," she said scornfully. She made the name of the Lord of Olympus sound like an obscenity.

We finished eating and I paid the check and we went outside into the mild, breezy Mykonos night, strolling for fifteen or twenty minutes, winding up finally in a dark, deserted part of the town, a warehouse district down by the water, where the street was no more than five feet wide and empty shuttered buildings with whitewashed walls bordered us on both sides.

She turned to me there and pulled me abruptly up against her. Her eyes were bright with mischief. Her lips sought mine. With a little hissing sound she nudged me backward until I was leaning against a wall, and she was pressing me tight, and currents of energy that could have fried a continent were passing between us. I think there could have been no one, not man nor god, who would not have wanted to trade places with me just then.

"Quickly! The hotel!" she whispered.

"The hotel, yes."

We didn't bother to walk. That would have taken too long. In a flash we vanished ourselves from that incomprehensible tangle of maze-like streets and reappeared in her room at our hotel, and from then to dawn she and I generated such a delirium of erotic force that the entire island shook and shivered with the glorious sturm and drang of it. We heaved and thrust and moaned and groaned, and rivers of sweat ran from our bodies and our hearts pounded and thundered and our eyes rolled in our heads from giddy exhaustion, for we allowed ourselves the luxury of mortal limitations for the sake of the mortal joy of transcending those limitations. But because we *weren't* mortal we also had the option of renewing our strength whenever we had depleted it, and we exercised that option many a time before rosy-fingered dawn came tiptoeing up over the high-palisaded eastern walls.

Naked, invisible to prying eyes, Aphrodite and I walked then hand in hand along the morning-shimmering strand of the fish-swarming sea, and she murmured to me of the places we would go, the things we would experience.

"The Taj Mahal," she said. "And the summer palace at Udaipur. Persepolis and Isfahan in springtime. Baalbek. Paris, of course. Carcassonne. Iguazu Falls, and the Blue Mosque, and the Fountains of the Blue Nile. We'll make love in the Villa of Tiberius on Capri—and between the paws of the Sphinx—and in the snow on top of Mount Everest—"

"Yes," I said. "Yes. Yes. Yes. Yes."

And what I was thinking was, *Zeus. Zeus. Zeus. Zeus.*

And so we travel about the world together, Aphrodite and I, seeing the things in it that are beautiful, and there are many of those; and so she distracts me from my true task. For the time being. It is very pleasant, traveling with Aphrodite; and so I permit myself to be distracted this way.

But I have not forgotten my purpose. And this is my warning to the world.

I am a restless being, a mighty thrusting force. I was created that way. My adversary doesn't seem currently to be around. But Zeus is here somewhere. I know he is. He wears a mask. He disguises himself as a mortal, either because it amuses him to do so, or because he has no choice, for there is something in the world of which he is afraid, something from which he must hide himself, some god greater even than Zeus, as Zeus was greater than Cronus and Cronus was greater than Uranus.

But I will find him. And when I do, I will drop this body and take on my own form again. I will stand mountain-high, and you will see my hundred heads, and my fires will flash and range. And Zeus and I will enter into combat once more, and this time I will surely win.

It will happen.

I promise you that, O small ones. I warn you. It will happen.

You will tremble then. I'm sorry for that. The mind that came with this body I wear now has taught me something about compassion; and so I regret the destruction I will inevitably visit upon you, because it cannot be avoided, when Zeus and I enter into our struggle. You have my sincerest apologies, in advance. Protect yourselves as best you can. But for me there can be no turning away from my task.

Zeus? This is Typhoeus the Titan who calls you!

Zeus, where are you?

THE TREE THAT
GREW FROM THE SKY

*The behind-the-scenes story of this story will provide no astounding rev-
elations. It was the spring of 1996; I had just finished writing the enormous
novel* Sorcerers of Majipoor, *and somehow had a little creative vitality left
over; and Scott Edelman, the editor of* Science Fiction Age, *asked me on
the right day whether I might feel like contributing a longish story to his
magazine. I had been reading something about the artificer Daedalos at the
time, and also there was a beautiful comet with a hyphenated name that
I have now forgotten hanging in the night sky over our garden just then.
A little cross-pollination of the imagination took place and out came this
story, which Edelman happily published and which went on to be a Hugo
and Nebula nominee, though it won no awards.*

Science Fiction Age *was a magazine that bore all the dreadful stig-
mata of modern science-fiction publishing: strikingly ugly cover lettering,
gaudy and unpleasant full-page advertisements within for movies that I
would never have dreamed of going to see, classified ads in back for psy-
chics and pen-pal clubs and ghastly statuettes of dragons and elves. But
that is what you have to do, in this vulgar, tacky age, if you want to succeed in science-fiction publishing. It also happened that Edelman, a man of
wit and taste and much experience in science fiction, slipped a great many
superb science-fiction stories and science articles in among all that tacki-
ness. Nevertheless the magazine went out of business after five years or so.
Did it fail because it wasn't ugly enough, or because the stories were too*

good? We'll never know. I was sorry to see it disappear, anyway, though editor Edelman—surely a man for modern times—did manage to land on his feet, moving over to some Internet publication about science-fiction movies and television shows. I hope he returns to the world of print publications, such as it is, sooner or later, because I know that that's where his heart is.

1.

The visitor star, which the people foolishly think of as a tree, is growing larger overhead every night. Of course it is no sort of tree at all, but simply the kind of bright wandering star that star-watchers call a comet; but to the common folk it is a tree, a tree that is descending upon us from the heavens. They fear that it means to fall upon the world and bring about the destruction of all things.

It is easy enough to see why the people believe that. Through all the weeks of its presence above us the visitor star has steadily gotten bigger and brighter; it has become amazingly bright by now, astonishingly huge above us. But I know that it will not fall on us. I have plotted its position night by night; I see that it moves constantly to the north and east in the sky all the while that it is approaching us.

Plainly it will miss us by a goodly distance and sail onward through the cold empty spaces that surround us until it plummets into the sun. Or, what is more likely, it will not enter the sun but will swing on an arc about it like a pebble on a string, as comets of the past have been known to do, until finally it is caught in the hand of Maldaz, or perhaps one of the other gods that watch over us; and the god will hurl it back across the heavens to whatever place it came from.

All this week I have wanted to speak with the Alien about the comet and its movements—soon, before the king changes his mind again and decides to have him put to death after all.

The Alien, naturally, would understand these cometary matters much more deeply than I, because he has actually sailed across those dark seas of the night where the stars have their homes, and I have only looked up into them from below and wrestled with the gods for answers to my questions. During his years among us I have had many conversations with the Alien and he has taught me a great deal, but beyond doubt there will always be much more that I could learn from him.

At the moment there is, however, the problem of gaining access to him. He has been in a foul, sour mood for weeks, now—ever since the coming of the comet, in fact—sequestering himself, allowing no guests to come to him. The maze in which he dwells not only pens him in but keeps outsiders from entering unbidden. Since the comet came to take on its full brilliance we have sometimes seen him emerge at night, pacing high up along the inner wall of his enclosure with his face turned toward the sky, as well he might, for the comet is an extraordinary sight and he has few diversions in the course of his daily life. But on those occasions he has taken no notice of us; and when my daughter Theliane went to visit him the day before yesterday, as she so often has in the past, he turned her angrily from the gate, even her, his one true friend.

These moods have come to him often during his time among us, though not often with such intensity as at the present time. He has an angry heart, our Alien does. The burning poison of incurable loneliness and homesickness has spread through his veins in these fifteen years of his captivity.

The Alien fascinates me. His mere presence among us tells me that the sky is full of worlds, and those worlds are peopled, and some of those peoples go to and fro among the stars as easily as I would go from Kevorn to Stoi, from Stoi to Shagrool, from Shagrool to Kinipoil. That is a miracle to me. We thought we were alone in the universe until the Alien came. Now we see the folly of that belief: I do, at least.

How I would love to know all the things he knows! His head must be full of ideas and concepts never even dreamed by us, and what great wonders I might accomplish if I could call upon those ideas myself! His knowledge added to mine would allow me to achieve things never before attempted.

Nevertheless, I should not be too disparaging of my gifts or my accomplishments. My own mind, on its own, is far from a trivial thing. It is able to meet most intellectual tasks with distinction. I look; I see; I think; I comprehend. And so I understand this visitor star, and therefore it does not frighten me.

But the people will believe what they will believe, and how can I make them listen to me? I have never been able to make them listen to me. They respect me, yes. They employ my services and value my skills, yes. But to *listen*, when I tell them things?

No.

They will believe what they will believe. And the visitor star frightens them. The wide plain west of the city is bright with the fires of ghazul trees that they have set alight as offerings to the gods. They burn a tree to Maldaz, and nevertheless the visitor star draws ever nearer, and so they burn a tree to Kleysz, and one to Hayna, and one to Gamiridon; and still it comes toward us.

The ghazul trees are rare and very beautiful, and their sweet oil is precious for its seventy uses. It is a pity to waste them this way.

But the people will believe, and their beliefs make them afraid.

What can I do? Let them believe.

2.

At the beginning of the month, on a night when no moons were in the sky and the visitor star blazed out against the darkness like a river of light, the king sent word to me that I was to come to him in the Citadel, the great hilltop palace overlooking the Living Sea that I built for his father long ago, and explain to him the meaning of what was happening in the sky.

It always gives me great pleasure to behold the Citadel. It is not the cleverest of my buildings—the cleverest one is the maze that I built as the Alien's habitation and prison—but it is the largest and most magnificent. Still, the Citadel's design is not without a cleverness of its own. Outside, it is massive and grand. The great sloping walls of greenish-black stone, the enormous gray exterior columns that support the heavy blue-tiled roof, the awesome lifelike images of gods and goddesses that I spent four years carving with my own hands in high relief on the western facade: all these testify to the power and might of the dynasty that has governed us these nine hundred years past.

But once you are within the building, all is twisting and undulating and sly, and that testifies to the subtlety and vision of Kell the Artificer, who is the only man in the world who could have conceived such things. I am divine Tulabaratha's creature, he who is the builder of palaces for his fellow gods, and he, who is by far the most skillful of all the godly ones in the making of things, the Artificer of Artificers, has shared his understanding with me in generous measure.

The king was waiting for me in the Throne-Room of the Equinox. That is the long open hall on the second story at the palace's eastern end, facing the sea. There is a day in the spring every year when the sun in its northward journey crosses the celestial equator, and a day every autumn when it crosses that equator again going in the other direction, and on both of those days the hours of light and the hours of darkness are exactly equal. I have positioned the throne in that throne-room in such a way that at the moment of the equinoctial crossing a long shaft of golden-red sunlight penetrates the room and strikes a polished bronze pommel that rises above the center of the throne.

That was an easy enough effect to calculate; but King Thalk for whom I built the Citadel was so overwhelmed by his first sight of it that he paid me a bonus of five thousand pieces of gold, and King Hai-Theklon his son seats himself on the throne a day or two prior to the moment of the light-beam's semi-annual advent, for fear it might come early some year and he would miss it. And there he sits for hour after hour every spring and every autumn, despite my having advised him that it is not necessary to do so, until Maldaz has indeed hurled his golden shaft against the consecrated sphere of bronze.

I loved old King Thalk, but I have no great fondness for King Hai-Theklon his son. He was lazy and arrogant and unintelligent when he was a boy and I was his tutor; and though he is far from lazy now that he is king, he is still arrogant and unintelligent. Since he has kept those latter two qualities into his adult years, I wish he had kept his laziness as well: he would do less harm that way.

He was standing right at the brink of the throne-room's open side when I entered, hands clasped behind his back, head hunched forward, staring upward into the sky. One good shove from behind would have sent him down into the Living Sea. But I lack the blind courage of the assassin.

"Kell?" he said, without turning.

"I hail and obey, Majesty," I said, and made the formal gesticulation of submission even though he was not looking my way. Now that he is king, he demands these formalities and I am careful not to forget that. It was once easier between him and me. For many years I called him "Choyin," which was his father's pet name for him, after his fancied resemblance to the little glassy-legged serpent of the Great

Central Desert. If I dared to use that name for him now he would probably lock me up for the rest of my days in the maze where the Alien lives.

Still not deigning to glance at me, he beckoned me toward him with a flick of his hand. I came up close, and impatiently he ordered me closer yet, right to the edge. Red waves of dizziness swept through me, but I took up my place right beside him at the brink and clamped my two long anchor-toes tightly around the stone rim. My hsorn-sense is keener than most—too keen, perhaps—and therefore I have some fear of edges. To soar through the air like a bird would afford me intense delight, I like to think, but standing at the very edge of a steep drop makes me queasy. Still, I forced myself.

Just below us lay the roiling strangeness of the Living Sea. Which, to be accurate, is not exactly a sea at all, but rather an immense quivering pudding-like lake of a pale pink substance that is thicker than water but thinner than mud. It stretches eastward from this shore as far as anyone can imagine. Some say it goes halfway around the world.

I have studied it for many years: I know that it is a live creature, a single tremendous entity that has some sort of intelligent mind, though of what quality that intelligence is, not even I can say. By day and by night a flickering pink radiance rises from it, and warmth. The people believe that anyone who enters it will instantly die.

Despite the competing brightness that came from the sea, the visitor star stood out clearly and vividly against the dark moonless sky. The reason why the people spoke of it as a "tree" was obvious even to me, for the tail that splayed out behind it across much of the sky was particularly long and thick, indeed somewhat like the trunk of a tree, and terminated in a multitude of twisted curling streamers of light that could be construed as bearing some resemblance to a tree's roots. Ignorant but imaginative folk might well think that what they saw was a great tapering narrow-headed tree tumbling crown-foremost toward the world.

"This new star," said the king. "Is it a tree or is it a comet, Kell?"

"A comet that looks something like a tree, Majesty."

"A comet. You're certain of that?"

"A very bright and large comet, yes. A thing of dust and ice that comes out of the cold distant darkness trailing a white stream of light, crosses our course in the heavens, and vanishes again back into the darkness from which it came."

"'No comets are seen when a poor man dies, but the fall of kings is blazoned in the skies,'" he intoned, in that dreadful pumped-up over-theatrical way that I had never succeeded in persuading him to abandon. "You know those lines, Master Kell?"

"They are from my play *Heyolf the Bold*, Sire." He had quoted the passage with uncharacteristic accuracy.

"Yes. The wise old man Vithak speaks them. And then the young wizard Greyborn replies, *'Comets, aye! Famine and pestilence pour down from them like rain from a cloud.'* The fall of kings, Kell. Famine and pestilence." He still had not looked at me so much as once. His voice was hollow, sepulchral. "If your poetry has any truth to it, Master Kell, the coming of this comet means that the realm is in great danger."

"My poetry is only poetry. My play is just a play."

"All just a fabric of lies, is it, this great masterpiece of yours which once you forced me to commit to memory down to its final word?"

"The play in its totality is a thing of wisdom and truth, Majesty. But it is the sum of its differing parts. Individual characters speak according to their individual ways of thinking, and those are not necessarily ones with which the author agrees. Old Vithak believes that comets are omens of evil, and so does the young wizard Greyborn. But the era in which they purportedly lived was long ago, when men were ignorant. It is a mistake to think that Kell the Master of Sciences, who created Vithak and Greyborn and put those words in their mouths, believes everything that they happen to believe."

"So I am mistaken, am I, Kell?"

There was an ominous tone in his voice. The king is slight of build, and I am a heavy-set man; but it would have been easy enough for him to fling me into the sea with one petulant push. I found myself wondering if I would try to take him with me if he did.

"It is not a useful policy to interpret the words of characters in a play as statements of scientific verities," I said carefully. "Poetry is poetry and science is science."

"You are both a scientist and a poet, Kell. I have always assumed that your poetry is scientific."

"That is not a safe thing to assume, Majesty."

He was silent for a time, considering that. Then he said, "Is this comet going to crash into us, do you think?"

"It will pass to the north and east, traveling toward the sun, and leave us in peace."

"Am I to take that answer as science or poetry, Kell?"

"I have made observations every night since the comet appeared in the sky. It grows larger, yes, but also it travels upward and outward. Last week it was there; tonight it is here; next week it will be *there*." I pointed far to the northeast.

"Unless it decides to smash through the roof of this Citadel instead, and kill the king, and bring famine and pestilence to the world, as your wise men say in that play of yours."

"Comets make no decisions, Majesty. They follow the inexorable laws of nature. Just as a river will not suddenly decide to flow uphill, this comet will not decide to turn from its path and descend into our midst."

"The people think it will. I've sent men out into the city to listen to what they say. They think that the comet is a great tree that Kleysz has placed in the sky, or perhaps it was Hayna who put it there, and it grows downward from the heavens all the time, getting bigger and heavier, and eventually its roots will lose their hold on the sky and it will drop upon us in a terrible catastrophe. That is what they believe."

"I know that. Believing a thing doesn't make it so."

"But what am I to do, Kell?"

"About their beliefs? Very little can be done about those, I would expect. Go before them and tell them that their fears are needless, that the visitor star cannot possibly do us any—"

"Any harm, yes," he cut in, drawling the words derisively, before I could finish the sentence. "And next you will say that time will prove me right and the people will rejoice. Fine. And if the comet falls upon us anyway, what then?"

"Why, then, we will all be dead. But it is not going to happen."

"You are the great artificer, Kell. You are Tulabaratha's own likeness come to dwell among us. Fashion something for me that will blow this thing, this tree, this comet, from the skies before it can do any injury to us. Some great projectile hurled from a mighty catapult, for example, that will shatter it into a million harmless fragments."

"That is not only unnecessary, Sire—I can show you mathematical proof that the comet will pass us by—it also happens to be impossible."

"A word you rarely use," he said, and laughed.

"But appropriate in this case."

"How am I to trust these mathematical proofs of yours? What if they mean no more than the words of the characters in that play of yours?"

"We could get the Alien out of his prison and question him about these matters. He has traveled between the stars; very likely he has seen comets journeying in their courses; he will know the law by which they must abide. And they will be exactly as I have told you they are."

"The Alien," said the king moodily. "I should take him out of that maze and have his throat cut on the high altar."

I gave him a look of horror. "Sire?"

"I've felt since I was a boy that letting him live among us is dangerous. The place he comes from is one where the gods we love are unknown. He owes them no allegiance, indeed probably denies their very existence. His coddled existence here is a mockery in their faces. For fifteen years they've waited for us to destroy him; and, since we don't do it, they've hurled this tree at him to do the job. The fact that the tree will smash *us* up too is unimportant to them, I suppose."

"A comet, Sire. Not a tree."

"Whatever. If it should collide with the world—"

"It will not. And the Alien is a poor stranded wayfarer whose life among us is a misery of loneliness. He is here through no choice of his own, but while he is here he is our guest, and guests are sacred. If you were to kill him, the gods might indeed be annoyed enough to hurl something our way. I beg you, Majesty, put all thought of sacrificing him out of your mind."

"Well—"

"And your fears as well. No harm will come to us from this comet."

"Well," he said again. "Perhaps so, Master Kell."

3.

I backed most humbly and properly out of the royal presence then, even though the king still stood with his face turned from me, looking outward to the sky, and made my way through the splendors of the palace that I had so cunningly built for his father—through the Room of Nine Metals, and past the Pool of Nine Waters, and down the spiral staircase that I had fashioned so that it drills like an auger into the Nine Levels of the world's core, far below the Citadel itself. It may be blasphemy to say so, but the divine Tulabaratha by whose grace I have attained all my skills could not have done better. And then I passed beneath the bronze dragons with which I had bedecked the

Lesser Gate and was outside in the night, and saw the comet hanging overhead, a dazzling shaft of cool white fire in the sky, bright as the sword of Gamiridon.

The king's anxieties had been allayed, for the moment, and all was well.

But with Hai-Theklon all was never well for long. He is just intelligent enough to be restless of mind, but not sufficiently intelligent to know when he is putting that restlessness to a foolish purpose. It is hard for him to hold to a steady course. Would he think once again, tomorrow, that it was a good idea to have me build a catapult with which to destroy the comet as it hovers above us? Would he begin toying again with the notion of sacrificing the Alien as an offering to the angry gods? Or sacrificing me, for that matter, if the panic among the common folk continued to grow? I am more useful to him than any ten thousand of them could ever be; but logic has never prevented kings from acting against their own best interests. They usually have the luxury of surviving their mistakes and continuing as before. I though, have only one life.

Confident though I was of my own conclusions concerning the comet, I resolved to check and recheck all my calculations to make absolutely certain that this comet, unusually big as it is, would behave like all previous ones known to history and swing past the world at a comfortable distance. A conversation on that subject with the Alien would be in order, too, I thought. I have, and never have made any secret about it, high regard for my own powers of mind; but I am wise enough to know that I am not infallible. That is one of the ways in which I am different from a king.

I was positive that the comet would not hit us. But what if it came very close, much closer than I expected it to, and swept like an avenging scimitar above the tops of our tallest buildings? The people would doubtless go berserk. In their terror they would surely burn the city and perhaps try to kill the king; and the king, as the wild mobs approached the Citadel, very likely would turn his anger on me.

So my figures had to be utterly trustworthy. If I saw any possibility of error in them, it would probably behoove me to disappear from the capital until the comet had passed by, or even, perhaps, to seek permanent service with some other king. There are many who would have me, and gladly.

I would set to work on my recalculations at once, that very night.

The quickest route from the Citadel to the compound where I have my observatory and workshop passes through the Great Plaza of the Kings. That is where the Tower of the Alien, which long ago had carried its lone passenger across the great sea of suns to our world, had made its landing on the astounding day when it came hurtling down through the sky, and that was where it had stood ever since, precisely in the center of the plaza, on the grassy lawn where King Mosa-Bodrik slew his fifty brothers in the time of the myths. The grass for a considerable distance around it was badly charred, but has long since grown back. "How I marvel at the elegant way you came down in the one open space in the midst of our city without harming a thing," I told the Alien once; to which he replied, not at all flattered, "Elegant? It was outrageous idiocy. I had no business landing in the city at all. But the ship was out of control and I was doing the best I could. It was just blind luck that I didn't kill fifty thousand people."

The Tower has never ceased to fascinate me. It summons for me a deep and shivering sense of the vastness and wondrousness of the universe; and never had I crossed the Great Plaza of the Kings without pausing a moment or two to stare at it in awe. And, sometimes, not simply to stare; on many occasions I had actually entered it, clambering up the winding staircase within it in order to study the array of mysterious devices in the cabin at its summit. No one else, to my knowledge, ever went into it. No one would dare.

They utterly baffled me, those devices. But just as one will probe with one's tongue at a sore tooth, so had I gone back again and again into the Tower to stare in bewilderment at those perplexing banks of mechanisms. I am not accustomed to bewilderment, nor to perplexity. Solutions to problems, even the hardest ones, have a way of presenting them to me, after a time. But not these. The devices in the Tower were alien mechanisms and the problems they offered were alien problems; and my mind, for all its versatility, is deeply rooted in the things of this world.

This night the Tower seemed more wondrous even than usual. Rust, over the years, has flecked its battered metal skin with a coating of brilliant colors, ochre and auburn and scarlet and emerald, but now, lit by the comet's white glare, it had taken on a whole host of unfamiliar and wonderful new hues.

As I stood then before it there leaped into my mind's eye the thought of making a painting of what I beheld at that moment, the comet splitting the sky with its light and the Tower beneath it all ablaze with the colors engendered by the reflection of that light. It would be a considerable challenge to reproduce the myriad interwoven coruscating tones of the Tower and the cool contrasting brilliance of the comet with mere pigment on canvas; but when had I ever turned away from challenge?

There was, however, no time for making paintings just now. So that night I merely walked entirely around it, briefly stopping several times to admire the eerie starlit beauty of its patina, and after a few moments of that I went on my way.

When I reached my observatory I made that night's measurements and etched them on the screen that gives me my comparative locations of the comet; and I saw that it had continued to move in the direction in which I believed it should be traveling, and at the requisite velocity. I held up to the sky the instrument that tells me the size of heavenly objects, and saw that the tail had once more extended its length. This, too, was completely in accordance with my prediction.

Then I took out the calculating machine that I had fabricated from strips of reed and slivers of copper wire, and went through all my numbers from the very first, plotting the actual course of the comet across the sky against my original predictions of them. And I confirmed, to my great satisfaction, that I had been correct at every step.

These things took me all night. Just before dawn Theliane came to me, sleepy and puzzled-looking, a candle in her hand.

"Father? I awoke and saw a light in here. Is there anything wrong?"

"Only in King Hai-Theklon's head," I answered. "He's been reading old plays of mine and something he found in one of them made him start to think the comet was going to hit us after all. So I've been rechecking my calculations. It's taken me a while. The figures are right."

Of Hai-Theklon's notion of putting the Alien to death to propitiate angry gods, I said nothing. I knew of the deep love she bore for that creature from another world. And I suspected that Hai-Theklon, like his father before him, both dreaded and to some degree revered the Alien, and would not dare to harm him, so why arouse needless apprehension in her?

"Only he would doubt that your figures are right!" she said indignantly. "But it does seem so close, all the same. And constantly getting closer. I can see why he'd be worried. The whole city's muttering, you know."

"It isn't close at all," I said.

"It isn't?"

"When the comet comes into the sky each night, it's in approximately the same place as the night before, right? It's moved a little to the north, a little to the east, but you still see the same stars in the background behind it, Ligur, Izka, Semilgat, Vroz. Yes?"

"Well—yes."

"The world turns, and the comet goes out of view as morning nears, and the next night it's back again. Ligur, Izka, Semilgat, Vroz. Whereas the moons, which everybody agrees are very close to us, go whizzing across the sky from horizon to horizon. If the position of the comet against the background of the stars doesn't change very much, it must be farther away than the moons, is that not so? A good deal farther, as a matter of fact. And no one worries about the moons colliding with us. Nor should we worry about the comet. It's well out there in space, and though it's going to get closer to us before it starts going away, it's not going to hit us. I promise you that, Theliane. There are laws that all comets obey—laws not made by kings, but by the gods themselves—and this comet will behave the way all the others have."

"So it's definitely a comet, then, and not some kind of gigantic tree that's dropping down on us?"

"*Theliane!*"

"Did I say something stupid again, father? You know I'm not really stupid. But I suppose to you everybody, even someone with a reasonable amount of intelligence, must seem not much better than a moron."

"Hardly so," I told her.

And I scarcely need observe that Theliane was not stupid at all: simply not a genius. Not being a genius is no sin, though, or the priests would be busy kindling absolution-offerings all day and all night. But Theliane's mind was agile enough, as the minds of ordinary folk go, and her beauty was so remarkable that I often wondered how such a creature as she could have come from the loins of one like me.

I must concede, however, that I had assistance in the fashioning of her. In the distribution of parental traits Theliane may have received only a portion of her father's boiling intelligence, but a full measure of her mother's beauty. Better that, I suppose, than the other way around; and had she been given intellectual gifts on a par with her physical ones, the gods would have had to destroy her out of sheer envy.

She said, peering through the observatory window at the paling sky, from which the comet had vanished some hours before, "Do you know, father, I wish that it really *was* a tree with a great solid trunk, and that it would come close enough for me to climb up into it."

"You do? You would?"

One other trait of mine that had not been inherited by her was my overriding caution.

"Wouldn't you, father? No, perhaps you wouldn't. But I'd do it in a flash. It must be half as big as the world, wouldn't you say? And I'd climb right to the top of it. Imagine the view from up there! All the stars at once, and moons that no one can see from down here. And the other planets practically within my reach. Just stretch out my arm, like this— and touch—"

She laughed. Her eyes were bright with yearning. She was twenty years old, and still had a child's eager desire to enfold the universe in her arms.

"It's not a tree," I said. "And ninety-nine percent of what you see up there is nothing but a bright stream of gas. You'd have a hard time climbing *that*."

"That's too bad," she said. "If I could, I would. Maybe somehow I will."

I smiled and set about putting my instruments away, and she, perhaps already beginning to plan the scheme that would cause me so much grief, went off to bring me my morning meal. She was always solicitous in that way. None of my wives ever cared for me the way Theliane did. I have had no luck in my choice of women, not even once, except that one of them, sullen and cold though she was, gave me Theliane.

As she spread the food-bowls before me I said to her, "I need to talk with the Alien. But he's been so peculiar, lately. You said he wouldn't let even you visit him the other day."

The Alien had always regarded Theliane with great warmth, ever since she was a small child. There is no one in the world who has ever been closer to him than she. He was often surly and curt, but never with her. His skill in our language was something he owed to her, the long hours she had spent cloistered with him in his prison cell across fifteen years. Now that she was grown, she would have become his lover, I suppose, if such a thing had been physically possible between a man of his race and a woman of ours.

"It must be the sky-tree that agitates him so," she said. "The comet, I mean to say. Ever since it first came into view he's been getting edgier and edgier. What can that mean?"

I had no idea. Nor did she. But she promised to try again to get him to allow her through the gate, and to win his permission for me to enter also.

I slept from dawn to mid-morning, which is all the sleep I need. When I awakened, I heard Theliane moving about on the lower level of my chambers, singing prettily to herself as she tidied and dusted. She told me, when I went downstairs to her, that she had been to the Alien, who seemed more calm today; that he had admitted her to the maze in friendly enough fashion; that he was willing to let me speak with him that very afternoon.

I clasped her in my arms and tenderly touched my forehead to hers. "What would I do without you?" I asked her. "What would I ever do?"

4.

The maze of the Alien, as I have said, is my most ingenious creation. Old King Thalk, may the gods ever caress him, told me to spare no expense: to make it a monument that would stand for the ages, a work of wonder that would outlast him and me both and the Alien as well, and by its unique distinction of design and elegance of artifice to announce to all the world in centuries to come that it was our city that had been singled out by the gods to be the home for this extraordinary being from the far stars.

It is a building fashioned out of spirals, a great many of them, some of which go upward and some down. They interlock and overlap in an artful way that dizzies the mind: you will be carefully following a downward-sloping spiral that seems to be a direct route inward, and, though you are diligently ignoring the temptations of dead-end side-passages and brightly lit major corridors that clearly go nowhere, it will suddenly occur to you from the effort of your movements that you have somehow ceased to descend and begun to climb a steep ramp, all the while thinking you were continuing down, and that you now are heading toward the perimeter of the maze rather than toward its center. Or you will be under the impression that you are ascending until you find out that you are not, and so forth.

There are, naturally, dozens of passages that double back in short order upon themselves and return you swiftly and mockingly to your starting point. There are some that seem agreeably straightforward until they terminate in impassable walls. There are high-vaulted galleries flanked with five or six doorways of which two or three appear to lead onward in useful directions, but none of which in fact go anywhere. And so on and so on, a delicious little city of mysteries. Though many paths will take you easily and encouragingly inward through the outer third of the maze, only a few will carry you very far into the middle third, and only one will bring you to the innermost zone.

I made the maze beautiful, too, though few in our lifetimes would have a chance to appreciate its beauty. The floors of the great galleries are decorated with a host of eerie little tapering mounds of carved white stone, much like the stalagmites one finds in caves. From certain angles they have the look of animals, or people, or gods; but then when you walk around to the other side of them they become incomprehensible lumps of shapeless rock, and you wonder how you could have recognized any sort of form in them whatever.

Then there are chambers where I built canopies and draperies all of a much finer white stone cut with a myriad little openings, so that they have the appearance of the most costly of woven fabrics; and also I constructed reflecting pools and walls that have the gleam of mirrors, and long mysterious openings in the ceilings of the lower rooms that seem to look upward into other worlds, and many another decorative feature that gives evidence of my skill as an artificer. And the entire structure is run through with ventilating pipes and concealed sources of illumination, all of the most artful inventiveness. I also designed a system of speaking-tubes by which those outside the maze can communicate with the Alien, and he with us. There is nothing like these tubes anywhere else in the world, not even at the king's own Citadel.

The apartments of the Alien are at the very center of all this, and they are comfortable enough, essentially the sort of lodging one might provide for a prince of the royal house. His spacious rooms are arranged on five levels, forming a discrete structure within the structure that rises up like a thrusting arm through the heart of the maze and culminates in a flat peak surrounded by an open circular gallery, thus giving him a lofty promenade where he can enjoy a fresh-air stroll, or look outward on the joyous light of day and the brilliance of the stars. It is possible to see him from outside the wall of the maze when he appears on his balcony, a distant tiny figure outlined against the sky, and when he does so appear the people often gather to peer at him, though by this time he is far from a novelty here.

I used six different sub-architects to build the maze, and each one employed his own team of workmen, and no members of any team were given any knowledge of the plans that the other five groups were following. As a result, no one understands the secret of how to reach the inner apartments, except for three people. I am one and the king is another—Thalk insisted on that—and the third is the official known as the Guardian of the Alien, who is the blind eunuch Kataphrazes. I taught Kataphrazes the route myself, placing his probe-fingers on each key landmark along the way until he knew them all by touch-memory. His sense of hsorn is exceedingly powerful, very likely because of his blindness: he was amazingly quick to master the correct path and was able almost at once to make his way through the passages errorlessly and with unfaltering step.

Each morning Kataphrazes leads the servitors who bring the Alien his food to the inner barrier, never taking the same approach twice the same month, nor using the same servitors. If the Alien is to have guests, Kataphrazes will lead them inward in the same ever-varying fashion, and they are blindfolded besides, more for the theatrical pomp of the thing than as a real precaution, for nobody could ever learn the way simply by observing it just one single time.

There was a fourth who knew the route, who was Theliane. With King Thalk's permission I taught it to her when she was a child, at her urgent request, for there was little I would ever refuse Theliane.

The Alien's inner apartments are surrounded by a gated wall of sharp-tipped iron spars: the Alien alone has control over who passes through that gate. It is a little privilege that we bestowed on him to pre-serve the fiction that he is our guest, not our prisoner. When he feels gloomy and withdrawn, which is often, he denies entry to those who desire access to him, and so be it.

In any event he does not ordinarily have many visitors other than Theliane, who has been by far his most frequent guest, and myself; until his recent spell of unsociability I had gone to him every few weeks, and we had enjoyed long, far-ranging talks about the nature of the world and the cosmos. Other than us, he has had little company. The four high priests of the city pay him ceremonial calls every now and then, since he is regarded officially as an emissary from the gods. For the same reason King Thalk used to go to him every month or two; King Hai-Thelkon, though, finds him troublesome to look upon, indeed, downright hideous, and I think has entered the maze no more than twice in the five years of his reign. And sometimes high priests from other cities, when their travels bring them to us, are taken by Kataphrazes to see the Alien, by way of reminding them that his presence among us confers on us the status of a city honored above all others in the world.

It was months since I had last visited the Alien and this day, when I went to him, I was startled by the changes in his appearance. He is, obviously, not very much like us in form, other than in such superficial ways as having two legs on which he stands upright, and two arms, and a head set between his shoulders to bear his eyes and breathing-holes and mouth. I have long since grown accustomed to all the little oddities of his appearance, the flatness of his face, and the fact that his fingers are more or less all of the same size and so are his toes, and that his skin is pale and soft, and that his head is shaped the way it is and his eyes are the color and shape that they are, and so forth and so forth.

But the fur atop his head, which had changed its color from black to gray in the past few years, now seemed suddenly much more sparse than I remembered. I found that pleasing; it made him seem less like a beast of the fields. His face looked broader, as though the soft flesh of it were spreading and sagging. His flat inhuman eyes had a new look that seemed to me to speak not merely of the sadness of his soul but of a deep, inescapable weariness. Even his posture was different, his shoulders now slumping forward as if he found it an increasing effort to stand erect.

"Well, what do you expect, Kell?" he said, as I stood there gaping at him while he opened the gate that gave admission to his private apartments. There was an abruptness in his tone, a whipcrack rhythm, that I knew connoted anger. "Do you think I'm going to look the same way forever? I've spent a quarter of my entire life living in this labyrinth of yours. And now I'm starting to get old."

I had not said a thing, only stared. He often responds to unspoken statements that way, as though he can see into your mind and read your hidden thoughts.

For a long while I wondered whether the Alien might actually have that ability; since he has little or no hsorn, perhaps other senses of his are correspondingly hyper-keen. But later I realized that he merely has a highly developed capacity for interpreting facial expressions. It is, I suppose, a skill that his race cultivates and we do not, though I have given some effort to mastering it since learning from him that one can discover a great deal about the thoughts of others simply by studying their faces while they speak to you.

I told him that I knew that something had been troubling him lately which had caused him to shun my company and that of my daughter, and I asked whether it could be this, the onset of age, the distress that that was causing in him.

He merely lifted his shoulders a little way at that and turned his hands outward, the gesture he calls a "shrug," which is meant to convey indifference.

Why, he asked, did I think that growing old would be upsetting to him? To the contrary: the older he became, the closer he was to dying; and death for him meant only the end of captivity, the end of exile.

To these words I made no direct reply. They had been spoken in a flat, emotionless way that seemed to me to connote just as much anger as his earlier harshness. And I could see from his stance and a certain look about his mouth and eyes that he was speaking insincerely. A long silence prevailed between us.

"Is it the coming of the visitor star, then?" I asked, finally.

"You mean the comet?"

"Yes. I've seen you on the roof gallery, staring at it for hours."

"Well, why not? It's a colossal sight, a comet that brilliant. I've never seen one quite that grand. But what would be troublesome to me about a comet?" We had reached his sitting-room, now. In shelves on every wall were the multitude of things we had brought to him from his Tower, his books, his entertainment-cubes, the various machines with which he looks after his medical needs, and so forth. We are a civilized nation; we had tried to make his captivity as tolerable as possible. He beckoned me to my usual seat and said, "Do you people know what comets are, Kell?—You understand that they aren't actually stars, don't you?"

"We call them 'visitor stars,' but only because they are so conspicuous and move so much faster than true stars. But we know that comets are different from stars in some way, or we would not have the other word for them. For my own part, I think a comet is more like a little planet, is that not so?"

"Bravo, Kell! A little planet, yes! One that travels around and around the solar system just as the big planets do, only in a much more eccentric orbit."

"But the big planets will endure for all eternity," I said. "Comets must eventually exhaust their substance and disappear, or else falter in their orbits and tumble into the sun."

"You know that much, do you, Kell?"

"Am I not correct?" I asked him.

I knew that I was, but I was holding my breath all the same while awaiting confirmation from him. And I was leaning forward in the posture of expectation, pupil to master. Thirty years had gone by since I had last adopted that posture toward any person of my own species; but when in the company of the Alien I usually found myself taking such a stance within a matter of moments.

He said, "I've read your textbooks of astronomy. They're full of myth and fantasy."

"My ideas do not come from textbooks, but rather from direct observation of the phenomena."

"Ah, Kell, Kell, you're a special one, aren't you? Then tell me: why is it that you think comets will—what did you say?—exhaust their substance and disappear?"

"Because," I said, "they seem to be small hard balls of solid matter with a great cloak of light streaming out behind them. That cloak grows brighter and longer as the comet approaches the sun. What else can it be, but the comet's own substance, boiling forth from it in the form of gas as the sun's energy heats it? That substance can never be replaced, and so the comet must inevitably dwindle with each of its journeys around the sun, until there is nothing left of it."

I knew from the gleam of approval in his eyes that what I was saying was correct. Not that I had had any serious doubt of it.

"And as for how I know that the comets travel around the sun like planets, why, I have consulted the records. Not all of our astronomy is myth and fantasy, Alien. There are comets that have come back again and again, always at regular intervals for many centuries, and thus must be locked into permanent orbits as planets are. One comet has come every fifty years, one every sixty-two, and so on. It is in the records."

He pointed toward the ceiling. "This one, too?"

"Not this one. It has never been seen by us before."

"Causing great excitement out there, is it?"

"The people find it terrifying. They're afraid that it's going to collide with us and destroy the world. It looks like a tree to them, a huge tree that's falling from the sky, perhaps as a manifestation of the anger of the gods against us. I know that they're wrong, but when an irrational idea like that takes possession of people's minds, nothing I could say or do will lift it from them. They'll simply have to wait and see that nothing bad is going to happen."

"It's a lonely business, isn't it, Kell, to be as smart as you are."

I imitated his shrug-gesture. "I have adapted to it. I will accept the loneliness, if that's the price of the intelligence."

"And you aren't completely lonely. Apparently you've managed to find a wife, at any rate."

"I have had several wives. What I have never had is a mate."

He considered that for a moment.

"You've been blessed with a wonderful daughter, at least," he said, after a little while.

"So I have, yes. I thank the gods for her each day."

We fell into another spell of silence.

Then the Alien said, "Some comets do collide with planets, you know."

"They do?"

"It's been known to happen. For one thing, their orbits are dynamically unstable. Gravitational perturbations can make changes in a comet's path as it travels, and send it heading off on a collision course with something nearby. Do you know what I'm talking about, Kell? And even without that happening, the fact remains that the orbits of comets cross those of the planets. It's altogether possible, sooner or later, for a comet and a planet to arrive at the same place at the same time as they make their separate orbital journeys around the sun."

"This comet will not hit us," I said.

The Alien made his alien equivalent of a smile. "You say that with absolute confidence."

"I feel absolute confidence."

"Yes. It's the mark of a superior mind, isn't it? But also the mark of a completely closed and rigid one."

"I have calculated the orbit of this comet. Bright and large as it is, it will pass by us at a safe distance."

"I'd like to see those calculations," he said.

"I have brought them with me," I told him, and presented my portfolio of nightly observations.

That amused him, that I should be so well prepared for this discussion. For what seemed like a very long time he looked through my pages of notes, whistling occasionally, tapping the tips of his stubby little fingers against his teeth. I will not say that I felt serious self-doubt during this time, for I was sure that I had done my calculations properly; but I am not so foolish as to think I am a perfect being, and, as I have already said, this man's knowledge of the stars and heavens must by definition be greater than mine, because he has had direct experience of interstellar travel. So I allowed for the possibility that he would find some *qualitative* error in my assumptions, something that stemmed not from my observations and calculations (which I knew to be correct) but from some lack of understanding in me of the fundamental workings of the universe.

Then he looked up and said, "Very nice, Kell. You never cease to astonish me."

"The savage who walks on his hind legs once more demonstrates his unexpectedly capable mind, eh?"

"Don't be sarcastic. I feel great affection for you, do you know that? We're two of a kind, you and I. You're nearly as much out of place here as I am."

A curious remark. But I saw the truth in it, and I could not help but be flattered.

We talked then for a time about the nature of comets. He confirmed much that I had discovered on my own, and told me a few things I had not known, such as the existence of great swarms of comets at the outer edges of most solar systems, millions and millions of them clustering together far beyond the outermost planets. Only a few of these comets, he said, ever detach themselves from their fellows and undertake journeys past the inner worlds. Which explained to me why, since the world is at least half a million years old and perhaps very much older than that, there still are comets for us to see. The ones our remote ancestors saw have long since evaporated and vanished, but there are always new ones breaking loose from that enormous population of them out beyond the orbit of the farthest planet and coming our way.

We became silent yet again, after we had talked awhile.

Then abruptly he said, "What I told you when you arrived was untrue. The thing that's been troubling me is the comet."

His sudden reversal mystified me. "It is? And why is that?"

"I don't mean that it's the comet itself that's troublesome to me. As I told you, it's the most spectacular one I've ever seen, an extraordinary thing, and so I've been up there looking at it most nights like everybody

else. But I'm *not* like everybody else. When I look up at the comet, I also
see the stars."

"Ah."

"I've tried not to think about the stars, Kell. Or the planets that go
around them. Especially the one I came from."

"I see," I said.

"My native star isn't visible from this hemisphere, anyway. But, all
the same, when I look toward the heavens—"

"I understand."

The terrible anguish of his solitude leaped out at me like a beacon-
light shining from his flat alien eyes.

I tried, as I had tried a million times before, to imagine what his
home world was like, the world he had left so long ago and never would
see again. To me it seemed outlandish, fantastic, even frightening. But
to him it was home.

He had described it all to me again and again, so that I sometimes
could almost make myself believe I had been there myself. But I knew
that that was a delusion. I had no real idea of the nature of his world. I
never would. My mind stretches farther than that of anyone I have ever
known; but the home world of the Alien would always be inconceivably *other* to me. All those myriads of flat-faced people; the remarkable
green trees; the unthinkably bizarre animals; the vast seas of blue-
green water. A host of great cities, each one made up of buildings taller
than our mountains, and having more people in it than we have on
our entire world; machines beyond my comprehension, machines that
sent pictures instantly from continent to continent, machines that
enable one to fly from one planet to another and one star to another, all
manner of miraculous machines.

They were like gods, those people, if his tales of his home world
had any truth to them.

He said, "This was supposed to be a three-year exploratory mission.
Three of *my* years—that's only two of yours. Come out, look around, go
home and file my report. Equipment failure wasn't part of the mission
plan. Neither was shipwreck. Neither was capture and imprisonment
by an alien species."

"You are not our prisoner. You are our guest."

"Spare me the sophistry, Kell. We know each other too well for
that. Sweet old King Thalk was well aware that the priests would hang
his skin on the balcony of his palace if he let me get away from here,

because I am the messenger of the gods, and so long as I'm here, the gods will smile on your city. How that fits together with the notion that the gods are currently in the process of dropping a celestial tree on your city because I'm a resident in it is not something that needs close examination, is it?—Kell, I'm not going to live forever. I want to go home." The last few words came forth in a desperate blurt.

I ached for him. I am not a man of stone.

But I said, "You know that that's impossible."

"Is it? I thought 'impossible' is a word that isn't in your vocabulary."

"There is a difference between things that are merely difficult to accomplish and things that cannot be accomplished at all."

"Yes, I know. But this one isn't of that sort." He gave me a curious look, fierce and sharp, like winter lightning out of nowhere. In a tone of voice that was oddly constricted, as though a band had tightened about his throat, he said, "Do you ever go into my ship, Kell?"

"Sometimes, yes."

"I thought you might. What condition is it in, inside?"

I wondered at this. He rarely spoke of his ship: not at all, that I could remember, in several years. "It is as it was. We preserve it with care, as a holy monument. Grown somewhat rusty, perhaps, on the outside—"

"And the inside?"

"As it was on the day you last saw it."

"Sealed, is it, against rain, and insects, and general decay?"

"Sealed, yes."

"Is it, now?" He fixed his gaze on me as though he were pinning me to a board with a dagger. He said, speaking with great precision and clarity in that same tight tone of voice, "It often crosses my mind, Kell, that it might not be difficult to put the ship back into good working order, if it hasn't deteriorated since the time of my landing. And you lead me to think that it hasn't."

Those quiet words rocked me like an earthquake.

Hoarsely I said, "Can that be true?"

"I'm sure of it." The new intensity of his features was truly disturbing. There was a glow about him. It was as though fire streamed from his eyes. "The fundamental mechanisms were still intact when I made my landing. Certain components had broken down, others had become decalibrated, but the essential instrumentation was all right. Otherwise I couldn't ever have made my landing. If nothing in it has suffered further damage since I was imprisoned here, it ought to be fixable. You and I, working together, could put everything back together."

It is the comet, I thought, that has aroused these thoughts in him. Awakening yearnings that have long lain dormant within his soul.

"If my ship were to be repaired, I'd be able at the very least to get as far as one of the survey buoys ten or fifteen light-years from here and send a signal that would bring a rescue team to pick me up. And my ship *can* be repaired, Kell. By you. I'm certain of that."

I said nothing. I could scarcely bear to look at him.

His strange five-fingered hands reached toward me in what could only have been an imploring gesture. They were shaking in agitation. His voice grew louder. "It's not impossible. It isn't! I know what kind of skills you have, Kell. You're one of those amazing universal geniuses that come along maybe every five hundred years in a race's history. No, don't turn your head away like that—you know it's true as well as I do, and this is no moment for false modesty. You're an engineer and an architect, and you have an master artisan's technical abilities and the mind of a great physicist, and you paint and sculpt and write plays and poetry as well, and I don't know how many other things you can do, but the list probably includes just about everything.—Help me escape. Help me, Kell."

I stared at him. I begged him with my eyes not to go on.

But he was merciless. "There's no way you can refuse me. A man like you, Kell, with such a roving, questing, insatiable spirit: it surely can't be hard for you to imagine what it would be like to be locked away like this for the rest of your life!"

No. It was not hard at all. I shivered at the thought. But still I did not reply.

He took my silence for assent. The agitation that had taken hold of him subsided somewhat, and his entire posture grew more relaxed. "Well, then. Are we agreed? The two of us, Kell, working side by side, would be able in a matter of months, maybe even only weeks, to—"

"No," I said, at last, and held up my hand to stem the fervid flow of his words. "Wait. Please. No more of this. I told you it isn't possible, and I meant just that."

The light went from his face.

"What would stand in the way?" he asked.

I forced myself to speak calmly. "Alien, you have no comprehension of the realities of the situation. Do you seriously think that we could simply tell the king that you have decided that you would like to go home, whereupon the king would blithely release you from this maze and allow you to instruct me in how to make it possible for you to escape? Why would he be any more willing to do that than his father was?"

"I understand that. But certainly you of all people must know how to get me out of this place. We could go to the ship secretly by night, and—"

"Secretly. Yes. I drug the guards, let us say, and we sneak over there every night and work, and at dawn I bring you back here with no one the wiser. And finally one day the work is done and the ship is fixed and you get into your Tower and fly away to the stars, and what do you think will happen to me, when you have gone from here? Think, Alien, think! Will the king believe that you escaped from this maze by yourself, by means of some magical conjuration you knew? That you repaired your ship unaided? No, Alien, you will fly away home, and once you are gone I will die the most terrible death that any mind could invent. And that is why I say that what you ask is impossible. You want me to commit suicide for you. That is something I will not do."

5.

Ultimately it did not greatly surprise him, I suspect, that I was unwilling to help. He knew what risks it would involve for me. But he would have had no peace if he had not asked.

And I had no peace now that he had.

I left him soon afterward. A deep and abiding melancholy had come over me and I needed to be alone. I walked through the streets of the city looking neither to the left nor the right, and responding not at all to such greetings as came my way, until I had left the paved streets behind and found myself on the earthen path that leads down to the shore of the Living Sea.

Twilight was coming on, now. Two or three of the smaller moons had risen in the eastern sky. I stood beneath the cliff on which the royal Citadel sits and its long shadow stretched far out before me into the sea.

In the changing light of the waning day the sea itself was taking on its evening colors, a deeper radiance, a stronger pink hue shot through with hints of crimson and aquamarine. The phantasmagorical giant creature that is the Living Sea is more active by night. It stirs and tosses and ripples; small spiky projections and scalloped turrets rise from its surface and are quickly reabsorbed; little bubbling mouths appear, gape two or three times, and vanish.

I stood for a long while staring intently outward as if somehow I could see across to the mythical lands on its far shore, where the ones we call the Other Folk are said to dwell, those who subsist on nothing but stone and sand, and speak in whistling tones, and sacrifice three thousand wild song-birds to their sun-god every morning. They have a third eye set in the middle of their forehead, so we are told, and dozens of fingers clustering at the ends of their arms, and blue skin pockmarked everywhere with deep circular craters. But who knows if any of these things are true? Nobody in ten thousand years has crossed the Living Sea to visit the Other Folk; and tales ten thousand years old are no more to be trusted than the books we read in our dreams.

Such a great sadness had taken hold of me after my visit to ther Alien that for a time I considered giving myself up to the sea then and there. I had felt that temptation often enough before, for I had long been curious about the occult transformative powers the mysterious substance of the sea was rumored to possess, and what better way to understand those powers than to experience them directly?

But this was different. What was surging through me now was a yearning not for knowledge but for oblivion. Perhaps the sea would dissolve and consume me, as everyone believed it would consume any creature foolhardy enough to enter it; or perhaps I would simply drown the way one might drown in a lake or river of ordinary water; or maybe the current would carry me eastward, on and on, until at last I came ashore in the land of the Other Folk, who would hail me as a god. Whatever happened, I would be relieved of the feelings of shame and guilt that gripped me now.

But I knew what foolish, useless thoughts those were, and I put them from my mind.

I put, indeed, everything from my mind. I turned myself into a statue of myself, and stood empty of thought, while the sky grew dark and the long glowing tree-shaped streak of white that was the comet came out of the southwest and took up its place high above me. And I remained that way for an hour, or perhaps two, or three, or maybe it was only a couple of minutes.

I must have begun to walk along the shore, after a time, for when consciousness and volition returned to me I found myself far down at the southern end of the beach, where the Tree of Purple Flame stands in its great solitary splendor at the edge of the Living Sea.

It is a marvelous thing, that mighty tree. Its roots go deep down into the bed of the sea and its trunk is a smooth white unbranching shaft that rises nearly as high as the cliffs that border the shore. I think the tree is made of sea-stuff too, for strange ghostly purple light emanates from it, and the shadow that it casts is blue, and its great spreading crown is in constant motion, everything writhing, swarming, changing, never the same for a moment. You can see eyes in that writhing crown, faces, beating wings, long serpentine shapes that coil about each other to form intricate knots.

The tree surges and quivers with the constant transformation that is the essence of life. No one that I know of has ever dared to go close to it. Even the shadow that it casts is said to be deadly. But I have pondered that tree ever since I was a boy. To me it is a tree of magic. Now, standing nearer to it than I had ever been before, I pondered its nature yet again, for a time. There I stood, with one strange tree in front of me, another of a very different sort plunging through the dark sky overhead; and gradually my gloom and my pain went from me, and I was myself again, and I turned and went up the steep path that led from the seashore to the town.

A message from the Citadel was waiting for me at my chambers. The king had sent for me again: I was to come at once.

This time I found him not in his usual haunt, the Equinox throne-room, but rather in the Grand Council-Hall, which is the great room that occupies most of the third level of the building. That was a disturbing thing in itself, for the Grand Council-Hall is a huge and awesome place, and Hai-Theklon tends to go to it whenever some huge and awesome thought is rattling around in his mind. Which usually presages trouble for me.

He was seated at the far end of the room, which obliged me to walk its entire considerable length before I could make my gesture of obeisance. A great fire was burning in each of the fire-pits down there, so that his kingly grandeur was enhanced by the impressive and dramatic shadows of him that flickered on the blank white wall behind him.

He is fond of that effect. I spent five months painting vivid scenes from the lives of the gods all up and down the other walls of the Grand

Council-Hall—I used a process I invented myself, grinding dry pigments into powder and applying them to the wall with a wet brush while the undercoating of freshly applied lime-plaster was still drying, so that the colors would set with the plaster and remain forever bright—but I deliberately left the rear wall unpainted, as though anticipating that King Thalk's successor would want to magnify his own importance with this sort of shadow-show. I wonder if Hai-Theklon realizes that.

He said right away, before I could rise from my deep genuflection, "I have thought of a way of defending ourselves against the comet, Kell."

"Did I not explain, Sire, that there is no need for—"

He waved me to silence.

"The metal tower, Master Kell, in which the Alien flew from his world to ours: is it not the case that it could be repaired, and made to fly through the heavens once again?"

That stunned me, coming so soon after my conversation on the same subject with the Alien himself.

Fumblingly I said, "Well, Majesty—it may well be that that can be done, but it is just as likely—that is—if the mechanisms that operate it—we know that they were already somewhat damaged when the Alien came, and the passage of time could well have—but—on the other hand—perhaps—"

I have never sounded like such an idiot in all my life.

The king cut serenely into my blathering babble. "No matter what the difficulties are, Kell, you can deal with them. I know that you can."

I said, making a desperate effort to recover some fragment of my poise, "I lack your assurance of that, Sire. But possibly—just possibly—" A hopeful, cajoling note came into my voice now. "Perhaps, Majesty, it could be done, yes. If the Alien were allowed to be with me in the Tower as I worked at the repairs—if he were to instruct and direct me, and even to assist me, let us say—"

"No. He must not leave the maze, not now or ever."

"But how, then, will I be able—?"

"He can tell you what must be done, and you can go there and do it, and when you are done the ship will fly again."

I closed my eyes and nodded solemnly. Then after a moment I said, very gently, "And may I ask, Sire, what connection this has with defending ourselves from the comet?"

"Why, that ought to be obvious, Kell! Don't you see, you can cause the ship to go aloft on a course that will send it crashing into the comet. Thus destroying it as it passes overhead, before it can do us any harm!"

He was serious. It was all I could manage to keep from laughing aloud at this grotesque multiplication of absurdities.

But I maintained a certain degree of gravity, and soberly told the king that I would give his plan the most careful consideration; and then I extricated myself from his presence as quickly as I could, before I betrayed my true opinion of his splendid idea.

I hurried home and told Theliane of my conversations with the Alien and the king. She reacted with the greatest excitement and enthusiasm for the project. This, in my folly, I misinterpreted as growing entirely out of her affection for the hapless prisoner in the maze.

The next day I told the Alien also of the king's eagerness to have the ship repaired. The irony of the coincidence amused him greatly. He laughed—it has always seemed remarkable to me that the Alien's way of showing amusement should be so much like our own—and shook his head in a sidewise fashion again and again, which is his sign of bemused disbelief. Then he turned his head away from me and put his hands over his face. His shoulders moved in an odd convulsive way, and a low muffled sound came from him, out of his throat and chest, that I had never heard him make before.

"Are you all right?" I asked.

"Yes."

"What are you doing?"

He swung around to face me. There was the sheen of fresh moisture on his cheeks, as if some unusual gland had discharged a substance from his eyes.

"Expressing my happiness at the thought of going home," he said.

6.

The comet grew even brighter in the days immediately following, so that it seemed to fill half the sky and obscured the light of the stars and the moons.

And as it waxed ever more brilliant overhead, the mood in the city, already sufficiently ugly, turned much uglier still.

Burning ghazul trees as offerings to the gods had been bad enough, I thought; but now the people began burning temples also. The gods, it now was widely declared, had withdrawn their favor from the city, and they must be informed that we were displeased by that. If they would threaten us with a comet, well, then, we would retaliate by threatening them with the loss of our love. And so there was a serious fire at the House of the Ceremonies and a lesser one, though still very destructive, at the lovely little Shrine of Kleysz. Two priests of the cult of Hayna were beaten in the streets, and one of them died. The sanctuary of Gamiridon was looted of its treasures by an angry mob. An animal was slaughtered in a sacrilegious way at the foot of the golden statue of Maldaz in Pelathas Square.

I would have told them, if anyone had been willing to listen to me, that the continuing increases in the comet's brightness and apparent size were normal and not at all dangerous. I would have explained to them that the comet had not yet reached its closest point of approach to the world and would grow brighter yet in the days ahead before it grew smaller, but that it was still embarked on a course that would take it safely past us and out into the darkness of space again.

But no one was willing to listen to me, nor in any case did I feel much desire to go forth expounding on these matters to those who do not have the capacity to understand them.

Besides, it appeared that going out among the populace would have been dangerous for me. Theliane reported that she had heard tales circulating in the streets that blamed me, not the gods, for bringing the comet—"the tree," they kept calling it, with idiotic persistence—down upon the world. It was all my fault; supposedly I had engaged in some grandiose scientific experiment that had gone awry and as a result the "tree" had been pulled toward our world from some other part of the heavens.

"They have started speaking of it as 'Kell's tree,'" Theliane told me, trembling. I had never seen her show fear before. But it was for me, not herself, that she trembled.

It was easy enough for me to keep out of sight. By day I was safe in the heart of the maze, receiving instruction from the Alien on the location and workings of his ship's controls. And by night I was in the ship itself, striving to find some way of making the vessel functional again.

The first few days there were purely exploratory ones. I made careful sketches of the panels and dials and levers that had puzzled me for so long, and took them to the Alien, who pored over them and tried to identify the role of each piece of equipment and determine whether it still might be capable of operation. Of course he had not been inside the ship for fifteen years, and much had grown unclear to him; but gradually the details started to return to his mind.

It was on the fifth day that I first felt the emotion, unusual to me, of despair. The control mechanisms of the Alien's ship had been defective to some degree in the first place, or he would never have had to make his forced landing here. They had been further damaged in that very landing, and afterward had suffered fifteen years of natural deterioration; and here was I, a man of a civilization entirely different from the one that had built this ship, trying to undo all those various kinds of damage without any knowledge of the underlying technology! It was the wildest sort of fantasy to think that I could succeed.

I have not had much experience of despair in my life. I felt it as a leaden weight within my throat, and an aching behind my eyes, and a griping of my gut that left me unable for a day or more at a time to take sustenance.

Theliane was dismayed by the darkness of my mood. "Perhaps I can help you with your work, father," she suggested.

I saw no way that she could. But she so fervently wanted to take part, and I was so reluctant to rebuff her in any way, that I began bringing her into the Tower with me. She stood at my side, she shined lights for me into the dusty crannies, she handed me tools as I requested them. Her very presence compelled me to moderate the pessimism that continued each night to mount in me. But I could not conceal from myself the reality of the situation, which was that I was making no progress.

The intensity of the comet's light was baleful now and disconcerting even to me. It illuminated the night sky almost like a second sun, though it was a sun that emitted no heat, only a cold terrible glow.

One could see, even with the naked eye, the huge rocky sphere that was its head, jagged and ominous, with thick masses of luminous smoke streaming away behind it. The color of its long tail had changed, now, from its earlier pure white to a kind of frightful yellowish-green, with a hard metallic forcefulness to it that struck the eye the way the clangor of a bell strikes the ear. That change of color troubled me. Could the comet be closer than I had calculated, so close that the stream of gaseous matter that it threw off was reacting with the gases that make up our atmosphere? It was a terrible hour for me. Yet again I doubted my own figures; but I checked and rechecked, and came away convinced once more that I had made no error.

The king called me to him once more. This time I found him in his private quarters in the Citadel, surrounded by the sculptures and paintings and tapestries I had so lovingly made for his father long ago.

"Was it you that summoned the comet to our world, Kell?" he asked sternly.

"You give me too much credit, Majesty. I have many skills, but drawing comets down from the skies is not among them."

"The people speak of it now as 'Kell's tree.' Are you aware of that, Kell?"

I sighed. "I am, yes. The people say many things, Sire, and not all of them are founded in fact. The comet is not a tree, and it is not mine."

"Finish the job of fixing the Alien's ship," he said, "and hurl it against this comet, and let us have an end to this thing. How goes the work?"

"It goes very well, Majesty. I hope to have excellent news for you very soon."

That was an utter lie, not the first I had told this king. It is often necessary for an ordinarily trustworthy man to provide some sort of shady response to the peremptory demands of unreasonable people.

But on that very night I made the first breakthrough toward success.

By baleful comet-light I crossed from the Citadel to the Plaza of the Kings and entered the Tower of the Alien, and ascended the spiraling metal ramp to the control cabin at the top. Theliane was not with me on this particular evening; she had gone to the maze, to the Alien.

I laid my hands against the plates and dials of the control panel, which I had inspected without avail so many times before. But this time, because of things the Alien had explained to me about functions and capacities that had suddenly begun to cohere in my mind, I began to see the pattern. I saw only its corner at first, and even that was shrouded in mist; but I am such that even if I see only the corner of a pattern, I often can in time make out the whole of it, and that was what happened now.

I drew new sketches and brought them to the Alien, and he studied them and nodded and drew some sketches of his own, and asked certain questions of me and sent me back to the Tower to find the answers. And I found them; and that led to more questions, and more answers still. And one night a few days later I began to pull broken sections free from the master panel, and to set about the task of designing and forging replacements for them.

So did the real work of repair begin, and so did it proceed. I will not claim that I understood all of what I was doing, or even a great deal of it. The mind that directed the work was the Alien's, from a distance, guiding me from his prison as though he was standing by my shoulder and whispering instructions in my ear; what I contributed were the eyes and the hands, and the metallurgy, and the intuitive skills. It was as though a god had taken hold of me and was bringing forth wonders from me as I lay in his grasp.

Theliane was of no small assistance. Her mind did not have the wide-ranging perception of mine, the ability to make sudden swooping leaps of comprehension and connection, but even so her learning and skills were far from trifling. She had helped me before; she knew why metals behave as they do, how they respond to temperature and pressure, how they are refined and annealed. She had learned more than a little of the purifying arts of melting and reducing and fusing.

She worked with me step by step, phase by phase. She asked sensible and useful questions; she made keen observations. I was proud of her.

I should have burned that Tower to the ground. Instead, with the aid of the Alien's instructions and Theliane's faithful help, and working as ever under the benevolent guidance of my patron god Tulabaratha who is the special deity of artificers, I succeeded in restoring it to working order. It was a triumphant demonstration of my skill. I never knew before that one might live to regret a triumph.

7.

On a day when I saw beyond any doubt that success was within my reach, that the completion of the task was at hand, I began to give some thought once again to the predicament I had been creating for myself.

The king had ordered me to repair the Tower for the sake of using it to shatter the encroaching comet; but that, of course, was nonsense. What the ship would be used for was to facilitate the Alien's escape from our world.

And what would happen to me, once the Tower went roaring up into the sky with the Alien on board?

Why, very likely the king would hold me responsible for his departure. I understood the workings of Hai-Theklon's mind only too well. No matter that I had repaired the ship at the king's own direct order; no

matter that I had no apparent motive for aiding the Alien to flee; someone had to be the scapegoat, and I was the one who had done the work.
The king would also probably hold me to blame for the coming of the
comet, as so many others already were doing. So I would die in some
ghastly fashion and the king's anger would be assuaged, and sooner or
later the comet would leave the vicinity of our world and Hai-Theklon
would take credit for that, too. But I would still be dead.

So the thought occurred to me that it might be a sensible thing for
me to be on board that ship when the Alien took off for his home.

I played with that idea as if it were some wondrous new toy that I had
fashioned for myself. To rise into the heavens atop a bellowing column of
flame; to soar across the darkness, looking down on our world from on
high until it dwindled to the size of a grain of sand; to plunge outward
into that infinity of stars of which the Alien had so often spoken—what
joy that would be!

And then one day to arrive at the Alien's own world! To behold that
prodigiously fantastic landscape with my own eyes!

The mere contemplation of that dizzied me. The blue-green water
and the green-leafed trees; the gleaming titanic buildings rising like
arrows into the cloud-flecked sky; the hordes of flat-faced people moving through the streets; the vehicles that go forward with no beasts to
draw them, the air-ships that stay aloft without movement of their wings;
the mountains that give forth bursts of flame and rivers of molten rock;
the flakes of frozen water falling from the skies. I have traveled widely
on this world of ours and I have seen many of its famous wonders, the
wheel-beasts of the western plains and the phosphorescent lakes of
Gemborionta and the voriagar hives of the Velk Peninsula and the trees
of salt that grow in Domrin Land, and much else. I have been to the chapel of Kleysz at Galfi and the bottomless pools of Grelf, and I have seen
what there is to see at Pangu and Rorm and Glay. But all those things
would not be a patch on the marvels of the world of the Alien. Endless
astonishments would await me there, all the days of my life.

So much to see! So much to learn! The strangenesses, the wonders,
the inexplicable enigmas with which I would wrestle. Things that were
utterly unfamiliar, that had only shape and color, but no meaning. Things
that were fascinating because they were incomprehensible: things whose
purposes were unguessable, because they filled needs that were themselves beyond the compass of my mind. What ecstasy to confront such
things! What delight to find in every hour of every day the necessity to

struggle to understand the simplest things of that other world! I would be like a child again, wandering breathless through a world of mysteries, finding and solving puzzle after puzzle until the larger patterns began to connect themselves and overwhelming revelations came rushing in on my ever-avid mind.

And then I thought of Theliane, and the whole fantasy collapsed into ashes.

I could never leave her. She was the joy of my life, the music of my heart. Without her I would be nothing but a strange lonely old man with an unusual mind and an empty soul.

But to bring her with me: how could I do that? To rip her away from all that was familiar to her, and carry her off to a world of unutterable alienness where every moment of every day would confront her with a bewildering jumble of insoluble riddles, and where she would grow old and die without ever having known the touch of a loving mate or heard the laughter of her own children?

No. No. It was impossible. Insane. I banished the idea from my mind.

The ship was ready, though, for testing. I had no idea what to do.

And while I hesitated—concealing for the moment the extent of the recent progress I had made, both from the Alien and, of course, the king—catastrophe came down upon me.

It was night. I was in my observatory, measuring the position of the comet. So concerned with my work was I that although I was aware of a curious booming sound, quite loud, and saw out of the corner of my eye an odd flash of red light passing just above the rooftops, it was thirty seconds, at least, before I reacted. By that time I could hear the first sounds of uproar in the city.

"Theliane?" I called. "What's going on out there?"

No answer came. The noises from the street grew louder and more agitated: wild shouts, hysterical outcries of fear. Out of the midst of chaotic yelling came one man's voice, loud and clear as a god's, crying over and over, "The tree is falling into the city! We all are doomed! The tree! The tree! The tree!"

The tree, yes. I knew what he meant by that. But the comet was still in its proper place in the sky, a fiercely bright yellowish-green slash across the belly of the darkness. It was not falling on us. It would not fall on us.

I looked for Theliane downstairs, running from room to room, calling her name. She was nowhere in the house. But tacked to the inside of the front door was a note in her handwriting:

Father—

I have gone up into the sky to look at the tree. I must see; I must know.
You understand what I am saying.

I love you.

Gods, no! No!

A reverberating drumbeat of thunder rolled in my head. White fire
flashed. I heard a loud buzzing as of ten thousand insects all at once,
marching through my brain. For a moment everything grew disjointed,
and I was unable to see. The faces of mocking gods whirled about me
in a pulsating circle.

Then I collected myself a little and stepped outside the house, and
saw throngs running through the streets, hundreds of people, thousands, perhaps, many of them wild-eyed and screaming as they ran, and
every one heading in the same direction, eastward, toward the cliffs, the
shore, the Living Sea. It was a raging river of panicky humanity; and
like a man caught up in some terrible nightmare I allowed myself to be
engulfed by that river and borne along by it on its inexorable journey to
the sea.

Long before I reached the shore I was able to see what it was that
was drawing them there. From the high rim of the cliff I saw it, by pale
pink sea-glow and yellow comet-light. I would gladly have screened my
eyes from the sight. But there was no hiding from it, none.

Theliane's flight in the starship had been very brief. The rust-
flecked Tower of the Alien was lying on its side, a short distance out in
the Living Sea, jutting up at an angle with perhaps half its length above
the surface. Theliane had succeeded in getting the ship aloft, which was
miraculous enough, but evidently she had been unable to control it,
and it had executed a wobbly, erratic flight lasting no more than a matter of moments, during which it traveled just above rooftop level across
the width of the city from its starting point in the Great Plaza of the
Kings, over the temple district and the residential quarter and out past
the hill of the royal Citadel, and onward a short distance over the sea.

But there it had reached the end of its journey. The ship's power
must have cut off when Theliane was barely beyond the edge of the
shore: in my mind's eye I saw the vessel halting in mid-air, standing
upright and seemingly motionless above the sea for a moment, and
then toppling in a steady downward plunge.

I tell you all this by putting one word after another, in calm, dispassionate, orderly fashion. But I assure you that I was neither calm

nor dispassionate nor orderly as I went running down that sloping earthen path from the top of the cliff to the shore of the sea. Nothing was in my mind but the fact that the Tower had gone aloft and that it had crashed and that my daughter was in it, out there in the unknown and threatening substance that is the Living Sea. No: not even that. My only thought was that Theliane was in danger and I must rescue her.

The crowd on the shore melted away to either side of me like mist before the piercing rays of the summer sun as I ran past. Do you know how you seem to move in a dream, as though floating, your feet not touching the ground? That was how I moved then.

I reached the edge of the sea and I did not pause at all. In that dreamlike drifting way I moved out onto the strand of steaming pink mud that forms at the border between land and not-land, and, without breaking my stride, I continued unhesitatingly on out into the body of that great unknown thing that no one had ever entered before.

What did I expect to happen to me? I expected nothing. I hoped only that I would survive the short journey out to the fallen ship, and bring Theliane forth from it alive.

The sea was warm and steaming, and very shallow even when I was fifty or sixty paces out from shore, no more than chest-deep for me. It did not seem to grow deeper at all as I proceeded outward. Its strange odor, sweet and not unpleasant, struck my nostrils. I felt its pink substance warm about me, rising past my calves, my knees.

It had a thick consistency, oddly agreeable to the touch. A quiet hissing sound came from it, a burbling, a kind of gentle squeak. Each step I took produced a soft sucking effect as I lifted my feet. Small wriggling protrusions rising from the surface of the sea danced playfully about me like little serpents standing on their tails.

Was there pain? No. Were my legs dissolving? No. Was I being transformed into something unimaginably strange? No. I was still myself, still alive, still moving forward. The sea's grasp was like a sly caress, unseen slithering tendrils sliding over my body, across my thighs, my belly, my loins. Sea-stuff was in my mouth, my eyes, my ears. A strand of it had wrapped itself around my throat.

Colors flashed everywhere. There was purple haze all around me. I saw ghosts circling in a shimmering golden aura in the air, faces that seemed almost familiar, one that might have been my father's, and one that resembled King Thalk, and one that could have been Theliane's.

I felt no fear. The sea was too warm, too welcoming, too comforting for that.

What I did feel was a strange sense of *contact*, with the sea, with the sky, with everything that existed in the world. I was immensely extended; I was infinite; I understood what it must be like to be a god.

It seemed to me that I could stretch out my arms and touch the fingertips of one hand to the cliffs behind me and those of the other to the coast of the distant unreachable eastern continent halfway around the world, where the three-eyed whistling Other Folk live. It seemed to me also that my head rose high above the clouds, so that I could stare face to face at the gleaming pockmarked visage of the comet, and it could stare at me. And I felt the roots of the planet beneath my feet, the tumbling, churning fires of the core, where the toiling god Manibal sweats eternally over the forge of creation.

I touched a myriad souls at once: the soul of the king, and the soul of the Alien, and the souls of all the people who were clustered along the beach. I made contact with everyone in the world at once. Everyone except one; the only soul I could not find was that of my daughter.

Once I glanced back toward the shore. It was surprisingly far away, a black line against the comet-riven sky. The multitude of townspeople who had gathered there now looked to me like so many insects. They stood motionless, watching, watching, watching, as Kell the lunatic artificer went striding ever farther into the Living Sea.

From the cliff, the starship had seemed only a little way from shore, but the actual distance was greater than I had thought. An endless time went by until at last I came to the ship.

It had fallen into the sea in such a way that the entry hatch was on the underside, beneath the sea's surface. I would have had to submerge myself completely in order to reach it, and that gave me pause for the first time since I had gone out from the shore; but also I realized that Theliane, intending a flight into the cold and darkness of the farther sky, would have dogged the hatch shut before taking off. I would never be able to enter it from without.

Instead I began to clamber up the side of the ship, crawling hand to hand along its ridged skin. There were hand-holds there, perhaps for the use of maintenance personnel on that faraway planet from which it had been launched. Bright droplets of sea-stuff fell away from my hands and arms like glistening pearls as I emerged into the air.

Near the top of the vessel is a porthole made of something like glass, though it is not glass, that provides a view for the occupant of the control cabin. In a desperate plodding way I pulled myself up the ship until I was looking in that porthole, and I looked upon the face of my daughter Theliane.

Her eyes were open, but she was dead.

I had no doubt of that, from the moment I first saw her. Her eyes, those lovely glowing eyes whose color was the delicate color of thyrla eggs, were glassy and unblinking, and filmed over with the unmistakable film of death. Her finely tapered nostril-slits were slack; her mouth drooped and sagged to one side. The posture of her body as she sat in the straps of the pilot's cradle was the posture of the dead.

The shock of the landing impact, no doubt, had killed her. I could not accept that thought, but neither could I deny it. I hammered my hands against the side of the ship until I thought my bones would break. I pressed my face against that porthole and shouted her name again and again, knowing that no sound from outside could possibly penetrate those metal walls. But in any case she could never have heard me.

Then my strength failed me and I dropped away from the ship's skin, falling free of the vessel's flank and landing in the sea. My landing was soft and easy. The sea seemed to reach up to catch me and it drew me down gently into itself. Quietly I lay just beneath the surface, unmoving, not even bothering to breathe, cushioned by the density of the strange warm fluid. I floated. I drifted. I was in the caressing arms of a vast mother.

It embraced me and enfolded me and very soon, I think, it would have begun to digest me. I imagined my skin and my flesh peeling painlessly away, and soon afterward my bones as well. The particles that had composed me would distribute themselves through the body of the sea, and I would be part of it forever.

But that did not happen. Numbly, unthinkingly, I began to paddle with my arms, and after a moment more to drop my feet to the shallow bottom and to push myself forward, and step by step I made my way toward shore.

I came to land close by the Tree of Purple Flame, far down the beach from the place where I had entered the sea. I saw the bright shaft of its smooth white trunk and the ghostly flickering of its unceasing purple radiance, and they drew me onward. The tree was singing, too, a low, gentle, soothing, wordless song of comfort and strength, and as I drew close to it I began to sing also.

Its gnarled roots rose above the surface of the sea. I seized one and clung to it and pulled myself across its smooth slippery sides until I was up out of the sea entirely. I lay there for a time, gasping, looking up into the crown of the tree, seeing the faces there, the eyes, the coiling shapes, the beating wings. Then I rose and walked down the narrow ridge of the root's upper face until I arrived at the trunk itself, and I embraced it, stretching out my arms as wide as they would go. But that was hardly enough to reach one-fiftieth of the way around that great trunk.

People had come down the beach toward me. But they would not go close to the tree; they stood back, gaping, eyes very wide, whispering among themselves.

I saw that the king himself was among them.

"Majesty," I said in a voice that was like a voice from the next world, and let go of the tree-trunk and took a few tottering steps toward him. "Majesty, I repaired the ship, and my daughter rode it into the sky without my knowledge or permission. She wanted to see the great comet at close range. And now the ship is in the Living Sea and she is dead within it."

For once there was no bluster about him and no foolishness either. His face was sad and solemn. "She had the same hunger for knowledge that burns in you, Kell."

"Yes. And a great deal more courage."

"She was very brave, yes."

I sank down on the sand before him and tried to make the gesture of obeisance, but I was trembling too much from my exertions to manage it. Hai-Theklon, bending, caught me by the elbows and lifted me to my feet. His eyes stared into mine.

"What will you do now?" he asked me.

"I will build a machine that will go out into the sea and bring the Tower back to shore," I told him. "And I'll open it up and take her from it, and carry her out of the city to the burial-place and do the things that are done there. And then—then—"

I went faltering into silence. To my great surprise a wrenching sound came from me, from deep down in my throat, a sound that was something like the sound that the Alien had made that time when his face had become moist and he told me that he was expressing his happiness at the thought of going home. It had not seemed like a sound of happiness then. It was not a sound of happiness when it came from me now.

"She was very brave," said the king again. "And very beautiful, I am told."

"Very beautiful, yes, Sire," I said. "She was that. And much more."

8.

The next day I designed, and over the following week, under my direction, fifty artisans constructed, the machine that is to pull the Tower of the Alien from the place where it lies half submerged in the Living Sea. It is a great wooden framework on wheels, a kind of giant wagon, equipped at its front end with a large and sturdy leather hoop that can be tightened by the operation of an arrangement of cogs and wheels.

Pulleys and levers connect the machine to a large and sturdy iron band that I have caused to be set into the face of the cliff along the shore. Pressure on the levers induces the pulleys to tighten, moving the wagon-wheels and thrusting the machine outward into the sea. Reversing the action of the levers will draw the wagon back toward land. It is a cunning device. The old artificer may have been shattered by grief, but he has not yet lost his skills.

I will ride the wagon tomorrow as it goes into the sea. Despite my demonstration that it is possible for us to go into the Living Sea and return unharmed, there is still no one else who will venture close to its pink surf. But that is all right. I should be the one who brings Theliane back from the sea, and I will be the one who does it. From my seat atop the wagon, I will operate the controls that bring the hoop into place around the ship and tighten it; and then I will give the signal and the men on shore will pull the wagon and the ship up onto the land.

And what will happen after that?

"Do you think the ship can be repaired again?" I asked the Alien, the day before yesterday. I have gone to visit him every day, since Theliane's death. He is nearly as deeply moved by it as I am.

He said, "I think the ship will turn out not to be very seriously damaged, despite the crash."

"But it fell down into the sea!"

"Not because of any mechanical failure, I think, but simply because she gave it the wrong commands," the Alien said. "She must have become confused. She was speaking a foreign language, after all."

"Speaking?"

"The ship responds to spoken commands. In the language of my planet."

"How would Theliane have known the language of your planet?"

"I taught her," he said quietly. "Years ago. She asked me to. It gave me great pleasure, being able to speak again with someone in my native language. And so she knew how to tell the ship what to do. But once it was aloft she must have become confused. If you give the ship conflicting commands, or say something that makes no sense to it, it might very well tumble out of control."

"Ah," I said. There were signs of anguish plainly visible on his face again; and, I suspect, on mine. Together we had conspired to kill her, he and I, and we had not understood what we were doing at all.

He held out his hands, his odd little stubby-fingered hands, and clasped my larger ones within them, and we stood like that for a while, face to face, one mourner to another. He made a small sound deep in his throat again; and I made one also. It gives some relief from sorrow, that sound.

Then I said, "In two or three days we will pull the ship out of the sea, and after I have taken Theliane from it and sent her to her eternal rest, I will go into back it and do whatever has to be done to make sure that it is still in working order. And then, Alien, I will come for you here in the maze."

Color came into his long pallid face, and light. "Will you, then?"

"By night, yes, when the guards are sleeping or drunk. And if your official guardian Kataphrazes the eunuch happens to be here, I will take him and turn him and turn him and turn him in circles until his hsorn-sense is altogether befuddled, and I will lock him up here in your apartment and bring you forth out of this maze that long ago I built for you, and we will go to the ship, you and I, and this time it will receive the proper instructions and it will take you into the sky."

"And you, Kell? Won't the king punish you for that, as you said he would, once I've disappeared? He'll know it was you that was responsible."

"The king will have to find me, first," I said. "And I will be in the sky with you."

"*What?*"

"Yes," I said. "That is my plan."

Why not?
Why not?

Nothing holds me here now. I will go with him to his world, and let whatever may happen to me there happen. It will be my turn to be the Alien, there. Let them build a maze for me to live in, if that is what they want. Will that be any worse than the way I live here among my own people? I have always been a stranger in their midst. So I will leave, and I will be an alien among the aliens of the Alien's world, and everything will be new and fresh and strange to me, and so be it.

So be it.

The comet, I noticed when I took my measurements last night, has passed its point of maximum brightness and soon will begin to fade. Day by day now it will grow ever dimmer, until at last it cannot be seen at all, and then it will be gone from our skies, perhaps for a hundred years, perhaps for a hundred thousand. And I will be gone with it, and gone forever.

So I make my farewell now to this world, and even to its gods, for they will not go with me where I am going. I had faith in them: and what sort of faith did they keep with me, to take me from my only child? Kleysz, goodbye. Goodbye to you, Gamiridon of the bright sword. Maldaz who rules the sun, Hayna, ever-toiling Manibal, goodbye. And you also, Tulabaratha, you greatest of artificers. You served me well, even as I was serving you. I will take something of you with me, wherever it is that I go now. But I say farewell even to you.

Perhaps the people, not knowing what has become of me, will tell one another gravely that the comet has carried me off to some place in the stars. I like that. Let them say it. "Kell's Tree," they always called it, in their invincible ignorance. The tree that grew from the sky. "The tree reached down to us to get him," they will say. "And he has climbed it and vanished into the sky." But no. No. Whatever they say, it was never a tree. A comet is what it is, and nothing else: my comet, Kell's Comet. And now its brightness fades. It begins to take its leave of them. And so does the Artificer Kell.

THE CHURCH AT
MONTE SATURNO

I generally learn quickly from my mistakes and therefore don't often repeat them, but I am also a very stubborn man, and sometimes those two character traits turn out to be incompatible. I refer you to my introduction to "Diana of the Hundred Breasts," in which I tell how I decide to write a story for Alice K. Turner of Playboy *based on things I had seen on my recent trip to Turkey, and she turns it down, as she has turned down several previous stories of mine set in foreign lands, calling it an "IRS story" because she thinks my prime motivation for writing it is to establish a tax deduction for the trip.*

Now watch me do it all over again.

It is June 12, 1996—almost exactly a year after I wrote the "Diana" story. Once again, uncharacteristically, I feel like doing some writing in the summer months, something I have avoided fairly assiduously for a long time. I will try another one for Alice, and, yes, it will be another IRS story, and this time I give her fair warning:

"What I'd like to try," I tell her, "is something in the direction of fantasy. (Not necessarily horror fantasy.) Probably one growing out of my travels & my interest in archaeology. Whenever I've offered you something in the past along those lines—one that was set in Mexico, and another in Israel, I recall, and the one last year in Ephesus, "Diana of the Hundred Breasts"— you've turned it down, whereas my batting average with you on science fiction is better than Ted Williams's. I begin to wonder whether you've been

implicitly telling me to stick to what I'm best known for....Or maybe it's just the particular fantasy stories I've sent you that were the problem, not the fact that they were fantasies."

Alice replies a couple of days later that she has no objection to seeing fantasy from me, if it's the right kind of fantasy. "I don't think historical fantasy is a good bet for us, but if it was lively enough I might change my mind. What I definitely don't want is one of those IRS stories of yours, all sightseeing and no plot."

So I have had fair warning too. And on July 16, 1996, I sent her "The Church at Monte Saturno," with these comments appended:

"So here's the story. I figured it would turn out a fantasy (or a ghost story, or whatever) and so it has. I will undoubtedly write more science fiction one of these days, but it is not where my head, as they used to say, is at right this minute.

"You will probably call it an IRS story. You keep calling them that, but it just isn't so. The reality of the situation is that IRS will let me deduct overseas travel even if I don't write stories about the places where I go, because the possibility always exists that I might, someday. There's no telling what a writer might do, sooner or later, with material he's gathered. In 39 years of deducting foreign travel I've never been challenged on this. So I have no sense of needing to write something about where I went on my last vacation purely to justify the writeoff.

"The real situation is that I find the theme of the American who goes overseas and gets out of his depth in some spooky situation very appealing, and I keep playing with it, and I tend to set those stories in places where I've already been, because that makes more sense to me than trying to set them in places that I know about only from the National Geographic. Justifying a tax deduction never enters into my mind. You don't want me to set everything in San Francisco, do you, or on some planet of Goofus IX? So I write about places I know something about where I don't happen actually to live.

"Here it is, anyway. May it meet a better fate at your hands than its predecessors. But stop hocking me about the IRS already, okay?"

You can see from this that Alice and I have a very unusual author-editor relationship. You can probably see, also, that I am skating on very thin ice, and back to me almost immediately comes Alice's letter of rejection:

"OK, I promise not to make any more cracks about IRS stories, though I reserve the right to my private opinions. And of course I don't want you to set everything in San Francisco, though I have no objections to the planet Goofus IX—it's been a long time between visits.

"But, that said, I'm going to reject this story. Very little happens in it, and it's just not interesting or energetic enough, for me at any rate. Schematically, it's man goes to strange place, sees strange thing, strange thing goes away, he goes away. Bye....Of course, it's as smoothly done as ever, and I'm sure it will quickly find a home. But I'd prefer to wait for something a little more gripping. I'm sure it won't be a long wait."

Ah, me. It's the "Diana" outcome all over again, one year later. Once more Alice and I agree to disagree, and once more I take my story to Shawna McCarthy of Realms of Fantasy, *who has no objections to it at all, and she publishes it in her April, 1997 issue. The next time I write a story for Alice Turner, I set it in such places as Istanbul, Rome, and Paris, all of which I have visited many times, writing off some of the cost of each trip as a research expense, and Alice buys it quickly without saying a word about the IRS.*

Serafina said, "You are English, no?"

"American, actually," Gardiner told her.

"I would say English. The studious look. The glasses. The bad hair-cut. The way you dress. Like you have money but don't think it's nice to spend it. Very English, I think."

True enough. Only he wasn't. And he had taken her at first glance for a simple Sicilian peasant girl, but obviously that was wrong also. There was nothing simple about her. Both of them, it seemed, had instantly invented imaginary identities for each other and were working their way backward now to the actual ones.

"I'm a professor. An associate professor, actually. History of art." Who had taught at three different universities in fourteen years, and still was only an associate professor. Who did not even have his doctorate. And now was roaming the edges of the classical world peering at Byzantine mosaics in the hope they would somehow rescue him. "Associate professors often tend to seem a little English. I dress like this because it's what I can afford. It's also very comfortable."

They were sitting under a gnarled old oak on a summer-parched brown hillside at the edge of the little town of Monte Saturno in central Sicily, looking southward into a steep gorge densely covered on both slopes with tough, leathery-looking gray-green shrubs. The sky was a hot iron dome, painted a pale blue. Even at this early hour of the day the air was stifling. Gardiner felt a little dizzy. This was a dizzying place, Sicily. The air, rich with lemon and herbs. The heat. The dark fissures of decay everywhere. The beauty. The taint of antiquity, the unfathomable mysteries lurking in every narrow alleyway, behind every crumbling facade.

He had arrived in town late the night before, driving down from Palermo, and had known her for less than half an hour. He was just finishing breakfast at the little *albergo* where he was staying when she came in to chat with the proprietor, her uncle. Gardiner had lured her out for a stroll: past the low lopsided cathedral, the scruffy and padlocked municipal museum, the ancient windowless building that was the post office. Almost at once they were in the open countryside, staring out into the island's immense empty hinterland. She was long and lean, nearly as tall as he was, with prominent cheekbones, a long sharp nose, dark penetrating eyes. She had been born in this village, she told him, but lived in Palermo and had spent considerable time in Rome; she had come here a few days before to visit her grandfather, who was ninety. Gardiner found her attractive, and also oddly forward, flirtatious. But of course he knew better than to indulge in any fantasies. This was Sicily, after all.

"The history of art? You come to *Sicily* to study Italian art? There is some confusion here, I think. You should be in Florence, Venice, Rome."

"Not Italian art, especially. Byzantine. I'm writing a doctoral thesis on the transition from the Roman style of mosaic work to the Byzantine." How tidy that sounded! But he hardly wanted to tell her that he had come to Italy seeking something that he could not define, that his life, though satisfying in some ways, seemed fundamentally static and insubstantial: that he yearned for a coup, a grand achievement that would establish him before the world. Serafina sat leaning toward him, listening intently, with her long legs crossed, her hands outstretched on her knees. "You understand what that is, a doctoral thesis?" he asked.

"*Capisco, si.*" She was speaking mostly in English, which she handled well, though she dropped into Italian now and then for emphasis. Gardiner, fairly fluent in Italian, had begun the conversation in that language but something about her expression made him think that she found that condescending, and he had cut it out. She could be, he suspected, a prickly, difficult woman. "You write your thesis, they make you a *dottore della filosofia*, and then you become a real professor, that is how it works, no?"

"A *full* professor."

"Ah. *Si*. So you are here to see our mosaics. Already you have seen the mosaics in Palermo? The Capella Palatina, the church of La Martorana, the cathedral at Monreale?"

"All of them. Plus the one at Cefalu. They're all later than the ones I'm studying, really, but how could I pass them up?" Gardiner loved mosaics with a powerful passion. Not for the religious scenes they depicted, which had no real importance or significance to him beyond an esthetic one. He was in no way a religious man. The holy saints and martyrs of the Christian mosaics and the gods and goddesses of the older, pagan ones were simply just so much mythology for him, quaint, mildly amusing. But the mosaics themselves—their plasticity of design, their glinting surfaces, their inner light—that was what excited him. It was nearly impossible for him to put his feelings into words: an almost sexual yearning, focused on bits of colored tile glued to walls. He was possessed, and he knew it.

"And now?"

"Today I'll head down to Piazza Armerina, the Villa Romana, the palace of the Roman emperor. With absolutely wonderful mosaics."

"I have never been there," she said.

Never? That was odd. Piazza Armerina was, he calculated, no more than an hour's drive away. But New Yorkers never went to the Statue of Liberty or Parisians to the Eiffel Tower, either. Gardiner toyed with the idea of inviting Serafina to accompany him. "From Piazza Armerina I'll continue on south to Agrigento for a look at the Greek temples, and then up along the coast to Trapani, where I can catch the ferry for Tunis. The Bardo Museum in Tunis has one of the finest collections of mosaics in the world." Into his mind now there sprang the wild notion of asking her to join him for the Tunisian expedition too, and he was startled by the sudden throbbing beneath his breastbone at the idea. On half an hour's acquaintance, though? At best she would laugh; she might spit in his face. The old days of impenetrably guarded chastity might be gone here, but at the outset she would want him at least to pretend that he thought of her as a respectable woman. He looked guiltily away, as if fearing that his intentions were visible on his face.

I should ask her now, he thought, about herself: where she went to school, what she does, how it happens that she speaks English so well. But he hesitated, momentarily unwilling to plod through the standard conversational gambits. A sharp silence fell between them. Gardiner heard the buzz and click of insects all around, and a peculiar ticking coming from a nearby tree, as though the heat were shrinking its bark. The sudden tension sharpened his senses, and he became aware of a tumult of Mediterranean scents assailing him on all sides, lavender, maybe, rosemary, the fragrance of prickly-pear blossoms and lemon leaves.

A hawk drifted diagonally across the sky. Gardiner, idly following its path with his eyes, watched it descend abruptly into the gorge as if diving to seize a rabbit. As his gaze traveled downward with the plunging hawk he noticed for the first time what appeared to be a small isolated building on the far side of the valley, all but hidden in the scrubby brush. Not much more than the curving arc of its low white dome was visible. Something about the shape of that dome aroused his attention. He had seen buildings like that before. But not in Sicily.

"What is that across the way?" he asked her, pointing.

She knew what he meant. "A ruin. Not important."

His guidebook had said nothing about ruins in Monte Saturno. So far as he knew there was nothing of that sort here, neither Greek, Roman, Byzantine, nor Norman, none of the multitudinous layers upon layers of superimposed realities out of which this island was built. He had stopped here last night simply because he had had a late start out of Palermo and decided en route not to risk driving on into Piazza Armerina after dark on this rough country road. It had been pure luck that the town's one *trattoria* maintained a few upstairs rooms for tourists passing through.

"A church of some sort, is it?"

"Of some sort, yes. Not Catholic. A Greek church, the Orthodox faith. Empty a long time. Not a holy place any more."

"Empty how long?"

A shrug. "A long time?"

"Five hundred years? A thousand?"

"Who knows? But a long time. It is very ruined. Nobody goes there except goats. And young *innamorati*. You know, lovers looking for a place to be alone."

Gardiner felt a slow stirring of excitement.

"A Greek church," he said slowly. "Byzantine, you mean?"

"That may be." Serafina laughed. "Ah, you think there are mosaics there? You think you have made a great artistic discovery? There is nothing. Dirt. Ghosts."

"Ghosts?"

"It is very haunted there. Yes."

She sounded almost serious. He had, for a moment, a sense that a door had opened into a dark place forever inaccesible to him and Serafina was standing on the far side of the threshold. He knew that many of the villagers here lived on the interface between modern civilization and that shadowy realm of antiquity that was beyond his understanding; but Serafina, he had thought, was entirely of his world. He saw now that he might have been wrong about that. But then she grinned and was a contemporary woman again.

He said, forcing a grin of his own, "I'd be interested in seeing it, haunted or not. Is there any way of getting to it?"

"A road. Very bad, very rough."

"Could you take me there? I very much would like to have a look at it."

Anger flashed like summer lightning in her eyes. "Ah, you are so subtle, you *inglesi!*"

"American," he said. And then, comprehending: "And you misunderstand me, if you think I'm trying in some roundabout fashion to engineer a rendezvous with you. *Lei capisce,* 'rendezvous'?" She nodded. "But as long as I'm here—a Byzantine church that isn't even in the guidebook—"

Another eyeflash, this one more mischievous. She still seemed angry, but in a different way now.

"Truly, *Professore,* you are interested only in the architecture of this dirty abandoned church? You take me to this rendezvous for lovers merely to see stone walls? Ah, I think I misjudge the kind of man you are. A beautiful woman means nothing to you, I think."

Gardiner sighed. He was caught in a no-win situation. Bluntness seemed the best tactic.

"They mean a great deal. And you are extremely beautiful. But I know better than to proposition a *Siciliana* five minutes after I've met her, and in any case there's a bed in my hotel room, if that's what I was after. I don't need to take you to an abandoned building full of goatshit and straw. But I would like to see the church. Honestly."

Serafina's expression softened. She looked merely amused now.

"You want to go?" she said. "Really? *Allora.* We go, then." She snapped her fingers under his nose. "Come! Up! We get ready, we go, at once, *subito!*"

But of course they didn't go *subito*. Nothing ever happened *subito* in Sicily. They had to prepare themselves properly for the expedition, sturdy boots, jackets to ward off brambles and wide-brimmed hats for the sun, plus a bottle of wine, some bread and cheese and salami and fruit, as if they were going on a long journey, not just down the side of one nearby hill and up another. The preparations mysteriously stretched on for hours. He had a suitable jacket and even a hat but no hiking boots, only sneakers, which Serafina glanced at with contempt. Her cousin Gino would lend him a pair of boots.

Cousin Gino was twenty-three or so, sullenly handsome, a swarthy, bull-necked bushy-haired man with enormous forearms and bright, fierce eyes, unexpectedly blue in this land of dark-eyed people. Though Gardiner was a big man himself, broad-shouldered and ruggedly athletic of build, who looked more like a football coach than an assistant professor of the history of art, it appeared likely to him that in any kind of fight Gino would twirl him around his wrist like spaghetti. And just now Gino was glowering at Gardiner with what looked very much like unconcealed hostility, bringing to mind all of Gardiner's stereotyped notions of the way the men of this island defended their women's chastity. Serafina said something to him in the transmogrified and deformed dialect of Italian, both clipped and slurred, that was Sicilian—a patois which Gardiner found utterly opaque. Gino, replying with an equally unintelligible stream of brusque, sputtering words, gave them both a furious glare and went whirling away from them.

"What's bothering him?" Gardiner asked, still inventing Gino's proprietary rage, imagining dire warnings, threats of vendetta.

"He says your feet are too big, they will stretch his boots."

"That's all?" Gardiner felt something close to disappointment. "Well, tell him not to worry. If anything, his feet look bigger than mine."

"Maybe yes, maybe no. He will get the boots anyway, he said. As a special favor for me. We are very good friends, Gino and I."

The image came unbidden to Gardiner's mind of Serafina and her brutish cousin, over there across the gorge one languid summer night seven or eight years ago, lying naked in each other's arms, ferociously entwined in the incestuous embraces that he assumed were altogether customary among the rural adolescents of this backward country. He doubted that any such thing had ever happened between them; but if it had, no wonder Gino was pissed off over her taking this *straniero* to their special place, and in his own best boots, yet.

Gardiner smiled at his own foolishness. He was capable of engendering an ethnic cliche for any occasion. It was a habit, he told himself, that he needed to break.

Eventually Gino came back with a pair of huge clodhoppers dangling from one immense hand. To Gardiner's surprise, and apparently Gino's, the boots were a perfect fit.

It was a little before noon when they finally set out. The sun filled half the sky, blazing like a permanent atomic explosion, and the hot, shimmering air was full of madly dancing bugs that sang manic droning songs in his ears. There was a sort of a road at first, but it morphed into a narrow untidy trail after a few hundred yards and then, a little while later, became nothing more than a faint exiguous track through the dry stiff-branched chaparral.

Despite the heat and the difficulties of the route, long-legged Serafina set a brisk pace. Gardiner kept up with her without much effort, but he was marinating in his own sweat under the jacket that she had insisted he wear. At the bottom of the Monte Saturno side of the gorge they came to a campsite, a flat rock and a fire-pit and enough discarded wine bottles to keep future archaeologists amused for centuries, and she said crisply, "We make the lunch here."

"*Va bene.*" He welcomed the break. The climb ahead looked formidable.

Serafina assembled sandwiches while he opened the wine. As they ate and drank she offered snippets of autobiography. She had lived here until she was sixteen, she told him, and then was taken away to Rome by her uncle, not the same one who owned the *trattoria*, to be educated. There was a bit of extra spin about the way she said "uncle" and "educated," and Gardiner flamboyantly hypothesized all manner of sinister iniquities, some wealthy waxed-mustachioed stranger buying the beautiful girl from her impoverished parents to be put to the most depraved uses in his elegant baroque apartment overlooking the Spanish Stairs. But she talked instead of learning English at a genteel Roman academy whose name meant nothing to Gardiner but sounded quite elite; then a stint in the Roman office of a big British investment bank; an affair, apparently, with a young British bond trader that brought her a transfer to the London office, a dizzying taste of the international high life, and, so she appeared to be saying, the inevitable accidental pregnancy and concomitant mess, letdown, and heartbreak. Her fair-haired bond trader operated out of Prague now and she, having had her fill of banking, worked at the Hertz Rent-a-Car office in Palermo. She was fluent in English, French, Spanish, and German, as well as Italian and the local dialect. So much for her being a simple peasant girl, he thought. He guessed that she was around twenty-nine. He was nine years older. In the thick afternoon warmth the aura of her lean sleek Mediterranean attractiveness expanded into the hazy air around him, dazzling and mesmerizing him, enveloping him in an unexpected and astonishing explosion of impulsive speculation. How it would startle everyone at the college, Gardiner told himself, if he came back from his summer research trip not only with material for his thesis but with a beautiful and cosmopolitan Italian wife!

"*Andiamo*," she said, the moment the bottle was empty. "Now I show you the fabulous Byzantine church."

The hill on the southern side of the gorge was steep, all right, and the heat was unthinkable now, and Serafina moved with jackrabbit energy up the slope, as though deliberately testing his endurance; but, fortified by the good red wine of Monte Saturno and his own implacable curiosity about the ruin ahead and now, also, this absurd but amusing new bit of romantic fancy of his, he matched her step for step, a couple of yards behind her with his gaze fixed steadily on the taut, tantalizing seat of her jeans.

Suddenly they were in a little scraggly clearing, and the ruined church lay right in front of them.

"*Ecco*," she said. "Behold your heart's desire."

The building was a little one, no bigger than a garage and half concealed in tangles of brush, but it was pure late-Byzantine in form, a squared-off Greek cross of a structure with a squat dome perched atop its four blocky walls. He knew of no other building of this sort in Sicily. It reminded him of nothing so much as the eleventh-century church at Daphni, outside Athens. But Daphni was world-famous for its luminous mosaics.

It was impossible, Gardiner thought, that mosaics like those of Daphni could have gone unnoticed all this time, even in this obscure hilltop village.

"Let's go in," he said hoarsely.

"*Si, si*." She beckoned to him. "*Venga di qua*."

The main entrance was sealed by a dense barrier of interwoven woody shrubs, but a smaller door stood slightly ajar on the northern side, a crudely made wooden one, cracked and crazed, that looked as though it had been tacked on about a hundred years ago by some farmer using this place as a barn. Serafina, with a surprising show of strength, levered it open just far enough to let them slip inside.

The church was rank, musty, dismal, a claustrophobe's nightmare. When Gardiner switched on his flashlight he saw that over the centuries enough sandy dirt had blown in through the narrow windowgrates and through crevices in the walls to lift the floor level at least eight feet in most places, so that he was standing practically within arm's reach of the dome. Heaps of ancient mildewed straw were piled everywhere: a barn, yes. The pungent aroma of innumerable copulations hovered in the air. For how many generations had the passionate young of Monte Saturno committed sins of the flesh in this bedraggled former house of God?

He aimed his beam upward, praying that he would see the stark somber face of Christ the Pantocrator scowling down at him, as at Daphni and other Byzantine churches. No. The dome was bare. He had not really expected anything else. Probably this had been some simple chapel for wayfarers, in use for perhaps fifty years a thousand years ago, then abandoned, forgotten.

"You are satisfied?" Serafina asked.

"I suppose."

"I myself parted with my virtue here," she said, in a bold, cool, self-mocking tone. He looked at her, taken aback, angered and repelled by her unsolicited revelation. The idea that Serafina had ever engaged in any sexual event in this grim squalid place was sickening to him. She and some clumsy village Romeo sprawling on a scratchy tick-infested blanket, his shaggy eager body pressing down on hers, her splendid slender legs spraddled wide, toes pointed at the dome: the thrusts, the grunts, the gasps. "I was fifteen. We thought we were being very brave coming here, because of the ghosts. But every young couple in town is brave like that when the time comes. Some things are so urgent that even ghosts are unimportant. The ghosts must be defied."

Gardiner shook his head. "Ghosts?" he muttered, roaming the edges of the building, scuffing at the mounded straw. That door into the unknown opening again. This damned island, he thought: level after level of superstition, evil, and madness. You were forever toppling down through the detritus of all its many occupiers to the jolting incomprehensibilities beneath.

He was no good at dealing with such stuff. It forever amazed him when he came running up against some apparently rational person's firmly held belief in the irrational, the impossible, the altogether inexplicable. For Gardiner there was nothing inexplicable, only phenomena that had not yet been properly explained; anything that seemed to be truly and eternally inexplicable was, he suspected, something that had either been badly misinterpreted or had simply never in fact occurred.

He prodded and kicked at the ground along the perimeter of the building with the tip of Gino's boot. "Who was the lucky boy?" he asked, after a time, amazed at himself for keeping the distasteful subject open.

"Does it matter?" she said. "His name was Calogero. He is dead now."

"I'm sorry," said Gardiner automatically. He continued to kick and scuff. Then came a surprise. "Hold on. What's this?"

A forehead of glistening tile was showing along the wall, just at the debris line. He dropped to his knees and scrabbled at it, hurling handfuls of sand behind him. Other things came into view. Eyebrows. Eyes. A serene face, nearly complete; a halo. He trembled. There was a mosaic here after all.

"It is not easy to believe," she said, as they made their way wearily back to town at dusk after a long breathless afternoon of clearing away debris. "All those years, and those beautiful things on the wall, and no one ever thought to look under the dirt, until you."

Gardiner barely heard her. He was lost in a feverish dream of academic triumph. There would be articles in the journals; there would be a book; he would waltz to his doctorate. The mosaics were not of the first rank, hardly that, but they were undeniably late-Byzantine, a continuous band of them that circled the walls just below the surface of the intrusive fill, saints and pilgrims and Biblical figures in bright, intense reds and greens and golds and blacks. The tesserae, the bits of colored glass out of which the mosaic patterns were fashioned, were large and crude and not always perfectly fitted together—this was not Monreale or Cefalu, not Ravenna's San Vitale, not the Keriye Djami in Istanbul—and the figures were awkward and often poorly arranged; but there was a purity about them, an innocence, that made them very beautiful in their own less sophisticated manner.

Schemes, plans, were swiftly unfolding now. He would use his meager funds to hire workmen in town; he would clear out all the fill; he would photograph, he would analyze, he would compare and contrast, he would publish, he would publish, he would publish—

As he and Serafina entered the town's central *piazza* Gardiner saw that the entire population had turned out, making the nightly promenade, families moving in clustered groups, old men walking arm in arm, young couples holding hands. Some glanced at them, smiling. It seemed to him that everyone was remarking knowingly on their dusty, sweaty look, speculating vividly, lubriciously, on what they had been up to all afternoon in the church across the gorge. And not one with any idea of the truth.

Gardiner had been thinking of inviting her into the *trattoria* for a celebratory dinner, candles and a fine bottle of red Regeleali *riserva* with the meal, and then, perhaps, a night of glorious celebratory delights upstairs: all the way back, he had seen that as a natural and inevitable sequel to the day's triumphant events. But here in town he perceived instantly the impossibility of any such thing. Sweep her grandly into the inn with everybody watching, his carnal notions as manifest to all as if he had exposed himself in the street, and she not to be seen again until morning? Hardly. Whatever destiny awaited him with this woman, and Gardiner was convinced now that some sort of destiny did, it would not be consummated in this tiny and hermetic village. Not tonight, at any rate, virtually in public, as it were.

She appeared to have figured all that out long before him. "Well," she said, hardly pausing a moment outside the little inn before turning away, "I congratulate you on your good fortune. I am happy to have been of service." She touched the tips of her fingers to his, and then she was gone, walking in long strides across the *piazza* to greet a pair of hatchet-faced old women who were clad in the traditional somber costume of an earlier era.

There was no bath in his room, only a washbasin. Gardiner stripped, quickly splashed himself clean, lay down on the creaking bed to reflect on the day's achievement and perhaps enjoy a little repose. Instantly he was asleep. When he woke, with a start, it was past ten. He dressed hastily. As he descended the stairs, he met someone coming upward, a sturdy-looking, black-bearded, youngish man in a priest's black robe, who smiled and saluted him when they passed each other. So the *albergo* had acquired a new guest during the day. Two guests at once: a booming tourist season for them, Gardiner supposed.

The *padrona* was in the dining room, reading a newspaper. She seemed untroubled by his tardiness, and immediately went about putting together dinner for him, pasta with sardines, some roasted pork, a carafe of the red *vino di casa*. "It was a good day for you?" she asked.

"Fine. Splendid." His glow could leave no doubt.

"You stay here tomorrow?"

"Certainly. Even past tomorrow."

This time, when he settled down on his bed again after dinner, sleep was impossible for a long time. He stared up at the low fly-specked ceiling and saw mosaics on the screen of his wearied mind, stylized mosaic figures, angels, patriarchs, sheep, frolicking dogs. It was too good to be true: much too good. Perhaps he had imagined the whole thing. The heat, the wine, the enchanting proximity of Serafina—

No. No. No. No. They had really been there. His discovery, his mosaics. He had touched them with his own hands. Felt their smooth shining surfaces.

He slept, finally. It was a night of strange frightening dreams, masked figures dancing around him as he lay strapped to a smoldering pyre in the middle of the *piazza*.

At nine he awakened, breakfasted downstairs on cheese and figs and rolls, and peered out into the town square, which was utterly empty except for a couple of elderly dogs. He had no idea where Serafina was and felt uncomfortable about asking; and in any case he and she had made no arrangements for today. He equipped himself with his hat, his jacket, and Gino's ponderous boots, and tucked a bottle of wine from the display on the dining room table into his backpack, along with enough rolls and cheese and fruit to last him through lunch, and, armed with flashlight, notebook, camera, went capering off alone toward the ravine.

He dug all morning, using as his shovel a slab of gray slate that was lying in the clearing outside the church. As the layer of loose fill retreated, and he laid bare more and more of the band of mosaic ornament that rimmed the walls, Gardiner grew increasingly excited by his find. The work was on the crude side, yes, but it had a raw power that marked it as an important stylistic mode in its own right. The background in particular was an intense bluish-white, giving the newly exposed parts of the wall a fierce brilliance that flamed wondrously as the sun came slanting occasionally in through the narrow windows and the cracks in the dome, fading when it moved along. Each moment of brightness was the occasion for a hasty flurry of photographs, and soon all his film was gone. It was a giddy, magical few hours.

He postulated some tenth or eleventh-century craftsman traveling down from Palermo, perhaps to do a job of interior decoration at some baron's palazzo along the island's south shore, being inveigled en route into spending a few weeks touching up this little chapel. And really getting into it, seeing it as an opportunity to experiment with an individual style of work, perhaps slipping into a little romantic entanglement with one of the town girls that gave him motivation to linger a little while longer, now a real labor of love, so that months went by, maybe even a year or two of solitary toil, preparing the little colored cubes and painstakingly mortaring them into place, his own private masterpiece. All too soon to be forgotten, the building allowed to go derelict, a habitation for donkeys, the brilliant mosaics covered in time by an accretion of wind-blown rubble many feet deep.

There was more than a thesis to be had here. There was an entire scholarly reputation.

At midday, unable to move another molecule of dirt, Gardiner slipped outside into the stupefying heat for his wine and cheese. As soon as he had finished, sleep came over him, in an instant, as though a thick velvet curtain had been dropped on him.

Awakening just as instantly some ninety minutes later, he went back into the church and beheld something so bewildering that his mind could not at first encompass it, and he thought he might still be dreaming. But he knew that he had to be awake. The evidence of physical sensation was compelling. The heavy, shimmering, almost tangible air, the penetrating heat, the myriad of musty pungent smells left behind by vanished centuries: all of that was too vividly real.

And the mosaics had undergone a bizarre transformation. The saints had grown leering faces with forked tongues, and their haloes glowed and pulsated with a neon fury. The peasants tending their flocks had been rearranged into obscene configurations, and looked back jeeringly over their shoulders at him while buggering bat-winged monstrosities. Placid sheep and bounding dogs had been replaced by grotesque reptilian horrors. Colors everywhere clashed garishly.

Impossible.

Impossible.

There was no conceivable explanation for this. Gardiner was shaken, stunned. He felt physically ill. A wild vertigo assailed him. Numbed, half dazed, his heart racing wildly, he backed out of the building, cautiously returned, looked again. Monsters, nightmares, abominations. Frightful sights, all. But what frightened him more than the ghastliness on the walls was the feeling of utter destabilization that whirled through him, the sense that his mind had lost its moorings. He had never experienced any kind of dislocation like this. Never.

He fought himself into calmness. It must be the heat, Gardiner told himself carefully. He had to be hallucinating. His photographs would show the truth.

With unsteady hands he lifted his camera, remembering only after the shutter's first click that he had used up all his film. He shrugged. For a long moment he stood staring at the hideous things on the walls.

All I need now, he thought, is for one of them to wink at me.

All I need—

Abruptly all his hard-won calmness dissolved and something close to panic overcame him.

Turning, he fled down the side of the gorge, ran with superhuman energy up the far side into town, arriving panting and dizzied, and found Serafina on the porch of her grandparents' decrepit old stone house behind the post office. "Come with me," he said. "The mosaics—I was just there, and they looked all *changed*. You've got to come and tell me it isn't so."

"Changed?"

"Into something horrible. Monsters and demons all over the wall. I couldn't believe it."

"Ah," she said, smiling amiably, a calm knowing smile as old as Zeus. "So the ghosts are at work."

Gardiner felt a shiver run along his back. The ghosts, again.

"It was the ghosts, yes," he said harshly. "Or the heat making me crazy. Or something I ate. Whatever it is, you've got to go back there with me. To check those mosaics out with your own eyes. I need to prove to myself that I didn't actually see what I saw. Will you come? Right now?"

She hesitated only a beat. "Yes," she said, still looking more amused than anything else. "Of course."

This time he led the way. It was the hottest part of the afternoon; but Gardiner was in the grip of a crazy adrenaline surge, and moved so quickly that Serafina was hard pressed to match his speed.

He entered the church first and switched on his flashlight, bracing himself for the worst. But what he saw were the scenes he had uncovered that morning. Benign golden-haloed saints, looking back at him with gazes of sappy medieval sanctity. Smiling dull-eyed shepherds stood amidst their patient sheep. Innocent dogs performed mindless leaps. He was limp with relief.

Serafina, following him in, glanced around at the mosaics, and said, smiling, "Yes, well, so tell me: where are all these horrible things?"

Gardiner peered at the walls, baffled.

"I swear, Serafina, I was absolutely certain that they were there. A completely convincing hallucination, as real as—as real as these walls. The saints had turned into demons. The farm animals had become monsters. The colors—"

She gave him a queer look. "You drank a whole bottle of wine with your lunch, yes? And slept in the sun. And then you dreamed. Ah, yes, yes, *caro*, a very bad dream. Which the oh-so-devilish ghosts of this place playfully put into your sleeping mind to perplex you. Look, look, there are no monsters here. It would be a good story if there were, but there are not.—They are very pretty, your mosaics, I think."

Yes. Yes, they were. Gentle scenes, lovely, innocuous.

Perplexed indeed, altogether lost in bewilderment, Gardiner said almost nothing while they trudged back to town. Already that panoply of monsters was becoming unreal to him. But what he could not put aside was his conviction that he had, at least for a moment, truly seen those things with his own sober eyes, though he knew, *knew*, that it was impossible that he had.

As they came up the path into the *piazza* Serafina said, "You should take the Greek priest over to see the church. He will find it a very exciting surprise."

"Who?"

"Father Demetrios. He is Eastern Orthodox, of the Martorana church in Palermo. He is visiting here since yesterday."

Gardiner recalled, now, the other guest at the hotel, the black-bearded young priest of the night before.

An *Orthodox* priest, though? The Greek rite? All thoughts of ghosts and monsters, and of his own possibly wobbling sanity, fled from Gardiner at once. He was seized by sudden overmastering practical fear. The priest, if he found out about the mosaics, would surely claim the derelict church on behalf of his sect and take control of any scholarly use of the art within it. Gardiner would be shut out, his rights of discovery overridden by the assertion of the higher right of prior ownership.

"No," he said. "I'd rather not show the mosaics to anybody just yet.—You haven't already told him about them, have you?"

"No," she said, "of course not."

Was she telling the truth? There was something almost petulant about that *of course*, and something ambivalent about the shake of the head.

The town square was deserted. The villagers were still enjoying their siesta, the whole town torpid in the late-day heat. Serafina accompanied him as far as the porch of his inn, and lingered there a moment, long enough for him to wonder whether he should invite her upstairs. But even now, with no one to spy on them, it felt somehow inappropriate, even sordid, to make such an overture to her out of the blue. Their frantic jog over to the ruin had hardly been a proper romantic prelude, and his strange hallucination, his babbling account of imagining that he had witnessed a demonic transformation of the mosaics, left him feeling abashed and demeaned now. He offered no invitation.

"Well, then, *ciao, amico.* I will be seeing you," she added formally, and turned away.

Was that a touch of disappointment in her tone? So it seemed to him, for a moment. But it was too late to call her back. Already, moving swiftly as always, she was halfway across the *piazza*.

Gardiner went to his room, rinsed himself perfunctorily, unloaded his camera and buried the roll of film deep in his suitcase. For a long time he sat by his fly-specked window, staring into the square below, pondering many strangenesses. It was half past seven, now; the day was cooling, the townsfolk were coming forth for their pre-dinner stroll.

Without warning a desperate reckless desire to see the mosaics again, to confirm the reality of them, overcame him. He seized his camera and in a few minutes found himself once more laboring down the now-familiar path into the gorge.

In the grayness of early evening he saw what he took to be bats flitting about the little domed church. Brushing impatiently past them, Gardiner marched inside, grim-faced, and cast his flashlight beam on the walls.

The mosaics were in nightmare mode again. Everything was fangs, claws, tentacles, jutting swollen penises, jagged blurts of discordant color.

He felt like sobbing. Why did the damned things keep oscillating in this maddening way? Why couldn't they keep to one form or the other?

"*Serafina!*" he howled, as if expecting her to be able to hear him across the canyon. "It's happened again!"

This time he had had no wine. The day's heat had relented. He believed himself to be sane. What explanation could there be for this?

There was none. He was staring into the abyss of the incomprehensible.

Waves of nausea went sweeping through him. He was trembling, and his teeth were chattering, which was something he could not remember having experienced ever before, that convulsive spastic movement of his jaws, that terrible eerie clacking of his teeth. He steadied himself with an immense effort. This must be recorded, he thought. Yes. Yes. Aiming his camera at the ghastliest of the designs, Gardiner pressed and pressed again, but the flash attachment would not operate. He had no idea why. Fear gave way to rage. He spat, slapped the camera, pressed once more. Nothing. Fumblingly he took some photos by flashlight illumination alone, knowing they would never come out.

He gave the things on the wall one long last hard look. Then he turned and ran from the building, struggling at every step through the tangled knots of brambles that blocked the path and were so much harder to see, this late in the day. He moved like a machine, never pausing. A void had taken possession of his mind; it was empty now of all thought, all speculation. He dared not even try to think.

Darkness had fallen when he entered the town. His legs were aching mercilessly from the uphill run. His powerful thighs, of which he was so proud, the product of endless miles of dawn jogging, throbbed with pain. As he rounded the corner by the museum, a figure stepped out of the shadows and struck him a terrible blow in the stomach. His eyeglasses went flying. Astounded, Gardiner staggered back, doubling over, gagging and choking and reeling, though in some reflexive way he managed to put his fists up anyway to ward off another punch.

It was Gino, Serafina's cousin. He loomed over Gardiner, swollen with wrath, rocking from side to side as he prepared his next swing. His blue eyes were ablaze with rage. Gardiner slapped at the balled fist confronting him.

"Hey, hold it," he said. "I'll give you back your goddamn boots, if that's what you want."

"It is not the boots," said Gino venomously, speaking remarkably precise Italian now. He swung again. Gardiner pivoted so that he took the punch on the meaty part of his left arm instead of in the middle of his chest. It went through him like a bolt of electricity.

He could not remember when he had last been in a fist-fight: not since he was twelve, most likely. But he was no weakling. He would fight back, if he had to. Automatically he dropped into a boxer's crouch and weave, and when Gino swung again he ducked and threw a punch of his own, which Serafina's cousin batted away with a contemptuous swipe, as though he were swatting at a mosquito. Gino's next punch caught Gardiner just below his right clavicle, landing with thunderbolt force and sending him sprawling to the ground.

Through a mist of pain and humiliation he became aware that Serafina had emerged from somewhere and was pounding her fists furiously against Gino's chest. *"Pazzo!"* she cried. *"Cretino! Imbecile!"*

"Tell him I'm finished with his precious boots," Gardiner muttered feebly.

"The boots are not the issue," she said, in English. "He is enraged because you have not slept with me. Because you have rejected me two nights twice."

Gardiner, still on the ground, gaped. "What the hell are you saying? I thought Sicilian men were supposed to *defend* the honor of their women, not to—"

"It is because he thinks you think you are too good for me. He wants you to take me to bed, and then he will make you marry me, and you will settle a fortune on the entire family, because you are American and Americans are rich. In his mind it is my job to seduce you. In this, he believes, I have failed, and so he is angered." Serafina extended her hand to Gardiner and pulled him to his feet. "Angered with you," she said, "not me. Of me he is afraid." She turned to Gino, standing to one side like a fettered ox, and unleashed on him a torrent of fiery Sicilian. Gardiner was unable to understand a word of it. When at last she fell silent, Gino went slinking wordlessly away into the night.

"Come," she said, picking up Gardiner's glasses and handing them to him. Still befogged, he put them in his shirt pocket. "Are you badly hurt?"

"Nothing broken. Only bent."

She led him into the *albergo*, pausing at the bar to pick up a bottle of grappa. Upstairs, in his room, she poured a drink for him, helped him get his backpack off, gently probed his chest and shoulders for damage. "You will live," she said, and measured out some grappa for herself. "Gino is very stupid, but he means well. I apologize on his behalf." Then, with a sly smile: "You are much more handsome without your glasses, *Professore*. A strong face, like a Roman emperor, hard, virile. All beveled planes and stony angles. The glasses destroy your face completely, do you know?" She was wearing a thin green cardigan and a flimsy purple skirt, and now she began to unbutton the cardigan. "You do not have to marry me, only to be nice," she said. "You went to the mosaics again tonight?"

"Yes."

"And?"

"What I saw—it makes no sense, Serafina. They'd gone all strange again." He felt abashed even to say such a thing. "I'm sorry. That's how they were."

"The ghosts have you in their grip," she said. "I am sorry for you for that. But come. Lie down with me. You want to, don't you?" She was narrow through the hips and small-bottomed, not at all Italian that way, and her arms and shoulders were almost distressingly thin, but her breasts were agreeably full. They stayed in his room for two hours. The bed was too small for two, and creaked loudly enough to be heard all over town, but they coped, and coped well. In the close humid atmosphere of the little room Gardiner forgot entirely the pain of Gino's punches and, in Serafina's arms, even for a time succeeded in exorcising the nightmarish threat to his sense of his own sanity that his most recent visit to the ruined church had awakened in him.

Afterward they went downstairs. The *padrone* and his wife appeared to have gone to sleep, but Serafina went into the kitchen of the trattoria and put together a dinner for the two of them out of whatever she could find there, some leftover pasta with anchovies and a cold shoulder of lamb and a platter of broiled tomatoes and garlicky mushrooms, along with what was left in several open bottles of wine. When they had eaten Gardiner asked her to go back up to his room with him again, but this time she declined with a polite smile, explaining it would not be wise for her to stay the night with him. "Until tomorrow," she said. "And you should not go to the church again alone. *Buona notte, caro.*" Blew him a fingertip-kiss and was gone.

This has been a very weird day, Gardiner thought.

In the morning, as he was finishing breakfast, Serafina appeared at the *albergo* and said, "Let us make another visit to your mosaics. I still would like to see them, these horrors of yours."

"Most likely they'll have changed back overnight," Gardiner said, almost jauntily. "But let's go anyway." He realized that he was becoming obsessed by the improbability of all this: an encounter with the absurd, his very first. There was a certain charm to its very inexplicability, even. But behind the charm lay something truly scary that would not relinquish its hold on him: the terrifying possibility that the hinges of his mind had begun to loosen. It was either that or ghosts; and he had never been very successful at believing in ghosts.

He was stiff and sore, not only from Gino's onslaught but from all of yesterday's runnings to and fro, and Serafina had to pause several times to wait for him to catch up as they crossed the valley. But at last they were at the church. "Let me go in first," he said grandly, which brought the sly knowing smile from her once again. She waved him forward.

He expected everything to be normal again, that they would see nothing more than gentle pastoral scenes. But no—no, almost with gratitude he saw that the walls of the chapel this morning were still full of terrifying hideosities. But they were different ones from last night's. Today's carnival of abominations featured savage carnivorous things with rows of red glaring eyes, extraterrestrial-looking spindly-headed satyrs in full spate, pious pilgrims with melting slimy faces. Hieronymus Bosch on acid. He was surprised at how little dismay he felt. He was becoming almost resigned to these metamorphoses, he thought. The trick was not to search for explanations. "Take a look," he called hoarsely to her. She came in and stood for a moment by his side as he shined his beam here and there and there. He heard her soft little gasp: plainly she had not really expected to see the things that she was seeing here now. She slipped her arm through his and pressed close against him, shivering. When he attempted once more to take photographs, the flash attachment again refused to function.

"This is the work of demons," Serafina said, in a tone an octave deeper than normal. *"Andiamo! Fuori!"* They went swiftly outside. With a visibly shaky hand she crossed herself three times. All that ballsy cosmopolitan pizzazz had been stripped from her in an instant; she was a country girl again, and a terrified one. "You should tell Father Demetrios about this right away," she said. Her eyes were wide rigid disks.

"Why?"

"This church formerly belonged to his faith. It is his responsibility to drive these things away."

"To—drive them away—?"

She was talking about an exorcism, this very modern young Sicililan woman. Gardiner stared. Moment by moment he could feel himself being drawn backward into the opaque, inscrutable medieval past.

She said, as though explaining to a child, "You and I both saw saints and shepherds here yesterday afternoon, but in the morning and the evening, alone, you saw monsters. This morning, the monsters are still there, and now I see them too. So we are both hallucinating or else it is real, and I do not think we are hallucinating. It is easier for me to believe in demons than in shared hallucinations."

"I suppose."

"Look, strange things have occurred in this church for many years. Although not like this, not that I have ever heard. It is a serious thing, this deception in a place that once was holy. If nothing is done to cure it, who can say what harm might befall to others who come here?"

"Let me think about all this a little."

"What is there to think?"

The unreality of it all was overwhelming. But Gardiner struggled to keep things in a practical perspective. "I can't predict what might happen to the mosaics once Father Demetrios knows about them. Suppose he insists on destroying them? I found them, Serafina. They're important to me."

"This is my village, *caro*. It is important to me."

Gardiner had no answer for that. He had no answers for any of this.

They returned to town in silence. Serafina grew perceptibly less tense the farther they got from the ruined church, as though they were returning not from a searing glimpse into the pit but only from some spooky horror film, and by the time they entered the village she was her familiar lively self again, whistling, joking, walking with easy free strides. "We will go to see Father Demetrios now, all right?" she said. "He will be at the cathedral, with Father Giuseppe, I think. They are great friends, Father Demetrios and Father Giuseppe. Father Demetrios comes here every few months to play chess with him, and to argue doctrinal matters, whether the Holy Spirit proceeds from the Father alone or from the Father and the Son, and matters like that which will never be settled if they argue about them for ten million years."

"Does that mean Father Giuseppe will have to be told about the mosaics too?" Gardiner asked.

"No. No. This matter is not the business of his church, only of the Greek Orthodox people. Let Father Demetrios handle it. If we tell Father Giuseppe, we will have the Pope here by next Tuesday, and the reporters and the television people, and everybody else. Look, here is Father Demetrios now." She pointed across the *piazza* toward the pathetic little cathedral, the only badly designed one Gardiner had ever seen, a shallow-vaulted asymmetrical structure fashioned from rough-hewn blocks of dark stone ineptly fitted together. "He is very sexy, I think, Father Demetrios," said Serafina slyly, giving Gardiner a playful nudge. "It is a great waste, a man like that in the priesthood. Come." He was swept along in her wake, unable to protest.

Father Demetrios was garbed in black from head to toe, even now in the blowtorch blast of midday heat: cylindrical flat-topped black hat, long high-collared black robe sweeping down to shining black shoes. A heavy golden cross lay on his breast, its upper half vanishing into the dense coils of his long, thick, square-cut beard. He was about thirty-five, a handsome man, stocky and deep-chested, youthfully vigorous, with glossy, intelligent eyes buried in networks of little precocious wrinkles.

"The building has a bad history," he said, speaking in passable English, over a cold bottle of white wine at the *trattoria*, when Gardiner had finished telling his tale. "I myself have never entered it. The mosaics, be they holy or otherwise, are a surprise to me. But the tradition is that a murder was done there, a priest struck down by a furious Norman knight. It was then deconsecrated. You will take me there now?"

"The road is very bad, father," Serafina said, indicating the priest's flowing robe, his gleaming shoes.

He grinned broadly. "No problem," he said, and winked. Sexy, yes. Gardiner could see that. "I will be right back." He went up to his room and returned quickly in khaki trousers, a light windbreaker over a T-shirt, and sturdy boots. All that remained of his clerical garb was the cross and the black cylindrical hat.

When they reached the church, Gardiner made as though to enter first, but Father Demetrios asked for the flashlight and waved him aside. Entering the building a step behind Father Demetrios, Gardiner saw that the mosaics had reverted to their original innocuous form: shepherds and patriarchs, Abraham and Isaac, the Nativity, the journey to Bethlehem.

"Quite remarkable," said Father Demetrios. "You have photographs of the other state?"

"I tried. The camera flash wouldn't go off."

"That is to be expected. Let us go outside and wait a little while."

For ten minutes they stood in the clearing; then the priest sent Gardiner into the church alone. This time the walls were covered with a wild conglomeration of diabolic filth: a gory massacre, a bestial orgy, a witches' sabbath, and more. He ran to the doorway. "Father! *Father!* Come and see!" The priest hurried in, followed by Serafina. When Gardiner turned to illuminate the mosaics again, they were as they had been before, pure, holy.

He felt his face flaming. "I swear to you, father—"

"Yes. I understand. They are great masters of roguery. We will wait once again." But, though they went in and out of the church several times over the next hour, the mosaics were unchanged. They would not revert to the hideous apocalyptic form. Gardiner found that maddening. He wanted to see the demons again, with the priest as witness. He *needed* to see the demons again.

But the demons would not appear, and finally they gave up. On the way back to town Gardiner studied the priest carefully, wondering if the man suspected him of being some kind of lunatic. But Serafina had seen the distorted mosaics too. Thank God for that, he thought. He would be just about ready to sign up with a shrink by now, otherwise.

"I must think profoundly about this," said Father Demetrios, and went to his room. Serafina said she had to go to her grandmother: she told Gardiner she would join him for dinner. Gardiner stood by himself in the empty *piazza*, watching solid-looking heat-shimmers go spiraling upward. This was the hottest day yet. The town was like an oven.

In late afternoon, unable to bear any of this any longer, Gardiner went back across to the church yet again, and found its walls once more bright with capering loathsomenesses. They no longer frightened him; they simply made him sad. He could weep with the sadness of it all. He had found such lovely sweet mosaics in this unexpected place, such marvels of naive medieval art. Why wouldn't they stay that way? Why did they have to assail him like this, striking at the foundations of his sanity? For a long time he stood swaying in the midst of this den of horrors, looking with distaste and disbelief from scene to scene. The chapel seemed airless in the pounding heat, as though every atom of oxygen had fled from it into the sky.

The figures appeared to be moving. That was a new phenomenon, and an awful one. He blinked at them. His hand quivered as he moved the flashlight beam from place to place. The leering dancers—the unthinkable shapes—

Somehow the flashlight fell from his hand, and went out as it hit the ground. Gardiner knelt, groping for it in the stifling darkness. He was unable to find it, nor did he have the strength to make his way out of the church. He simply crouched where he was, kneeling, head downward, wearily resting both his palms on the sandy soil.

He felt a hand on his shoulder. A calm voice: "Let us go outside, my friend." Father Demetrios.

"I fell asleep, I guess," said Gardiner.

"No," said the priest. "Not really."

Father Demetrios had a flashlight of his own, a dim one. Gardiner pointed at the walls. They were still covered with monsters.

"Do you see them?" Gardiner asked raggedly.

"I see them, yes. You wanted to find mosaics here, and you found them, eh? But I think you wanted it a little too hard. This is what happens, when they know you want something too hard."

"When *they* know? What *they*? Who?"

"Come," the priest said. "Outside."

Father Demetrios led him from the building and sat him down in the clearing. Dusk had come. Serafina was not there. Gardiner noticed that the priest had placed a number of lighted candles on the ground all about the building. He was taking things from a backpack: a crucifix, a couple of small silver chalices, a Bible.

"Are you going to do an exorcism?" Gardiner asked.

"A reconsecration," said Father Demetrios. "I have not the authority to do exorcisms. The effect will be the same, though. You will please say nothing of this to anyone, yes? There is some irregularity in my proceeding on my own this way." He was going about the building, now, anointing it with oil from one of the chalices. "This is all to be our little secret, do we agree?"

Gardiner's head was swimming. He heard the priest chanting in Greek and saw him raising and lowering candles and making the sign of the cross on the walls with the holy oil. It went on and on. Then he knelt a long time in prayer. "We are done," Father Demetrios said at last. "Let us go back to the village, now."

"Shall we look inside the church, first?" Gardiner asked.

"I think not. Let us simply go."

"No. I have to see," said Gardiner. He took one of the candles out of the ground and used it to light his way.

The walls were as blank as if Father Demetrios had whitewashed them. After a moment's hesitation he put out his forefinger and rubbed. A rough stucco surface; no hint of the smoothness of mosaic tile anywhere. Even in this asphyxiating heat, Gardiner felt a chill spreading over him. This was the last straw, this newest mutation. He knew he had to flee, not just the church but the town itself. There was nothing solid here, only abysses beneath abysses.

He went stumbling out. "There's nothing there, father. An hour ago there were mosaics all over those walls!"

"There were?" Father Demetrios said.

Serafina met him at the hotel and said, "Will we have dinner together tonight?"

"I think not," Gardiner said. "I'm going to leave."

"Leave? Now? But it is already dark, and you have not eaten!"

"That's all right. I think I should go."

"Ah. Do you?"

"This is no place for me. You've got too many different kinds of reality here, I think. A little retreating is in order, a little regrouping. There are other places, other mosaics, elsewhere, you know. Best to try my luck at one of those. A place without any ghosts."

She considered that for a moment. "Yes. Maybe you're right." She gave him a sad smile. "Do you blame me for this, what happened here?"

"You? Why should I blame *you*?"

"Good," she said. "I would like you to have at least one happy memory of my village."

He thought he saw an unstated appeal in her eyes. "Will I see you again somewhere?" he asked. "In Palermo, maybe? If I ask for you at the Hertz office?"

"You could do that, yes," she said. "Yes. Please do."

They stood a little while together, neither of them speaking. Then she leaned forward and kissed him lightly, a quick brush against his lips, and took his hand and squeezed it, and smiled, not so sadly this time; and then she was gone.

Gardiner went to his room and packed, and found the *padrone* and settled his bill, and started off down the road, southward into the sultry night, heading for the coast, not daring to look back at dwindling Monte Saturno in his mirror, as though fearing that he would see some titanic winged figure standing with folded arms above the town, grinning at his departure. Was there any place on this island, he wondered, that had no ghosts? Maybe not. But he knew that he needed a change of air. Different ghosts. Less volatile, less mischievous. Relicts of an older, cooler realm, one where reason had held sway at least for a little while. Monte Saturno's mysteries had been too much for him—immense, unanswerable.

He reached Agrigento on the southern shore just before dawn. The ancient Agrigentum, it was, where the clear-minded, logic-loving old Greeks had built a dozen elegant temples whose austere remains still could be seen. It was cooler, here. A fresh breeze was blowing from the sea. Gardiner felt a measure of steadiness returning. Amidst the clean, stark, tranquil ruins of the calm and rational classical era he watched, with tears of happiness and relief streaming down his face, the sun come up over the shattered columns of the Temple of Olympian Zeus.

HANOSZ PRIME
GOES TO OLD EARTH

Up to this point, all of the stories in the nine volumes of this collection have been arranged in strict chronological order of writing, beginning with September 1953's "Gorgon Planet" and plodding on, decade after decade, to July 1996's "The Church at Monte Saturno." But putting "Hanosz Prime Goes to Old Earth" in its proper chronological place is something of a puzzle.

Most of it was written in March of 1992—but not as a short story. It began life as an early chapter of what I think is my one and only abandoned novel—an epic of the far future, the first volume of a trilogy, no less, with which I struggled in an agonized way for seven or eight weeks before deciding that it would take me a thousand pages to tell the story I had in mind for the first volume alone, and it was quite possible that the book would make no sense even if I lived long enough to finish it. The novel, or at least the 150 pages that I managed to write before giving up, was written in an experimental, impressionistic style, of which this, the opening paragraph, is a fair sample:

Heigh-ho! It's time to sing of the ending of time! Yes, the death of worlds, the crumbling of the continuum, the great Folding-In of the Gloriously Unfolded. Here is how it came about: this is what befell in the Time of the Falling of the Stars, which led to the Crossing of the Dark, which brought about the Birth of the Universe. For what we are gathered here to pay homage to today is the Grand Circularity of Everything.

First things first and last things last, that's the way of the worlds—
but also last things first, as you will be amply shown. That's how it
always goes: how it always has gone, how it always must. The cosmos
is a serpent with its tail in its mouth, and who is to say which is the
beginning and which the end? Not I, not you, not any of us.

*If I had been able to keep that up for the whole length of the book, I
might have had something interesting, I suppose. But instead things went off
in all directions, and then in no direction at all, leaving me with a collection
of fancy set-pieces that didn't add up to a good start for a novel. After much
internal huffing and puffing I began to see that I needed to give the thing up as
a failure, and I did. Over the years that followed I grabbed some of the interesting scenes from the torso of the thing and welded them into various other
things I was writing, and, no, I won't tell you which they are, partly because I
don't really remember any more. Take it on faith that I made good use of them
and that my travail over that unfinished book eventually paid off.*

*Now we jump to July of 1997. John R. Fultz, one of the pioneering e-pub-
lishers, has started an online publishing company and an online magazine
called* Cosmic Visions, *and gets in touch with me about publishing some of
my work in electronic form. In 1997 my house is still modem-free and the
only computer I have uses the already antiquated DOS operating system,
but I am willing to dip a toe or two in the e-publishing lake nevertheless. I
agree to let Fultz distribute two of my novels on the Internet and, when he
asks me for a short story for* Cosmic Visions, *I remember my abandoned
novel and carve out a 4000-word chunk that follows one of the many story-
lines of the book, taking a bit from this scene and a bit from that one until I
have something that looks like a coherent short story.*

*I don't know whether Fultz ever published it in any real sense of the
word. Since I didn't have Internet access in 1997, he sent me a neat printout
of the October 1997 issue of* Cosmic Visions, *and there indeed is "Hanosz
Prime." But soon afterward I learned from Fultz that cosmicvisions.com
had come to the end of its days. Since I have no record of being paid for my
story, perhaps his site didn't last long enough to put it out on the Internet.*

*Meanwhile I had met Luis Ortiz, another of the pioneers of modern-
style s-f publishing, though what he was involved with then was a desktop-
publishing endeavor rather than an online magazine. In 1993 K.J. Cypret
had founded* Non-Stop, *which described itself as a magazine of "alternative science fiction," and by way of establishing its credentials had run a
lovely short story in its first issue by Paul Di Filippo, surely one of the most
alternative of alternative s-f writers. The second issue, which appeared*

two years after the first one, had fiction by the equally alternative Barry Malzberg in it, and an essay by Di Filippo on the narrative art. There was a third issue somewhat later, which I've never seen. Ortiz, originally the art director of Non-Stop and later its editor, sent me the first two issues and asked if I would contribute a story for the forthcoming fourth one. Since Malzberg and Di Filippo are both good friends of mine, I thought it would be fun to join them on the contents page of this lively, irreverent magazine, and, having just been told by John Fultz that all rights in "Hanosz Prime" had reverted to me, I let Ortiz know about its existence. He accepted it immediately and I was paid $190 for it in February, 1998, after which Non-Stop went instantly out of business and "Hanosz Prime Goes to Old Earth" dropped completely from my mind.

The next jump takes us to the early months of 2005. I am, by then, an Internet user like everyone else, and I belong to a science-fiction discussion group called Fictionmags, where, suddenly, a bibliographer is asking me questions about "Hanosz Prime." I post an account of its history with Cosmic Visions and Non-Stop and add, "I have no idea who owns the rights to the story now, but maybe I do, and I ought to dig out the contract and see if I can get it into print somewhere." Luis Ortiz saves me the trouble of doing that. He is a member of Fictionmags too, and he informs me that with Non-Stop long defunct, the rights to "Hanosz Prime" were all mine.

Cold-eyed professional that I am, I whip off an e-mail to Sheila Williams of Asimov's Science Fiction, telling her that I have unearthed a perfectly good short story that may or may not have been published on-line eight years previously and then had been bought but not used by an obscure and vanished desktop mag. Sheila replies that she's interested in seeing it. I bring it up on screen for a once-over, rewrite it to make it seem more like a short story and less like an excerpted fragment, and she publishes it in the April-May 2006 issue of Asimov's.

So there you have the saga: part of an unfinished novel in 1992, transformed into a short story of sorts in 1997 and accepted by two ephemeral publications, one of which may have published it and one which did not, and then, rewritten again in the spring of 2005, finally put into print. I think it's a lively item, but, I gather from some quick Googling around the blogs, many of Asimov's readers found it incomprehensible. Perhaps it's all for the best that I decided, back there in 1992, not to finish that novel.

The whole thing got arranged, with surprising ease, in short order at long range.

Hanosz Prime of Prime—young again and feeling restless, beginning his new life in startling new ways, eager to travel, suddenly desirous of seeing historic Old Earth while it was still there to be seen—caused word to be sent ahead by hyperwave, using diplomatic channels, in order to get himself invited to be a house-guest at the palatial home of one of the grandest and most famous of Earth's immortal aristocrats, the distinguished and celebrated Sinon Kreidge. Prime had good social connections in more than one galaxy.

And so the message went forth, pretty much instantaneously across two million light-years, through an elaborate interface of official intermediaries spanning half a dozen stellar systems, and the answer came back in a trice—a favorable one. *Sinon Kreidge and his daughter Kaivilda have heard a great deal about the distinguished and celebrated Hanosz Prime of Prime, or at any rate they claim that they have, and will be happy to entertain him during his stay on Earth.* And so the visit was arranged. Quick, quick, back and forth across the galaxies!

It's an age of miracles, the Ninth Mandala that is the era of Prime and Sinon Kreidge. Our own accomplishments are as nothing beside theirs, *nothing*. To the people of the Ninth Mandala, all we are is pathetic ignorant smelly primitives, mere shaggy shambling creatures from the dawn of time—computers, color televisions, space satellites, and all.

By the time of Hanosz Prime of Prime, nine mandalas and a bunch of cycles and encompassments from now, they'll have faster-than-light starships powered by devices that don't exist even in concept right now. It'll be a simple deal to travel quickly and cheaply and easily not just between cities or continents or planets or solar systems but between whole galaxies, faster than it would be for you or me to get from New York to Kansas City. Diplomats and tourists will pop back and forth across millions of light-years in hardly any time at all, say a week or two from here to the quasar 3C 279 without giving it a second thought. Intergalactic messages will move even more quickly—by sub-etheric telephone, let's say, or hyperwave communicator, or some such thing.

I know, it all sounds pretty damned improbable. But stop to think a moment. We're talking about millions of years from now. The Ninth Mandala may very well be a lot farther in our future than the dinosaurs are in our past. A lot of impossible things can get to be possible in that many years.

The dinosaurs, remember, didn't know anything about anything. They were masters of the planet, but they didn't have the simplest form of technology, not a smidgeon. Hell, they couldn't even spell their own names. Look how far we've come, technologically speaking, in a mere 65,000,000 years. We have computers and color television and orbiting space satellites, all of them invented just a microsecond or two ago on the geological scale of things.

And for us the age of miracles is only just beginning.

So now Hanosz Prime is on his way to the threatened planet that once again calls itself Earth. Great wonders and strangenesses await him on the mother world of all humans.

His departure was uneventful. We see him now aboard his elegant little ship as it plunged Earthward at incomprehensible velocity. Manned by an invisible crew, it has swiftly made its tumble through windows and wormholes, sliding down the slippery planes, through the thin places of the cosmos, descending by sly side-passages and tricksy topological evasions across the vast reaches of the dusty intergalactic darkness. Onward it goes across the light-years (or around them, whenever possible) skimming through nebulas aglow with clotted red masses of hydrogen gas, through zones where the newest and hottest stars of the ancient universe—latecomers, lastborn of the dying galaxy, never to run their full cycle of life—valiantly hurled their fierce blue radiance into the void; and now the journey is almost over.

The small golden sun of Earth lay dead ahead. Around it danced Earth's neighboring planets, whirling tirelessly through the changeless darkness along their various orbits, filling his screens with the brilliance of their reflected light.

"Is that Earth?" he asked. "That little blue thing?"

"That is exactly what it is," replied the voice of Captain Tio Patnact, who had traveled from Aldebaran to Procyon and from Procyon to Rigel in the time of the Fifth Mandala, when that was a journey worth respecting. Captain Tio Patnact was what we would call software now, or what an earlier age than ours would probably have called a ghost. "It isn't all that little, either. You'll see when you get there."

"You've been there, right?"

"Quite a while ago, yes."

"But it hasn't changed much since your time, has it?"

"It will have changed in small details," said Captain Tio Patnact, after a time. "But not in any of the large ones, I suspect. They are a fundamentally conservative people, as very wealthy people who know they are going to live forever tend to be."

Hanosz Prime of Prime considered that. He regarded himself as wealthy, as anyone who had ruled and essentially owned most of an entire planet might be thought justified in doing. Was Captain Tio Pacnact being sarcastic, then, or patronizing, or simply rude?—or trying to prepare him for the shock of his life?

"How wealthy are they?" he asked, finally.

"They are all grand lords and ladies. Every one of them. And every one of them lives in a magnificent castle."

And yet they are doomed, Prime thinks. The grand immortals of glittering Earth, living under the shadow of unanticipated destruction. Prime is fascinated by that idea. It seems so appropriate, somehow—so interestingly perverse. Earth, of all places, going to be sucked into some mysterious and absolutely unstoppable vacancy that has opened in the middle of nowhere! What is it like, he wonders, if you are one of those immortal ones—envied by all, the high aristocracy of the cosmos!—and you suddenly discover that you *are* going to die after all, immortal or not, when your part of the galaxy gets swallowed up by this hungry hole?

(The truth is that the curiosity he feels about precisely this thing is one of the motives that has pulled him across two million light-years to Earth. He wants to see how the immortals are handling their death sentence. Will they flee? Can they flee? Or will they—*must* they—remain on Earth to its very last moments, and go bravely down with the ship?

"So it's true, the stories people tell about the Earthfolk, how rich and splendid they all are. And they're all perfect, too, aren't they?" said Hanosz Prime of Prime. "That's what I've been hearing about them forever. Everything in balance, harmonious and self-regulating. A perfect world of perfect people who never have to die unless they want to, and even then it's not necessarily permanent. Isn't that so, Tio Patnact?"

"In a manner of speaking, yes."

"What does that mean?"

"It means that they think they are perfect, and that you may very well think so too."

"Ah," said Hanosz Prime, ex-ruler of Prime. He never knew when Captain Tio Patnact was having some fun with him. That was one of the problems of being only a couple of centuries old, more or less, in a time when most people tended to be very long-lived indeed and certain highly privileged ones like the people of Earth were capable of living forever.

Brooding, Prime paces the length and breadth of the ship. It's quite a fine ship, but it isn't very big. Prime keeps it for his personal use, for jaunts between the planets of the Parasol system and occasionally to nearby star-groups. He's never taken it this far before.

Curving inlays of silver and burnished bronze brighten the walls. Heavy draperies of azure velvet flocked with gold add that little extra touch of regal splendor. Along the sides of the main cabin are holographic portraits of previous members of the royal family, twenty or thirty of them selected at random from the royal portrait gallery. Prime hadn't put them there; they came with the ship, and he had always felt it would be rude to pull them down. The most impressive portrait of the bunch is that of Prime's formidable grandfather, the fierce old undying tyrant who had finally relented and sired an heir in his six thousandth year, and then had lived another thousand anyway, so that Prime's father had had the throne hardly more than a cycle or two. The old man's deep-set eyes burn like suns: he seems ready to step down from the wall and take command of the ship.

"But even *you* had to die eventually, you old bastard," Prime says, staring at the ferocious, implacable holographic face. "You fought and kicked all the way to the end, but the end couldn't be avoided forever. Whereas the great lords and ladies of Earth—"

Prime can't stop thinking about them. Immortals who have to die! What a dirty joke the universe has played on them! What a nasty sense of irony the gods must have!

Prime activated Captain Tio Patnact again.

"If the Earthfolk are the perfect creatures that you say they are, and immortal besides," he said, "what I want to know is, how do you think they feel about learning that they're going to die when the stars fall into the Center of Things? Are they furious? Depressed? Trying desperately to find a way out of their trouble? Are they so calm and perfect and god-like that the thought of their planet's being gobbled up by some kind of black hole doesn't bother them at all? Or is it driving them out of their minds?"

"Wouldn't it bother you?" asked the captain, and vanished into silence.

Standing by the screen, Prime watched Earth grow rapidly larger and larger. The shapes of the continents were visible now, great wedge-shaped chunks of deckle-edged brownness arranged like the spokes of a fan in the middle of an immense sea. At sparse intervals bright spots of heat and light rose from them, glaring out of the infrared, the spectral fingerprint of the fires of life: emanations of the settled areas, the magnificent castles of the grand and immortal Earthfolk.

Prime felt a flicker of awe, a shiver of something close to fear. He caught his breath and clenched his fists. There was a pressure at his throat, a heaviness in his chest, a throbbing in his skull.

Earth! The eternal mother of us all!—the ancestral world—the home of civilization for billions of years, layer upon layer of epochs going back through all nine mandalas and the disorganized forgotten eras that had preceded them.

An encapsulated pulse of Earth's enormous history came squirting out of his midbrain to bedazzle the outer lobes of his whirling mind. He struggled desperately to embrace the totality of that dizzying blurt, the knowledge of all those different races and civilizations and cultures and empires of mankind, rising up and falling down and being replaced by others that in turn would disappear, wave after wave of endlessly changing but still somehow identifiably human forms over uncountable spans of time, the Originals and the Basics and the Radiants and Serenities, the Masks and the Spinners and the Sorcerers and the Thrones, the Wanderers replacing the Star-Scriers and the Moon-Sweepers driving out the Wanderers and the Hive Folk overwhelming the Moon-Sweepers, and on and on and on, eon after eon, a great continuity of change, the whole thing forming the mountainous and incomprehensible agglomeration that was the turbulent history of the mother world. Most of which had been lost: what remained, names and dates and eras and annals, was only a tiny fragment of the whole, Hanosz Prime knew, only a snippet, only a slice, a faint film with most of the substance behind it gone.

Prime was stunned, staggered, overwhelmed by the proximity of this ancientmost planet of the human realm, standing as it was atop the throne of its own gigantic past.

"Help me," he said. "I'm overloading. The whole weight of human history is falling on me. I'm choking under it."

The ship's medic—Farfalla Vlinder was his name, a native of Boris in the Borboleta system, still alive there, as a matter of fact, but duplicated under contract for use in starships—said quickly, "Don't try to take in all of Earth, its whole outrageous past and present, in a single gulp. No one can absorb all that. There's too much, much too much."

"Yes—but—"

"Think of now and nothing but now. Think just of a single district, a single town, a single house. Think of Sinon Kreidge's great palace. And think of his daughter Kaivilda. Especially Kaivilda. How beautiful she is. How eager you are to see her."

"Yes. Yes."

Yes. Prime will allow himself to think only of Kaivilda.

He has no idea at this point what she looks like, other than that she is beautiful. In his dreams she is formless, nothing more than a golden aura stippled with amethyst and bright ruby. Her colors and textures call to him across the endless night of space.

Of the real Kaivilda, though, Prime knows almost nothing.

So Prime does the best he can. He summons up an ideal construct of Beauty, telling himself that it represents Kaivilda, and concentrates on that. A column of pure music shimmers in his mind. The lines of the full spectrum pulsate at its core. Umbrellas of cool light descend upon him.

"Shall we begin landing procedures?" asks Captain Tio Pacnact.

"Begin them, yes. Immediately."

The screen brightens. Earth rushes forward until it seems that the whole planet is leaping into his hands.

The tiny scarlet teardrop that is his starship arches across the orbit of ponderous swirling Hjentiflir, which you would call Jupiter, and plunges past the great flower-shaped pattern of eternally blazing matter which the Star-Scrier people of the 104th Encompassment had fabricated for their amusement and pleasure from the otherwise useless clutter which we know as the asteroid belt, and swoops toward the landing stage of Sinon Kreidge's Keep on the eastern coast of Earth's great central continent.

Prime steps from his ship. And instantly he sees that this is indeed a planet of wonders and miracles.

Golden sunlight runs in rivers across the iron-blue sky, dazzling him. Stars shine at midday in the firmament. It is warm here, even on this mountaintop, much warmer than on snowy Prime. The sweet unfamiliar air of Earth, thin but not harsh, sweeps about him and as he sucks it in it seems to him that he is drinking down the mellowed wine of antiquity, thousands of cycles old. There is magic in that strange air. Ancient sorceries, floating dissolved in the fragrant atmosphere like flecks of gold in a rare elixir, penetrate his being.

Prime looks around, numbed, dazed. A figure materializes out of the shimmering haze and gestures to him.

It is Kaivilda. She has been waiting at the rim of the landing stage to greet him when he arrives; and now she moves toward him with heartrending grace, as though she is drifting weightless through the strange thin air.

To his great relief Hanosz Prime, stepping from his ship into the warm alien air of Earth, was instantly struck by the perfection of Kaivilda's beauty. It's the good old *click!* we all know so well, still operating up there in the remote Ninth Mandala. For him, for her. *Click!* Ninth Mandala love is nothing very much like love as we understand the term, nor is sex, as you'll see, nor is marriage. But the *click!*—the good old pheromonal *click!*—that hasn't changed at all.

Prime had known a little of what to expect, but Kaivilda goes far beyond anything he had imagined from the advance reports. She is wondrous—flawless—superb. She inspires in him immediately dreams of the activity that *they* call rapport and that you can't really understand at all, which is the Ninth Mandala equivalent of love and sex and much more besides. And she is equally charmed by him. The mere sight of him has set her glowing all up and down the spectrum.

Young love! At first sight, no less! In any era, it's something to admire and envy.

(But what an odd pair our young couple would seem to us to be! For them it's love at first sight—sheer physical attraction. You, on the other hand, would probably find her exceedingly weird-looking and not in the least attractive, and him terrifying and downright repellent.)

For this journey Hanosz Prime had had himself done up as an Authentic, awesome and swaggering and virile. As for Kaivilda, she had lately adopted the modularity known as the Serenity, which had come into fashion only recently. Like most of the modularities that were popular in this decadent age it was of an antiquarian nature: a resurrection of one of the many vanished forms through which the human species had passed in the course of its long voyage through time. The original Serenities, a long-vanished human species that had been dominant in the peaceful and cultivated period known as the Fifth Mandala, had been oval in form, tender and vulnerable in texture: tapering custardy masses of taut cream-hued flesh equipped with slender supporting limbs and ornamented along their upper surfaces with a row of unblinking violet eyes of the keenest penetration. The motions of a Serenity were heartbreakingly subtle, a kind of vagrant drifting movement that had the quality of a highly formal antique dance. All this had been quite accurately reproduced in the modern recreation.

So neither Prime nor Kaivilda would appear to be in any way human to you, nor did either one look remotely like the other. But why should they? For one thing, there's been all that time for evolutionary change to take place (not to mention a lot of deliberate genetic fiddling-around for cosmetic purposes) in the thousands of centuries that separate their time from ours. In the Ninth Mandala—when the various races of humanity were spread across billions of worlds and millions of light-years, and just about anything was technologically possible—you could, as we've already noted, take on any physical form you cared to; or none at all, for that matter. (The disembodied form— for those who liked to travel light—was still a minority taste, but not really rare.) No reasons existed for everyone to look like everyone else. Everybody understood this. Nobody was troubled by it.

To you, then, Kaivilda would seem like a gigantic boiled egg, peeled of its shell, adorned with a row of blue eyes and a slit of a mouth and a few other external features like arms and a pair of spindly legs.

It would be hard for you to find much physical appeal in that, I suspect. No matter how kinky you like to think you are, Kaivilda just wouldn't be your type.

But you aren't Hanosz Prime of Prime, and this isn't the 1111th Encompassment of the Ninth Mandala. Your tastes aren't relevant to what turns Prime on, and vice versa. So maybe you'd be better off to forget what I've just told you about what she looks like. If you're a man, you'll have a lot simpler time of it if you try to see her as your own ideal of present-day feminine beauty, whatever that may be—a tall willowy blonde or a petite brunette or a voluptuous redhead, whatever kind of

woman turns you on the most. And if you're female you may find that it
will also help to forget all I said about Hanosz Prime's oppressive bulk
and mass, the sharp bony quills jutting from his upper back, the other
lethal-looking spurs and crests of bone sticking out elsewhere on his
body, and those fleshy yellow frills dangling from his neck. Think of
him as a lanky, good-looking young guy of about twenty-five who went
to a nice Ivy League school, wears expensive sweaters, and drives a neat
little Mercedes-Benz sports car.)

(I suppose you may argue that that would be cheating. Okay: go
ahead, then, and get yourself into a proper Ninth Mandala mind-set.
Hanosz Prime looks like a cross between a compact two-legged dinosaur
and a small battle-tank, and Kaivilda like a giant boiled egg mounted on
a pair of very spindly legs. And each one thinks right away that the other
is tremendously sexy, as that concept is understood in Ninth Mandala
times, though I assure you that sex as we understand it is definitely not a
custom of the era. There you are. Cope with it any way you can.)

As Prime stood frozen and gaping with delight and awe, Kaivilda
moved smoothly to his side and said, speaking softly with her fingertips,
"Welcome to Kalahide Keep, Hanosz Prime."

"How beautiful it is to be here," said Hanosz Prime. It was an effort
for him to frame words at first, but he managed. "What a marvelous
house. And what a glorious planet this is. How delighted I am to look
upon its ancient hills and valleys."

(Meaning: *How pleased I am to be near you. How satisfactory a
being you seem to be. What a splendid challenge you are.* Both of them
understood this.)

And now he comprehends the thing that he has come here to learn.
The Earth will be destroyed, before very long on the cosmic scale of
things, of that there is no doubt. Its immortal folk will surely perish
with it. The galaxies themselves will crumble, sooner or later, although
more likely later than sooner. But none of that matters today, to these
happy people of Old Earth, for today is today, the finest day that ever
was, and who, on a day like this, could fret about the morrow? Hanosz
Prime understands that fully, now, for he is here with Kaivilda of Old
Earth, and even if the universe were to end tomorrow, that makes no difference to him today. Let the future look after itself, he tells himself. We
all live in the present, do we not, and isn't the present a glorious place?

"Come," Kaivilda said. She took him by one of his bony wrist-spurs
and gently drew him into the Keep.

THE MILLENNIUM EXPRESS

Do you remember the great Y2K crisis?

We have to go all the way back to the closing years of the last century for the grim details. Western industrial civilization had made itself wholly dependent on computers; and, so we were told late in the final decade of the twentieth century, those computers hadn't been properly programmed for the gigantic shift from years beginning in "19" to years beginning in "20". As a result, on the stroke of midnight on December 31, 1999, every computer would be paralyzed: planes in flight would crash, trains would leave their tracks, power stations would shut down, et cetera, et cetera.

In the hysteria that followed the Y2K revelations, billions of dollars were spent to upgrade everybody's computer; and, as a result, the vast apocalyptic consequences that the new millennium was supposed to bring never occurred. But one consequence that did occur was a general focusing of everybody's attention on the fact that we were about to enter a new millennium, and that led the editors of Playboy to make their January, 2000 issue a Special Millennium Issue.

That meant, of course, a futuristic angle to most of the articles: a feature by Ray Bradbury about cities on the moon, William F. Buckley and his son Christopher discussing the future of vice and the future of virtue, Harry Dent forecasting Dow-Jones 41,000 in the upcoming millennium, and, well, a story by Robert Silverberg, who had been Playboy's most prolific science-fiction contributor over the previous ten or twelve years.

Alice K. Turner, Playboy's redoubtable fiction editor, e-mailed me on September 17, 1998 to tell me about the planned special issue and to invite me to write something for it. "You have lots of time, about 9 months, to think about it," she said, "and I trust you to come up with something terrific."

Crusty pedant that I am, I didn't even think January 1, 2000 would mark the coming of the new millennium. (Pedants like me think that new centuries begin in years that end with the digit 1—1701, 1801, 1901, 2001— and that new millennia begin with the first year of the new century, since the first millennium had begun that way. But our modern civilization is not kind to pedants and their pedantry, and it was easy to see, well in advance of the actual event, that almost everybody else was going to hail January 1, 2000, as the first day of the third millennium.

I decided not to fight it. I would celebrate the dawning of Y2K with the rest of the populace that day, reserving to myself a private conviction that it wasn't really going to arrive for another year. And I certainly wasn't going to let mere pedantry stand in my way of a sale to the highest-paying market in the business. I e-mailed back right away, accepting the assignment, and from Alice came a description of what I ought to write: "No alternate history, no aliens, no time-travel. It should be an 'if this goes on' story rather than a 'what if.' Upbeat would be better, if possible—I think the issue in general will be upbeat—so the consequences of over-population, the AIDS epidemic, the trashing of the rainforests, the overfishing of the oceans, the consequences of pollution might not be ideal subjects. Unless, of course, you solve these problems!"

All that seemed pretty limiting, despite Alice's cheery last sentences: "I'm sure you won't feel constricted by these parameters. You'll come up with something interesting, and I look forward to it." But I replied, "I have no problem with upbeat—I can even do comic—and I will start thinking seriously about the story as soon as the weather stops being so goddamn Californian."

Perhaps they were expecting me to write about the Y2K crisis, but I had no intention of doing a story that would be obsolete and irrelevant by January 2, 2000, and also I had my private doubts that Y2K was going to be as big a deal as the doomsayers were telling us. So later that fall I told Alice that I was going to write a story set on the eve of the fourth millennium, not the upcoming third one, and she found that a pleasing switcheroo. I did the story around Christmas week of 1998, tinkered with it for a little while, and sent it to her on January 14, 1999, with a covering letter saying, "Story herewith. I think it qualifies as upbeat. (Wouldn't you say that having lovely villas with gardens of tropical palms near the summit of the Matterhorn is an upbeat interpretation of the greenhouse effect?")

"Upbeat" is a subjective term, I guess. To me, a story that ends with tears of joy streaming from a character's eyes and a new era beginning with a clean slate is about as upbeat as a story needs to be. To my dismay, Alice didn't agree, at least not on first reading. She reported herself "puzzled" by the story. I wrote back, "In all our various interactions over the decades, the one thing don't think I've ever managed to is puzzle you, although I confess a couple of your rejections have puzzled me," and, since she had also said her perceptions were a bit blurry because of the flu, I asked her to take a second look when she felt a little better. And so she did, and, she wrote me, she "decided that I had definitely been affected by flu crankiness, and that you had figured out a clever way to look at our past century as well as the future." So I got my check—a very nice one—and the story ran as planned in Playboy's *first issue of what most people considered to be the new millennium.*

Though Playboy *itself had some doubts about that. The opening sentence of the editorial introduction to the issue declared, "The millennium at last—or is it? Depends on how you want to divvy up the calendar." But there it was, a big, glorious special issue, with my story on page 102, splendidly illustrated with a color plate of Messrs. Picasso, Einstein, Hemingway, and Cleversmith standing in front of the good old Louvre with, surprisingly, palm trees in its courtyard.*

As things turned out, it would be my last contribution to Playboy *after a twenty-year run. Alice Turner left the magazine soon after, and its fiction policies changed, and, with the fun of meeting Alice's lofty editorial standards taken away and my own story output diminishing from year to year anyway, I saw no reason to continue submitting stories there. I even let my subscription lapse, around the time of my 70th birthday. A time comes, I guess, when even a hearty lad like me decides he's done with* Playboy.

———

In a quiet moment late in the tranquil year of 2999 four men are struggling to reach an agreement over the details of their plan to blow up the Louvre. They have been wrangling for the last two days over the merits of implosion versus explosion. Their names are Albert Einstein (1879-1955), Pablo Picasso (1881-1973), Ernest Hemingway (1899-1961), and Vjong Cleversmith (2683-2804).

Why, you may wonder, do these men want to destroy the world's greatest repository of ancient art? And how does it come to pass that a man of the 28th century, more or less, is conspiring with three celebrities of a much earlier time?

Strettin Vulpius (2953-), who has been tracking this impish crew across the face of the peaceful world for many months now, knows much more about these people than you do, but he too has yet to fathom their fondness for destruction and is greatly curious about it. For him it is a professional curiosity, or as close to professional as anything can be, here in this happy time at the end of the Third Millennium, when work of any sort is essentially a voluntary activity.

At the moment Vulpius is watching them from a distance of several thousand meters. He has established himself in a hotel room in the charming little Swiss village of Zermatt and they are making their headquarters presently in a lovely villa of baroque style that nestles far above the town in a bower of tropical palms and brightly blossoming orchids on the lush green slopes of the Matterhorn. Vulpius has succeeded in affixing a minute spy-eye to the fleshy inner surface of the room where the troublesome four are gathered.

It provides him with a clear image of all that is taking place in there.

Cleversmith, who is the ringleader, says, "We need to make up our minds." He is slender, agile, a vibrant long-limbed whip of a man. "The clock keeps on pulsing, you know. The Millennium Express is roaring toward us minute by minute."

"I tell you, implosion is the way for us to go," says Einstein. He looks to be about forty, smallish of stature, with a great mop of curling hair and soft thoughtful eyes, incongruous above his deep chest and sturdy athletic shoulders. "An elegant symbolic statement. The earth opens; the museum and everything it contains quietly disappears into the chasm."

"Symbolic of what?" asks Picasso scornfully. He too is short and stocky, but he is almost completely bald, and his eyes, ferociously bright and piercing, are the antithesis of Einstein's gentle ones. "Blow the damn thing up, I say. Let the stuff spew all around the town and come down like snow. A snowfall of paintings, the first snow anywhere in a thousand years."

Cleversmith nods. "A very pretty image, yes. Thank you, Pablo.—Ernest?"

"Implode," says the biggest of the men. "The quiet way, the subtle way." He lounges against the wall closest to the great curving window with his back to the others, a massive burly figure, holding himself braced on one huge hand that is splayed out no more than five centimeters from the spy-eye as he stares down into the distant valley. He carries himself like a big cat, graceful, loose-jointed, subtly menacing. "The pretty way, eh?—Your turn, Vjong."

But Picasso says, before Cleversmith can reply, "Why be quiet or subtle about welcoming the new millennium? What we want to do is make a splash."

"My position precisely," Cleversmith says. "My vote goes with you, Pablo. And so we are still deadlocked, it seems."

Hemingway says, still facing away from them, "Implosion reduces the chance that innocent passers-by will get killed."

"Killed?" cries Picasso, and claps his hands in amusement. "Killed? Who worries about getting killed, in the year 2999? It isn't as though dying is forever."

"It can be a great inconvenience," says Einstein quietly.

"When has that ever concerned us?" Cleversmith says. Frowning, he glances around the room. "Ideally we ought to be unanimous on this, but at the very least we need a majority. It was my hope today that one of you would be willing to switch his vote."

"Why don't you switch yours, then?" Einstein says. "Or you, Pablo: you of all people ought to prefer to have all those paintings and sculptures sink unharmed into the ground rather than having them be blown sky-high."

Picasso grins malevolently. "What fallacy is this, Albert? Why should I give a damn about paintings and sculptures? Do you care about—what was it called, physics? Does our Ernest write little stories?"

"Is the Pope Catholic?" Hemingway says.

"Gentlemen—gentlemen—"

The dispute quickly gets out of hand. There is much shouting and gesticulation. Picasso yells at Einstein, who shrugs and jabs a finger at Cleversmith, who ignores what Einstein says to him and turns to Hemingway with an appeal that is met with scorn. They are all speaking Anglic, of course. Anything else would have been very strange. These men are not scholars of obsolete tongues.

What they are, thinks the watching Vulpius, is monsters and madmen. Something must be done about them, and soon. As Cleversmith says, the clock is pulsing ceaselessly, the millennium is coming ever nearer.

It was on a grassy hilltop overlooking the ruins of sunken Istanbul that he first had encountered them, about a year and a half earlier. A broad parapet placed here centuries ago for the benefit of tourists provided a splendid view of the drowned city's ancient wonders, gleaming valiantly through the crystalline waters of the Bosporus: the great upjutting spears that were the minarets of Hagia Sophia and the Mosque of Suleyman the Magnificent and the other great buildings of that sort, the myriad domes of the covered bazaar, the immense walls of Topkapi Palace.

Of all the submerged and partly submerged cities Vulpius had visited—New York, San Francisco, Tokyo, London, and the rest—this one was one of the loveliest. The shallow emerald waters that covered it could not fully conceal the intermingling layers upon layers of antiquity here, white marble and colored tile and granite slabs, Constantinople of the Byzantine Emperors, Stamboul of the Sultans, Istanbul of the Industrial Age: toppled columns, fallen friezes, ponderous indestructible fortifications, the vague chaotic outlines of the hilly city's winding streets, the shadowy hints of archaic foundations and walls, the slumping mud-engulfed ruins of the sprawling hotels and office buildings of a much later era that itself was also long gone. What a density of history! Standing there on that flower-bedecked hillside he felt himself becoming one with yesterday's seven thousand years.

A mild humid breeze was blowing out of the hinterland to the east, bearing the pungent scent of exotic blooms and unidentifiable spices. Vulpius shivered with pleasure. It was a lovely moment, one of a great many he had known in a lifetime of travel. The world had gone through long periods of travail and over the centuries, but now it was wholly a garden of delight, and Vulpius had spent twenty years savoring its multitude of marvels, with ever so much still ahead for him.

He was carrying, as he always did, a pocket mnemone, a small quasi-organic device, somewhat octopoid in form, in whose innumerable nodes and bumps were stored all manner of data that could be massaged forth by one who was adept in the technique. Vulpius aimed the instrument now at the shimmering sea below him and squeezed it gently, and in its soft, sighing, semi-sentient voice it provided him with the names of the half-visible structures and something of their functions in the days of the former world: this had been the Galata Bridge, this the Castle of Roumeli Hissar, this the Mosque of Mehmet the Conqueror, these were the scattered remnants of the great Byzantine imperial palace.

"It tells you everything, does it?" said a deep voice behind him. Vulpius turned. A small bald-headed man, broad-shouldered and cocky-looking, grinning at him in a powerfully insinuating way. His obsidian eyes were like augers. Vulpius had never seen eyes like those. A second man, much taller, darkly handsome, smiling lazily, stood behind him. The little bald one pointed toward the place in the water where six graceful minarets came thrusting upward into the air from a single vast building just below the surface. "What's that one, for instance?"

Vulpius, who was of an obliging nature, massaged the mnemone. "The famous Blue Mosque," he was told. "Built by the architect Mehmet Aga by order of Sultam Ahmet I in the seventeenth century. It was one of the largest mosques in the city and perhaps the most beautiful. It is the only one with six minarets."

"Ah," said the small man. "A famous mosque. Six minarets. What, I wonder, could a mosque have been? Would you know, Ernest?" He looked over his shoulder at his hulking companion, who merely shrugged. Then, quickly, to Vulpius: "—But no, no, don't bother to find out. It's not important. Those things are the minarets, I take it?" He pointed again. Vulpius followed the line of the pointing hand. It seemed to him, just then, that the slender towers were gently swaying, as though they were mere wands moving in the breeze. The effect was quite weird. An earthquake, perhaps? No: the hillside here was altogether steady. Some hallucination, then? He doubted that. His mind was as lucid as ever.

The towers were definitely moving from side to side, though, whipping back and forth now as if jostled by a giant hand. The waters covering the flooded city began to grow agitated. Wavelets appeared where all had been calm. A huge stretch of the surface appeared almost to be boiling. The disturbance was spreading outward from a central vortex of churning turmoil. What strange kind of upheaval was going on down there?

Two minarets of the Blue Mosque tottered and fell into the water, and three more went down a moment later. And the effect was still expanding. Vulpius, stunned, appalled, scanned the sunken metropolis from one side to the other, watching the fabled ruins crumble and collapse and disappear into the suddenly beclouded Bosporus.

He became aware then of two more men clambering up to the observation parapet, where they were exuberantly greeted by the first pair. The newcomers—one of them short, bushy-haired, soft-eyed, the other long and lean and fiercely energetic—seemed flushed, excited, oddly exhilarated.

Much later, it was determined that vandalous parties unknown had placed a turbulence bomb just off shore, the sort of device that once had been used to demolish the useless and ugly remains of the half-drowned urban settlements that had been left behind in every lowland coastal area by the teeming populace of Industrial times. A thing that had once been employed to pulverize the concrete walls and patios of hideous tract housing and the squat squalid bulks of repellent cinderblock factory buildings had been utilized to shake to flinders the fantastic fairy-tale towers of the great imperial capital by the Golden Horn.

Vulpius had no reason to connect the calamity that had befallen sunken Istanbul with the presence of the four men on the hillside across the way. Not until much later did that thought enter his mind. But the event would not leave him: he went over and over it, replaying its every detail in a kind of chilled fascination. He was deeply unsettled, of course, by what he had witnessed; but at the same time he could not deny having felt a certain perverse thrill at having been present at the moment of such a bizarre event. The shattering of the age-old city was the final paragraph of its long history, and he, Strettin Vulpius, had been on the scene to see it written. It was a distinction of a sort.

Other equally mysterious disasters followed in subsequent months.

The outer wall of the Park of Extinct Animals was breached and many of the inner enclosures were opened, releasing into the wilderness nearly the entire extraordinary collection of carefully cloned beasts of yesteryear: moas, quaggas, giant ground sloths, dodos, passenger pigeons, aurochses, oryxes, saber-toothed cats, great auks, wisents, cahows, and many another lost species that had been called back from oblivion by the most painstaking manipulation of fossil genetic material. Though the world into which they now had been so brusquely set loose was as close to a paradise as its human population could imagine, it was no place for most of these coddled and cherished creatures, for in their resuscitated existences at the Park they never had had to learn the knack of fending for themselves. All but the strongest met swift death in one fashion or another, some set upon by domestic cats and dogs, others drowned or lost in quagmires, a few killed inadvertently during attempts at recapturing them, many perishing quickly of starvation even amidst the plenty of the garden that was the world, and still others expiring from sheer bewilderment at finding themselves on their own in unfamiliar freedom. The loss was incalculable; the best estimate was that it would take a hundred years of intense work to restock the collection.

The Museum of Industrial Culture was attacked next. This treasury of medieval technological artifacts was only perfunctorily guarded, for who would care to steal from a place that was everyone's common storehouse of quaint and delightful objects? Society had long since evolved past such pathetic barbarism. All the same, a band of masked men broke into the building and ransacked it thoroughly, carrying off a mountain of booty, the curious relics of the harsh and bustling age that had preceded the present one: devices that had been used as crude computers, terrifying medical implements, machines that once had disseminated aural and visual images, weaponry of various sorts, simple vision-enhancing things worn on hooks that went around one's ears, instruments used in long-distance communication, glass and ceramic cooking vessels, and all manner of other strange and oddly moving detritus of that vanished day. None of these items was ever recovered. The suspicion arose that they had all gone into the hands of private holders who had hidden them from sight, which would be an odd and troublesome revival of the seeking and secret hoarding of possessions that had caused so much difficulty in ancient times.

Then came the undermining of the Washington Monument; the nearly simultaneous aerial explosion that ruptured the thousands of gleaming windows that still were intact in the gigantic abandoned buildings marking the watery site where Manhattan Island had been in the days before the Great Warming; the destruction through instantaneous metal fatigue of the Great Singapore Tower; and the wholly unexpected and highly suspicious eruption of Mount Vesuvius that sent new lava spilling down over the excavations at Pompeii and Herculaneum.

By this time Vulpius, like a great many other concerned citizens all over the world, had grown profoundly distressed by these wanton acts of desecration. They were so primitive, so crass, so horrifyingly atavistic. They negated all the great achievements of the Third Millennium.

After all those prior centuries of war and greed and unthinkable human suffering, mankind had attained true civilization at last. There was an abundance of natural resources and a benevolent climate from pole to pole. Though much of the planet had been covered by water during the time of the Great Warming, humanity had moved to higher ground and lived there happily in a world without winter. A stable population enjoyed long life and freedom from want of any kind. One respected all things living and dead; one did no harm; one went about one's days quietly and benignly. The traumas of previous epochs seemed unreal, almost mythical, now. Why would anyone want to disrupt the universal harmony and tranquility that had come to enfold the world here in the days just before the dawning of the thirty-first century?

It happened that Vulpius was in Rome, standing in the huge plaza in front of St. Peter's, when a great column of flame sprang into the sky before him. At first he thought it was the mighty basilica itself that was on fire. But no, the blaze seemed to be located to the right of the building, in the Vatican complex itself. Sirens now began to shriek; people were running to and fro in the plaza. Vulpius caught at the arm of a portly man with the florid jowly face of a Roman Caesar. "What's going on? Where's the fire?"

"A bomb," the man gasped. "In the Sistine Chapel!"

"No," cried Vulpius. "Impossible! Unthinkable!"

"The church will go next. Run!" He broke free of Vulpius's grasp and went sprinting away.

Vulpius, though, found himself unable to flee. He took a couple of wobbly steps toward the obelisk at the center of the plaza. The pillar of fire above the Vatican roof was growing broader. The air was stiflingly hot. It will all be destroyed, he thought, the Chapel, the Rooms of Raphael, the Vatican library, the entire dazzling horde of treasures that he had visited only a few hours before. They have struck again, it seems. They. *They.*

He reached the steps at the base of the obelisk and paused there, panting in the heat. An oddly familiar face swam up out of the smoky haze: bald head, prominent nose, intensely penetrating eyes. Unforgettable eyes.

The little man from Istanbul, the day when the ruins had been destroyed.

Beside him was the other little man, the one with the thick bushy hair and the moody, poetic gaze. Leaning against the obelisk itself was the very big one, the handsome man with the immense shoulders. And, next to him, the wiry, long-legged one.

The same four men that Vulpius had seen at Istanbul. Staring wide-eyed, transfixed by the sight of the burning building. Their faces, red with the reflection of the fiery glow overhead, displayed a kind of grim joy, an almost ecstatic delight.

Another catastrophe, and the same four men present at it? That went beyond the possibilities of coincidence.

No. No.

Not a coincidence at all.

He has been pursuing them around the world ever since, traveling now not as a tourist but as a secret agent of the informal governmental police that maintains such order as is still necessary to be enforced in the world. He has seen them at their filthy work, again and again, one monstrous cataclysm after another. The trashing of the Taj Mahal; the attack on Tibet's lofty Potala; the tumbling of the Parthenon, high on its acropolis above the lake that once was Athens. They are always present at these acts of pre-millennial vandalism. So is he, now. He has taken care, though, not to let them see him.

By this time he knows their names.

The little one with the terrifying staring eyes is called Pablo Picasso. He had been cloned from the remains of some famous artist of a thousand years before. Vulpius has taken the trouble to look up some of the original Picasso's work: there is plenty of it in every museum, wild, stark, garish, utterly incomprehensible paintings, women shown in profile with both eyes visible at once, humanoid monsters with the heads of bulls, jumbled gaudy landscapes showing scenes not to be found anywhere in the real world. But of course *this* Picasso is only a clone, fabricated from a scrap of the genetic material of his ancient namesake; whatever other sins he may have committed, he cannot be blamed for the paintings. Nor does he commit new ones of the same disagreeable sort, or of any sort at all. No one paints pictures any more.

The other little man is Albert Einstein, another clone fashioned from a man of the previous millennium—a thinker, a scientist, responsible for something called the theory of relativity. Vulpius has been unable to discover precisely what that theory was, but it hardly matters, since the present Einstein probably has no idea of its meaning either. Science itself is as obsolete as painting. All that was in need of discovering has long since been discovered.

The big husky man's name is Ernest Hemingway. He too owes his existence to a shred of DNA retrieved from the thousand-years-gone corpse of a celebrated figure, this one a writer. Vulpius has retrieved some of the first Hemingway's work from the archives. It means very little to him, but perhaps it has lost something in translation into modern Anglic. And in any case the writing and reading of stories are diversions that are no longer widely practiced. The twentieth-century historical context that Vulpius consults indicates that in his own time, at least, Hemingway was considered an important man of letters.

Vjong Cleversmith, the fourth of the vandals, has been cloned from a man dead a little less than two hundred years, which means that no grave-robbing was necessary in order to obtain the cells from which he was grown. The ancestral Cleversmith, like nearly everyone else in recent centuries, had left samples of his genetic material on deposit in the cloning vaults. The record indicates that he was an architect: the Great Singapore Tower, brought now to ruination by his own posthumous gene-bearer, was regarded as his masterwork.

The very concept of cloning makes Vulpius queasy. There is a ghoulishness about it, an eerieness, that he dislikes.

There is no way to replicate in clones the special qualities, good or bad, that distinguished the people from whom they were drawn. The resemblance is purely a physical one. Those who specify that they are to be cloned after death may believe that they are attaining immortality of a sort, but to Vulpius it has always seemed that what is achieved is a facsimile of the original, a kind of animated statue, a mere external simulation. Yet the practice is all but universal. In the past five hundred years the people of the Third Millennium have come to dislike the risks and burdens of actual childbearing and childrearing. Even though a lifetime of two centuries is no longer unusual, the increasing refusal to reproduce and the slow but steady emigration to the various artificial satellite planetoids have brought the number of Earth's inhabitants to its lowest level since prehistoric times. Cloning is practiced not only as an amusement but as a necessary means of fending off depopulation.

Vulpius himself has occasionally played with the notion that he too is a clone. He has only vague memories of his parents, who are mere blurred elongated shadows in his mind, faceless and unknowable, and sometimes he thinks he has imagined even those. There is no evidence to support this: his progenitors' names are set down in the archives, though the last contact he had with either of them was at the age of four. But again and again he finds himself toying with the thought that he could not have been conceived of man and woman in the ancient sweaty way, but instead was assembled and decanted under laboratory conditions. Many people he knows have this fantasy.

But for this quartet, these men whom Vulpius has followed across the world all this year, clonehood is no fantasy. They are genuine replicas of men who lived long ago. And now they spend their days taking a terrible revenge against the world's surviving antiquities. Why was that? What pleasure did this rampage of destruction give them? Could it be that clones were different from naturally conceived folk, that they lacked all reverence for the artifacts of other times?

Vulpius wants very much to know what drives them. More than that: they must be stopped from doing further mischief. The time has come to confront them directly, straightforwardly, and command them in the name of civilization to halt.

To do that, he supposes, he will have to hike up the flank of the Matterhorn to their secluded lodge close to the summit. He has been there once already to plant the spy-eye, and found it a long and arduous walk that he is not eager to make a second time. But luck is with him. They have chosen to descend into the town of Zermatt this bright warm afternoon. Vulpius encounters Hemingway and Einstein in the cobbled, swaybacked main street, outside a pretty little shop whose dark half-timbered facade gives it an look of incalculable age: a survivor, no doubt, of that long-ago era when there were no palm trees here, when this highland valley and the mighty Alpine peak just beyond it were part of winter's bleak realm, a land eternally imprisoned in ice and snow, a playground for those who thrived on chilly pleasures.

"Excuse me," Vulpius says, approaching them boldly.

They look at him uneasily. Perhaps they realize that they have seen him more than once before.

But he intends to be nothing if not forthright with them. "Yes, you know me," he tells them. "My name is Strettin Vulpius. I was there the day Istanbul was destroyed. I was in the plaza outside St. Peter's when the Vatican burned."

"Were you, now?" says Hemingway. His eyes narrow like a sleepy cat's. "Yes, come to think of it, you do look familiar."

"Agra," Vulpius says. "Lhasa. Athens."

"He gets around," says Einstein.

"A world traveler," says Hemingway, nodding.

Picasso now has joined the group, with Cleversmith just behind him. Vulpius says, "You'll be departing for Paris soon, won't you?"

"What's that?" Cleversmith asks, looking startled.

Hemingway leans over and whispers something in his ear. Cleversmith's expression darkens.

"Let there be no pretense," says Vulpius stonily. "I know what you have in mind. The Louvre must not be touched."

Picasso says, "There's nothing in it but a lot of dusty junk, you know."

Vulpius shakes his head. "Junk to you, perhaps. To the rest of us the things you've been destroying are precious. I say, enough is enough. You've had your fun. Now it has to stop."

Cleversmith indicates the colossal mass of the Matterhorn above the town. "You've been eavesdropping on us, have you?"

"For the past five or six days."

"That isn't polite, you know."

"And blowing up museums is?"

"Everyone's entitled to some sort of pastime," says Cleversmith. "Why do you want to interfere with ours?"

"You actually expect me to answer that?"

"It seems like a reasonable question to me."

Vulpius does not quite know, for the moment, how to reply to that. Into his silence Picasso says, "Do we really need to stand here discussing all this in the public street? We've got some excellent brandy in our lodge."

It does not occur to Vulpius except in the most theoretical way that he might be in danger. Touching off an eruption of Mount Vesuvius, causing the foundation of the Washington Monument to give way, dropping a turbulence bomb amidst the ruins of Byzantium, all these are activities of one certain sort; actually taking human life is a different kind of thing entirely. It is not done. There has not been an instance of it in centuries.

The possibility exists, of course, that these four might well be capable of it. No one has destroyed any museums in a long time either, perhaps not since the savage and brutal twentieth century in which the originals of three of these four men lived their lives. But these are not actual men of the twentieth century, and, in any case, from what Vulpius knows of their originals he doubts that they themselves would have been capable of murder. He will take his chances up above.

The brandy is, in fact, superb. Picasso pours with a free hand, filling and refilling the sparkling bowl-shaped glasses. Only Hemingway refuses to partake. He is not, he explains, fond of drinking.

Vulpius is astonished by the mountaintop villa's elegance and comfort. He had visited it surreptitiously the week before, entering in the absence of the conspirators to plant his spy-eye, but stayed only long enough then to do the job. Now he has the opportunity to view it detail. It is a magnificent eyrie, a chain of seven spherical rooms clinging to a craggy outthrust fang of the Matterhorn. Great gleaming windows everywhere provide views of the surrounding peaks and spires and the huge breathtaking chasm that separates the mountain from the town below. The air outside is moist and mild. Tropical vines and blossoming shrubs grow all about. It is hard even to imagine that this once was a place of glittering glaciers and killing cold.

"Tell us," Cleversmith says, after a while, "why it is you believe that the artifacts of the former world are worthy of continued preservation. Eh, Vulpius? What do you say?"

"You have it upside down," Vulpius says. "I don't need to do any defending. *You* do."

"Do I? We do as we please. For us it is pleasant sport. No lives are lost. Mere useless objects are swept into nonexistence, which they deserve. What possible objection can you have to that?"

"They are the world's heritage. They are all we have to show for ten thousand years of civilization."

"Listen to him," says Einstein, laughing. *"Civilization!"*

"Civilization," says Hemingway, "gave us the Great Warming. There was ice up here once, you know. There were huge ice packs at both poles. They melted and flooded half the planet. The ancients caused that to happen. Is that something to be proud of, what they did?"

"I think it is," Vulpius says, with a defiant glare. "It brought us our wonderful gentle climate. We have parks and gardens everywhere, even in these mountains. Would you prefer ice and snow?"

"Then there's war," Cleversmith says. "Battle, bloodshed, bombs. People dying by tens of millions. We barely *have* tens of millions of people any more, and they would kill off that many in no time at all in their wars. That's what the civilization you love so much accomplished. That's what all these fancy temples and museums commemorate, you know. Terror and destruction."

"The Taj Mahal—the Sistine Chapel—"

"Pretty in themselves," says Einstein. "But you get behind the prettiness and you find that they're just symbols of oppression, conquest, tyranny. Wherever you look in the ancient world, that's what you find: oppression, conquest, tyranny. Better that all of that is swept away, wouldn't you think?"

Vulpius is speechless.

"Have another brandy," Picasso says, and fills everyone's glass unasked.

Vulpius sips. He's already had a little too much, and perhaps there's some risk in having more just now, because he feels it already affecting his ability to respond to what they are saying. But it is awfully good.

He shakes his head to clear it and says, "Even if I were to accept what you claim, that everything beautiful left to us from the ancient world is linked in some way to the terrible crimes of the ancients, the fact is that those crimes are no longer being committed. No matter what their origin, the beautiful objects that the people of the past left behind ought to be protected and admired for their great beauty, which perhaps we're incapable of duplicating today. Whereas if you're allowed to have your way, we'll soon be left without anything that represents—"

"What did you say?" Cleversmith interrupts. "'Which perhaps we're incapable of duplicating today,' wasn't it? Yes. That's what you said. And I quite agree. It's an issue we need to consider, my friend, because it has bearing on our dispute. Where's today's great art? Or great science, for that matter? Picasso, Einstein, Hemingway—the original ones—who today can match their work?"

Vulpius says, "And don't forget your own ancestor, Cleversmith, who built the Great Singapore Tower, which you yourself turned to so much rubble."

"My point exactly. He lived two hundred years ago. We still had a little creativity left, then. Now we function on the accumulated intellectual capital of the past."

"What are you talking about?" Vulpius says, bewildered.

"Come. Here. Look out this window. What do you see?"

"The mountainside. Your villa's garden, and the forest beyond."

"A garden, yes. A glorious one. And on and on right to the horizon, garden after garden. It's Eden out there, Vulpius. That's an ancient name for paradise. Eden. We live in paradise."

"Is there anything wrong with that?"

"Nothing much gets accomplished in paradise," Hemingway says.

"Look at the four of us: Picasso, Hemingway, Einstein, Cleversmith. What have we created in our lives, we four, that compares with the work of the earlier men who had those names?"

"But you aren't those men. You're nothing but clones."

They seem stung by that for an instant. Then Cleversmith, recovering quickly, says, "Precisely so. We carry the genes of great ancient overachievers, but we do nothing to fulfill our own potential. We're superfluous men, mere genetic reservoirs. Where are our great works? It's as though our famous forebears have done it all and nothing's left for us to attempt."

"What would be the point of writing Hemingway's books all over again, or painting Picasso's paintings, or—"

"I don't mean that. There's no need for us to do their work again, obviously, but why haven't we even done our own? I'll tell you why. Life's too easy nowadays. I mean that without strife, without challenge—"

"No," Vulpius says. "Ten minutes ago Einstein here was arguing that the Taj Mahal and the Sistine Chapel had to be destroyed because they're symbols of a bloody age of tyranny and war. That thesis made very little sense to me, but let it pass, because now you seem to be telling me that what we need most in the world is a *revival* of war—"

"Of challenge," says Cleversmith. He leans forward. His entire body is taut. His eyes now have taken on some of the intensity of Picasso's. In a low voice he says, "We are slaves to the past, do you know that? Out of that grisly brutal world that lies a thousand years behind us came the soft life that we all lead today, which is killing us with laziness and boredom. It's antiquity's final joke. We have to sweep it all away, Vulpius. We have to make the world risky again.—Give him another drink, Pablo."

"No. I've had enough."

But Picasso pours. Vulpius drinks.

"Let me see if I understand what you're trying to say—"

Somewhere during the long boozy night the truth finds him like an arrow coursing through darkness: these men are fiercely resentful of being clones, and want to destroy the world's past so that their own lives can at last be decoupled from it. They may be striking at the Blue Mosque and the Sistine Chapel, but their real targets are Picasso, Hemingway,

Cleversmith, and Einstein. And, somewhere much later in that sleepless night, just as a jade-hued dawn streaked with broad swirling swaths of scarlet and topaz is breaking over the Alps, Vulpius's own resistance to their misdeeds breaks down. He is more tipsy than he has ever been before, and weary almost to tears besides. And when Picasso suddenly says, "By the way, Vulpius, what are the great accomplishments of *your* life?" he collapses inwardly before the thrust.

"Mine?" he says dully, blinking in confusion.

"Yes. We're mere clones, and nothing much is to be expected from us, but what have *you* managed to do with your time?"

"Well—I travel—I observe—I study phenomena—"

"And then what?"

He pauses a moment. "Why, nothing. I take the next trip."

"Ah. I see."

Picasso's cold smile is diabolical, a wedge that goes through Vulpius with shattering force. In a single frightful moment he sees that all is over, that the many months of his quest have been pointless. He has no power to thwart this kind of passionate intensity. That much is clear to him now. They are making an art-form out of destruction, it seems. Very well. Let them do as they please. Let them. Let them. If this is what they need to do, he thinks, what business is it of his? There's no way that his logic can be any match for their lunacy.

Cleversmith is saying, "Do you know what a train is, Vulpius?"

"A train. Yes."

"We're at the station. The train is coming, the Millennium Express. It'll take us from the toxic past to the radiant future. We don't want to miss the train, do we, Vulpius?"

"The train is coming," says Vulpius. "Yes." Picasso, irrepressible, waves yet another flask of brandy at him. Vulpius shakes him off. Outside, the first shafts of golden sunlight are cutting through the dense atmospheric vapors. Jagged Alpine peaks, mantled in jungle greenery reddened by the new day, glow in the distance, Mont Blanc to the west, the Jungfrau in the north, Monte Rosa to the east. The gray-green plains of Italy unroll southward.

"This is our last chance to save ourselves," says Cleversmith urgently. "We have to act now, before the new era can get a grasp on us and throttle us into obedience." He looms up before Vulpius, weaving in the dimness of the room like a serpent. "I ask you to help us."

"Surely you can't expect me to take part in—"

"Decide for us, at least. The Louvre has to go. That's a given. Well, then: implosion or explosion, which is it to be?"

"Implosion," says Einstein, swaying from side to side in front of Vulpius. The soft eyes beg for his support. Behind him, Hemingway makes vociferous gestures of agreement.

"No," Picasso says. "Blow it up!" He flings his arms grandly outward. "Boom! Boom!"

"Boom, yes," says Cleversmith, very quietly. "I agree. So, Vulpius: you will cast the deciding vote."

"No. I absolutely refuse to—"

"Which? Which? One or the other?"

They march around and around him, demanding that he decide the issue for them. They will keep him here, he sees, until he yields. Well, what difference does it make, explode, implode? Destruction is destruction.

"Suppose we toss a coin for it," Cleversmith says finally, and the others nod eager agreement. Vulpius is not sure what that means, *tossing a coin*, but sighs in relief: apparently he is off the hook. But then Cleversmith produces a sleek bright disk of silvery metal from his pocket and presses it into Vulpius's palm. "Here," he says. "You do it."

Coinage is long obsolete. This is an artifact, hundreds of years old, probably stolen from some museum. It bears a surging three-tailed comet on one face and the solar-system symbol on the other. "Heads we explode, tails we implode," Einstein declares. "Go on, dear friend. Toss it and catch it and tell us which side is up." They crowd in, close up against him. Vulpius tosses the coin aloft, catches it with a desperate lunge, claps it down against the back of his left hand. Holds it covered for a moment. Reveals it. The comet is showing. But is that side heads or tails? He has no idea.

Cleversmith says sternly, "Well? Heads or tails?"

Vulpius, at the last extremity of fatigue, smiles benignly up at him. Heads or tails, what does it matter? What concern of his is any of this?

"Heads," he announces randomly. "Explosion."

"Boom!" cries jubilant Picasso. "Boom! Boom! Boom!"

"My friend, you have our deepest thanks," Cleversmith says. "We are all agreed, then, that the decision is final? Ernest? Albert?"

"May I go back to my hotel now?" Vulpius asks.

They accompany him down the mountainside, see him home, wish him a fond farewell. But they are not quite done with him. He is still asleep, late that afternoon, when they come down into Zermatt to fetch him. They are leaving for Paris at once, Cleversmith informs him, and he is invited to accompany them. He must witness their deed once more; he must give it his benediction. Helplessly he watches as they pack his bag. A car is waiting outside.

"Paris," Cleversmith tells it, and off they go.

Picasso sits beside him. "Brandy?" he asks.

"Thank you, no."

"Don't mind if I do?"

Vulpius shrugs. His head is pounding. Cleversmith and Hemingway, in the front seat, are singing raucously. Picasso, a moment later, joins in, and then Einstein. Each one of them seems to be singing in a different key. Vulpius takes the flask from Picasso and pours some brandy for himself with an unsteady hand.

In Paris, Vulpius rests at their hotel, a venerable gray heap just south of the Seine, while they go about their tasks. This is the moment to report them to the authorities, he knows. Briefly he struggles to find the will to do what is necesary. But it is not there. Somehow all desire to intervene has been burned out of him. Perhaps, he thinks, the all-too-placid world actually needs the goad of strife that these exasperating men so gleefully provide. In any case the train is nearing the station: it's too late to halt it now.

"Come with us," Hemingway says, beckoning from the hallway.

He follows them, willy-nilly. They lead him to the highest floor of the building and through a narrow doorway that leads onto the roof. The sky is a wondrous black star-speckled vault overhead. Heavy tropic warmth hangs over Paris this December night. Just before them lies the river, glinting by the light of a crescent moon. The row of ancient bookstalls along its rim is visible, and the gray bulk of the Louvre across the way, and the spires of Notre Dame far off to the right.

"What time is it?" Einstein asks.

"Almost midnight," says Picasso. "Shall we do it, Vjong?"

"As good a time as any," says Cleversmith, and touches two tiny contacts together.

For a moment nothing happens. Then there is a deafening sound and a fiery lance spurts up out of the glass pyramid in the courtyard of the museum on the far side of the river. Two straight fissures appear in the courtyard's pavement, crossing at ninety-degree angles, and very quickly the entire surface of the courtyard peels upward and outward along the lines of the subterranean incision, hurling two quadrants toward the river and flipping the other two backward into the streets of the Right Bank. As the explosion gathers force, the thick-walled medieval buildings of the surrounding quadrangle of the Louvre are carried high into the air, the inner walls giving way first, then the dark line of the roof. Into the air go the hoarded treasures of the ages, Mona Lisa and the Winged Victory of Samothrace, Venus de Milo and the Codex of Hammurabi, Rembrandt and Botticelli, Michelangelo and Rubens, Titian and Brueghel and Bosch, all soaring grandly overhead. The citizenry of Paris, having heard that great boom, rush into the streets to watch the spectacle. The midnight sky is raining the billion fragments of a million masterpieces. The crowd is cheering.

And then an even greater cry goes up, wrung spontaneously form ten thousand throats. The hour of the new millennium has come. It is, very suddenly, the year 3000. Fireworks erupt everywhere, a dazzling sky-splitting display, brilliant reds and purples and greens forming sphere within sphere within sphere. Hemingway and Picasso are dancing together about the rooftop, the big man and the small. Einstein does a wild solo, flinging his arms about. Cleversmith stands statue-still, head thrown back, face a mask of ecstasy. Vulpius, who has begun to tremble with strange excitement, is surprised to find himself cheering with all the rest. Unexpected tears of joy stream from his eyes. He is no longer able to deny the logic of these men's madness. The iron hand of the past has been flung aside. The new era will begin with a clean slate.

TRAVELERS

The first science-fiction magazine I ever read was the February, 1949 issue of Amazing Stories, *which appeared on the newsstands of Brooklyn, where I was born and raised, in December, 1948.* Amazing, *then, was owned by Ziff-Davis Publications of Chicago. By then the magazine had a long history behind it—it was the first of all s-f magazines, founded in 1926 by Hugo Gernsback—but by 1948 it was an uncouth-looking pulp magazine with gaudy cover illustrations that featured slam-bang adventure fiction, mostly of pretty feeble literary quality. To me, though, back there in Junior High School 232, the stories in* Amazing *were utterly wonderful, and I lost no time submitting (terrible) ones of my own to the magazine.* Amazing *lost no time in sending them back, either, for, as I discovered a year or two later, it was entirely written by a small in-house staff and unsolicited manuscripts were returned unread.*

Toward the end of 1949 Ziff-Davis moved its headquarters to New York. A couple of years later it experimented with turning Amazing *from a shaggy-looking pulp into an attractive little slick magazine, dropping the old staff of hired hands and replacing their simple action stories with high-quality work by the likes of Robert A. Heinlein, Theodore Sturgeon, Arthur C. Clarke, and a hot new writer named Philip K. Dick. But the new policy was a commercial failure, and before long* Amazing *reverted to its old arrangement of using staff-written fiction only, though it remained in the digest-size format it had adopted during its brief slick phase. Once again a little group of writers turned out all the stories in every issue, each one having a quota of so many words a month to deliver. The editors didn't bother reading the stories before accepting them, because they knew they could trust the staff writers to stay close to the standard pulp formula. You handed your work in, you got paid, and you went home to bang out the next story. Now that the magazine's owners had moved to New York, a new group of staffers—Milton Lesser and Paul W. Fairman, primarily—came in to replace of the Chicago writers.*

But Lesser and Fairman couldn't write the whole magazine, plus Amazing's companion magazine Fantastic, *all by themselves, and editor Howard Browne cast about for a couple of other New York-based contributors. And so, in the summer of 1955, somewhat to my own amazement, I found myself joining the* Amazing *staff. Bear in mind that this was less than seven years since I had begun reading the magazine in junior high school. Now I was a college senior, but I was also a precocious professional writer, and thanks to the good offices of an older writer—Randall Garrett—with whom I had struck up a collaborative partnership, I was taken aboard. My first story for* Amazing *appeared in the January, 1956 issue, and thereafter, either in collaboration with Garrett or flying solo, I sold the magazine dozens of stories under all sorts of pseudonyms.*

Editors came and went over the following years, editorial policies changed again and again, but throughout it all I remained a regular contributor. Eventually Ziff-Davis sold its fiction magazines to an outfit called the Ultimate Publishing Company, and Amazing *staggered on through a decade and a half of diminishing sales under the successive editorships of Joseph Ross, Harry Harrison, Barry Malzberg, Ted White, and Eleanor Mavor. I wrote stories for* Amazing, *did book reviews occasionally, and, in the Mavor days, briefly transferred my long-running opinion column to it. When Ultimate Publishing gave up the ghost in 1982 it looked as though the venerable magazine was finished at last, but no, it was bought by TSR Hobbies, a big publisher of fantasy games, and I remained a regular contributor under the newest editor, George Scithers, and his successor, Patrick Lucien Price.*

In 1991 this ever-mutating magazine underwent its most startling transformation yet. TSR brought in Kim Mohan to replace Pat Price, and under Mohan's guidance Amazing *turned into a glorious large-size slick magazine with color illustrations, probably the most handsome science-fiction magazine ever published. I was there in the first transmogrified issue with a short story ("A Tip on a Turtle") and an installment of my regular column in which I described the magazine's long history and many of the details of my own involvement with it that I've just set down here.*

I never could understand the economic underpinnings of the Mohan Amazing. It sold for $3.95 a copy and probably cost $5 a copy to produce. But it went on for one magnificent issue after another until 1994, when TSR finally pulled the plug on it in a two-stage process: first it reverted to the digest-size format it had had between 1952 and 1991, getting rid of the slick paper and the color illustrations, and then, after limping on a few issues more, it expired altogether. This time it looked like the end, but no, no, back it came three and a half years later, published now by Wizards of the Coast, another game-playing company that had absorbed TSR. It still was edited by Kim Mohan, and was back in large slick format, nearly as glamorous as it had been before. Mohan called me and asked if I would write a new story to celebrate this latest revival of the seemingly unkillable Amazing. "But of course," I replied, and, dipping into the virtually inexhaustible background material of my galaxy-spanning 1986 novel, I came up with "Travelers" in April of 1999. Mohan ran it in Amazing's 597th issue, dated Summer, 1999.

Eventually, though, someone at Wizards of the Coast noticed the gap between production costs and cover price, and suspended publication of Amazing with issue 602, Summer 2000. This time it really did seem that the magazine was finished after a 74-year run under at least eight different publishers. But, as we'll see a couple of stories farther along in this book, it had one more life left in it, nor was my decades-long involvement with the magazine quite at an end either.

Are we all ready, then?" Nikomastir asks. He has fashioned a crown of golden protopetaloids for himself and gleaming scarlet baubles dangle from his ears: the bright translucent shells of galgalids, strung on slender strands of pure gold. His long pale arms wave in the air as though he is conducting a symphony orchestra. "Our next destination is—" and he makes us wait for the announcement. And wait. And wait.

"Sidri Akrak," says Mayfly, giggling.

"How did you know?" cries Nikomastir. "Sidri Akrak! Yes! Yes! Set your coordinates, everybody! Off we go! Sidri Akrak it is!"

A faint yelp of dismay comes from Velimyle, and she shoots me a look of something that might almost have been fear, though perhaps there is a certain component of perverse delight in it also. I am not at all happy about the decision myself. Sidri Akrak is a nightmare world where gaudy monsters run screaming through the muddy streets. The people of Sidri Akrak are cold and dour and inhospitable; their idea of pleasure is to wallow in discomfort and ugliness. No one goes to Sidri Akrak if he can help it, *no* one.

But we must live by our rules; and this day Nikomastir holds the right of next choice. It is devilish of Mayfly to have put the idea of going to Sidri Akrak into his head. But she is like that, is Mayfly. And Nikomastir is terribly easily influenced.

Will we all perish on hideous Sidri Akrak, victims of Mayfly's casual frivolity?

I don't think so, however nasty the visit turns out to be. We often get into trouble, sometimes serious trouble, but we always get out of it. We lead charmed lives, we four travelers. Someday Mayfly will take one risk too many, I suppose, and I would like not to be there when she does. Most likely I will be, though. Mayfly is my mask-sister. Wherever she goes, I go. I must look after her: thoughtful, stolid, foolish me. I must protect her from herself as we four go traveling on and on, spinning giddily across the far-flung worlds.

Sidri Akrak, though—

The four of us have been to so many wondrous lovely places together: Elang-Lo and the floating isle of Vont, and Mikni and Chchikkikan, Heidoth and Thant, Milpar, Librot, Froidis, Smoor, Xamur and Iriarte and Nabomba Zom, and on and on and on. And now—Sidri Akrak? Sidri Akrak?

We stand in a circle in the middle of a field of grass with golden blades, making ourselves ready for our relay-sweep departure from Galgala.

I wouldn't have minded remaining here a few months longer. A lovely world indeed is Galgala the golden, where myriads of auriferous microorganisms excrete atoms of gold as metabolic waste. It is everywhere on this planet, the lustrous pretty metal. It turns the rivers and streams to streaks of yellow flame and the seas to shimmering golden mirrors. Huge filters are deployed at the intake valve of Galgala's reservoirs to strain the silt of dissolved gold from the water supply. The plants of Galgala are turgid in every tissue, leaf and stem and root, with aureous particles. Gold dust, held in suspension in the air, transforms the clouds to golden fleece.

Therefore the once-precious stuff has grievously lost value through-out the galaxy since Galgala was discovered, and on Galgala itself a pound of gold is worth less than a pound of soap. But I understand very little about these economic matters and care even less. Only a miser could fail to rejoice in Galgala's luminous beauty. We have been here six weeks; we have awakened each morning to the tinkle of golden chimes, we have bathed in the golden rivers and come forth shining, we have wrapped our bodies round with delicate golden chains. Now, though, it is time for us to move along, and Nikomastir has decreed that our new destination is to be one of the universe's most disagreeable worlds. Unlike my companions I can see nothing amusing about going there. It strikes me as foolish and dangerous whimsy. But they are true sophisticates, untrammeled creatures made of air and light, and I am the leaden weight that dangles from their soaring souls. We will go to Sidri Akrak.

We all face Nikomastir. Smiling sweetly, he calls out the coordinate numbers for our journey, and we set our beacons accordingly and dou-blecheck the settings with care. We nod our readiness for departure to one another. Velimyle moves almost imperceptibly closer to me, Mayfly to Nikomastir.

I would have chosen a less flighty lover for her than Nikomastir if matters had been left to me. He is a slim elegant youth, high-spirited and shallow, a prancing fantastico with a taste for telling elaborate fanciful lies. And he is very young: only a single rebirth so far. Mayfly is on her fifth, as am I, and Velimyle claims three, which probably means four. Sembiran is Nikomastir's native world, a place of grand valleys and lofty snow-capped mountains and beautiful meadows and thriving cities, where his father is a minor aristocrat of some sort. Or so Nikomastir has said, although we have learned again and again that it is risky to take anything Nikomastir says at face value.

My incandescent mask-sister Mayfly, who is as small and fair as Nikomastir is tall and dark, encountered him while on a visit to Olej in the Lubrik system and was immediately captivated by his volatile impulsive nature, and they have traveled together ever since. Whither Mayfly goeth, thither go I: that is the pledge of the mask. So do I trudge along now from world to world with them, and therefore my winsome, sly, capricious Velimyle, whose psychosensitive paintings are sought by the connoisseurs of a hundred worlds but who belongs to me alone, has willy-nilly become the fourth member of our inseparable quartet.

Some people find relay-sweep transport unlikable and even frightening, but I have never minded it. What is most bothersome, I suppose, is that no starship is involved: you travel unprotected by any sort of tangible container, a mere plummeting parcel falling in frightful solitude through the interstices of the continuum. A journey-helmet is all that covers you, and some flimsy folds of coppery mesh. You set up your coordinates, you activate your beacon, and you stand and wait, you stand and wait, until the probing beam of some far-off sweep-station intersects your position and catches you and lifts you and carries you away. If you've done things right, your baggage will be picked up and transported at the same time. Most of the time that is so.

It is a stark and unluxurious mode of travel. The relay field wraps you in cocooning bands of force and shoots you off through one auxiliary space and another, kicking you through any convenient opening in the space-time lattice that presents itself, and while you wait to be delivered to your destination you drift like a bauble afloat in an infinite sea, helpless, utterly alone, bereft of all power to override the sweep. Your metabolic processes are suspended but the activity of your consciousness is not, so that your unsleeping mind ticks on and on in the most maddening way and there is nothing you can do to quiet its clamor. It is as though you must scratch your itching nose and your hands are tied behind your back. Eventually—you have no idea whether it has been an hour, a month, a century—you are plunked unceremoniously down into a relay station at the planet of your choice and there you are. Relay-sweep transport is ever so much more efficient than any system requiring vast vessels to plough the seas of space from world to world; but all the same it is a disquieting and somewhat degrading way to get around.

So now we depart. Mayfly is the first to be captured by the sweep-beam. Perhaps half an hour later Nikomastir disappears, and then, almost immediately after, Velimyle. My own turn does not arrive for many long hours, which leaves me fidgeting gloomily in that golden meadow, wondering when, if ever, I will be taken, and whether some disjunction in our routes will separate me forever from my three companions. There is that risk—not so much that we would fail to arrive on Sidri Akrak at all, but that we might get there many years apart. I find that a melancholy thought indeed. More than that: it is terrifying.

But finally the dazzling radiance of the sweep aura engulfs me and hurls me out into the Great Dark, and off I go, dropping freely through hundreds of light-years with nothing but an invisible sphere of force to protect me against the phantoms of the auxiliary spaces through which I fall.

I hang in total stasis in a realm of utter blackness for what feels like a thousand centuries, an infinity of empty space at my elbow, as I go my zigzag way through the wormholes of the adjacent continua.

Within that terrible passivity my hyperactive mind ponders, as it all too often does, the deep questions of life—issues of honor, duty, justice, responsibility, the meaning of existence, subjects about which I have managed to learn nothing at all, basically, either in this life or the four that preceded it. I arrive at many profound conclusions during the course of my journey, but they fly away from me as fast as I construct them.

I begin to think the trip will never end, that I will be one of those few unfortunate travelers, the one out of a billion who is caught in some shunt malfunction and is left to dangle in the middle of nowhere for all eternity, or at least for the ten or twenty thousand realtime years it will take for his metabolically suspended body to die. Has this actually ever happened to anyone? There are only rumors, unfounded reports. But there comes a time in every sweep-jump when I am convinced that it has happened to me.

Then I see a glare of crimson and violet and azure and green, and my mask-sister Mayfly's voice purrs in my ear, saying, "Welcome to Sidri Akrak, darling, welcome, welcome, welcome!"

Nikomastir stands beside her. A moment later Velimyle materializes in a haze of color. The four of us have made a nearly simultaneous arrival, across who knows how many hundreds of light-years. We definitely do lead charmed lives, we four.

Everyone knows about Sidri Akrak. The place was settled at least a thousand years ago and yet it still has the feel of a frontier world. Only the main streets of the half-dozen big cities are paved and all the rest are mere blue dirt that turn into rivers of mud during the rainy season. The houses are ramshackle slovenly things, lopsided and drafty, arrayed in higgledy-piggledy fashion as though they had been set down at random by their builders without any regard for logic or order. After all this time the planet is mostly jungle, a jungle that doesn't merely encroach on the settlements but comes right up into them. Wild animals of the most repellent sorts are permitted to rampage everywhere, wandering about as they please.

The Akrakikans simply don't care. They pretend the animals—monstrous, appalling—aren't there. The people of Sidri Akrak are a soulless bloodless bunch in the main, altogether indifferent to such things as comfort and beauty and proper sanitation. Primitive squalor is what they prefer, and if you don't care for it, well, you're quite free to visit some other world.

"Why, exactly, did we come here?" I ask.

It is a rhetorical question. I know perfectly well why: because Nikomastir, clueless about our next destination, had opened a void that Mayfly had mischievously filled with one of the most unappealing suggestions possible, just to see what Nikomastir would do with it, and Nikomastir had as usual given the matter about a thousandth of a second of careful consideration before blithely leaping headlong into the abyss, thereby taking the rest of us with him, as he has done so often before.

But Nikomastir has already rearranged the facts in what passes for his mind.

"I absolutely had to come here," he says. "It's a place I've always felt the need to see. My daddy was born on Sidri Akrak, you know. This is my ancestral world."

We know better than to challenge Nikomastir when he says things like that. What sense is there in arguing with him? He'll only defend himself by topping one whopper with another twice as wild, building such a towering edifice of spur-of-the-moment fantasy that he'll end up claiming to be the great-grandson of the Fourteenth Emperor, or perhaps the reincarnation of Julius Caesar.

Velimyle whispers at my side, "We'll just stay here two or three days and then we'll move along."

I nod. We all indulge Nikomastir in his whims, but only up to a point.

The sky of Sidri Akrak is a sort of dirty brown, broken by greasy, sullen green clouds. The sunlight is greenish too, pallid, tinged with undertones of dull gray. There is a sweet, overripe, mildly sickening flavor to the warm, clinging air, and its humidity is so intense that it is difficult to distinguish it from light rain. We have landed within some city, apparently—in a grassy open space that anywhere else might have been called a park, but which here seems merely to be a patch of land no one had bothered to use for anything, vaguely square and a couple of hundred meters across. To our left is an irregular row of bedraggled two-story wooden shacks; on our right is a dense clump of ungainly asymmetrical trees; before and behind us are ragged aggregations of unpainted buildings and scruffy unattractive shrubbery.

"Look," says Mayfly, pointing, and we have our first encounter with the famous wildlife of Sidri Akrak.

An ugly creature comes bounding toward us out of the trees: a bulky, round-bodied thing, dark and furry, that rises to a disconcerting height atop two scrawny hairless legs covered with bright yellow scales. Its face is something out of your worst dreams, bulging fiery eyes the size of saucers and dangling red wattles and jutting black fangs, and it is moving very quickly in our direction, howling ferociously.

We have weapons, of course. But it swiftly becomes apparent that the thing has no interest in us, that in fact it is fleeing an even more ghastly thing, a long bristle-covered many-legged monster built close to the ground, from whose spherical head emerge three long horn-like projections that branch and branch again, terminating in scores of writhing tendrils that are surely equipped with venomous stings. First one vile creature and then the other runs past us without seeming to notice us and they lose themselves in the shrubbery beyond. We can hear wild shrieking and hissing in there, and the sound of cracking branches.

Nikomastir is smiling benignly. All this must be delightful to him. Mayfly too looks entranced. Even Velimyle, who is closest to me in temperament, almost normal in her desires and amusements, claps her hands together in fascination. I alone seem to be troubled by the sight of such creatures running about unhindered on what is supposedly a civilized world.

But it is ever thus in our travels: I am fated always to stand a little to one side as I follow these three around the universe. Yet am I linked irrevocably to them all the same.

Mayfly was my lover once, two lives back. That was before we took the mask together. Now, of course, it would be unthinkable for anything carnal to happen between us, though I still cherish cheerful memories of her pixy breasts in my hands, her slim sleek thighs about my hips. Even if we have forsworn the sexual part of our friendship, the rest is deeper than ever, and in truth we are still profoundly a couple, Mayfly and I, despite the rich and rewarding relationship I maintain with Velimyle and the frothy, sportive one Mayfly has built with Nikomastir. Above and beyond all that, there is also the bond that links us all. The lines of attraction go this way and that. We are inseparables. They are my world; I am a citizen only of our little group. Wherever we go, we go together. Even unto Sidri Akrak.

In a little while two immigration officers show up to check us out. Sidri Akrak is an Imperium world and therefore the local immigration scanners have been automatically alerted to our arrival.

They come riding up in a sputtering little snub-nosed vehicle, a man and a woman in baggy brown uniforms, and begin asking us questions. Nikomastir does most of the answering. His charm is irresistible even to an Akrakikan.

The questioning, brusque and hard-edged, is done in Imperial, but from time to time the immigration officers exchange comments with each other in their own dialect, which sounds like static. The woman is swarthy and squat and flat-faced and the man is even less lovely, and they are not at all obliging; they seem to regard the arrival of tourists on their planet simply as an irritating intrusion. The discussion goes on and on—do we plan to remain here long, are we financially solvent, do we intend to engage in political activity in the course of our stay? Nikomastir meets every query with glib easy reassurances. During our interrogation a slimy rain begins to fall, oily pink stuff that coats us like grease, and a massive many-humped blue-green beast that looks like an ambulatory hill with purple eyes appears and goes lolloping thunderously past us with utter unconcern for our presence, leaving an odor of decay and corruption in its wake. After a time I stop listening to the discussion. But finally they flash bright lights in our faces—passports are validated retinally on Sidri Akrak—and Nikomastir announces that we have been granted six-month visas. Lodgings are available three streets away, they tell us.

The place they have sent us to turns out to be a dismal rickety hovel and our innkeeper is no more friendly than the immigration officials, but we are grudgingly allowed to rent the entire upper floor. The rooms I am to share with Velimyle face the rear garden, a patch of uncouth tangled wilderness where some slow-moving shaggy monster is sluggishly browsing about, nibbling on the shrubbery. It lifts its head in my direction and gives me a cold glare, as though to warn me away from the plants on which it's feeding. I signal it that it has nothing to worry about and turn away from the window. As I unpack I see a procession of glassy-shelled snail-like things with huge bulbous red eyes crawling diagonally across the bedroom wall. They too stare back at me. They seem almost to be smirking at me.

But Nikomastir and Mayfly claim to be delighted to be here, and Velimyle seems to have no complaints. I feel outnumbered by them. Velimyle announces that she would like to do a painting of Nikomastir in the hotel garden. She only paints when she's in a buoyant mood. Buoyant, *here*? They run off together downstairs, hand in hand like happy children. I watch from above as Velimyle sets up her easel outside and goes about the task of priming the psychosensitive surface of her canvas. She and Nikomastir are as untroubled as any Akrakikan by the shambling shaggy thing that grazes noisily nearby. How quickly they have acclimated.

"Are you very miserable here, darling?" Mayfly asks, running her fingertips lightly along my cheeks.

I give her a stoic smile. "I'll be all right. We'll find things to amuse us, I'm sure. It's all for the best that Nikomastir brought us to this place."

"You don't mean that, do you? Not really."

"Not really, no."

Yet in some sense I do. I often tell myself that it's important not to live as though life is just a perpetual holiday for us, even though in fact it is. It would be too easy to lose ourselves, if we aren't careful, in the nightmare that is perfection.

This is an era when all things are possible. We have godlike existences. We have every imaginable comfort close at hand. Beauty and long life are ours for the asking; we are spared the whole dreary business of sagging flesh and spreading waistlines and blurry eyesight and graying hair and hardening arteries that afflicted our remote ancestors. And all the incredible richness of the galaxy lies open to us: key in your coordinates, snap your fingers, off you go, any world you choose to visit instantly available. Never in the history of the universe has any species lived such a life as ours.

I fear the terrible ease of this existence of ours. I think sometimes that we'll eventually be asked to pay a great price for it. That thought engulfs me in secret terror.

Mayfly, who knows me almost as well as I know myself, says, "Think of it this way, love. There's something to be learned even from ugliness. Isn't it true that what we're trying to get out of all this travel is experience that has meaning? If that's what we want, we can't just limit ourselves to the beautiful places. And maybe a horrid place like Sidri Akrak has something important to teach us."

Yes. She's right. Is she aware that she's voicing my own most private thoughts, or is she just being playful? Perhaps it's all self-delusion, but I do indeed seek for meaning as we travel, or at least think that I do. These furtive broodings in which I indulge in the hidden places of my soul are, so it seems to me, the thing that sets me apart from Nikomastir and Mayfly and Velimyle, who take life as it comes and ask no questions.

Velimyle and Nikomastir return from the garden a little while later. She puts the rolled canvas away without showing it to me. There is an uncharacteristically somber expression on Velimyle's face and even giddy Nikomastir seems troubled. Plainly something has gone awry.

I know better than to ask for details.

We eat at our hotel that night. The surly innkeeper slams the dishes down before us almost angrily: a thin greenish gruel, some sort of stewed shredded meat, a mess of overcooked vegetables. The meat tastes like cooked twine and the vegetables have a dank swampy flavor. I pretend we are back on Iriarte, where food is the highest art and every meal is a symphony. I pretend we have returned to Nabomba Zom, to that wondrous palatial hotel by the shore of the scarlet sea, the waters of which at dawn would reverberate as if struck by a hammer as the first blue rays of morning fell upon it.

But no, no, we are on Sidri Akrak. I lie sleepless through the night with Velimyle breathing gently beside me, listening to the fierce honkings and roarings and screechings of the wild beasts that roam the darkness beyond our windows. Now and again then the sounds of the lovemaking of Mayfly and Nikomastir come through the thin walls that separate our bedroom from theirs, giggles and gasps and long indrawn sighs of pleasure.

In the morning we go out exploring.

This city, we have learned, is called Periandros Andifang. It has a population of just under one hundred thousand, with not a single building of the slightest architectural distinction and a year-round climate of clamminess and drizzle. The plant life is, generally speaking, strikingly unsightly—a preponderance of *gray* leaves, *black* flowers— and the air is full of clouds of little stinging midges with malevolent purple beaks, and of course one has to deal with the fauna, too, the fiend's gallery of grisly monstrosities, seemingly no two alike, that greet you at every turn: huge beasts with beady eyes and slavering fangs and clacking claws, things with pockmarked pustulent skins or writhing furry tentacles or clutching many-jointed arms. Almost always they appear without warning, galloping out of some clump of trees uttering banshee shrieks or ground-shaking roars. I begin to understand now the tales of unwary travelers who have total mental breakdowns within an hour of their arrival on Sidri Akrak.

It quickly becomes clear to us, though, that none of these horrendous creatures has any interest in attacking us. The only real risk we run is that of getting trampled as they go charging past. Very likely it is the case that they find humanflesh unpalatable, or indigestible, or downright poisonous. But encountering them is an unnerving business, and we encounter them again and again and again.

Nikomastir finds it all fascinating. Painstakingly he searches out the ill-favored, the misshapen, the feculent, the repulsive—not that they are hard to find. He drifts ecstatically from one eyesore of a building to the next, taking an infinite number of pictures. He adores the plants' sooty foul-smelling blossoms and sticky blighted-looking leaves. The rampaging animals give him even greater pleasure; whenever some particularly immense or especially abhorrent-looking loathsomeness happens to cross our path he cries out in boyish glee.

This starts to be very irritating. His callow idiocy is making me feel old.

"Remember, sweet, he's not even seventy yet," Mayfly reminds me, seeing my brows furrowing. "Surely you were like that yourself, once upon a time."

"Was I? I'd like to think that isn't so."

"And in any case," says Velimyle, "Can't you manage to find that enthusiasm of his *charming*?"

No. I can't. Perhaps it's getting to be time for my next rebirth, I think. Growing old, for us, isn't a matter so much of bodily decay—that is fended off by efficient processes of automatic bioenergetic correction—as of increasing inward rigidity, a creakiness of the soul, a corrugation of the psyche, a stiffening of the spiritual synapses. One starts to feel sour and petty and crabbed. Life loses its joy and its juice. By then you begin to become aware that it is time to clamber once more into the crystal tank where an intricate spiderweb of machinery will enfold you like a loving mother, and slip off into sweet oblivion for a while, and awaken to find yourself young again and ready to start all over. Which you can do over and over again, until eventually you arrive at the annoying point, after the eleventh or twelfth rebirth, where the buildup of solar poisons in your system has at last become ineradicable under any circumstances, and that is the end of you, alas. Even gods have to die eventually, it would seem.

Nikomastir is a young god, and I am, evidently, an aging one. I try to make allowances for that. But I find myself fervently hoping, all the same, that he will tire of this awful place very soon and allow us to go onward to some happier world.

He does not tire of it, though.

He loves it. He is in the grip of what some ancient poet once called the fascination of the abomination. He has gone up and down every street of the city, peering at this building and that one in unstinting admiration of their imperfections. For several days running he makes it clear that he is searching for some building in particular, and then he finds it: a rambling old ruin of great size and formidable ugliness at the very edge of town, standing apart from everything else in a sort of private park.

"Here it is!" he cries. "The ancestral mansion! The house where my father was born!"

So Nikomastir still clings to the claim that he is of Akrakikan descent. There is no way that this can be true; the natives of this world are a chilly bloodless folk with mean pinched hard souls, if they have souls at all and not just some clicking chattering robotic mechanisms inside their skulls. Indeed I have known robots with personalities far more appealing than anyone we have met thus far on Sidri Akrak. Nikomastir, bless him, is nothing at all like that. He may be silly and frivolous and empty-headed, but he also is sweet-natured and lively and amiable and vivacious, terms that have never yet been applied to any citizen of Sidri Akrak, and never will be.

Velimyle has tried to paint him again. Again the attempt was a failure. This time she is so distressed that I dare to breach the wall of privacy behind which she keeps her art and ask her what the difficulty is.

"Look," she says.

She unrolls the second canvas. Against the familiar swirling colors of a typical Velimyle background I see the slender, angular form of Nikomastir, imprinted there by the force of Velimyle's mental rapport with the psychosensitive fabric. But the features are all wrong. Nikomaster's perpetual easy smile has given way to a dreadful scowling grimace. His lip curls backward menacingly; his teeth are the teeth of some predatory beast. And his eyes—oh, Velimyle, those harsh, glaring eyes! Where is his cheerful sparkle? These eyes are hard, narrow, fierce, and above all else *sad*. The Nikomastir of Velimyle's painting stares out at the universe with tragic intensity. They are the eyes of a god, perhaps, but of a dying god, one who knows he must give up his life for the redemption of his race.

"The first one was almost as bad," Velimyle says. "Why is this happening? This isn't Nikomastir at all. I've never had something like this happen."

"Has he seen either of the paintings?"

"I wouldn't let him. All I told him was that they didn't come out right, that they would depress him if I showed them to him. And of course he didn't want to see them after that."

"Something about this planet must be shading your perceptions," I say. "Burn this, Velimyle. And the other one too. And forget about painting him until we've left here."

Nikomastir wants to have a look inside the crumbling, lurching pile that he says is his family's ancestral home. But the place, ruinous though it is, happens to be occupied by Akrakikans, a whole swarm of them, and when he knocks at the front door and grandly introduces himself to the major-domo of the house as Count Nikomastir of Sembiran, who has come here on a sentimental journey to his former paternal estate, the door is closed in his face without a word. "How impolite," Nikomastir says, not seeming very surprised. "But don't worry: I'll find a way of getting in."

That project gets tabled too. Over the next few days he leads us farther and farther afield, well out into the uninhabited countryside beyond the boundaries of Periandros Andifang. The land out here is swampy and uningratiating, and of course there are the animals to contend with, and the insects, and the humidity. I can tell that Mayfly and Verimyle are growing a little weary of Nikomastir's exuberance, but they both are as tolerant of his whims as ever and follow him loyally through these soggy realms. As do I—partly, I suppose, because we agreed long ago that we would journey everywhere as a single unit, and partly because I have been stung, evidently, by various hints of Mayfly's and Velimyle's that my recent crochetiness could mean I might be getting ready for my next rebirth.

Then he turns his attention once more to the old house that he imagines once belonged to his family. "My father once told me that there's a pool of fire behind it, a phosphorescent lake. He used to swim it when he was a boy, and he'd come up dripping with cool flame. I'm going to take a swim in it too, and then we can head off to the next planet. Whose turn is it to pick our next planet, anyway?"

"Mine," I say quickly. I have Marajo in mind—the sparkling sands, the City of Seven Pyramids. "If there's a lake behind that house, Nikomastir, I advise you very earnestly to stay away from it. The people who live there don't seem to look favorably on trespassers. Besides, can't you imagine the kind of nastinesses that would live in a lake on this world?"

"My father went swimming in that one," Nikomastir replies, and gives me a defiant glare. "It's perfectly safe, I assure you."

I doubt, of course, that any such lake exists. If it's there, though, I hope he isn't fool enough to go swimming in it. My affection for the boy is real; I don't want him to come to harm.

But I let the matter drop. I've already said too much. The surest way to prod him into trouble, I know, is oppose him in one of his capricious fancies. My hope is that Nikomastir's attention will be diverted elsewhere in the next day or two and all thought of that dismal house, and of the fiery lake that may or may not be behind it, will fly out of his mind.

It's generally a good idea, when visiting a world you know very little about, to keep out of places of unknown chemical properties. When we toured Megalo Kastro, we stood at the edge of a cliff looking down into the famous living sea, that pink custardy mass that is in fact a single living organism of gigantic size, spreading across thousands of kilometers of that world. But it did not occur to us to take a swim in that sea, for we understood that in a matter of hours it would dissolve and digest us if we did.

And when we were on Xamur we went to see the Idradin crater, as everyone who goes to Xamur does. Xamur is the most perfect of worlds, flawless and serene, a paradise, air like perfume and water like wine, every tree in the ideal place, every brook, every hill. It has only one blemish—the Idradin, a huge round pit that reaches deep into the planet's primordial heart. It is a hideous place, that crater. Concentric rings of jagged cooled lava surround it, black and eroded and bleak. Stinking gases rise out of the depths, and yellow clouds of sulfuric miasma belch forth, and wild red shafts of roaring flame, and you peer down from the edge into a roiling den of hot surging magma. Everyone who goes to Xamur must visit the Idradin, for if you did not see perfect Xamur's one terrible flaw you could never be happy on any other world. And so we stared into it from above, and shivered with the horror we were expected to feel; but we were never at all tempted to clamber down the crater's sides and dip our toes into that realm of fire below.

It seems unlikely to me that Nikomastir will do anything so stupid here. But I have to be careful not to prod him in the wrong direction. I don't mention the lake to him again.

Our exploration of Sidri Akrak proceeds. We visit new swamps, new groves of fetid-smelling malproportioned trees, new neighborhoods of misshapen and graceless buildings. One drizzly disheartening day succeeds another, and finally I am unable to bear the sight of that brown sky and greenish sun any longer. Though it is a violation of our agreements, I stay behind at the hotel one morning and let the other three go off without me.

It is a quiet time. I spend the hours reflecting on our travels of years past, all the many worlds we have seen. Icy Mulano of the two suns, one yellow, one bloody red, and billions of ghostly electric life-forms glimmering about you in the frigid air. Estrilidis, where the cats have two tails and the insects have eyes like blue diamonds. Zimbalou, the sunless nomad world, where the cities are buried deep below the frozen surface. Kalimaka, Haj Qaldun, Vietoris, Nabomba Zom—

So many places, so many sights. A lifetime of wonderful experiences; and yet what, I ask myself, has it all meant? How has it shaped me? What have I learned?

I have no answers, only to say that we will continue to go onward, ever onward. It is our life. It is what we do. We are travelers by choice, but also by nature, by destiny.

I am still lost in reverie when I hear Velimyle's voice outside my window, calling to me, telling me that I must come quickly. "Nikomastir—" she cries. "Nikomastir!"

"What about him?"

But she can only gesture and wave. Her eyes are wild. We run together through the muddy streets, paying no heed to the bulky and grotesque Akrakikan monstrosities that occasionally intersect our path. I realize after a time that Velimyle is leading me toward the tumbledown house at the edge of town that Nikomastir has claimed as his family's former home. A narrow grassy path leads around one side of it to the rear; and there, to my amazement, I see the phosphorescent lake of Nikomastir's fantasies, with Mayfly beside it, leaping up and down in agitation that verges on frenzy.

She points toward the water. "Out there—there—"

On this ugly world even a phosphorescent lake can somehow manage to be an unlovely sight. I saw one once on Darma Barma that flashed like heavenly fire in rippling waves of cobalt and amethyst, magenta and gold, aquamarine and emerald and jade. But from this lake emanates the most unradiant of radiances, a dull, prosaic, sickly gleam, dark-toned and dispiriting, except in one place off toward the farther shore where a disturbance of some sort is setting up whirlpools of glinting metallic effects, swirls of eye-jabbing bright sparkles, as though handfuls of iron filings are being thrown through a magnetic field.

The disturbance is Nikomastir. He—his body, rather—is tossing and heaving at the lake's surface, and all about him the denizens of the lake can be seen, narrow scaly jutting heads popping up by the dozens, hinged jaws snapping, sharp teeth closing on flesh. A widening pool of blood surrounds him. They, whatever they are, are ripping him to shreds.

"We have to get him out of there," Mayfly says, her voice congested with horror and fear.

"How?" I ask.

"I told him not to do it," says trembling Velimyle. "I told him, I told him, I told him. But he plunged right in, and when he was halfway across they began to break the surface, and then—then he began screaming, and—"

Mayfly plucks urgently at my sleeve. "What can we do? How can we rescue him?"

"He's beyond rescuing," I tell her hollowly.

"But if we can get his body back," she says, "there'll be a way to revive him, won't there? I know there is. Scientists can do anything nowadays." Velimyle, more tentatively, agrees. Some kind of scientific miracle, Nikomastir gathered up and repaired somehow by the regeneration of tissue—

But tissue is all that's left of him now, frayed sorry scraps, and the creatures of the lake, frantic now with blood-lust, are devouring even those in furious haste.

They want me to tell them that Nikomastir isn't really dead. But he is: really, really, really dead. Dead forever. What has been played out on this shore today was not a game. There is nothing that can be saved, no way to regenerate. I have never seen the death of a human being before. It is a dizzying thing to contemplate: the finality, the utterness. My mind is whirling; I have to fight back convulsions of shock and horror.

"Couldn't you have stopped him?" I ask angrily, when I am able to speak again.

"But he wanted so badly to do it," Mayfly replies. "We couldn't have stopped him, you know. Not even if we—"

She halts in midsentence.

"Not even if you had wanted to?" I say. "Is that it?" Neither of them can meet my furious gaze. "But you didn't want to, did you? You thought it would be fun to see Nikomastir swim across the phosphorescent lake. Fun. Am I right? Yes. I know that I am. What could you have been thinking, Mayfly? Velimyle?"

There is no sign of Nikomastir at the surface any longer. The lake is growing still again. Its phosphorescence has subsided to a somber tarnished glow.

For a long time, minutes, hours, weeks, none of us is capable of moving. Silent, pale, stunned, we stand with bowed heads by the shore of that frightful lake, scarcely even able to breathe.

We are in the presence of incontrovertible and permanent death, which to us is a novelty far greater even than the living sea of Megalo Kastro or the blue dawn of Nabomba Zom, and the immense fact of it holds us rooted to the spot. Was this truly Nikomastir's ancestral world? Was his father actually born in that great old falling-down house, and did he really once swim in this deadly lake? And if none of that was so, how did Nikomastir know that the lake was there? We will never be able to answer those questions. Whatever we do not know about Nikomastir that we have already learned, we will never come to discover now. That is the meaning of death: the finality of it, the severing of communication, the awful unanswerable power of the uncompromising curtain that descends like a wall of steel. We did not come to Sidri Akrak to learn about such things, but that is what we have learned on Sidri Akrak, and we will take it with us wherever we go henceforth, pondering it, examining it.

"Come," I say to Mayfly and Velimyle, after a time. "We need to get away from here."

So, then. Nikomastir was foolish. He was bold. He has had his swim and now he is dead. And why? Why? For what? What was he seeking, on this awful world? What were we? We know what we found, yes, but not what it was that we were looking for. I wonder if we will ever know.

He has lived his only life, has Nikomastir, and he has lost it in the pursuit of idle pleasure. There is a lesson in that, for me, for Velimilye, for Mayfly, for us all. And one day I will, I hope, understand what it is.

All I do know after having lived these hundreds of years is that the universe is very large and we are quite small. We live godlike lives these days, flitting as we do from world to world, but even so we are not gods. We die: some sooner, some later, but we do die. Only gods live forever. Nikomastir hardly lived at all.

So be it. We have learned what we have learned from Nikomastir's death, and now we must move on. We are travelers by nature and destiny, and we will go forward into our lives. Tomorrow we leave for Marajo. The shining sands, the City of Seven Pyramids. Marajo will teach us something, as Xamur once did, and Nabomba Zom, and Galgala. And also Sidri Akrak. Something. Something. Something.

THE COLONEL RETURNS
TO THE STARS

Many of science fiction's best editors were top-flight writers also—John W. Campbell, Jr., H.L. Gold, Frederik Pohl, and Anthony Boucher are four who come to mind right away. They had varying attitudes about selling stories to themselves. John Campbell, who was one of the leading s-f writers of the 1930s, let it be known quite publicly that editing a monthly science fiction magazine was a job that didn't leave much time over for writing stories, and in any case selling stories to yourself was a bit like shooting fish in a barrel. Therefore he announced that he was giving up writing when he took over Astounding *in 1937, and would turn any good story ideas he might have thenceforth over to one of his regular writers; and so he did. Anthony Boucher published half a dozen or so of his own stories in* Fantasy & Science Fiction *in the 1950s, but nobody minded that, because Boucher wrote splendid short stories. Horace Gold had three or four stories in his* Galaxy Science Fiction *in the same era, but sent most of his work elsewhere. On the other hand, Fred Pohl, who had had plenty of stories in* Galaxy *when Gold was editing it, continued selling fiction to it after he took over the magazine himself in 1961—again, a sensible move, because Pohl had been one of* Galaxy's *most popular writers almost since its inception.*

I never edited a monthly science-fiction magazine—nobody ever asked me to, and I wouldn't have accepted if someone had, because I wouldn't have wanted such a huge distraction from my primary career as a writer. I did, for a decade or so beginning in 1969, edit the annual original-fiction anthology New Dimensions, *but I never ran anything of my own in it, since I had plenty of markets for my work elsewhere and didn't want to occupy space in the anthology that I could be devoting to fiction by talented new writers. (I did, though, use plenty of my own stories in the various reprint anthologies I edited over the years, but always because I felt they fitted the theme of the anthology at least as well as something I might have chosen by another writer.)*

By 2003 I had pretty much given up editing anthologies on a regular basis, having done dozens of the things over the previous 37 years and regarding them as a sufficient statement of what I considered excellence in science fiction to be. Except for the occasional big item like the two Legends *books and* Far Horizons, *I withdrew to the sidelines and let whippersnappers like Gardner Dozois and Martin H. Greenberg take over the anthology franchise. But when Doubleday's Science Fiction Book Club came around to me with a proposal that I edit a collection of six original novellas dealing with the exploration of worlds beyond our solar system, I found the idea too appealing to resist.*

I rounded up a bunch of colleagues—Nancy Kress, James Patrick Kelly, Mike Resnick, Walter Jon Williams, and Stephen Baxter—pressed money into their hands, and set them to work. And, fond as I am of writing about the great interstellar spaces, I decided to grab one of the six slots for myself, even though I had been becoming less and less active as a writer and was muttering about retiring entirely (something I still haven't quite managed to achieve.)

And so the novella "The Colonel Returns to the Stars" came into being in December, 2003—my first new story in a year and a half. Since it's a story about someone who thinks he has retired from active practice of his profession but finds himself dragged helplessly back into it, some have seen a certain autobiographical component to the plot, and I will not try to deny that. The anthology that contains it, Between Worlds, *was published by the Science Fiction Book Club in 2004.*

———

O n the day that the Colonel found himself seized by circumstances and thrust back against his will into active service he had risen early, as usual, he had bathed in the river of sparkling liquid gold that ran behind his isolated villa in a remote corner of the Aureus

Highlands, he had plucked a quick handful of dagger-shaped golden leaves from the quezquez tree for the little explosive burst of energy that chewing them always provided, and he had gone for his morning stroll along the glimmering crescent dunes of fine golden powder that ran off down toward the carasar forest, where the slender trunks of the long-limbed trees swayed in the mild breeze like the elongated necks of graceful lammis-gazelles. And when the Colonel got back to the villa an hour later for his breakfast the stranger was there, and everything began to change for him in the life that he had designed to be changeless forever more.

The stranger was young—*seemed* young, anyway; one never could really tell—and compactly built, with a tightly focused look about him. His eyes had the cold intensity of a fast-flowing river of clear water; his lips were thin, with deep vertical lines at their sides; his thick, glossy black hair was swept backward against his head like the wings of a raven. The little silver badge of the Imperium was visible on the breast of his tunic.

He was standing on the open patio, arms folded, smiling a smile that was not really much of a smile. Plainly he had already been inside. There was nothing to prevent that. One did not lock one's doors here. The Colonel, looking past him, imagined that he could see the fiery track of the man's intrusive footsteps blazing up from the green flagstone floor. He had entered; he had seen; he had taken note. The Colonel kept about himself in his retirement the abundant memorabilia of a long life spent meddling in the destinies of worlds. In his sprawling house on golden Galgala he had set out on display, for his eyes alone, a vast array of things, none of them very large or very showy—bits of pottery, fossils, mineral specimens, gnarled pieces of wood, coins, quaint rusted weapons, all manner of ethnographic artifacts, and a great number of other tangible reminders of his precise and devastating interventions on those many worlds.

Most of these objects—a scrap of bone, a painted stone, a bit of tapestry, a blunted knife, a tattered banner that bore no emblem, a box of sullen-looking gray sand—had no obvious significance. They would have been baffling to any visitor to the Colonel's Galgala retreat, if ever a visitor were to come, although there had not been any in many years, until this morning. But to the Colonel each of these things had special meaning. They were talismans, touchstones that opened a century and a half of memories. From Eden, from Entrada, from Megalo

Kastro, from Narajo of the Seven Pyramids, from snowy Mulano, from unhappy Tristessa, even, and Fenix and Phosphor and some two dozen others out of mankind's uncountable string of planets had they come, most of them collected by the Colonel himself but some by his pinch-faced limping father, the Old Captain, and even a few that had been brought back by his swaggering buccaneer of a grandfather, who had carved a path through the universe as though with a machete five hundred years before him.

The Colonel now was old, older than his father had lived to be and beginning to approach the remarkable longevity of his grandfather, and his days of adventure were over. Having outlived the last of his wives, he lived alone, quietly, seeking no contact with others. He did not even travel any more. For the first two decades after his retirement he had, more from habit than any other motive, gone off, strictly as a tourist, on journeys to this world and that, planets like Jacynth and Macondo and Entropy and Duud Shabeel that he had never found occasion to visit during the course of his long professional career. But then he had stopped doing even that.

In his time he had seen enough, and more than enough. He had been everywhere, more or less, and he had done everything, more or less. He had overthrown governments. He had headed governments. He had survived a dozen assassination attempts. He had carried out assassinations himself. He had ordered executions. He had refused a kingship. He had lived through two poisonings and three marriages. And then, growing old, old beyond the hope of many further rejuvenations, he had put in for retirement and walked away from it all.

When he was young, restless and full of insatiable hungers, he had dreamed of striding from world to world until he had spanned the entire universe, and he had leaped with savage eagerness into the shining maw of each new Velde doorway, impatient to step forth onto the unknown world that awaited him. And no sooner had he arrived but he was dreaming of the next. Now, though, obsessive questing of that sort seemed pointless to him. He had decided, belatedly, that travel between the stars as facilitated by the Velde doorways or by the other and greater system of interstellar transport, the Magellanic one, was too easy, that the ease of it rendered all places identical, however different from one another they might actually be. Travel should involve travail, the Colonel had come to think. But modern travel, simple, instantaneous, unbounded by distance, was too much like magic. Matters had been different for the ancient explorers of ancient Earth, setting out on their arduous voyages of discovery across the dark unfriendly seas of their little planet with almost incomprehensible courage in the face of impossible odds. Those men of so many thousands of years ago, staking their lives to cross uncharted waters in tiny wooden ships for the sake of reaching alien and probably hostile shores on the very same world, had been true heroes. But now—now, when one could go almost anywhere in the galaxy in the twinkling of an eye, without effort or risk, did going anywhere at all matter? After the first fifty worlds, why not simply stay home?

The visitor said, "Your home is fascinating, Colonel." He offered no apology for trespassing. The Colonel did not expect one. With the smallest of gestures he invited the man inside. Asked him, in a perfunctory way, if he had had a good journey. Served him tea on the terrace overlooking the river. Awaited with formal politeness the explanation for the visit, for surely there had to be some explanation, though he did not yet know that it was ultimately going to break the atoms of his body apart once again, and scatter them once more across the cosmos, or he would have shut the man out of his house without hearing another word.

The man's surname was one that the Colonel recognized, one that had long been a distinguished one in the archives of the Imperium. The Colonel had worked with men of that name many years ago. So had his father. Men of that name had pursued his buccaneering grandfather across half the galaxy.

"Do you know of a world called Hermano?" the man asked. "In the Aguila sector, well out toward the Core?"

The Colonel searched his memory and came up with nothing. "No," he said. "Should I?"

"It's two systems over from Gran Chingada. The records show that you spent some time on Gran Chingada ninety years back."

"Yes, I did. But two systems over could be a dozen light-years away," said the Colonel. "I don't know your Hermano."

The stranger described it: an ordinary-sounding world, a reasonably pleasant world-shaped world, with deserts, forests, oceans, flora, fauna, climate. One of six planets, and the only habitable one, around a standard sort of star. Apparently it had been colonized by settlers from Gran Chingada some thirty or forty years before. Its exports were medicinal herbs, precious gems, desirable furs, various useful metals. Three years ago, said the stranger, it had ejected the Imperium commissioners and proclaimed itself independent.

The Colonel, listening in silence, said nothing. But for a moment, only a moment, he reacted as he might have reacted fifty years earlier, feeling the old reflexive stab of cold anger at that clanging troublesome word, *independent*.

The stranger said, "We have, of course, invoked the usual sanctions. They have not been effective." Gran Chingada, itself not the most docile of worlds, had chosen to people its colony-world by shipping it all the hard cases, its most bellicose and refractory citizens, a rancorous and uncongenial crowd who were told upon their departure that if they ever were seen on Gran Chingada again they would be taken to the nearest Velde doorway and shipped out again to some randomly chosen destination that might not prove to be a charming place to live, or even one that was suitable for human life at all. But the Hermano colonists, surly and contentious though they were, had found their new planet very much to their liking. They had made no attempt to return to their mother world, or to go anywhere else. And, once their settlement had reached the point of economic self-sufficiency, they had blithely announced their secession from the Imperium and ceased remitting taxes to the Central Authority. They had also halted all shipments of the medicinal herbs and useful metals to their trading partners throughout the Imperium, pending a favorable adjustment in the general structure of prices and tariffs.

A familiar image had been ablaze in the Colonel's mind since the first mention of Hermano's declaration of independence: the image of a beautiful globe of brilliantly polished silver, formerly flawless, now riven by a dark hideous crack. That was how he had always seen the Imperium, as a perfect polished globe. That was how he had always seen the attempts of one world or another to separate itself from the perfection that was the Imperium, as an ugly crevasse on the pure face of beauty. It had been his life's work to restore the perfection of that flawless silvery face whenever it was marred. But he had separated himself from that work many years ago. It was as though it had been done by another self.

Now, though, a little to his own surprise, a flicker of engagement leaped up in him: he felt questions surging within him, and potential courses of action, just as if he were still on active duty. Those medicinal herbs and useful metals, the Colonel began to realize, must be of considerably more than trifling significance to interstellar commerce. And, over and beyond that, there was the basic issue of maintaining the fundamental integrity of the Imperium. But all that was only a flicker, a momentarily renewed ticking of machinery that he had long since ceased to use. The maintenance of the fundamental integrity of the Imperium was no longer his problem. The thoughts that had for that flickering moment sprung up reflexively within him subsided as quickly as they arose. He had devoted the best part of his life to the Service, and had served loyally and well, and now he was done with all that. He had put his career behind him for good.

But it was clear to him that if he wanted to keep it that way he must be prepared to defend himself against the threat that this man posed, and that it might not be easy, for obviously this man wanted something from him, something that he was not prepared to give.

The stranger said, "You know where I'm heading with this story, Colonel."

"I think I can guess, yes."

The expected words came: "There is no one better able to handle the Hermano problem than you."

The Colonel closed his eyes a moment, nodded, sighed. Yes. What other reason would this man have for coming here? Quietly he said, "And just why do you think so?"

"Because you are uniquely fitted to deal with it."

Of course. Of course. They always said things like that. The Colonel felt a prickling sensation in his fingertips. It was clear now that he was in a duel with the Devil. Smiling, he said, making the expected response, "You say this despite knowing that I've been retired from the Service for forty years." He gestured broadly: the villa, the display of souvenirs of a long career, the garden, the river, the dunes beyond. "You see the sort of life I've constructed for myself here."

"Yes. The life of a man who has gone into hiding from himself, and who lives hunkered down and waiting for death. A man who dies a little more than one day's worth every day."

That was not so expected. It was a nasty thrust, sharp, brutal, intended to wound, even to maim. But the Colonel remained calm, as ever. His inner self was not so easily breached, and surely this man, if he had been briefed at all properly, knew that.

He let the brutality of the words pass unchallenged. "I'm old, now. Hunkering down is a natural enough thing, at my age. You'll see what I mean, in a hundred years or so."

"You're not *that* old, Colonel. Not too old for one last round of service, anyway, when the Imperium summons you."

"Can you understand," the Colonel said slowly, "that a time comes in one's life when one no longer feels an obligation to serve?"

"For some, yes," said the stranger. "But not for someone like you. A time comes when one *wishes* not to serve, yes. I can understand that. But the sense of obligation—no, that never dies. Which is why I've come to you. As I said, you are uniquely fitted for this, as you will understand when I tell you that the man who has made himself the leader of the Hermano rebellion is a certain Geryon Lanista."

Lanista?

It was decades since the Colonel had last heard that name spoken aloud. It crashed into him like a spear striking his breast. If he had not already been sitting, he would have wanted now to sink limply into a seat.

He controlled himself. "How curious. I knew a Geryon Lanista once," he said, after a moment. "He's long dead, that one."

"No," said the stranger. "He isn't. I'm quite sure of that."

"Are we talking about Geryon Lanista of Ultima Thule in the San Pedro Cluster?" The Colonel was struggling for his equilibrium, and struggling not to let the struggle show. "The Geryon Lanista who was formerly a member of our Service?"

"The very one."

"Well, he's been dead for decades. He killed himself after he bungled the Tristessa job. That was probably long before your time, but you could look it all up. He and I handled the Tristessa assignment together. Because of him, we failed in a terrible way."

"Yes. I know that."

"And then he killed himself, before the inquiries were even starting. To escape from the shame of what he had done."

"No. He *didn't* kill himself." Profoundly unsettling words, spoken with quiet conviction that left the Colonel a little dizzied.

"Reliable sources told me that he did."

Calm, the Colonel ordered himself. Stay calm.

"You were misinformed," the visitor said, in that same tone of deadly assurance. "He is very much alive and well and living on Hermano under the name of Martin Bauer, and he is the head of the provisional government there. The accuracy of our identification of him is beyond any doubt. I can show him to you, if you like. Shall I do that?"

Numbly the Colonel signalled acquiescence. His visitor drew a flat metal case from a pocket of his tunic and tapped it lightly. A solido figure of a man sprang instantly into being a short distance away: a stocky, powerfully built man, apparently of middle years, deep-chested and extraordinarily wide through the shoulders, a great massive block of a man, with a blunt-tipped nose, tight-clamped downturned lips, and soft, oddly seductive brown eyes that did not seem to be congruent with the bulkiness of his body or the harshness of his features. The face was not one that the Colonel remembered having seen before, but time and a little corrective surgery would account for that. The powerful frame, though, was something that no surgery, even now when surgery could achieve almost anything, could alter. And the eyes—those strange, haunted eyes—beyond any question they were the eyes of Geryon Lanista.

"What do you think?" the visitor asked.

Grudgingly the Colonel said, "There are some resemblances, yes. But it's impossible. He's dead. I know that he is."

"No doubt you want him to be, Colonel. I can understand that, yes. But this is the man. Believe me. You are looking at your old colleague Geryon Lanista."

How could he say no to that? Surely that was Lanista, here before him. Surely. Surely. An altered Lanista, yes, but Lanista all the same. What was the use of arguing otherwise? Those eyes—those freakishly wide shoulders—that barrel of a chest—

But there was no way that Lanista could be alive.

Clinging to a stubborn certainty that he was beginning not to feel was really solid the Colonel said, "Very well: the face is his. I'll concede that much. But the image? Something out of the files of fifty years ago, tarted up with a few little tweaks here and there to make him look as though he's tried recently to disguise himself? What's here to make me believe that this is a recent image of a living man?"

"We have other images, Colonel." The visitor tapped the metal case again, and there was the stocky man on the veranda of an imposing house set within a luxurious garden. Two small children, built to the same stocky proportions as he, stood beside him, and a smiling young woman. "At his home on Hermano," said the visitor, and tapped the case again. Now the stocky man appeared in a group of other men, evidently at a political meeting; he was declaiming something about the need for Hermano to throw off the shackles of the Imperium. He tapped the case again—

"No. Stop. You can fake whatever scene you want. I know how these things are done."

"Of course you do, Colonel. But why would we bother? Why try to drag you out of retirement with a bunch of faked images? Sooner or later a man of your ability would see through them. But we *know* that this man is Geryon Lanista. We have all the necessary proof, the incontrovertible genetic data. And so we've come to you, as someone who not only has the technical skills to deal with the problem that Lanista is creating, but the personal motivation to do so."

"Incontrovertible genetic data?"

"Yes. Incontrovertible. Shall I show you the genomics? Here: look. From the Service files, sixty years back, Geryon Lanista, his entire genome. And here, this one, from the Gran Chingada immigration records, approximately twenty years old, Martin Bauer. Do you see?"

The Colonel glanced at the images, side by side in the air and identical in every respect, shook his head, looked away. The pairing was convincing, yes. And, yes, they could fake anything they liked, even a pair of gene charts. There wasn't all that much difficulty in that. But to fake so *much*—to go to such preposterous lengths for the sake of bamboozling one tired old man—no, no, the logic that lay at the core of his soul cried out against the likelihood of that.

His last resistance crumbled. He yielded to the inescapable reality. Despite everything he had believed all these years, this man Martin Bauer *was* Geryon Lanista. Alive and well, as this stranger had said, and conspiring against the Imperium on a planet called Hermano. And the Service wanted him to do something about that.

For an instant, contemplating this sudden and disastrous turn of events, the Colonel felt something that wasn't quite fear and not quite dismay—both of them feelings that he scarcely understood, let alone had ever experienced—but was certainly a kind of discomfort. This had been a duel with the Devil, all right, and the Devil had played with predictably diabolical skill, and the Colonel saw that here, in the very first moments of the contest, he had already lost. He had not thought to be beaten so easily. He had lived his life, he had put in his years in the Service, he had met all dangers with bravery and all difficulties with triumphant ingenuity, and here, as the end of it all approached, he had come safely to rest in the harbor of his own invulnerability on this idyllic golden world; and in a moment, with just a few quick syllables, this cold-eyed stranger had ripped him loose from all of that and had tumbled him back into the remorseless torrents of history. He ached to refuse the challenge. It was within the range of possibility for him to refuse it. It was certainly his right to refuse it, at his age, after all that he had done. But—even so—even so—

"Geryon Lanista," the Colonel said, marveling. "Yes. Yes. Well, perhaps this really is him." There was a touch of hoarseness in his tone.— "You know the whole story, Lanista and me?"

"That goes without saying. Why else would we have come to you?"

The odd prickling in the Colonel's fingertips began to give way to an infuriating trembling. "Well, then—"

He looked across the table and it seemed to him that he saw a softening of those icy eyes, even a hint of moisture in them. An upwelling of compassion, was it, for the poor old man who had been so cruelly ensnared in the sanctity of his own home? But was that in any way likely, coming from *this* particular man, who had sprung from *those* ancestors. Compassion had never been a specialty of that tribe. Perhaps they are making them softer nowadays, the Colonel thought, yet another example of the general decadence of modern times, and felt renewed pleasure in the awareness that he was no one's ancestor at all, that his line ended with him. And then he realized that he was wrong, that there was no compassion in this man at all, that those were simply the jubilant self-congratulatory tears of triumph in the other man's eyes.

"We can count on you?" the visitor asked.

"If you've been lying to me—"

"I haven't been lying," said the visitor, saying it in a flat offhanded way that conveyed more conviction than any number of passionate oaths might have done.

The Colonel nodded. "All right. I give in. You win. I'll do what I can do," he said, in a barely audible voice. He felt like a man who had been marched to the edge of a cliff and now was taking a few last breaths before jumping off. "Yes. Yes. There are, I hardly need to say, certain practical details that we need to discuss, first—"

There was something dreamlike about finding himself making ready for a new assignment after so many years. He wouldn't leave immediately, of course, nor would the journey to Hermano be anything like instantaneous. The maintenance of the villa during his absence had to be arranged for, and there was the background information of the Hermano situation to master, and certain potentially useful documents to excavate from the archives of his career, and then he would have to make the long overland journey to Elsinore, down on the coast, where the nearest Velde doorway was located. Even after that he still would have some traveling to do, because Gran Chingada and its unruly colony-world Hermano, both of them close to the central sector of the galaxy, were beyond the direct reach of Velde transmission. To complete his journey he would have to shift over to the galaxy's other and greater teleportation system, the ancient and unfathomable one that had been left behind by the people known as the Magellanics.

He had not expected ever to be jaunting across the universe again. The visit to Duud Shabeel, two decades before, had established itself in his mind as the last of all his travels. But plainly there was to be one more trip even so; and as he prepared for it, his mind went back to his first journey ever, the one his ferocious fiery-eyed grandfather had taken him on, in that inconceivably remote epoch when he was ten years old.

He had lived on Galgala even then, though not in the highlands but along the humid coast, where liquid gold came bubbling up out of the swamps. His grandfather had always had a special love for Galgala, the planet that had ruined the value of gold for the entire galaxy. Gold was everywhere there, in the leaves of the trees, in the sands of the desert, in the stones of the ground. Flecks of gold flowed in the veins of Galgala's native animals. Though it had been thousands of years since the yellow metal had passed as currency among humankind, the discovery of Galgala had finished it for all eternity as a commodity of value. But the old pirate who had engendered the Colonel's father was a medieval at heart, and he cherished Galgala for what its gold might have meant in the days when the whole of the human universe was just the little blue world that was Earth. He had made it his headquarters during his privateering career, and when he was old he had gone there to dwell until the end of his days. The Colonel's father, who in his parsimonious pinch-faced way claimed only the honorary title of Captain, was in the Service then, traveling constantly from world to world as need arose and only rarely coming to rest, and, not knowing what to do with the boy who would some day become the Colonel, had sent him to Galgala to live with his grandfather.

"It's time you learned what traveling is like," the old man said one day, when the boy who would become the Colonel was ten.

He was already tall and sturdy for his age, but he was still only ten, and his grandfather, even then centuries old—no one knew exactly how old he was, perhaps not even he himself—rose up and up beside him like a great tree, a shaggy-bearded tree with furious eyes and long black coils of piratical hair dangling to his shoulders and horrendous jutting cheekbones sharp as blades. The gaunt, bony old man had spent the many years of his life outside the law, the law that the Captain and later the Colonel would serve with such devotion, but no one in the family ever spoke openly of that. And although he had finally abandoned his marauding ways, he still affected the showy costume of his trade, the leather jerkin and the knee-high boots with the tapered tips and the broad-brimmed hat from which the eternally black coils of his long hair came tumbling superabundantly down.

They stood before the doorway, the future Colonel and his formidable grandfather, and the old man said, "When you step through it, you'll be scanned and surveyed, and then you'll be torn apart completely, down to the fragments of your atoms, altogether annihilated, and at the same moment an exact duplicate of you will be assembled at the other end, wherever that may be. How do you like that?"

The old man waited, then, searching for signs of fear or doubt on his grandson's face. But even then the boy understood that such feelings as fear or doubt ought not to be so much as felt, let alone displayed, in the presence of his grandfather.

"And where will we come out, then?" the boy who would be the Colonel asked.

"At our destination," said the old pirate, and casually shoved him toward the doorway. "You wait for me there, do you hear me, boy? I'll be coming along right behind."

The doorway on Galgala, like Velde doorways everywhere in the considerable sector of the galaxy where Velde-system terminals had been established, was a cubicle of black glass, four meters high, three meters wide, three meters deep. Along its inner walls a pair of black-light lenses stared at each other like enigmatic all-seeing eyes. On the rear wall of the cubicle were three jutting metal cones from which the Velde force emanated whenever a traveler crossed the threshold of the cubicle.

The theory of Velde transmission was something that everyone was taught when young, the way the law of gravity is taught, or the axioms of geometry; but one does not need to study Newton or Euclid very deeply in order to know how to descend a staircase or how to calculate the shortest way to get across a street, and one could make a fifty-light-year Velde hop without any real understanding of the concept that the universe is constructed of paired particles, equal masses of matter and antimatter, and that matter can decay spontaneously into antimatter at any time, but each such event must invariably be accompanied by the simultaneous conversion of an equivalent mass of antimatter into matter somewhere else—anywhere else—in the universe, so that the symmetry of matter is always conserved.

Velde's Theorem had demonstrated the truth of that, long ago, millennia ago, back in those almost unimaginable primeval days when Earth and Earth alone was mankind's home. Then Conrad Wilf, free-booting physicist, provided a practical use for Velde's equations by showing how it was possible to construct containment facilities that could prevent the normally inescapable mutual annihilation of matter and antimatter, thereby making feasible the controlled conversion of particles into their antiparticles. Matter that was held within a Wilf containment field could be transformed into antimatter and stored, without fear of instant annihilation, while at the same moment a corresponding quantity of antimatter elsewhere in the universe was converted into matter and held in a corresponding Wilf field far away.

But Wilf conversions, contained though they were, still entailed a disconcerting randomness in the conservation of symmetry: when matter was destroyed here and a balancing quantity of antimatter was created elsewhere, *elsewhere* could be at any point at all in the universe, perhaps ten thousand kilometers away, perhaps ten billion light-years; everything was open-ended, without directionality or predictability. It remained for Simtow, the third of the three great pioneers of interstellar transport, to develop a device that tuned the Velde Effect so that the balancing transactions of Wilf conversions took place not randomly but within the confines of a specific closed system with Wilf containment fields at both ends. At the destination end, antimatter was stored in a Wilf containment vessel. At the transmission end, that which was to be transmitted would undergo a Velde transformation into antimatter, a transformation that was balanced, at the designated destination end, by the simultaneous and equivalent transformation of the stored antimatter into a quantity of matter identical to that which had been converted by the transmitter. The last step was the controlled annihilation of the antimatter that had been created at the transmission end, thereby recapturing the energy that had powered the original transmission. The effect was the simultaneous particle-by-particle duplication of the transmission matter at the receiving end.

The boy who would become the Colonel comprehended all this, more or less, at least to the extent of understanding that one was demolished *here* and reassembled instantaneously *there*. He knew, also, of the ancient experiments with inanimate objects, with small animals and plants, and finally with the very much living body of the infinitely courageous pioneering voyager Haakon Christiansen, that showed that whatever went into a transmission doorway would emerge unharmed at its destination. All the same it was impossible for him to avoid a certain degree of uncertainty, even of something not very different from terror, in the moment when his grandfather's bony hand flung him toward the waiting doorway.

That uncertainty, that terror, if that is what it was, lasted only an instant's part of an instant. Then he was within the doorway and, because Velde transmission occurs in a realm where relativistic laws are irrelevant, he found himself immediately outside it again, but he was somewhere else, and it all looked so completely strange that there was no point in being frightened of it.

Where he found himself was a world with a golden-red sun that cast a hard metallic light altogether unlike the cheerful yellow light of Galgala's sun, which was the only sunlight he had ever seen. He was on a barren strip of flat sandy land with a lofty cliff at his back and what looked like a great oceanic expanse of pink mud in front of him. There were no living creatures in sight, no plants, no trees. He had never been in the presence of such utter emptiness before.

That sea of pink mud at whose border he stood stretched out as far as the horizon and, for all he knew, wrapped itself around it and kept going down the other side of the planet. It was indeed an ocean of mud: quivering, rippling mud, mud that seemed almost to be alive. Perhaps it *was* alive, a single living organism of colossal size. He could feel warmth radiating from it. He sensed a kind of sentience about it. Again and again some patch of its surface would begin throbbing spasmodically, and then it would send up odd projections and protuberances that slowly wriggled and writhed like questing tentacles before sinking down again into the huge sluggish mass from which it had arisen. He stared at it for a long while, fascinated by its eerie motions.

After a time he wondered where his grandfather was.

He should have followed instantly, should he not? But it didn't appear that he had. Instead the boy discovered himself alone in a way that was completely new to him, perhaps the only human being on a vast strange planet whose name he did not even know. At least twenty minutes had gone by. That was a long time to be alone in a place like this. He was supposed to wait here; but for how long? He wondered what he would do if, after another hour or two, his grandfather still had not arrived, and decided finally that he would simply step through the doorway in the hope that it would take him back to Galgala, or at least to some world where he could get help finding his way home.

Turning away from the sea, he looked backward and up, and then he understood where it was that his grandfather had sent him, for there on the edge of that towering cliff just in back of him he was able to make out the shape of a monumental stone fortress, low and long, outlined sharply against the glowering greenish sky like a crouching beast making ready to spring. Everyone in the galaxy knew what that fortress was. It was the ancient gigantic ruined building known as Megalo Kastro, from which this planet took its name—the only surviving work of some unknown extinct race that had lived here eight million years ago. There was nothing else like it in the universe.

"What do you say?" his grandfather said, stepping through the doorway with the broad self-congratulatory smile of someone arriving exactly on time. "Are you ready to climb up there and have a look around?"

It was an exhausting climb. The old man had long legs and a demon's unbounded vitality, and the boy had a ten-year-old's half-developed muscles. But he had no choice other than to follow along as closely as possible, scrambling frantically up the rough stone blocks of the staircase, too far apart for a boy's lesser stride, that had been carved in the face of the cliff. He was breathless by the time he reached the top, fifty paces to the rear of his grandfather. The old man had already entered the ruin and had begun to saunter through it with the proprietorial air of a guide leading a party of tourists.

It was too big to see in a single visit. They went on and on, and still there was no end to its vaulted chambers. "This is the Equinox Hall," his grandfather said, gesturing grandly. "You see the altar down at that end? And this—we call it the Emperor's Throne Room. And this—the Hall of Sacrifices. Our own names for them, you understand. Obviously we'll never know what they really were called." There were no orderly angles everywhere. Everything seemed unstable and oppressively strange. The walls seemed to waver and flow, and though the boy knew it was only an illusion, it was a profoundly troublesome one. His eyes ached. His stomach felt queasy. Yet his heart pounded with fierce excitement.

"Look here," said his grandfather. "The handprint of one of the builders, maybe. Or a prisoner's." They had reached the cellar level now. On the wall of one of the dungeon-like rooms was the white outline of a large hand, a hand with seven fingers and a pair of opposable thumbs, one on each side. An *alien* hand.

The boy who would become the Colonel shivered. No one knew who had built this place. Some extinct race, surely, because there was no known race of the galaxy today that could have done it except the human race—no others encountered thus far had evolved beyond the most primitive level—and mankind itself had not yet evolved when Megalo Kastro had been built. But it was not likely to have been the work of the great unknown race that humans called the Magellanics, either, because they had left their transporter doorways, immensely more efficient and useful than Velde doorways, on every world that had been part of their ancient empire, and there was no Magellanic doorway, nor any trace of one, on Megalo Kastro. So they had never been here. But *someone* had, some third great race that no one knew anything about, and had left this fortress behind, millions of years ago.

"Come," said his grandfather, and they descended and returned to the doorway, and went off to a world with an amber sky that had swirls of blue in it, and a dull reddish sun lying like a lump of coal along the horizon with a second star, brighter, high overhead. This was Cuchulain, said the old man, a moon of the subluminous star Gwydion, the dark companion of a star named Lalande 21185, and they were only eight light-years from Earth, which to the boy's mind seemed just a snap of the fingers away. That amazed him, to be this close to Earth, the almost legendary mother world of the whole Imperium. The air here was thick and soft, almost sticky, and everything in the vicinity of the doorway was wrapped in furry ropes of blue-green vegetation. In the distance a city of considerable size gleamed through the muzzy haze. The boy felt heavy here: Cuchulain's gravity nailed him to the ground.

"Can we go on from here to Earth?" the boy asked. "It's so near, after all!"

"Earth is forbidden," said the old man. "No one goes to Earth except when Earth does the summoning. It is the law."

"But you have always lived outside the law, haven't you?"

"Not this one," his grandfather said, and put an end to the discussion.

He was hurt by that, back then in his boyhood. It seemed unfair, a wanton shutting out of the whole universe by the planet that had set everything in motion for the human race. They should not close themselves off to their descendants this way, he told himself. But years later, looking back on that day with his grandfather, he would take a different view. They are right to keep us out, he would tell himself later. That is how it should be. Earth is long ago, Earth is far away. It should remain like that. We are the galactic people, the people born in the stars. We are the future. They are the past. They and we should not mingle. Our ways are not their ways, and any contact between them and us would be corrupting for both. For better or for worse they have turned us loose into the stars and we live a new kind of life out here in this infinite realm, nothing at all like theirs, and our path must forevermore be separate from theirs.

His grandfather had taken him to Cuchulain only because it was the contact point for a world called Moebius, where four suns danced in the sky, pearly-white triplets and a violet primary. The boy imagined that a world that had a name like Moebius would be a place of sliding dimensions and unexpected twisted vistas, but no, there was nothing unusual about it except the intricacy of the shadows cast by its quartet of suns. His grandfather had a friend on Moebius, a white-haired man as frail and worn as a length of burned rope, and they spent a day and a half visiting with him. The boy understood very little of what the two old men said: it was almost as if they were speaking some other language. Then they moved on, to a wintry world called Zima, and from there to Jackal, and from Jackal to Tycho, and from Tycho to Two Dogs, world after world, most of them worlds of the Rim where the sky was strangely empty, frighteningly black at night with only a few thousand widely spaced stars in view, not the bright, unendingly luminous curtain that eternally surrounded a Core world like Galgala, a wall of blazing light with no break in it anywhere; and then, just as the boy was starting to think that he and the old man were going to travel forever through the Imperium without ever settling down, they stepped through the doorway once more and emerged into the familiar warm sunlight and golden vegetation of Galgala.

"So now you know," his grandfather said. "Galgala is just one small world, out of many."

"How great the Imperium is!" cried the boy, dazzled by his journey. The vastness of it had stunned him, and the generosity of whatever creator it was that had made so many stars and fashioned so many beautiful worlds to whirl about them, and the farsightedness of those who had thought to organize those worlds into one Imperium, so that the citizens of that Imperium could rove freely from star to star, from world to world, without limits or bounds. For the first time in his life, but far from the last, he saw in his mind the image of that flawless silver globe, shining in his imagination like the brightest of all possible moons. His grandfather had worked hard to instill a love for anarchy in him, but the trip had had entirely the opposite effect. "How marvelous that all those different worlds should be bound together under a single government!" he cried.

He knew at once that it was the wrong thing to say. "The Imperium is the enemy, boy," said his grandfather, his voice rumbling deep down in his chest, his scowling face dark as the sky before a thunderstorm. "It strangles us. It is the chain around our throats." And went stalking away, leaving him to face his father, who had come back from a mission in the Outer Sector during his absence, and who, astonishingly, struck him across the cheek when the boy told him where he had been and what he had seen and what his grandfather had said.

"The enemy? A chain about our throats? Oh, no, boy. The Imperium is our only bulwark against chaos," his father told him. "Don't you ever forget that." And slapped him again, to reinforce the lesson. The boy hated his father in that moment as he had never hated him before. But in time the sting of the slaps was gone, and even the memory of the indignity of them had faded, and when the hour came for the boy to choose what his life would be, it was the Service that he chose, and not the buccaneering career of his demonic grandfather.

When the preparations for the start of his journey to rebellious Hermano were complete, the Colonel traveled by regular rail down to the coastal city of Elsinore, where, as he had done so many times in the distant past, he took a room in the Grand Terminus Hotel while the agents of the Imperium worked out his Velde pathway. He had not been in Elsinore for many years and had not thought ever to see it again. Nothing much had changed, he saw: wide streets, bustling traffic, cloudless skies, golden sunlight conjuring stunning brilliance out of the myriad golden flecks that bespeckled the paving-stones. He realized, contemplating now a new offworld journey when he had never expected to make any again, how weary he had become of the golden sameness of lovely Galgala, how eager—yes, actually eager—he was once more to be confronting a change of scene. They gave him a room on the third floor, looking down into a courtyard planted entirely with exotic chlorophyll-based plants, stunningly green against the ubiquitous golden hue of Galgala.

Three small purple dragons from some world in the Vendameron system lay twined in a cage at the center of the garden, as always. He wondered if these were the same dragons who had been in that cage the last time, years ago. The Colonel had stayed in this very room before, he was sure. He found it difficult to accept the fact that he was staying in it again, that he was here at the Terminus waiting to make one more Velde jump, after having put his time of traveling so thoroughly behind him. But the cold-eyed emissary from the Imperium had calculated his strategy quite carefully. Whatever vestigial sense of obligation to the Imperium that might still remain in the Colonel would probably not have been enough to break him loose from his retirement in order to deal with one more obstreperous colony. The fact that Geryon Lanista, his one-time protege, his comrade, his betrayer, was the architect of the Hermano rebellion was another matter entirely, though, one that could not be sidestepped. To allow himself to miss a chance to come face to face with Geryon Lanista after all these years would be to act as though not just his career in the Service but his life itself had come to its end.

The emissary who had come to him at his villa was gone. He had done his work and was on to his next task. Now, at the Grand Terminus Hotel, the Colonel's liaison man was one Nicanor Ternera, who had the gray-skinned, pudgy-faced look of one who has spent too much of his life in meetings and conferences, and who could not stop staring at the Colonel as though he were some statue of an ancient emperor of old Earth that had unaccountably come to life and walked out of the museum where he was on exhibit.

"These are your papers," Nicanor Ternera told him. "You'll hold formal ambassadorial accreditation as head of a trade legation that's based on Gavial, which as I think you know is a planet of the Cruzeiro system. You will not be going as a representative of the Imperium itself, but rather as a diplomat affiliated with the regional government of the Cruzeiro

worlds. As you are already aware, the rebels won't at present allow officials of the Imperium to arrive on Hermano, but they're not otherwise
closed to visitors from outside, even during the present period of trade
embargo, which they describe as a temporary measure while they await
recognition by the Imperium of their independent status."

"They'll wait a long time," said the Colonel. "Especially if they won't
allow anyone from the Imperium to go in and explain the error of their
ways to them." He glanced at the papers. "For the purpose of this mission
my name is Petrus Haym?"

"Correct."

"Lanista will recognize me instantly for who I am. Or is this going
to be the sort of mission I'll be doing in disguise?"

"You'll be disguised, to some degree, for the sake of being able to
obtain entry. Once you've succeeded in getting access to Hermano as
Petrus Haym of Gavial, you can decide for yourself when and how to
reveal yourself to Lanista, which beyond any doubt you will at some
point find necessary to do in order to bring the mission to a successful
conclusion. From that point on you'll be functioning openly as an agent
of the Imperium."

"And what leverage am I to have over them?" the Colonel asked.

"The ultimate," said Nicanor Ternera.

"Good," said the Colonel. He had expected no less. He would have
accepted no less. Still, it was better to have it offered readily than to
have to demand it.

Nicanor Ternera said, "You'll be accompanied on the trip by three
genuine government people out of Gavial and another Imperium agent,
a woman from Phosphor named Magda Cermak, who'll have the official
rank of second secretary to the mission. She's been in the Service for a
dozen years and has a good grasp of the entire situation, including your
prior relationship with Geryon Lanista."

"You don't think I'd be better off handling this project entirely on
my own?"

"It's altogether possible that you could. But we'd rather not take
the risk. In any case it's essential to maintain the fiction of a trade delegation at least until you're safely on Hermano and have made contact
with Lanista, and a properly plausible delegation involves five or six
members, at least." Ternera looked to the Colonel for approval, which
he reluctantly gave. "As these documents will show you, the crux of
Gavial's issue is Hermano's termination of the export of a drug called

cantaxion, the properties of which are beneficial to people suffering from a manganese deficiency, something that's chronic on Gavial. You'll find all the details in the attached documents. Gavial has already asked for an exception to the embargo, which you are now going to try to negotiate. Ostensibly the Hermanans are willing to discuss resumption of cantaxion exports in return for military weapons to be manufactured on Bacalhao, another of the Cruzeiro worlds."

"Which would be, of course, in complete violation of Imperium law, since the Imperium has placed an embargo of its own on doing business with Hermano. Am I supposed to conclude that Gavial is considering rebelling against the Imperium also?"

"Most definitely not. At our strong urging Gavial has indicated that it's at least open to the idea of entering into such transactions, provided they can be kept secret. That doesn't mean it actually would. How far you want to proceed with any of this once you make contact with Lanista himself is entirely up to you, naturally. I doubt that he'll find the idea that this is simply a trade mission very credible, once he realizes that it's you that he's dealing with, but of course that won't matter at that point."

"Of course," said the Colonel, who was already six moves ahead in the game that had to be played once he reached Hermano, and wished that Nicanor Ternera would hand over the rest of the briefing papers and disappear, which eventually he did, though not as swiftly as the Colonel would have preferred.

The first stop on his journey to Hermano was Entrada, where the Service's main operational center was located. Going to Entrada would be to make what could be thought of as a long jump in the wrong direction. Hermano, like Galgala, was a Core world, close to the center of the galaxy, whereas Entrada was one of what had once been called the Inner Worlds, and therefore was actually out on the Rim, because all distances had been measured from Earth in those early days. Earth itself was a Rim world, and Entrada, just a couple of dozen light-years distant from it, was off in the same obscure corner of the galaxy, far from the galactic core, as the original mother planet. But stellar distances had no significant meaning in Velde transmission and Entrada was where the Service had its most important base. Here the Colonel would undergo his transformation into Petrus Haym, diplomat from Gavial.

He had undergone so many transformations in his time that the Service had a better idea of what his baseline self looked like than he did himself. He knew that he was slightly above the median in height, that he was of mesomorphic build with longer-than-average limbs, and that the natural color of his eyes was olive-green. But his eyes had been blue and brown and violet and even scarlet on various occasions, his hair had been tinted every shade in the book and sometimes removed entirely, and his teeth and nose and ears and chin had been subjected to so much modification over the years that he no longer remembered their exact original configuration. When he had retired from the Service they had restored him, so they claimed, to baseline, but he was never entirely sure that the face he saw in the mirror each morning, the pleasant, thoughtful, agreeably nondescript face of a man who was certainly no longer young but nowhere near the end of his days, was really anything like the one that had looked back at him in the days before all the modifications had begun.

The concept of a baseline self was pretty much obsolete, anyway. Short of making fundamental rearrangements in a person's basic skeletal structure—and they were working on that one—it had, for many hundreds of years, been feasible to give anyone any appearance at all. Rebuilds were standard items for everyone, not just operatives of the Service. You could look young or old, benign or cruel, open-hearted or brooding, as you wished, and when you tired of one look you could trade it in for another, just as, up to a point, you could roll back the inroads of the aging process by fifty years or so every now and then. That sort of mutability had been available even in the Colonel's grandfather's day, and by now everyone took it for granted. It was only his sheer obstinate perversity of will that had led the Colonel's father to insist on retaining, for the last seventy years of his life, the limp that he had acquired while carrying out an assignment on one of the worlds of the Magnifico system and that he had proudly displayed forever after.

The Colonel hesitated only the tiniest part of a moment when finally he stood before the Elsinore doorway. Some fraction of him still did not want to do this, but it was, he knew, only an extremely small fraction. Then he stepped through and was annihilated instantly and just as instantly reconstituted at the corresponding doorway on Entrada.

It was close to a century since the Colonel had last been to the operations center on Entrada. Entrada was a place he had hoped never to see again. He remembered it as a tropical world, much too hot from pole to pole, humid and jungly everywhere, with two potent white suns that were set close together in the sky and went whirling around each other three or four times a day, giving the appearance of a single weird egg-shaped mass. Only Entrada's great distance from those two sizzling primaries made the planet habitable at all. The Colonel hated its steambath heat, its thick, almost liquid greenish-gold atmosphere, its lunatic profusion of vegetation, the merciless round-the-clock glare of those twin suns. And also it was a world severely afflicted by the presence of a strong lambda field, lambda being a force that had been unknown until the early days of Velde travel. In those days anyone making the transition from a low-lambda world to a high-lambda world found himself knocked flat on his back during a period of adaptation that might stretch across several months. The problem of lambda differential had been conquered over a thousand years ago, but even now some minor effects could be felt by new arrivals to a high-lambda world, a lingering malaise, a sense of spiritual heaviness, that took days or even weeks to shake off.

But the Colonel, having come once more to Entrada despite all expectation, found it easy enough to shrug off all its discomforts. This would be only a brief stop, and there would never be another, of that he was certain beyond all question. He went through it as one goes through a bad dream, waiting for the release that morning brings.

Obsequious Service officers met him at the transit station, greeting him in an almost terrified way, with a kind of heavy-handed stifling reverence, the way one might greet some frightful spectre returned from the tomb, and conveyed him to the operations center, which was ten times the size of the building the Colonel remembered. Once he was inside its windowless mass he might have been on any planet at all: Entrada and all its tropic hyperabundance had no presence within these well insulated halls.

"Colonel, this is how you are going to look," they told him, and a full-size image of Petrus Haym sprang into view in the air before him.

They had conceived Petrus Haym as a stolid burgher, round-cheeked, complacent, with heavy-lidded sleepy eyes, full lips, a short thick neck, a fleshy body, the very model and essence of what he was supposed to be, a man who had devoted his life to issues of tariff regulation and balances of trade. Indifferently the Colonel gave his approval, offering no suggestions whatever for revisions in the Haym format, though they seemed to be expecting them. He didn't care. The format they had conceived would do. To look like an animated stereotype of a trade commissioner would make it all the simpler for the Colonel to assume the identity he was supposed to take on.

That he would be able to operate convincingly as the accredited leader of a trade delegation from a planet he knew nothing about was not anything that he doubted. He was a quick study. In his time he had assumed all kinds of roles: he had been a priest of the Goddess, an itinerant collector of zoological specimens, an organizer of disenfranchised laborers, a traveling musician, a deeply compassionate counselor to the bereaved, and many other things, whatever was required to fit the task at hand, which was always, ultimately, the engineering of consent. Preserving the integrity of the Imperium had been his constant goal. The Imperium's scope verged on the infinite; so too, then, must his.

When they had done all that they needed to do with him at the operations center, and he had done all that he needed to do as well, he went on to the next stop on his journey, Phosphor, where the rest of his team was awaiting him.

Like many of the worlds of the Imperium, Phosphor was a planet of a multiple-sun system. The Colonel had visited it once before, early in his career, but all he remembered of the visit was that he had gone there to seek out and eliminate a veteran agitator who was living there in exile from his home world and laying plans to return home to engage in a fresh round of destabilizing activities. The Colonel recalled carrying out the job successfully, but the planet itself he had forgotten. Seeing it now, he still did not remember much about his earlier stay there. He had seen so many worlds, after all. Here, a huge cool red sun, old and dying, lay like an angry blemish in the east by day, and a hot blue one that was at least a couple of hundred units away blazed out of the west, bright as a beacon in the sky. Even at night—the unnerving, intensely black night of a Rim world that the Colonel had never learned to like— stray tendrils of light from one sun or the other streamed into view at the hemisphere's darkside edge.

The people of Phosphor did not seem to go in for somatic modification. The likeness they bore toward one another indicated that they seemed to cling almost defiantly to the somatotypes of the original handful of settlers of thousands of years ago, who must predominantly have been short, sinewy, broad-based folk, swarthy-skinned, beady-eyed. Magda Cermak, who was waiting for the Colonel at the Velde station, was the perfect exemplar of her people, a dark-haired sharp-nosed woman who stood only chest-high to the Colonel but who was so solidly planted atop her thick, sturdy legs that a rolling boulder could not have knocked her down. She seemed about fifty, no more than that, and perhaps she actually was. She welcomed the Colonel in an efficient, uneffusive way, addressing him as Petrus Haym, inquiring without real curiosity about his journey, and introducing him to the three delegates from Gavial, two men and a woman, who stood diffidently to one side, a well-nigh invisible trio of pallid bureaucrats, fidgety, self-effacing, like the supernumeraries that in fact they were in the drama to come.

His point of arrival on Phosphor was its capital city, a sprawling, untidy place that bore the ancient historical name of Jerusalem. At the Imperium headquarters there, Magda Cermak provided the Colonel with an update on the activities of Geryon Lanista—Martin Bauer, as he was now—since their paths had last crossed on that ill-starred world, Tristessa, half a century before.

"The one part of the trail we don't have," Cermak said, "covers the period between his escape from Tristessa's companion planet and his arrival in the Aguila sector. The period in the immediate aftermath of the faked suicide, that is. We figure that he spent about twenty years as far out of sight as he could keep himself. Our best guess is that he may have been moving around in the Rim worlds during those years. One informant insists that he even spent a certain amount of time on Earth itself."

"Could that be so?" asked the Colonel.

Magda Cermak shrugged. "There's no way of knowing. He's probably capable of managing it, wouldn't you say? But if he did get to Earth, Earth doesn't know anything about it, and Lanista isn't going to tell us either."

"All right. That's twenty blank years. What about the next thirty?"

"He first turns up under the name of Paul Thurm as a grape farmer on Iriarte, but he doesn't last long there. A legal problem arises, Thurm vanishes, and at that point a couple of years are gone from the record. When we pick up the trail again we find him in one of the Aguila Sector systems as Heinrich Bauer, supposedly an expert on land reclamation. He spends four years on a planet called Thraka, teaching the locals how to drain swamps, and then he moves on to Alyatta, a world of an adjacent system, where he shows the people how to irrigate a desert."

"A highly versatile man," the Colonel said.

"Very. He's on Alyatta for six or seven years, apparently marrying and having a couple of children and acquiring substantial properties. Then once again he vanishes abruptly, leaving his family behind, and shows up on Gran Chingada, where his name now is *Martin* Bauer. We don't know the motive for the switch. Something to do with the abandonment of his family, perhaps, although why he didn't change the surname too is hard to understand. Possibly the 'Heinrich' entry was erroneous all along. Keeping detailed track of a whole galaxy full of people is only approximately possible, you know.—You have been to Gran Chingada, I understand."

"A long time ago. It's a rough place."

"It's quieter now. They got rid of their worst malconents thirty years back."

"Shipping them off to Hermano, two star-systems away, I'm told."

"Correct."

"Was Martin Bauer among those who was sent into exile?"

"No. He emigrated voluntarily, a dozen years ago, after the settlement on Hermano was fairly well established. Supposedly he was brought in by the plantation owners who grow the herb from which cantaxion is made, on account of his old specialty, land reclamation. He became a plantation owner himself in a major way, and involved himself very quickly in politics there, and before long he had won election to the Council of Seven, the oligarchy that was the ruling body on Hermano before its declaration of independence from the Imperium."

"An oligarchy whose members are *elected*?" said the Colonel. "Isn't that a little unusual?"

Magda Cermak smiled. "'Politics' on Hermano doesn't mean that they have universal suffrage. The richest land-owners have run the place from the beginning. In the days of the Council of Seven, new members of the Council were chosen by the existing ones whenever a vacancy developed. It appears that Bauer got very rich very fast and was able to buy his way onto the Council. From what I hear, he was always an extremely persuasive man."

"Quite," the Colonel said.

"The last report of the Imperium commissioners before their expulsion indicates that he quickly made himself the dominant figure on it. He was the one, as I expect you've already guessed, who maneuvered Hermano into breaking with the Imperium."

"And what is he now, King of Hermano? Emperor of Hermano?"

"First Secretary of the Provisional Government is his title. He and four other members of the old Council of Seven make up the provisional government."

"An oligarchy of five being more manageable than an oligarchy of seven, I suppose. The next phase in the process being the replacement of the provisional government with an even more manageable one-man dictatorship."

"No doubt," said Magda Cermak.

She had more to tell him, little details of Martin Bauer's life on Hermano—he had married again, it seemed, and had had another set of children, and lived in monarchical splendor on a great estate on the southern coast of Hermano's one settled continent. The Colonel paid no more attention to what she was saying than professional courtesy required. It came as no surprise to hear that Geryon Lanista was looking after himself well. That had always been a specialty of his.

What occupied the center of the Colonel's attention was the fact of the rebellion on Hermano itself. That the person formerly known as Geryon Lanista was the instrument by which that rebellion had come about concerned him only in an incidental way now; it was a purely personal datum that had succeeded nicely in entangling him, at a time when he had thought he had completely shed his identity as a functionary of the Service, in this enterprise. If he could settle the score with Geryon Lanista after all this time, so be it. That would not be a trivial thing, but it was nevertheless a peripheral one. It was the existence of the rebellion, rather than Lanista's involvement in it, that had in these recent days brought powerful old emotions up from the center of the Colonel's being, had reawakened in him that sense of the necessity of protecting the Imperium that had been the essential driving factor of his personality through his entire adult life.

A rebellion was an act of war, nothing else. And in a galaxy of many thousands of inhabited worlds war could not be allowed to come back into existence.

There had been strife once, plenty of it, in the early years of the great galactic expansion. There had been trade wars and there had been religious wars and there had been real wars, in which whole worlds had been destroyed. The immensity of the spaces that separated one planet from another, one solar system from another, one stellar cluster from another, meant nothing at all in a civilization in which the far-flung Velde system and the even more expansive network of Magellanic gateways rendered travel over unthinkable distances a simpler and faster and safer process than a journey from one city to the next on the same continent had been in that era, many thousands of years in the past, when all of mankind had been confined to a single small world of the galaxy.

In those ancient days war between cities, and then between states when states had evolved, had been commonplace events. Schoolchildren on a million worlds still studied the history and literature of Earth as if they themselves were citizens of that little planet. They would not be able to find Earth's sun on a chart of the skies if they searched for thirty centuries, but they could recite the names of a dozen or more of Earth's famous wars, going back even into dim prehistory to the oldest war of all, the great war between the Greeks and the Trojans, when men had fought with clanging swords.

That had been a small war fought by great men. Later, millennia later, when humanity had spilled forth into all the galaxy, had come great wars fought by small men, wars not between tiny cities but between worlds, and there had been raging chaos in the stars, terrible death, terrible destruction. And then the chaos had at last burned itself out and there had come peace, fragile at first, then more certain. The galaxy-spanning institution known as the Imperium maintained that peace with iron determination.

The Imperium would not allow war. The age of chaos was over forever. That was universally understood, understood by all—or nearly all—

"Well, then, shall we start out on our way to Hermano, and get on with the job?" said the Colonel, when Magda Cermak had finished her briefing at last.

❂

The first segments of the Velde system had been constructed at a time when Earth was all there was to the human galaxy and no one seriously expected that the multitudinous stars of the galactic center would ever come within mankind's reach. Though Velde transmission itself was non-relativistic, the setting up of the original system had had to be carried out under the constraints of the old Einsteinian rules, in which the speed of light was the limiting velocity.

And so, piece by piece, the necessary receiving equipment was put in place by conventional methods of delivery on one after another of the so-called Inner Worlds, those that orbited stars lying within a sphere a hundred light-years in diameter with Earth at its center. Even though the equipment was shipped out aboard vessels traveling close to the Einsteinian limit, unmanned starships journeying outward with great sails unfurled to the photonic winds, finding potentially habitable worlds, releasing robots that would set the Velde receivers in position, then going on to the next world and the next, extending the highway of receiving stations from one star system to another, it took centuries to get the job done. And by then the Magellanics' transit system had been discovered, impinging—just barely—on the tiny segment of the galaxy where Earth had managed to set up its little network of Velde stations.

Nobody knew how old the Magellanic system was, nor who had built it, nor even how it worked. That their builders had originated in the nearby galaxy known as the Greater Magellanic Cloud was only a guess, which somehow everyone had embraced as though it were a proven fact. They might just as readily have come from the Andromeda galaxy, or the great spiral galaxy in Eridanus, or some other stellar cluster ten or twelve billion light-years away, whose component stars and all the inhabitants of its many worlds had perished back in the ungraspable remoteness of the distant past. No one knew; no one expected to find out. The only thing that was certain was that the so-called Magellanics had traveled freely through the galaxy that one day would be mankind's, roaming it some unknowable number of years ago, using a system of matter transmission to journey from world to world, and that among the artifacts they had left behind on those worlds were their matter-transmitters, still in working order, apparently designed to function through all of eternity to come.

They operated more or less as the Velde transmitters did—you stepped through *here* and came out *there*—but whether they worked on similar principles was also something that was unknowable. There was nothing to analyze. Their doorways had no moving parts and drew on no apparent power source. Certain brave souls, stumbling upon these doorways during the early days of exploration on the outer worlds of humanity's sphere of expansion, had stepped through them and emerged on other planets even farther out, and eventually some working knowledge of the network, which doorway led to what other world, had been attained. How many lives had been lost in the course of attaining that knowledge was another thing that could never be known, for only those explorers who had survived their trips through the doorways could report on what they had done. The others—instantly transported, perhaps, to some other galaxy, or to the heart of a star, or to a world of intolerable gravitational force, or one whose doorway had been surrounded, over the millennia, by a sea of molten lava—had not been able to send back useful information about their trips.

By now, though, humankind had been making use of the Magellanic doorways for upwards of ten thousand years. The usable routes had all been tested and charted and the doorways had played a determining role in mankind's expansion across immense galactic distances that otherwise might not have been crossed until some era unimaginably far off in the future. The little sphere of planets that once had been known as the Inner Worlds was now thought of as the Rim, out there on the edge of galactic civilization; Earth, the primordial world where everything had begun, had become almost a legend, unvisited and shrouded in myth, that had very little reality for most of the Imperium's trillions of citizens; the essential life of galactic mankind long ago had moved from the Rim to the close-packed worlds of the Core. Though Velde stations still were an important means of travel within local sectors of the galaxy, and new Velde links were being constructed all the time, most long-hop travel now was carried out via the Magellanic system, which required no input of energy and maintained itself free of cost to those who used its gateways. The Colonel's journey to Hermano would involve the use of both systems.

The first jump took him via Velde transmission from Phosphor to nearby Entropy, a world that the Colonel had visited as a tourist forty years before, in the early days of his retirement. He did not remember it as a particularly interesting place. He had gone there only to gain access to the Magellanic doorway on Trewen, fifty light-years away, where he could leap across the galaxy to lovely Jacynth, his intended destination back then.

Entropy was no more interesting now: a yellow-green sun, mild weather, a few small cities, three big moons dangling in a row across the daytime sky. Magda Cermak preceded him there, and his three Gavial associates followed along behind. When the whole group was assembled they did a Velde hop to Trewen, now as before a virtually uninhabited world, cool and dry and bleak, notable only because the Magellanics had chosen to plant one of their doorways on it. Transit agents from the Service were waiting there to conduct the Colonel and his party to the doorway, which was tucked away within a deep cave on a rocky plateau a few hundred meters from the Velde station.

It seemed like only the day before yesterday that the Colonel had made his previous visit to this place. There on the right side of the cave was the sleek three-sided doorway, tapering upward to a sharp point, framing within itself a darkness so intense that it made the darkness of a Rim-world night seem almost inconsequential. Along each of its three sides was a row of gleaming hieroglyphs, an incomprehensible message out of a vanished eon. The doorway was wide enough for several to go through at a time. The Colonel beckoned the three Gavial people through first, and then stepped through himself, with Magda Cermak at his side. There was no sensation of transition: he walked through the darkness and came out of another doorway on Jacynth, one of the most beautiful of all worlds, as beautiful, almost, as lost Tristessa: a place of emerald meadows and a ruby-red sky, where great trees with feathery silver leaves and scarlet trunks sprang up all about them and a milky waterfall went cascading down the side of an ebony mountain that rose in serried pinnacles just ahead. The Colonel would have been happy to end the journey at that point and simply remain on Jacynth, where even the most troubled soul could find contentment for a while, but there was no hope of that, for more Service personnel awaited him there to lead him on to the next doorway, and by day's end the Colonel had arrived on Gavial of the Cruzeiro system, halfway across the galaxy from that morning's starting point at the Grand Terminus Hotel on Galgala.

Not even a Colonel in the Service was able to know everything about every one of the worlds of the Imperium, or even very much about very many of them. The galaxy was simply too big. Before the dark-haired intruder had enmeshed him in this undertaking the Colonel had been aware of Cruzeiro only because it was that rare thing, a solar system that had more than one world—four, in fact—that was inhabitable by human beings without extensive modification. Of Gavial itself, or its neighbor Bacalhao, or the other two worlds of the Cruzeiro system, he knew nothing at all. But now he was going to be masquerading as a native of the place, no less, and so he needed to acquire some first-hand familiarity with it. He had carried out the usual sort of research in the days before leaving home, and that had given him all the background on Gavial that he needed, though not a fully three-dimensional sense of what sort of world it was. For that you had to spend a little time there. He did know how large Gavial was, though, its climatic and geographical details, the history of its colonization, its major products, and a host of other things that he was probably not going to need to draw upon during his stay on Hermano, but which, simply by being present in some substratum of his mind, would allow him to make a convincing pretense of being Gavialese. As part of that he had learned to speak in the thick-tongued Gavialese way, spitting and sputtering his words in a fashion that accurately mimicked the manner of speech of his three Gavialese companions.

At first Magda Cermak, who spoke Galactic with the sharp-edged precision that seemed to be typical of the natives of Phosphor, could be seen smothering laughter every time the Colonel began to speak.

"Is it so comic, then?" he asked her.

"You sound like a marthresant," she said, giggling.

"Remind me of what a marthresant is," said the Colonel.

It was, she explained, one of her world's marine mammals, a huge ungainly creature with a wild tangle of bristly whiskers and long flaring tusks, which made coarse whooping snorts that could be heard half a kilometer away when it came up for air. Saying that he sounded like a marthresant did not appear to be a compliment. But he thanked her gravely for the explanation and told her that he was happy that his accent provided her with a little reminder of home.

That seemed to amuse her. But perhaps she was wondering whether she had offended him, for she made a point of telling him that she found his own accent, the accent of Galgala, extremely elegant. Which obliged the Colonel to inform her that his accent was not Galgalan at all, that he had lived on Galgala only during his boyhood and in the years since his retirement, and that in the years between he had spent so much time on so many different worlds, counterfeiting so many different accents, that he had lost whatever his original manner of speech had been. What he normally spoke now was actually a kind of all-purpose pan-Galactic, a randomly assorted mixture of mannerisms that would baffle even the most expert student of linguistics.

"And will you have some Gavialese in the mix when this is all over?" she asked.

"Perhaps nothing worse than a little snorting and whooping around the edges of the consonants," he told her, and winked.

She appeared to be startled by his sudden playfulness. But it had emerged only in response to hers, when she had begun giggling over his accent. The Colonel had been aware from the first that she felt an almost paralyzing awe for him, which she had been attempting to conceal with great effort. Nothing unusual about that: he was a legendary figure in the Service, already famous throughout the galaxy long before she was born, the hero of a hundred extravagantly risky campaigns. Everyone he had come in contact with since taking on this assignment had regarded him in that same awe-stricken way, though some had been a little better at hiding it than others. There were times, looking back at all he had done, that he almost felt a twinge of awe himself. The only one who had seemed immune to the power of his fame was the cold-eyed man who had gone to him in the first place, someone, obviously, who was so highly placed in the modern Service that he was beyond all such emotion. All the others were overwhelmed by the accumulated grandeur of his reputation. But it would only make things more difficult all around as this project unfolded if Magda went on thinking of him as some sort of demigod who had condescended to step down from the heavens and move among mortals again this one last time. He was relieved that she was professional enough to shake some of that off.

They remained on Gavial for a week while he soaked up the atmosphere of the place, did a little further research, and endured a round of governmental banquets and tiresome speeches that were designed to help him believe that he really *was* a trade representative from this planet whose only purpose in visiting Hermano was to get the flow of a vitally needed medicine going again. By the time that week was nearing its end Magda's attitude toward him had loosened to the extent that she was able to say, "It must be strange to think that in a few days you're finally going to get a chance to come face to face with the man you hate more than anyone else in the universe."

"Lanista? I don't even know if that's really him, over there on Hermano."

"It is. There's no question that it is."

"The Service says he is, and says it has the proof, but I've had too much experience with the way the Service creates whatever evidence it needs to buy a hundred percent of anything the Service claims. But suppose that *is* Lanista on Hermano. Why do you think I would hate him? I don't even know what the word means, really."

"The man who was working against you behind your back on one of your most important projects, and who, when things were heading toward an explosion that he himself had set up, went off without giving you a word of warning that you were very likely to get killed? What do you call that, if not treachery?"

"Treachery is exactly what I would call it, indeed," said the Colonel.

"And yet you don't hate him for that?" She was floundering now.

"I told you," the Colonel said, trying to choose his words with great care, "that 'hate' isn't a word I understand very well. Hate seems so useless, anyway. My real concern here is that I could have misjudged that man so completely. I *loved* him, you know. I thought of him almost as a son. I brought him into the Service, I taught him the craft, I worked with him on a dozen jobs, I personally insisted on his taking part in the Tristessa thing. And then—then—then he—he—"

His throat went dry. He found himself unable to continue speaking. He was swept by feelings that he could only begin to comprehend.

Magda was staring at him in something close to horror. Perhaps she feared that she had pushed into territory that she had had no right to be exploring.

But then, as though trying to repair whatever damage she had caused, she pressed desperately onward.

"I didn't realize that you and Lanista were actually that—close. I thought he was just your partner on an assignment. Which would be bad enough, selling you out like that. But if in fact he was almost like—your—"

She faltered.

"My protege," the Colonel said. "Call him my protege." He went to the window and stood with his back to her, knotting his hands together behind him. He wished he had never let this conversation begin.

The sun, Cruzeiro, was starting to set, an unspectacular yellowish sun tinged with pale pink. A hard-edged crescent moon was edging upward in the sky. Behind it lay two sharp points of brilliant light, two neighboring worlds of this system. Bacalhao and Coracao, their names were. He thought that Bacalhao was the one on the left, but wasn't entirely sure which was which. You could usually see them both in the twilight sky here. The odd names, he supposed, were derived, as so many planetary names were, from one of the ancient languages of Earth, a world where, so it was said, they had had a hundred different languages all at once, and people from one place could scarcely understand what people from another place were saying. It was a wonder they had been able to accomplish anything, those Earthers, when they wouldn't even have been able to make themselves understood if they went as much as five hundred kilometers away from home. And yet they had managed to make the great leap out into space, somehow, and to spread their colonies over thousands of solar systems, and to leave their words behind as the names of planets, although no one remembered any more what most of those words once meant.

"My protege," he said again, without turning to face her. "Who betrayed me, yes. That has always mystified me, that he would have done such a thing. But do I hate him for it? No."

Yes, he told himself. *Of course you do.*

Tristessa. A magical place, the Colonel had once thought. On Tristessa your eye encountered beauty wherever it came to rest. He remembered everything about it down to the finest detail: the sweet fragrance of its soft, moist atmosphere, the bright turquoise/emerald glory of its double sun, the throngs of magnificent winged reptiles soaring overhead, the glistening smoothness of the big, round white pebbles, like the eggs of some prehistoric monster, that formed the bed of the clear rushing stream that ran past his lodging. The pungent flavor of a triangular yellow fruit that dangled in immense quantities from nearby trees. The many-legged crab-like things, glossy black carapaces criss-crossed with jagged blood-red streaks, that roamed the misty forests searching in the dark rich loam for food, and looked up from their foraging to study you like solemn philosophers with a multitude of faceted amber eyes.

Its name, someone had told him once, was derived from a word of one of the languages of ancient Earth, a word that carried a connotation of "sadness," and certainly sadness was appropriate in thinking of Tristessa now. But how could they have known, when giving such a melancholy name to such a beautiful world, what sort of destiny was awaiting it five thousand years in the future?

For the Colonel, who was in the late prime of his career as an arch-manipulator of worlds, the Tristessa affair had begun as a routine political intervention, the sort of assignment he had dealt with on more occasions than he could count. He saw no special challenge in it. He expected that Geryon Lanista, whom he had been grooming for a decade or so to be his successor in the Service, would do much of the real work; the Colonel would merely supervise, observe, confirm in his own mind that Lanista was fully qualified to take things over from him.

Tristessa, lovely, underpopulated, economically undeveloped, had a companion world, Shannakha, less than thirty million kilometers away. Shannakha had been settled first. Its climate, temperate rather than tropical, wasn't as appealing as Tristessa's, nor was its predominantly sandy, rocky landscape anywhere near as beautiful. But it offered a wider range of natural resources—pretty little Tristessa had nothing much in the way of metals or fossil fuels—and it was on Shannakha that cities had been founded and an industrial economy established. Tristessa, colonized by Shannakha a few hundred years later, became the holiday planet for its neighbor in the skies. Shannakha's powerful merchant princes set up plantations where Tristessa's abundant fruits and vegetables could be raised and shipped to eager markets on the other world, and created great estates for themselves in the midst of those plantations; Shannakha's entrepreneurs built grand resort hotels for middle-class amusement on the beautiful island archipelagoes of Tristessa's tropical seas; and thousands of less fortunate Shannakhans settled on Tristessa to provide a labor force for all those estates, plantations, and hotels. It all worked very well for hundreds of years, though of course it worked rather better for the absentee owners on Shannakha than it did for their employees on Tristessa, since the Shannakhans prohibited any kind of ownership of Tristessan real estate or other property by Tristessans, kept payrolls as low as possible, and exported all profits to Shannakha.

But, as any student of history as well informed as the Colonel was would certainly know, the unilateral exploitation of one world by another does not work well forever, any more than the unilateral exploitation of one city or state by another had worked well in that long-ago era when all the human race was confined to that one little world called Earth. At some point a malcontent will arise who will argue that the assets of a place belong to the people who dwell in that place, and should not be tapped for the exclusive benefit of a patrician class living somewhere else, far away. And, if he is sufficiently persuasive and charismatic, that malcontent can succeed in finding followers, founding a movement, launching an insurrection, liberating his people from the colonial yoke.

Just that was in the process of happening when the Colonel was called in. Tristessa's charismatic malcontent had arisen. His name was Ilion Gabell; he came from a long line of farmers who raised and grew the agreeably narcotic zembani leaf that was the source of a recreational drug vastly popular on Shannakha; and because his natural abilities of leadership were so plainly manifest, he had been entrusted by a group of the plantation owners with the management of a group of adjacent zembani tracts that stretched nearly halfway across Tristessa's primary continent. That, unfortunately for the plantation owners, gave him access to clear knowledge of how profitable the Tristessa plantations really were. And now—so reliable informants had reported—he was on the verge of launching a rebellion that would break Tristessa free of the grasp of its Shannakhan owners. It was the Colonel's assignment to keep this from happening. He had chosen Geryon Lanista to assist him.

Lanista, who was fond of exploring both sides of an issue as an intellectual exercise, said, "And why, exactly, should this be any concern of the Imperium? Is it our job to protect the economic interests of one particular group of landowners against its own colonial employees? Are we really such conservatives that we have to be the policemen of the status quo all over the universe?"

"There would be wider ramifications to a Tristessa uprising," the Colonel said. "Consider: this Ilion Gabell gives the signal, and in a single night every Shannakhan who happens to be on Tristessa is slaughtered. Such things have occurred elsewhere, as you surely know. The Imperium quite rightly deplores wholesale murder, no matter what virtuous pretext is put forth for it. Next, a revolutionary government is proclaimed and transfers title to all Shannakhan-owned property on Tristessa to itself, to be held in the name of the citizenry of the Republic of Tristessa. What happens after that? Will Shannakha, peace-loving and enlightened, simply shrug and say that inasmuch as war between planets is illegal by decree of the Imperium, it therefore has no choice but to recognize the independence of Tristessa, and invites the Tristessans to enter into normal trade relationships with their old friends on the neighboring world?"

"Maybe so," said Lanista. "And that might even work."

"But the down side—"

"The down side, I suppose, is that it would send a signal to other planets in Tristessa's position that a rebellion against the established property interests can pay off. Which will create a lot of little Tristessa-style uprisings all over the galaxy, one of which might eventually explode into actual warfare between the mother world and its colony. Therefore a great deal of new toil for the Service will be required in order to keep those uprisings from breaking out, in which case it might be better to snuff out this one before it gets going."

"It might indeed," said the Colonel. "Now, the opposite scenario—"

"Yes. Shannakha, infuriated by the expropriation of its properties on Tristessa, retaliates by sending an armed expedition to Tristessa to get things under control. Thousands of Tristessans die in the first burst of hostilities. Then a guerrilla war erupts as Gabell and his insurrectionists are driven underground, and in the course of it the plantations and resorts of Tristessa are destroyed, perhaps with unusually ugly ecological consequences, and many additional casualties besides. Shannakha wrecks its own economy to pay for the war and Tristessa is ruined for decades or centuries to come. And at the end of it all we either wind up with something that's worse than the status quo ante bellum, Shannakha still in charge of Tristessa but now perhaps unable to meet the expense of rebuilding what was there once, or else with two devastated planets, Tristessa independent but useless and Shannakha bankrupt."

"And therefore—" the Colonel said, waiting for the answer that he knew would be forthcoming.

Lanista provided it. "Therefore we try to calm Ilion Gabell down and negotiate the peaceful separation of Tristessa and Shannakha by telling Gabell that we will obtain better working conditions for his people, while at the same time leading the Shannakhans to see that it's in their own best interest to strike a deal before a revolution can break out. If we can't manage that, I'd say that the interests of Tristessa, Shannakha, and the Imperium would best be served by suppressing Ilion Gabell's little revolution out of hand, either by removing him permanently or by demonstrating to him in a sufficiently persuasive way that he stands no chance of success, and simultaneously indicating to the Shannakhans that they'd better start treating the Tristessans a little more generously or they're going to find themselves faced with the same problem again before long, whether the revolution is led by Gabell or by someone else with the same ideas. Yes?"

"Yes," said the Colonel.

So it was clear, then, what they had to try to achieve, and what they were going to do to achieve it. All scenarios but one led to a violent outcome, and violence was a spreading sore that if not checked at its source could consume an entire civilization, even a galactic one. The problems on Tristessa, which were easily enough identified, needed to be corrected peacefully before a worse kind of correction got under way. The Colonel was as skillful an operative as there was and Geryon Lanista was nearly as shrewd as he was, and he still had all the energy of youth, besides. Why, then, had it all gone so terribly wrong?

And then it was time at last to make the last jump in the sequence, the one from Gavial to Hermano, where, despite all that the Colonel had believed for the last fifty years, Geryon Lanista was very much alive and at the head of his own insurrectionist government.

Despite the general trade embargo, the Velde link between Hermano and certain worlds of the galaxy, such as Gavial, was still operational. Only the wildest of insurrectionists would take the rash step of cutting themselves completely off from interstellar transit, and Lanista was evidently not that wild. Velde connections required two sets of tuned equipment, one at each end of any link, and once a planet chose to separate itself from Velde travel it would need the cooperation of the Imperium to re-establish the linkage. Lanista hadn't cared to risk handing the Imperium a unilateral stranglehold over his planet's economy. There had been other rebellions, as he of all people would have known very well, in which the Imperium had picked a time of its own choosing to restore contact once it had been broken off by the rebels.

The Colonel was completely composed as they set out on this final hop of the long journey. He searched for anxiety within himself and found none. He realized that it must have been destined all along that before the end of his life he would once again come face to face with Geryon Lanista, so that there might be a settlement of that troublesome account at last.

And why, he asked himself, should there be any immediate cause for anxiety? For the moment he was Petrus Haym, emissary plenipotentiary from the Cruzeiro system to the provisional government of independent Hermano, and Lanista was Martin Bauer, the head of that provisional government. Whatever meeting there was to be between the two of them would be conducted, at least at first, behind those masks.

Hermano, the Colonel saw at once, was no Tristessa. Perhaps he had arrived in this hemisphere's winter: the air was cool, even sharp, with hardly any humidity at all. He detected a hint of impending snow in it. The sky had a grayish, gloomy, lowering look. There was an odd acrid flavor to the atmosphere that would require some getting used to. The gravity was a little above Standard Human, which was going to exacerbate the task of carrying the extra flesh of Petrus Haym.

Everything within immediate view had a thrown-together, improvised appearance. The area around the Velde station was one of drably utilitarian tin-roofed warehouses, with an unprepossessing medium-sized town of low, anonymous-looking buildings visible in the distance against a backdrop of bleak stony hills. Tufts of scruffy vegetation, angular and almost angry-looking, sprang up here and there out of the dry, sandy soil. There was nothing to charm the eye anywhere. The Colonel reminded himself that this planet had been settled only about forty years before by a population of exiles and outcasts. Its people probably hadn't found time yet for much in the way of architectural niceties. Perhaps they had little interest in such things.

Somber-faced port officials greeted him in no very congenial way, addressing him as Commissioner Haym, checking through his papers and those of his companions, and unsmilingly waving him and his four companions aboard a convoy of antiquated lorries that took them down a ragged, potholed highway into town. Alto Hermano, the place was called. A signpost at the edge of town identified it grandiosely as the planetary capital, though its population couldn't have been much over twenty or thirty thousand. The vehicles halted in a stark open square bordered on all four sides by identical five-story buildings with undecorated mud-colored brick facades. An official who introduced himself as Municipal Procurator Tambern Collian met them there. He was a gray-eyed unsmiling man, just as dour of affect as everyone else the Colonel had encountered thus far here. He did not offer the expectable conventional wishes that Commissioner Haym had had an easy journey to Hermano nor did he provide pleasantries of any other sort, but simply escorted the delegation from Cruzeiro into one of the buildings on the square, which turned out to be a hotel, grimly functionalist in nature, that the government maintained for the use of official visitors. It was low-ceilinged and dim, with the look of a third-class commercial hotel on a backwater world. Municipal Procurator Collian showed the Colonel to his quite modest suite without apologies, indifferently wished him a good evening, and left, saying he would call again in the morning to begin their discussions.

Magda Cermak's room was adjacent to his. She came by to visit, rolling her eyes, when the Municipal Procurator was gone. The coolness of their welcome plainly hadn't been any cause of surprise to her, but she was irritated all the same. A dining room on the ground floor of the hotel provided them with a joyless dinner, choice of three sorts of unknown meat, no wine available of any kind. Neither of them had much to say. Their hosts were all making it very clear that Hermano was a planet that had declared war on the entire universe. They were willing to allow the delegation from the Cruzeiro system to come here to try to work out some sort of trade agreement, since they appeared to see some benefit to themselves in that, but evidently they were damned if they were going to offer the visitors much in the way of a welcome.

Municipal Procurator Collian, it developed, was to be Commissioner Haym's primary liaison with the provisional government. Precisely what Collian's own role was in that government was unclear. There were times when he seemed to be just the mayor of this starkly functional little city, and others when he appeared to speak as a high functionary of the planetary government. Perhaps he was both; perhaps there was no clear definition of official roles here at the moment. This was, after all, a provisional government, one that had seized power only a few years before from a previous government that had itself been mostly an improvisation.

It was clear, at any rate, that First Secretary Bauer himself did not plan to make himself a party to the trade talks, at least not in their initial stages. The Colonel did not see that as a problem. He wanted a little time to take the measure of this place before entering into what promised to be a complex and perhaps dangerous confrontation.

Each morning, then, the Colonel, Magda, and the three Gavialese would cross the plaza to a building on the far side that was the headquarters of the Ministry of Trade. There, around a squarish conference table of the sort of inelegant dreary design that seemed especially favored by the Hermanan esthetic, they would meet with Municipal Procurator Collian and a constantly shifting but consistently unconvivial assortment of other Hermanan officials to discuss the problem of Hermano's embargo on all foreign trade, and specifically its discontinuation of pharmaceutical exports to Gavial that Gavial regarded as vital to the health of its citizens.

The factor behind the unconviviality soon became clear. The Hermanans, a prickly bunch inexperienced in galactic diplomacy, apparently were convinced that Commissioner Haym and his companions were here to accomplish some sort of trickery. But the Hermanans had no way of knowing that and had been given no reason to suspect it. And the faintly concealed animosity with which they were treating the visitors from Gavial would surely get in the way of reaching any agreement on the treaty that the Gavialese had ostensibly come here to negotiate, a treaty that would be just as beneficial to Hermano as it would to Gavial.

So it became the Colonel's immediate job—in the role of Petrus Haym, envoy from the Cruzeiro system, not as a functionary of the

Imperium—to show the Hermanans that their own frosty attitude was counterproductive. For that he needed to make himself seem to be the opposite of deceitful: a good-hearted, willingly transparent man, open and friendly, a little on the innocent side, maybe, not in any way a fool but so eager to have his mission end in a mutually advantageous agreement that the Hermanans would think he might allow himself to be swayed into becoming an advocate for the primary interests of Hermano. Therefore, no matter the provocation, he was the soul of amiability. The technicians of the Service had designed him to look stout and sleepy and unthreatening, and he spoke with a comic-opera Gavialese accent, which was helpful in enabling him to play the part of an easy mark. He spoke of how much he longed to be back on Gavial with his wife and children, and he let it be perceived without explicitly saying so that for the sake of an earlier family reunion he might well be willing to entertain almost any proposal for a quick settlement of the negotiations. He made little mild jokes about the discomforts of his lodgings here and the inadequacies of the food to underscore his desire to be done with this job and on his way. When one of the authentic Gavialese betrayed some impatience with the seeming one-sidedness of the talks in their early stage, Commissioner Haym rebuked him good-naturedly in front of the Hermanans, pointing out that Hermano was a planet that had chosen an exceedingly difficult road for itself, and needed to be given the benefit of every doubt. And gradually the Hermanans began to thaw a bit.

The sticking point in the discussions was Hermano's request that the Cruzeiro worlds serve as Hermano's advocate before the Imperium in its quest for independence. What the Cruzeiro people knew, and Hermano probably knew it as well, was that the Imperium was never going to permit any world to secede. The only way that Gavial was going to get the pharmaceuticals that it wanted from Hermano, and for Hermano to get the weapons it wanted from the Cruzeiro worlds, was for the two groups to cook up a secret and completely illegal deal between them, in utter disregard not just of the wishes of the Imperium but of its laws.

Gavial had already signaled, disingenuously, that it was willing to do this—urged on by the Imperium, which had pledged that it would provide them with a continued supply of cantaxion in return for its cooperation. But Hermano, perhaps because it quite rightly was mistrustful of Gavial's willingness to enter into a secret illegal deal or perhaps because of the obstinate naivete of its leaders, was continuing to hold out for official recognition by Gavial and the other Cruzeiro worlds of Hermanan independence.

By prearrangement the Colonel and Magda Cermak took opposite positions on this issue. Magda—stolid, brusque, rigid, unsmiling—bluntly told the Hermanan negotiators the self-evident truth of the situation, which was that Gavial was not going to align itself with the Hermanan independence movement because nobody's requests for independence from the Imperium were ever going to get anywhere, that the Imperium would never countenance any kind of official recognition of any member world's independence. Such a thing would set a wholly unacceptable precedent. It was out of the question; it was scarcely worth even discussing. If Gavialese recognition of Hermanan independence was the price of reopening trade relations between Gavial and Hermano, she said coldly, then the Gavialese trade delegation might as well go home right now.

Meanwhile her associate, Commissioner Haym—genial, placid, undogmatic, a trifle lacking in backbone, maybe, and therefore readily manipulable—sadly agreed that getting the Imperium to allow a member world, no matter how obscure, to pull out of the confederation would be a very difficult matter to arrange, perhaps impossible. But he did point out that that it was the belief of the rulers of Gavial that the current philosophy of the Imperium was strongly nonbelligerent, that the Central Authority was quite eager to avoid having to launch military action against unruly members. For that reason, Commissioner Haym suggested, certain highly influential officials in the government of Gavial felt that the Imperium might be willing under the right circumstances to forget about Hermano entirely and look the other way while Hermano went right on regarding itself as independent. "I am not, you realize, speaking on behalf of the Imperium," Commissioner Haym said. "How could I? I have no right to do that. But we of Gavial have been given to understand that the Imperium is inclined toward leniency in this instance." The essential thing was that Hermano would have to keep quiet about its claim to independence, though it could go on behaving as though it were independent all the same. That is, in return for that silence, Commissioner Haym indicated, the Central Authority might be willing to overlook Hermano's refusal to pay taxes to it, considering that those taxes were a pittance anyway. And Hermano would be free to strike whatever private deals with whatever Imperium worlds it liked, so long as it kept quiet about those too—such as, he said, the proposed weapons-for-drugs arrangement that would get a supply of cantaxion flowing to Gavial once again and allow Hermano to feel capable of protecting itself against possible Imperium aggression.

Commissioner Haym communicated these thoughts to Procurator Collian at a time when Magda Cermak was elsewhere. Demanding immediate independence, he reiterated, was probably going to achieve nothing. But independence for Hermano might just be achievable in stages. Accepting a kind of de facto independence now might well clear the way for full independence later on. And he offered—unofficially, of course—Gavial's cooperation in persuading the Imperium to leave Hermano alone while it went on along its present solitary way outside the confederation of worlds.

Collian looked doubtful. "Will it work? I wonder. And how can you assure me the cooperation of your planet's government when not even your own colleague Commissioner Cermak is in agreement with you on any of this?"

"Ah, Commissioner Cermak. Commissioner Cermak!" Commissioner Haym favored Procurator Collian with a conspiratorial smile. "A difficult woman, yes. But not an unreasonable one. She understands that our fundamental goal in coming here, after all, is to restore trade between Gavial and Hermano by any means possible. Which ultimately should be Hermano's goal, too." Commissioner Haym allowed a semblance of craftiness to glimmer in his heavy-lidded eyes. "This is, of course, a very ticklish business all around, because of the Imperium's involvement in our dealings. You and I understand how complicated it is, eh?" A wink, a nudge of complicity. "But I do believe that your planet and mine, working toward our mutual interests, can keep the Imperium out of our hair, and that Gavial will stand up for Hermano before the Imperium if we commissioners bring back a unanimous report. And do you know how I think I can swing her over to the position that you and I favor?" he asked. "If I could show her that we have the full backing of First Secretary Bauer—that he sees the plan's advantages for both our worlds, that he wholeheartedly supports it—I think we can work out a deal."

Municipal Procurator Collian seemed to think that that was an interesting possibility. He proposed that Commissioner Haym quickly prepare a memorandum setting forth all that they had discussed between themselves, which he could place before the First Secretary for his consideration. Commissioner Haym, though, replied mildly that Municipal Procurator Collian did not seem to have fully understood his point. Commissioner Haym was of the opinion that he could most effectively make his thoughts clear to the First Secretary during the course of a personal meeting. Collian was a bit taken aback by that. The evasive look that flitted across his chilly features indicated that very likely one was not supposed to consume the time of the First Secretary in such low-level things as meetings with trade commissioners. But then—the Colonel watched the wheels turning within the man—Collian began, so it seemed, to appreciate the merits of letting First Secretary Bauer have a go at molding with his own hands this extremely malleable envoy from Gavial. "I'll see what I can do," he said.

Not all of Hermano was as bleak as the area around the capital city, the Colonel quickly discovered. The climate grew moister and more tropical as he headed southward, scraggy grasslands giving way to forests and forests to lush jungles in the southernmost region of the continent, the one continent that the Hermanans had managed to penetrate thus far. The view from the air revealed little sign of development in the southern zone, only widely scattered plantations, little isolated jungle domains, separated from one another by great roadless swaths of dense green vegetation. He did not see anything amounting to continuous settlement until he was nearly at the shores of the ocean that occupied the entire southern hemisphere of this world, stretching all the way to the pole. Here, along a narrow coastal strip between the jungle and the sea, the elite of Hermano had taken up residence.

First Secretary Bauer's estate was situated at the midpoint of that strip, on a headland looking out toward the green, peaceful waters of that southern sea. It was expectably grand. The only surprising thing about it was that it was undefended by walls or gates or even any visible guard force: the road from the airstrip led straight into the First Secretary's compound, and the estatehouse itself, a long, low stone building rising commandingly on the headland in a way that reminded the Colonel of the fortress at Megalo Kastro, seemed accessible to anyone who cared to walk up to its door.

But the Colonel was taken instead to one of the many outbuildings, a good distance down the coastal road from the First Secretary's villa itself, and there he was left in comfortable seclusion for three long days. He had a five-room cottage to himself, with a pretty garden of flowering shrubs and a pleasant view of the sea. No one kept watch over him, but even so it seemed inappropriate and perhaps unwise to wander any great distance from his lodgings. His meals were brought to him punctually by silent servants: seafood of various kinds, mainly, prepared with skill and subtlety, and accompanied by pale wines that were interestingly tangy and tart. A small library had been provided for him, mostly familiar classics, the sort of books that Geryon Lanista had favored during their years of working together. He inspected the garden, he strolled along the beach, he ventured a short way into the dense forest of scrubby little red-leaved trees with aromatic bark on the inland side of the compound. The air here was soft and had a mildly spicy flavor, not at all bitter like the air up at Alto Hermano. The water of the sea, into which he ventured ankle-deep one morning, was warm and clear, lapping gently at the pink sands. Even the strong pull of this world's gravity was less oppressive here, though the Colonel knew that that was only illusion.

On the fourth day the summons to the presence of the First Secretary came to him.

The dispassionate tranquility that had marked the Colonel's demeanor since his departure from Gavial remained with him now. He had brought himself to his goal and whatever was fated to happen next would happen; he faced all possibilities with equanimity. He was taken into the great villa, conveyed down long silent hallways floored with gleaming panels of dark polished wood, led past huge rooms whose windows looked toward the sea, and delivered, finally, into a much smaller room, simply furnished with a desk and a few chairs, at the far end of the building. A man who unquestionably was Geryon Lanista waited for him there, standing behind the desk.

He was greatly altered, of course. The Colonel was prepared for that. The face of the man who stood before him now was the one he had seen in the solido that the dark-haired visitor had shown him in his villa on Galgala, that day that now seemed so long ago: that blunt-tipped nose, those downturned lips, the flaring cheekbones, the harsh jutting jaw, all of them nothing like the features of the Geryon Lanista he once had known. This man looked only to be sixty or so, and that too was unsurprising, though actually Lanista had to be close to twice that age; but no one ever looked much more than sixty any more, except those few who preferred to let a few signs of something approaching their true age show through to the surface. Lanista had had every reason to transform himself beyond all recognition since the debacle on Tristessa. The surprising thing, the thing that forced the Colonel for an instant to fight against allowing an uncontrolled reaction to make itself visible, was how easy it was for him to see beyond the cosmetic transformations to the real identity behind them.

Was it the hulking frame that gave him away, or the expression of the eyes? Those things had to be part of it, naturally. Very few men were built on such a massive scale as Lanista, and not even the canniest of cosmetic surgeons could have done anything about the breadth of those tremendous shoulders and that huge vault of a chest. His stance was Lanista's stance, the rock-solid stance of a man of enormous strength and physical poise: one's habitual way of holding one's body could not be unlearned, it seemed. And the eyes, though they were brown now and the Colonel remembered Lanista to have had piercingly blue ones, still had that eerie, almost feminine softness that had given such an odd cast to the old Lanista's otherwise formidably masculine face. Surely a surgeon could have done something about that. But perhaps one had tried, and even succeeded, and then the new eyes had come to reveal the innate expression of Lanista's soul even so, shining through inexorably despite everything: for there were the veritable eyes of Geryon Lanista looking out at him from this unfamiliar face.

The eyes—the stance—and something else, the Colonel thought, the mere intangible presence of the man—the inescapable, unconcealable essence of him—

While the Colonel was studying Martin Bauer and finding Geryon Lanista behind the facade, Martin Bauer was studying Commissioner Petrus Haym, giving him the sort of close scrutiny that any head of state trying to evaluate a visiting diplomat of whom he intended to make use could be expected to give. Plainly he was reading Petrus Haym's bland meaty face to assure himself that the Gavialese commissioner was just as obtuse and pliable as the advance word from Procurator Collian had indicated. The precise moment when Lanista made the intuitive leap by which he saw through the mask of Commissioner Petrus Haym to the hidden Colonel beneath was difficult for the Colonel to locate. Was it when the tiniest of muscular tremors flickered for an instant in his left cheek? When there was that barely perceptible fluttering of an eyelid? That momentary puckering at the corner of his mouth? The Colonel had had a lifetime's training in reading faces, and yet he wasn't sure.

Perhaps it was all three of those little cues that signalled Lanista's sudden stunned realization that he was in the presence of the man he had looked to as his master and mentor, or perhaps it was none of them; but somewhere in the early minutes of this encounter Lanista had identified him. The Colonel was certain of that.

For a time neither man gave any overt indication of what he knew about the other. The conversation circled hazily about the ostensible theme of an exchange of arms for medicine and how that could be arranged in conjunction with Hermano's desire to break free from the political control of the Central Authority of the Imperium. The Colonel, as Haym, took pains to radiate an amiability just this side of buffoonery, while always drawing back from full surrender to the other man's wishes. Lanista, as Bauer, pressed Haym ever more strongly for a commitment to his cause, though never quite pouncing on him with a specific demand for acquiescence. Gradually it became clear to the Colonel that they were beginning to conduct these negotiations in the voices of Lanista and the Colonel, not in those of First Secretary Bauer and Commissioner Haym. Gradually, too, it became clear to him that Lanista was just as aware of this as he was.

In the end it was Lanista who was the one who decided to abandon the pretense. He had never been good at biding his time. It had been his besetting flaw in the old days that a moment would always come when he could no longer contain his impatience, and the Colonel saw now that no surgery could alter that, either. Commissioner Haym had been moving through the old circular path once more, asking the First Secretary to consider the problems that Gavial faced in weighing its need for cantaxion against the political risks involved in defying the decrees of the Central Authority, when Lanista said abruptly, in a tone of voice far more sharply focused and forceful than the woolly diplomatic one he had been using up until then, "Gavial doesn't have the slightest intention of speaking up for us before the Imperium, does it, Colonel? This whole mission has been trumped up purely for the sake of inserting you into the situation so you can carry out the Imperium's dirty work here, whatever that may be. Am I not right about that?"

"Colonel?" the Colonel said, in the Haym voice.

"Colonel, yes." Lanista was quivering, now, with the effort to maintain his composure. "I can see who you are. I saw it right away.— I thought you had retired a long time ago."

"I thought so too, but I was wrong about that. And I thought you were dead. I seem to have been wrong about that too."

✸

For half a century the Colonel had lived, day in, day out, with the memories of his last two weeks on the paradise-world that Tristessa once had been. Like most bad memories, those recollections of the Tristessan tragedy, and his own narrow escape from destruction, had receded into the everyday background of his existence, nothing more now than the dull, quiet throbbing of a wound long healed, easily enough ignored much of the time. But in fact the wound had never healed at all. It had merely been bandaged over, sealed away by an act of sheer will. From time to time it would remind him of its existence in the most agonizing way. Now the pain of it came bursting upward once again out of that buried part of his consciousness in wave upon wave.

He was back on Tristessa again, waiting for Lanista to return from his mission to Shannakha. Lanista had gone to the companion world ten days before, intending to see the minister who had jurisdiction over Tristessan affairs and make one last effort to head off the conflict between the two planets that had begun to seem inevitable. He was carrying with him documents indicating that the Tristessa colonists were ready to launch their rebellion, and that only the promulgation by Shannakha of a radical program of economic reform could now avoid a costly and destructive struggle. Recent developments on Shannakha had given rise to hope that at least one powerful faction of the government was willing to offer some significant concessions to the Tristessan colonists. The Colonel, meanwhile, was holding talks with Ilion Gabell, the rebel leader, in an attempt to get him to hold his uprising off a little while longer while Lanista worked out the details of whatever concessions Shannakha might offer.

Gabell's headquarters were on the floating island of Petra Hodesta, five hundred hectares of grasses thick as hawsers that had woven themselves tightly together long ago and broken free of the mainland. The island, its grassy foundation covered now with an accretion of soil out of which a forest of slender blue-fronded palms had sprouted, circled in a slow current-driven migration through the sparkling topaz waters of Tristessa's Triple Sea, and Gabell's camp was a ring of bamboo huts along the island's shore. The Colonel had arrived five days earlier. He had a good working relationship with Gabell, who was a man of commanding presence and keen intelligence with a natural gift for leadership, forty or fifty years old and still in the first strength and flourish of his early manhood. The Colonel had laid out in great detail and more than customary forthrightness everything that Lanista had gone to the mother world to request; and Gabell had agreed to wait at least until he saw what portion of the things Lanista was asking for would be granted. He was not a rash or hasty man, was Gabell. But he warned that any kind of treachery on Shannakha's part would be met with immediate and terrible reprisals.

"There will be no treachery," the Colonel promised.

Petra Hodesta's wandering route now was taking it toward the northernmost of Triple Sea's three lobes, the one adjacent to Gespinord, the Tristessan capital province. Since Lanista was due back from Shannakha in a few more days, it was the Colonel's plan to go ashore on the coast of Gespinord and make his way by airtrain to the main Velde terminal, two hundred kilometers inland at the capital city, to await his return. But he was less than halfway there when the train came spiraling down to its track with the sighing, whistling sound of an emergency disconnect and someone in uniform came rushing through the cars, ordering everyone outside.

Tristessa was under attack. Without warning Shannakhan troops had come pouring through every Velde doorway on the planet. Gespinord City, the capital, had already been taken. All transit lines had been cut. The Colonel heard distant explosions, and saw a thick column of black smoke rising in the north, and another, much closer, to the east. They were hideous blotches against the flawless emerald-green of the Tristessan sky; and there in the west the Colonel saw a different sort of blemish, the harsh dark face of stark stony Shannakha, low and swollen and menacing on the horizon. What had gone wrong up there? What—even while they were in the midst of delicate negotiations—had led the Shannakhans to break the fragile peace?

The train had halted at some provincial station bordered on both sides by rolling crimson meadows. Somehow the Colonel found a communications terminal. Reaching Lanista on Shannakha proved impossible: no outgoing contact with other worlds was being allowed. But against all probability he did manage to get a call through to the rebel headquarters on Petra Hodesta, and, what was even less probable than that, Ilion Gabell himself came to the screen. His handsome features now had taken on a wild, almost bestial look: the curling golden mane was greasy and disheveled, the luminous, meditative eyes had a frenzied glaze, his lips were drawn back in a toothy grimace. He gave the Colonel a look of searing contempt. "No treachery, you said. What do you call this? They've invaded us everywhere at once. Without warning, without any declaration of hostilities. They must have been planning it for years."

"I assure you—"

"I know what your assurance is worth," Gabell said. "Well, mine is worth more. The reprisals have already begun, Colonel. And as for you—"

A blare of visual static sliced across the screen and it went black. "Hello?" the Colonel shouted. "Hello? Hello?"

The stationmaster, bald and plump and nearly as wild-eyed as Gabell had looked, appeared from a back room. The Colonel identified himself to him. He gaped at the Colonel in amazement and blurted, "There's an order out for your arrest. You and that other Imperium agent, both. You're supposed to be seized by anyone who finds you and turned over to the nearest officers of the republic."

"What republic is that?"

"Republic of Tristessa. Proclaimed three hours ago by Ilion Gabell. All enemies of the republic are supposed to be rounded up and—"

"Enemies of the republic?" the Colonel said, astonished. He wondered if he was going to have to kill him. But the plump stationmaster clearly had no appetite for playing policeman. He let his eye wander vaguely toward the open door to his left and shrugged, and made an ostentatious show of turning his attention away from the Colonel, busying himself with important-looking papers on his desk instead. The Colonel was out through the door in a moment.

He saw no option but to make his way to the capital and find whatever was left of the diplomatic community, which no doubt was attempting to get off Tristessa as quickly as possible, and get himself off with them. Something apocalytic was going on here. The sky was black with smoke in every direction, now, and the drumroll of explosions came without a break, and frightful tongues of flame were leaping up from a town just beyond the field on his left. Was the whole planet under Shannakhan attack? But that made no sense. This place was Shannakha's property; destroying it by way of bringing it back under control was foolishness.

Gabell had spoken of reprisals. Was *he* the one behind the explosions?

It took the Colonel a week and a half to cover the hundred kilometers from the train station to the capital, a week and a half of little sleep and less food while he traversed a zigzag route through the devastated beauty of Gespinord Province, dodging anyone who might be affiliated with the rebels. That could be almost anybody, and was likely to be nearly everybody. A woman who gave him shelter one night told him of what the rebels were doing, the broken dams and torched granaries and poisoned fields, a war of Tristessa against itself that would leave the planet scarred for decades and worse than useless to its Shannakhan masters. At dawn she came to him and told him to go; he saw men wearing black rebel armbands entering the house on one side as he slipped away from it on the other.

He had three more such narrow escapes in the next four days. After the last of them he stayed away from inhabited areas entirely. He hurt his leg badly, slogging across a muddy lake. He cut his hand on a sharp palm frond and it became infected. He ate some unknown succulent-looking fruit and vomited for a day and a half. Skulking northward through swamps and over fresh ashheaps still warm from the torching, he started to experience the breaking down of his innate unquenchable vitality. The eternal self-restoring capacity of his many-times-rejuvenated body was no longer in evidence. A great weariness came over him, a sense of fatigue that approached a willingness to cease all striving and lie down forever. That was a new experience for him, and one that shocked him. He began to feel his true age and then to feel older than his true age, a thousand years older, a million. He was ragged and dirty and lame and his throat was perpetually parched and there was a pounding against the right side of his skull in back that would not stop; and as he grew weaker and weaker with the passing days he began to think that he was going to die before much longer, not from some rebel's shot but only from the rigors of this journey, the fever and the chill and the hunger. He cursed Geryon Lanista a thousand times. Whatever Lanista had been up to on Shannakha, could he not have taken a moment to send his partner on Tristessa some warning that everything was on the verge of blowing up? Evidently not.

And then, at last, he stumbled into Gespinord City, where uniformed soldiers of Shannakha patrolled every street. He identified himself to one of them as a representative of the Imperium, and was taken to a makeshift dormitory in a school gymnasium where members of the diplomatic corps were being given refuge. There were about a dozen of them from five or six worlds, consular officials, mainly, who in ordinary times looked after the interests of tourists from their sectors of the galaxy that were holidaying on Tristessa. All the tourists were long gone, and the few officials who remained had stayed behind only to supervise the final stages of the evacuation of the planet. One of them, a woman from Thanda Bandanareen, saw to it that the Colonel was washed and fed and medicated, and afterward, when he had rested awhile, explained that the Tristessan Authority, which was the name under which the invaders from Shannakha were going, had ordered all outworlders to leave Tristessa at once. "I've been shippping people out for five days straight," she said, and the Colonel perceived for the first time that she was not much farther from exhaustion than he was himself. "There's no time to set coordinates. You go to the doorway and you step through and you work things out for yourself on the other side. Are you ready to go?"

"Now?"

"The sooner I get the last few stragglers out of here, the sooner I can go myself."

She led him to the doorway and, offering a word or two of thanks for her help, he entered its Velde field, a blind leap to anywhere, and came out, to his relief, on that glorious planet, Nabomba Zom, identifiable instantly by the astounding scarlet sea before him, which was shimmering with a violet glow as the first blue rays of morning struck its surface. There, in a guest lodge of the Imperium at the base of pale green mountains soft as velvet, the Colonel learned from a fellow member of the Service what had taken place on Shannakha.

It seemed that Geryon Lanista had badly overplayed his hand. For the sake of persuading the Shannakhans to adopt a more lenient Tristessa policy, Lanista had shown them forged documents indicating that Ilion Gabell's revolutionary army would not simply launch a rebellion on Tristessa if concessions weren't granted but would invade Shannakha itself. The Shannakhans had taken this fantasy seriously, much *too* seriously. Lanista had meant to worry them with it, but instead he terrified them; and in a frantic preemptive overreaction they hurriedly shipped an invading army to Tristessa to bring the troublesome colonists to heel. The worst-case scenario that Lanista had foreseen as a theoretical possibility, but did not seem to believe could happen, was going to occur.

The Colonel shook his head in disbelief. That Lanista—his own protege—would have done anything so stupid was next to impossible to accept; that he would have done so without telling him that he had any such crazy tactic in mind was an unpardonable breach of Service methodology. That he had not sent word to the fellow officer whom he had left behind in harm's way on Tristessa that events in this planetary system had begun to slide toward a ghastly cataclysm as a result of his bizarrely clumsy maneuver was unforgivable for a different reason.

It seemed Gabell had been anticipating an invasion from Shannakha and had had a plan all ready for it: a scorched-earth program by which everything on Tristessa that was of value to Shannakha would be destroyed within hours after the arrival of Shannakhan invaders. One overreaction had led to another; by the end of the first week of war Tristessa was utterly ruined. Between the furious destructiveness of the rebels and the brutal repression of the rebellion by the invaders that had followed, nothing was left of Tristessa's plantations, its great estates, its hotels, its towns and cities, but ashes.

"And Lanista?" the Colonel asked leadenly. "Where is he?"

"Dead. By his own hand, it would seem, though that isn't a hundred percent certain. Either he was trying to get away from Shannakha in a tremendous hurry and accidentally made a mess out of his Velde coordinates, or else he deliberately scrambled up the coding so that he wouldn't be reassembled alive at his destination. Whichever it was, there wasn't very much left of him when he got there."

"You really believed I was dead?" Lanista asked.

"I *hoped* you were dead. I *wanted* you to be dead. But yes, yes, I believed you were dead, too. Why wouldn't I? They said you had gone into a doorway and come out in pieces someplace far away. Considering what you had managed to achieve on Shannakha, that was a completely appropriate thing to have done. So I accepted what they told me and I went on believing it for the next fifty years, until some bastard from the Imperium showed up at my house with proof that you were still alive."

"Believe me, I thought of killing myself. I imagined fifty different ways of doing it. Fifty *thousand*. But it wasn't in me to do a thing like that."

"A great pity, that," the Colonel said. "You allowed yourself to stay alive and you lived happily ever after."

"Not happily, no," said Lanista.

He had fled from Shannakha in a desperate delirious vertigo, he told the Colonel: aware of how badly awry it all had gone, frantic with shame and grief. There had been no attempt at a feigned suicide, he insisted. Whatever evidence the Service had found of such a thing was its own misinterpretation of something that had nothing to do with him. Fearing that the truth about the supposed Tristessan invasion would emerge, that the Shannakhans would discover that he had flagrantly misled them, he had taken advantage of the confusion of the moment to escape to the nearest world that had a Magellanic doorway and in a series of virtually unprogrammed hops had taken himself into some shadowy sector of the Rim where he had hidden himself away until at last he had felt ready to emerge, first under the Heinrich Bauer name, and then, as a result of some kind of clerical error, as *Martin* Bauer.

In the feverish final hours before the Shannakhan invasion began he had, he maintained, made several attempts to contact the Colonel on Tristessa and urge him to get away. But all communications lines between Shannakha and its colony-world had already been severed, and even the Imperium's own private communications channels failed him. He asked the Colonel to believe that that was true. He *begged* the Colonel to believe it. The Colonel had never seen Geryon Lanista begging for anything, before. Something about the haggard, insistent look that came into his eyes made his plea almost believable. He himself had been unable to get any calls through to Lanista on Shannakha; perhaps the systems were blocked in the other direction too. That was not something that needed to be resolved just at this moment. The Colonel put the question aside for later consideration. For fifty years the Colonel had believed that Lanista had deliberately left him to die in the midst of the Tristessa uprising, because he could not face the anger of the Colonel's rebuke for the clumsiness of what he had done on Shannakha. Perhaps he didn't need to believe that any longer. He would prefer not to believe it any longer; but it was too soon to tell whether he was capable of that.

"Tell me this," he said, when Lanista at last had fallen silent. "What possessed you to invent that business about a Tristessan invasion of Shannakha in the first place? How could you ever have imagined it would lead to anything constructive? And above all else, why didn't you try the idea out on me before you went off to Shannakha?"

Lanista was a long while in replying. At length he said, in a flat, low, dead voice, the voice of a headstrong child who is bringing himself to confess that he has done something shameful, "I wanted to surprise you."

"What?"

"To surprise you and to impress you. I wanted to out-Colonel the Colonel with a tremendous dramatic move that would solve the whole crisis in one quick shot. I would come back to Tristessa with a treaty that would pacify the rebels and keep the Shannakhans happy too, and everything would be sweetness and light again, and you would ask me how I had done it, and I would tell you and you would tell me what a genius I was." Lanista was looking directly at the Colonel with an unwavering gaze. "That was all there was to it. An idiotic young subaltern was fishing for praise from his superior officer and came up with a brilliant idea that backfired in the most appalling way. The rest of my life has been spent in an attempt to atone for what I did on Shannakha."

"Ah," the Colonel said. "That spoils it, that last little maudlin bit at the end of the confession. 'An attempt to atone'? Come off it, Geryon. Atoning by starting up a rebellion of your own? Against the Imperium, which you once had sworn to defend with your life?"

Icy fury instantly replaced the look of intense supplication in Lanista's eyes. "We all have our own notions of atonement, Colonel. I destroyed a world, or maybe two worlds, and since then I've been trying to build them. As for the Imperium, and whatever I may have sworn to it—"

"Yes?"

"The Imperium. The Imperium. The universal foe, the great force for galactic stagnation. I don't owe the Imperium a thing." He shook his head angrily. "Let it pass. You can't begin to see what I mean.—The Imperium has sent you here, I gather. For what purpose? To work your old hocus-pocus on our little independence movement and bring me to heel the way you were trying to do with Ilion Gabell on Tristessa?"

"Essentially, yes."

"And how will you do it, exactly?" Lanista's face was suddenly bright with expectation. "Come on, Colonel, you can tell me! Consider it the old pro laying out his strategy one more time for the bumptious novice. Tell me. Tell me. The plan for neutralizing the revolution and restoring order."

The Colonel nodded. It would make no real difference, after all. "I can do two things. The evidence that you are Geryon Lanista and that you were responsible for the catastrophic outcome of the Tristessa rebellion is all fully archived and can quickly be distributed to all your fellow citizens here on Hermano. They might have a different view about your capability as a master schemer once they find out what a botch you made out of the Tristessa operation."

"They might. I doubt it very much, but they might.—What's the other thing you can do to us?"

"I can cut Hermano off from the Velde system. I have that power. The ultimate sanction: you may recall the term from your own Service days. I pass through the doorway and lock the door behind me, and Hermano is forever isolated from the rest of the galaxy. Or isolated until it begs to be allowed back in, and provides the Imperium with proof that it deserves to be."

"Will that please you, to cut us off like that?"

"What would please me is irrelevant. What would have pleased me would have been never to have had to come here in the first place. But here I am.—Of course, now that I've said all this, you can always prevent me from carrying any of it out. By killing me, for example."

Lanista smiled. "Why would I want to kill you? I've already got enough sins against you on my conscience, don't I? And I know as well as you do that the Imperium could cut us off from the Velde system from the outside any time it likes, and would surely do so if its clandestine operative fails to return safely from this mission. I'd wind up in the same position but with additional guilt to burden me. No, Colonel, I wouldn't kill you. But I do have a better idea."

The Colonel waited without replying.

"Cut us off from the Imperium, all right," Lanista said. "Lock the door, throw away the key. But stay here on the inside with us. There's no reason for you to go back to the Imperium, really. You've given the Imperium more than enough of your life as it is. And for what? Has serving the Imperium done anything for you except twisting your life out of shape? Certainly it twisted mine. It's twisted everybody's, but especially those of the people of the Service. All that meddling in interstellar politics—all that cynical tinkering with other people's governments—ah, no, no, Colonel, here at the end it's time for you to give all that up. Start your life over here on Hermano."

The Colonel was staring incredulously, wonderingly, bemusedly.

Lanista went on, "Your friends from Gavial can go home, but you stay here. You live out the rest of your days on Hermano. You can have a villa just like mine, twenty kilometers down the coast. The perfect retirement home, eh? Hermano's not the worst place in the universe to live. You'll have the servants you need. The finest food and wine. And an absolute guarantee that the Imperium will never bother you again. If you don't feel like retiring, you can have a post in the government here, a very high post, in fact. You and I could share the top place. I'd gladly make room for you. Who could know better than I do what a shrewd old bird you are? You'd be a vital asset for us, and we'd reward you accordingly.—What do you say, Colonel? Think it over. It's the best offer you'll ever get, I promise you that."

*

It was easiest to interpret what Lanista had said as a grotesque joke, but when the Colonel tried to shrug it away Lanista repeated it, more earnestly even than before. He realized that the man was serious. But, as though aware now that this conversation had gone on too long, Lanista suggested that the Colonel return to his own lodgings and rest for a time. They could talk again of these matters later. Until then he was always free to resume the identity of Petrus Haym of the Gavialese trade mission, and to go back to his four companions and continue to hatch out whatever schemes they liked involving commerce between Gavial and the Free Republic of Hermano.

He was unable to sleep for much of that night. So many revelations, so many possibilities. He hadn't been prepared for that much. None of the usual adjustments would work; but toward dawn sleep came, though only for a little while, and then he awoke suddenly, drenched in sweat, with sunlight pouring through his windows. Lanista's words still resounded in his mind. *The Imperium has twisted your life out of shape*, Lanista had said. Was that so? He remembered his grandfather saying, hundreds of years ago—thousands, it felt like—*The Imperium is the enemy, boy. It strangles us. It is the chain around our throats.* The boy who would become the Colonel had never understood what he meant by that, and when he came to adulthood he followed his father, who had said always that the Imperium was civilization's one bulwark against chaos, into the Service.

Well, perhaps his father had been right, and his grandfather as well. He had strapped on the armor of the Service of the Imperium and he had gone forth to do battle in its name, and done his duty unquestioningly throughout a long life, a very long life. And perhaps he had done enough, and it was time to let that armor drop away from him now. What had Lanista said of the Imperium? *The universal foe, the great force for galactic stagnation.* An angry man. Angry words. But there was some truth to them. His grandfather had said almost the same thing. An absentee government, enforcing conformity on an entire galaxy—

On that strange morning the Colonel felt something within him breaking up that had been frozen in place for a long time.

"What do you say?" Lanista asked, when the Colonel had returned to the small office with the desk and the chairs. "Will you stay here with us?"

"I have a home that I love on Galgala. I've lived there ever since my retirement."

"And will they let you live in peace, when you get back there to Galgala?"

"Who?"

"The people who sent you to find me and crush me," Lanista said. "The ones who came to you and said, *Go to a place called Hermano, Colonel. Put aside your retirement and do one more job for us.* They told you that a man you hate was making problems for them here and that you were the best one to deal with him, am I not right? And so you went, thinking you could help the good old Imperium out yet again and also come to grips with a little private business of your own. And they can send you out again, wherever else they feel like sending you, whenever they think you're the best one to deal with whatever needs dealing with."

"No," the Colonel said. "I'm an old man. I can't do anything more for them, and they won't ask. After all, I've failed them here. I was supposed to destroy this rebellion, and that won't happen now."

"Won't it?"

"You know that it won't," the Colonel said. He wondered whether he had ever intended to take any sort of action against the Hermano rebels. It was clear to him now that he had come here only for the sake of seeing Lanista once again and hearing his explanation of what had happened on Shannakha. Well, now he had heard it, and had managed to persuade himself that what Lanista had done on Shannakha had been merely to commit an error of judgment, which anyone can do, rather than to have sought to contrive the death of his senior officer for the sake of convering up his own terrible blunder. And now there was that strange sensation he was beginning to feel, that something that had been frozen for fifty years, or maybe for two hundred, was breaking up within him. He said, "Proclaim your damned independence, if you like. Cut yourselves off from the Imperium. It makes no difference to me. They should have sent someone else to do this job."

"Yes. They should have.—Will you stay?"

"I don't know."

"We're no longer of the Imperium and neither are you."

Lanista spoke once again of the villa by the sea, the servants, the wines, the place beside him in the high administration of the independent world of Hermano. The Colonel was barely listening. It would be easy enough to go home, he was thinking. Lanista wouldn't interfere with that. Hop, hop, hop, and Galgala again. His lovely house beside that golden river. His collection of memorabilia. The souvenirs of a life spent in the service of the Imperium, which is a chain about our throats. Home, yes, home to Galgala, to live alone within the security of the Imperium. The Imperium is the enemy of chaos, but chaos is the force that drives evolutionary growth.

"This is all real, what you're offering me?" he asked. "The villa, the servants, the government post?"

"All real, yes. Whatever you want."

"What about Magda Cermak and the other three?"

"What do you want done with them?"

"Send them home. Tell them that the talks are broken off and they have to go back to Gavial."

"Yes. I will."

"And what will you do about the doorways?"

"I'll seal them," Lanista said. "We don't need to be part of the Imperium. There was a time, you know, when Earth was the only world in the galaxy, when there was no Imperium at all, no Velde doorways either, and somehow Earth managed to get along for a few billion years without needing anything more than itself in the universe. We can do that too. The doorways will be sealed and the Imperium will forget all about Hermano."

"And all about me, too?" the Colonel asked.

"And all about you, yes."

The Colonel laughed. Then he walked to the window and saw that night had fallen, the radiant, fiery night of the Core, with a million million stars blazing in every direction he looked. The doorways would be sealed, but the galaxy still would be out there, filling the sky, and whenever he needed to see its multitude of stars he needed only to look upward. That seemed sufficient. He had traveled far and wide and the time was at hand, was more than at hand, for him to bring an end to his journeying. Well, so be it. So be it. No one would ever come looking for him here. No one would look for him anywhere; or, if looking, would never find. At the Service's behest he had returned to the stars one last time; and now, at no one's behest but his own, he had at last lost himself among them forever.

THE EATER OF DREAMS

The details of my long relationship with the oldest of all science fiction magazines, Amazing Stories, beginning with the first copy of it that I bought, late in 1948, and ending with its suspension of publication in 2000, are amply outlined in the introduction to "Travelers." But, as I indicated there, Amazing had not quite reached its end even then.

After a six-year hiatus, Amazing returned yet again, this time under the aegis of a company unknown to me, Paizo Publishing. That is to say, Paizo was listed on the contents page as the publisher, but the magazine was copyrighted in the name of Wizards of the Coast, the gaming company that had been Amazing's publisher in its previous incarnation. What relationship, if any, existed between Paizo and Wizards of the Coast, I never knew. But the important fact was that Amazing had returned from the dead once again, and once again was being published as a large-size slick magazine.

Having been entangled with Amazing Stories first as avid reader and then as prolific contributor through so many of its various incarnations, I couldn't resist contacting the Paizo people, up near Seattle, and asking them if there might be some role for me to play in their version of the magazine. Yes, certainly, replied editor Dave Gross. Every issue was featuring a 1000-word story by some well-known s-f writer. Would I care to do a short-short of my own for the series?

My favorite story form is the novella, the story of 20,000 to 40,000 words. I like to develop background and character in an unhurried way and to set in motion a fairly elaborate plot that gradually reaches an inevitable though unexpected conclusion. The short-short, the quick vignette with a

291

snapper ending, has never been a speciality of mine, though I've written some, naturally, in the course of a long career. The thousand-worders the Paizo Amazing *had already published included work by such commendable pros as Jack Williamson, David Gerrold, and Joe Haldeman. It seemed like an interesting challenge. (And I would be well compensated for the trouble of compressing a story idea into a thousand-word span.)*

So I wrote "The Eater of Dreams" in December of 2004 and sent it in and duly received my satisfactory paycheck...and almost immediately Amazing *went out of business again. A sad little letter from the publisher told me that the magazine was going into yet another hiatus, and, at least as of the day I write this, no new rescuer has appeared this time. The rights to my mini-story thus reverted to me, and I offered it to Sheila Williams, the editor of* Asimov's Science Fiction, *and she published it in her April-May 2007 issue. And thus it was that* Amazing Stories *and I finally came to a parting of the ways. Or so it seems, anyway.*

The Queen-Goddess feels another dream coming to her tonight, and she knows it will be a dark one. So I am summoned to her, masked in the mask of my profession, and I crouch by her pallet, awaiting the night. The Queen-Goddess sleeps, lying asprawl like a child's discarded doll. At the foot of the bed lurks the Vizier in his horned mask: our chaperone. No man, not even the royal Eater of Dreams, may enter the Queen-Goddess' bedchamber unescorted.

Her spirit flutters and trembles. Her eyes move quickly beneath their lids. She is reaching the dream-world now.

Her dreams are always true visions. Therefore she suffers when a dark one comes, for such dreams acquaint her with pain and grief, and we suffer when she suffers, since all things flow to us through the spirit of the Queen-Goddess. What she will bring us after such a dream is pain and grief. We cannot abide pain or grief; and so I must take her dark dreams from her as swiftly as I can.

Last night she dreamed—she could not communicate it well to me—of ashes and ruin, of ugliness and shame, of strife and sadness. From her vague description I knew that she has been ranging through ancient times again. She often makes contact with some epoch of the distant pre-Imperial past, that era of apocalyptic nightmare out of which our own shining civilization emerged. Last night's dream, for which, alas, I was not summoned in time, has cast its shadow over today's flow of beneficial energy. If another like it comes tonight, I will be here to guard her majesty against it.

And, yes, yes, the dream is coming, and it is the same.

Surely her majesty has slipped once more into the black abyss of time past. I say the words that unlock the portals of her spirit, link my mind with hers, and see a fearful strangeness. The stars, of which she gives me just the most fleeting of glimpses before her gaze turns away from them, seem to have an unfamiliar look: the constellations I so quickly see do not appear to be the constellations we know today. They must be those of some long-ago epoch. The stars in their courses travel great distances over time.

And what I behold under these strange skies is bleakness and horror. We are in a hideous city. It is an era I have never seen in her dreams before, an awful one. The buildings are brutal towers, looming inexorably. On myriad interlacing roadways vehicles move like swarming beetles. I see an ashen sky; I see stunted trees with blackened leaves; I see hordes of people with faces twisted in anguish. The air itself has a poisonous-looking pall. It is the past, yes; it is one of those dark predecessor civilizations, ridden with pain and error, out of which we have emerged into sunlight and joy. What can this terrible ancient era be, if not the dreadful world of eight, ten, twelve thousand years ago, that grim time so proud of the frenzied, furious industriousness that its builders mistook for wealth, from which the benevolence of her majesty's dynasty has emancipated us all forever?

"Majesty," I say softly. "Give me this dream."

I utter the words of transfer and the dream enters me in all its fury. For a moment I recoil; but I am skilled in my art, and quickly I engulf the images, neutralize them, dissipate them, and then it is over and I am rising, trembling, drenched in sweat, fighting nausea. It will take me a while to recover. But I am used to that. Her majesty's face is tranquil. She sleeps like a happy child. The Vizier comes to me and we embrace, mask against mask. "Well done," he says. "But I fear this is not the last of them."

The day that follows is a happy one. Strength and joy flow from her majesty from dawn to dusk. It is a day of golden sunlight, of cloudless skies, of unfolding blossoms and rising fragrance. The great lawns sweeping down to the river have never looked greener; the river's pure flow is a celestial blue. We are a blessed people. We will not make the mistakes of yesteryear. Our civilization will endure eternally.

But at midnight the Vizier summons me again.

"Another," he says. "The third night. This one will be the worst."

Smiling, I tell him, "Whatever it is, I am ready."

Indeed I am. For sixty years now I have guarded her majesty against the terrors of the night, and we have moved together from triumph to triumph. In the privacy of my soul I flatter myself with the thought that I am essential to the realm, that without my diligence and skill the Queen-Goddess would be ridden nightly by horror and torment and all the world would be the worse for that.

I don my mask. The Vizier dons his. The Queen, ever youthful, ever beautiful, is asleep. Signs of tension are visible on her brow. The dream is coming. I say the words. The link is formed.

It comes now, the dream.

Her wandering mind has entered that same ancient era, but this night there are significant differences. The brutal towers now are shattered: charred stumps are everywhere. Those interlacing roads are twisted and broken. Vehicles lie piled in rusting heaps along their margins. The air is black and oily. The citizens—there are just a few in the ruined streets—have a dazed, stunned look. Some dreadful thing has happened. The dreaming mind of the Queen-Goddess must have found the very end of the former era, the disastrous climactic time of the Great Collapse, when all assumptions were overthrown and the corrosive prosperity of the day tumbled overnight into that dreary poverty out of which, after so many centuries, our Imperial government created the serene, lovely epoch in which we live today.

It is a much more powerful vision than last night's, and I know that afterward I will reverberate with it for hours, but so be it. I will take it from her and all will be well.

"Majesty," I say, as ever. "Give me—"

But then her head shifts, and she murmurs in her sleep, and the perspective changes and she shows me the sky, not the brief glimpse of last night but a long, slow, clear view, and everything is wrong. The moon, our familiar pockmarked moon, is a chipped and broken thing, and the stars whose patterns I have studied so well are not the stars of some vanished yesterday nor the stars of today but stars strung across the sky in some utterly unknown configuration. And in that moment all my strength leaves me, for I know this dream to be too huge to swallow.

It is the future, not the past, through which the Queen-Goddess walks tonight, and what it shows is that the cycle of destruction will come round again, that our green and golden era that we thought to be invulnerable will not last eternally after all, that we too will be swept away as all earlier civilizations of Earth have been swept away. I can protect her against the past, but there is no way I can stave off the onrushing future, and I fling my mask aside and crouch and weep while the Vizier, maskless and stunned as well, comes hurrying to my side.

A PIECE OF THE
GREAT WORLD

After publishing my anthology Between Worlds, *for which I had writ-ten the novella "The Colonel Returns to the Stars," Andrew Wheeler of the Science Fiction Book Club asked Gardner Dozois to edit a similar anthol-ogy of novellas, this one dealing with tales of the far future, and in the summer of 2004 Gardner invited me to write a story for it.*

The far-future tale had held a particular fascination for me ever since I was a small boy discovering H.G. Wells' The Time Machine. *I had written plenty of them myself—the novels* Son of Man *and* At Winter's End *are the most significant of them, I think—and I had edited several anthologies of stories with far-future themes by other writers. So I told Dozois at once that I would be happy to take part.*

As it happened, I had been looking just then at At Winter's End *and its sequel,* The Queen of Springtime, *which were about to be reissued by the University of Nebraska Press.* At Winter's End, *a long, intricate book that I had written in 1986 and early 1987, is set in a post-apocalyptic world nearly a million years in the future. The Earth has been bombarded by a cloud of comets that sent it into a 700,000-year-long ice age. The vastly evolved human beings of that era have fled to another world, leaving behind an assortment of artificially created successor races: a reptilian one (the "sapphire-eyes folk"), an insectoidal one (the "hjjks,") a dolphin-derived one (the "sea-lords,") a plant-derived one (the "vegetals"), and a robotic one (the "mechanicals,") plus an anthropoid race derived from one of the species of higher apes, who call themselves the People. The People have waited out the long winter in subterranean cocoons, and several of the other races have survived the catastrophe in one way or another, and now, with warmth returning to the world, the People are emerging into a vastly changed environment.*

I had planned it as a trilogy. At Winter's End *would tell the story of the emergence from the underground cocoons and the founding of the first new surface settlements;* The Queen of Springtime, *which I wrote in 1988, would describe the evolution of those primitive settlements into an advanced urban culture; and the third volume,* The Summer of Homecoming, *would bring the vanished humans back to Earth and explain many of the mysteries I had set up in the first two books. But my publisher of that time—Warner Books—was in a state of perpetual upheaval, and the two long books, which had cost me an enormous effort to produce, were not particularly successful commercially, and when the time came to write the third of the trilogy the current Warner editor not only had his own idea of how I should write the book, radically different from what I was proposing, but also offered me a radically reduced advance for writing it. I turned the deal down. I wanted to write my novel, not his, and, since the first two books had been so difficult to write, I was not interested in spending close to a year writing the third one for a very much smaller guarantee.*

That third book will never be written, now. Publishers are not interested in buying the third volume of a broken trilogy that was begun by some other house twenty years before, and in any case I no longer feel I have the stamina to write that third volume, which would have been at least as challenging to do as the troublesome first two volumes were. So all that the world will ever see of The Summer of Homecoming *is the lengthy outline that the University of Nebraska Press printed as an appendix to its edition of* The Queen of Springtime.

With one exception. I was reading through that outline just as Gardner Dozois' request for a far-future novella reached me, and I saw right away that one section of my proposed book could be reshaped into a stand-alone story of the right length. Thus "A Piece of the Great World," which I wrote in the closing months of 2004 and the early days of 2005, came into being, and Dozois included it, along with five other tales of the distant future, in his anthology One Million A.D., *which the Science Fiction Book Club published in December, 2005.*

The expedition to the ancestral cocoon would be setting out very soon now. Nortekku was still deep in the task of preparing for it, studying up on the accounts of the events of two centuries before. For weeks he had been poring over the accounts of the emergence of the People from the cocoons when the Long Winter had finally ended—out into that strange, empty world, where the debris flung up by the death-stars still hovered in the upper levels of the atmosphere and a rippling mesh of color streamed in the sky, rainbow nets of amethyst, copper, topaz, crimson, radiant green. He had read too of the famous trek across the continent to the ruins of ancient Vengiboneeza, and of the founding of the first cities of the New Springtime. By then he had become so caught up in the story that he kept pushing his research backward and ever backward across the ages, digging hungrily, compulsively.

There was so much to absorb. He wondered if he would ever master it all. The years fluttered before him, going in reverse. He moved step by step from the tale of the Time of Going Forth back to the era of the cocoons itself, the seven hundred thousand years of life underground during the Long Winter that had preceded the Going Forth, and from there to the dire onslaught of the death-stars that had brought on the deep snows and black winds of the Long Winter. Then he went farther back yet, to the glorious civilization known as the Great World that the winter of the death-stars had destroyed, when all was in motion and great caravels circled the globe laden with merchandise of fabulous richness and splendor, and onward even into what little was known of that shadowy era, millions of years before the Great World had existed, when the vanished human race had dominated the world.

Nortekku had never cared much about all that before—he was an architect by profession, looking toward the future, not the past. But Thalarne, who was an archaeologist, did, and he cared very much about Thalarne, with whom he was about to go off on an expedition of the highest archaeological significance. So for her sake he went tunneling deep into these historical matters that he had not thought about since his schoolboy days.

He studied the way of life of the cocoon era until he began to feel like a cocoon-dweller himself. Those snug cozy burrows, insulated chambers deep in the ground, self-sufficient, sealed away from the cold, carved out by the patient labor of generations—what marvels of architecture they must have been! A maze of passageways twisting and forking like serpents, a network of intricate ventilation shafts providing fresh air, clusters of luminescent glowberries for lighting, water pumped up from streams far underground, special chambers for raising crops and livestock—

Soon he and Thalarne would be venturing into the holiest cocoon of all, the one from which Hresh and Koshmar and the rest of the great city-builders had come. When all of the planning was complete, a week or ten days from now, they would set out from Yissou in a cavalcade of motor vehicles on a journey that would take them halfway across the continent in search of the supposed site of the ancestral cocoon. Together they would uncover its buried secrets. Thalarne would be at his side, a woman like no woman he had ever known, beautiful slender Thalarne of the emerald eyes and the dark sleek fur, Thalarne of the quick, questing mind and the elegant vibrant body—Thalarne—oh, how he loved her!

But then everything fell apart.

First, practically on the eve of departure, they quarreled. It was over a trifle, an absurd trifle. And then, just as Nortekku was beginning to believe that everything had been patched up, Thalarne's mate Hamiruld came to him unexpectedly with news that the expedition was cancelled.

"Cancelled?" Nortekku said, amazed. "But I'm almost finished with all the arrangements! How—why—?"

Hamiruld shrugged. He appeared scarcely to care. Hamiruld was marvelously indifferent to almost everything, up to and including Nortekku's months-long romance with his mate. "She asked me to tell you that something else has come up, something more important. That's all I know."

"All because of that stupid argument we had?"

Another shrug. Hamiruld's bland reddish-gray eyes seemed to be gazing into some other dimension. Idly he patted down a tangle in his fur. "I wouldn't know about that. Something more important, she said."

Nortekku felt as though he had been punched. Cancelled? *Cancelled?* Just like that?

"If that's so," he said to Hamiruld, "I've got to talk to her right now. Where is she? At home, or at the Institute?"

"Neither one," Hamiruld said.

"Neither?"

"I'm afraid she's gone," said Hamiruld mildly.

"Gone? Where?" This was bewildering. Nortekku wanted to shake him.

"I don't actually know," said Hamiruld, giving Nortekku a quick, pallid little smile. "She left very quickly, last night, without telling me where she was going. I didn't see her. All there was was this message, asking me to let you know that the expedition was off." There seemed to be a glint of malice behind the smile. *Perhaps Hamiruld isn't quite as indifferent to things as he leads one to believe*, Nortekku thought.

Cancelled. Something more important has come up.

What do I do now, he wondered?

It was his engagement to the Princess Silina of Dawinno—or, rather, an indirect consequence of his impulsive breaking off of that engagement—that had brought Nortekku into contact with Thalarne in the first place. Giving him not the slightest hint of his intentions, Nortekku's father had arranged a marriage for his only child with the vapid but highborn Silina, whose ancestral line went back to some helmet-wearing chieftain of the Beng tribe that had played such a key part in the early days of the city-founding era.

The elder Nortekku was one of the wealthiest and most successful members of the merchant class that was coming to wield the real economic and political power in Dawinno. For him the mating would provide his family with the touch of aristocracy that was the only asset it lacked. To his son, though, it felt like an intolerable intrusion on his freedom of choice. He had never been involved with any one woman for very long, had never even considered taking any of them as his mate, had not even been thinking about such things. And he had seen enough of silly Silina over the years, in the course of the regular social round of the Dawinnan upper classes, to know that she was close to the last woman he would want as his mate, assuming he wanted one at all.

He tried to keep those feelings hidden. He did try. But then, with plans for the nuptials already far along, it all suddenly overflowed in him. Angrily Nortekku told his father that he rejected the entire arrangement and was indignant that it had been set up without consulting him. He would never marry, he said, never, never, never—not the Princess Silina, not anyone. All of which was met, just as heatedly, with a blazing glare, a snarl of fury, and a quick, explicit threat of disinheritance.

"As you wish," Nortekku replied, without a moment's hesitation. He had never had any interest in his father's wealth or in the dreary commercial pursuits that had created it. He had taken up architecture as his profession instead of going into the family firm because he wanted to accomplish something in his own right, not simply become the passive beneficiary of the older man's boundless riches. Yearning to penetrate deep secrets, he had aspired originally to be an astronomer; but although there was poetry in him there was not quite enough mathematics, and so the choice had fallen upon architecture instead. "Keep your money, father. Give it to the poor. I'm not for sale."

"So you'll go to her family, then, and tell them to their faces that you're breaking off the betrothal? Just like that, sorry, it was all a mistake, goodbye, *poof*! What do you think Prince Vuldimin will say?"

That was a difficult one. Prince Vuldimin, the shrewd and powerful cousin of King Falid of Yissou, was Nortekku's most important client at the moment, and Nortekku's whole professional relationship with him was an outgrowth of the marital negotiations. Vuldimin had come to Dawinno earlier in the year in search of an architect to design a new palace for him in the countryside outside Yissou, a palace that would favor the bright, airy, swooping look of modern Dawinnan architecture rather than the crabbed and somber style typical of Yissou.

That project fell to Nortekku because Vuldimin was distantly related to Silina's father, who was, for all his lofty ancestry, an impoverished aristocrat eager to see Silina married off to a man of wealth and importance. He saw the job of designing Vuldimin's palace as a useful step in the building of his future son-in-law's career, and arranged a meeting between Nortekku and the prince. It went very well: Vuldimin spelled out his ideas for the new palace, Nortekku dared to make some suggestions for bettering them, and Vuldimin showed what appeared to be unfeigned enthusiasm. And so two contracts were drawn up, one pledging the troth of Silina and Nortekku, the other engaging Nortekku as the architect of Vuldimin's palace. The voiding of one contract now might well cause the other to be be broken as well, with disastrous results for Nortekku's career.

Well, there was no helping any of it. If his father refused to name him as his heir, if Vuldimin withdrew the commission for designing the palace, so be it. Nortekku wasn't going to spend the rest of his life listening to the Princess Silina's whinnying laughter and mindless girlish chatter.

The day he went to pay the ceremonial call on Silina's family to explain his reluctance to undertake the mating, it happened, just to make everything worse, that Prince Vuldimin was there. But there was no turning back. Silina's parents and brothers and cousins and uncles, perhaps anticipating what he was about to say, stood arrayed before him like a court of inquisition, every one of them glaring at him with those eerie crimson Beng eyes of theirs, while he lamely told them that he had looked into the depths of his soul in the past few weeks and seen how hastily, carried away by his infatuation with Silina's great beauty and fascinating personality, he had allowed himself to plunge into the marriage contract.

He understood now how rash that decision had been, he said.

He did not see how the marriage could be a success.

He told them that he felt unready for mating, that he was too callow and flighty to be able to offer a splendid woman like Silina the sort of life she deserved, that he felt covered with shame and chagrin but saw no alternative but to withdraw from the contract. It was his hope, he said, that the Princess Silina would before long find a mate more worthy of her than he could possibly be.

This produced an immediate uproar, loud and intense. Nortekku considered the possibility that there might even be violence. Silina, sobbing, rushed from the room. Her parents puffed up in rage like infuriated adders. The brothers and cousins and uncles shook fists and shouted. Threats of legal action were uttered.

There was something almost comic about it, Nortekku thought, although he knew that the developments following upon his repudiation of Silina were not likely to be in any way amusing. He stood stock-still in the midst of the clamor, pondering how he was going to manage to make his escape.

In the end it was Prince Vuldimin, who had witnessed the whole scene from the side, who rescued him. The prince, a short, stocky older man of almost regal presence and authority, cut through the hubbub with a few quick pacifying words, delivered in a tone that could not fail to gain attention, and in the moment of shocked calm that ensued took Nortekku by the elbow and led him swiftly from the room.

When they were outside, Nortekku saw that the prince was smiling, even choking back a giggle. A great flood of relief washed over him.

I have an ally here, he realized.

The prince, who must understand his kinsmen here as well as anyone, had plainly sized up the situation in a moment and his sympathies were all with Nortekku. Thanks be to all the gods for that, Nortekku told himself.

"What a pack of buffoons," Vuldimin murmured. "How did you ever get entangled with them, anyway? Were you really so very infatuated with the princess?"

"Not for a second," Nortekku said. "It was all my father's doing. He arranged it and told me about it afterward.—But I'm in trouble now, aren't I? What do you think will happen next?"

"Nothing that you're going to like. If they're wise, they'll hush the whole thing up and try to find another husband for their girl before she gets branded as unmarriageable. But, as you see, they aren't wise. So there'll probably be a noisy lawsuit, breach of contract, defamation of character, the gods only know what else. They'll want to portray you as a worthless adventurer, an evil seducer, a shameless social climber—"

"I seduced no one here. And if I'm such a shameless social climber, why would I back out of a mating with a Beng princess, however much of a ninny she may be? There's no sense to any of that."

"Maybe so. But there'd be plenty of sense to suing you if the real goal is to squeeze a couple of million units out of your father to settle the suit."

Nortekku gasped. "He's already threatened to disinherit me if I don't go through with the wedding. He's certainly not going to pay my legal bills. And I don't have a unit of my own to my name."

Vuldimin seemed to know that already. There was an almost fatherly warmth in his golden eyes as he looked up toward the much taller Nortekku and said, "Then the best thing for you is to get out of town for a while. Come up to Yissou; stay at my estate for a month or two. We'll say that you need to begin surveying the site of the country palace. There's truth in that, after all. And process-servers from Dawinno have no jurisdiction up there, so the lawsuit will be stalled for however much time you're out of town, and perhaps in your absence I can talk my kinsmen here into forgetting about the whole unfortunate event without making it even worse by suing. Once they realize that your father isn't going to underwrite any settlement they may be willing to be rational about things. But in the meanwhile, get yourself to my place in Yissou and wait it out. What do you say?"

"I couldn't be more grateful, your grace," said Nortekku, and thought for one wild moment that he was about to burst into tears.

That night he left for Yissou, not aboard the regular evening train but—at Vuldimin's suggestion—as a passenger on a freight caravan, where no Dawinno bailiff would be likely to look for him. In Yissou he was given lavish quarters at Vuldimin's sprawling dark-walled palace just off an enormous square known as the Plaza of the Sun, and during the succeeding weeks was treated by the prince's huge staff of servants as though he were a visiting member of some royal house. Vuldimin himself returned from Dawinno shortly, assured Nortekko that his problems with Silina's family would in one way or another be overcome, and made it clear that his breaking of the marriage contract would in no way affect the commission to build the new palace.

Nortekku had never cared much for Yissou, which was far to the north of Dawinno and had a much colder climate, especially now, in winter. One's first view of the city was utterly off-putting. Its entire core was surrounded by a colossal, brooding wall of black stone, a wall of enormous height and breadth that had been constructed nearly two centuries before by one of the earliest kings of the city, who feared all manner of enemies both real and unreal and had devoted a reign of many decades to raising that wall ever higher and higher, until its implacable shadow came to dominate almost the whole of the city within.

Once you were inside the wall things were no prettier. Nortekku's architect's eye was offended by the cramped and twisting alleyways that passed for streets and the squat, ungraceful, ponderous stone buildings that filled them, each jammed up against the next, low thick-walled ground-hugging boxes with the narrowest of slits to serve as windows. Marketplaces had been situated with seeming randomness throughout the city, so you were assailed everywhere by the smell of produce that was no longer fresh and seafood that had spent too many days away from the sea. And one whole quarter of the city was populated by Hjjks, those giant yellow-and-black insect-creatures that were the only one of the Six Peoples of the Great World that had survived the cataclysm of the death-stars. Nortekku had no great fondness for Hjjks, even though the ancient threat of warfare between the hive-dwellers and the People had subsided more than a century ago. He was displeased by the look of them, their dry, harsh, chittering voices, their icy alien reserve. But there were very few of them in Dawinno, far to the south, and he rarely encountered one there. Here in Yissou, much closer to the bleak Hjjk homeland that spanned the northern half of the continent, one saw them everywhere, tall menacing-looking six-legged creatures with formidable claws and beaks. He greatly disliked rubbing shoulders with them in the streets.

Still, life in Yissou had its compensations. Vuldimin's palace was handsome and comfortable, and so long as Nortekku stayed indoors the ugliness and dank coldness of the city were no problem for him. Vuldimin himself was warm and friendly in a quasi-paternal way, and clearly had taken a liking to him. Nortekku, who had never known much in the way of affection from his own blustering, churlish father, found that very welcome. And it was the prince, rather than Yissou's monarch, his gloomy cousin Falid, who was at the center of Yissou's social and political life. Vuldimin was a man of great cultivation and progressive ideas, unarguably superior in intellect and vision and charisma to the cautious, reactionary king, and it was to him that Yissou's brightest and most interesting people flocked. Thus it came to pass that Nortekku, at one of the regular assemblages of industrialists and scientists and artists one evening at Prince Vuldimin's palace, found himself face to face with the brilliant young archaeologist Thalarne and had his life turned upside down between one moment and the next.

He had noticed her from the far side of the room, engaged in an animated conversation with six or seven persons who, Nortekku observed, all happened to be men. She was an instaneously compelling sight: tall, nearly as tall as Nortekku himself, with a fine figure and a thick, gleaming pelt of dark fur spotted here and there by oval splotches of dazzling white.

Every aspect of her commanded attention. Her eyes were of a rich emerald color, glistening with an inner light; her features were delicately and beautifully formed, her expression a searching, mobile one; her stance was alert and dynamic. She wore the vivid yellow sash that Nortekku knew indicated membership in Yissou's Institute of Scientific Study, the counterpart of his own city's great research center, the House of Knowledge. Several of the men surrounding her wore the yellow sash also.

Nortekku drifted closer.

She was speaking of the tendency of sophisticated people in Yissou nowadays to regard the stories of the People's past as just that—stories, mere myth. Indeed Nortekku had encountered the same phenomenon among his friends in Dawinno, who brushed the popular historical tales aside as the stuff of legend. Had there ever really been a Long Winter? Did the People actually live once upon a time in underground cocoons? Had the Great World truly been as magnificent as the legends would have it?

"We have the evidence of the Chronicles, of course," one of the men said.

"So we do," said another, "but how do we know that they represent actual history? They may be no more reliable than the history plays we see in the theater."

"Yes. *Torlyri and Trei Husathirn*, said a third man. "*The Boyhood of Hresh. Hresh at the Nest of Nests.*"

"And there's that play about Nialli Apuilana and her captivity among the Hjjks, and how she faced down the Hjjk Queen and defeated Her," said another.

"You speak of them as though they're just fiction," the first man said. "These people actually existed. They really did the things that they're credited with doing. Otherwise, how did we get here? Who led us from the cocoon, if not Koshmar and Torlyri? Who founded the cities, if not Hresh and Harruel and Salaman? Who drove back the Hjjks when they wanted to take over all our land? Why, Thalarne here is a direct descendant herself of Taniane, Hresh, Thu-Kimnibol—"

"They were real, yes," said the second man. "But can we be sure that any of their great deeds actually took place? What if it's all just a bunch of children's fables?"

It was at that point, by which time Nortekku had brought himself to the very edge of the circle around Thalarne and was standing directly opposite her, that she said, in a deep, throaty voice that made him tingle with delight, "Which is exactly why all the evidence of the Chronicles needs to be challenged, reviewed, subjected to modern scientific examination. And the first step in that, I think, is to retrace the great trek, eastward all the way to the Hallimalla, and find the original Koshmar cocoon. Which is what I intend to do."

"How soon will you be leaving?" one of the other sash-wearers asked.

"Two months, maybe three," she said. "However long it takes to get the funding together and acquire the equipment."

"Excuse me," Nortekku said then. "I couldn't help overhearing your discussion. I'm Nortekku of Dawinno, an architect, here to design a palace outside the wall for Prince Vuldimin." He was addressing himself directly to her, as though the others weren't there at all.

"Thalarne Koshmar," she said.

His name, his link to his father's vast wealth, didn't seem to mean anything to her. But she was looking straight back at him, very intently indeed. He knew what an intense stare like that usually meant. He knew, also, that he was probably staring at her the same way.

"And did I hear correctly that you're planning an expedition to the original cocoon?"

"Yes," she said. "Yes, I most certainly am."

"Well, then," said Nortekku at once. "I wonder if there might be room in your group for someone who isn't himself an archaeologist, but who—"

The words were out of his mouth before he had given the thing half a thought. He had no idea what use an architect would be to a bunch of archaeologists, but that hardly mattered. Four or five weeks, even a couple of months, perhaps, out there in the back woods with this wondrous Thalarne—why would he hesitate for so much as a moment?

"Are you serious?" she asked, with a little flurrying show of surprise.

"Positively! To be part of a project like that—why, it's the most fascinating idea I've heard in years, Thalarne!" Shamelessly he said, almost believing it for the moment, "History has always been one of my great interests, as a matter of fact."

"Ah, has it? Why, that's wonderful!" she said, as though she might not be entirely sure of his sincerity, but wanted to be.

"And to be on hand when scientists enter the original Koshmar cocoon—to help recover whatever artifacts our forefathers might have left behind at the Time of Going Forth—to gain new knowledge of the early days of the People—!"

His mind went racing ahead, looking for reasons that might make his presence on the expedition plausible. As an architect, he would be well equipped to map and sketch the intricate layout of the underground chambers that had been inhabited so long. They surely went great distances into the earth. He might even be able to provide technical aid with the excavations. And he could offer financial support too, if that was needed—by way of his father's many business enterprises he was well connected among the princes and great merchants of Dawinno, many of whom claimed to have a profound interest in matters of antiquity.

But it was unnecessary to muster any of those arguments. He could see right away, from the sudden brightness in Thalarne's eyes and the sudden quivering of her sensing-organ and the unmistakable rising of her lustrous black fur, that Thalarne wanted him on the expedition as much as he wanted to be on it, and for the same reasons, which had very little, actually, to do with archaeology.

Over the weeks that followed his mind dwelled on the adventure to come to the exclusion of almost everything else. Enamored of her and newly enraptured by the science to which she had devoted her life, he flung himself into his belated study of antiquity, the better to understand her.

She loaned him books. Worlds were revealed to him: worlds piled on worlds, worlds without end—the world of the humans, of which not the slightest speck remained, and the Great World, whose merest outlines alone survived, and the hidden world of the now abandoned cocoons in which the People, created out of simple apelike animals by the humans to be the successors to the Great World, had waited out the Long Winter. And now, rising atop those strata of antiquity, the brave new world that the People had created for themselves since the Time of Going Forth. Was that, too, destined to thrive awhile and decay and vanish, and be replaced by another, Nortekku wondered? Probably. The earth changes, he thought. Mountains rise, are ground to dust, give way to plains and valleys. Shorelines are drowned; new islands are thrust upward out of the sea. Civilizations are born, die, are forgotten. The planet alone abides, and all that dwells upon it is transient.

Contemplating these things, he felt much the richer for all his freshly acquired knowledge. He felt that for the first time he comprehended, at least in some small way, the great chain of existence, stretching across time from misty past to unborn future. And in the months ahead, he told himself, that comprehension would only grow and deepen as Thalarne and he made their way, side by side, into the ancestral cocoon.

These months in Yissou were the happiest of his life. He and Thalarne had become lovers almost immediately, and soon after that became twining-partners also, even before he discovered that she already had a mate, a certain Hamiruld, who was yet another kinsman of the king of Yissou and of Prince Vuldimin. The fact that Thalarne was married did not appear to be a serious obstacle. Nortekku quickly came to see Hamiruld as a sly and effete man, who appeared to have no particular interest in Thalarne and displayed no overt signs of love for her. Why he had married her, the gods alone knew, but he seemed not to be in any way possessive. Indeed, he seemed to go beyond complaisance into indifference. Quite likely he would step aside if asked; for Nortekku, for the first time ever, had mating on his mind. Thalarne's stunning beauty, her soaring spirit, her keen intelligence—

But that was for later. Finishing the plans for the expedition was the central thing now. Nortekku busied himself putting together the financial backing and purchasing the necessary equipment—Prince Til-Menimat, the famous collector of antiquities, provided most of the money—while Thalarne assembled her team of fellow archaeologists and worked out the details of the route to the ancestral cocoon.

Her ancestral cocoon, anyway, for Thalarne was highborn, not just a member of the aristocratic Koshmar line but of the House of Hresh that was the leading family of that line. Therefore she could trace a direct line of descent from several of the leaders of the little band of People that had come forth at the end of the Long Winter to found both Yissou and Dawinno. Nortekku himself had no clear idea of his own ancestry. All that his father had ever been able to discover was that they had sprung from one of the minor People groups—he wasn't sure which one, maybe the Stadrains, maybe the Mortirils—that had been eking out a scruffy existence in the hinterlands at the time when Hresh and Koshmar and Harruel and the rest of those heroes of long ago, semi-mythical by now, had made their epic trek westward to found the two great city-states of the coastal strip.

They were ten days or so away from the departure date. And then came the quarrel.

It was a preposterous thing: a new opera was having its premiere, *Salaman*, about the tempestuous life of the second king of Yissou, he who had built the great wall. Tickets were scarce—it would be the social event of the winter season—but Prince Vuldimin was able to obtain a dozen of them and gave a pair to Nortekku, who offered one to Thalarne. He thought she would be pleased. She had already spoken of the new opera in some excitement, and Hamiruld, who notoriously had branded opera as a decadent amusement on several recent occasions, was unlikely to want to attend. Nortekku was excited too: it would be their first public outing as a couple.

"But surely you realize that I'll be going to the opera with Hamiruld!" Thalarne said.

Nortekku was taken aback by that, and let it show.

She gave him a puzzled look. "Why do you seem so surprised, Nortekku?"

"That you should be going with Hamiruld? He doesn't have any more interest in opera than that chair over there!"

"But we have tickets. He feels that he ought to go. It's an important evening. He's a direct descendant of King Salaman, you know."

"So is half the nobility of the city. What does that have to do with it?—He's deliberately doing this because he doesn't want us to be seen here in public together, isn't he?"

Her expression darkened into annoyance. "That's ridiculous, Nortekku. Has he ever shown any sort of jealousy? But he's my mate, don't forget. If he wants to go to the opera with me, why shouldn't he? And why should you read all sorts of dark motives into it? He sees it as a social obligation. And if he does, it's simply a matter of good form that I be seen attending the opera with my husband instead of with my—my—"

"Your lover," he supplied, as she faltered into silence.

"My lover, yes," she said, and Nortekku could not mistake the frosty edge that she had put on the word.

He suspected that he was getting ever deeper into trouble, but he drove recklessly onward, unable to hold himself back. "The whole city knows about us already. Everybody is aware that you and I are about to set out on a trip lasting many months and that Hamiruld doesn't care in the slightest. So what difference can it make if you happen to be sitting next to me in the opera house one night next week?"

"What I might be doing next month along the banks of the Hallimalla, far from this city and all its busybodies, is very different from what I choose to do next week in the opera house of Yissou."

"Nevertheless—"

"No. Listen to me, Nortekku."

"You listen to me."

"Please, Nortekku—"

"You know he hates opera." He waved the tickets about. "I insist—"

"You *insist*?"

It got worse from there. Very quickly they were shouting at each other; then they grew more calm, but it was the calmness of cold fury, and then she turned and walked out. Nortekku realized instantly how stupid he had been. Hamiruld and Thalarne were husband and wife; this was their native city, where they were people of some importance; he was an interloper in their marriage and so long as they were still living together he had no claim on her. And what did next week's opera matter, anyway? She herself had reminded him that soon enough he and Thalarne would be far from Yissou and Hamiruld, with time aplenty for making love. To be raising such a fuss over a purely symbolic thing like a night at the opera together now was completely idiotic.

He sent her a letter of apology, and a gift. When no reply came, he sent a second letter, not quite so abject as the first but definitely conciliatory. She agreed to meet with him and gave convincing signs of having accepted his expressions of contrition. Even then there was still some distance between them, which at the moment he made no attempt to bridge, but it seemed to him that the damage was well on the way toward being repaired.

He had to spend the next two days doing the final surveying work out at the site of Vuldimin's new palace in the country. When he came back, Hamiruld was waiting for him with the news that the expedition was off and Thalarne had left the city for points unknown, and the realization that he had no choice but to take himself back to Dawinno and face whatever it was that Silina's people, or his father, or both, had in store for him.

He was still pondering his dilemma that evening when a burly, deep-chested man of middle years, with coarse thick fur and a fierce, glowering visage, hailed him by name in the street. Only after he had actually walked a few steps past him did the preoccupied Nortekku recognize him as Khardakhor, one of his father's great commercial rivals, a dealer in metals and precious stones.

Once, many years back, Khardakhor and Nortekku's father had been partners. Something had gone wrong between them, though. There had been a bitter and vindictive dispute and a court battle of some sort, and the name of Khardakhor was no longer mentioned in Nortekku's house. But Nortekku had never known or cared very much about any of that and he saw no reason to snub Khardakhor now, this far from home. He halted and acknowledged the other man.

Khardakhor seemed amiable enough. He proved to be not nearly so fierce as he looked, greeting Nortekku like a long-lost nephew rather than as the son of an enemy. Evidently he had come north on business, and evidently, too, he had spent some time recently with Prince

Vuldimin, because he knew about Nortekku's having been hired to design a palace for the prince, and—wink, nudge, hearty grin—he knew about Nortekku's affair with the beautiful Thalarne as well. "Quite a choice piece, that one is," he said. "Saw her at Vuldimin's a year or two ago, one of those dinner parties of his. If I were a little younger I'd have gone for her myself. I understand you and she have been cutting quite a swathe lately.—But why haven't you gone off to Bornigrayal with her?"

"Bornigrayal?" Nortekku said blankly. What did Bornigrayal have to do with anything? He wondered whether he had heard correctly. Bornigrayal was a city on the other coast. He knew practically nothing about it, only its name and that it was one of the Five Cities back there. Everyone knew their names—Cignoi, Gharb, Gajnsiuelem, Thisthissima, Bornigrayal—but rarely did anyone from the two western city-states have any reason to visit one. Unknown tribes, emerging from unknown cocoons on the far side of the Hallimalla, had founded them after the Long Winter. For citizens of Dawinno or Yissou, they were all so distant that they might just as well have been on some other planet. "I don't follow you. We didn't have any plans for going to Bornigrayal. What we were about to do was to set out for the Hallimalla, to hunt for the old Koshmar-tribe cocoon."

"Yes, of course. I heard about that project from Til-Menimat back in Dawinno. He expects you to find all sorts of marvels for his collection, I understand. But that's been called off, hasn't it? I ran into Thalarne's husband Hamiruld yesterday"—wink, nudge, grin—"and he told me that he had put Thalarne aboard an airwagon bound for Bornigrayal, a few days back. There's been some kind of discovery out that way that completely puts the cocoon thing in the shade."

Nortekku shook his head. He felt as though a thick mist had wrapped itself about him. It seemed to him that he was moving from bafflement to bafflement these past few days, hardly having a chance to absorb one confusing thing before two or three more presented themselves.

"Well, maybe so. But Hamiruld didn't say anything to *me* about her going to Bornigrayal," Nortekku muttered, after a moment. He had difficulty articulating the words, like someone one who was just coming up from sleep. "He told me she was gone, but he didn't know *where* she had gone. Didn't have any idea, is what he said."

"Which is what he told *you*, anyway," said Khardakhor, grinning broadly. "To me, he said something different. I can't see where he'd have had any reason to lie to me. Maybe he just didn't want you going off to

Bornigrayal after her." The fierce eyes narrowed a bit. "Well, you didn't hear it from me, did you? But the girl's in Bornigrayal. I have it on the best authority."

This was incomprehensible. Nortekku felt a heavy pounding in his chest. Carefully he said, "And what could be in Bornigrayal that might interest her, do you think?"

"How would I know? Never been there, never thought much about the place. I don't do any business there." Khardakhor was studying him very closely. In the narrow glinting eyes Nortekku saw amusement, pity, even, perhaps, just a little envy. "Odd that she didn't say anything to you, if you and she were really as thick with each other as all the rumors around town had it. But if that was how you and she really were, shouldn't you be heading off to Bornigrayal to look for her?"

"Bornigrayal," Nortekku said, hopelessly befuddled. The other end of the continent. It was frightening to think that she was that far from him, and frightening also to contemplate the notion of going there after her. It was an unimaginable distance. He had never traveled anywhere except up and down the Western Coast between Dawinno and Yissou. The journey to the banks of the Hallimalla would have been the grandest peregrination of his life. Why Bornigrayal? What could have possibly taken her there, on the spur of the moment, giving him no warning? To get away from him and all the complexities he had introduced into her marriage? It would hardly have been necessary to go to the ends of the Earth for that. Simply telling him it was over would have sufficed.

Bornigrayal, he thought, in wonder. Why? Why?

"I should go, yes," he said. "Find her. Talk to her. Get all of this straightened out."

Khardakhor was beaming now. "Absolutely, boy. Absolutely! Go to Bornigrayal. Do you know our ambassador there, Samnibolon? He'll help you. He's a very good man, is Samnibolon. You tell him you're a friend of mine, that you're looking for your girlfriend, that I told you she's in Bornigrayal. Go, boy. Waste no time. Bornigrayal may be only the first stop for her. She may be planning to go even farther than that."

It was all becoming something very dreamlike. He felt himself being drawn onward and onward, surrendering all volition. If this man

Khardakhor thought he should go to Bornigrayal after Thalarne, who was he to say no? *Go, boy. Waste no time.*

Prince Vuldimin appeared to feel the same way. The prince knew nothing about Thalarne's hasty departure and had no idea whatever of what could have drawn her to Bornigrayal, though he too seemed to know that that was where she had gone. Unhesitatingly he provided Nortekku with money for the trip. He provided a coachman, too, the following morning, who took Nortekku out to Yissou Sky Harbor, an enormous barren expanse of land far beyond the city walls, with two great concrete runways down its center and a huge gray airwagon sitting at the end of one of them. And within an hour Nortekku, who had never flown anywhere, who had never so much as thought of undertaking a journey by air, found himself aboard that great vessel as it made ready for takeoff.

The airwagon was a very large elongated metal box with wings, a thing of gigantic size. There must have been two or three dozen other passengers on board, perhaps even more. Nortekku was unable to understand how anything this massive could ever be capable of rising into the air. It was only about thirty years since the first experimental flying wagons had made the first tiny uncertain hops between one village and another, and already they were able to traverse the entire continent, which was impressive progress indeed; but for Nortekku transcontinental travel by air was simply something that one might read about, one more of the many technological miracles of modern times, not anything that had any any real relevance to one's own life.

Would he survive the voyage, he asked himself? Did it matter?

He had no assurance that he would be able find Thalarne at all when he got there, or if he did, that she would welcome his having pursued her across all this great distance. It might well be that this whole enterprise would prove destructive to the very thing he hoped to accomplish. Maybe, he thought, she had gone off like this to sort out her feelings about him, and his going after her would serve only to convince her that he was still an adolescent in some ways, an interesting choice for a brief fling but too troublesome to remain involved with for very long.

From beneath him rose a terrifying rumble. From each side of the airwagon came a low throbbing sound that rapidly expanded into a deafening roar.

Without even pausing to consider the incongruity of what he was doing Nortekku, who had never had a moment of religious feeling in his life, murmured a quick spontaneous prayer to all the ancient tribal gods. He called upon Yissou the Protector to look after him, and then asked Mueri the Comforter to ease his journey, and then, for good measure, begged the surveillance of Friit the Healer and Emakkis the Provider as well, and even Dawinno himself, the deity of destruction and transformation.

The airwagon began to move forward. And suddenly, astonishingly, unbelievably, it was aloft.

Nortekku had no clear sense of the point at which the wagon made the transition from ground to sky. But there could be no doubt that it *had* made the transition, for he was looking down at treetops and the metal-roofed sheds of Yissou Sky Harbor, and then, as the wagon banked and wheeled eastward, he saw Yissou City far below, a clenched fist of a place, an ugly huddled maze of tangled streets held in a constricting grasp by the formidable medieval wall that encircled them, with a chaotic sprawl of latter-day suburbs spreading outward from it. From this height it was possible clearly to make out the perfectly circular outline of the city: the first settlers had built the place inside the rim of one of the giant craters that had been formed when the death-stars struck the Earth.

Yissou diminished quickly and was lost to sight somewhere behind them.

In its jarring, lurching way the airwagon sped on through the sky. Red sparks streamed by the windows like frantic scarlet insects. The steady metallic screaming of the engines, disconcerting at first, came to seem familiar and almost welcome. Below, all was a green wilderness, with great blankets of snow on the highest elevations. From time to time Nortekku saw a great circular scar, a brown-walled cicatrice in the midst of the greenness: one of the innumerable pockmarks left on the face of the Earth by the falling death-stars.

As he looked down he was struck by an inrushing awareness of the vastness of the world, and of its antiquity, and of the succession of races that had come and gone upon this planet. Down below there was nothing at all, now, but trees and stones. But once all that wilderness had been inhabited, he knew, by the myriad denizens of the long-lost Great World civilization, the unthinkably rich and glorious era of the Six Peoples whom he had studied in school long ago and then again lately in the first flush of his affair with Thalarne: the Hjjks, the Sea-Lords, the Vegetals, the reptilian race known as the Sapphire-Eyes people, the

Mechanicals, and the most enigmatic ones of all, the Dream-Dreamers, who might perhaps have been the last vestiges of the humans who once had ruled this world in a previous epoch.

For some unknowable length of time—half a million years, a million?—the huge cities of the Great World, full of quivering vitality, astounding in their opulence and size, their myriad windows sparkling in the sun, had covered the landscape below. They had come, they had flourished, they had disappeared, he thought. And it will be the same with us, as it was for others who had lived before them. More strongly than ever before he understood that we are all just visitors here. Though our time of stay may last for millions of years, we are merely temporary residents all the same.

As Nortekku passed high above that landscape he sought with second sight to pry open the eons and thrust his mind into that ancient world, and the worlds that had lived before it, but without success. Nothing remained of it now except some vague traceries of foundation-lines and a few ruined structures. Now and again he thought he could make out the spidery outlines of one of those lost ancient cities below, but perhaps that was only an illusion. Those cities were long gone, right down to their roots. The death-stars had come, dropping in swarms from the sky to stir up dark clouds of debris that blotted out the sun and brought on a winter seven hundred thousand years long, and the all the Great World peoples had perished, all but the Hjjks, who manifestly could survive anything, even the end of the world.

There were half a dozen Hjjks aboard this very wagon. Nortekku saw their bristling antennae rising from seats not very far in front of his. He wondered what they were thinking and feeling as they looked down toward the uninhabited plains where their ancestors had dwelled in the Great World's time of majesty. Nostalgia for that vanished epoch? Pride at its accomplishments? Grief over its destruction? Nothing at all, perhaps. Who could say what sort of emotions a Hjjk might have? They kept their feelings to themselves, if they had any.

But his own feelings were in turmoil again. Contemplating the antiquity of the world had stirred fresh yearnings for Thalarne in him. He wanted to sweep into his arms all those millions of lost years whose faint traces he imagined he could see down there, all that richness of a vanished world, as though to embrace the whole of Earth's past, because by embracing that incomprehensible past he was embracing Thalarne, whose goal it was to comprehend it. And for him Thalarne was the future.

Bornigrayal would tell the tale.

He was surprised at how swiftly the day grew darker as they continued eastward. It was winter, of course, and days were short; but the airwagon had taken off in the morning, and already the sky had the dull cast of afternoon, though they had been aloft only a couple of hours. Such a foreshortening of the day perplexed him for a time. But then Nortekku realized that the sun, rising out of the east, was in motion just as they were, already past him and rushing off beyond the cities of the west into the Western Ocean even as they went roaring on in the opposite direction toward the gathering night. The hour must be later the farther east one went; in some places out there, night had already fallen. In Bornigrayal, Thalarne might even now be sitting down to her evening meal, while for him it was not much past midday. Strange, he thought, that it should be early afternoon here, and night already there. He had never considered such matters before.

A meal was served; and then the wagon began to descend. Landing at Bornigrayal so soon? Fine. He had already had more than enough of this trip. But no, no, not Bornigrayal: it was a place called Kundalimon, they told him, a town he had never heard of, somewhere in the middle of nowhere. Three passengers disembarked; seven new passengers came on board, five People and two Hjjks. The airwagon, he realized, must not have the capacity to fly all the way across the continent in a single burst, and, in any case, the inhabitants of places like Kundalimon must sometimes need to travel also. Within fifteen minutes the wagon was aloft again.

The hours went past. The sky became ashen with dusk and then grew entirely dark. Sometimes isolated villages came into view below, little sprinklings of lights, thin white rivulets of smoke curling upward. Otherwise he could no longer see anything down there. For all he knew they had already by this time passed above the Hallimalla, the great southward-flowing river that cut the continent in half. They might have gone right over the ancestral cocoon, even. But all was blackness below. Nortekku fell into a doze, and dreamed that he was wandering through a fabulous city, a place of gigantic shining towers and gleaming bridges that looped through the air without apparent means of support. In his dream he understood it to be Vengiboneeza, the one city of the Great World that had survived the Long Winter almost intact, and in which the Koshmar tribe of People, Thalarne's ancestors, had dwelled for a few years after the Time of Going Forth. Dreaming about

Vengiboneeza was nothing new for Nortekku; every architect specu-lated about Vengiboneeza, trying to reconstruct in his imagination how it must have looked. The descriptions left of it by those who had seen it while it still existed led one to think that its buildings were unparalleled for beauty and brilliance of design, crystalline cloud-piercing towers, arrayed on grand boulevards. But nothing remained of the place now. The Hjjks had occupied it after the People had moved on south to found Yissou and Dawinno, two centuries back, and in the war that soon fol-lowed between the Hjjks and the People the great Koshmar warrior Thu-Kimnibol had pounded those priceless ruins into oblivion, using potent Great World weapons that his brother, the famed wise man Hresh, had obtained for him by excavating ancient sites. Those two, Thu-Kimnibol, Hresh, were directly ancestral to Thalarne, Nortekku knew. He wondered whether her passion for archaeology was in some way a means of atoning for the destruction of great Vengiboneeza that her famous ancestors had brought about.

The airwagon made another stop, and another. Another meal was served. Nortekku slept again, and when he awakened the morning sunlight was in the sky and the wagon was landing once more.

Another brief stop, he thought. We will go on and on, for days, for weeks, for months, until this machine finally brings us to Bornigrayal. If ever it does.

But no: this place was Bornigrayal, even now, here, actually, truly, journey's end. Rumpled and blinking, he joined the line of passengers leaving the wagon, descended the staircase that took him to the run-way, shaded his eyes against the sudden flinty brightness of the day. This was the northernmost of the Five Cities of the Eastern Coast, and it was cold here, very cold, colder even than in Yissou. The Bornigrayal sky-harbor was situated practically at the shore of what must surely be the Eastern Ocean. A ferocious brutal wind, knife-sharp, came roaring in off the dull gray surface of that immeasurable body of water. The chill was like a bit of the Long Winter, long after its time, obstinately lingering here in these high latitudes. That wind cut right through Nortekku's dense covering of fur and struck at the skin beneath, so that he began to shiver. None of the other debarking passengers seemed to be affected by the cold, not just the Hjjks, who were impervious to cold, but the various People too. Yissouans, naturally, were accus-tomed to hard winters, and so also must be the passengers who had boarded in mid-flight. But Nortekku had grown up in golden Dawinno of the balmy breezes, where true winter never came, where the only distinction between one season and another was that during the winter months the days were shorter and there was occasionally a little rain. For love of Thalarne he had subjected himself to a winter in Yissou, and now, it seemed, still for love of Thalarne, he was going to have to endure even worse weather than that.

Carriages were waiting to take the arriving passengers to the Bornigrayal proper, which could be seen against the western horizon as a distant row of white flat-topped towers glinting in the hard morning light. On the eve of his departure Nortekku had mentioned to Prince Vuldimin that the merchant Khardakhor had advised him to seek out the Dawinnan ambassador, Samnibolon, upon his arrival, and Vuldimin had at once given him a letter of introduction. The ambassador was, he said, an old friend of his. It was amazing how everybody of any importance in the two city-states of the Western Coast turned out to be an old friend of Vuldimin's, if not an actual kinsman. But it should hardly be surprising that close ties of kinship would unite most of the highborn of both cities, since their ancestors had all come out of just two cocoons, the Koshmar one and the Beng, and Koshmars and Bengs had intermarried steadily since the union of the two tribes in the early days of the Going Forth.

"I should warn you," Prince Vuldimin had said, "in case you're not already aware of it, that Prince Samnibolon is connected by marriage to the family of the Princess Silina. Quite probably he doesn't know a thing about your unfortunate little interaction with them. But I wouldn't go out of my way to mention it, if I were you."

"I wouldn't think of it," said Nortekku. "Not to him, not to anyone, not ever."

Prince Samnibolon was a small-framed man, gray-furred, whose office in the embassy quarter of the city was as elegantly appointed as any prince's chamber should be, with painted scrolls on the wall and glass cases that contained the sort of small Great World artifacts that so many highborns were fond of collecting. The ambassador sat at a circular desk fashioned of strips of rare woods, raised on a gleaming bronze dais. Nortekku knew him to be a member of the House of Hresh, Dawinno's dominant family, who held most of the highest posts in Dawinno's government. He was reputed to be a suave and subtle man, a diplomat of diplomats. Through the Hresh connection he was related in some way to Thalarne.

The ambassador skimmed quickly through Nortekku's letter of introduction and said, "Building a new palace for Vuldimin, are you? He does have a taste for comfort and luxury, that man!" Then, with a knowing smile: "But if I had to live in a ghastly place like Yissou, I suppose that I would too.—You've been up north for quite some time, then?"

"Most of this past year. I bring you greetings from your friend the merchant Khardakhor, who is currently in Yissou. It was at his suggestion that I came to you."

Samnibolon delicately raised one eyebrow in a brief show of surprise. He would know, certainly, about the bitter commercial rivalry between Khardakhor and the elder Nortekku. But he said nothing of that now, merely murmuring a word or two about hearty old rough-hewn Khardakhor and moving smoothly on to ask what it was that had brought Nortekku to Bornigrayal. To which Nortekku responded that he had come to have a small role in an archaeological project under the direction of Thalarne Koshmar of Yissou's Institute of Scientific Study. She was currently here in Bornigrayal on a matter of family business, he said; and, since certain unexpected problems now had arisen regarding their project, he needed to locate her and apprise her of the new developments. It was a story that he had carefully rehearsed all morning and he delivered it unfalteringly.

"Ah, Thalarne!" the ambassador said. "One of the great ornaments of the Yissouan branch of my family, so everyone says."

"You know her, do you?"

"Alas, no. I haven't had the pleasure. But I've heard many good things of her: said to be a most attractive woman—most! And brilliant and learned as well. As no doubt I hardly need to tell you." Samnibolon pointed out that as a citizen of Yissou she was outside his official sphere of responsibility, and therefore she would not have had any reason to contact him since her arrival. So he could not confirm that she was actually in Bornigrayal at this very time, but if Nortekku wished him to make inquiries about her at the Yissouan Embassy, he definitely would. Nortekku did so wish. He gave the ambassador the address of the hostelry where he had found lodgings, and, after a few pleasant minutes of exchanging gossip about certain high figures of Dawinno who were known to them both—Nortekku noticed that throughout the interview Samnibolon had made no mention of Nortekku the elder; he must be aware of their estrangement—he took his leave.

Late the next day a courier from the Embassy came to him bearing the address of the place where Thalarne was living.

It was, Nortekku learned, halfway across the city from his own place. Which meant a considerable distance, for Bornigrayal had turned out to be a diffuse, far-flung city, endlessly proliferating itself over a succession of islands linked by bridges as it sloped down toward the ocean. Because of the cold, he had not cared to explore the city at all thus far—indeed he failed to understand why anyone had been mad enough to found a city in such a chilly site—but he saw now, as a hired carriage took him on what proved to be an hour-long journey to Thalarne's lodgings, that considerable ingenuity and skill had been expended on the layout and construction of this place, and in fact it was a city of some grandeur, in every way the equal of grand Dawinno itself. One might regard all those tall flat-topped white buildings as stark and monotonous; but, just as readily, one might find great power in them, much rugged strength.

According to the message from Samnibolon, Thalarne had found rooms for herself in the faculty lodge of Bornigrayal University. Nortekku, apprehensive over the meeting, had not sent word ahead to Thalarne that he was coming to see her. He realized that he half hoped she would be somewhere else when he arrived.

The University was dramatically situated on a high craggy outcropping rising above the city's central island. His driver dropped him off in the wrong place, and Nortekku needed to do much dreary trudging about from building to building before he located the right one.

That same apprehension, that same uneasiness about coming face to face with her, still gripped him as he knocked at her door. How would she react to his showing up like this on her doorstep? With amazement, no doubt, that he had followed her all the way across the continent. But then what? Displeasure, resentment, irritation, anger?

He heard footsteps. The door opened. For a moment, standing there facing her, Nortekku had to fight back the temptation to turn and flee. But then he saw that she was smiling. Her eyes were warm and bright with surprise and pleasure.

"So you got here at last!" she cried. "Oh, Nortekku, what could have taken you so long?"

And drew him quickly across the threshold, and enfolded him in her arms, and touched her sensing-organ to his in a greeting of unqualified delight.

He was too befuddled to be able to speak at all. Fearing the worst, he had never dared to expect anything like this. For a long while they embraced in silence; then, as she released him, he stepped back and looked at her in wonder, and said, finally, "What—took—me—so—long? Thalarne, what can you possibly mean? I had to find out where you had gone, first. And then make arrangements to get here. And then—you know how long the trip takes—then I had to track you down.—You aren't upset that I came, then?"

"Upset?" She sounded mystified. "I've been waiting for you all week. If you hadn't turned up in another couple of days, I would have had to continue on without you. The ship is due to sail at the end of the week, and—"

"The ship?" he said. "What ship?" There was a lot to sort out here. "Wait a minute, Thalarne. This isn't making sense. Can we back things up a little? Hamiruld came to me and told me that you had left town without saying a word to him about where you were going, and that he was instructed to simply inform me that our expedition was off."

"No. That isn't true, Nortekku."

"What isn't true? That he told me—"

"No. That I left any such message for you." Something close to panic flared in her eyes. "Oh, Nortekku, Nortekku, this is all so badly garbled! What I asked him to let you know was that there's been a new discovery, something that has a much higher priority than anything you and I could have done at the cocoon site, and that I was leaving straightaway for Bornigrayal. You were supposed to take the next flight out."

He felt numb. "He said nothing whatever like that. Only that you had gone off somewhere, and the expedition was cancelled. And I thought—that perhaps, because of that imbecilic quarrel I had with you—"

"The quarrel was over and done with."

"I thought so too."

"Hamiruld lied to you," Thalarne said. She seemed to be trembling. "Deliberately and cold-bloodedly lied to you. I can hardly believe it."

By second sight Nortekku felt waves of sincerity radiating from her. To use second sight on another person without permission was improper in Dawinno, always had been, but the Yissouans had no such prohibition, and he and Thalarne had allowed themselves that communion almost from the beginning. He felt it now. There could be no doubt.

He said, "I thought he had no feelings of jealousy about us. But that isn't so, is it? I wanted to think so, but obviously that isn't true. He deliberately withheld the key part of your message and distorted the rest of it, hoping to cause trouble between us. I see now that I've never really understood your relationship with Hamiruld."

She was silent a moment, frowning a little, as though debating how much she wanted to tell him. Then she said, "Hamiruld has no physical interest in women, Nortekku. He never has. I don't know why: that's just how he is. But he claims to love me, and I think he does. I'm a kind of trophy for him, perhaps: something to be proud of, a woman whom every man in Yissou seems to desire for one reason or another, most, I guess, for my looks, maybe some for my mind. Or both. And so he's been willing to countenance my—affairs, provided I'll go on living with him."

My affairs. Well, he thought, of course he hadn't been the first. Of course not.

"And you?" he said. "You're perfectly willing to have that kind of marriage? Do you love him, Thalarne?"

Something close to evasiveness crossed her features. "Love? How can I say? It was never an issue, before you came along. We were, well, happy. We got on well together. We enjoyed each other's company. We went to the year's social events as a couple. To the parties at court. To the opera—you saw what a problem it created when you wanted to take me. He didn't get in the way of my research. If I felt like amusing myself with another man, he didn't interfere."

"Up to a point, it would seem."

"Up to a point, yes. But clearly he was unhappy about the proposed cocoon expedition, or at least with your being a part of it, and even unhappier when I announced I was going to come out here. And so he suppressed my message to you, which I find tremendously distressing. He's never done anything like that before. It's a complete violation of the rules of our marriage."

Nortekku glanced away from her. All of this, this series of unwanted glimpses into the intimacies of their life together, was beginning to make him exceedingly uncomfortable.

The less he knew of the rules of their marriage, the less he knew about their marriage at all, the better, he thought. He had taken care never to question her about any aspect of it. It had seemed unlikely to him that they coupled—indeed Hamiruld didn't appear to be the sort of man who cared much about bodily passion—but Nortekku had not presumed to pry. Did they twine? He certainly had not wanted to know that. And now—having heard everything that had just poured out of her—

We got on well together. We enjoyed each other's company.

Hoarsely he said, "We've taken ourselves completely off the track with this discussion of how Hamiruld handled that message of yours. The important thing is that I still don't know why it is that you went to Bornigrayal, or wanted me to come here. A new discovery, you said—a higher priority than excavating the cocoon site—"

"Yes." She looked relieved to be changing the subject also. "Do you know where the Inland Sea is, Nortekku?"

"Approximately, yes."

From the uncertainty of his tone she must have realized how approximate that knowledge was. Nortekku knew that there were other continents in the world, of course, somewhere on the far side of the Eastern Ocean, and that two of them were separated by a great land-rimmed sea that was almost a third ocean in itself. But that was all. One never thought much about the other side of the world. The Five Cities of this coast were remote enough; the continents of the other hemisphere were beyond consideration.

She sketched a quick map for him. "Our continent, here. Yissou, Dawinno." A line down the middle for the Hallimalla River. Five dots along the eastern seaboard for the Five Cities. Then emptiness—the Eastern Ocean—and then, far off at the left end of the sheet, two amorphous land-masses, one above the other, with another emptiness, this one long and oval, between them. "The Inland Sea," Thalarne said, tapping the sheet. "And here, on its southern coast, where the weather is very warm, a little colony of Sea-Lords has been living ever since the Long Winter began."

She said it quite calmly, as though telling him that she had learned of some interesting new inscription that had been discovered there, or some unusual Great World artifact. But for him it was like an earthquake. Sea-Lords? Still living somewhere, a little colony of them on the far side of the Eastern Ocean? There were no Sea-Lords anywhere, he thought. The Sea-Lords were gone, every last one of them, like all the rest of the Great World except the Hjjks.

Nortekku's recent historical studies had told him very little about the Sea-Lords. One of the Six Peoples of the Great World, yes, a race of intelligent amphibious mammals, sea-going merchant princes who had held sway over the extensive maritime commerce that had flourished in Great World times. That was all he knew of them, other than that they were all supposed to have perished when the darkness and cold of the Long Winter fell upon the Earth. The books that Hresh and other historians had written about that era had dealt mainly with the reptilian Sapphire-Eyes, the dominant race of their time, and provided some knowledge of their servants the Mechanicals, and of the floral Vegetals, and, in abundance, of the Hjjks, whose subterranean hives had sheltered them without difficulty throughout the interminable icy years. But of the Sea-Lords virtually nothing was known. They were the most mysterious of the Great World races, other than the totally baffling Dream-Dreamers.

"You mean to say they're still there? Living as they always did?"

"Still there, yes. Living as they always did, no. From what I've been told, I suspect that they're pitiful impaired creatures, decadent, degenerate, whatever word you want to use—half crazy, most of them. Bestial. Sad. They've retrogressed, gone some distance backward toward the animals they once were."

That saddened him. Attuned to ancient history as he had lately become, he had often longed for some miracle that would restore at least a part of the Great World to life, in all its wonder, for him to see and experience. Still, the fact that they had survived at all—

"They're definitely Sea-Lords, though? Not just some contemporary species of marine mammal?"

"Oh, yes. Definitely Sea-Lords. They speak what is thought to be a Great World language, or at least a debased version of it. The Hjjks who were in the discovery party claim to be able to communicate with them. Legends of the Great World have survived among them. They know what they once were, it seems."

"This stands everything that we know about the end of the Great World on its head, doesn't it?" Nortekku said.

"Much of it, anyway. We thought that the oceans everywhere had grown so cold that it became impossible for the Sea-Lords to survive. Apparently not so. And if there's a band of them still alive on the coast of that southern continent, who can say what still survives farther south? A bunch of Sapphire-Eyes, maybe? Vegetals? It's only two hundred years since we came out of the cocoons, Nortekku. We think we've achieved a lot, with our cities and our universities and our airwagons and all of that. But the truth is we've only just begun, really, to explore the world around us. Off in Dawinno and Yissou, it seems to us that cities of the Eastern Coast like Bornigrayal and Thisthissima are worlds unto themselves, far off beyond our ken. Actually we should look upon them as being next door to us, though. There's a whole huge continent south of us that we know just about nothing about—"

"South?"

"South, yes. Going on and on, right on down to the Pole, maybe. There have been some voyages to it from Cignoi, but the Cignese haven't been saying anything about whatever they may have found there. And in the east, across this ocean here, there are two continents far larger than this one, with cities of the People on them—we know the names of two or three—with which Bornigrayal has regular commerce, though they haven't been talking much about that either. Beyond those two—"

"Even more continents?" Nortekku said. This was dizzying.

"Who knows? Nobody's ever been there. But it's a round planet, Nortekku. You keep going east, sooner or later you reach the Western Ocean's far side, and if we could sail across it we'd be back at our own coast again. I find it hard to believe that there's nothing but empty ocean west of us."

"The Sea-Lords," he said. "Come back to the Sea-Lords. You told me, when I first came in, that there's a ship due to sail from here at the end of the week, and you're planning to be on it. To go and look for that colony of Sea-Lords, is that it? And you want me to accompany you?"

"Of course," Thalarne said.

It was too much, flooding in all in a single moment like this. His head was swimming. One day he had simply been trying to repair a spat with his lover, and the next, practically, he found himself aboard an airwagon heading for the other side of the continent, and then—new continents—living Sea-Lords—a voyage to the eastern hemisphere, to the shores of the Inland Sea—

She sat him down and poured wine for him, and she told him a little about the arrangements she had made for the new expedition and her hopes of what they would find out there across the ocean, and her fears, too, and of a good deal else, while he listened spellbound, though only partly convinced that any of this was really happening. Perhaps, Nortekku thought, he was still back in Yissou, lost in some fever-dream. Perhaps he had never even left Dawinno.

But the whiplash sound of an icy wind against the window reminded him that he really was in wintry Bornigrayal, and that the dark, emerald-eyed woman beside him actually was Thalarne, whom he had not lost after all, and that he and she were talking quite seriously about taking passage aboard some ocean-going vessel and crossing the sea in quest of survivors of a race that had thought to be extinct for seven hundred thousand years. He moved closer to her. By imperceptible stages they found themselves embracing, and then, after only a moment of shared uncertainty—shall we couple first? Or twine?—they made their choice and slid to the floor and were hard at it, coupling for the first time in—what, two weeks? Three? She arched her back against his chest, pressing herself close, and awaited him. How good it was to reunite with her now! First the coupling, the simpler communion, the basic one, the old primitive thing that all creatures enjoyed. And then later, he hoped, they would twine. But for now he lost himself in her rich scent, in the warmth of her. He clasped her tight, and cupped her breasts in his hands, and from her came a gasp of joy as he thrust himself into her.

And afterward, when they had coupled, and rested, perhaps even dozed a little while, their sensing-organs came into contact, idly, nudging playfully, at first, and then touching in what was not a playful way at all, and they entered twining mode, made ready for the true union of souls, the joining that only the People could do, the linking of their perceptors in the deepest, most intense, most intimate contact that was possible between one person and another. The essence that was Thalarne came flooding into him, and all that was Nortekku into her. He felt her love—no question of it—and her excitement at everything that was opening before them now, the new quest and their own companionship in the weeks to come.

They slept, then. They rose and put together a sort of a meal. They coupled a second time. No twining, this time—one did not twine often; it was too intense—and then they slept again, and when Nortekku woke just after dawn there was a light carpeting of shining snow over the grounds outside the building. Nortekku had never seen snow at such close range before. Snow was wholly unknown in and around Dawinno, certainly, where it was summer all year round, and even up by chillier Yissou it was a once-in-a-decade event, so they said. Since the end of the Long Winter the world had grown warmer year by year, and, having spent his whole life in the benign climate of the Western

Coast, Nortekku had come to assume that all the world now enjoyed similar temperate weather. Not true, it seemed. Here on the other side of the continent things were different. They were not as distant yet in Bornigrayal from the days of the Long Winter as were those who lived on the other coast.

Since Thalarne was still asleep, he went downstairs and walked in the snow for a time. Scooped some up in his hand: it burned like flame against his bare skin. He shivered and wrapped his arms about himself. This must have been what the Long Winter was like, he thought, something like this snowy morning, though on a much greater scale. Snow-drifts many times higher than a man's head; vast expanses of blinding whiteness, stretching off as far as anyone could see; black icy winds, relentless, remorseless, raking the land like scythes. No leaf in sight, no blade of grass. How awful!

He cast his mind back across the ages, tried once again, as he had so many times before, to imagine the Long Winter's onset: the death-stars plummeting from the sky—the legend had it that they came every twenty-six million years, clusters of jagged stones falling out of the heavens, crashing down to engender such clouds of dust and smoke that the sky turned black and there was darkness on the face of the Earth and its inhabitants were cut off from the warmth of the sun for century after century. Whole races had died out in that terrible winter and those that survived did so by creeping off into safe hiding-places until the agony of the planet was over. And when it was over the Great World was gone and the inheritors of the planet were the simpler folk who called themselves the People.

The Great World peoples could have saved themselves, so said the Book of Hresh that that great wise man had set down toward the end of his life, in the first generation after the Time of Going Forth. Their wisdom would have been equal to that task. But they had calmly chosen to die instead, all but the Hjjks, who, like insects of every sort, seemed to intend to endure until the end of time. According to Hresh, though, the others had convinced themselves that it was the great design of divine Dawinno to replace old races by new ones from time to time in the course of the world's history: the ancient humans had given way to the peoples of the Great World, and now it was the turn of the Great World peoples to vanish in favor of the furry folk of the cocoons, whose turn it would be, so Hresh supposed, to yield the stage eventually themselves some day. Dawinno was the deity of transformations, was he not? He destroyed and then he created, all in the service of eternal change and renewal.

So the Sapphire-Eyes and the Vegetals, who were not in any way fitted to withstand cold, had done nothing to protect themselves against it, and the Mechanicals, those intelligent machines, saw that they would have no purpose once the others had died, and let themselves be overtaken by the snowfall in open country, where their rusted remains could still be found all these many years later, and the Dream-Dreamer race disappeared somewhere also, except for those few who settled among the People in the cocoons, and those did not outlast the Long Winter. And, though scientists knew that the oceans themselves had not completely frozen over during the Long Winter, it was believed that the Sea-Lords, too, had found the new climate too much for them.

Evidently not, if Thalarne's tale of that degenerate band on the southern shore of the Inland Sea had any substance to it. To some small extent they had defied Dawinno's great plan of extinction, just as the Hjjks had done. What, Nortekku wondered, would old Hresh have made of that?

He had had enough of walking through the snow. He went back inside and found that Thalarne had awakened.

"Did you enjoy it, the snow?" she asked.

He rubbed his tingling hands together. "An interesting experience, I suppose. But a little of it goes a long way."

"You'll find it much warmer where we're going. More like your own city."

"Good," he said. "Excellent."

While they breakfasted she told him more of the details of the the venture on which they were about to embark.

The sea voyage would take two weeks, possibly three. That was staggering in itself: cooped up for such a long time in what he envisioned as some sort of wooden container, tossing on the turbulent breast of an ocean so great in size that his imagination was unable to encompass it. He was restless by nature. It would be difficult, he knew, to get through the days and nights of such a long voyage without growing a little fretful, maybe more than a little. But he did not share his anxiety about that with her.

And he would have to prepare himself, Thalarne said, for a certain amount of discomfort. Did he know what seasickness was? The winter seas in these latitudes were not easy. Nortekku brushed that part of it aside also, making a fine show of not thoroughly heartfelt bravado. They would be together: what could a few bothersome storms matter? Their initial destination, she said, was Sempinore, a port city on the southern coast of the northern continent. There they would spend a week or so replenishing their supplies, and then they would set out southward across the Inland Sea, a journey of only a few days, to the secret location of the Sea-Lord colony on the northern shore of the other continent.

It was all going to take much longer than he had expected, he saw. Nortekku fidgeted a bit, thinking about the expenses. After a time he said, "I hate to bring this up, but I'm not sure how I'm going to deal with the cost of this much traveling. You ought to know, Thalarne, that I'm not a rich man. My father is, yes, but he and I—"

"There won't be any expense," she said crisply. "The entire expedition is being underwritten by a syndicate of wealthy and prominent Western Coast individuals, both from Dawinno and Yissou, which is how I happened to learn about the project at all. Our friend Prince Til-Menimat, for one."

"So he's behind this one, too? How did *he* get to be part of it?"

"He's currently financing the excavations in Thisthissima, right down the coast from Bornigrayal. The Bornigrayan archaeologists who made the Sea-Lord discovery are connected with that work too. Thisthissima, you know, is built right on top of a major Great World city, and some very fruitful digging has been going on the past couple of years. So the Bornigrayal people came to Til-Menimat and said, 'Listen, your grace, we're on to something very big over across the Eastern Ocean, but we need serious funding in order to go ahead with it, and therefore—'"

Nortekku began to feel just a little dazed. He understood the hunger to unearth the buried remnants of the world's forgotten epochs, here in these constantly burgeoning years of the New Springtime. But only since becoming involved with Thalarne had he come to understand how fierce that hunger was. There was something ugly about it. Highborns from every city seemed to be competing frenziedly with one another in the race to uncover the secrets of all those lost yesterdays. Til-Menimat was a charming, cultured man, but in his lust to own pieces of the Great World he seemed to have greedy tentacles outstretched everywhere.

He walked to the window. The morning sun was high, now, painting a fiery orange track across the snowy fields below.

"So this is just an artifact-hunting operation, then?" he asked.

"Not *just* an artifact-hunting operation. That part of it won't be any concern of yours or mine. But we'll be there to do scientific work. Studying the Sea-Lords."

"While these other archaeologists do the treasure-hunting. These Bornigrayal people."

"Yes," she said. "A man and a woman, Kanibond Graysz and his mate Siglondan. I've had a little correspondence with them, and I met them for the first time the other day, but I don't really know much about them. It seems that they were in Sempinore consulting the archives there when some local Hjjks came to them and said that they had made a very interesting discovery over on the other side of the Inland Sea. So Kanibond Graysz and Siglondan went over with them to have a look, and there were the Sea-Lords. They hurried back to Bornigrayal, and then down to Thisthissima when they heard that Prince Til-Menimat happened to be back east touring the Thisthissima excavations just then. And that was when they told him about the discovery and got him to put up the money for this new expedition."

Nortekku nodded distantly. One aspect of the story had begun to bother him as this part of her story unfolded. "But you were right on the verge of setting out on our cocoon expedition, which Til-Menimat was also underwriting. Why would he have wanted to pull you off that and send you flying out to Bornigrayal?"

"He didn't," Thalarne said. All resonance had suddenly fled from her tone, and her voice sounded hollow and dead. "It was Hamiruld who got me mixed up in this."

"Hamiruld?" he said, in a voice as suddenly leaden as hers.

So he was in this too. The revelation came with the force of a blow. Every one of these highborns seemed linked to each of the rest in their worldwide dealings. They were all over the place. You came upon one where you didn't expect him and then you saw that there was another of his kind standing right next to him. For all he knew, Prince Samnibolon was part of the group too. And had been quietly smiling within while Nortekku went on and on, the other day at the Embassy, about Thalarne's having come to Bornigrayal on "family business."

Speaking a little too quickly, Thalarne said, "Prince Til-Menimat invited him into the syndicate, you see. They've gone into a lot of these things together. But Hamiruld pointed out that an out-and-out artifact-collecting expedition would raise some ethical problems, considering that what was involved was a bunch of actual living Sea-Lords. I mean, it's one thing to dig up artifacts on an uninhabited site a million years old, and another thing entirely to take them from living people. Some archaeologist whose interests were purely scientific ought to go along also, Hamiruld said, for the sake of keeping an eye on the two Bornigrayans and make sure that everything was carried out in an appropriate way."

"Someone like you," Nortekku said.

"Someone like me, yes."

"Even though the artifacts are going to get taken anyway, whether you're keeping an eye on things or not?"

She gave him a pained look. "Don't press me too hard on this, Nortekku. If I want to be part of the expedition at all, I can't make myself too much of an obstacle. I know there are problems here. I'll do whatever I can."

Everything was falling into place now for him. Hamiruld not only had known all along about her running off that way to Bornigrayal, he had engineered her leaving town himself. Unwilling, despite his pretense of indifference, to have Thalarne and Nortekku spend cozy weeks or even months digging things up together out by the Hallimalla, Hamiruld had maneuvered her into a place on this Sea-Lord expedition. Til-Menimat would surely have seen the importance of the discovery, and it might not have been hard to convince him that the cocoon venture could always wait for some other time, that the Sea-Lord journey must come first, and that Thalarne's presence on it was necessary to provide scientific cover for the real purposes of the project. And then, after having shipped Thalarne safely off to the other side of the world, presumably far beyond Nortekku's reach, Hamiruld would prevent Nortekku from finding out where she was by coolly pretending to him that he had no information whatever about where she had gone.

Nortekku could understand all that easily enough. Hamiruld must have been more annoyed by Thalarne's affair with him than he wanted to admit. Any man, even one who had countenanced the sort of things in his marriage that Hamiruld evidently had, might be expected to react in that way to an affair that gave the appearance of going well beyond the previously defined bounds of their arrangement.

Well, he had thwarted Hamiruld's scheme—but only because Hamiruld had been careless enough to tell Khardakhor that Thalarne had gone to Bordigrayal, never dreaming that Khardakhor would share the news with the son of his worst enemy. What still disturbed him, though, was the agitation Thalarne had displayed when she discovered that Hamiruld had blatantly altered the message she had given him about going to Bornigrayal, and the hesitation she had shown in revealing to him that Hamiruld was actually a key player in this Sea-Lord enterprise.

In his quiet way Hamiruld held plenty of power over her, he saw. On some level she must still be uneasy about his presence as a third partner in her marriage—that the marriage itself still had more of a hold on her than she would like him to think, that she seemed eager to gloss swiftly over anything that might demonstrate to him that Hamiruld still played a significant role in her life. It was clear now that Hamiruld intended to fight to keep his marriage intact; what was not so clear, Nortekku thought, was what Thalarne's own position on the future of that marriage might be.

"You're very quiet," Thalarne said, in something more like her normal tone of voice.

"You've given me a lot to think about."

"The risks of the trip? The part about collecting artifacts? The fact that Hamiruld is involved?"

"All of it."

"Oh, Nortekku—"

They stood facing each other across the room for a moment. He had no idea what to say. Neither, it seemed, did she.

But only for a moment. The same bright glow came into her eyes that he had seen at their first meeting, back in Yissou, what felt like eons ago. She stretched her arms toward him.

"Come here," she said.

The ship was much smaller than Nortekku had expected—a tubby, wide-bodied vessel, oddly square-looking, fashioned from thick planks of some kind of blackish wood, that sat low in the water along a weatherbeaten pier at the harbor of Bornigrayal. It was hard to believe that a clumsy little craft like that, which seemed scarcely big enough to pass as a riverboat, would be able to carry them all the way across the immensities of the Eastern Ocean in anything less than a lifetime and a half.

Once he was aboard, though, he saw that he had greatly underestimated the vessel's size. There was much more of it below the water line than was visible from dockside. Two parallel corridors ran its length, with a host of small low-ceilinged cabins branching off from them, and a series of spacious cargo holds at front and back. Nortekku and Thalarne were going to share a cabin near the ship's bow. "This will be a little complicated," she told him. "Kanibond Graysz knows that I'm the wife of one of the backers of the expedition. I've booked only one cabin, and they've let me know that they can't or won't make another one available. But I don't dare try to pass you off as Hamiruld."

"Shall we just say we're very good friends?" Nortekku asked.

"Don't joke. I've let it be known that we're brother and sister. When we're in public, make sure you behave that way."

"I hate telling lies, Thalarne. You know that."

"Tell this one. For me."

"Can we at least be a particularly friendly brother and sister, then?"

"Please, Nortekku."

"What if anyone passing our cabin at night happens to hear sounds coming out of it that might not be considered appropriate for a brother and sister to be making?"

"*Please,*" Thalarne said, as irritated as he had ever heard her sound. "You know how badly I wanted you to accompany me on this expedition. But stirring up a scandal won't achieve anything for anybody. I don't think anybody's going to care, but we need to observe the forms, anyway. Is that clear, brother?"

He forced a grin. "Completely, sister."

Their cabin was ridiculously tiny. The two narrow bunks, one above the other, took up more than half of it. They had one small cabinet for their possessions, and a washbasin. There was scarcely room to turn around in the middle of the floor. The atmosphere in the room was pervaded by the thick, piercing odor of some caulking compound, close to nauseating at first, though Nortekku found himself rapidly getting used to it. A single slitlike opening, not even a hand's-breadth wide, was their window to the outside world. When he pushed the shutter aside a harsh stream of cold air, salty and acrid and unpleasant, drifted in through it, filling the room with a rank, heavy smell that cut through the other one. The smell of the sea, he thought. Of multitudes of fishes, of seaweed, of scuttling sea-creatures moving about just beyond the hull. He had never smelled anything like it before, insistent, commanding, hostile.

The Bornigrayans, Kanibond Graysz and Siglondan, had the cabin just across the corridor. They would have made a far more plausible brother-sister pair than Nortekku and Thalarne: indeed they might almost have been twins. They both were small and fine-boned, both were white-furred, though not from age, both had small alert close-set eyes, his a sharp yellow, hers blue-green. Their faces were cold and pinched, and when they looked at you out of those small bright eyes it was in what struck Nortekku as a shifty, calculating way, as though they were measuring you for some kind of swindle. He found himself taking an instant irrational dislike to them.

But they were affable enough. They greeted Thalarne warmly and showed no sign of surprise that she had suddenly produced a brother as a traveling companion. Wisely, she introduced him as the architect that he was, rather than as any sort of archaeologist, but explained that he had a deep and abiding interest in Great World history—a hobby of his since childhood, she said—and had begged her to be taken along. If they had any misgivings about that, they said nothing about them. They talked mostly about the excitement of what lay ahead, the great discoveries that were certain to be made. Not that Nortekku had an easy time understanding them: the language spoken in Bornigrayal was essentially no more than a dialect of that of the West Coast, but the pronunciation and placing of accents differed in a number of significant ways, words were often slurred, other words were entirely unfamiliar, and at all times the two Bornigrayans spoke so quickly that Nortekku found himself lagging a sentence or two behind. Still, they produced a flask of superb Bornigrayan brandy, of a truly extraordinary smoothness and tang, and the four of them solemnly raised a toast to each other and to the success of the expedition. No one who would share brandy of that quality with people they barely knew could be altogether bad, Nortekku decided.

As the Bornigrayans poured a second round there came the shattering sound of the ship's horn, three mighty blasts. Then the whole vessel began to quiver and from somewhere far below came the drumbeat pounding of the engines. The journey was beginning.

Within moments Nortekku heard a frightful creaking sound that he realized must be the first movements of the ship's two great paddlewheels. They went up on deck to watch as the ship pulled out. There was room for perhaps eight people up there, along with a couple of lifeboats, a sputtering oil lamp, a bell hanging in the bow. The planks were stained and unevenly laid. A flimsy-looking rail was all that guarded the deck's margin.

The day was cold, the sky bleak, a few wisps of snow swirling about. Ominous green lightning was crackling far out at sea. Quickly, but with a troublesome sidewise swaying motion, not quite sickening but distinctly unsettling, the ship moved away from Bornigrayal and on into the gray, unwelcoming ocean. This close to land the water was fairly calm, but dismaying-looking waves were curling along the surface out by the horizon. There would surely be worse to come. The sea is very wide, Nortekku thought, and our ship is so small.

"You look unhappy," Thalarne murmured at his side.

"I think this is scarier than flying, and flying is scary enough. But if your airwagon falls out of the sky you die right away. I suspect that drowning is slow and hideous."

"No doubt it is. So let's try not to drown, all right?"

Gloomily he said, "Wouldn't one good wave be sufficient to turn this ship upside down?"

She looked entirely unperturbed about that: amused, even, by his fears. By way of dismissing them she invented even worse ones for him, slimy sea-monsters rising from the depths and swarming across the deck, or gigantic ocean-going birds swooping down from on high to carry off unsuspecting passengers, or a sudden whirlpool in the sea that would suck the ship down like a ravening monster. He admired her casual attitude—outwardly casual, at least—toward the perils of the sea, and felt abashed for his own faintheartedness. But he went on feeling miserable all the same, and before long returned to their cabin, pleading chill.

At twilight the eastern sky dimmed swiftly, deep blue streaked with red, then a brooding grayish purple, then black. All sight of land had disappeared. They were alone in a seemingly endless expanse of water.

But as one day slid into the next no sea-monsters turned up, nor whirlpools or other menaces, and though a storm swept over them on the fourth or fifth day out, lifting awesome waves that went crashing across the ship's bow, the crewmen behaved as though they were unconcerned and nothing untoward occurred. Nortekku felt himself sliding into the rhythm of the voyage. His fears subsided. Despite all the constraints that their brother-sister masquerade entailed, it was delightful to have Thalarne close beside him all the time, delightful to know that night after night he could climb down from his upper berth and find her welcoming arms outstretched to him.

He was discovering, though, that that closeness was not without its drawbacks. In the cramped cabin they got on each other's nerves all too easily. She had brought a little collection of books, as much as she could gather on short notice about the Great World and Sea-Lords in particular the day she had left for Bornigrayal. During the long hours of the day Nortekku studied them avidly, for what little good that did: they all had the same information, most of it sketchy and speculative. Often, though, Thalarne wanted to consult them too. Somehow whichever book he happened to be reading was the one she needed to look at, right now—or the other way around. Often that led to sharpness between them.

They would heal these little conflicts, frequently, with bouts of coupling. But even that was hampered by the need not to be vocal in their taking of pleasure with each other lest they reveal to the Bornigrayans across the hall, or to some passing member of the crew, that their relationship was somewhat more intimate than that of brother and sister ordinarily should be.

Not that it was at all certain that they had anyone fooled. On a morning when the sea was especially rough Nortekku was passing the time in the ship's little lounge, and Thalarne had gone above—they tried now to give each other as much space as they could—when a couple of crewmen came down the stairs and one said to him, in that thick-tongued Bornigrayan dialect that Nortekku still had so much difficulty understanding, "You ought to go up. Your woman is sick on deck, pretty bad."

There was nothing unusual about that. The weather had mostly been stormy, eternally gray and windy, with much rain and sometimes sleet, and one or another of them had had a bout of seasickness practically every day. But Nortekku took exception to the phrasing.

"My *sister*, you mean."

"Your sister, yes." There was mockery in the man's unfriendly blue eyes. "Up there, sick, your sister, on deck." He winked suggestively. The other began to laugh.

Well, let them laugh, Nortekku thought. Having to pass himself off as Thalarne's brother hadn't been *his* idea.

He went up on deck. She was finished being sick, by then, but she looked dreadful. Nortekku laid his hand on her wrist and lightly rubbed the thick fur up and down by way of comfort, and she managed a faint, unconvincing smile.

"Bad?" he asked.

"Worse than seeing five sea-monsters crawling up on deck. But it's over now."

Just then the sea bucked beneath them, though, and the ship seemed to skip and hop above it, and from Thalarne came a dry ratcheting sound, followed almost at once by a little moan. She turned away from him, huddling miserably into herself. He held her, gently stroking her shoulders, and the spasm passed without further incident. With a game little grin she said, "I wonder how much longer this voyage is supposed to last."

"Only another four years or so," he told her. "Maybe three, if we remember to say our prayers every night."

Seasickness did not seem to afflict him. But as the days went by the restlessness that had plagued him since boyhood grew to a level that was barely tolerable. He prowled constantly from deck to deck, up, down, up, down, standing a long while in the sleety air abovedecks, and then, half frozen, descending to their cabin, where Thalarne sat poring over some map of Great World sites and looked anything but pleased to see him, and then up again, down again to the tiny lounge in the stern, up, down.

The time did pass, somehow. And it became evident, not many days later, that the worst of the voyage was behind them. Each day winter yielded a little more to spring, and the path of the ship had been trending all the while toward the southeast, so that now the skies were a clear blue the whole day long, no more rain fell, and the air was taking on some warmth. Birds were common sights overhead. Siglondan, who appeared to know something about natural history, said that they were shore-birds, coming out from the eastern continent just ahead of them.

She and Kanibond Graysz, with whom Thalarne and Nortekku took their meals every day, were speaking more openly now about the approaching fulfillment of the goals of the expedition. They seemed more slippery than ever, still cagy about what was actually supposed to be achieved. But what was becoming clear was that they had been bought, that their chief interest lay not in what could be learned about this handful of Sea-Lords that had so surprisingly endured beyond their supposed time of extinction, but in how much profit they could turn by prying loose rare artifacts for which the sponsors of the venture would pay extremely well. From something careless that Kanibond Graysz had let slip, Nortekku concluded that whatever collectible objects they brought back with them would be distributed among Til-Menimat and Hamiruld and the other backers according to some prearranged system, and the two Bornigrayan archaeologists would be given bonuses according to the quantity and quality of what they brought back for them.

A grimy business, Nortekku thought. And he knew what Thalarne thought of it as well. But she seemed able to balance her qualms against the advantage of being able to gain access to these improbable survivors from antiquity. He only hoped that she would emerge from the project with her own scientific reputation still untarnished.

The ship moved on, into warmer and warmer weather. Then there was a darkness on the horizon, which rapidly resolved itself into the skyline of a city.

"That's Sempinore there," Siglondan said. They had completed their crossing of the ocean; they were staring out at another continent, at a totally new world.

The city of Sempinore occupied a long looping crescent around a curving bay of sparkling blue water under a warm, inviting sun. He was unable to see either its beginning or its end. Its population, he thought, must be enormous. He felt awed and overwhelmed.

A grand boulevard ran along the shore parallel to the wharves, with swarms of wheeled vehicles moving swiftly up and down it, and porters guiding patient-looking red-furred beasts of burden that moved heedlessly among them. The air was sweet and fragrant, laden with the aroma of strange spices. There was noise everywhere, the shouts of the porters, the rhythmic chants of peddlers pushing heavily laden carts, the dissonant clash of unfamiliar music. Nortekku counted six wide, straight avenues radiating from the shoreline boulevard into different parts of the city: the main arteries, it would seem.

It was good to eat fresh tender meat that night, to drink sweet young wine again, and cool water from a nearby mountain spring, to fill one's mouth with the flavors of fruits and vegetables that hadn't spent weeks stored in casks. Good, also, to be at rest in a place solidly rooted in the ground, that didn't sway or pitch or heave on the bosom of the sea. At the hotel Nortekku and Thalarne were given separate rooms, as befitted brother and sister; but he came to her after dinner and they slept that night side by side, in an actual bed, in one another's arms. He left before dawn and returned to his own room, taking care not to be seen, though he doubted that any of their fellow travelers believed any longer that their relationship was what they had claimed it to be.

During the idle week they spent in Sempinore Nortekku devoted much time to a study of the city's architecture. The place had a profoundly alien look, and though he knew he should have expected that, it was a source of constant amazement for him.

Its buildings—whitewashed clusters of high domes, spidery aerial bridges high above the ground linking spiky-tipped towers, massive dark octagonal stone structures surrounded by the delicate traceries of pink fretwork walls—had a kind of consistency of style from one block to the next, but it was an alien consistency, a style that reminded him curiously of the imaginary Vengiboneeza that he had seen once in his dreams. They had been designed and built by people whose experiences had been nothing like those of his own people, whose history was in every way different, other than that they too had waited out the Long Winter in cocoons.

Those who dwelled here were folk who knew not Hresh, nor Koshmar nor Torlyri nor Thu-Kimnibol, nor any of the great Bengs, and they spoke a different language, a sibilant, whispering thing of which Nortekku couldn't comprehend a single word, and when they had reached the city-building stage of civilization they had built a city that reflected all those differences. There are only certain ways one can handle the enclosing of space, Nortekku knew—that was what architecture was primarily about, he believed, the enclosing of space. And there are only certain things one can do with light, with form, with proportion. And yet, given all that, many sorts of variants were possible within those basics: variant materials, variant strategies of structural support, and variant kinds of ornament, of cornices, windows, façades, pediments, colonnades. Wherever he looked here, he saw variants from what he considered the norm. Everything, *everything*, was different here. Yissou was different from Dawinno, yes, and Bornigrayal different from both of those in other ways, but this place was—does the phrase make sense, he wondered?—more different still. He felt a kind of vertigo of the soul, walking among its infinity of strange build-ings. This too was like a dream, the oddest kind of dream, in which one could not only see but also touch, and feel.

Thalarne sometimes accompanied him on these walks, sometimes not. When she was with him he tried to make clear the impact that this place was having on him. Sempinore had produced an odd rever-sal in their relationship: when the center of their discourse had been the world's ancient past, she was the teacher, he the novice, but now he was leading the way, endlessly analyzing and explaining the unfamiliar and sometimes almost unbelievable structural assumptions by which the buildings of Sempinore had been put together, and she followed his discourses as well as she could.

At last the reprovisioning job was complete and the time had come for the next stage of their journey.

Two Hjjks had come on board now. Nortekku glumly watched them arrive: like all their kind they were towering figures, taller than any man, with long gleaming bodies marked horizontally with bands of yellow and black, fearsome-looking beaks, narrow tapering heads topped by great feathery antennae, glittering blue-black eyes, deep constrictions marking the boundaries between head and thorax, tho-rax and abdomen. They were, he supposed, their guides, the two who had discovered the Sea-Lord colony across the Inland Sea. Apparently they were going to sleep on the main deck. They laid out a little Hjjk domain for themselves there, nailing talismans of plaited grass to the planks, setting up small wooden shrines that contained some smooth egg-shaped white stones, installing a cupboard that held a stock of the dried fruit and sun-parched meat that was their food.

He knew he would never understand Hjjks, nor come to have any liking for them. It was, he supposed, some kind of inherent racial ani-mosity, something that had run through him from birth, inbred in blood and bone. To him they were unsightly, ominous things, dry and cold of soul, alien, remote, dangerous. Some of that feeling was a legacy of the things he had been taught in school about the early wars between People and Hjjks for territory in the first years of the New Springtime, but that was just history now. The Hjjks posed no sort of menace at all. The old system of dominance by a central Queen operating out of a central Nest had been shattered by a civil war; the Queen of Queens had been put to death by her own military caste, in a punitive action typical of the icy Hjjk mentality, after a rebellion by the lesser Queens.

Now, Nortekku knew, each Nest was independent and the People's old sense of the Hjjks as an implacable monolithic entity had been replaced by an awareness that, divided as they were, they could no longer be any sort of threat. The two species lived together, not exactly in friendship—never that—but with a sort of cool mutual toleration. There was commerce now, not warfare, between the two species. Hjjks moved freely through the cities of the People and had taken up residence in certain sectors of them. It was too warm and humid for them in Dawinno, but you saw them wherever you went in Yissou, and there had been many of them in Bornigrayal, too. Even so, Nortekku still felt a reflexive stiffening of his spine whenever he was near one; and now there would be two of them as his companions for the rest of the voyage.

Kanibond Graysz and Siglondan could be seen up on deck with them most of the day, huddling in close conversations conducted in low, conspiratorial tones, the two Bornigrayans muttering in their rapid-fire Bornigrayan way and the Hjjks answering in their own harsh, chittering manner. Nortekku saw much sketching of diagrams, and handing of them back and forth, and a good deal of gesturing and pointing. There was something oddly secretive, almost unsavory, about these discussions that Nortekku found very puzzling. They made no attempt to draw their fellow archaeologist Thalarne into them, let alone Nortekku. He never even learned the names of the two Hjjks, if indeed—he had never been sure on that point—Hjjks had individual names. Well, he thought, whatever the Hjjks and the Bornigrayans had to say to each other was no concern of his. He was here to see the Sea-Lords; that, and to be with Thalarne.

The second voyage was wholly different from the first one. The Inland Sea was the most placid body of water imaginable, waveless, tideless, a shimmering blue pathway offering no challenges of any sort. The whole day long the sun filled the sky like a beacon, bright, huge, astonishingly warm, drawing them on to the south. From the side of the deck Nortekku could see the creatures of the depths in all their abundance, great schools of silvery fish swarming almost at the surface, occasional solitary giants hanging motionless nearby like underwater balloons and feeding, it seemed, on the great wads of seaweed that lay in clumps all about, and swift predators with the fins along their backs raised up into view like swords cutting the air. Once a mountainous turtle paddled close beside the ship, extended its long neck to stare at him in a glassy, unintelligent way, and slowly closed one eye in a grotesque parody of a wink. Such a profusion of maritime life, Nortekku realized, could not have developed just in the relatively few years since the thawing of the world. Whatever havoc the Long Winter had worked among the citizens of the Great World, it must not have brought complete devastation to these denizens of this warm sea.

In just a few days the shore came into view ahead of them, a long low line of sand and trees. The air was warm and soft. It was easy to believe that in this blessed place the Long Winter had never come, or, if it had, that it had brushed the land with only the gentlest of touches. They coasted westward past white beaches lined with trees of a kind Nortekku had never seen before, thick stubby brown trunks jutting upward from the sand to culminate in a single amazing explosion of long, jagged green leaves at the summit, like a crown of feathers. Farther back he saw wild tangles of vines all snarled together, blooming so profusely that they formed great blurts of color, a solid mass of magenta here, a burst of brilliant orange there, a huge spread of scarlet just beyond.

Late that afternoon they pulled into a protected cove where steamy mist was hovering above the water. Bubbles were visible along the western curve of the little bay, suggesting that a stream of heated water must be rising here from some volcanic furnace below the sea.

Large brown animals, perhaps as many as ten of them, were splashing about in the surf, diving, surfacing, beating the water with their flipperlike limbs, uttering loud trumpeting snorts. Nortekku assumed at first, carelessly, unthinkingly, that they were nothing more than seagoing mammals—akin, perhaps, to the good-natured barking bewhiskered beasts that often could be seen frolicking off the coast near Dawinno. But then, as the ship's dinghy carried him closer to the shore, he saw the luminous glow of what had to be intelligence in their sea-green eyes, and realized with a quick hard jolt of understanding and something not far from terror what these beings actually were.

It was if a doorway in time had rolled suddenly open and a segment of the ancient world had come jutting through.

Of course the two Hjjks who stood distressingly close by him in the dinghy were survivors of the Great World themselves, but one took the survival of the Hjjks for granted: they had never gone away, they had been part of the landscape from the first moment when the People began coming forth from their cocoons. Sea-Lords, though, were a dead race, extinct, the next thing to legendary. Yet here they were, seven, eight, ten of them close at hand in the steamy pinkish water of this cove, and more appearing now on shore, emerging from the trees that lined the beach and clumsily moving down toward the edge of the water on their flipperlike hind legs.

They displayed no sign of fear. The ones that had been in the water ceased to splash and snort, and now had gathered in a silent group to watch the dinghy's approach, but they seemed quite calm. So too did the ones on shore, collecting now in five or six groups just at the fringe of the sea. They were handsome animals, Nortekku thought, telling himself instantly that he must not call them animals, must never think of them that way. Their kind had been among the rulers of the world when his own ancestors had been apes chattering in the trees.

There might have been sixty of them all told, though others, possibly, might be lingering on the far side of the line of shallow dunes that rose just behind the trees, or out of sight at sea. They were gracefully tapering creatures, sturdily built, bigger and obviously stronger than men, with powerful, robust bodies that had a dense layer of sleek brown fur plastered close to their skin. Both their upper and lower sets of limbs were flipperlike, though Nortekku saw that their hands had capable-looking fingers with opposable thumbs. Their heads too were tapered, long and narrow, but with high-domed foreheads that indicated the force and capacity of the minds housed within.

"Such sadness," Thalarne said softly. "Do you see it, Nortekku? That look in their eyes—that misery, that pain—"

Yes. It was impossible not to perceive it, even from a distance: a look of the deepest sorrow, almost of grief. Those big glossy eyes, so close in color to her own, seemed without exception disconsolate, desolate, shrouded in lamentation. There was a touch of anger in those eyes, too, he thought, a hot blast of fury plainly visible behind that sadness. He asked himself whether he had any right to project emotion of any sort on these beings of another species, whose true feelings probably could not be read with any accuracy. And then he looked again, and it was the same as before: sorrow, grief, heartbreak, rage. They were strong, agile, handsome, graceful beings: they should have been happy creatures on this happiest of coasts. But that did not appear to be the case.

The dinghy came to rest in the shallows. "Is there a village here?" Thalarne asked Siglondan, as they scrambled ashore.

"We didn't find one last time, if by a village you mean permanent structures. They live mostly in the water, though they come up on shore for some part of every day and settle down for naps under the trees."

"Then they have no tools, either? Nothing that we'd call a culture?"

"Not any more. But they have language. They have a knowledge of their own race's history. We think that they may keep some shrines containing objects of Great World provenance somewhere not very far inland. They've pretty much reverted to a natural existence, but there's no doubt that they're genuine Sea-Lords." Pretentiously Siglondan added, "It's almost impossible for one to comprehend the full awesomeness of the discovery."

"Awesome, yes," Thalarne said. "And sad. So very sad. These pitiful creatures."

The Bornigrayan woman gave her an odd look. "Pitiful, did you say?" But Thalarne had already begun to wander off. Nortekku moved along after her. He glanced down toward the group of Sea-Lords by the shore; then, hastily, he glanced away. The thought of transgressing on the privacy of these beings whom he had come such a great distance to behold made him ill at ease. That expression of deep-seated melancholy mingled with rage that he imagined he saw in those huge glossy green eyes, whether it was really there or not, was something that suddenly he could not bear to see.

He considered what small stock of information he had about the Sea-Lord civilization of the Great World days. About all there was was the account in the book that Hresh had written, he who so many years ago had penetrated the ruined cities of the ancients and looked with his own eyes on their way of life by means of machines of theirs, no longer functional now, that had given him glimpses of their actual time.

The Sea-Lords, Hresh said, had been created by the humans out of some species of intelligent sea-going mammal, just as they had created the People out of apes. Like all mammals they breathed air, not water, but they were much more at home in the sea than on land, where they moved about with some degree of difficulty. When they were on land they traveled in cunningly made chariots that moved on silver treads, controlling them with manipulations of their flipper-fingers. Mainly, though, they lived at sea, guiding the vessels that carried all manner of costly merchandise from one part of the Great World to another. The other Great World races depended heavily on them. When they were in port, Hresh said, in the taverns and shops and waterfront restaurants that they frequented, they behaved like the bold, swaggering princes of the sea that they were.

And now—to have retrogressed to the simple life of water-going beasts—

The crewmen were putting up tents under the trees. Nortekku watched them for a while. Not that the sight of tents being raised was so fascinating, but just now he wanted to avoid coming close to the Sea-Lords, or even to look in their direction.

Siglondan and Kanibond Graysz didn't appear to feel any such inhibition. They and their two Hjjk confederates went quickly down to the nearest Sea-Lord group and involved themselves in what looked very much like a conversation with them. Nortekku could hear the clicking, buzzing sound of Hjjk-speak, then the quick chatter of the Bornigrayans, and then the Hjjks again, speaking in brief outbursts with long spans of silence between them. From time to time the Sea-Lords seemed to reply, with a sort of clipped grunting that had the cadence and phrasing of language. After each burst of it the Hjjks spoke again to the two Bornigrayans, as if interpreting what had just been said.

But how had the Hjjks learned the Sea-Lord language? By second sight, perhaps. Hjjks, Nortekku knew, had a kind of second sight that was much more powerful than that of the People. They were able to speak directly to minds with it: that was how they had first communicated with the newly emerged People in the early days of the Going Forth. Perhaps they had used it to develop some understanding of Sea-Lord speech, too.

Thalarne now had joined the group and was listening attentively. Curiosity overcame Nortekku's uneasiness: it felt foolish to hang back like this. He took himself down the sloping strand to the place close by the water where the others were gathered but the gathering broke up just as he arrived. The Sea-Lords headed into the water and the two Bornigrayans, with the pair of Hjjks, went off up the beach. Thalarne alone remained.

She gave him a stricken look as he approached.

"What was all that about?" Nortekku asked.

She seemed to be struggling to shape an answer. Then she said, "There's something very bad going on here, but I'm not altogether sure what it is. All I can tell you is that we aren't just imagining what we think we see in their eyes. One good look will tell you that. It's very clear that these people are aware of their own tragedy. They know what they once were; they know what they are now. You just have to look into those eyes and you know that they're the eyes of people who can't understand why they're still alive, and don't want to be any more. People who wish they were dead, Nortekku."

Who wish they were dead? For a moment Nortekku made no reply. He had never seen her look so deeply unnerved. It was easy enough to believe that there was something tragic about the expression in these creatures' eyes: he had seen it himself, from far away. But how could she be certain of this startling interpretation of it? The grunting speech of the Sea-Lords and the mind-speech of the Hjjks were closed books to her, Nortekku knew.

"You heard the Hjjks tell this to Kanibond Graysz and Siglondan?"

She shook her head. "I got there too late to hear anything important. It was all winding down by then. I'm speaking purely intuitively."

"Ah. I see. And you trust that intuition, Thalarne?"

"Yes. I do." She was steadier now. "I looked into those eyes, Nortekku. And what they were saying was, *We want to die. Show us how to do it. You are great ones who can cross the mighty sea; surely you can give this little thing to us. Surely. Surely. Surely.*"

That was going much too far, Nortekku told himself. This was hardly the method of science, as he understood that concept. The look in their eyes: was something like that a sufficient basis for so fantastic a theory? But Thalarne seemed wholly carried away by it. He had to be careful here. Cautiously he said, "You may be right. But I just can't help but think that you're making an awfully big intuitive leap."

"Of course I am. And I've already told you I'm not fully sure of it myself. Just go and stand close to them, though, and you can see for yourself. Those eyes are sending a message without any ambiguity at all. They're pleading for it, Nortekku. They're crying out for it."

"For death."

"For death, yes. For the extinction that somehow was denied them when the rest of the Great World was destroyed. They want to die, Nortekku, but they don't know how to manage it. It's almost as if they're saying they want us to kill them. To put them out of their misery."

"But that's insane!" Nortekku said, brushing at the air as though to push the concept away.

"Well, then, so they're insane. Or half insane, anyway. Or perhaps they're so terribly sane that to us they seem crazy."

"Asking to be killed—asking to be made extinct—"

Perhaps there was something to it. He had seen those eyes himself. She was simply guessing, but the guess had a cold plausibility about it. But was Thalarne hinting, then, that she felt that their wish ought to be granted?

Surely not.

The idea was repellent, unthinkable, horrifying. It was a violation of all she believed, and he as well. She was a scientist, not an executioner. She had come here to investigate this surprising remnant of the Great World, to learn all that could be learned about it, not to extirpate it. And for him the survival of these Sea-Lords was a marvelous boon, a miraculous restoration of a small piece of a vanished world.

With short, quick, troubled steps he began to pace back and forth, ankle-deep, at the margin of the gentle surf. Thalarne, moving along beside him, said, "Their whole context is gone. They're all alone in a world they are no longer part of, one that they don't like or understand. They have the intelligence their race had in the old days, or nearly so, but there's nothing to apply it to, no framework to fit into, no world to belong to. So they swim and copulate and catch fish all day. Does that sound good to you? Then try it. Try it for ten, twenty, fifty years. Watch your parents growing old in such a life. Watch your children entering into it. They live a long time, Nortekku. They try not to bring new generations into being, but it happens. They think their gods have forgotten them. Their life is meaningless, and it goes on and on and on. It's driven them halfway to madness. And so they want to die. If only they knew how."

"Well, maybe so. We can't really know. But of course, even if that's what they want, we couldn't possibly—"

"No. Of course not," she said quickly. "How could we even consider it?"

That much was a relief, he thought.

"But that's why this situation, if I'm right about it, is so tragic," she went on. "And that's why we need to find out much more about them."

"Yes," Nortekku said. "Yes, definitely." He would have said anything, just then. He wanted to get away from this whole subject as fast as he could.

"Come with me," Thalarne said abruptly. "Up there, behind those dunes, where Siglondan thinks there may be shrines. Places where artifacts are kept."

That made him uneasy too. "Should we go there, do you think? Wouldn't it be sacrilege?"

"Just to look. Siglondan and Kanibond Graysz surely will, before very long."

Getting over the dunes was no trivial task. Very little vegetation of any kind grew on them, and the loose sand slipped and slid beneath their feet. Thalarne pointed out places where the Sea-Lords themselves had worn deep tracks, compacting the dunes with their flippers, and they followed those. On the far side the air was still and very warm, heavy with the stifling interior heat of this continent: nowhere could they feel the sea breeze that made the strip by the shore so pleasant. Strange spiky plants were growing here, tall, stiff-armed, leafless, bristling with spines. These stood everywhere about, like guardians in the sandy wasteland. It was hard to follow the track here, but after a little searching Nortekku found something that had the look of a path, and they took it.

By trial and error they made their way to a place where, no question about it, many flippered feet had passed. The sand was packed down hard. There was a second row of dunes here, much more stable ones, tightly bound by low sprawling shrubs interwoven with gray clumps of tough, sharp-edged grass.

"Look here," Thalarne said.

Three bare metal frameworks sat in a row at the foot of the dunes: mere shapes, the fragile outlines of things rather than the things themselves. But from those shapes it seemed clear that these were the remnants of three of the vehicles—"chariots," Hresh had called them—by which the ancient Sea-Lords had traveled when ashore. The ghostly hints of levers, of wheels, of seats, all gave credence to that idea.

There was a sign, also, of a passageway into the dune, a tunnel roofed over by wooden arches. Nortekku and Thalarne exchanged glances. He saw her eagerness.

"No," he said. "We mustn't. Not without their permission."

"Even though Kanibond Graysz and Siglondan will—"

"Let them. We can't. This has to be a sacred place."

He knew that Thalarne conceded the strength of that argument. But in any case the decision was taken from their hands, for a Sea-Lord had appeared from somewhere, an elderly one, it seemed, a male, stooped and bowed, with silvered fur and veiled, blinking eyes, who came shuffling up to them and took up a stance between them and the three chariots. The custodian of this place, perhaps—a priest, maybe. He had the sadness in his eyes too, and possibly also the anger that Nortekku believed lay behind it, but mainly they were tired eyes, very old, very weary. The Sea-Lord said something in a barely audible tone, low and husky, and, after a brief silence, said it again.

"He wants us to leave, I think," Nortekku said. But of course the old Sea-Lord could have been saying almost anything else.

Thalarne agreed, all too readily. "Yes. Yes, that has to be it."

She smiled at the Sea-Lord and turned her hands outward, apologetically, and the two of them moved away, back toward the encampment by the water. The Sea-Lord remained where he was, watching them go.

"Will you tell the Bornigrayans about this?" Nortekku asked.

"I have to," said Thalarne. "We're not here as competitors. They've shared a lot of things with me. They'll find it by themselves before long, anyway. You know that."

"Yes," he said. "I imagine they will."

The eyes of that old Sea-Lord haunted him as they picked their way back over the outer dune. Thinking of him, Nortekku felt again a sense of the great age of the world into which his own people had erupted so recently. *His* world was new and young, only two centuries old, bursting with the vigor that came with having been let free of the cocoons after seven hundred thousand years in hiding. But now he saw more clearly than ever that the world of the New Springtime was but a thin overlay masking the dead, used-up world that had preceded it—masking a whole succession of dead, used-up worlds, going back to who knew what pre-human mysteries.

So you are back to that, he thought. The transience of everything, the eternal cycle of decay and extinction. That is a grim and cheerless way of looking at things, he told himself. It is a vision devoid of all hope.

But in that same bleak moment came once again the opposite thought, the compensating and comforting one, the thought that the world is a place of constant renewal through billions of years, and that that renewal was a never-ending process that held out the promise of eternal life. World after world, world without end.

I will cling to that idea, Nortekku told himself. I must. I must.

❋

The next morning Thalarne led the two Bornigrayan archaeologists to the site on the far side of the dunes. Nortekku was still displeased about that, but grudgingly he accepted her argument that it would be unethical for one member of the expedition to conceal an important find from the others. He had to bear in mind, she reminded him, that she was here—and he as well—only because they had invited her along.

There was something wrong with that line of reasoning, but Nortekku did not feel like taking the matter up with her. She was here, in fact, because her husband had wanted to send her somewhere far away, someplace where her lover wouldn't be able to find her: it was for that reason, and no other, that Hamiruld had arranged to have her included in what was fundamentally an expedition designed to produce new plunder for those wealthy highborn collectors of antiquities who were paying the venture's expenses. Whatever scientific information might be gathered was strictly incidental. And so, even though it struck Nortekku as folly to be worrying about ethical issues when dealing with such people as Siglondan and Kanibond Graysz, he wasn't in a good position to be urging her to conceal finds from them. The truth of the situation was, he conceded, that he and Thalarne were fundamentally helpless here.

Helplessly, therefore, they accompanied the Bornigrayans to the place of the chariots. The old Sea-Lord custodian was nowhere in sight. That was a blessing, Nortekku thought. Helplessly they looked on as Kanibond Graysz, using a power torch, went slithering into the tunnel that entered the dune. Helplessly they watched him emerge with objects: a rusted helmet that had an air of immense age about it, a knobby-tipped rod of scabby yellow metal that might have been a scepter, a battered bronze box inscribed with curvilinear writing of a Great World sort.

"Nothing else in there," Kanibond Graysz reported. "Just these three things, scattered about at random. But it's a start. We'll need to excavate to see if other things are buried beneath the floor. Tomorrow, perhaps."

Little was said by anybody as they returned to camp. But once Nortekku and Thalarne were back in the tent that they shared—the pretense that they were brother and sister had long since been abandoned—he found, to his horror, that he could not keep himself from raising the issue that he knew he must not raise with her.

"That made me sick, what happened today. It's theft, Thalarne. You said yourself, back in Bornigrayal, that it's one thing to collect objects from a site that's been abandoned for a million years, and something very different to steal them from living people."

"Yes. That's true."

"And yet you just stood there while he went in and took those things. Even leaving the ethical issues out of the question, I ask you, Thalarne: is that good archaeological technique, just to walk in and pick up objects, without recording stratification or anything else?—But then there are the ethical issues too."

She made no attempt to hide her anguish. "Let me be, Nortekku. I don't have any answers for you."

He pressed onward anyway. "Is it your position that since these people don't care a hoot whether they live or die, it doesn't matter what we do with the things that belong to them? We aren't sure that that's how they feel, you know. It's just a speculation."

"A very likely one, though."

"Well, then—granting that you're right—can we really feel free to help ourselves to their possessions while they're still alive?"

"Let me be, Nortekku," Thalarne said again, tonelessly. "Can't you see that I'm caught between all sorts of conflicting forces, and there's nothing I can do? *Nothing.*"

He saw that it was dangerous to push her any further. There was nothing she could do, nor he, for that matter. Nor would she allow any further debate about this. It was as though she had pulled an impenetrable curtain down around herself.

The days went by. Nortekku stayed away, most of the time, when the Bornigrayans went over the dunes to poke in the caches of hidden artifacts back there. Usually Thalarne went with them, sometimes not, but when she did go she had little to report to Nortekku about anything they might have found there. It couldn't have been much, he knew: Kanibond Graysz said something about that, one night at dinner, remarking on how scrappy and insignificant most of their finds had been. The sponsors of the expedition were going to be disappointed. Too bad, Nortekku thought, but he kept his opinions to himself.

He still could not bring himself to go near the Sea-Lords. They spent much of their time in the water, often far out from shore where it would not have been possible to go, but when they returned to the beach he kept his distance from them. The unhappiness that they emanated was too contagious: being near them plunged him into gloom. Now and then he would see one of them looking toward him with that poignant, yearning stare of theirs. He would always look away.

His estrangement from Thalarne saddened him as much as what the archaeologists were doing in the dunes. They still shared a tent, they still would couple from time to time, but there was no lifting of the invisible barrier that had fallen between them. Since he was unable to discuss anything with her involving the Sea-Lords, about all that was left to talk about was the weather, and the weather was unchanging, warm and sunny and calm day after day.

It surprised him not at all when the two Bornigrayans returned from a trip to the inner dune one morning, accompanied by their two Hjjks, who were carrying one of the Great World Sea-Lord chariots on an improvised litter of planks that had been brought from the ship. Of course they would take one of the chariots: of course. There had been so little else of any note to bring back. The chariot was a major prize, worthy of the finest collection.

The Sea-Lords who were nearby didn't seem to be in any way upset as the chariot was stowed aboard the dinghy and transported to the ship. Shouldn't they be protesting this flagrant theft of one of their most sacred objects? Apparently they didn't care. They looked on in the same uninvolved, passive way they had greeted everything else since the landing of the expedition on their shore. Either the chariot wasn't really sacred to them, or, as Thalarne believed, they had so thoroughly divested themselves of all will to live that its removal couldn't possibly make any difference to them. If so, then he had been wrong to berate Thalarne after the Bornigrayans' initial intrusion into the artifact cache, and he needed to tell her that. Even if the Sea-Lords didn't care, though, he did, and it saddened him greatly to watch what was happening.

Siglondan herself admitted to some vestigial guilt over the removal of the chariot. In a rare moment of openness she said to Nortekku, as they stood together by the shore watching the dinghy return, "I can't help feeling that this is hurting them. That chariot is practically all that they have left to remember their ancestors by. We haven't ever excavated a site that still has living descendants of the ancients on it before. But Kanibond Graysz thinks it's such an important object that we simply have to take it. It's not as though it's their only one."

It was the first sign Nortekku had seen of any compassion for the Sea-Lords in her, or of the slightest disagreement on a policy issue between Siglondan and her mate. Kanibond Graysz seemed all greed, all ice. Siglondan, at least, had revealed some flickerings of conscience just now.

He said, feeling some elusive need to reassure her, "Well, if they just don't care about anything, if they even regret that they're alive at all—"

It was the wrong thing to say. The Bornigrayan woman shot him a peculiar look. "That wild fantasy of Thalarne's, eh? That they want to die? That they're a bitter people who think their gods have forgotten them? That they're looking for a way to get us to put them out of their misery? You believe it too, do you?"

"I don't know what I believe. I have no evidence to work with."

"Neither does she."

"So you think she's wrong?"

"Of course I do. Kanibond Graysz and I have had conversations with them, you know."

"But everything gets filtered through the Hjjks, and who knows what distortions the things that they're saying pick up along the way?"

She shrugged. "This isn't a matter of translation. This is a matter of understanding the realities that are right here around us. The notion Thalarne is trying to put forth is crazy, Nortekku, completely crazy. The Sea-Lords have given us no indication whatever of a death-wish. If she tries to propose such an idea publicly, we'll oppose her at every step." He could feel Siglondan drawing back, closing down. The openness of a few moments before was gone now. Her voice had taken on a cold, formal intonation. She was angry and defensive. "Has your—*sister*— told you that she not only believes they want to die, she's willing to help them achieve it?"

"She told me that we mustn't even consider it."

"Well, she *is* considering it, regardless of anything she might have told you. I know that she is. But even if her theory about them is right, and there's no reason to think that it is, we couldn't possibly allow any such thing to happen. You understand that, I hope. These beings are infinitely precious. They're the last few of their kind, so far as we know, the only survivors of a great ancient culture. We have to protect their lives at all cost. We're preservers of the past, Nortekku, not destroyers." And with a barren little smile she moved on toward her tent.

He stood looking after her, bewildered. He had no idea where he stood in any of this. After hearing Siglondan's scornful dismissal, Thalarne's theory did indeed seem wild, fantastic, almost frightening in its arbitrary assumptions. And yet, when you studied a Sea-Lord's eyes, when you saw that terrible look that could only be an expression of intolerable grief and rage and longing and despair, it didn't seem all that arbitrary. But as for enabling the Sea-Lords to die, as an act of compassion, if that was what Thalarne was advocating—and she had denied that, had she not?—the concept was too absurd even to consider. To kill the very creatures they had come here to find—no—no—

As he struggled with these matters Nortekku became aware of figures moving up the beach toward him—a couple of Sea-Lords, females, by the size of them, and one of the Hjjks trailing along a few paces behind. Automatically he turned to go. Even less than ever, now, did he want to be in any sort of proximity to a Sea-Lord.

But before he could take more than a few steps the bigger of the two Sea-Lords, moving with surprising swiftness, closed the distance between them in a few long sliding strides. One of its flippers shot out and grabbed his arm. The webbed fingers tightened around his wrist. Grunting, barking, it pulled him roughly toward it, swinging him around so that they stood face to face.

He was too amazed even to feel afraid. For a moment he was conscious only of the fishy reek of the creature, and of the great shining bristles that jutted from its muzzle, and—yes—of its huge glistening eyes, close to his own, staring at him with a frightful intensity. There was no way he could break its grip. The Sea-Lord was as big as he was, and much stronger. He leaned away as far as he could, holding himself rigid, averting his head. A further series of low barking grunts came from it.

"Tell it to let go of me," Nortekku said to the Hjjk, who was standing by in utter unconcern.

"It will release you when it is ready to release you," said the Hjjk in that dispassionate Hjjk way of theirs. "First it will finish what it is saying."

Saying? Yes. Nortekku observed now that those grunts had a structured rhythm to them, the balance and even the audible punctuation of what must surely be a language. It was indeed trying to say something to him. But what?

"I can't understand you," Nortekku told the Sea-Lord futilely. "Let me go! Let go!" And, to the Hjjk: "What's it saying, then?"

The Hjjk replied, evasively, in the clickings and chitterings of its own tongue, which Nortekku had never mastered.

He glared at the insect-man's great-beaked face. "No," he said. "Tell it so I can understand."

"What it is is the usual thing," said the Hjjk, after a moment. "It is asking for your help."

"My—help?" Nortekku said, and a monstrous realization began to dawn in him. "What kind of help?"

The Sea-Lord was finished with its oration, now. It loosed its hold on Nortekku's wrist and stepped back, watching him expectantly. Nortekku turned once more to the Hjjk.

"What kind of help?" he demanded again.

Once again the Hjjk answered him, maddeningly, in Hjjk.

Nortekku snatched up a driftwood log that was lying near his right foot and brandished it under the Hjjk's jutting beak. "Tell it the right way, or by all the gods, I'll pull you apart and feed your fragments to the fishes!"

The Hjjk showed no sign of alarm. Crossing its uppermost arms across its thorax in what might have been a gesture of self-protection, but which had more of an aura of unconcern, it said blandly, "It would like to end its life. It wishes that you would teach it how to die. This is the thing that they always are saying, you know."

Yes. Yes, of course. *Teach it how to die.* Precisely what he had not wanted to hear, precisely what he would prefer not to face. Precisely what Thalarne had already guessed. *It is the thing that they are always saying.*

Thalarne did not seem surprised at all, when he told her of his encounter with the Sea-Lord. It was as if she had been expecting vindication of this kind to come at any moment.

"It *had* to be, Nortekku. I felt it from my first glimpse of them." Wonderingly she said, "It wants us to teach it how to die! Which means they can't achieve it on their own—they probably don't even have the *concept* of suicide. So they've been asking and asking, ever since we got here. And of course those two have been suppressing it. The Sea-Lords are their big asset, their key to fame and fortune and scientific glory. They'd never permit anything to happen to them."

"And you would?"

"No. You know I wouldn't. Couldn't. It isn't possible to take a responsibility like that into one's own hands."

He nodded. He wished he could hear more conviction in her voice.

She went on, "What I would do—what I *will* do—is file a report with the Institute about all this when I get back. And with the government of Yissou, and I suppose with the Presidium of Dawinno also. And let *them* decide what to do about the Sea-Lords."

"You know that Kanibon Graysz and Siglondan will file a dissenting report."

"Let them. The powers that be can hire their own Hjjk interpreters and send their own expedition out here and find out themselves what the Sea-Lords do or don't want. The decision's not up to us. But how good it is, Nortekku, that you discovered what you did. I was sure of it, but I had no proof. And now—"

"Proof? All you have, Thalarne, is the word of a Hjjk that that's what the Sea-Lord was saying.

"It's a step toward understanding what's happening here," she said. "A very important one. And why would a Hjjk invent anything so fantastic? The Hjjks aren't famous for their great imaginations. I don't think they tell a lot of lies, either. Neither one of them would have volunteered a word about this on its own, but when you asked for a translation—"

"It gave me one. Yes. And an accurate one, I suppose. They're too indifferent to want to tell lies, aren't they?"

It wishes that you would teach it how to die.

No. No. No. No.

He and Thalarne agreed to say nothing more about any of this, neither to each other nor, certainly, to the Bornigrayans, until they had returned to their home continent. Siglondan had made it quite clear where she and her mate stood on the subject of Thalarne's Sea-Lord theory. There was nothing to gain but trouble by debating it with them now.

Later in the week, as it became clear that the visit was winding down, Nortekku heard the sound of hammering coming from the ship as it sat at anchor off shore. The ship's carpenters must be doing some remodeling on board. Then came Kanibond Graysz's announcement that the ship would leave the next morning: the only thing that remained, he said, was to round up the Sea-Lord specimens that they were taking back, and put them on board the—

"*What* did you say?" Thalarne asked incredulously.

"To round up the Sea-Lord specimens," the Bornigrayan said again. And then, in a droning, official tone: "Our charter empowers us to bring up to four Sea-Lords back with us to Bornigrayal, where they will be placed in a congenial environmental situation so that they can undergo careful study in the most sympathetic surroundings possible."

"I don't believe this," Thalarne said. Her whole body had gone taut. "You're going to take *prisoners*? Intelligent autonomous beings are going to be collected by you and brought home and turned into zoological exhibits?"

"That is in our charter. It was the understanding from the beginning. I can show you the authorization we have—the signatures of such important figures as Prince Samnibolon of Dawinno, and Prince Til-Menimat—"

"No," Thalarne said. "This can't be."

"And of your own husband, lady, Prince Hamiruld of Yissou—"

"Hamiruld doesn't have the rank of prince," said Thalarne, absurdly, in the faintest of voices. She looked stunned. Turning from the Bornigrayan as if he had uttered some vile obscenity, she hurried off up the beach toward the tents. Nortekku went running after her. He caught up with her just outside the tent.

"Thalarne—"

Panting, wild-eyed, she whirled to face him. "Did you hear that? This is outrageous! We can't let them do it, Nortekku!"

"We can't?"

"We could make a case out for *killing* the Sea-Lords, if that's what they genuinely want. But to put them on display in a zoo? Coddled, peered at, *imprisoned*? Their lives will be even more nightmarish than they already are."

"I agree. This is very ugly."

"Worse than ugly: criminal. We won't allow it."

"And just how will we stop it, then?"

"Why—why—" She paused only briefly. "We'll explain to the captain and his men that what these two want to do is illegal, that he and his whole crew will be making themselves accessories to a crime—"

"They'll laugh in our faces, Thalarne. Their pay comes from Kanibond Graysz, not from us. The captain takes his orders from Kanibond Graysz."

"Then we'll prevent the ship from setting out if it has any Sea-Lords aboard."

"How?" Nortekku asked again.

"We'll figure something out. Damage the engine, or something. We *can't* let this happen. We *can't*."

"If we make any sort of trouble," Nortekku said quietly, "they'll simply throw us overboard. Or at best put us in irons and keep us chained up until the ship has docked at Bornigrayal. Believe me, Thalarne: there's isn't any way we can stop this. None. None. None."

He made her see it, finally, though it took some time. He got her to see, also, that he was as horrified by Kanibond Graysz' scheme as she was, that he was in no way condoning it when he said they must simply abide by what was going to occur. There were just the two of them against a whole crew of burly Bornigrayan sailors who weren't going to collect their pay until they had fulfilled their obligations under their contract with their employers. And it struck him as far from implausible that he and Thalarne would be dumped into the middle of the ocean if they made themselves sufficiently obstreperous. Kanibond Graysz could tell any sort of story he pleased. *The woman fell overboard during rough weather*, he could say, *and the man jumped in to rescue her, and then—they were surrounded by flesh-eating fish—there was nothing we could do to save them—nothing—*

It was a shameful affair, hideous, morally repugnant. But it couldn't be halted. He and Thalarne would have to stand by and watch it happen, which in effect turned them into accomplices. He had never felt so powerless in his life.

This is Hamiruld's revenge, he thought.

Helpless once more, he watched stonily as Kanibond Graysz pointed out four of the Sea-Lords on the beach, two males, two females, to the crewmen of the ship. Eight or ten of the crewmen, wielding electric prods, surrounded one of the female Sea-Lords and hustled her into the water and aboard the dinghy. Nortekku expected her to resist, to fling the crewmen away from her as though they were discarded dolls—even the females, smaller than the males, were powerfully muscular creatures—but, no, the prods never were needed, there was no resistance at all, not even when the Bornigrayans produced a thick rope and swiftly wrapped it about her upper flippers to prevent her from escaping. She remained quiescent as they heaved her into the dinghy, as they rowed back to the ship, as they pulled her up on deck. It went the same way with the other three. Neither the other female nor the two males, huge and brawny though they were, gave any indication of being aware of what was taking place.

It is true, then, about their wanting to die, Nortekku realized. Life is already over for them; nothing remains but the actual moment of termination. What happens to them between now and then is of no concern to them whatever.

Still, it had been sickening to watch the capture. The Sea-Lords might not care, but *he* did, and, of course, Thalarne, who was so strongly affected by it that it was several days before she came up far enough from her depression even to feel like speaking.

By then they were well out to sea. The continental coast behind them dwindled to the most imperceptible line and then vanished altogether. The course was a straight westerly one: they would not be going back to Sempinore, either to reprovision or to drop off the two Hjjk guides, but would, rather, leave the Inland Sea as soon as possible and head right across the Eastern Ocean to Bornigrayal with their booty.

Nortekku knew now what the hammering aboard the ship had been. They had converted the two storage holds at the ship's stern into one large tank for the Sea-Lords. Some kind of siphon arrangement brought fresh ocean water up into the tank each day. Thus the four captives would have access to the environment in which they preferred to spend most of their time. At mid-morning each day they were brought out for exercise on the desk—a solemn ritual in which they flapped up and back for half an hour or so—and then they lay basking until it was time for them to return to their cabins. The ropes with which they had been pinioned had been removed. It would have been simple enough for them to leap over the rail and make their way back to their home at the edge of the southern continent; but either they believed that they were already too far from home to be able to accomplish the journey, or, what was more probable, their being prisoners here aboard the ship was of no consequence to them. All four seemed to be living in some private world. They paid no attention to their captors. Mostly they were silent; occasionally they spoke with one another in their language of grunts and barks, but once, when Thalarne asked one of the Hjjks for a translation, the Hjjk merely stared at her as though her own language were unintelligible to it.

The westward crossing was far easier than the eastward voyage had been. Spring had come to the ocean, now, and the air was nearly as warm as it was when they were in the region of the Inland Sea. There were no storms, only occasional gentle showers. An easy wind came from behind them, helping them along.

Nortekku and Thalarne were standing on the deck as the ship docked at Bornigrayal Harbor. Suddenly she caught her breath as though in shock, and grasped his wrist tightly with both her hands. He turned to her, amazed.

"Look! Look! Down there, Nortekku!"

He glanced down, toward the quay, where the deckhands were tying up the ship.

Hamiruld was standing there.

Thalarne could barely speak. Only choked monosyllables came from her. "How—why—"

"Easy, Thalarne. Easy."

Struggling to regain her self-control, she said, "But what's he *doing* here? What does he want? He should be back in Yissou. He's got no business being here!"

Nortekku, feeling shaken also by the presence of Thalarne's mate here, so far from their home, stared toward the slight, wiry figure of Hamiruld and was appalled to see him cheerily smiling and waving at them. The loving husband showing up at the pier to welcome his wife and a friend of hers as they returned from a little trip, yes. How sweet of him.

This is very bad, Nortekku thought.

As calmly as he could he said, "He's come to claim you back, I suppose. Someone must have told him I flew out to Bornigrayal after you. Khardakhor, perhaps. Or even Prince Vuldimin." Could that be, he wondered? Would he have cared that much? A more reasonable possibility presented itself.—"Or perhaps he's just here to represent the syndicate. I suspect they'd want to check up on our two Bornigrayan friends, and make sure that when the ship is unloaded they don't go walking off with any Sea-Lord finds that don't belong to them."

Either way, it was the worst finish to the voyage he could imagine, except, possibly, if the ship had gone down at sea with the loss of all aboard. First to discover the dolorous state of the little Sea-Lord colony, then to have to participate, however involuntarily, in the capture of the four who had come back with them, and now to be confronted in the moment of their arrival by Thalarne's mean-souled, spiteful little husband—

Hamiruld was courtesy itself, though, as they landed. He came sprinting up on deck as soon as the boarding ramp had been laid down, saluted the captain, warmly embraced Thalarne—she held herself stiffly away from him as he hugged her—and even clapped Nortekku exuberantly on the shoulder. He proffered no explanation for being here on this side of the continent. He let them know that had already heard reports of the great success of the expedition and that he wanted to hear all the details, that night, at the hotel in town where they would all be staying. He had rented the finest rooms; there would be a grand celebratory feast.

"I will be spending the night aboard the ship, I think," said Nortekku coolly. He assumed that Hamiruld would sweep Thalarne up into his own luxurious suite at the hotel, and the last thing he wanted was to be under the same roof. "There are a few details I have to finish up— I need to organize my notes, to do some final packing—"

Hamiruld looked a little surprised at that, but not greatly troubled. All his attention was focused on Thalarne.

She, though, said just as coolly, "I will be staying aboard the ship tonight also, Hamiruld."

At that a flash of quick fury came up into his eyes, like a goblin-face appearing at a window. Then, just as quickly, he grew calm again. "You will? And why is that, Thalarne?"

"I'd rather speak with you privately about that," she said.— "Nortekku? Would you excuse us for a moment?"

She was in full command, now. Obediently Hamiruld allowed her to march him off toward the ship's bow, and just as obediently Nortekku swung around and walked to the other side of the ship, where he could look outward into the harbor instead of having to observe their conversation from a distance.

It went on a very long while. It was one of the longest moments of his life. Then she returned, grim-faced, her jaw tightly set. Glancing across, Nortekku saw that Hamiruld was gone from the deck, that he had descended once again to the pier.

"Well?" Nortekku asked.

"I told him that we had brought four living Sea-Lords back with us, and that I wanted him to have them released. I told him that I would leave him, if he didn't."

The conditional nature of that threat left Nortekku feeling chilled. But all he said, when she did not continue, was: "And then?"

"And then he shrugged. He said, 'You're going to leave me anyway, aren't you? So why should I let them go?' And that was all. He's going back to the hotel now. I'll stay with you aboard the ship."

In the night Thalarne awakened him and said, "Do you hear noises, Nortekku?"

"Noises?" He had been in the deepest of sleeps.

"Thumps. Shouts. A scream, maybe."

Nortekku pushed himself upward through the fog that shrouded his mind. Yes, there *were* noises. Muffled thumpings. A panicky outcry. Another. Then deep-voiced grunting sounds that could only be the bellowings of Sea-Lords.

"Someone's in there with them in the tank," she said. "Listen—that sound's coming from a Sea-Lord. But that one isn't."

"Hamiruld?" Nortekku suggested, pulling the idea out of the blue. "Could it be that he's come on board, and—"

But she was already up and on her way out of the cabin. Nortekku ran madly after her, down the corridor, up the little flight of well-worn stairs, and down the upper corridor that led toward the stern of the ship and the tank of the captive Sea-Lords. The door of their hold was open. The light was on inside.

Hamiruld, yes.

What was he doing on board? Who knew? Here to gloat over his invaluable prisoners, maybe? Or simply making sure that Thalarne and Nortekku weren't going to release them in the night?

But he seemed to be under attack. He was at the back of the hold, up on the narrow boardwalk that ran along three sides of the room around the edges of the tank, and the four Sea-Lords stood crowding around him, jostling him roughly. They were clustered close, pushing fiercely at him with their shoulders, buffeting him from one to another, and Hamiruld, crying out in terror and pain, was trying to get out from among them. The two big males seemed to be letting the females do most of the shoving, but even they were bigger than Hamiruld, and when they thrust themselves against him he went ricocheting back like a flimsy toy.

"They'll kill him!" Thalarne cried.

Nortekku nodded. It was hard to believe, these gentle, passive creatures wanting to kill, but surely the rough sport they were having with

Hamiruld was doing great injury. And very likely they would kill any-one who tried to intervene, too. He hesitated, uncertain of what to do, looking around for something he could use to push the Sea-Lords back from him.

Then came footsteps in the corridor. Crewmen appearing, five or six of them, the night watch belatedly putting in its appearance.

Nortekku pointed. "Don't you see what's happening?"

They could see it, yes, and, seizing electric prods from a case mounted just inside the door, they ran into the room and headed down the boardwalk.

At the sight of them, the Sea-Lords closed in even more tightly. Hamiruld was completely hidden by them now. Out of the center of the group came a single horrible shriek, high-pitched, cracking at the end. Then the crewmen were in the midst of the melee themselves, jab-bing at the Sea-Lords with the prods, trying to push them back into the water of the tank. One of the males swung a broad flipper at the nearest crewman and knocked him on a high curving arc into the tank. The other men danced backward, then approached with their prods again. There came the hissing sound of electrical discharges—the bright flash of light at the tips of the prods—

"No!" Thalarne called. "Not maximum! Don't use maximum!"

Everything dissolved into confusion, then—Sea-Lords and crewmen lurching back and forth on the narrow platform, prods hissing, lights flashing, Hamiruld nowhere to be seen—and then, abruptly, it was over.

Two of the crewmen were in the tank. The rest stood gasping against the wall. All four of the Sea-Lords lay sprawling on the board-walk, motionless. The crumpled figure of Hamiruld, broken and bent, was face-down at the edge of the tank, motionless also.

Nortekku and Thalarne, who had remained in the doorway through-out the struggle, moved out along the boardwalk now. Thalarne knelt beside Hamiruld. She touched his shoulder with the tip of a finger, very gently. Then she looked up.

"Dead, I think."

"I imagine he is," said Nortekku. He had reached one of the Sea-Lord females. "This one is, too. And this. They all are, all four. These idiots did have their prods turned to maximum!"

"Dangerous animals," one of the crewmen mumbled. "Gone berserk. Anything could have happened. Look, they killed that man who came from the city—"

"Yes. So they did. And they're dead too."

So four of them, at least, had had their wish. The Sea-Lords at rest were awesome, mysterious, calm. There was a rightness, he thought, about their death. They were creatures out of place in time, who should have died when the Great World ended. They had carried on their backs the whole burden of the world's past ages, and now they had relinquished it at last.

Nortekku looked toward Thalarne. "That was what they wanted most, wasn't it? To die? It's why they attacked him. They did it deliberately, to set things in motion. So that someone would come rushing in to defend him, someone who would kill them for the sake of protecting Hamiruld. Don't you think so?"

"I think you're right," Thalarne said, her voice hardly more than a whisper. She was still kneeling by Hamiruld, holding his limp arm at the wrist. Letting go of it, she rose and looked about, surveying the carnage. "What a ghastly scene, though. Dead, all of them. And Hamiruld too."

"He shouldn't have been in here," said Nortekku. "He had no right to be aboard." But that only made it all the worse, blaming Hamiruld for his own death.

Some ungovernable impulse made him ask her, as he had asked her once before, "Did you love him, Thalarne?"

"I suppose I must have, once. In some way, yes, I did. After a fashion. But what difference does that make? I told him this afternoon I could never forgive him. For lying to you, for sponsoring this expedition, for agreeing to the capture of the Sea-Lords. I told him I wanted nothing more to do with him. Maybe that was why he came here tonight."

"We'll never know what really went on in this room, will we?"

"No," she said. "We'll never know."

"Come. Let's get out of here."

He led her up on deck. The night air was warm, the moon was high and nearly full. The ship rocked gently against the pier. Out here it was as though none of the horror below had really happened.

He felt very strange. He had never been in the presence of violent death before. And yet, shocked and dazed as he was, he felt that what had happened had not entirely been a thing of horror, that some necessary act of liberation had taken place this night. Those four Sea-Lords would not now go onward to a humiliating life as exhibits in a zoo; and whatever forces had driven the tormented Hamiruld were at rest now also. Perhaps all of them, Hamiruld and the Sea-Lords both, had found in that terrible melee in the tank room that which they had been seeking most.

And for him everything that he thought he believed had been transformed in one moment of violence.

What now? Now, Nortekku thought, it is up to us to finish the job.

Thalarne moved close up beside him. He slipped one arm around her and they stood that way in silence.

"You said you'd file a report with the governments of Yissou and Dawinno, and let them decide what to do with the Sea-Lords," he said, after a long time had passed. "But you know who has the last word in what those governments decide: Prince Til-Menimat, and Prince Samnibolon, and maybe Prince Vuldimin, and Prince This-and-That, all the rest of them who paid for this expedition so they could add Sea-Lord artifacts to their collections. Do you know what they'll do, when they find out that the first try at bringing some live Sea-Lords back has failed? They'll organize another expedition right away."

"Yes. That's exactly what they'll do."

"We have to get there first, don't we?" He looked at her. "Tomorrow morning," he said, "we'll speak to the captain, and ask him if his ship is available for making a voyage right back to where we just came from."

She nodded. She understood. "Yes. We should go back there."

"And we will," he said. "We have to. Because now we have to show the rest of those Sea-Lords how to die."

AGAINST THE CURRENT

Because I started so young—I was in my late teens when I began getting stories professionally published—my career as a science-fiction writer has been one of the longest on record, if you leave aside such probably unmatchable ones as those of Jack Williamson (who began writing in 1928 and went right on for 75 years plus, until his death a few years ago at the age of 98) and Frederik Pohl (whose earliest published story dates from 1939 and who was still at it more than 65 years later.) Ray Bradbury, whose career got under way in 1941, is another whose career span exceeds mine by quite some distance. But it is now some 56 years since editors began saying yes to my s-f stories, and through a lucky combination of longevity and precocity I have been able to exceed in the duration of my writing career those of such major figures of the field as Isaac Asimov, Robert A. Heinlein, Theodore Sturgeon, and Poul Anderson, and, though I don't expect to break the flabbergasting Williamson record, I do intend to keep heading toward it for some while longer.

The nine volumes of this series have demonstrated some changes along the route of my six-decade career. Not only has there been some growth in literary ability, I hope, but there's been a steady slowdown in productivity from what was, at the beginning, a virtually inhuman pace. If you look at the introductions I wrote for the stories in Volume One, To Be Continued, you will find an ongoing subtext of eerie high-volume production: "Despite the rigors of college work, I wrote short stories steadily throughout 1954—one in April, two in May, three in June, two in October after the summer break...and by June of 1955 I was writing a story a week." A pace of a story a week would add up to fifty or so stories a year. But then we find, "I wrote ['Alaree'] in March of 1956—one of eight stories that I managed to produce that month, while still carrying a full class load in college." And then the topper: "June of 1956: the new college graduate, in his first official month as a full-time professional writer, turns out no less than eighteen stories plus two small nonfiction pieces—an average of just about one a day, considering that I always took Saturdays and Sundays off—and sells them all."

Well, that had to stop. Not only weren't there enough science-fiction magazines in existence to absorb eighteen stories a month by one writer, but I wasn't going to be 21 forever, either, and no writer even of first-magnitude prolificity has ever been able to manage to keep up an eighteen-story-a-month pace for very long. As can be seen, volume after volume, my output of short stories gradually dropped to a more normal sort, partly because I had begun writing novels as well, partly because many of the old-line magazines that had encouraged my voluminous production had gone out of business, and partly because I just couldn't keep hammering away at that frantic rate indefinitely. Writers, like everybody else, want to take things a little easier as the years mount up. Shakespeare and Hemingway didn't write anything in their sixties. (They were dead by then.) Asimov, Heinlein, Pohl, and Bradbury all slowed down some as time went along. So did I. And, as was more fully discussed in the introduction to this book, I had other reasons for cutting back on my output also. Gradually, then, over the years, I have come to write less and less, though I've continued to write steadily, by and large, except for the sabbatical years from 1974 to 1978. Volume Two of this series includes just twenty-one stories to represent the years 1962 to 1969, respectable enough productivity but a very far cry from the eighteen of June, 1956 alone. A similar slowing of pace is evident in the volumes that follow, and by the time we get to the present volume, we find just a dozen stories emerging from the entire decade beginning in 1995, and nearly all of those were the result of some direct request from an editor rather than my own burning desire to add one more short story to my long list. Indeed, I wrote no short stories at all between "The Church at Monte Saturno" in the summer of 1996 and "The Millennium Express" in December, 1998, except for a couple related to my Majipoor and Roma Eterna story sequences that are not included in this collection because their proper place is with the others of their kind. And my next four stories—"Travelers," "The Colonel Returns to the Stars," "The Eater of Dreams," and "A Piece of the Great World"—all were instigated by editorial request rather than by some inner hunger to write.

But even an aging writer who feels that he has said just about all he wants to say in the way of science fiction over the many decades of his career still does occasionally feel the irresistible pull of a story that demands to be written. At least, that was my experience one sunny day in the fall of 2006 when, while reading a fifty-year-old anthology of fantasy stories that Ray Bradbury had edited, the idea of writing a story about a man who gets into his car and drives off into the past popped into my mind.

. I wasn't looking for story ideas. I had not let myself get drawn into any new writing obligations since finishing "A Piece of the Great World" early in 2005, and the rest of that year and most of 2006 had glided by without any new Silverberg fiction entering the world. But suddenly the story that I would call "Against the Current" was taking shape willy-nilly in my mind, and the only response that seemed appropriate was, "Why not write it?" So I did. Over the next week or so it came forth virtually of its own accord, an experience that has been, I have to confess, exceedingly rare for me in modern times. I didn't stop to ask myself how it might be possible to get into one's car and drive into one's past. That would have spoiled the fun. All I wanted to do was tell the story as it told itself to me, and whether the story was science fiction (i.e. the car has been rigged to act as a sort of time machine) or fantasy (i.e. the car simply does what it does, no explanations offered) was irrelevant to me. I figured this story was a gift from the gods, and I wasn't minded to look a gift story in the mouth.

The magazine most receptive to out-of-genre stories like this, over the years, has been Fantasy and Science Fiction. *I had been an infrequent but regular contributor to F&SF since 1957, when the brilliant Anthony Boucher was its editor. It had published such stories of mine as "Sundance" and "Born with the Dead," and it had serialized my novels* The Stochastic Man *and* Lord Valentine's Castle. *Its editor and publisher now was Gordon van Gelder, with whom I had come to strike up a pleasant and curious friendship. (We are both involuntary early risers, and we have breakfast together at the World Science Fiction Convention each year in the dawn hours, while the rest of the convention-goers are still fast asleep.) I sent it to Gordon and he published it in his October-November 2007 issue.*

About half past four in the afternoon Rackman felt a sudden red blaze of pain in both his temples at once, the sort of stabbing jab that you would expect to feel if a narrow metal spike had been driven through your head. It was gone as quickly as it had come, but it left him feeling queasy and puzzled and a little frightened, and, since things were slow at the dealership just then anyway, he decided it might be best to call it a day and head for home.

He stepped out into perfect summer weather, a sunny, cloudless day, and headed across the lot to look for Gene, his manager, who had been over by the SUVs making a tally of the leftovers. But Gene was nowhere in sight. The only person Rackman saw out there was a pudgy salesman named Freitas, who so far as he recalled had given notice a couple of weeks ago. Evidently he wasn't gone yet, though.

"I'm not feeling so good and I'm going home early," Rackman announced. "If Gene's around here somewhere, will you tell him that?"

"Sure thing, Mr. Rackman."

Rackman circled around the edge of the lot toward the staff parking area. He still felt queasy, and somewhat muddled too, with a slight headache lingering after that sudden weird stab of pain. Everything seemed just a bit askew. The SUVs, for instance—there were more of the things than there should be, considering that he had just run a big clearance on them. They were lined up like a whopping great phalanx of tanks. How come so many? He filed away a mental note to ask Gene about that tomorrow.

He put his card in the ignition slot and the sleek silver Prius glided smoothly, silently, out of the lot, off to the nearby freeway entrance. By the time he reached the Caldecott Tunnel twenty minutes later the last traces of the pain in his temple were gone, and he moved on easily through Oakland toward the bridge and San Francisco across the bay.

At the Bay Bridge toll plaza they had taken down all the overhead signs that denoted the FasTrak lanes. That was odd, he thought. Probably one of their mysterious maintenance routines. Rackman headed into his usual lane anyway, but there was a tolltaker in the booth—why?—and as he started to roll past the man toward the FasTrak scanner just beyond he got such an incandescent glare from him that he braked to a halt.

The FasTrak toll scanner wasn't where it should be, right back of the tollbooth on the left. It wasn't there at all.

Feeling a little bewildered now, Rackman pulled a five-dollar bill from his wallet, handed it to the man, got what seemed to be too many singles in change, and drove out onto the bridge. There was very little traffic. As he approached the Treasure Island tunnel, though, it struck him that he couldn't remember having seen any of the towering construction cranes that ran alongside the torso of the not-quite-finished new bridge just north of the old one. Nor was there any sign of them— or any trace of the new bridge itself, for that matter, when he glanced into his rear-view mirror.

This is peculiar, Rackman thought. Really, really peculiar.

On the far side of the tunnel the sky was darker, as though dusk were already descending—at 5:10 on a summer day?—and by the time he was approaching the San Francisco end of the bridge the light was all but gone. Even stranger, a little rain was starting to come down. Rain falls in the Bay Area in August about once every twenty years. The morning forecast hadn't said anything about rain. Rackman's hand trembled a little as he turned his wipers on. I am having what could be called a waking dream, Rackman thought, some very vivid hallucination, and when I'm off the bridge I better pull over and take a few deep breaths.

The skyline of the city just ahead of him looked somehow diminished, as though a number of the bigger buildings were missing. And the exit ramps presented more puzzles. A lot of stuff that had been torn down for the retro-fitting of the old bridge seemed to have been put back in place. He couldn't find his Folsom Street off-ramp, but the long-gone Main Street one, which they had closed after the 1989 earthquake, lay right in front of him. He took it and pulled the Prius to curbside as soon as he was down at street level. The rain had stopped—the streets were dry, as if the rain had never been—but the air seemed clinging and clammy, not like dry summer air at all. It enfolded him, contained him in a strange tight grip. His cheeks were flushed and he was perspiring heavily.

Deep breaths, yes. Calm. Calm. You're only five blocks from your condo.

Only he wasn't. Most of the high-rise office buildings were missing, all right, and none of the residential towers south of the off-ramp complex were there, just block after block of parking lots and some ramshackle warehouses. It was night now, and the empty neighborhood was almost completely dark. Everything was the way it had looked around here fifteen, twenty years before. His bewilderment was beginning to turn into terror. The street signs said that he was at his own corner. So where was the thirty-story building where he lived?

Better call Jenny, he thought.

He would tell her—delicately—that he was going through something very baffling, a feeling of, well, disorientation, that in fact he was pretty seriously mixed up, that she had better come get him and take him home.

But his cell phone didn't seem to be working. All he got was a dull buzzing sound. He looked at it, stunned. He felt as though some part of him had been amputated.

Rackman was angry now as well as frightened. Things like this weren't supposed to happen to him. He was 57 years old, healthy, solvent, a solid citizen, owner of a thriving Toyota dealership across the bay, married to a lovely and loving woman. Everyone said he looked ten years younger than he really was. He worked out three times a week and ran in the Bay-to-Breakers Race every year and once in a while he even did a marathon. But the drive across the bridge had been all wrong and he didn't know where his condo building had gone and his cell phone was on the fritz, and here he was lost in this dark forlorn neighborhood of empty lots and abandoned warehouses with a wintry wind blowing— hey, hadn't it been sticky and humid a few minute ago?—on what had started out as a summer day. And he had the feeling that things were going to get worse before they got better. If indeed they got better at all.

He swung around and drove toward Union Square. Traffic was surprisingly light for downtown San Francisco. He spotted a phone booth, parked nearby, fumbled a coin into the slot, and dialed his number. The phone made ugly noises and a robot voice told him that the number he had dialed was not a working number. Cursing, Rackman tried again, tapping the numbers in with utmost care. "We're sorry," the voice said again, "the number you have reached is not—"

A telephone book dangled before him. He riffled through it—Jenny had her own listing, under Burke—but though half a dozen J Burkes were in the book, five of them lived in the wrong part of town, and when he dialed the sixth number, which had no address listed, an answering machine responded in a birdlike chirping voice that certainly wasn't Jenny's. Something led him then to look for his own listing. No, that wasn't there either. A curious calmness came over him at that discovery. There were no FasTrak lanes at the toll plaza, and the dismantled freeway ramps were still here, and the neighborhood where he lived hadn't been developed yet, and neither he nor Jenny was listed in the San Francisco phone book, and therefore either he had gone seriously crazy or else somehow this had to be fifteen or even twenty years ago, which was pretty much just another way of saying the same thing. If this really is fifteen or twenty years ago, Rackman thought, then Jenny would be living in Sacramento and I'd be across the bay in El Cerrito and still married to Helene. But what the hell kind of thing was that to be thinking, *If this really is fifteen or twenty years ago?*

He considered taking himself to the nearest emergency room and telling them he was having a breakdown, but he knew that once he put himself in the hands of the medics, there'd be no extricating himself: they'd subject him to a million tests, reports would be filed with this agency and that, his driver's license might be yanked, bad things would happen to his credit rating. It would be much smarter, he thought, to check himself into a hotel room, take a shower, rest, try to figure all this out, wait for things to get back to normal.

Rackman headed for the Hilton, a couple of blocks away. Though night had fallen just a little while ago, the sun was high overhead now, and the weather had changed again, too: it was sharp and cool, autumn just shading into winter. He was getting a different season and a different time of day every fifteen minutes or so, it seemed. The Hilton desk clerk, tall and balding and starchy-looking, had such a self-important manner that as Rackman requested a room he felt a little abashed at not having any luggage with him, but the clerk didn't appear to give a damn about that, simply handed him the registration form and asked him for his credit card. Rackman put his Visa down on the counter and began to fill out the form.

"Sir?" the desk clerk said, after a moment.

Rackman looked up. The clerk was staring at his credit card. It was the translucent kind, and he tipped it this way and that, puzzledly holding it against the light. "Problem?" Rackman asked, and the clerk muttered something about how unusual the card looked.

Then his expression darkened. "Wait just a second," he said, very coldly now, and tapped the imprinted expiration date on the card. "What is *this* supposed to be? Expires July, 2010? *2010*, sir? *2010*? Are we having a little joke, sir?" He flipped the card across the counter at Rackman the way he might have done if it had been covered with some noxious substance.

Another surge of terror hit him. He backed away, moving quickly through the lobby and into the street. Of course he might have tried to pay cash, he supposed, but the room would surely be something like $225 a night, and he had only about $350 on him. If his credit card was useless, he'd need to hang on to his cash at least until he understood what was happening to him. Instead of the Hilton, he would go to some cheaper place, perhaps one of the motels up on Lombard Street.

On his way back to his car Rackman glanced at a newspaper in a sidewalk rack. President Reagan was on the front page, under a headline about the invasion of Grenada. The date on the paper was Wednesday, October 26, 1983. Sure, he thought. 1983. This hallucination isn't missing a trick. I am in 1983 and Reagan is President again, with 1979 just up the road, 1965, 1957, 1950—

In 1950 Rackman hadn't even been born yet. He wondered what was going to happen to him when he got back to a time earlier than his own birth.

He stopped at the first motel on Lombard that had a VACANCY sign and registered for a room. The price was only $75, but when he put two fifties down on the counter, the clerk, a pleasant, smiling Latino woman, gave him a pleasant smile and tapped her finger against the swirls of pink coloration next to President Grant's portrait. "Somebody has stuck you with some very funny bills, sir. But you know that I can't take them. If you can pay by credit card, though, Visa, American Express—"

Of course she couldn't take them. Rackman remembered, now, that all the paper money had changed five or ten years back, new designs, bigger portraits, distinctive patches of pink or blue ink on their front sides that had once been boringly monochromatic. And these bills of his had the tiny date "2004" in the corner.

So far as the world of 1983 was concerned, the money he was carrying was nothing but play money.

1983.

Jenny, who is up in Sacramento in 1983 and has no idea yet that he even exists, had been 25 that year. Already he was more than twice her age. And she would get younger and younger as he went ever onward, if that was what was going to continue to happen.

Maybe it wouldn't. Soon, perhaps, the pendulum would begin to swing the other way, carrying him back to his own time, to his own life. What if it didn't, though? What if it just kept on going?

In that case, Rackman thought, Jenny was lost to him, with every-thing that had bound them together now unhappened. Rackman reached out suddenly, grasping the air as though reaching for Jenny, but all he grasped was air. There was no Jenny for him any longer. He had lost her, yes. And he would lose everything else of what he had thought of as his life as well, his whole past peeling away strip by strip. He had no reason to think that the pendulum *would* swing back. Already the exact details of Jenny's features were blurring in his mind. He struggled to recall them: the quizzical blue eyes, the slender nose, the wide, generous mouth, the slim, supple body. She seemed to be drifting past him in the fog, caught in an inexorable current carrying her ever farther away.

He slept in his car that night, up by the Marina, where he hoped no one would bother him. No one did. Morning light awakened him after a few hours—his wristwatch said it was 9:45 P.M. on the same August day when all this had started, but he knew better now than to regard what his watch told him as having any meaning—and when he stepped outside the day was dry and clear, with a blue summer sky overhead and the sort of harsh wind blowing that only San Francisco can manage on a summer day. He was getting used to the ever-changing weather by now, though, the swift parade of seasons tumbling upon him one after another. Each new one would hold him for a little while in that odd *enclosed* way, but then it would release its grasp and nudge him onward into the next one.

He checked the newspaper box on the corner. *San Francisco Chronicle*, Tuesday, May 1, 1973. Big front-page story: Nixon dismisses White House counsel John Dean and accepts the resignations of aides John Ehrlichman and H.R. Haldeman. Right, he thought. Dean, Ehrlichman, Haldeman: Watergate. So a whole decade had vanished while he slept. He had slipped all the way back to 1973. He wasn't even surprised. He had entered some realm beyond all possibility of surprise.

Taking out his wallet, Rackman checked his driver's license. Still the same, expires 03-11-11, photo of his familiar 50-something face. His car was still a silver 2009 Prius. Certain things hadn't changed. But the Prius stood out like a shriek among the other parked cars, every last one of them some clunky-looking old model of the kind that he dimly remembered from his youth. What we have here is 1973, he thought. Probably not for long, though.

He hadn't had anything to eat since lunchtime, ten hours and thirty-five years ago. He drove over to Chestnut Street, marveling at the quiet old-fashioned look of all the shopfronts, and parked right outside Joe's, which he knew had been out of business since maybe the Clinton years. There were no parking meters on the street. Rackman ordered a salad, a Joe's Special, and a glass of red wine, and paid for it with a ten-dollar bill of the old black-and-white kind that he happened to have. Meal plus wine, $8.50, he thought. That sounded about right for this long ago. It was a very consistent kind of hallucination. He left a dollar tip.

Rackman remembered pretty well what he had been doing in the spring of 1973. He was 22 that year, out of college almost a year, working in Cody's Books on Telegraph Avenue in Berkeley while waiting to get into law school, for which he had been turned down the first time around but which he had high hopes of entering that autumn. He and Al Mortenson, another young Cody's clerk—nice steady guy, easy to get along with—were rooming together in a little upstairs apartment on Dana, two or three blocks from the bookshop.

What ever had happened to old Al? Rackman had lost touch with him many years back. A powerful urge seized him now to drive across to Berkeley and look for him. He hadn't spoken with anyone except those two hotel clerks since he had left the car lot, what felt like a million years ago, and a terrible icy loneliness was beginning to settle over him as he went spinning onward through his constantly unraveling world. He needed to reach out to someone, anyone, for whatever help he could find. Al might be a good man to consult. Al was levelheaded; Al was unfluster-able; Al was *steady*. What about driving over to Berkeley now and looking for Al at the Dana Street place?—"I know you don't recognize me, Al, but I'm actually Phil Rackman, only I'm from 2008, and I'm having some sort of bad trip and I need to sit down in a quiet place with a good friend like you and figure out what's going on." Rackman wondered what that would accomplish. Probably nothing, but at least it might provide him with half an hour of companionship, sympathy, even understanding. At worst Al would think he was a lunatic and he would wind up under seda-tion at Alta Bates Hospital while they tried to find his next of kin. If he really was sliding constantly backward in time he would slip away from Alta Bates too, Rackman thought, and if not, if he was simply unhinged, maybe a hospital was where he belonged.

He went to Berkeley. The season drifted back from spring to late winter while he was crossing the bridge: in Berkeley the acacias were in bloom, great clusters of golden yellow flowers, and that was a January thing. The sight of Berkeley in early 1973, a year that had in fact been the last gasp of the Sixties, gave him a shiver: the Day-Glo rock-concert posters on all the walls, the flower-child costumes, the huge, bizarre helmets of shaggy hair that everyone was wearing. The streets were strangely clean, hardly any litter, no graffiti. It all was like a movie set, a careful, loving reconstruction of the era. He had no business being here. He was entirely out of place. And yet he had lived here once. This street belonged to his own past. He had lost Jenny, he had lost his nice condominium, he had lost his car dealership, but other things that he had thought were lost, like this Day-Glo tie-dyed world of his youth, were coming back to him. Only they weren't coming back for long, he knew. One by one they would present themselves, tantalizing flashes of a returning past, and then they'd go streaming onward, lost to him like everything else, lost for a second and terribly final time.

He guessed from the position of the pale winter sun, just coming up over the hills to the east, that the time was eight or nine in the morning. If so, Al would probably still be at home. The Dana Street place looked just as Rackman remembered it, a tidy little frame building, the landlady's tiny but immaculate garden of pretty succulents out front, the redwood deck, the staircase on the side that led to the upstairs apartment. As he started upward an unsettling burst of panic swept through him at the possibility that he might be going to come face to face with his own younger self. But in a moment his trepidation passed. It wouldn't happen, he told himself. It was just *too* impossible. There had to be a limit to this thing somewhere.

A kid answered his knock, sleepy-looking and impossibly young, a tall lanky guy in jeans and a t-shirt, with a long oval face almost completely engulfed in an immense spherical mass of jet-black hair that covered his forehead and his cheeks and his chin, a wild woolly tangle that left only eyes and nose and lips visible. A golden peace-symbol amulet dangled on a silver chain around his neck. My God, Rackman thought, this really is the Al I knew in 1973. Like a ghost out of time. But *I* am the ghost. *I* am the ghost.

"Yes?" the kid at the door said vaguely.

"Al Mortenson, right?"

"Yes." He said it in an uneasy way, chilly, distant, grudging.

What the hell, some unknown elderly guy at the door, an utter stranger wanting God only knew what, eight or nine in the morning: even the unflappable Al might be a little suspicious. Rackman saw no option but to launch straight into his story. "I realize this is going to sound very strange to you. But I ask you to bear with me.—Do I look in any way familiar to you, Al?"

He wouldn't, naturally. He was much stockier than the Phil Rackman of 1973, his full-face beard was ancient history and his once-luxurious russet hair was close-cropped and gray, and he was wearing a checked suit of the kind that nobody, not even a middle-aged man, would have worn in 1973. But he began to speak, quietly, earnestly, intensely, persuasively, his best one-foot-in-the-door salesman approach, the approach he might have used if he had been trying to sell his biggest model SUV to a frail old lady from the Rossmoor retirement home. Starting off by casually mentioning Al's roommate Phil Rackman—"he isn't here, by any chance, is he?"—no, he wasn't, thank God—and then asking Al once again to prepare himself for a very peculiar tale indeed, giving him no chance to reply, and swiftly and smoothly working around to the notion that he himself was Phil Rackman, not Phil's father but the actual Phil Rackman who been his roommate back in 1973, only in fact he was the Phil Rackman of the year 2008 who had without warning become caught up in what could only be described as an inexplicable toboggan-slide backward across time.

Even through that forest of facial hair Al's reactions were readily discernible: puzzlement at first, then annoyance verging on anger, then a show of curiosity, a flicker of interest at the possibility of such a wild thing—hey, man, far out! Cool!—and then, gradually, gradually, gradually bringing himself to the tipping point, completing the transition from skepticism verging on hostility to mild curiosity to fascination to stunned acceptance, as Rackman began to conjure up remembered episodes of their shared life that only he could have known. That time in the summer of '72 when he and Al and their current girlfriends had gone camping in the Sierra and had been happily screwing away on a flat smooth granite outcropping next to a mountain stream in what they thought was total seclusion, 8000 feet above sea level, when a wide-eyed party of Boy Scouts came marching past them down the trail;

and that long-legged girl from Oregon Rackman had picked up one
weekend who turned out to be double-jointed, or whatever, and showed
them both the most amazing sexual tricks; and the great moment when
they and some friends had scored half a pound of hash and gave a party
that lasted three days running without time out for sleep; and the time
when he and Al had hitchhiked down to Big Sur, he with big, cud-
dly Ginny Beardsley and Al with hot little Nikki Rosenzweig, during
Easter break, and the four of them had dropped a little acid and gone
absolutely gonzo berserk together in a secluded redwood grove—

"No," Al said. "That hasn't happened yet. Easter is still three months
away. And I don't know any Nikki Rosenzweig."

Rackman rolled his eyes lasciviously. "You will, kiddo. Believe me,
you will! Ginny will introduce you, and—and—"

"So you even know my own future."

"For me it isn't the future," Rackman said. "It's the long-ago past.
When you and I were rooming together right here on Dana Street and
having the time of our lives."

"But how is this possible?"

"You think I know, old pal? All I know is that it's happening. I'm
me, really me, sliding backward in time. It's the truth. Look at my face,
Al. Run a computer simulation in your mind, if you can—hell, people
don't have their own computers yet, do they?—well, just try to age me
up, in your imagination, gray hair, more weight, but the same nose, Al,
the same mouth—" He shook his head. "Wait a second. Look at this."
He drew out his driver's license and thrust it at the other man. "You see
the name? The photo? You see the birthdate? *You see the expiration date?*
March 2011? Here, look at these fifty-dollar bills! The dates on them.
This credit card, this Visa. Do you even know what a Visa is? Did we
have them back in 1973?"

"Christ," Al said, in a husky, barely audible whisper. "Jesus Christ,
Phil.—It's okay if I call you Phil, right?"

"Phil, yes."

"Look, Phil—" That same thin ghostly whisper, the voice of a man
in shock. Rackman had never, in the old days, seen Al this badly shaken
up. "The bookstore's about to open. I've got to get to work. You come in,
wait here, make yourself at home." Then a little manic laugh: "You *are*
at home, aren't you? In a manner of speaking. So wait here. Rest. Relax.
Smoke some of my dope, if you want. You probably know where I keep
it. Meet me at Cody's at one, and we can go out to lunch and talk about

all this, okay? I want to know all about it. What year did you say you came from? 2011?"

"2008."

"2008. Christ, this is so wild!—You'll stay here, then?"

"And if my younger self walks in on me?"

"Don't worry. You're safe. He's in Los Angeles this week."

"Groovy," Rackman said, wondering if anyone still said things like that. "Go on, then. Go to work. I'll see you later."

The two rooms, Al's and his own just across the hall, were like museum exhibits: the posters for Fillmore West concerts, the antique stereo set and the stack of LP records, the tie-dyed shirts and bell-bottom pants scattered in the corner, the bong on the dresser, the macrame wall-hangings, the musty aroma of last night's incense. Rackman poked around, lost in dreamy nostalgia and at times close to tears as he looked at this artifact of that ancient era and that one, *The Teachings of Don Juan, The White Album, The Whole Earth Catalog.* His own copies. He still had the Castaneda book somewhere; he remembered the beer stain on the cover. He peered into the dresser drawer where Al kept his stash, scooped up a pinch of it in his fingers and sniffed it, smiled, put it back. It was years since he had smoked. Decades.

He ran his hand over his cheek. His stubble was starting to bother him. He hadn't shaved since yesterday morning on Rackman body time. He knew there'd be a shaver in the bathroom, though—he was pretty sure he had left it there even after he began growing his Seventies beard—and, yes, there was his old Norelco three-headed job. He felt better with clean cheeks. Rackman stuffed the shaver into his inside jacket pocket, knowing he'd want it in the days ahead.

Then he found himself wondering whether he had parked in a tow-away zone. They had always been very tough about illegally parked cars in Berkeley. You could try to assassinate the president and get off with a six-month sentence, but God help you if you parked in a tow-away zone. And if they took his car away, he'd be in an even worse pickle than he already was. The car was his one link to the world he had left behind, his time capsule, his home, now, actually.

The car was still where he had left it. But he was afraid to leave it for long. It might slip away from him in the next time-shift. He got in, thinking to wait in it until it was time to meet Al for lunch. But although it was still just mid-morning he felt drowsiness overcoming him, and almost instantly he dozed off. When he awakened he saw that it was dark outside. He must have slept the day away. The dashboard clock told him it was 1:15 P.M., but that was useless, meaningless. Probably it was early evening, too late for lunch with Al. Maybe they could have dinner instead.

On the way over to the bookstore, marveling every step of the way at the utter weirdness of everybody he passed in the streets, the strange beards, the flamboyant globes of hair, the gaudy clothing, Rackman began to see that it would be very embarrassing to tell Al that he had grown up to own a suburban automobile dealership. He had planned to become a legal advocate for important social causes, or perhaps a public defender, or an investigator of corporate malfeasance. Everybody had noble plans like that, back then. Going into the car business hadn't been on anyone's screen.

Then he saw that he didn't have to tell Al anything about what he had come to do for a living. It was a long story and not one that Al was likely to find interesting. Al wouldn't care that he had become a car dealer. Al was sufficiently blown away by the mere fact that his former roommate Phil Rackman had dropped in on him out of the future that morning.

He entered the bookstore and spotted Al over near the cash register. But when he waved he got only a blank stare in return.

"I'm sorry I missed our lunch date, Al. I guess I just nodded off. It's been a pretty tiring day for me, you know."

There was no trace of recognition on Al's face.

"Sir? There must be some mistake."

"Al Mortenson? Who lives on Dana Street?"

"I'm Al Mortenson, yes. I live in Bowles Hall, though."

Bowles Hall was a campus dormitory. Undergraduates lived there. This Al hadn't graduated yet.

This Al's hair was different too, Rackman saw now. A tighter cut, more disciplined, more forehead showing. And his beard was much longer, cascading down over his chest, hiding the peace symbol. He might have had a haircut during the day but he couldn't have grown four inches more of beard.

There was a stack of newspapers on the counter next to the register, the *New York Times*. Rackman flicked a glance at the top one. *November 10, 1971.*

I haven't just slept away the afternoon, Rackman thought. I've slept away all of 1972. He and Al hadn't rented the Dana Street place until after graduation, in June of '72.

Fumbling, trying to recover, always the nice helpful guy, Al said, "You aren't Mr. Chesley, are you? Bud Chesley's father?"

Bud Chesley had been a classmate of theirs, a jock, big, broad-shouldered. The main thing that Rackman remembered about him was that he had been one of about six men on campus who were in favor of the war in Vietnam. Rackman seemed to recall that in his senior year Al had roomed with Chesley in Bowles, before he and Al had known each other.

"No," Rackman said leadenly. "I'm not Mr. Chesley. I'm really sorry to have bothered you."

✸

So it was hopeless, then. He had suspected it all along, but now, feeling the past tugging at him as he hurried back to his car, it was certain. The slippage made any sort of human interaction lasting more than half an hour or so impossible to sustain. He struggled with it, trying to tug back, to hold fast against the sliding, hoping that perhaps he could root himself somehow in the present and then begin the climb forward again until he reached the place where he belonged. But he could feel the slippage continuing, not at any consistent rate but in sudden unpredictable bursts, and there was nothing he could do about it. There were times when he was completely unaware of it until it had happened and other times when he could see the seasons rocketing right by in front of his eyes.

Without any particular destination in mind Rackman returned to his car, wandered around Berkeley until he found himself heading down Ashby Avenue to the freeway, and drove back into San Francisco. The toll was only a quarter. Astonishing. The cars around him on the bridge all seemed like collector's items, with yellow-and-black license plates, three digits, three letters. He wondered what a highway patrolman would say about his own plates, if he recognized them as California plates at all.

Halfway across the bridge Rackman turned the radio on, hoping the car might be able to pick up a news broadcast out of 2008, but no, no, when he got KCBS he heard the announcer talking about President

Johnson, Secretary of State Rusk, Vietnam, Israel refusing to give back Jerusalem after the recent war with the Arab countries, Dr. Martin Luther King calling for calm following a night of racial strife in Hartford, Connecticut. It was hard to remember some of the history exactly, but Rackman knew that Dr. King had been assassinated in 1968, so he figured that just in the course of crossing the bridge he probably had slid back into 1967 or even 1966. He had been in high school then. All the sweaty anguish of that whole lunatic era came swimming back into his mind, the Robert Kennedy assassination too, the body counts on the nightly news, Malcolm X, peace marches, the strident 1968 political convention in Chicago, the race riots, Nixon, Hubert Humphrey, Mao Tse-tung, spacemen in orbit around the moon, Lady Bird Johnson, Cassius Clay. *Hey hey hey, LBJ, how many kids did you kill today?* The noise, the hard-edged excitement, the daily anxiety. It felt like the Pleistocene to him now. But he had driven right into the thick of it.

The slippage continued. The long hair went away, the granny glasses, the Day-Glo posters, the tie-dyed clothes. John F. Kennedy came and went in reverse. Night and day seemed to follow one another in random sequence. Rackman ate his meals randomly too, no idea whether it was breakfast or lunch or dinner that he needed. He had lost all track of personal time. He caught naps in his car, kept a low profile, said very little to anyone. A careless restaurant cashier took one of his gussied-up fifties without demur and gave him a stack of spendable bills in change. He doled those bills out parsimoniously, watching what he spent even though meals, like the bridge toll, like the cost of a newspaper, like everything else back here, were astoundingly cheap, a nickel or a dime for this, fifty cents for that.

San Francisco was smaller, dingier, a little old 1950s-style town, no trace of the high-rise buildings now. Everything was muted, old-fashioned, the simpler, more innocent textures of his childhood. He half expected it all to be in black and white, as an old newsreel would be, and perhaps to flicker a little. But he took in smells, breezes, sounds, that no newsreel could have captured. This wasn't any newsreel and it wasn't any hallucination, either. This was the world itself, dense, deep, real. All too real, unthinkably real. And there was no place for him in it.

Men wore hats, women's coats had padded shoulders. Shop windows sparkled. There was a Christmas bustle in the streets. A little while later, though, the sky brightened and the dry, cold winds of San Francisco summer came whistling eastward at him again out of the Pacific, and then, presto jingo, the previous winter's rainy season was upon him. He wondered which year's winter it was.

It was 1953, the newspaper told him. The corner newspaper rack was his only friend. It provided him with guidance, information about his present position in time. That was Eisenhower on the front page. The Korean war was still going on, here in 1953. And Stalin: Stalin had just died. Rackman remembered Eisenhower, the president of his childhood, kindly old Ike. Truman's bespectacled face would be next. Rackman had been born during Truman's second term. He had no recollection of the Truman presidency but he could recall the salty old Harry of later years, who went walking every day, gabbing with reporters about anything that came into his head.

What is going to happen to me, Rackman wondered, when I get back past my own birthdate?

Maybe he would come to some glittering gateway, a giant sizzling special effect throwing off fireworks across the whole horizon, with a blue-white sheen of nothingness stretching into infinity beyond it. And when he passed through it he would disappear into oblivion and that would be that. He'd find out soon enough. He couldn't be much more than a year or two away from the day of his birth.

Without knowing or caring where he was going Rackman began to drive south out of San Francisco, the poky little San Francisco of this far-off day, heading out of town on what once had been Highway 101, the freeway that led to the airport and San Jose and, eventually, Los Angeles. It wasn't a freeway now, just an oddly charming little four-lane road. The billboards that lined it on both sides looked like ads from old National Geographics. The curving rows of small ticky-tacky houses on the hillsides hadn't been built yet. There was almost nothing except open fields everywhere, down here south of the city. The ballpark wasn't there—the Giants still played in New York in this era, he recalled—and when he went past the airport, he almost failed to notice it, it was such a piffling little small-town place. Only when a DC-3 passed overhead like a huge droning mosquito did he realize that that collection of tin sheds over to the left was what would one day be SFO.

Rackman knew that he was still slipping and slipping as he went, that the pace of slippage seemed to be picking up, that if that glittering gateway existed he had already gone beyond it. He was somewhere near 1945 now or maybe even earlier—they were honking at his car on the road in amazement, as though it was a spaceship that had dropped down from Mars—and now a clear, cold understanding of what was in store for him was growing in his mind.

He wouldn't disappear through any gateway. It didn't matter that he hadn't been born yet in the year he was currently traveling through, because he wasn't growing any younger as he drifted backward. And the deep past waited for him. He saw that he would just go endlessly onward, cut loose from the restraints that time imposed, drifting on and on back into antiquity. While he was driving southward, heading for San Jose or Los Angeles or wherever it was that he might be going next, the years would roll along backward, the twentieth century would be gobbled up in the nineteenth, California's great cities would melt away—he had already seen that happening in San Francisco—and the whole state would revert to the days of Mexican rule, a bunch of little villages clustered around the Catholic missions, and then the villages and the missions would disappear too. A day or two later for him, California would be an emptiness, nobody here but simple Indian tribes. Farther to the east, in the center of the continent, great herds of bison would roam. Still farther east would be the territory of the Thirteen Colonies, gradually shriveling back into tiny pioneering settlements and then vanishing also.

Well, he thought, if he could get himself across the country quickly enough, he might be able to reach New York City—Nieuw Amsterdam, it would probably be by then—while it still existed. There he might be able to arrange a voyage across to Europe before the continent reverted entirely to its pre-Columbian status. But what then? All that he could envisage was a perpetual journey backward, backward, ever backward: the Renaissance, the Dark Ages, Rome, Greece, Babylon, Egypt, the Ice Age. A couple of summers ago he and Jenny had taken a holiday in France, down in the Dordogne, where they had looked at the painted caves of the Cro-Magnon men, the colorful images of bulls and bison and spotted horses and mammoths. No one knew what those pictures meant, why they had been painted. Now he would go back and find out at first hand the answer to the enigmas of the prehistoric caves. How very cool that sounded, how interesting, a nice fantasy, except that if you gave it half a second's thought it was appalling. To whom would he impart that knowledge? What good would it do him, or anyone?

The deep past was waiting for him, yes. But would he get there? Even a Prius wasn't going to make it all the way across North America on a single tank of gas, and soon there weren't going to be any gas stations, and even if they were he would have no valid money to pay for gas, or food, or anything else. Pretty soon there would be no roads, either. He couldn't *walk* to New York. In that wilderness he wouldn't last three days.

He had kept himself in motion up until this moment, staying just ahead of the vast gray grimness that was threatening to invade his soul, but it was catching up with him now. Rackman went through ten or fifteen minutes that might have been the darkest, bleakest moments of his life. Then—was it something about the sweet simplicity of this little road, no longer the roaring Highway 101 but now just a dusty, narrow two-laner with hardly any traffic?—there came an unexpected change in his mood. He grew indifferent to his fate. In an odd way he found himself actually welcoming whatever might come. The prospect before him looked pretty terrifying, yes. But it might just be exciting, too. He had liked his life, he had liked it very much, but it had been torn away from him, he knew not how or why. This was his life now. He had no choice about that. The best thing to do, Rackman thought, was to take it one century at a time and try to enjoy the ride.

What he needed right now was a little breather: come to a halt if only for a short while, pause and regroup. Stop and pass the time, so to speak, as he got himself ready for the next phase of his new existence. He pulled over by the side of the road and turned off the ignition and sat there quietly, thinking about nothing at all.

After a while a youngish man on a motorcycle pulled up alongside him. The motorcycle was hardly more than a souped-up bike. The man was wearing a khaki blouse and khaki trousers, all pleats and flounces, a very old-fashioned outfit, something like a scoutmaster's uniform. He himself had an old-fashioned look, too, dark hair parted in the middle like an actor in a silent movie.

Then Rackman noticed the California Highway Patrol badge on the man's shoulder. He opened the car window. The patrolman leaned toward him and gave him an earnest smile, a Boy Scout smile. Even the smile was old-fashioned. You couldn't help believing the sincerity of it. "Is there any difficulty, sir? May I be of any assistance?"

So polite, so formal. *Sir.* Everyone had been calling him *sir* since this trip had started, the desk clerks, the people in restaurants, Al Mortenson, and now this CHP man. So respectful, everybody was, back here in prehistory.

"No," Rackman said. "No problem. Everything's fine."

The patrolman didn't seem to hear him. He had turned his complete attention to Rackman's car itself, the glossy silver Prius, the car out of the future. The look of it was apparently sinking in for the first time. He was staring at the car in disbelief, in befuddlement, in unconcealed jaw-sagging awe, gawking at its fluid streamlined shape, at its gleaming futuristic dashboard. Then he turned back to Rackman himself, taking in the look of his clothing, his haircut, his checked jacket, his patterned shirt. The man's eyes seemed to glaze. Rackman knew that there had to be something about his whole appearance that seemed as wrong to the patrolman as the patrolman's did to him. He could see the man working to get himself under control. The car must have him completely flummoxed, Rackman thought. The patrolman began to say something but it was a moment before he could put his voice in gear. Then he said, hoarsely, like a rusty automaton determined to go through its routine no matter what, "I want you to know, sir, that if you are having any problem with your—ah—your car, we are here to assist you in whatever way we can."

To assist you. That was a good one.

Rackman managed a faint smile. "Thanks, but the car's okay," he said. "And I'm okay too. I just stopped off here to rest a bit, that's all. I've got a long trip ahead of me." He started the car. Silently, smoothly, the Prius floated forward into the morning light and the night that would quickly follow it and into the random succession of days and nights and springs and winters and autumns and summers beyond, forward into the mysteries, dark and dreadful and splendid, that lay before him.

THE TRUE VINTAGE
OF ERZUINE THALE

In 1950 an exciting boom in new science-fiction magazines was getting under way. Such titles as Galaxy *and* Fantasy and Science Fiction *were challenging the long-time dominance of John W. Campbell's* Astounding Science Fiction, *and more were on the way. One of the most interesting new magazines was* Worlds Beyond, *published by Hillman Periodicals, a major magazine company of the time, and edited by the shrewd, demanding Damon Knight.*

The first issue of Worlds Beyond *came out late that year, dated December, 1950, and it was an elegant production indeed, with stories by Jack Vance, Poul Anderson, C.M. Kornbluth, Harry Harrison, and Richard Matheson. The second issue, a month later, was equally strong, as was the third. But for me—a high-school junior, looking ahead to college life and the hope of a career as a science-fiction writer after that—the most interesting thing about the magazine was the advertisement on the back cover of the first issue, promising that a novel by Jack Vance,* The Dying Earth, *would be "at your newsstand soon," as part of a new series of Hillman paperbacks.*

Even then, though it was still early days in his great career, Jack Vance had become one of my favorite authors. A handful of novelettes and novellas in such pulp magazines as Thrilling Wonder Stories *and its companion* Startling Stories *had excited me with their vivid, colorful style and sly, cynical manner of narration, and marked Vance for me as a writer to watch. And the theme of* The Dying Earth, *the last days of our world, had*

been one of special interest to me since I had discovered H.G. Wells's The
Time Machine *in my earliest days as a science-fiction reader. "Time had
worn out the sun," that back-cover Hillman advertisement declared, "and
earth was spinning quickly toward eternal darkness. In the forests strange
animals hid behind twisted trees, plotting death; in the cities men made constant revel and sought sorcery to cheat the dying world...."*

*There was a preview of the Vance book, just a tantalizing snippet, in
the first issue of* Worlds Beyond—*"The Loom of Darkness," a delicate tale
of wizardry and vengeance, which whetted my appetite for the actual book
with its images of decay and decline, tumbled pillars, slumped pediments,
crumbled inscriptions, the weary red sun looking down on the ancient cities
of humanity. I have rarely looked forward to the publication of a forthcoming novel so keenly. And so for week after week I searched the magazine
shops of Brooklyn, where I lived then, for Vance's* Dying Earth. *I had to
have a copy of it. It seemed to me that it would be everything I wanted in a
science-fiction novel.*

What I didn't know, though, is that Damon Knight's Worlds Beyond
*had been killed in its first days of existence. Discouraging early sales figures
led Hillman Periodicals to cancel the magazine soon after the release of its
initial issue, although issues two and three, since they were well along in
the production process, would be released anyway in a sort of posthumous
production. The Hillman paperback line was to be dropped also, once the
titles in the pipeline had been distributed, and no great effort was going to
be made to put those out on the newsstands.*

*All through the chilly weeks of November and December I looked with-
out success, and then, early in the new year, a friend who had been lucky
enough to find a copy gave me his: I have it still. And treasure that crude-
looking little book inordinately, for its rough, badly printed pages unlocked
unforgettable realms of wonder for me. I read it again every few years.
The effect on is always as powerful as it had been at first acquaintance in
January of 1951.*

*Here we are on an Earth where "ages of rain and wind have beaten
and rounded the granite, and the sun is feeble and red. The continents have
sunk and risen. A million cities have lifted towers, have fallen to dust. In
place of the old peoples a few thousand strange souls live." Vance shows
us "a dark blue sky, an ancient sun....Nothing in sight, nothing of Earth
was raw or harsh—the ground, the trees, the rock ledge protruding from
the meadow; all these had been worked upon, smoothed, aged, mellowed.
The light from the sun, though rich, and invested every object of the land,*

the rocks, the trees, the quiet grasses and flowers, with a sense of lore and ancient recollection."

Wonderful. Wonderful.

Imagine my delight and astonishment, then, when in the spring of 2007 Gardner Dozois asked me to write something for a book that he was editing with George R.R. Martin of stories set in the world of...Jack Vance's The Dying Earth! How splendid, I thought, to be allowed to borrow that lyrical tone of voice and that dry, sly wit and enter Vance's world for myself. I accepted the offer at the speed of light and, in October, 2007, wrote "The True Vintage of Erzuine Thale" for the book that would be called Songs of the Dying Earth. It was a happy experience. My only regret is that I can't go back and write another one set in that world, at least not without being asked, because the world of the Dying Earth belongs to Jack Vance. But what a delight it was to share it, if only for a little while.

Puillayne of Ghiusz was a man born to every advantage life offers, for his father was the master of great estates along the favored southern shore of the Claritant Peninsula, his mother was descended from a long line of wizards who held hereditary possession of many great magics, and he himself had been granted a fine strong-thewed body, robust health, and great intellectual power.

Yet despite these gifts Puillayne, unaccountably, was a man of deep and ineradicable melancholic bent. He lived alone in a splendid sprawling manse overlooking the Klorpentine Sea, a place of parapets and barbicans, loggias and pavilions, embrasures and turrets and sweeping pilasters, admitting only a few intimates to his solitary life. His soul was ever clouded over by a dark depressive miasma, which Puillayne was able to mitigate only through the steady intake of strong drink. For the world was old, nearing its end, its very rocks rounded and smoothed by time, every blade of grass invested with the essence of a long antiquity, and he knew from his earliest days that futurity was an empty vessel and only the long past supported the fragile present. This was a source of extreme infestivity to him. By assiduous use of drink, and only by such use of it, he could succeed from time to time in lifting his gloom, not through the drink itself but through the practice of his art, which was that of poetry: his wine was his gateway to his verse, and his verse, pouring from him in unstoppable superiloquent abundance, gave him transient release from despond. The verse forms of every era were at his fingertips, be they the sonnet or the sestina or the villanelle or the free chansonette so greatly beloved by the rhyme-loathing poets of Sheptun-Am, and in each of them he displayed ineffable mastery. It was typical of Puillayne, however, that the gayest of his lyrics was invariably tinged with ebon despair. Even in his cups he could not escape the fundamental truth that the world's day was done, that the sun was a heat-begrudging red cinder in the darkening sky, that all striving had been in vain for Earth and its denizens, and those ironies contaminated his every thought.

And so, and so, cloistered in his rambling chambers on the heights above the metropole of Ghiusz, the capital city of the happy Claritant that jutted far out into the golden Klorpentine, sitting amidst his collection of rare wines, his treasures of exotic gems and unusual woods, his garden of extraordinary horticultural marvels, he would regale his little circle of friends with verses such as these:

The night is dark. The air is chill.
Silver wine sparkles in my amber goblet.
But it is too soon to drink. First let me sing.
Joy is done! The shadows gather!

Darkness comes, and gladness ends!
Yet though the sun grows dim,
My soul takes flight in drink.

What care I for the crumbling walls?
What care I for the withering leaves?
Here is wine!

Who knows? This could be the world's last night.
Morning, perhaps, will bring a day without dawn.
The end is near. Therefore, friends, let us drink!

Darkness....darkness....
The night is dark. The air is chill.
Therefore, friends, let us drink!
Let us drink!

"How beautiful those verses are," said Gimbiter Soleptan, a lithe, playful man given to the wearing of green damask pantaloons and scarlet sea-silk blouses. He was, perhaps, the closest of Puillayne's little band of companions, antithetical though he was to him in the valence of his nature. "They make me wish to dance, to sing—and also...." Gimbiter let the thought trail off, but glanced meaningfully to the sideboard at the farther end of the room.

"Yes, I know. And to drink."

Puillayne rose and went to the great sideboard of black candana overpainted with jagged lines of orpiment and gambodge and flake blue in which he kept the wines he had chosen for the present week. For a moment he hesitated among the tight-packed row of flasks. Then his hand closed on the neck of one fashioned from pale-violet crystal, through which a wine of radiant crimson glowed with cheery insistence.

"One of my best," he announced. "A claret, it is, of the Scaumside vineyard in Ascolais, waiting forty years for this night. But why let it wait longer? There may be no later chances."

"As you have said, Puillayne. 'This could be the world's last night.' But why, then, do you still disdain to open Erzuine Thale's True Vintage? By your own argument you should seize upon it while opportunity yet remains. And yet you refuse."

"Because," Puillayne said, smiling gravely, and glancing toward the cabinet of embossed doors where that greatest of all wines slept behind barriers of impenetrable spells, "This may, after all, *not* be the world's last night, for none of the fatal signs have made themselves apparent yet. The True Vintage deserves only the grandest of occasions. I shall wait a while longer to broach it. But the wine I have here is itself no trifle. Observe me now."

He set out a pair of steep transparent goblets rimmed with purple gold, murmured the word to the wine-flask that unsealed its stopper, and held it aloft to pour. As the wine descended into the goblet it passed through a glorious spectrum of transformation, now a wild scarlet, now deep crimson, now carmine, mauve, heliotrope shot through with lines of topaz, and, as it settled to its final hue, a magnificent coppery gold. "Come," said Puillayne, and led his friend to the viewing-platform overlooking the bay, where they stood side by side, separated by the great vase of black porcelain that was one of Puillane's most cherished treasures, in which a porcelain fish of the same glossy black swam insolently in the air.

Night had just begun to fall. The feeble red sun hovered precariously over the western sea. Fierce eye-stabbing stars already blazed furiously out of the dusky sky to north and south of it, arranging themselves in the familiar constellations, the Hoary Nimbus, the Panoply of Swords, the Cloak of Cantenax, the Claw. The twilight air was cooling swiftly. Even here in this land of the far south, sheltered by the towering Kelpusar range from the harsh winds that raked Almery and the rest of Grand Motholam, there was no escape from the chill of the night. Everywhere, even here, such modest daily warmth as the sun afforded fled upward through the thinning air the moment that faint light was withdrawn.

Puillayne and Gimbiter were silent a time, savoring the power of the wine, which penetrated subtly, reaching from one region of their souls to the next until it fastened on the heart. For Puillayne it was the fifth wine of the day, and he was well along in the daily defeat of his innate somberness of spirit, having brought himself to the outer borderlands of the realm of sobriety. A delightful gyroscopic instability now befuddled his mind. He had begun with a silver wine of Kauchique flecked with molecules of gold, then had proceeded to a light ruby wine of the moorlands, a sprightly sprezzogranito from Cape Thaumissa, and, finally, a smooth but compelling dry Harpundium as a prelude to this venerable grandissimus that he currently was sharing with his friend. That progression was a typical one for him. Since early manhood he had rarely passed a waking hour without a goblet in his hand.

"How beautiful this wine is," said Gimbiter finally.

"How dark the night," said Puillayne. For even now he could not escape the essentially rueful cast of his thoughts.

"Forget the darkness, dear friend, and enjoy the beauty of the wine. But no: they are forever mingled for you, are they not, the darkness and the wine. The one encircles the other in ceaseless chase."

This far south, the sun plunged swiftly below the horizon. The ferocity of the starlight was remorseless now. The two men sipped thoughtfully.

Gimbiter said, after a further span of silence, "Do you know, Puillayne, that strangers are in town asking after you?"

"Strangers, indeed? And asking for me?"

"Three men from the north. Uncouth-looking ones. I have this from my gardener, who tells me that they have been making inquiries of *your* gardener."

"Indeed," said Puillayne, with no great show of interest.

"They are a nest of rogues, these gardeners. They all spy on us, and sell our secrets to any substantial bidder."

"You tell me no news here, Gimbiter."

"Does it not concern you that rough-hewn strangers are asking questions?"

Puillayne shrugged. "Perhaps they are admirers of my verses, come to hear me recite."

"Perhaps they are thieves, come from afar to despoil you of some of your fabled treasures."

"Perhaps they are both. In that case, they must hear my verses before I permit any despoiling."

"You are very casual, Puillayne."

"Friend, the sun itself is dying as we stand here. Shall I lose sleep over the possibility that strangers may take some of my trinkets from me? With such talk you distract us from this unforgettable wine. I beg you, drink, Gimbiter, and put these strangers out of your mind."

"I can put them from mine," said Gimbiter, "but I wish you would devote some part of yours to them." And then he ceased to belabor the point, for he knew that Puillayne was a man utterly without fear. The profound bleakness that lay at the core of his spirit insulated him from ordinary cares. He lived without hope and therefore without uneasiness. And by this time of day, Gimbiter understood, Puillayne had further reinforced himself within an unbreachable palisade of wine.

The three strangers, though, were troublesome to Gimbiter. He had gone to the effort of inspecting them himself earlier that day. They had taken lodgings, said his head gardener, at the old hostelry called the Blue Wyvern, between the former ironmongers' bazaar and the bazaar of silk and spices, and it was easy enough for Gimbiter to locate them as they moved along the boulevard that ran down the spine of the bazaar quarter. One was a squat, husky man garbed in heavy brown furs, with purple leather leggings and boots, and a cap of black bearskin trimmed with a fillet of gold. Another, tall and loose-limbed, sported a leopardskin tarboosh, a robe of yellow muslin, and red boots ostentatiously spurred with the spines of the roseate urchin. The third, clad unpretentiously in a simple gray tunic and a quilted green mantle of some coarse heavy fabric, was of unremarkable stature and seemed all but invisible beside his two baroque confederates, until one noticed the look of smouldering menace in his deep-set, resolute, reptilian eyes, set like obsidian ellipsoids against his chalky-hued face.

Gimbiter made such inquiries about them at the hostelry as were feasible, but all he could learn was that they were mercantile travelers from Hither Almery or even farther north, come to the southlands on some enterprise of profit. But even the innkeeper knew that they were aware of the fame of the metropole's great poet Puillayne, and were eager to achieve an audience with him. And therefore Gimbiter had duly provided his friend with a warning; but he was sadly aware that he could do no more than that.

Nor was Puillayne's air of unconcern an affectation. One who has visited the mephitic shores of the Sea of Nothingness and returned is truly beyond all dismay. He knows that the world is an illusion built upon a foundation of mist and wind, and that it is great folly to attach oneself in any serious way to any contrary belief. During his more sober moments, of course, Puillayne of Ghiusz was as vulnerable to despair and anxiety as anyone else; but he took care to reach with great speed for his beloved antidote the instant that he felt tendrils of reality making poisonous incursions through his being. But for wine he would have had no escape from his eternally sepulchral attitudinizing.

So the next day, and the next, days that were solitary by choice for him, Puillayne moved steadfastly through his palace of antiquarian treasures on his usual diurnal rounds, rising at daybreak to bathe in the spring that ran through his gardens, then breakfasting on his customary sparse fare, then devoting an hour to the choice of the day's wines and sampling the first of them.

In mid-morning, as the glow of the first flask of wine still lingered in him, he sat sipping the second of the day and reading awhile from some volume of his collected verse. There were fifty or sixty of them by now, bound identically in the black vellum made from the skin of fiendish deodands that had been slaughtered for the bounty placed upon such fell creatures; and these were merely the poems that he had had sufficient sobriety to remember to indite and preserve, out of the scores that poured from him so freely. Puillayne constantly read and reread them with keen pleasure. Though he affected modesty with others, within the shelter of his own soul he had an unabashed admiration for his poems, which the second wine of the day invariably amplified.

Afterward, before the second wine's effect had completely faded, it was his daily practice to stroll through the rooms that held his cabinet of wonders, inspecting with ever-fresh delight the collection of artifacts and oddities that he had gathered during youthful travels that had taken him as far north as the grim wastes of Fer Aquila, as far to the east as the monster-infested deadlands beyond the Land of the Falling Wall where ghouls and deadly grues swarmed and thrived, as far west as ruined Ampridatvir and sullen Azederach on the sunset side of the black Supostimon Sea. In each of these places the young Puillayne had acquired curios, not because the assembling of them had given him any particular pleasure in and of itself, but because the doing of it turned his attention for the moment, as did the drinking of wine, from the otherwise inescapable encroachment of gloom that from boyhood on had perpetually assailed his consciousness. He drew somber amusement now from fondling these things, which recalled to him some remote place he had visited, summoning up memories of great beauty and enchanting peace, or arduous struggle and biting discomfort, it being a matter of no importance to him which it might have been, so long as the act of remembering carried him away from the here and now.

Then he would take his lunch, a repast scarcely less austere than his morning meal had been, always accompanying it by some third wine chosen for its soporific qualities. A period of dozing invariably followed, and then a second cooling plunge in the garden spring, and then—it was a highlight of the day—the ceremonial opening of the fourth flask of wine, the one that set free his spirit and allowed the composition of that day's verses. He scribbled down his lines with haste, never pausing to revise, until the fervor of creation had left him. Once more, then, he read, or uttered the simple spell that filled his bayside audifactorium with music. Then came dinner, a more notable meal than the earlier two, one that would do justice to the fifth and grandest wine of the day, in the choosing of which he had devoted the greatest of care; and then, hoping as ever that the dying sun might perish in the night and release him at last from his funereal anticipations, he gave himself to forlorn dreamless sleep.

So it passed for the next day, and the next, and on the third day after Gimbiter Soleptan's visit the three strangers of whom Gimbiter had warned him presented themselves at last at the gates of his manse.

They selected for their unsolicited intrusion the hour of the second wine, arriving just as he had taken one of the vellum-bound volumes of his verse from its shelf. Puillayne maintained a small staff of wraiths and revenants for his household needs, disliking as he did the use of living beings as domestic subordinates, and one of these pallid eidolons came to him with news of the visitors.

Puillayne regarded the ghostly creature, which just then was hovering annoyingly at the borders of transparency as though attempting to communicate its own distress, with indifference. "Tell them they are welcome. Admit them upon the half hour."

It was far from his usual custom to entertain visitors during the morning hours. The revenant was plainly discommoded by this surprising departure from habit. "Lordship, if one may venture to express an opinion—"

"One may not. Admit them upon the half hour."

Puillayne used the interval until then to deck himself in formal morning garb: a thin tunic of light color, a violet mantle, laced trousers of the same color worn over underdrawers of deep red, and, above all the rest, a stiff unlined garment of a brilliant white. He had already selected a chilled wine from the Bay of Sanreale, a brisk vintage of a shimmering metallic-gray hue, for his second wine; now he drew forth a second flask of it and placed it beside the first.

The house-wraith returned, precisely upon the half hour, with Puillayne's mysterious guests.

They were, exactly as Gimbiter Soleptan had opined, a rough-hewn, uncouth lot. "I am Kesztrel Tsaye," announced the shortest of the three, who seemed to be the dominant figure: a burly person wrapped in the thick shaggy fur of some wild beast, and topped with a gold-trimmed cap of a different, glossier fur. His dense black beard encroached almost completely on his blunt, unappealing features, like an additional shroud of fur. "This is Unthan Vyorn"—a nod toward a lanky, insolent-looking fellow in a yellow robe, flamboyantly baroque red boots, and an absurd betasseled bit of headgear that displayed a leopard's spots—"and this," he said, glancing toward a third man, pale and unremarkably garbed, notable mainly for an appearance of extreme inconsequence bordering on nonpresence, but for his eyes, which were cold and brooding, "is Malion Gainthrust. We three are profound admirers of your great art, and have come from our homes in the Maurenron foothills to express our homage."

"I can barely find words to convey the extreme delight I experience now, as I stand in the very presence of Puillayne of Ghiusz," said lanky Unthan Vyorn in a disingenuously silken voice with just the merest hint of sibilance.

"It seems to me that you are capable of finding words readily enough," Puillayne observed. "But perhaps you mean only a conventional abnegation. Will you share my wine with me? At this hour of the morning I customarily enjoy something simple, and I have selected this Sanreale stuff."

He indicated the pair of rounded gray flasks. But from the depths of his furs Kesztrel Tsaye drew two globular green flasks of his own and set them on the nearby table. "No doubt your choice is superb, master. But we are well aware of your love of the grape, and among the gifts we bring to you are these carboys of our own finest vintage, the celebrated azure ambrosia of the Maurenrons, with which you are, perhaps, unfamiliar, and which will prove an interesting novelty to your palate."

Puillaine had not, in truth, ever tasted the so-called ambrosia of the Maurenrons, but he understood it to be an acrid and deplorable stuff, fit only for massaging cramped limbs. Yet he maintained an affable cordiality, studiously examining the nearer of the two carboys, holding it to the light, hefting it as though to determine the specific gravity of its contents. "The repute of your wines is not unknown to me," he said diplomatically. "But I propose we set these aside for later in the day, since, as I have explained, I prefer only a light wine before my midday meal, and perhaps the same is true of you." He gave them an inquisitive look. They made no objection; and so he murmured the spell of opening and poured out a ration of the Sanreale for each of them and himself.

By way of salute Unthan Vyorn offered a quotation from one of Puillayne's best-known little pieces:

What is our world? It is but a boat
That breaks free at sunset, and drifts away
Without a trace.

His intonation was vile, his rhythm was uncertain, but at least he had managed the words accurately, and Puillayne supposed that his intentions were kindly. As he sipped his wine he studied this odd trio with detached curiosity. They seemed like crude ruffians, but perhaps their unpolished manner was merely the typical style of the people of the Maurenrons, a locality to which his far-flung travels had never taken him. For all he knew, they were dukes or princes or high ministers of that northern place. He wondered in an almost incurious way what it was that they wanted with him. Merely to quote his own poetry to him was an insufficient motive for traveling such a distance. Gimbiter believed that they were malevolent; and it might well be that Gimbiter, a shrewd observer of mankind, was correct in that. For the nonce, however, his day's intake of wine had fortified him against anxiety on that score. To Puillayne they were at the moment merely a puzzling novelty. He would wait to see more.

"Your journey," he said politely, "was it a taxing one?"

"We know some small magics, and we had a few useful spells to guide us. Going through the Kelpusars there was only one truly difficult passage for us," said Unthan Vyorn, "which was the crossing of the Mountain of the Eleven Uncertainties."

"Ah," said Puillayne. "I know it well." It was a place of bewildering confusion, where a swarm of identical peaks confronted the traveler and all roads seemed alike, though only one was correct and the others led into dire unpleasantness. "But you found your way through, evidently, and coped with equal deftness with the Gate of Ghosts just beyond, and the perilous Pillars of Yan Sfou."

"The hope of attaining the very place where now we find ourselves drew us onward through all obstacles," Unthan Vyorn said, outdoing even himself in unctuosity of tone. And again he quoted Puillayne:

> *The mountain roads we traveled rose ten thousand cilavers high.*
> *The rivers we crossed were more turbulent than a hundred demons.*
> *And our voices were lost in the thunder of the cataracts.*
> *We cut through brambles that few swords could slash.*
> *And then beyond the mists we saw the golden Klorpentine*
> *And it was as if we had never known hardship at all.*

How barbarously he attacked the delicate lines! How flat was his tone as he came to the ecstatic final couplet! But Puillayne masked his scorn. These were foreigners; they were his guests, however self-invited they might be; his responsibility was to maintain them at their ease. And he found them diverting, in their way. His life in these latter years had slipped into inflexible routine. The advent of poetry-quoting northern barbarians was an amusing interlude in his otherwise constricted days. He doubted more than ever, now, Gimbiter's hypothesis that they meant him harm. There seemed nothing dangerous about these three except, perhaps, the chilly eyes of the one who did not seem to speak.

His friend Gimbiter evidently had mistaken bumptiousness for malversation and malefic intent.

Fur-swathed Kesztrel Tsaye said, "We know, too, that you are a collector of exotica. Therefore we bring some humble gifts for your delight." And he, too, offered a brief quotation:

Let me have pleasures in this life
For the next is a dark abyss!

"If you will, Malion Gainthrust—"

Kesztrel Tsaye nodded to the icy-eyed silent man, who produced from somewhere a sack that Puillayne had not previously noticed, and drew from it a drum of red candana covered with taut-stretched thaupin-hide, atop which nine red-eyed homunculi performed an obscene dance. This was followed by a little sphere of green chalcedony out of which a trapped and weeping demon peered, and that by a beaker which overflowed with a tempting aromatic yellow liquid that tumbled to the floor and rose again to return to the vessel from which it had come. Other small toys succeeded those, until gifts to the number of ten or twelve sat arrayed before Puillayne.

During this time Puillayne had consumed nearly all the wine from the flask he had reserved for himself, and he felt a cheering dizziness beginning to steal over him. The three visitors, though he had offered them only a third as much apiece, had barely taken any. Were they simply abstemious? Or was the shimmering wine of Sanreale too subtle for their jackanapes palates?

He said, when it appeared that they had exhausted their display of gewgaws for him, "If this wine gives you little gratification, I can select another and perhaps superior one for you, or we could open that which you have brought me."

"It is superb wine, master," Unthan Vyorn said, "and we would expect no less from you. We know, after all, that your cellar is incomparable, that it is a storehouse of the most treasured wines of all the world, that in fact it contains even the unobtainable wine prized beyond all others, the True Vintage of Erzuine Thale. This Sanreale wine you have offered us is surely not in a class with that; but it has much merit in its own way and if we drink it slowly, it is because we cherish every swallow we take. Simply to be drinking the wine of Puillayne of Ghiusz in the veritable home of Puillayne of Ghiusz is an a honor so extreme that it constringes our throats with joy, and compels us to drink more slowly than otherwise we might."

"You know of the True Vintage, do you?" Puillayne asked.

"Is there anyone who does not? The legendary wine of the Nolwaynes who have reigned in Gammelcor since the days when the sun had the brightness of gold—the wine of miracles, the wine that offers the keenest of ecstasies that it is possible to experience—the wine that opens all doors to one with a single sip—" Unshielded covetousness now gleamed in the lanky man's eyes. "If only we could enjoy that sip! Ah, if only we could merely have a glimpse of the container that holds that wondrous elixir!"

"I rarely bring it forth, even to look at it," said Puillayne. "I fear that if I were to take it from its place of safekeeping, I would be tempted to consume it prematurely, and that is not a temptation to which I am ready to yield."

"A man of iron!" marveled Kesztrel Tsaye. "To possess the True Vintage of Erzuine Thale, and to hold off from sampling it! And why, may I ask, do you scruple to deny yourself that joy of joys?"

It was a question Puillayne had heard many times before, for his ownership of the True Vintage was not something he had concealed from his friends. "I am, you know, a prodigious scribbler of minor verse. Yes," he said, over their indignant protests, "minor verse, such a torrent of it that it would fill this manse a dozen times over if I preserved it all. I keep only a small part." He gestured moodily at the fifty volumes bound in deodand vellum. "But somewhere within me lurks the one great poem that will recapitulate all the striving of earthly history, the epic that will be the sum and testament of us who live as we do on the precipice at the edge of the end of days. Someday I will feel that poem brimming at the perimeters of my brain and demanding release. That feeling will come, I think, when our sun is in its ultimate extremity, and the encroaching darkness is about to arrive. And then, only then, will I broach the seal on the True Vintage, and quaff the legendary wine, which indeed opens all doors, including the door of creation, so that its essence will liberate the real poet within me and in my final drunken joy I will be permitted to set down that one great poem that I yearn to write."

"You do us all an injustice, master, if you wait to write that epic until the very eve of our doom," said Unthan Vyorn in a tone of what might almost have been sorrow sincerely framed. "For how will we be able to read it, when all has turned to ice and darkness? No poems will circulate among us as we lie there perishing in the final cold. You deny us your greatness! You withhold your gift!"

"Be that as it may," Puillayne said, "the time is not yet for opening that bottle. But I can offer you others."

From his cabinet he selected a generous magnum of ancient Falernian, which bore a frayed label, yellowed and parched by time. The great rounded flask lacked its seal and it was obvious to all that the container was empty save for random crusts of desiccated dregs scattered about its interior. His visitors regarded it with puzzlement. "Fear not," said Puillayne. "A mage of my acquaintance made certain of my bottles subject to the Spell of Recrudescent Fluescence, among them this one. It is inexhaustibly renewable." He turned his head aside and gave voice to the words, and within moments miraculous liquefaction commenced. While the magnum was filling he summoned a new set of goblets, which he filled near to brimming for his guests and himself.

"It is a wondrous wine," said Kesztrel Tsaye after a sip or two. "Your hospitality knows no bounds, master." Indeed such parts of his heavily bearded face that were visible were beginning to show a ruddy radiance. Unthan Vyorn likewise displayed the effects of the potent stuff, and even the taciturn Malion Gainthrust, sitting somewhat apart as though he had no business in this room, seemed to evince some reduction of his habitual glower.

Puillayne smiled benignly, sat back, let tranquility steal over him. He had not expected to be drinking the Falernian today, for it was a forceful wine, especially at this early hour. But he saw no harm in somewhat greater midday intoxication than he habitually practiced. Why, he might even find himself producing verse some hours earlier than usual. These uncouth disciples of his would probably derive some pleasure from witnessing the actual act of creation. Meanwhile, sipping steadily, he felt the walls around him beginning to sway and glide, and he ascended within himself in a gradual way until he felt himself to be floating slightly outside and above himself, a spectator of his own self, with something of a pleasant haze enveloping his mind.

Somewhat surprisingly his guests, gathered now in a circle about him, appeared to be indulging in a disquisition on the philosophy of criminality.

Kesztrel Tsaye offered the thought that the imminence of the world's demise freed one from all the restraints of law, for it mattered very little how one behaved if shortly all accounts were to be settled with equal finality. "I disagree," said Unthan Vyorn. "We remain responsible for our acts, since, if they transgress against statute and custom, they may in truth hasten the end that threatens us."

Interposing himself in their conversation, Puillayne said dreamily, "How so?"

"The misdeeds of individuals," Unthan Vyorn replied, "are not so much offenses against human law as they are ominous disturbances in a complex filament of cause and effect by which mankind is connected on all sides with surrounding nature. I believe that our cruelties, our sins, our violations, all drain vitality from our diminishing sun."

Malion Gainthrust stirred restlessly at that notion, as though he planned at last to speak, but he controlled himself with visible effort and subsided once more into remoteness.

Puillayne said, "An interesting theory: the cumulative infamies and iniquities of our species, do you say, have taken a toll on the sun itself over the many millennia, and so we are the architects of our own extinction?"

"It could be, yes."

"Then it is too late to embrace virtue, I suspect," said Puillayne dolefully. "Through our incorrigible miscreancy we have undone ourselves beyond repair. The damage is surely irreversible in this late epoch of the world's long existence." And he sighed a great sigh of unconsolable grief. To his consternation he found the effects of the long morning's drinking abruptly weakening: the circular gyration of the walls had lessened and that agreeable haze had cleared, and he felt almost sober again, defenseless against the fundamental blackness of his intellective processes. It was a familiar event. No quantity of wine was sufficient to stave off the darkness indefinitely.

"You look suddenly troubled, master," Kesztrel Tsaye observed.

"Despite the splendor of this wine, or perhaps even because of it, I see that some alteration of mood has overtaken you."

"I am reminded of my mortality. Our dim and shriveled sun—the certainty of imminent oblivion—"

"Ah, master, consider that you should be cheered by contemplation of the catastrophe that is soon to overcome us, rather than being thrust, as you say, into despond."

"Cheered?"

"Most truly. For we each must have death come unto us in our time—it is the law of the universe—and what pain it is as we lie dying to know that others will survive after we depart! But if all are to meet their end at once, then there is no reason to feel the bite of envy, and we can go easily as equals into our common destruction."

Puillayne shook his head obstinately. "I see merit in this argument, but little cheer. My death inexorably approaches, and that would be a cause of despair to me whether or not others might survive. Envy of those who survive is not a matter of any moment to me. For me, it will be as though all the cosmos dies when I do, and the dying of our sun adds only an additional layer of regret to what is already an infinitely regrettable outcome."

"You permit yourself to sink into needless brooding, master," said Unthan Vyorn airily. "You should have another goblet of wine."

"Yes. These present thoughts of mine are pathetically insipid, and I shame myself by giving rein to them. Even in the heyday of the world, when the bright yellow sun blazed forth in full intensity, the concept of death was one that every mature person was compelled to face, and only cowards and fools looked toward it with terror or rage or anything else but acceptance and detachment. One must not lament the inevitable. But it is my flaw that I am unable to escape such feelings. Wine, I have found, is my sole anodyne against them. And even that is not fully satisfactory."

He reached again for the Falernian. But Kesztrel Tsaye, interposing himself quickly, said, "That is the very wine that has brought this adverse effect upon you, master. Let us open, instead, the wine of our country that was our gift to you. You may not be aware that it is famed for its quality of soothing the troubled heart." He signalled to Malion Gainthrust, who sprang to his feet, deftly unsealed the two green carboys of Maurenron ambrosia, and, taking fresh goblets from Puillayne's cabinet, poured a tall serving of the pale bluish wine from one carboy for Puillayne and lesser quantities from the other for himself and his two companions.

"To your health, master. Your renewed happiness. Your long life."

Puillayne found their wine unexpectedly fresh and vigorous, with none of the rough and sour flavor he had led himself to anticipate. He followed his first tentative sip with a deeper one, and then with a third. In very fact it had a distinctly calmative effect, speedily lifting him out of the fresh slough of dejection into which he had let himself topple.

But another moment more and he detected a strange unwelcome furriness coating his tongue, and it began to seem to him that beneath the superficial exuberance and openheartedness of the wine lay some less appetizing tinge of flavor, something almost alkaline that crept upward on his palate and negated the immediately pleasing effect of the initial taste. Then he noticed a heaviness of the mind overtaking him, and a weakness of the limbs, and it occurred to him first that they had been serving themselves out of one carboy and him out of another, and then that he was unable to move, so that it became clear to him that the wine had been drugged. Fierce-eyed Malion Gainthrust stood directly before him, and he was speaking at last, declaiming a rhythmic chant which even in his drugged state Puillayne recognized as a simple binding spell that left him trussed and helpless.

Like any householder of some affluence Puillayne had caused his manse to be protected by an assortment of defensive charms, which the magus of his family had assured him would defend him against many sorts of inimical events. The most obvious was theft: there were treasures here that others might have reasons to crave. In addition one must guard one's house against fire, subterranean tremors, the fall of heavy stones from the sky, and other risks of the natural world. But also Puillayne was given to drunkenness, which could well lead to irresponsibility of behavior or mere clumsiness of movement, and he had bought himself a panoply of spells against the consequences of excessive intoxication.

In this moment of danger it seemed to him that Citrathanda's Punctilious Sentinel was the appropriate spirit to invoke, and in a dull thick-tongued way Puillayne began to recite the incantation. But over the years his general indifference to jeopardy had led to incaution, and he had not taken the steps that were needful to maintain the potency of his guardian spirits, which had dimmed with time so that his spell had no effect. Nor would his household revenants be of the slightest use in this predicament. Their barely corporeal forms could exert no force against tangible life. Only his gardeners were incarnate beings, and they, even if they had been on the premises this late in the day, would have been unlikely to heed his call. Puillayne realized that he was altogether without protection now. Gently his guests, who now were his captors, were prodding him upward out of his couch. Kesztrel Tsaye said, "You will kindly accompany us, please, as we make our tour of your widely reputed treasury of priceless prizes."

All capacity for resistance was gone from him. Though they had left him with the power of locomotion, his arms were bound by invisible but unbreakable withes, and his spirit itself was captive to their wishes. He could do no other than let himself be led through one hall after another of his museum, staggering a little under the effect of their wine, and when they asked him of the nature of this artifact or that, he had no choice but to tell them. Whatever object caught their fancy they removed from its case, with Malion Gainthrust serving as the means by which it was carried back to his great central room and added to a growing heap of plunder.

Thus they selected the Crystal Pillow of Carsephone Zorn, within which scenes from the daily life of any of seven subworlds could be viewed at ease, and the brocaded underrobe of some forgotten monarch of the Pharials, whose virility was enhanced twentyfold by an hour's wearing of it, and the Key of Sarpanigondar, a surgical tool by which any diseased organ of the body could be reached and healed without a breaching of the skin. They took also the Infinitely Replenishable Casket of Jade, once the utmost glory of the turban-wearing marauders of the frigid valleys of the Lesser Ghalur, and Sangaal's Remarkable Phoenix, from whose feathers fluttered a constant shower of gold dust, and the Heptachromatic Carpet of Kypard Segung, and the carbuncle-encrusted casket that contained the Incense of the Emerald Sky, and many another extraordinary object that had been part of Puillayne's hoard of fabulosities for decade upon decade.

He watched in mounting chagrin. "So you have come all this way merely to rob me, then?"

"It is not so simple," said Kesztrel Tsaye. "You must believe us when we say that we revere your poetry, and were primarily motivated to endure the difficulties of the journey by the hope of attaining your actual presence."

"You choose an odd way to demonstrate your esteem for my art, then, for you would strip me of those things which I love even while claiming to express your regard for my work."

"Does it matter who owns these things for the upcoming interim?" the bearded man asked. "In a short while the concept of ownership itself will be a moot one. You have stressed that point frequently in your verse."

There was a certain logic to that, Puillayne admitted. As the mound of loot grew, he attempted to assuage himself by bringing himself to accept Kesztrel Tsaye's argument that the sun would soon enough reach its last moment, smothering Earth in unending darkness and burying him and all his possessions under an obdurate coating of ice twenty marasangs thick, so what significance was there in the fact that these thieves were denuding him today of these trifles? All would be lost tomorrow or the day after, whether or not he had ever admitted the caitiff trio to his door.

But that species of sophistry brought him no surcease. Realistic appraisal of the probabilities told him that the dying of the sun might yet be a thousand years away, or even more, for although its inevitability was assured, its imminence was not so certain. Though ultimately he would be bereft of everything, as would everyone else including these three villains, Puillayne came now to the realization that, all other things being equal, he preferred to await the end of all things amidst the presence of his collected keepsakes rather than without them. In that moment he resolved to adopt a defensive posture.

Therefore he attempted once more to recite the Punctilious Sentinel of Citrathanda, emphasizing each syllable with a precision that he hoped might enhance the power of the spell. But his captors were so confident that there would be no result that they merely laughed as he spoke the verses, rather than making any effort to muffle his voice, and in this they were correct: as before, no guardian spirit came to his aid. Puillayne sensed that unless he found some more effective step to take he was about to lose all that they had already selected, and, for all he knew, his life as well; and in that moment, facing the real possibility of personal extinction this very day, he understood quite clearly that his lifelong courtship of death had been merely a pose, that he was in no way actually prepared to take his leave of existence.

One possibility of saving himself remained.

"If you will set me free," Puillayne said, pausing an instant or two to focus their attention, "I will locate and share with you the True Vintage of Erzuine Thale."

The impact of that statement upon them was immediate and unmistakable. Their eyes brightened; their faces grew flushed and glossy; they exchanged excited glances of frank concupiscence.

Puillayne believed he understood this febrile response. They had been so overcome with an access of trivial greed, apparently, once they had had Puillayne in their power and knew themselves free to help themselves at will to the rich and varied contents of his halls, that they had forgotten for the moment that his manse contained not only such baubles as the Heptochromatic Carpet and the Infinitely Replenishable

Casket, but also, hidden away somewhere in his enormous accumulation of rare wines, something vastly more desirable, the veritable wine of wines itself, the bringer of infinitely ecstatic fulfillment, the elixir of ineffable rapture, the True Vintage of Erzuine Thale. Now he had reminded them of it and all its delights; and now they craved it with an immediate and uncontrollable desire.

"A splendid suggestion," said Unthan Vyorn, betraying by his thickness of voice the intensity of his craving. "Summon the wine from its place of hiding, and we will partake."

"The bottle yields to no one's beck," Puillayne declared. "I must fetch it myself."

"Fetch it, then."

"You must first release me."

"You are capable of walking, are you not? Lead us to the wine, and we will do the rest."

"Impossible," said Puillayne. "How do you think this famed wine has survived so long? It is protected by a network of highly serviceable spells, such as Thampyron's Charm of Impartial Security, which insures that the flask will yield only to the volition of its inscribed owner, who at present is myself. If the flask senses that my volition is impaired, it will refuse to permit opening. Indeed, if it becomes aware that I am placed under extreme duress, the wine itself will be destroyed."

"What do you request of us, then?"

"Free my arms. I will bring the bottle from its nest and open it for you, and you may partake of it, and I wish you much joy of it."

"And then?"

"You will have had the rarest experience known to the soul of man, and I will have been cheated of the opportunity to give the world the epic poem that you claim so dearly to crave; and then, I hope, we will be quits, and you will leave me my little trinkets and take yourselves back to your dreary northern caves. Are we agreed?"

They looked at one another, coming quickly and wordlessly to an agreement, and Kesztrel Tsaye, with a grunt of assent, signalled to Malion Gainthrust to intone the counterspell. Puillayne felt the bonds that had embraced his arms melting away. He extended them in a lavish stretching gesture, flexed his fingers, looked expectantly at his captors.

"Now fetch the celebrated wine," said Kesztrel Tsaye.

They accompanied him back through chamber after chamber until they reached the hall where his finest wines were stored. Puillayne made a great show of searching through rack after rack, muttering to himself, shaking his head. "I have hidden it very securely," he reported after a time. "Not so much as a precaution against theft, you realize, but as a way of making it more difficult for me to seize upon it myself in a moment of drunken impulsiveness."

"We understand," Unthan Vyorn said. "But find it, if you please. We grow impatient."

"Let me think. If I were hiding such a miraculous wine from myself, where would I put it? The Cabinet of Meritorious Theriacs? Hardly. The Cinnabar Vestibule? The Chrysochlorous Benefice? The Tabulature? The Trogonic Chamber?"

As he pondered he could see their restiveness mounting from one instant to the next. They tapped their fingers against their thighs, they moved their feet from side to side, they ran their hands inside their garments as though weapons were hidden there. Unheeding, Puillayne continued to frown and mutter. But then he brightened. "Ah, yes, yes, of course!" And he crossed the room, threw open a low door in the wall at its farther side, reached into the dusty interior of a service aperture.

"Here," he said jubilantly. "The True Vintage of Erzuine Thale!"

"This?" said Kesztrel Tsaye, with some skepticism.

The bottle Puillayne held forth to them was a gray tapering one, dust-encrusted and unprepossessing, bearing only a single small label inscribed with barely legible runes in faint grayish ink. They crowded around like snorting basilisks inflamed with lust. Each in turn puzzled over the writing; but none could decipher it.

"What language is that?" asked Unthan Vyorn.

"These are Nolwaynish runes," answered Puillayne. "See, see, here is the name of the maker, the famed vintner Erzuine Thale, and here is the date of the wine's manufacture, in a chronology that I fear will mean nothing to you, and this emblem here is the seal of the king of Gammelcore who was reigning at the time of the bottling."

"You would not deceive us?" said Kesztrel Thale. "You would not fob some lesser wine off on us, taking advantage of our inability to read these scrawls?"

Puillayne laughed jovially. "Put all your suspicions aside! I will not conceal the fact that I bitterly resent the imposition you are enforcing on me here, but that does not mean I can shunt aside thirty generations of family honor. Surely you must know that on my father's side I am the Eighteenth Maghada of Nalanda, and there is a geas upon me as hereditary leader of that sacred order that bans me from all acts of deceit. This is, I assure you, the True Vintage of Erzuine Thale, and nothing else. Stand a bit aside, if you will, so that I can open the flask without activating Thampyron's Charm, for, may I remind you, any hint that I act under duress will destroy its contents. It would be a pity to have preserved this wine for so long a time only to have it become worthless vinegar in the moment of unsealing."

"You act now of your own free will," Unthan Vyorn said. "It was your choice to offer us this wine, nor was it done at our insistence."

"This is true," Puillayne responded. He set out four goblets and, contemplating the flask thoughtfully, spoke the words that would breach its seal.

"Three goblets will suffice," said Kesztrel Tsaye.

"I am not to partake?"

"If you do, it will leave that much less for us."

"You are cruel indeed, depriving me even of a fourth share of this wine, which I obtained at such expense and after negotiations so prolonged I can scarcely bear to think of them. But so be it. I will have none. As you pointed out, what does it matter, or anything else, when the hour of everlasting night grows ineluctably near?"

He put one goblet aside and filled the other three. Malion Gainthrust was the first to seize his, clutching it with berserk intensity and gulping it to its depths in a single crazed ingurgitation. Instantly his strange chilly eyes grew bright as blazing coals. The other two men drank more judiciously, frowning a bit at the first sip as though they had expected some more immediate ebullition, sipping again, frowning again, now trembling. Puillayne refilled the goblets. "Drink deep," he abjured them. "How I envy you this ecstasy of ecstasies!"

Malion Gainthrust now fell to the floor, thrashing about oddly, and a moment later Kesztrel Tsaye did the same, toppling like a felled tree and slapping his hands against the tiles as though to indicate some extreme inward spasm. Long-legged Unthan Vyorn, suddenly looking deathly pale, swayed erratically, clutched at his throat, and gasped, "But this some poison, is it not? By the Thodiarch, you have betrayed us!"

"Indeed," said Puillayne blandly, as Unthan Vyorn joined his writhing fellows on the floor. "I have given you not the True Vintage of Erzuine Thale, but the Efficacious Solvent of Gibrak Lahinne. The strictures of honor placed upon me in my capacity as Eighteenth Maghada of Nalanda do not extend to a requirement that I ignore the need for self-defense. Already, I believe, the bony frame of your bodies has begun to dissolve. Your internal organs must also be under attack. You will shortly lose consciousness, I suspect, which will spare you from whatever agonies you may at the moment be experiencing. But do you wonder that I took so harsh a step? You thought I was a helpless idle fool, and quite likely that scornful assessment was correct up until this hour, but by entering my sanctum and attempting to part me from the things I hold precious, you awakened me from my detachment and restored me to the love of life that had long ago fled from me. No longer did the impending doom of the world enfold me in paralysis. Indeed, I chose to take action against your depredations, and so—

But he realized that there was no reason for further statements. His visitors had been reduced to puddles of yellow slime, leaving just their caps and boots and other garments, which he would add to his collection of memorabilia. The rest required only the services of his corps of revenants to remove, and then he was able to proceed with a clear mind to the remaining enterprises of a normal afternoon.

"But will you not now at last permit yourself to enjoy the True Vintage?" Gimbiter Soleptan asked him two nights later, when he and several other of Puillayne's closest friends had gathered in a tent of sky-blue silk in the garden of the poet's manse for a celebratory dinner. The intoxicating scent of calavindra blossoms was in the air, and the pungent odor of sweet nargiise. "They might so easily have deprived you of it, and who knows but some subsequent miscreant might have more success? Best to drink it now, say I, and have the enjoyment of it before that is made impossible for you. Yes, drink it now!"

"Not quite yet," said Puillayne in a steadfast tone. "I understand the burden of your thought: seize the moment, guarantee the consumption while I can. By that reasoning I should have guzzled it the instant those scoundrels had fallen. But you must remember that I have reserved a higher use for that wine. And the time for that use has not yet arrived."

"Yes," said Immiter of Glosz, a white-haired sage who was of all the members of Puillayne's circle the closest student of his work. "The great epic that you propose to indite in the hour of the sun's end—"

"Yes. And I must have the unbroached True Vintage at hand to spur my hand, when that hour comes. Meanwhile, though, there are many wines here of not quite so notable a puissance that are worthy of our attention, and I propose that we ingest more than a few flasks this evening." Puillayne gestured broadly at the array of wines he had previously set out, and beckoned to his friends to help themselves. "And as you drink," he said, drawing from his brocaded sleeve a scrap of parchment, "I offer you the verses of this afternoon."

The night is coming, but what of that?
Do I not glow with pleasure still, and glow, and glow?
There is no darkness, there is no misery
So long as my flask is near!

The flower-picking maidens sing their lovely song by the jade pavilion.
The winged red khotemnas flutter brightly in the trees.
I laugh and lift my glass and drain it to the dregs.
O golden wine! O glorious day!

Surely we are still only in the springtime of our winter
And I know that death is merely a dream
When I have my flask!

DEFENDERS OF THE FRONTIER

Hardly had I agreed to write a Dying Earth *story for the editorial team of Gardner Dozois and George R.R. Martin but they were back at me to do something for a second anthology they were assembling, a book called* Warriors.

This wasn't specifically a science-fiction anthology. Ultimately it would include some s-f stories by Joe Haldeman, David Weber, S.M. Stirling, editor Dozois, and other stalwarts of the genre, but it was intended to cut across genre lines to take in stories of all sorts that were linked only by the theme of warfare, and the contributors represented a broad range of fields and a stellar conglomeration of writers, Lawrence Block and Peter S. Beagle and Robin Hobb and Cecelia Holland and many more.

As George R.R. Martin says in his introduction, "We asked each of them for the same thing—a story about a warrior. Some chose to write in the genre they're best known for. Some decided to try something different. You will find warriors of every shape, size, and color in these pages, warriors from every epoch in human history, from yesterday and today and tomorrow, and worlds that never were...."

I am no warrior myself. I am a quiet, somewhat reserved man who dislikes confrontation and violence, and I have had no experience with military service, having been born too late for World War II, having spent the time of the Korean War in college, and being too old for Vietnam and all the wars that have followed. But I haven't visited the worlds of Alpha Centauri, either, nor have I been an android, a time traveler, the monarch of a gigantic planet of the far future, or a telepath, and that hasn't stopped *me from writing about them with, I think, some conviction and plausibility. So, although "Defenders of the Frontier" has no battle scenes in it, no technical descriptions of armaments and the way to use them, no elaborate demonstrations of the strategy of warfare, it is quite definitely a story about warriors and the stresses they face on a distant frontier, to which I applied the same sort of imaginative thinking that produced* Dying Inside, Lord Valentine's Castle, *and* "Sailing to Byzantium." *I wrote the story relatively quickly and with considerable pleasure in December, 2007, and George and Gardner published it in their anthology in March, 2010.*

S eeker has returned to the fort looking flushed and exhilarated. "I was right," he announces. "There is one of them hiding quite close by. I was certain of it, and now I know where he is. I can definitely feel directionality this time."

Stablemaster, skeptical as always, lifts one eyebrow. "You were wrong the last time. You're always too eager these days to find them out there."

Seeker merely shrugs. "There can be no doubt," he says.

For three weeks now Seeker has been searching for an enemy spy—or straggler, or renegade, or whatever he may be—that he believes is camped in the vicinity of the fort. He has gone up to this hilltop and that one, to this watchtower and that, making his solitary vigil, casting forth his mind's net in that mysterious way of his that none of us can begin to fathom. And each time he has come back convinced that he feels enemy emanations, but he has never achieved a strong enough sense of directionality to warrant our sending out a search party. This time he has the look of conviction about him. Seeker is a small, flimsy sort of man, as his kind often tends to be, and much of the time in recent months he has worn the slump-shouldered look of dejection and disappointment. His trade is in finding enemies for us to kill. Enemies have been few and far between of late. But now he is plainly elated. There is an aura of triumph about him, of vindication.

Captain comes into the room. Instantly he sizes up the situation. "What have we here?" he says brusquely. "Have you sniffed out something at last, Seeker?"

"Come. I'll show you."

He leads us all out onto the flat roof adjacent to our barracks. To the right and left, the huge turreted masses of the eastern and western redoubts, now unoccupied, rise above us like vast pillars, and before us lies the great central courtyard, with the massive wall of tawny brick that guards us on the north beyond it. The fort is immense, an enormous sprawling edifice designed to hold ten thousand men. I remember very clearly the gigantic effort we expended in the building of it, twenty years before. Today just eleven occupants remain, and we rattle about it like tiny pebbles in a colossal jug.

Seeker gestures outward, into the gritty yellow wasteland that stretches before us like an endless ocean on the far side of the wall. That flat plain of twisted useless shrubs marks the one gap in the line of precipitous cliffs that forms the border here between Imperial territory and the enemy lands. It has been our task these twenty years past—we were born to it; it is an obligation of our caste—to guard that gap against the eventual incursion of the enemy army. For two full decades we have inhabited these lonely lands. We have fortified that gap, we have patrolled it, we have dedicated our lives to guarding it. In the old days entire brigades of enemy troops would attempt to breach our line, appearing suddenly like clouds of angry insects out of the dusty plain, and with great loss of life on both sides we would drive them back. Now things are quieter on this frontier, very much quieter indeed, but we are still here, watching for and intercepting the occasional spies that periodically attempt to slip past our defenses.

"There," says Seeker. "Do you see those three little humps over to the northeast? He's dug in not very far behind them. I know he is. I can feel him the way you'd feel a boil on the back of your neck."

"Just one man?" Captain asks.

"One. Only one."

Weaponsmaster says, "What would one man hope to accomplish? Do you think he expects to come tiptoeing into the fort and kill us one by one?"

"There's no need for us to try to understand them," Sergeant says. "Our job is to find them and kill them. We can leave understanding them to the wiser heads back home."

"Ah," says Armorer sardonically. "Back home, yes. Wiser heads."

Captain has walked to the rim of the roof and stands there with his back to us, clutching the rail and leaning forward into the dry, crisp wind that eternally blows across our courtyard. A sphere of impenetrable chilly silence seems to surround him. Captain has always been an enigmatic man, solitary and brooding, but he has become stranger than ever since the death of Colonel, three years past, left him the ranking officer of the fort. No one knows his mind now, and no one dares to attempt any sort of intimacy with it.

"Very well," he says, after an interval that has become intolerably long. "A four-man search party: Sergeant to lead, accompanied by Seeker, Provisioner, and Surveyor. Set out in the morning. Take three days' food. Search, find, and kill."

It has been eleven weeks since the last successful search mission. That one ended in the killing of three enemies, but since then, despite Seeker's constant efforts, there have been no signs of any hostile presence in our territory. Once, six or seven weeks back, Seeker managed to convince himself that he felt emanations coming from a site along the river, a strange place for an enemy to have settled because it was well within our defense perimeter, and a five-man party led by Stablemaster hastened out to look. But they found no one there except a little band of the Fisherfolk, who swore that they had seen nothing unusual thereabouts, and the Fisherfolk do not lie. Upon their return Seeker himself had to admit that he no longer felt the emanations and that he was now none too certain he had felt any in the first place.

There is substantial feeling among us that we have outlived our mission here, that few if any enemies still occupy the territory north of the gap, that quite possibly the war has long since been over. Sergeant, Quartermaster, Weaponsmaster, and Armorer are the chief proponents of this belief. They note that we have heard nothing whatsoever from the capital in years—no messengers have come, let alone reinforcements or fresh supplies—and that we have had no sign from the enemy, either, that any significant force of them is gathered anywhere nearby. Once, long ago, war seemed imminent, and indeed real battles often took place. But it has been terribly quiet here for a long time. There has been nothing like a real battle for six years, only a few infrequent skirmishes with small enemy platoons, and during the past two years we have detected just a few isolated outliers, usually no more than two or three men at a time, whom we catch relatively easily as they try to infiltrate our territory. Armorer insists that they are not spies but stragglers, the last remnants of whatever enemy force once occupied the region to our north, who have been driven by hunger or loneliness or who knows what other compulsion to take up positions close to our fort. He argues that in the twenty years we have been here, our own numbers have dwindled from ten thousand men to a mere eleven, at first by losses in battle but later by the attrition of age and ill health, and he thinks it is reasonable that the same dwindling has occurred on the other side of the border, so that we few defenders now confront an enemy that may be even fewer in number than ourselves.

I myself see much to concur with in Armorer's position. I think it might very well be the case that we are a lost platoon, that the war is over and the Empire has forgotten us, and that there is no purpose at all in our continued vigilance. But if the Empire has forgotten us, who can give the order that withdraws us from our post? That is a decision that only Captain can make, and Captain has not given us the slightest impression of where he stands on the issue. And so we remain, and may remain to the end of our days. What folly that would be, says Armorer, to languish out here forever defending this forlorn frontier country against invaders that no longer choose to invade! And I half agree with him, but only half. I would not want to spend such time as remains to me working at a fool's task; but equally I do not wish to be guilty of dereliction of duty, after having served so long and so honorably on this frontier. Thus I am of two minds on the issue.

There is, of course, the opposite theory that holds that the enemy is simply biding its time, waiting for us to abandon the fort, after which a great army will come pouring through the gap at long last and strike at the Empire from one of its most vulnerable sides. Engineer and Signalman are the most vocal proponents of this viewpoint. They think it would be an act of profound treason to withdraw, the negation of all that we have dedicated our lives to, and they become irate when the idea is merely suggested. When they propound this position I find it hard to disagree.

Seeker is the one who works hardest to keep our mission alive, constantly striving to pick up threatening emanations. That has been his life's work, after all. He knows no other vocation, that sad little man. So day by day Seeker climbs his hilltops and haunts his watchtowers and uses his one gift to detect the presence of hostile minds, and now and then he returns and sounds the alarm, and off we go on yet another search foray. More often than not they prove to be futile, nowadays:

either Seeker's powers are failing or he is excessively anxious to interpret his inputs as the mental output from nearby enemies.

I confess I feel a certain excitement at being part of this latest search
party. Our days are spent in such terrible empty routine, normally. We
tend our little vegetable patch, we look after our animals, we fish and
hunt, we do our regular maintenance jobs, we read the same few books
over and again, we have the same conversations, chiefly reminiscing
about the time when there were more than eleven of us here, recalling
as well as we can the robust and earthy characters who once dwelled
among us but are long since gone to dust. Tonight, therefore, I feel a
quickening of the pulse. I pack my gear for the morning, I eat my dinner with unusual gusto, I couple passionately with my little Fisherfolk
companion. Each of us, all but Seeker, who seems to know no needs of
that sort, has taken a female companion from among the band of simple people who live along our one feeble river. Even Captain takes one
sometimes into his bed, I understand, although unlike the rest of us he
has no regular woman. Mine is called Wendrit. She is a pale and slender
creature, surprisingly skillful in the arts of love. The Fisherfolk are not
quite human—we and they are unable to conceive children together, for
example—but they are close enough to human to serve most purposes,
and they are pleasant, unassuming, uncomplaining companions. So I
embrace Wendrit vigorously this night, and in the dawn the four of us
gather, Sergeant, Provisioner, Seeker, and I, by the northern portcullis.

It is a bright, clear morning, the sun a hard, sharp-edged disk in the
eastern sky. The sun is the only thing that comes to us from the Empire,
visiting us each day after it has done its work back there, uncountable
thousands of miles to the east. Probably the capital is already in darkness by now, just as we are beginning our day. The world is so large,
after all, and we are so very far from home.

Once there would have been trumpeters to celebrate our departure as we rode through the portcullis, hurling a brassy fanfare for us
into the quiet air. But the last of our trumpeters died years ago, and
though we still have the instruments, none of us knows how to play
them. I tried once, and made a harsh squeaking sound like the grinding of metal against metal, nothing more. So the only sound we hear as
we ride out into the desert is the soft steady thudding of our mounts'
hooves against the brittle sandy soil.

In truth this is the bleakest of places, but we are used to it. I still
have memories from my childhood of the floral splendor of the capital,

great trees thick with juicy leaves, and shrubs clad in clusters of flowers, red and yellow and orange and purple, and the dense green lawns of the grand boulevards. But I have grown accustomed to the desert, which has become the norm for me, and such lush abundance as I remember out of my earlier life strikes me now as discomfortingly vulgar and excessive, a wasteful riot of energy and resources. All that we have here in the plain that runs out to the north between the wall of hills is dry yellow soil sparkling with the doleful sparkle of overabundant quartz, small gnarled shrubs and equally gnarled miniature trees, and occasional tussocks of tough, sharp-edged grass. On the south side of the fort the land is not quite so harsh, for our little river runs past us there, a weak strand of some much mightier one that must pour out of one of the big lakes in the center of the continent. Our river must be looking for the sea, as rivers do, but of course we are nowhere near the sea, and doubtless it exhausts itself in some distant reach of the desert. But as it passes our outpost it brings greenery to its flanks, and some actual trees, and enough fish to support the tribe of primitive folk who are our only companions here.

Our route lies to the northeast, toward those three rounded hillocks behind which, so Seeker staunchly asserts, we will find the campsite of our solitary enemy. The little hills had seemed close enough when we viewed them from the barracks roof, but that was only an illusion, and we ride all day without visibly diminishing the span between them and us. It is a difficult trek. The ground, which is merely pebbly close by the fort, becomes rocky and hard to traverse farther out, and our steeds pick their way with care, heedful of their fragile legs. But this is familiar territory for us. Everywhere we see traces of hoofprints or tire tracks, five years old, ten, even twenty, the scars of ancient forays, the debris of half-forgotten battles of a decade and more ago. Rain comes perhaps twice a year here at best. Make a mark on the desert floor and it remains forever.

We camp as the first lengthening of the shadows begins, gather some scrubby wood for our fire, pitch our tent. There is not much in the way of conversation. Sergeant is a crude, inarticulate man at best; Seeker is too tense and fretful to be pleasant company; Provisioner, who has grown burly and red-faced with the years, can be jovial enough after a drink or two, but he seems uncharacteristically moody and aloof tonight. So I am left to my own resources, and once we have finished our meal I walk out a short way into the night and stare, as I often do, at the glittering array of stars in this western sky of ours, wondering, as ever, whether each has its own collection of worlds, and whether those worlds are peopled, and what sort of lives the peoples of those worlds might lead. It is a perverse sort of amusement, I suppose: I who have spent half my life guarding a grim brick fort in this parched isolated outpost stare at the night sky and imagine the gleaming palaces and fragrant gardens of faraway worlds.

We rise early, make a simple breakfast, ride on through a cutting wind toward those three far-off hills. This morning, though, the perspective changes quickly: suddenly the hills are much closer, and then they are upon us, and Seeker, excited now, guides us toward the pass between the southernmost hill and its neighbor. "I feel him just beyond!" he cries. For Seeker, the sense that he calls directionality is like a compass, pointing the way toward our foes. "Come! This is the way! Hurry! Hurry!"

Nor has he led us wrongly this time. On the far side of the southernmost hill someone has built a little lean-to of twisted branches covered with a heaping of grass, no simple project in these stony ungenerous wastes. We draw our weapons and take up positions surrounding it, and Sergeant goes up to it and says, "You! Come out of there, and keep your hands in the air!"

There is a sound of stirring from within. In a moment or two a man emerges.

He has the classic enemy physiognomy: a short, stumpy body, sallow waxen skin, and heavy features with jutting cheekbones and icy blue eyes. At the sight of those eyes I feel an involuntary surge of anger, even hatred, for we of the Empire are a brown-eyed people and I have trained myself through many years to feel nothing but hostility for those whose eyes are blue.

But these are not threatening eyes. Obviously the man had been asleep, and he is still making the journey back into wakefulness as he comes forth from his shelter, blinking, shaking his head. He is trembling, too. He is one man and we are four, and we have weapons drawn and he is unarmed, and he has been taken by surprise. It is an unfortunate way to start one's day. I am amazed to find my anger giving way to something like pity.

He is given little time to comprehend the gravity of his situation. "Bastard!" Sergeant says, and takes three strides forward. Swiftly he thrusts his knife into the man's belly, withdraws it, strikes again, again.

The blue eyes go wide with shock. I am shocked myself, in a different way, and the sudden cruel attack leaves me gasping with amazement.

The stricken enemy staggers, clutches at his abdomen as though trying to hold back the torrent of blood, takes three or four tottering steps, and falls in a series of folding ripples. There is a convulsion or two, and then he is still, lying face downward.

Sergeant kicks the entrance of the shelter open and peers within. "See if there's anything useful in there," he tells us.

Still astounded, I say, "Why did you kill him so quickly?"

"We came here to kill him."

"Perhaps. But he was unarmed. He probably would have given himself up peacefully."

"We came here to kill him," Sergeant says again.

"We might have interrogated him first, at least. That's the usual procedure, isn't it? Perhaps there are others of his kind somewhere close at hand."

"If there were any more of them around here," Sergeant says scornfully, "Seeker would have told us, wouldn't he have? Wouldn't he have, Surveyor?"

There is more that I would like to say, about how it might have been useful or at any rate interesting to discover why this man had chosen to make this risky pilgrimage to the edge of our territory. But there is no point in continuing the discussion, because Sergeant is too stupid to care what I have to say, and the man is already dead, besides.

We knock the shelter apart and search it. Nothing much there: a few tools and weapons, a copper-plated religious emblem of the kind that our enemies worship, a portrait of a flat-faced blue-eyed woman who is, I suppose, the enemy's wife or mother. It does not seem like the equipment of a spy. Even to an old soldier like me it is all very sad. He was a man like us, enemy though he was, and he died far from home. Yes, it has long been our task to kill these people before they can kill us. Certainly I have killed more than a few of them myself. But dying in battle is one thing; being slaughtered like a pig while still half asleep is something else again. Especially if your only purpose had been to surrender. Why else had this solitary man, this lonely and probably desperate man, crossed this unrelenting desert, if not to give himself up to us at the fort?

I am softening with age, I suppose. Sergeant is right that it was our assignment to kill him: Captain had given us that order in the most explicit way. Bringing him back with us had never been part of the plan. We have no way of keeping prisoners at the fort. We have little enough food for ourselves, and guarding him would have posed a problem. He had had to die; his life was forfeit from the moment he ventured within the zone bordering on the fort. That he might have been lonely or desperate, that he had suffered in crossing this terrible desert and perhaps had hoped to win shelter at our fort, that he had had a wife or perhaps a mother whom he loved, all of that was irrelevant. It did not come as news to me that our enemies are human beings not all that different from us except in the color of their eyes and the texture of their skins. They are, nevertheless, our enemies. Long ago they set their hands against us in warfare, and until the day arrives when they put aside their dream of destroying what we of the Empire have built for ourselves, it is the duty of people like us to slay men like him. Sergeant had not been kind or gentle about it. But there is no kind or gentle way, really, to kill.

The days that followed were extremely quiet ones. Without so much as a discussion of what had taken place in the desert we fell back into our routines: clean and polish this and that, repair whatever needs repair and still can be repaired, take our turns working in the fields alongside the river, wade in that shallow stream in quest of water-pigs for our table, tend the vats where we store the mash that becomes our beer, and so on, so forth, day in, day out. Of course I read a good deal, also. I have ever been a man for reading.

We have nineteen books; all the others have been read to pieces, or their bindings have fallen apart in the dry air, or the volumes have simply been misplaced somewhere about the fort and never recovered. I have read all nineteen again and again, even though five of them are technical manuals covering areas that never were part of my skills and which are irrelevant now anyway. (There is no point in knowing how to repair our vehicles when the last of our fuel supply was exhausted five years ago.) One of my favorite books is *The Saga of the Kings*, which I have known since childhood, the familiar account, probably wholly mythical, of the Empire's early history, the great charismatic leaders who built it, their heroic deeds, their inordinately long lifespans. There is a religious text too that I value, though I have grave doubts about the existence of the gods. But for me the choice volume of our library is the one called *The Register of Strange Things Beyond the Ranges*, a thousand-year-old account of the natural wonders to be found in the outer reaches of the Empire's great expanse. Only half the book remains to us now—perhaps one of my comrades ripped pages out to use as kindling, once upon a time—but I cherish that half, and read it constantly, even though I know it virtually by heart by this time.

Wendrit likes me to read to her. How much of what she hears she is capable of understanding, I have no idea: she is a simple soul, as all her people are. But I love the way she turns her big violet-hued eyes toward me as I read, and sits in total attention.

I read to her of the Gate of Ghosts, telling her of the customs shed there that spectral phantoms guard: "Ten men go out, nine men return." I read to her of the Stones of Shao, two flat-sided slabs flanking a main highway that on a certain day every ten years would come crashing together, crushing any wayfarers who happened to be passing through just then, and of the bronze Pillars of King Mai, which hold the two stones by an incantation that forbids them ever to move again. I read to her of the Mountain of a Thousand Eyes, the granite face of which is pockmarked with glossy onyx boulders that gleam down upon passersby like stern black eyes. I tell her of the Forest of Cinnamon, and of the Grotto of Dreams, and of the Place of Galloping Clouds. Were such places real, or simply the fantasies of some ancient spinner of tall tales? How would I know, I who spent my childhood and youth at the capital, and have passed the rest of my years here at this remote desert fort, where there is nothing to be seen but sandy yellow soil, and twisted shrubs, and little scuttering scorpions that run before our feet? But the strange places described in *The Register of Strange Things Beyond the Ranges* have grown more real to me in these latter days than the capital itself, which has become in my mind a mere handful of vague and fragmentary impressions. So I read with conviction, and Wendrit listens in awe, and when I weary of the wonders of the *Register* I put it aside and take her hand and lead her to my bed, and caress her soft pale-green skin and kiss the tips of her small round breasts, and so we pass another night.

In those quiet days that followed our foray I thought often of the man Sergeant had killed. In the days when we fought battles here I killed without compunction, five, ten, twenty men at a time, not exactly taking pleasure in it but certainly feeling no guilt. But the killing in those days was done at a decent distance, with rifles or heavy guns, for we still had ammunition then and our rifles and guns were still in good repair. It was necessary now in our forays against the occasional spies who approached the fort to kill with spears or knives, and to kill at close range feels less like a deed of warfare to me and more like murder.

My mind went back easily to those battles of yesteryear: the sound of the sentry's alarm, the first view of the dark line of enemy troops on the horizon, the rush to gather our weapons and start our vehicles. And out we would race through the portcullis to repel the invaders, rushing to take up our primary defensive formation, then advancing in even ranks that filled the entire gap in the hills, so that when the enemy entered that deadly funnel we could fall upon them and slaughter them. It was the same thing every time. They came; we responded; they perished. How far they must have traveled to meet their dismal deaths in our dreary desert! None of us had any real idea how far away the country of the enemy actually was, but we knew it had to be a great distance to the north and west, just as our own country is a great distance to the south and east. The frontier that our own outpost defends lies on the midpoint between one desert and another. Behind us is the almost infinite terrain of sparse settlements that eventually culminates in the glorious cities of the Empire. Before us are equally interminable wastes that gives way, eventually, to the enemy homeland itself. For one nation to attack the other, it must send its armies far across an uncharted and unfriendly nothingness. Which our enemy was willing to do, the gods only knew why, and again and again their armies came, and again and again we destroyed them in the fine frenzy of battle. That was a long time ago. We were not much more than boys then. But finally the marching armies came no more, and the only enemies we had to deal with were those few infrequent spies or perhaps stragglers whom Seeker pinpointed for us, and whom we went out and slew at close range with our knives and spears, looking into their frosty blue eyes as we robbed them of their lives.

Seeker is in a bad way. He can go from one day to the next without saying a word. He still heads up to his watchtowers almost every morning, but he returns from his vigils in a black cloak of gloom and moves through our midst in complete silence. We know better than to approach him at such times, because, though he is a man of no great size and strength, he can break out in savage fury sometimes when his depressions are intruded upon. So we let him be; but as the days pass and his mood grows ever darker, we fear some sort of explosion.

One afternoon I saw him speaking with Captain out on the rooftop terrace. It appeared that Captain had initiated the conversation, and that Seeker was answering Captain's questions with the greatest reluctance, staring down at his boots as he spoke. But then Captain said something that caused Seeker to react with surprising animation, looking up, gesticulating. Captain shook his head. Seeker pounded his fists together. Captain made a gesture of dismissal and walked away.

What they were saying to each other was beyond all guessing. And beyond all asking, too, for if anyone is more opaque than Seeker, it is Captain, and while it is at least possible at certain times to ask Seeker what is on his mind, making such an inquiry of Captain is inconceivable.

In recent days Seeker has taken to drinking with us after dinner. That is a new thing for him. He has always disliked drinking. He says he despises the stuff we make that we call beer and wine and brandy. That is reasonable enough, because we make our beer from the niggardly sour grain of a weed that grows by the river, and we wrest our thin wine and our rough brandy from the bitter gray fruits of a different weed, and they are pitiful products indeed to anyone who remembers the foaming beers of the capital and the sweet vintages of our finest wine-producing districts. But we have long since exhausted the supplies of such things that we brought with us, and, of course, no replenishments from home ever come, and, since in this somber landscape there is comfort to be had from drinking, we drink what we can make. Not Seeker, no. Not until this week.

Now he drinks, though, showing no sign of pleasure, but often extending his glass for another round. And at last one night when he has come back with his glass more than once, he breaks his long silence.

"They are all gone," he says, in a voice like the tolling of a cracked bell.

"Who are?" Provisioner asks. "The scorpions? I saw three scorpions only yesterday." Provisioner is well along in his cups, as usual. His reddened, jowly face creases in a broad toothy smile, as if he has uttered the cleverest of witticisms.

"The enemy," says Seeker. "The one we killed—he was the last one. There's nobody left. Do you know how empty I feel, going up to the towers to listen, and hearing nothing? As if I've been hollowed out inside. Can you understand what sort of feeling that is? Can you? No, of course you can't. What would any of you know?"

He stares at us in agony. "The silence…the silence…."

Nobody seems to know how quite to respond to that, so we say nothing. And Seeker helps himself to yet another jigger of brandy, and full measure at that. This is alarming. The sight of Seeker drinking like this is as strange as the sight of a torrential downpour of rain would be.

Engineer, who is probably the calmest and most reasonable of us, says, "Ah, man, can you not be a bit patient? I know you want to do your task. But more of them will come. Sooner or later, there'll be another, and another after that. Two weeks, three, six, who knows? But they'll come. You've been through spells like this before."

"No. This is different," says Seeker sullenly. "But what would you know?"

"Easy," Engineer says, laying his strong hand across the back of Seeker's frail wrist. "Go easy, man. What do you mean, 'this is different?'"

Carefully, making a visible effort at self-control, Seeker says, "All the other times when we've gone several weeks between incursions, I've always felt a low inner hum, a kind of subliminal static, a barely perceptible mental pressure, that tells me there are at least a few enemies out there somewhere, a hundred miles away, five hundred, a thousand. It's just a kind of quiet buzz. It doesn't give me any directionality. But it's there, and sooner or later the signal becomes stronger, and then I know that a couple of them are getting close to us, and then I get directionality and I can lead us to them, and we go out and kill them. It's been that way for years, ever since the real battles stopped. But now I don't get anything. Not a thing. It's absolutely silent in my head. Which means that either I've lost my power entirely, or else there aren't any enemies left within a thousand miles or more."

"And which is it that you think is so?"

Seeker scans us all with a haggard look. "That there are no enemies out there any more. Which means that it is pointless to remain here. We should pack up, go home, make some sort of new lives for ourselves within the Empire itself. And yet we have to stay, in case they come. I must stay, because this is the only task that I know how to perform. What sort of new life could I make for myself back there? I never had a life. This is my life. So my choice is to stay here to no purpose, performing a task that does not need to be performed any longer, or to return home to no existence. Do you see my predicament?" He is shivering. He reaches for the brandy, pours yet another drink with a trembling hand, hastily downs it, coughs, shudders, lets his head drop to the tabletop. We can hear him sobbing.

That night marks the beginning of the debate among us. Seeker's breakdown has brought into the open something that has been on my own mind for some weeks now, and which Armorer, Weaponsmaster, Quartermaster, and even dull-witted Sergeant have been pondering also, each in his own very different way.

The fact is unanswerable that the frequency of enemy incursions has lessened greatly in the past two years, and when they do come, every five or six or ten weeks apart, they no longer come in bands of a dozen or so, but in twos or threes. This last man whom Sergeant slew by the three little hills had come alone. Armorer has voiced quite openly his notion that just as our own numbers have dwindled to next to nothing over the years, the enemy confronting us in this desert must have suffered great attrition too, and, like us, has had no reinforcement from the home country, so that only a handful of our foes remain—or, perhaps, as Seeker now believes, none at all. If that is true, says Armorer, who is a wry and practical man, why do we not close up shop and seek some new occupation for ourselves in some happier region of the Empire?

Sergeant, who loves the excitement of warfare, for whom combat is not an ugly necessity but an act of passionate devotion, shares Armorer's view that we ought to move along. It is not so much that inactivity makes him restless—restlessness is not a word that really applies to a wooden block of a man like Sergeant—but that, like Seeker, he lives only to perform his military function. Seeker's function is to seek and Sergeant's function is to kill, and Seeker now feels that he will seek forever here and nevermore find, and Sergeant, in his dim way, believes that for him to stay here any longer would be a waste of his capability. He too wants to leave.

As does Weaponsmaster, who has had no weapons other than knives and spears to care for since our ammunition ran out and thus passes his days in a stupefying round of makework, and Quartermaster, who once presided over the material needs of ten thousand men and now, in his grizzled old age, lives the daily mockery of looking after the needs of just eleven. Thus we have four men—Armorer, Sergeant, Weaponsmaster, Quartermaster—fairly well committed to bringing the life of this outpost to an end, and one more, Seeker, who wants both to go and to stay. I am more or less of Seeker's persuasion here myself, aware that we are living idle and futile lives at the fort but burdened at the same time with a sense of obligation to my profession that leads me to regard an abandonment of the fort as a shameful act. So I sway back and forth. When Armorer speaks, I am inclined to join his faction. But when one of the others advocates remaining here, I drift back in that direction.

Gradually it emerges in our circular nightly discussion that the other four of us are strongly committed to staying. Engineer enjoys his life here: there are always technical challenges for him, a new canal to design, a parapet in need of repair, a harness to mend. He also is driven by a strong sense of duty and believes it is necessary to the welfare of the Empire that we remain here. Stablemaster, less concerned about duty, is fond of his beasts and similarly has no wish to leave. Provisioner, who is rarely given to doubts of any sort, would be content to remain so long as our supply of food and drink remains ample, and that appears to be the case. And Signalman still believes, Seeker's anguish to the contrary, that the desert beyond the wall is full of patient foes who will swarm through the gap and march against the capital like ravening beasts the moment we relinquish the fort.

Engineer, who is surely the most rational of us, has raised another strong point in favor of staying. We have scarcely any idea of how to get home. Twenty years ago we were brought here in a great convoy, and who among us bothered to take note of the route we traversed? Even those who might have paid attention to it then have forgotten almost every detail of the journey. But we do have a vague general idea of the challenge that confronts us. Between us and the capital lies, first of all, a great span of trackless dry wasteland and then forested districts occupied by autonomous savage tribes. Uncharted and, probably, well-nigh impenetrable tropical jungles are beyond those, and no doubt we would encounter a myriad other hazards. We have no maps of the route. We have no working communications devices. "If we leave here, we might spend the rest of our lives wandering around hopelessly lost in the wilderness," Engineer says. "At least here we have a home, women, something to eat and a place to sleep."

I raise another objection. "You all speak as though this is something we could just put to a vote. 'Raise hands, all in favor of abandoning the fort.'"

"If we did take a vote," Armorer says, "We'd have a majority in favor of getting out of here. You, me, Sergeant, Quartermaster, Weaponsmaster, Seeker—that's six out of eleven, even if Captain votes the other way."

"No. I'm not so sure I'm with you. I don't think Seeker is, either. Neither of us has really made up his mind." We all looked toward Seeker; but Seeker was asleep at the table, lost in winy stupor. "So at best we're equally divided right now, four for leaving, four for staying, and two undecided. But in any case this place isn't a democracy and how we vote doesn't matter. Whether we leave the fort is something for Captain to decide, and Captain alone. And we don't have any idea what his feelings are."

"We could ask him," Armorer suggests.

"Ask my elbow," Provisioner says, guffawing. "Who wants to ask Captain anything? The man who does will get a riding crop across the face."

There is general nodding around the table. We all have tasted Captain's unpredictable ferocity.

Quartermaster says, "If we had a majority in favor of going home, we could all go to him and tell him how we feel. He won't try to whip us all. For all we know, he might even tell us that he agrees with us."

"But you don't have a majority," Engineer points out.

Quartermaster looks toward me. "Come over to our side, Surveyor. Surely you see there's more merit in our position than in theirs. That would make it five to four for leaving."

"And Seeker?" Engineer asks. "When he sobers up, what if he votes the other way? That would make it a tie vote again."

"We could ask Captain to break the tie, and that would settle the whole thing," Armorer says.

That brings laughter from us all. Captain is very sensitive to anything that smacks of insubordination. Even the dullest of us can see that he will not react well to hearing that we are trying to determine a serious matter of policy by majority vote.

I lie awake for hours that night, replaying our discussion in my mind. There are strong points on both sides. The idea of giving up the fort and going home has great appeal. We are all getting along in years; at best each of us has ten or fifteen years left to him, and do I want to spend those years doing nothing but hunting water-pigs in the river and toiling over our scrawny crops and rereading the same handful of books? I believe Seeker when he says that the man we killed a few weeks ago was the last of the enemy in our territory.

On the other hand there is the question of duty. What are we to say when we show up in the capital? Simply announce that by our own authority we have abandoned the outpost to which we have devoted our lives, merely because in our opinion there is no further need for us to stay on at it? Soldiers are not entitled to opinions. Soldiers who are sent to defend a frontier outpost have no option but to defend that outpost until orders to the contrary are received.

To this argument I oppose another one, which is that duty travels both ways. We might be abandoning our fort, an improper thing for soldiers to be doing, but is it not true that the Empire has long ago abandoned us? There has been no word from home for ages. Not only have we had no reinforcements or fresh supplies from the Empire, there has not been so much as an inquiry. They have forgotten we exist. What if the war ended years ago and nobody at the capital has bothered to tell us that? How much do we owe an Empire that does not remember our existence?

And, finally, there is Engineer's point that going home might be impossible anyway, for we have no maps, no vehicles, no clear idea of the route we must follow, and we know that we are an almost unimaginable distance from any civilized district of the Empire. The journey will be a terrible struggle, and we may very well perish in the course of it. For me, in the middle of the night, that is perhaps the most telling point of all.

I realize, as I lie there contemplating these things, that Wendrit is awake beside me, and that she is weeping.

"What is it?" I asked. "Why are you crying?"

She is slow to answer. I can sense the troubled gropings of her mind. But at length she says, between sobs, "You are going to leave me. I heard things. I know. You will leave and I will be alone."

"No," I tell her, before I have even considered what I am saying. "No, that isn't true. I won't leave. And if I do, I'll take you with me. I promise you that, Wendrit." And I pull her into my arms and hold her until she is no longer sobbing.

❊

I awaken knowing that I have made my decision, and it is the decision to go home. Along with Armorer, Sergeant, Weaponsmaster, and Stablemaster, I believe now that we should assemble whatever provisions we can, choose the strongest of our beasts to draw our carts, and, taking our women with us, set out into the unknown. If the gods favor our cause we will reach the Empire eventually, request retirement from active duty, and try to form some sort of new lives for ourselves in what no doubt is a nation very much altered from the one we left behind more than twenty years ago.

That night, when we gather over our brandy, I announce my conversion to Armorer's faction. But Seeker reveals that he, too, has had an epiphany in the night, which has swung him to the other side: weak and old as he is, he fears the journey home more than he does living out the rest of his life in futility at the fort. So we still are stalemated, now five to five, and there is no point in approaching Captain, even assuming that Captain would pay the slightest attention to our wishes.

Then there is an event that changes everything. It is the day of our weekly pig-hunt, when four or five of us don our high boots and go down to the river with spears to refresh our stock of fresh meat. The water-pigs that dwell in the river are beasts about the size of cattle, big sleek purple things with great yellow tusks, very dangerous when angered but also very stupid. They tend to congregate just upriver from us, where a bend in the flow creates a broad pool thick with water-plants, on which they like to forage. Our hunting technique involves cutting one beast out of the herd with proddings of our spears and moving him downriver, well apart from the others, so that we can kill him in isolation, without fear of finding ourselves involved in a chaotic melee with seven or eight furious pigs snapping at us from all sides at once. The meat from a single pig will last the eleven of us a full week, sometimes more.

Today the hunting party is made up of Provisioner, Signalman, Weaponsmaster, Armorer, and me. We are all skilled hunters and work well together. As soon as the night's chill has left the air we go down to the river and march along its banks to the water-pig pool, choose the pig that is to be our prey, and arrange ourselves along the bank so that we will be in a semicircular formation when we enter the water. We will slip between the lone pig and the rest of his fellows and urge him away from them, and when we think it is safe to attack, we will move in for the kill.

At first everything goes smoothly. The river is hip-deep here. We form our arc, we surround our pig, we nudge him lightly with the tips of our spears. His little red-rimmed eyes glower at us in fury and we can hear the low rumblings of his annoyance, but the half-submerged animal pulls back from the pricking without attempting to fight, and we prod him twenty, thirty, forty feet downstream, toward the killing-place. As usual, a few Fisherfolk have gathered on the bank to watch us, though there is, as ever, a paradoxical incuriosity about their bland stares.

And then, catastrophe. "Look out!" cries Armorer, and in the same moment I become aware of the water churning wildly behind me, and I see two broad purple backs breaching the surface of the river, and I realize that this time other pigs—at least a couple, maybe more, who knows?—have followed on downstream with our chosen one and intend to defend their grazing grounds against our intrusion. It is the thing we have always dreaded but never experienced, the one serious danger in these hunts. The surface of the water thrashes and boils. We see pigs leaping frenetically on all sides of us. The river is murky at best, but now, with maddened water-pigs snorting and snuffling all about us, we have no clear idea of what is happening, except that we have lost control of the situation and are in great jeopardy.

"Out of the water, everybody!" Weaponsmaster yells, but we are already scrambling for the riverbank. I clamber up, lean on my spear, catch my breath. Weaponsmaster and Armorer stand beside me. Provisioner has gone to the opposite bank. But there is no sign of Signalman, and the river suddenly is red with blood, and great yellow-tusked pig-snouts are jutting up everywhere, and then Signalman comes floating to the surface, belly upward, his body torn open from throat to abdomen.

We carry him back borne on our shoulders, like a fallen hero. It is our first death in some years. Somehow we had come to feel, in the time that has elapsed since that one, that we eleven who still remain would go on and on together forever, but now we know that that is not so. Weaponsmaster brings the news to Captain, and reports back to us that that stony implacable man had actually seemed to show signs of real grief upon hearing of Signalman's death. Engineer and Provisioner and I dig the grave, and Captain presides over the service, and for several days there is a funereal silence around the fort.

Then, once the shock of the death has begun to ebb a little, Armorer raises the point that none of us had cared to mention openly since the event at the river. Which is, that with Signalman gone the stalemate has been broken. The factions stand now at five for setting out for home, four for remaining indefinitely at the fort. And Armorer is willing to force the issue on behalf of the majority by going to Captain and asking whether he will authorize an immediate retreat from the frontier.

For hours there is an agitated discussion, verging sometimes into bitterness and rage. We all recognize that it must be one way or another, that we cannot divide: a little group of four or five would never be able to sustain itself at the fort, nor would the other group of about the same size have any hope of success in traversing the unknown lands ahead. We must all stay together or assuredly we will all succumb; but that means that the four who would remain must yield to the five who wish to leave, regardless of their own powerful desires in the matter. And the four who would be compelled to join the trek against their wishes are fiercely resentful of the five who insist on departure.

In the end things grow calmer and we agree to leave the decision to Captain, in whose hands it belongs anyway. A delegation of four is selected to go to him: Engineer and Stablemaster representing those who would stay, and Armorer and me to speak for the other side.

Captain spends most of his days in a wing of the fort that the rest of us rarely enter. There, at a huge ornate desk in an office big enough for ten men, he studies piles of documents left by his predecessors as commanding officer, as though hoping to learn from the writings of those vanished colonels how best to carry out the responsibilities that the vagaries of time have placed upon his shoulders. He is a brawny, dour-faced man, thin-lipped and somber-eyed, with dense black eyebrows that form a single forbidding line across his forehead, and even after all these years he is a stranger to us all.

He listens to us in his usual cold silence as we set forth the various arguments: Seeker's belief that there are no more enemies for us to deal with here, Armorer's that we are absolved of our duty to the Empire by its long neglect of us, Engineer's that the journey home would be perilous to the point of foolhardiness, and Signalman's, offered on his behalf by Stablemaster, that the enemy is simply waiting for us to go and then will launch its long-awaited campaign of conquest in Imperial territory. Eventually we begin to repeat ourselves and realize that there is nothing more to say, though Captain has not broken his silence by so much as a single syllable. The last word is spoken by Armorer, who tells Captain that five of us favor leaving, four remaining, though he does not specify who holds which position.

Telling him that strikes me as a mistake. It implies—rightly—that a democratic process has gone on among us, and I expect Captain to respond angrily to the suggestion that any operational issue here can be decided, or even influenced, by a vote of the platoon. But there is no thunderstorm of wrath. He sits quietly, still saying nothing, for an almost unendurable span of time. Then he says, in a surprisingly moderate tone, "Seeker is unable to pick up any sign of enemy presence?" He addresses the question to Engineer, whom, apparently, he has correctly identified as one of the leaders of the faction favoring continued residence at the fort.

"This is so," Engineer replies.

Captain is silent once again. But finally he says, to our universal amazement, "The thinking of those who argue for withdrawal from the frontier is in line with my own. I have considered for some time now that our services in this place are no longer required by the Empire, and that if we are to be of use to the country at all, we must obtain reassignment elsewhere."

It is, I think, the last thing any of us had expected. Armorer glows with satisfaction. Engineer and Stablemaster look crestfallen. I, ambivalent even now, simply look at Captain in surprise.

Captain goes on, "Engineer, Stablemaster, make plans for our departure at the soonest possible date. I stipulate one thing, though: we go as a group, with no one to remain behind, and we must stay together as one group throughout what I know will be a long and arduous journey. Anyone who attempts to leave the group will be considered a deserter and treated accordingly. I will request that you all take an oath to that effect."

That is what we had agreed among ourselves to do anyway, so there is no difficulty about it. Nor do our four recalcitrants indicate any opposition to the departure order, though Seeker is plainly terrified of the dangers and stress of the journey. We begin at once to make our plans for leaving.

✷

It turns out that we do have some maps of the intervening territory after all. Captain produces them from among his collection of documents, along with two volumes of a chronicle of our journey from the capital to the frontier that the first Colonel had kept. He summons me and gives me this material, ordering me to consult it and devise a plan of route for our journey.

But I discover quickly that it is all useless. The maps are frayed and cracked along their folds, and such information as they once might have held concerning the entire center of the continent has faded into invisibility. I can make out a bold star-shaped marker indicating the capital down in the lower right-hand corner, and a vague, ragged line indicating the frontier far off to the left, and just about everything between is blank. Nor is the old Colonel's chronicle in any way helpful. The first volume deals with the organization of the expeditionary force and the logistical problems involved in transporting it from the capital to the interior. The second volume that we have, which is actually the third of the original three, describes the building of the fort and the initial skirmishes with the enemy. The middle volume is missing, and that is the one, I assume, that speaks of the actual journey between the capital and the frontier.

I hesitate to tell Captain this, for he is not one who receives bad news with much equanimity. Instead I resolve that I will do my best to improvise a route for us, taking my cues from what we find as we make our way to the southeast. And so we get ourselves ready, choosing our best wagons and our sturdiest steeds and loading them with tools and weapons and with all we can carry by way of provisions: dried fruit and beans, flour, casks of water, cartons of preserved fish, parcels of the air-dried meat that Provisioner prepares each winter by laying out strips of pig-flesh in the sun. We will do as we can for fresh meat and produce on the march.

The women placidly accept the order to accompany us into the wilderness. They have already crossed over from their Fisherfolk lives to ours, anyway. There are only nine of them, for Seeker has never chosen to have one, and Captain has rarely shown more than fitful interest in them. Even so we have one extra: Sarkariet, Signalman's companion. She has remained at the fort since Signalman's death and says she has no desire to return to her village, so we take her along.

The day of our departure is fair and mild, the sun warm but not hot, the wind gentle. Perhaps that is a good omen. We leave the fort without a backward glance, going out by way of the eastern gate and descending to the river. A dozen or so of the Fisherfolk watch us in their blank-faced way as we cross the little wooden bridge upstream of their village. Once we are across, Captain halts our procession and orders us to destroy the bridge. From Engineer comes a quick grunt of shock: the bridge was one of his first projects, long ago. But Captain sees no reason to leave the enemy any easy path eastward, should the enemy still be lurking somewhere in the hinterlands. And so we ply our axes for half a morning until the bridge goes tumbling down into the riverbed.

We have never had any reason in the past twenty years to venture very far into the districts east or south of the fort, but we are not surprised to find them pretty much the same as the region north and west of the fort that we have patrolled so long. That is, we are in a dry place of pebbly yellowish soil, with low hills here and there, gnarled shrubs, tussocks of saw-bladed grass. Now and again some scrawny beast scampers quickly across our path, or we hear the hissing of a serpent from the underbrush, and solitary melancholy birds sometimes go drifting high overhead, cawing raucously, but by and large the territory is deserted. There is no sign of water all the first day, nor midway through the second, but that afternoon Seeker reports that he detects the presence of Fisherfolk somewhere nearby, and before long we reach a straggling little stream that is probably another fork of the river whose other tributary runs close below our fort. On its farther bank we see a Fisherfolk camp, much smaller than the village on the banks of our river.

Wendrit and the other women become agitated at the sight of it. I ask her what the matter is, and she tells me that these people are ancient enemies of her people, that whenever the two tribes encounter each other there is a battle. So even the passive, placid Fisherfolk wage warfare among themselves! Who would have thought it? I bring word of this to Captain, who looks untroubled. "They will not come near us," he says, and this proves to be so. The river is shallow enough to ford; and the strange Fisherfolk gather by their tents and stand in silence as we pass by. On the far side we replenish our water-casks.

Then the weather grows unfriendly. We are entering a rocky, broken land, a domain of sandstone cliffs, bright red in color and eroded into jagged, fanciful spires and ridges, and here a hard, steady wind blows out of the south through a gap in the hills into our faces, carrying a nasty freight of tiny particles of pinkish grit. The sun now is as red as new copper in that pinkish sky, as though we have a sunset all day long. To avoid the sandstorm that I assume will be coming upon us I swing the caravan around to due east, where we will be traveling along the base of the cliffs and perhaps will be sheltered from the worst of the wind. In this I am incorrect, because a cold, inexorable crosswind arises abruptly, bringing with it out of the north the very sandstorm that I had hoped to avoid, and we find ourselves pinned down for a day and a half just below the red cliffs, huddling together miserably with our faces masked by scarves. The wind howls all night; I sleep very badly. At last it dies down and we hurry through the gap in the cliffs and resume our plodding southeastward march.

Beyond, we find what is surely a dry lake-bed, a broad flat expanse covered with a sparse incrustation of salt that glitters in the brutal sunlight like newly fallen snow. Nothing but the indomitable saw-grass grows here, and doubtless the lake has been dry for millennia, for there is not even a skeletal trace of whatever vegetation, shrubs and even trees, might have bordered its periphery in the days when there was water here. We are three days crossing this dead lake. Our supply of fresh water is running troublesomely low already, and we have exhausted all of our fresh meat, leaving only the dried stuff that increases our thirst. Nor is there any game to hunt here, of course.

Is this what we are going to have to face, week after week, until eventually we reach some kinder terrain? The oldest men, Seeker and Quartermaster, are showing definite signs of fatigue, and the women, who have never been far from their river for even a day, seem fretful and withdrawn. Clearly dismayed and even frightened, they whisper constantly among themselves in the Fisherfolk language that none of us has ever bothered to learn, but draw away whenever we approach. Even our pack-animals are beginning to struggle. They have had little to eat or drink since we set out and the effects are only too apparent. They snap listlessly at the tufts of sharp gray grass and look up at us with doleful eyes, as though we have betrayed them.

The journey has only just begun and already I am beginning to regret it.

One evening, when we are camped at some forlorn place near the farther end of the lake, I confess my doubts to Captain. Since he is our superior officer and I am the officer who is leading us on our route, I have come to assume some sort of equality of rank between us that will allow for confidential conversations. But I am wrong. When I tell him that I have started to believe that this enterprise may be beyond our powers of endurance, he replies that he has no patience with cowards, and turns his back on me. We do not speak again in the days that follow.

There are indications of the sites of ancient villages in the region beyond, where the river that fed that dry lake must once have flowed. There is no river here now, though my practiced eye detects the faint curves of its prehistoric route, and the fragmentary ruins of small stone settlements can be seen on the ledges above what once were its banks. But nowadays all is desert here. Why did the Empire need us to defend the frontier, when there is this gigantic buffer zone of desert between its rich, fertile territories and the homeland of the enemy?

Later we come to what must have been the capital city of this long-abandoned province, a sprawling maze of crumbled stone walls and barely comprehensible multi-roomed structures. We find some sort of temple sanctuary where devilish statues still stand, dark stone idols with a dozen heads and thirty arms, each one grasping the stump of what must have been a sword. Carved big-eyed snakes twine about the waists of these formidable forgotten gods. The scholars of our nation surely would wish to collect these things for the museums of the capital, and I make a record of our position, so that I can file a proper report for them once we have reached civilization. But by now I have arrived at serious doubt that we ever shall.

I draw Seeker aside and ask him to cast his mind forth in the old way and see if he can detect any intimation of inhabited villages somewhere ahead.

"I don't know if I can," he says. He is terribly emaciated, trembling, pale. "It takes a strength that I don't think I have any more."

"Try. Please. I need to know."

He agrees to make the effort, and goes into his trance, and I stand by, watching, as his eyeballs roll up into his head and his breath comes in thick, hoarse bursts. He stands statue-still, utterly motionless for a very long while. Then, gradually, he returns to normal consciousness, and as he does so he begins to topple, but I catch him in time and ease him to the ground. He sits blinking for a time, drawing deep breaths, collecting his strength. I wait until he seems to have regained himself.

"Well?"

"Nothing. Silence. As empty ahead as it is behind."

"For how far?" I ask.

"How do I know? There's no one there. That's all I can say."

We are rationing water very parsimoniously and we are starting to run short of provisions, too. There is nothing for us to hunt and none of the vegetation, such as it is, seems edible. Even Sergeant, who is surely the strongest of us, now looks hollow-eyed and gaunt, and Seeker and Quartermaster seem at the verge of being unable to continue. From time to time we find a source of fresh water, brackish but at any rate drinkable, or slay some unwary wandering animal, and our spirits rise a bit, but the environment through which we pass is unremittingly hostile and I have no idea when things will grow easier for us. I make a show of studying my maps, hoping it will encourage the others to think that I know what I am doing, but the maps I have for this part of the continent are blank and I might just as well consult my wagon or the beasts that pull it as try to learn anything from those faded sheets of paper.

"This is a suicidal trek," Engineer says to me one morning as we prepare to break camp. "We should never have come. We should turn back while we still can. At least at the fort we would be able to survive."

"You got us into this," Provisioner says, scowling at me. "You and your switched vote." Burly Provisioner is burly no longer. He has become a mere shadow of his former self. "Admit it, Surveyor: we'll never make it. It was a mistake to try."

Am I supposed to defend myself against these charges? What defense can I possibly make?

A day later, with conditions no better, Captain calls the nine of us together and makes an astonishing announcement. He is sending the women back. They are too much of a burden on us. They will be given one of the wagons and some of our remaining provisions. If they travel steadily in the direction of the sunset, he says, they will sooner or later find their way back to their village below the walls of our fort.

He walks away from us before any of us can reply. We are too stunned to say anything, anyway. And how could we reply? What could we say? That we oppose this act of unthinkable cruelty and will not let him send the women to their deaths? Or that we have taken a new vote, and we are unanimous in our desire that all of us, not just the women, return to the fort? He will remind us that a military platoon is not a democracy. Or perhaps he will simply turn his back on us, as he usually does. We are bound on our path toward the inner domain of the Empire; we have sworn an oath to continue as a group; he will not release us.

"But he can't mean it!" Stablemaster says. "It's a death sentence for them!"

"Why should he care about that?" Armorer asks. "The women are just domestic animals to him. I'm surprised he doesn't just ask us to kill them right here and now, instead of going to the trouble of letting them have some food for their trip back."

It says much about how our journey has weakened us that none of us feels capable of voicing open opposition to Captain's outrageous order. He confers with Provisioner and Stablemaster to determine how much of our food we can spare for them and which wagon to give them, and the conference proceeds precisely as though it is a normal order of business.

The women are unaware of the decision Captain has made. Nor can I say anything to Wendrit when I return to our tent. I pull her close against me and hold her in a long embrace, thinking that this is probably the last time.

When I step back and look into her eyes, my own fill with tears, and she stares at me in bewilderment. But how can I explain? I am her protector. There is no way to tell her that Captain has ordered her death and that I am prepared to be acquiescent in his monstrous decision.

Can it be said that it is possible to feel love for a Fisherfolk woman? Well, yes, perhaps. Perhaps I love Wendrit. Certainly it would cause me great pain to part from her.

The women will quickly lose their way as they try to retraverse the inhospitable desert lands that we have just passed through. Beyond doubt they will die within a few days. And we ourselves, in all likelihood, will be dead ourselves in a week or two as we wander ever onward in this hopeless quest for the settled districts of the Empire. I was a madman to think that we could ever succeed in that journey simply by pointing our noses toward the capital and telling ourselves that by taking one step after another we would eventually get there.

But there is a third way that will spare Wendrit and the other women, and my friends as well, from dying lonely deaths in these lonely lands. Sergeant had shown me, that day behind the three little hillocks north of the fort, how the thing is managed.

I leave my tent. Captain has finished his conference with Provisioner and Stablemaster and is standing off by himself to one side of our camp, as though he is alone on some other planet.

"Captain?" I say.

My blade is ready as he turns toward me.

Afterward, to the shaken, astounded men, I say quietly, "I am Captain now. Is anyone opposed? Good." And I point to the northwest, back toward the place of the serpent-wrapped stone idols, and the dry lake-bed beyond, and the red cliffs beyond those. "We all know we won't ever find the Empire. But the fort is still there. So come, then. Let's break camp and get started. We're going back. We're going home."

THE PRISONER

Sleep, supposedly, is restful. Knits up the raveled sleeve of care, etc., etc. My sleeves get just as raveled as anyone else's during the course of a busy day, and it it is with much gratitude that I put head to pillow at ten o'clock or thereabouts every night, and sleep usually comes upon me with welcome speed. But restful sleep? Alas, no. My mind, which over the decades has spawned more than a thousand stories and I know not how many hundreds of novels, keeps me occupied all night, but not necessarily amused, with an outpouring of vivid, detailed, and often quite disturbing dreams. Not just the standard dreams, either—the one in which you have to take a final exam and can't find the classroom, or the one in which you show up naked at the big party, or the one in which you discover that you can fly by jumping into the air and flapping your arms. I have had all of those, of course, but also a good many weird and grotesque ones, real horrors, inexplicable by anything so simple and obvious as mere anxiety or wish-fulfillment fantasy.

In my more active days as a writer I would often rise in the morning with some of those dreams still intact, and after breakfast I would turn them into salable fiction—which was some recompense, at least, for the uneasiness they had caused me in the night. Now and then I would even rise in the middle of the night and make notes on some dream that was too good a story to risk forgetting. I once assembled an entire novel—Son of Man, which I wrote in 1969—from three weeks' worth of dreams.

I'm not writing much fiction these days, so about all I can do with my dreams is tell them to my wife when she awakens (she does not awaken swiftly, and sometimes she mistakes my narration of a dream for some news report from the morning's paper) or e-mail them to a friend who was involved in them

447

(as in the case of the friend who advised me to turn my pet hippopotamus loose in our swimming pool to eat the water-weeds that had mysteriously begun to thrive there; we have neither a pet hippo nor a problem of weeds in the pool, but it all made sense in the dream, until the point when I found I was unable to get the damned beast out of the pool so that I could use it again myself.)

When the South African editor and critic Nick Gevers invited me in 2008 to turn some of my dreams into fiction for an anthology called The Book of Dreams that he was doing for Subterranean Press, I found the idea as irresistible as I had that earlier invitation to write a Dying Earth story for Gardner Dozois and George R.R. Martin. Simply to write one more story, after all the stories I've written since 1952 or so, does not set my pulse a-pounding. A story proposal that speaks to some special interest or quirk of mine is much more apt to arouse my interest; and I let Nick Gevers know by return email that I would contribute to his book. The basic idea for the story came to me almost at once, and in December, 2008 I began jotting down the details of some of my nastier dreams upon awakening each morning. (Some of the most sinister arrived during Christmas week.) Early in the new year I had enough for my needs, and I wrote the story in January, 2009; it appeared in the Gevers anthology the following year.

L ately his dreams have had great urgency. He is sprinting frantically up some bright windy beach from the edge of the surf, the cold rising tide licking at his heels, desperately trying to reach the dark rockpile at the foot of the nearby cliff where he can clamber up above the rapidly rising water. Or he is jogging through some nasty wasteland of spongy yellowish soil while narrow serpentine heads rise all about him out of little circular craters, snapping at his ankles with angry fangs. Or he is running uphill on a broad, steep urban boulevard, dodging the speeding cars that come rocketing downhill toward him.

He awakens from these dreams sweaty, panting, shivering with residual fear. They are only dreams, he tells himself, as he showers and shaves and dresses for work. They are strange dreams, they are unpleasant dreams, they are *very* unpleasant dreams, but all they are is dreams, after all, mere effluvia of the night, and they will fade and be gone swiftly in the bright light of morning.

The strange thing, though, is that they *don't* fade.

Through the first hour of the day's work they seem more real than the work itself. He stares into his screen and sees, not the gaily colored charts and graphs of the corporate ebb and flow, but the menacing images he thought he had left behind at the coming of dawn. Bristly antennae, slavering jaws, bulging green eyes, great jagged rocks bouncing down a hillside toward him, a roaring river in full spate above a dangling fractured bridge—whatever ugly terrifying scene had intruded on his sleeping mind the night before carries over into the day and churns and mills before him like some ghastly movie that has seized possession of his terminal.

His distress shows on his face. "Are you okay?" they ask. Or they say, "Big night out last night?" Or sometimes it is, "I'm beginning to think you're taking this job too seriously, Dave."

To which he replies such things as, "Bit of a headache this morning," or, "I look that bad, do I?" or, more usually, "No, really, I'm fine. Really."

But what they see is what there is. The face that looks back at him from the washroom mirror is unquestionably pale, haggard, tense. He splashes himself with cold water, briskly rubs the muscles of his cheeks and forehead to relax them, pulls his lips back in an idiotic forced grin that he hopes will seep inward so that he looks more at ease. Usually by lunchtime everything is normal again. He goes out with the gang, he does the standard banter, he swaps movie comments and sports chit-chat and stock predictions, and when he returns to the office the face in the washroom mirror is his ordinary everyday face again.

But then, come night—

It is two years and some months since his marriage broke up, and though he began going out again quickly enough afterward, he usually spends most nights of the week except Friday and Saturday alone. Which means that when dreams arrive, and if they are horrific ones, the sort of dreams that are beginning to become the norm for him, he has only his pillow to reach to for comfort when the sweaty anguish awakens him. Just as well, perhaps: more than once recently he has terrified some new Saturday-night companion with the four-a.m. scream and clutch, which he has found is a good way of transforming a promising new relationship into a one-night stand. "Sorry," he will say. "That was one lulu of a bad dream."

"It must have been," she says, and he can tell from her tone that she is already thinking of how soon she can get her clothes on and head for home.

Everybody dreams, he tells himself, and everybody has a nightmare once in a while. What he's going through now is a little unusual, perhaps, an odd spate of spectacularly grim stuff. But just a phase, he thinks. Maybe a temporary metabolic upheaval, or some short-lived digestive strangeness, a delayed reaction to the breakup of his marriage, or maybe some oblique reflection of ongoing challenges at the office. It will pass. It will pass.

Meanwhile he has started to dread going to sleep.

After three weeks he shares his troubles with Charlie, who is plump and balding and calm and likes to play the role of father confessor and amateur shrink around the office. Charlie has been through a lot of stuff himself, and he has read a lot of books, and he is the quickest hand anyone has seen at dredging up an Internet diagnosis for any sort of ailment.

"It's a normal biological process, dreaming," Charlie says. "The nocturnal shedding of daily stress through transformation of negative energy into randomly created imagery: a catharsis, a cleansing. We need the dreaming process in order to stay sane. You must be working your way through a lot of inner crap, things stored on some level that isn't even consciously accessible to you."

"And turning them into a nightly horror flick?"

"It's no use trying to understand the workings of your unconscious mind, Dave. There's no logic to it. It's not a rational entity. Almost by definition, what it pushes up into view passeth all understanding."

"But Freud—"

"Freud was a pioneer, and pioneers by definition don't know where the hell they're going. Columbus thought he'd landed in the Indies, remember? But they turned out to be the *West* Indies. What Freud said about dreams a hundred years ago was all well and good in its day, but it's not the last word on the subject. It's pretty much the *first* word."

"These dreams are disgusting. Appalling. Loathsome."

"So?"

"They're emerging out of my own mind. And they're the sickest, most revolting things. Charlie, I feel *ashamed* to be having dreams like that."

"Ashamed? Of what?"

"That I could be generating such garbage. That I could be capable of imagining things like that. How can I not take responsibility for that? These are my dreams, these hideous things, the products of my own personal mind, as much my own creation as a novelist's novel or a composer's song or a playwright's play is."

"Wrong. You're trying to compare art—conscious, dedicated craftsmanship—with the muck that comes drifting randomly up out of the sewers of your mind."

"Randomly? Freud said—"

"I told you: screw Freud," said Charlie. "Freud didn't know jack. It's all random. You aren't inventing this stuff, you're simply having it dumped on you by some impersonal inner force while you lie there asleep and defenseless. Why blame yourself for it? That's like somebody blaming himself for having cancer. For Christ's sake, you don't need to take responsibility for the flavor of your dreams. Isn't real life rough enough? Dave, there's no sense whatever beating yourself up over what goes on in your head when you aren't even conscious."

He is walking a tightrope stretching from one great midtown tower to another, eighty-odd floors above the ground. He knows that there is a crowd of people watching him from below, hundreds of people, maybe thousands, though he dares not look down. It is a cool sunny day, crisp and dry, and a brisk wind is blowing. He can feel the tightrope quivering against his bare feet. He has never done anything remotely like this before, and yet it was with great assurance that he had stepped out onto the rope, clutching his balance-pole lightly against his chest. At first it was easy. One step, another, another—

He realizes he is terrified. Nothing surprising about that; and yet he had felt no fear at the outset, and only now, perhaps a third of the way across, where he has gone too far to turn back, when it would be even more difficult to return to his starting point than to continue on to the opposite tower, do great sickening spasms of terror go curling upward through his body.

Keep going. Step. Step. Step. The rope sways. He adjusts his balance with the pole. Step. Step. Step. Yes! He is halfway across, now. Step. Step. He has never been so frightened in his life; but, then, he has never done anything as crazy as this before. And he is starting to think there's a chance he will make it. Step! Step! Step!

"Hey, schmuck!" calls a raucous voice from the roof of the tower behind him. "Schmuck, look at me!" And, like a schmuck, he does, twisting around and glancing up over his shoulder, and sways and grabs air and topples, and topples, and topples, and the pavement comes swooping up to meet him.

He begins to keep a diary of the dreams, searching for some common denominator in these calamitous scenarios. There is always danger in them, of course. Tension, dread, suspense. He is in dire peril. Each night he finds himself in some stark situation not of his own making, where external forces threaten to snuff him out. He has been out boating on the bay, and is swept overboard and carried out to sea, and bobs, alone in the cold trackless waters, unable even to see the shore, let alone reach it. He is hiking in the woods, disturbs a branch, is seized in the jaws of some remorseless metal trap. He is being frogmarched through the streets with a jeering mob swarming on both sides of him, led to a plaza where a stake and a great pile of logs and straw awaits him, and then a crackling blaze—

The rack—the thumbscrew—the garrotte—

He draws elaborate structural diagrams of the dreams. He makes charts. He devotes evening after evening to their analysis. He is an educated, thoughtful man, though his life has not worked out quite the way he had expected. His daily work is trivial and it bores him, but it is *his* work, and without it he would long ago have been lost. These days it is his bulwark against the nightly mysterious assault of these dreams. And now he applies the same sort of analytic techniques to the dreams that he uses each day in the office to sort and classify and draw conclusions from the information that he is paid to sort and classify and draw conclusions from.

An interesting pattern begins to emerge. He tells Charlie about it, his one confidant.

"It's starting to become clear," he says, "that I'm dreaming, not about myself, but about someone else. I'm not the protagonist—the victim—in all these various grisly events, but just a spectator. I'm there,

I'm plenty scared, but I'm not actually the one in jeopardy. I'm just standing to one side, watching, like somebody at a movie."

Charlie is puzzled. "Really? Are you be sure of that?"

"Sure? I'm not sure of anything. But that's how it starts to look as I write up my summaries of what I'm experiencing."

And he explains that as he replays each nightmare in his mind he has discovered that he has in fact displaced the center of the event. "We always assume that the central figure in our dreams, the consciousness through whom the dream is communicated to us, is ourself. We see him moving about before our mind's eye like an actor on a screen, but we attach our own identity to him, so that we are both watcher and performer. But that isn't actually how it is for me in these things."

It only *feels* to him, he says, as though he is the man desperately trying to outrun the rising tide, that he is the tottering trembler on the tightrope, that he is the panicky zigzagger darting between the traffic on that steep urban boulevard. In fact he has come to realize, as his analysis of the material proceeds, that he is merely looking on from one side, a witness to the sufferings of someone else.

Charlie is doubtful. Charlie still believes that when we dream, we dream about ourselves, even though we may think we are dreaming about someone else. For a man who has blown off Freud as not knowing jack, Charlie suddenly starts to seem very conventional indeed in his theory of dreams.

He decides not to argue the point. Let Charlie believe whatever he wants to believe. He has faith in his own analysis, and that faith grows stronger the longer he works with the material.

Of course there is no way for him to reexperience any one dream. None of the nightmares ever recurs in identical form; there is always a fresh one to torment him by night. But they remain with him as memories, all-too-vivid memories, and as he sets down synopses of them in his growing diary he starts to become more convinced than ever that his presence in each dream is in the role of an onlooker rather than a participant.

He was not the tightrope-walker; he may have been the man who shouts distractingly from the rooftop. He was not the man burned at the stake; he was somewhere in the midst of that jeering mob. He was not the drowning swimmer lost in the pathless expanse of a cold ocean; he was an observer floating somewhere high overhead, watching that bobbing head amongst the waves. In each dream the true protagonist is someone else, a hapless prisoner trapped in some extreme and frightening circumstance, and he himself is merely looking on.

Does that matter? The dreams are terrifying whether or not he perceives them as being about someone else's travail. The man in the dreams may be suffering terrible torment, but he is the one who awakens shaking with fear.

The days go by, and the nights, and nothing changes for the better. The man in the dreams has died a hundred horrible deaths, but is always restored to life in time for the next night's pitiless horrors.

He—or is it the unknown *he?*—is in a tiny stone-walled prison chamber in which he can neither sit nor lie down nor stand, but must remain in a sort of half-crouch against the rough clammy wall, his frozen knees screaming, his knotted back writhing perpetually in pain, and here he must huddle, month after month, year after year, with no hope of release.

He is in the intensive care unit, with a feeding tube in his stomach and a mechanical ventilator operating his lungs, and he is surrounded by a webwork of intravenous piping that feeds him sedatives, narcotics, anesthetics. The glittering-eyed diabolical nurse is ratcheting the flow higher, higher, higher. His brain is swimming in a chemical bath. His mind is starting to blur. He lifts one hand—struggles feebly to signal for help —

He is in the most comfortable of beds in the most luxurious of hotels. But as he awaits sleep the bedclothes turn into writhing tentacles and wrap themselves around his wrists and ankles, pinning him down. He lies there spreadeagled, helpless, and the ceiling slowly begins to descend. He tries to scream, but no sound will emerge, and all he can do is wait, eyes ablaze with dread, as that inexorable mass glides serenely down to crush him.

He is driving swiftly up a freeway entrance ramp, with another car beside him to the right, and a third car materializes abruptly, coming *down* the freeway ramp toward them both. The third car is moving swiftly, but nevertheless it takes hours for it to descend the ramp, the cars unable to turn from their courses, each driver looking at the other two in a sort of stasis, until at last there is the screech of brakes and the immense sound of metal hitting metal in the moment of impact.

All about him are the low squalid buildings of some medieval city. A scaffold has been erected against a rough brick wall at one side of a great public square. An expectant crowd watches as he ascends the scaffold, kneels, fights off the moment of panic that rises suddenly within him, sweeps his long hair back, and places his head on the block. The headsman lifts his shining axe—

A new theme now emerges. The man is not only in some horrible peril; he is calling actively for help.

There comes a dream in which he—or *he*—is hurrying down the platform of a railway station toward a waiting train, and the train's door closes in his face just as he reaches it, and he thrusts his his hand through the door, trying to wrench it apart again. And he is caught, trapped, and as the train begins to move he is carried along down the platform, unable to pull his arm free; and as he comes to comprehend his predicament and looks about him in shock, crying out to the others on the platform for aid, another man in a red sweatshirt appears from somewhere and runs alongside him, tugging at his arm, trying to help. But there is nothing he can do and at the platform's end he steps sadly back, watching in dull shock as the figure caught in the door is swept away to be battered to death against the walls of the railway tunnel a few hundred yards down the track.

He recognizes that red sweatshirt. It belongs to him, an old and familiar garment.

Then, another night, he sees a figure standing on a narrow ledge that runs along the outer wall of a lofty apartment building. Somehow the man has gone out on the ledge and now is trying to find his way back inside, but all the windows are closed to him, and he edges slowly along, clutching the brickwork with his fingertips to support himself and shunting his feet sideways inch by inch, moving along the building's façade, going to window after window, apartment after apartment, and suddenly they are looking at each other, face to face, the man on the ledge outside and the man within, and the eyes of the man outside are wide with terror and in them can be seen the mute appeal, *Help me, help me, help me.*

It is his own apartment building. Just such a ledge runs the length of the building on the sixth floor. But he is not the man outside. He is the onlooker within.

And on still another night the dream-figure is stranded on the icy white slope of a vast mountain, some Alp, some Himalayan peak, with a giant crevasse yawning behind him and another beginning to open just ahead, and the ice rumbling and cracking almost beneath his feet, and the first hints of an impending avalanche overhead; and he looks imploringly across the crevasse, gesturing toward someone who perhaps can toss him a rope, but who is either unable or unwilling to do it. And also he is looking back across that crevasse from the other side.

There is no mistaking that pleading look. He has seen it three times, at least, now. Quite probably he has failed to see it in earlier visitations, but it was there. He is certain now that the man in the dream is looking outward toward him across the wall of sleep, to him specifically, begging for rescue.

Help me. Help me. Help me.

"What can I do?" he asks Charlie. "How can I help him?"

But Charlie is beginning to lose interest in the whole problem. "You can't," he says, dismissively. "He doesn't exist. He's just a projection of yourself. In these dreams you've simply divided yourself in two, a watcher and a sufferer, but they're both the same person."

"I don't think so."

"What can I say? These are your dreams. He's a figment of your imagination. You want to believe he's someone else, well, okay, then he's somebody else. If you want to help him, reach in and pull him out, okay?"

The dreams do not let up. And he begins to understand that the world of dreams is another world, one that exists beside our own—a world where nothing is real and everything is possible. He has been staring into that world every night of his life without knowing what it is.

He is certain now, with the sort of strange certainty that comes in dreams, that the man in the dreams is a real person, trapped in that other world the way one of the dream-figures had become trapped on the ledge of that building, the way another had been seized by the door of that train. And he is sending messages asking for help.

How could he ignore that call? He sees that it is his task to reach into the other world and pull that poor sufferer forth, just as Charlie had jokingly suggested, or he will never have a night's peace again himself.

Mon semblable,—mon frère!

He had never been a particularly compassionate man—that may have been one of the reasons for the breakup of his marriage—but, chilly and aloof though he often was, he had never refused aid to someone in trouble. It was his saving grace.

He will not refuse now. He will offer help.

But how? How?

The dreams do not let up. And he begins to understand that the world of dreams is another world, one that exists beside our own—a world where nothing is real and everything is possible. He has been staring into that world every night of his life without knowing what it is.

He tells himself, as he makes ready for bed, that when that night's dreams come, he will do everything he can to initiate contact, to extend a hand across the border between the one world and the other.

Tonight the dream-figure is stumbling across an endless Sahara, tongue thick and blackened with thirst, eyes wild. He is plainly at the end of his endurance. Just beyond the next dune lies a fertile green oasis, but he lacks the strength to get there.

Keep going! Come on—come on—just a little way more!

No use. The man staggers, stumbles, falls face-forward into the hot sands.

And on another night he is lost in a city where the streets melt and flow before him as he walks, substantial avenues turning to water, great thoroughfares becoming flaccid ropy masses of dough. He knows he must get to the other side of the city before nightfall —the welfare of someone precious to him depends on it—but he can make no progress; all is fluid and indeterminate. He pauses, contemplating the possibility of some more stable route that would take him to his goal, and indeed the dreaming observer knows that there is such a route, just a few blocks ahead, but when he calls out to tell him that, the words are swept away by the wind. And as he stands there the pavement begins to move beneath his feet and he is swept backward as though by a relentless river. Darkness begins to descend; the city vanishes; he is swept by the wildest terror.

His real life, such as it had been, has nearly vanished altogether. He rises at the same hour as always, but instead of looking at the newspaper or watching the morning news he transcribes his notes on the night's dreams. He eats the same breakfast as ever, without tasting his food. He goes to the office by the usual route and does his work mechanically, competently, no more and no less engaged with it than he had ever been. During the lunch break he generally stays at his desk and eats a sandwich. He has almost no contact with his fellow workers. Charlie, plainly aware that something is amiss, comes over to inquire about the state of his health, but he replies with a shrug and a vague smile.

"Still having nightmares?" Charlie asks.

"Sometimes," he says.

He has stopped calling the few women he had been seeing. None of them call him. Just as well: even though he no longer awakens screaming from his darker dreams, now that they have become such a customary part of his existence, it would be a distraction to have someone lying beside him in bed at night. He wants to focus all his attention on the dreams themselves.

The thing to do, he has decided, is to try to redream one of the dreams he has already had, particularly one in which the dream-figure is obviously pleading for help. Since the scenario of the dream is already known to him, like the plot of some movie he has seen before, he believes that he will be able to intervene sooner, at some point where the situation has not yet become irrevocably catastrophic, and offer the dream-figure the succor he needs. The window-ledge dream, he thinks, would be a particularly fruitful one to employ. To be able to go immediately to the right window, to open it, to pull the man through to safety.

But deliberately to recapitulate some already dreamed dream is not such an easy thing to accomplish. In the hour before bedtime he lets his mind dwell on the images he hopes to conjure up; he goes to his own window-ledge, runs his hand along it, measures its width, imagines what it would be like to climb out onto it right now and sidle along the face of the building. Then, closing his eyes, he pictures the tormented figure he had seen out there, the frightened man despairingly struggling to keep his balance as he inches along. The picture is a vivid one. He can almost even make out the features of the man's face, something that he has not really succeeded in doing before: he thinks he has an idea of what the dream-figure's face looks like, he is certain that it is the same man in each and every dream, but the specific details elude him when he tries to describe them to himself. He could not have drawn a sketch of his face, nor even responded usefully to the expert questions of some police-department artist trying to guide him toward a description. Yet in these rehearsals for sleep it seems to him that he has envisioned the face in essence if not in specifics, that with only a little more effort he could come to see it clearly.

As he waits for sleep he keeps the window-ledge scene in mind; but when he drops off—and it has been taking him longer and longer to fall asleep each night—some other dream always comes, some dream of jeopardy, of course, but always a new one, as though the supply of these nightmares is infinite and none will ever recur. He is caught by surprise each time by the new surroundings in which the dream is set, unable to move himself into the right position to be helpful, unable to take the necessary steps to effect the desired rescue.

A month goes by, two, three. The sunny days of summer give way to the first rains of autumn.

And then, one night, the dream-state comes over him moments after he reaches his pillow and he realizes that at last he has been granted the recurrence of a dream. It is one in which the man is floating in a huge bottomless pool of chilly black water, unable to direct his own movements, simply drifting helplessly from one side to another across the face of that watery abyss like some bit of flotsam while sleek glossy monsters of the deep with gaping jaws and yellow eyes circle hungrily about him, closing in for the kill.

This is not a new dream. He has had it before, and he knows exactly what he must do. There is a stout coil of rope lying in a neat stack on the far side of the pool. The last time he dreamed this dream, the rope had been there also but he had simply remained where he was, watching as though in a stupor as the beasts unhurriedly closed in, surrounded their victim, toyed with him, and finally, in a frenzy of thrashing flukes, fell upon him and devoured him. This time he fights away that stupor. He wills himself around to the other side of the pool, crossing the great distance separating him from it with the speed of thought, and seizes one end of the coil of rope in a tight grasp, and, pivoting sharply, flings the other end far into the water.

"Quick!" he calls. "Grab hold of it!"

The man in the pool looks up, startled. Sees the rope; swims to it and seizes it; lets himself be drawn toward the edge of the pool. The man standing on the shore has no doubt of the other's face, now. The features are his own.

He reels the other in.

"Here," he says, kneeling by the water's edge, reaching his free hand down toward the other.

He extends his hand into that dark abyss, makes contact, grips and braces himself and pulls. Yanking with all his strength, he draws the other to him, draws him up and out and *through*, and in that same moment he feels a snap and a twist and a twirl of reciprocity, as though he is standing upon a moving turntable that is swinging him around into the mysterious realm beyond. He struggles to resist the force that is catapulting him onward; but resistance is impossible. He is powerless against that unyielding pressure. He is hurled through that invisible wall.

On the far side he finds himself alone in a soundless world.

And then he is sprinting frantically up some bright windy beach from the edge of the surf, the cold rising tide licking at his heels, desperately trying to reach the dark rockpile at the foot of the nearby cliff where he can clamber up above the rapidly rising water.

SMITHERS AND THE
GHOSTS OF THE THAR

I am not, of course, noted for writing ghost stories, but I have had a lifelong interest in them, going back to my discovery of the classic Wise & Fraser anthology Great Tales of Terror and the Supernatural when I was eleven or twelve years old. My unsurprising favorites have been, all these years, the stories of Algernon Blackwood, Arthur Machen, M.R. James, and Oliver Onions, whom I have read and re-read many times. A mere reference to a story title ("The Beckoning Fair One"…"O Whistle, and I'll Come to You, My Lad"…"The Willows") summons up memories of rainy evenings curled up in my chair, agreeable shivers, pleasingly uneasy dreams afterward.

Reading ghost stories has always been a sort of guilty pleasure for me. In my own life I am relentlessly logical, rational, sensible. I don't believe in ghosts or other sorts of supernatural manifestations. But a writer needs to know how to induce the willing suspension of disbelief in his readers, and I know how to induce it in myself as well. So I'm quite capable of a belief in spooks of various kinds for the duration of a story I'm reading, and perhaps for a little while afterward. And as the list of my favorite ghost-story writers indicates, I'm a bit of an Anglophile with a love for Victorian and Edwardian atmosphere: fog, carriages, the nineteenth-century architecture of London. The stories don't have to be set in London, though, so long as they have the right period flavor. Another favorite ghost-story writer of mine, from approximately the same period as Blackwood, Machen, James, and Onions, is Rudyard Kipling. Most of his best stories take place not in

London but in India, but they have that Victorian-Edwardian swing to them as well, and for me they provide a somewhat different but closely related sort of delight.

I haven't written ghost stories because no real market has existed for them over the past fifty years. I did dabble in the horror-story genre for a bit in the 1980s, and a couple of the things I wrote, like the Mexican-based "Not Our Brother," could probably be considered ghost stories. But that market, so far as I know, has gone away now, and I've written nothing ghostly in a couple of decades.

But when Nick Gevers and Jack Dann, an editorial team with one member based in South Africa and the other in Australia, asked me to contribute to an anthology of modern ghost stories paying homage to the British masters, the suggestion struck me exactly the right way and almost immediately I found myself sketching out a Kiplingesque tale of supernatural doings in remote and still mysterious Great Indian Desert, the Thar. I wrote the story in December of 2009 and it appeared in the 2011 anthology Ghosts by Gaslight.

What happened to Smithers out there in the Great Indian Desert, may seem a trifle hard to believe, but much that happens in Her Imperial Majesty's subcontinent is a trifle hard to believe, and yet one disbelieves it at one's peril. Unfortunately, there is nobody to tell the tale but me, for it all happened many years ago, and Yule has retired from the Service and is living, so I hear, in Palermo, hard at work on his translation of Marco Polo, and Brewster, the only witness to the tragic events in the desert, is too far gone in senility now to be of any use to anyone, and Smithers—ah, poor Smithers—

But let me begin. We start in Calcutta and the year is 1858, with the memory of the dread and terrible Mutiny still overhanging our dreams, distant though those bloody events were from our administrative capital here. That great engineer and brilliant scholar Henry Yule—Lieutenant-Colonel Yule, he was then, later to be Sir Henry—having lately returned from Allahabad, where he was in charge of strengthening and augmenting our defenses against the rebels, has now been made Secretary of the Public Works Department, with particular responsibility for designing what one day will be the vast railroad system that will link every part of India. I hold the title of Deputy Consulting Engineer for Railways. Our young friend Brewster is my right-hand man, a splendid draughtsman and planner. And as my story opens Brewster has come to us, looking oddly flushed, with the news that Smithers, our intense, romantic, excitable Smithers, whom we have sent off on a surveying mission to Jodhpur and Bikaner and other sites in the remote West, has returned and is on his way to us at this very moment with an extraordinary tale to tell.

"Is he now?" Yule said, without much sign of animation. Yule is a Scot, stern and outwardly dour and somewhat fierce-looking, though I am in a position to know that behind that grim bearded visage lies a lively mind keenly alert to the romance of exploration. "Did he find a railroad already in place out there, I wonder? Some little project of an enterprising Rajput prince?"

"Here he comes now," said Brewster. "You will hear it all from the man himself." And an instant later Smithers was among us.

Smithers was fairhaired and very pink-skinned, with gleaming blue eyes that blazed out from his face like sapphires. Though he was somewhat below middle height, he was deep-chested and wideshouldered, and so forceful was his physical presence that he could and did easily dominate a room of much taller men. Certainly he dominated his friend Brewster, who had known him since childhood. They had been to university together and they had entered the service of the East India Company together, taking appointment with the Bengal Engineers and making themselves useful in the Public Works Department, specializing in the building of bridges and canals. I could best describe the lanky, dark-complected Brewster as timid and cautious, one who was designed by Nature as a follower of stronger men, and Smithers, who in his heart of hearts looked upon himself as part of a grand English tradition of adventurous exploration that went back through Burton and Rawlinson and Layard to Walter Raleigh and Francis Drake, was the man to whom he had attached himself.

"Well, Smithers?" Yule asked. "What news from Bikaner?"

"Not from Bikaner, sir," said Smithers, "but from the desert beyond. The Thar, sir! The Thar!" His blazing blue eyes were wilder than ever and his face was rough and reddened from his weeks in the sun.

Yule looked startled. "You went into the Thar?" A reconnaissance of the vast bleak desert that lies beyond the cities of Rajputana had not been part of Smithers's immediate task.

"Only a short way, sir. But what I learned—what I have heard—!"

Yule, who can be impatient and irritable, made a swift circular beckoning gesture, as though to say, "Aye, out with it, man!" But Smithers needed no encouragement. Already a story was tumbling from him: how in the desert city of Bikaner he had fallen in with an itinerant Portuguese merchant newly returned from a venture into the Great Indian Desert—the Thar, as the natives call it, that immense waterless void 150 miles in breadth that stretches northeastward for some 400 miles from the swampy Rann of Cutch. Breathlessly Smithers retold the tale the Portuguese had told him: an unknown valley far out in the Thar, the sound of strange voices floating on the air, sometimes calling alluringly, sometimes wailing or sobbing, voices that could only be the voices of spirits or demons, for there was no one to be seen for miles around; the eerie music of invisible musicians, gongs and drums and bells, echoing against the sands; and above all a distinct sensation as of *summoning*, the awareness of some powerful force pulling one onward, deeper into that valley. The Portuguese had resisted that force, said Smithers, for he was a hard-nosed trader and was able to keep his mind on business; but from villagers at an oasis town the man had picked up fragmentary anecdotes of an entire ancient city hidden away in that valley, a lost civilization, a land of ghosts, in fact, from which that potent summons came, and into whose mysterious realm many a traveler had vanished, never to return.

I saw what I took to be the unmistakable glint of skepticism in Yule's eyes. He has never been a man to suffer foolishness gladly; and from the knotting of his bristling brows I interpreted his response to Smithers' wild fable as annoyance. But I was wrong.

"Singing spirits, eh?" Yule said. "Gongs and drums and bells? Let me read you something, and see if it sounds familiar."

He drew from his desk a sheaf of manuscript pages that were, we already knew, his translation of *The Book of Ser Marco Polo*—the earliest draft of it, rather, for Yule was destined to spend two decades on this magnum opus before giving the world the first edition in 1870, nor did he stop revising and expanding it even then. But even here in 1858 he had done a substantial amount of the work.

"Marco is in the Gobi," said Yule, "in the vicinity of the desert town of Lop, and he writes, 'The length of this desert is so great that 'tis said it would take a year and more to ride from one end of it to the other. Beasts there are none, for there is nought for them to eat. But there is a marvelous thing related of this desert, which is that when travelers are on the move by night, and one of them chances to lag behind or to fall asleep or the like, when he tries to gain his company again he will hear spirits talking, and will suppose them to be his comrades. Sometimes the spirits will call him by name; and thus shall a traveler ofttimes be led astray so that he never finds his party. And in this way many have perished.'"

"It is much like what the Portuguese told me," said Smithers.

Yule nodded. "I will go on. 'Sometimes the stray travelers will hear as it were the tramp and hum of a great cavalcade of people away from the real line of road, and taking this to be their own company they will follow the sound; and when day breaks they find that a cheat has been put upon them and that they are in an ill plight. Even in the daytime one hears those spirits talking. And sometimes you shall hear the sound of a variety of musical instruments, and still more commonly the sound of drums.'"

Smithers said, and his face grew even redder, "How I long to hear those drums!"

"Of course you do," said Yule, and brought out the whisky and soda, and passed around the cigars, and I knew that look in Yule's formidable glittering eyes had not been one of skepticism at all, but of complete and utter captivation.

He went on to tell us that such tales as Marco Polo's were common in medieval travel literature, and, rummaging among his papers, he read us a citation from Pliny of phantoms that appear and vanish in the deserts of Africa, and one from a Chinese named Hiuen Tsang six centuries before Marco that spoke of troops with waving banners marching in the Gobi, vanishing and reappearing and vanishing again, and many another tale of goblins and ghouls and ghostly dancers and musicians in the parched places of the world. "Of course," said Yule, "it is possible to explain some of this music and song merely as the noises made by shifting sands affected by desert winds and extreme heat, and the banners and armies as illusions that the minds of men traveling under such stressful conditions are likely to generate." He stared for a moment into his glass; he took a reflective puff of his cigar. "And then, of course, there is always the possibility that these tales have a rational origin—that somewhere in one of these deserts there does indeed lurk a hidden land that would seem wondrously strange to us, if only we could find it. The great age of discovery, gentlemen, is not yet over."

"I request leave, sir, to look into the Thar beyond Bikaner and see what might be found there," Smithers said.

It was a daring request. Smithers was our best surveyor, and the entire subcontinent needed measuring for the system of railways that we intended to create in its immense expanse, and nobody was planning to run track through the desert beyond Bikaner, for there was nothing there. Plenty of urgent work awaited Smithers between Delhi and Jodhpur, between Calcutta and Bombay, and elsewhere.

But Yule rose with that glitter of excitement in his eyes again and began pulling maps from a portfolio under his desk and spreading them out, the big thirty-two-miles-to-the-inch map and a smaller one of the Frontier, pointing to this place and that one in the Thar and asking if one of them might have been the one of which that Portuguese had spoken, and we knew that Smithers's request had been granted.

What I did not expect was that Brewster would be allowed to accompany him. Plainly it was a dangerous expedition and Smithers ought not to have been permitted to undertake it alone, but I would have thought that a subaltern or two and half a dozen native trackers would be the appropriate complement. Indeed Brewster was a strong and healthy young man who would readily be able to handle the rigors of the Thar, but an abundance of work awaited him right here in Calcutta and it struck me as remarkably extravagant for Yule to be willing to risk not one but two of our best engineers on such a fantastic endeavor at this critical time in the development of the nascent Indian railway system.

But I had failed to reckon with two traits of Yule's character. One was his insatiable scholarly curiosity, which had drawn him to the close study not only of Marco Polo's huge book but of the texts of many another early traveler whose names meant nothing to me: Ibn Battuta, for example, and Friar Jordanus, and Odoric of Pordenone. We were living at a time when the remaining unknown places of the world were opening before us, and the discovery—or rediscovery—of strange and marvelous regions of Asia held great fascination for him. Though he himself could not leave his high responsibilities in Calcutta, Smithers would serve as his surrogate in the far-off Thar.

Then, too, I had overlooked Yule's profound complexity of spirit. As I have already noted, he is not at all the grim, stolid, monolithic administrator that he appears to a casual observer to be. I have spoken of his irritability and impatience; I should mention also his bursts of temper, followed by spells of black depression and almost absolute silence, and also the—well, *eccentricity* that has led him, a man who happens to be color-blind, to dress in the most outlandish garb and think it utterly normal. (I have in mind his brilliant claret-colored trousers, which he always insisted were silver-gray.) He is complicated; he is very much his own man. So if he had taken it into his mind to send our highly valued Smithers off to look for lost cities in the Thar, nothing would stop him.

And when he asked Smithers what sort of complement he thought he would need, Smithers replied, "Why, Brewster and I can probably deal with everything all by ourselves, sir. We don't want a great silly crowd of bearers and trackers, you know, to distract us as we try to cope with those musical spectres in the desert."

Quickly I looked at Brewster and saw that he was as amazed as I was to find himself requisitioned for the expedition. But he made a quick recovery and managed a grin of boyish eagerness, as if he could think of nothing more jolly than to go trekking off into a pathless haunted desert with his hero Smithers. And Yule showed no reaction at all to Smithers's request: once again he demonstrated his approval simply through silence.

Of course, getting to the Thar would be no easy matter. It lies at the opposite side of the subcontinent from Calcutta, far off in the northwest, beyond Lucknow, beyond Agra, beyond Delhi. And, as I have said, all of this was taking place at a time before we had built the Indian railway system. Smithers had just made the round trip from Calcutta to Bikaner and back, fifteen hundred miles or more, by an arduous journey down the Grand Trunk Road, India's backbone before the railways existed. I have no idea how he traveled—by horse, by camel, by bullock-cart, by affiliating himself with merchant caravans, by any such means he could. And now he—and Brewster—would have to do it all over again. The journey would take months.

I should mention that Smithers had been engaged for the past year and a half to the Adjutant's daughter, Helena, a young woman as notable for her beauty as for her sweetness of temperament, and the wedding was due to take place in just another dozen weeks or so. I wondered how Smithers would be able to prevail on her for a postponement; but prevail he did, either through his own force of personality or the innately accommodating nature that is so typical of women, and the wedding was postponed. We held a grand farewell party for Smithers and Brewster at Fort William, where nothing was asked and nothing was volunteered about the reason for their departure, and in the small hours of the night we stood by the bank of the river with brandy-glasses in hand, singing the grand old songs of our native country so far away, and then in the morning they set out to find whatever it was that they were destined to find in the Great Indian Desert.

The weeks passed, and turned into months.

Helena, the Adjutant's lovely daughter, came to us now and again to ask whether there had been any word from her wandering fiancé. Of course I could see that she was yearning to get him back from the Thar and take him off to England for a lifetime of pink-faced fairhaired children, tea, cool fresh air, and clean linens. "I love him so," she would say.

The poor girl! The poor girl!

I knew that Smithers was India through and through, and that if she ever did get him back from the Thar there would be another quest after that, and another, and another.

I knew too that there had been an engagement before she had met Smithers, a Major invalided home from Lahore after some sort of dreary scandal involving drinking and gambling, about which I had wanted to hear no details. She was twenty-six, already. The time for making those pink-faced babies was running short.

The months went by, and Smithers and Brewster did not return from the Thar. Yule began to grow furious. His health was not good—the air of India had never been right for him, and Bengal can be a monotonous and depressing place, oppressively dank and humid much of the year—and he could see retirement from the Service not very far in his future; but he desperately wanted to know about that valley in the Thar before he left. And, for all that desperate curiosity of his, work was work and there was a railroad line to build and Smithers and Brewster were needed here, not drifting around in some sandy wasteland far away.

Yule's health gave way quite seriously in the spring of 1859 and he took himself home to Scotland for a rest. His older brother George, who had not been out of India for thirty years, went with him. They were gone three months. Since the voyage out and the voyage back took a month each, that left them only a month at home, but he returned greatly invigorated, only to be much distressed and angered by the news that Smithers and Brewster were still unaccounted for.

From time to time the Adjutant's daughter came to inquire about her fiancé. Of course I had no news for her.

"I love him so!" she cried.

The poor girl.

Then one day there was a stir in town, as there often is when a caravan from some distant place arrives, and shortly thereafter Brewster presented himself at my office at the Public Works Department. Not Brewster and Smithers: just Brewster.

I scarcely recognized him. He was decked out not in his usual khakis but in some bizarre native garb, very colorful and strange, flowing robes of rose, magenta, turquoise blue, but that was not the least of the change. The Brewster I had seen off, the year before, had been dark-haired and youthful, perhaps thirty-two years old at most. The man I saw before me now looked forty-five or even fifty. There were prominent streaks of gray in his thick black hair, and the underlying bony structure of his cheeks and chin seemed to have shifted about to some degree, and there was a network of fine lines radiating outward from the corners of his eyes that no man of thirty-two should have had. His posture had changed, too: I remembered him as upright and straight-backed, but he had begun to stoop a little, as tall men sometimes do with the years, and his shoulders seemed rounded and hunched in a way I did not recall. My first thought, which in retrospect shows an amazing lack of insight, was merely that the journey must have been a very taxing one.

"Welcome, old friend," I said. And then I said, carefully, "And Smithers—?"

Brewster gave me a weary stare. "He is still there."

"Ah," I said. And again: "Ah."

Brewster's reply could have meant anything: that Smithers had found something so fascinating that he needed more time for research, that he had fallen under the sway of some native cult and was wandering naked and ash-smeared along the ghats of Benares, or that he had perished on the journey and lay buried somewhere in the desert. But I asked no questions.

"Let me send for Yule," I said. "He will want to hear your story."

There had been a change in Yule's appearance, too, since Brewster's departure. He too had grown bowed and stooped and gray, but in his case that was no surprise, for he was nearly forty and his health had never been strong. But it was impossible not to notice Yule's reaction at the great alteration Brewster had undergone. Indeed, Brewster now looked older than Yule himself.

"Well," said Yule, and waited.

And Brewster began to tell his tale.

❋

They had set forth in the grandest of moods, Brewster said. Smithers was almost always exuberant and enthusiastic, and it had ever been Brewster's way, although he was of a different basic temperament, readily to fall in with his friend's customarily jubilant frame of mind. It had been their plan to go with the Spring Caravan heading for Aurangabad, but in India everything happens either after time or before time, and in this case the caravan departed before time, so they were on their own. Smithers found horses for them and off they went, westward along the Grand Trunk Road, that great long river-like highway, going back to the sixteenth century and probably to some prehistoric precursor, that carries all traffic through the heart of India.

It is a comfortable road. I have traveled it myself. It is perfectly straight and capably constructed. Trees planted on both sides of it give welcome shade the whole way. The wide, well-made middle road is for the quick traffic, the sahibs on their horses, and the like. It was on that road that the British armies moved swiftly out of Bengal to conquer the north Indian plain. To the left and right are the rougher roadbeds where the heavy carts with creaking wooden wheels go groaning along, the ones that bear the cotton and grain, the timber, the hides, the produce. And then there is the foot traffic, the hordes and hordes of moneylenders and holy men and native surgeons and pilgrims and peddlers, swarms of them in their thousands going about the daily business of India.

As traveling sahibs, of course, Smithers and Brewster encountered no problems. There are caravanserais at regular intervals to provide food and lodging, and police stations set close together so that order is maintained. When their horses gave out they rented others, and later they hired passage for themselves in bullock-carts until they could find horses once again, and after that they rode on camels for a time. From Durgapur to Benares they went, from Kanpur and Aligarh to Delhi, and there, although the Grand Trunk Road continues on northwestward to

Lahore and Peshawar to its terminus, they turned to secondary roads that brought them down via Bikaner to the edge of the desert.

The Thar, then! The vast unwelcoming Thar!

Brewster described it for us: the deep, loose, fine-grained sands, the hillocks that the winds have shaped, running from southwest to northeast, the dunes that rise two hundred feet or more above the dusty plain, the ugly gravel plains. As one might expect, there are no real rivers there, unless you count the Indus, which flows mostly to the west of it, and the Luri, which runs through its southern reaches. The Ghaggar comes down into it from the north but loses itself in the desert sands. There are some salt lakes and a few widely spaced freshwater springs. The vegetation, such as it is, is mostly thorny scrub, and some acacia and tamarisk trees.

Why anyone would plant a city in such a desolate place as the Thar is beyond my comprehension, but men will found cities anywhere, it seems. Most likely they chose sites along the eastern fringe of the desert, which is relatively habitable, because that great forbidding waste just beyond would protect them against invasion from the northwest. So along that fringe one finds the princely states of Rajasthan, and such royal capitals as Jodhpur, Jaipur, and Bikaner; and it was the walled city of Bikaner, famous for its carpets and blankets, that became expedition headquarters for Smithers and Brewster.

Brewster, who was something of a linguist, went among the people to ask about haunted valleys and invisible drum-players and the like. He did not quite use those terms, but his persistent questioning did get some useful answers, after a while. One old fakir thought that the place they sought might lie between Pakpattan and Mubarakpur. Smithers and Brewster bought some camels and laid in provisions and headed out to see. They did not find any lost civilizations between Pakpattan and Mubarakpur. But Smithers was confident that they would find something somewhere, and they went north and then west and then curved south again, tacking to and fro across a pathless sea of sand, making an intricate zigzagging tour through territory so forlorn, Brewster told us, that you felt like weeping when you saw it. And after a week or two, he said, as they plodded on between nowhere and nowhere and were close to thinking themselves altogether and eternally lost, the sound of strange singing came to them on the red-hot wind from the west.

"Do you hear it?" Smithers asked.

"I hear it, yes," said Brewster.

He told us that it was like no singing he had ever heard: delicate, eerie, a high-pitched chant that might have been made up of individual words, but words so slurred and blurred that they carried no meaning at all. Then, too, apart from the chanting they heard spoken words, a low incomprehensible whispering in the air, the urgent chattering conversation of invisible beings, and the tinkling of what might have been camel-bells in the distance, and the occasional tapping of drumbeats.

"There are our ghosts," Smithers said.

It was a word he liked to use, said Brewster. Like most of us Brewster had read a few ghost stories, and to him the word "ghosts" summoned up the creaking floorboards of a haunted house, shrouded white figures gliding silently through darkness, fluttering robes moving of their own bodiless accord, strangely transparent coaches traveling swiftly down a midnight road, and other such images quite remote from the chanting and drumming of desert folk in gaudy garb, with jingling anklets and necklaces, under a hot fierce sun. But the sounds of the Thar came from some invisible source, and to Smithers they were sounds made by ghosts.

Everything was as the Portuguese merchant had said it would be, even unto the mysterious *summoning* force that emanated from some location to the west. The Portuguese had fought against that pull and had won his struggle, but Smithers and Brewster had no wish to do the same, and they rode onward, wrapping their faces against the burning wind and the scouring gusts of airborne sand. The sounds grew more distinct. It seemed to them both that the voices they heard were those of revelers, laughing and singing in the marketplace of a populous city; but there could be no cities here, in this abysmal trackless wilderness of sand and thin tufts of grass and empty sky. There was nothing here whatever.

And then they entered a narrow canyon that showed a shadowy slit at its farther end. They went toward it—there was scarcely any choice, now, so strong was the pull—and passed through it, and, suddenly, without any sense of transition, they were out of the desert and in some new and altogether unexpected realm. It was more than an oasis; it was like an entire faery kingdom. Before them stretched groves of palms and lemon trees along gently flowing canals, and beyond those gardens were rows of angular, many-windowed buildings rising rank upon rank above a swiftly flowing river that descended out of low, softly rounded green hills in the west. Brewster and Smithers stared at each other in amazement and wonder. When they looked back they no longer could see the desert, for a thick gray film, a kind of solid vapor, stretched like an impenetrable band across the mouth of the canyon.

"A moment later," said Brewster, "we found ourselves surrounded by the inhabitants of this place. They rose up out of nowhere, like phantoms indeed, a great colorful horde of them, and danced a welcome about us in circles, singing and waving their arms aloft and crying out in what we could only interpret as tones of gladness."

The people of the hidden valley, Brewster told us, were a tall, handsome folk, plainly of the Caucasian race, dark-eyed but light-skinned, with sharp cheekbones and long narrow noses. They seemed rather like Persians in appearance, he thought. They dressed in loose robes of the most vibrant colors, greens, reds, brilliant yellows, the men wearing red or gold pointed skullcaps or beautiful soft-hued turbans striped with bright bands of lemon, pink, yellow, or white, and the women in voluminous mantles, filmy clouds of crepe, shawls shot through with gold brocade, and the like. Below their cascading robes both sexes wore white trousers of a ballooning sort, and an abundance of silver anklets. Their feet were bare. Of course throughout India one sees all manner of flamboyant exotic garb, varying somewhat from region to region but all of it colorful and almost magical in its beauty, and the way these people looked was not fundamentally different from the look of the dwellers in this district of Hindustan or that one, and yet there *was* a difference, a certain quaint touch of antique glamor, an element of the fantastic, that left the two travelers thinking that they had drifted not into some unknown valley but into the thousand-year-old pages of the *Thousand Nights and a Night*.

At no time did they feel as though they were in danger. Perhaps these people might be ghosts of some sort, but goblins, ghouls, demons, no. They were too amiable for that. The welcoming party, never ceasing its prancing and chanting, conducted them into the town, the buildings of which were of wattled mud plastered in white and overpainted with elaborate patterns of the same brilliant hues as the clothing. From there on it was all rather like entering into an unusually vivid dream. They were shown to a kind of caravanserai where they were able to rest and bathe. Their camels, which were the object of great curiosity, were taken away to be given provender and water, and they themselves were supplied with clothing of the native sort to replace the tattered garments in which they had crossed the desert.

"They fed us generously," said Brewster, "with an array of curried meats, and some fruits and vegetables, and a drink much like yoghourt, made of the fermented milk of I know not what creature." The flavor of the food was unfamiliar, rich with spices, particularly black pepper, but wholly lacking in the fiery red capsicums that we associate with the cuisine of the land. Of course the capsicum is not native to India—the Portuguese, I think, brought it here from the New World centuries ago—and perhaps it was impossible to obtain them here in the Thar; but their absence from the food was something that Brewster found especially notable.

He and Smithers were the center of all attention, day after day, as if they were the first to make their way into the valley from the outside world in many years, as most probably they were. Village notables came to them daily, men with flowing white beards and glorious turbans, one of them of particularly majestic bearing who was surely the rajah of the city, and pelted them with an endless flow of questions, none of which, of course, either man could understand. English was unknown here, and when Brewster and Smithers tried Hindustani or Rajasthani or such smatterings of Urdu and Sindhi that they knew, no connection was made. Gradually it dawned on Brewster, who was, as I have said, quite a good linguist, that they were speaking a primitive form of Hindi, something like the Marwari dialect that they speak in and around Bikaner, but as different from it as the English of Chaucer is from that of Queen Victoria's times. He did indeed manage to pick out a few words correctly, and achieved some few moments of successful communication with the valley folk, each time touching off a great gleeful volley of the local kind of applause, which involved stamping of the feet and jingling of the anklets.

In the succeeding weeks Smithers and Brewster became, to some degree, part of the life of the village. They were allowed to wander upriver by themselves, and found garden plots there where spices and vegetables were growing. They saw the workshops where cloth was laboriously woven and cut by women sitting crosslegged. They saw the dyers' tanks, great stone-walled pools of scarlet and mauve and azure and crimson. They saw the fields where livestock grazed.

It was a closed community, utterly self-sufficient, sealed away from the forbidding desert that surrounded it and completely able to meet all

SMITHERS AND THE GHOSTS OF THE THAR

its own needs, while outside the valley the world of kings and emperors and railroads and steam engines and guns and newspapers ticked on and on, mattering less than nothing to these oblivious people—these ghosts, as Smithers persisted in calling them.

And yet there was leakage: those sounds of gongs and drums and singing, drifting through that foggy barrier and into the wasteland beyond, and occasionally summoning some outsider to the valley. That was odd. Brewster had no explanation for it. I suppose no one ever shall.

Before long the irrepressible Smithers's innate exuberance came to the fore. He was full of ideas for transforming the lives of these people. He wanted to teach them how to build aqueducts, steam engines, pumps, looms. He urged Brewster, who even now could manage only a few broken sentences in their language, to describe these things to the rajah and his court. Brewster was not convinced that these folk needed aqueducts or pumps or any of the other things Smithers yearned to bestow on them, but he did his best, which was not nearly good enough. Smithers, impatient, began to try to learn their language himself. One of the women of the village—a girl, rather, a striking keen-eyed girl of about twenty, half a head taller than Smithers—seemed to have volunteered to be his tutor. Brewster often saw them together, pantomiming words, acting out little charades, laughing, gesturing. He might perhaps be learning something, Brewster thought.

But Brewster knew that they could not stay there long enough to build aqueducts. Fascinating though the place was, the time had come, he thought, to begin the journey back into the modern world. And so he said, one morning, to Smithers.

At that point in his narrative Brewster fell silent. He seemed entirely played out. "So you would call it truly a lost civilization?" Yule asked, when Brewster had said nothing for what might have been several minutes. "Cut off in the desert for hundreds of years or even more from all contact with the rest of India?"

"I would call it that, yes," said Brewster.

"And when the time came for you to leave, Smithers chose to remain?"

"Yes," said Brewster, showing some signs of uneasiness at the question. "That is exactly what happened."

He did not offer details, but merely said that after some weeks he felt that it was incumbent upon them to return to Calcutta and make their report, and, when Smithers insisted on remaining to conduct further studies, of the type that so many venturesome men of our nation have carried out in Africa and Asia and the Americas, Brewster, finding it impossible to shake his resolve, at last reluctantly resolved to leave without him. The valley people seemed distressed at the thought of his departure, and indeed made it so difficult for him to locate the camels that he thought they might intend to restrain him from going; but eventually he found them, and—this part was very difficult too— went back out of the canyon, blundering around in one direction and another in that thick band of vapor before finding the one and only exit into the desert. Getting back to Bikaner from there was another great challenge, and only by some lucky guesswork was he able to retrace his earlier path. And after a lengthy and evidently toilsome journey back across the subcontinent, a journey that he did not choose to describe, but which I thought must have been so exhausting that it had put that strange appearance of premature age upon him, here he was among us once more in Yule's office.

Yule said, when he was done, "And would you be able to find that place again, if you had to? If I were to ask you to go back there now to get Smithers?"

Brewster seemed stunned by the request.

He winced and blinked, like one stepping out of a dark room into Calcutta sunlight. I could see signs of a struggle going on within him. Yule's question had caught him completely by surprise; and plainly he was searching for the strength to refuse any repetition of the ordeal he had just been through. But the indomitable Yule was waiting grimly for a reply, and finally, in a barely audible voice, Brewster said, "Yes, I think that I could. I think so, sir. —But is it necessary that I do?"

"It is," said Yule. "We can hardly do without him. It was wrong of you to come away with him still there. You must go back and fetch him."

Brewster considered that. He bowed his head. I think I may have heard a sob. He looked ragged and pale and tired. He was silent a great while, and it seemed to me that he was thinking about something that he did not care to discuss with us.

Yule, waiting once again for a reply, appeared terribly tired himself, as though he wanted nothing more than a year's rest in some gentler clime. But the great strength of the man was still evident, bearing down on poor Brewster with full force.

After a long, an interminable silence, whatever resistance Brewster had managed to muster seemed to snap. I saw him quiver as it happened.

He said quietly, huskily, "Yes, I suppose I must." And planning for the return trip began forthwith.

I was with Brewster the next day when Helena came to inquire about her errant fiancé. Brewster told her that Smithers was making great discoveries, that his discovery of this lost land would assure him eternal fame in the annals of exploration. He has remained behind for a while to complete his notes and sketches, Brewster said. I noticed that he did not meet the Adjutant's daughter's eager gaze as he spoke; in truth, he looked past her shoulder as though she were a creature too bright to behold.

※

This time there was no grand farewell party. Brewster simply slipped away alone to the Grand Trunk Road. He had insisted that no one should accompany him, and he did so with such unBrewsterlike firmness that even Yule was taken aback, and yielded, though to me it seemed like madness to let the man make that trip by himself.

And so Brewster departed once more for that valley in the Thar. Soon Yule left us again also—he had another breakdown of his health, and went on recreational leave to Java—and, since we were now in the full throes of planning the Indian railway system and our staff was already undermanned, my own responsibilities multiplied manifold. In 1857 we had had only 200 miles of track in operation in all of India. Our task was to increase that a hundredfold, not only for greater ease in our own military operations, but also to provide India with a modern system of mass transportation that would further the economic development of that huge and still largely primitive land. As the months went along and my work engulfed me, I confess that I forgot all about Brewster and Smithers.

Yule returned from Java, looking much older. Before long he would resign from the Service to return to England, and then, as his wife's health weakened also, on to the more benevolent clime of Italy, where he would complete and publish his famous translations of Marco Polo and other medieval travelers in Asia. In his remaining time in Calcutta he said nothing about Brewster and Smithers either; I think they had fallen completely out of his mind, which had no room for the irresponsible Smitherses and feckless Brewsters of the world.

One day in 1861 or early 1862 I was hard at work, preparing a report for the Governor-General on the progress of the Bombay-Calcutta line, when an old man in faded robes was shown into my office. He was thin and very tall, with rounded shoulders and a bent, bowed posture, and his long, narrow face was deeply lined, so that his eyes looked out at me from a bewildering webwork of crevices. He was trembling as though palsied, though more likely it was just the tremor of age. Under his arm he carried a rectangular box of some considerable size, fastened with an ornate clasp of native design. Because his skin was so dark and he was wearing those loose robes I mistook him for a native himself at first, but then I began to think he might be a deeply tanned Englishman, and when he spoke his accent left no doubt of that.

"You don't recognize me, do you?" he asked.

I stared. "I'm sorry. I don't think I do." I was annoyed by the interruption. "Are you sure that the business you have is with the Public Works Department?"

"I am, in fact, an employee of the Public Works Department. Or was, at least."

His face was still unrecognizable to me. But the voice—

"Brewster?"

"Brewster, yes. Back at last."

"But this is impossible! You're—what, thirty-five years old? You look to be—"

"Sixty? Seventy?"

"I would have to say so, yes."

He studied me implacably.

"I am Brewster," he said. "I will be thirty-seven come January."

"This is impossible," I said, though aware of the foolishness of my words as soon as I spoke them. "For a man to have aged so quickly—"

"Impossible, yes, that's the word. But I am Brewster."

He set that box down on my desk, heedless of the clutter of blueprints and maps on which he was placing it. And he said, "You may recall that Lieutenant-Colonel Yule ordered me to return to a certain valley in the Thar and bring Major Smithers out of it. I have done so. It was not an easy journey, but I have accomplished it, and I have returned. And I have brought Smithers with me."

I peered expectantly at him, thinking that he would wave his age-withered arm and Smithers would come striding in from the hall. But no: instead he worked at the clasp of that big wooden box with those trembling fingers of his for what seemed like half an hour, and opened it at last, and lifted the lid and gestured to me to peer in.

Inside lay a bleached skull, sitting atop a jumble of other bones, looking like relics exhumed from some tumulus of antiquity. They were resting on a bed of sand.

"This is Smithers," he said.

For a moment I could find nothing whatever to say. Then I blurted, "How did he die?"

"He died of extreme age," Brewster said.

And he told me how, after expending many weeks and months crossing India and bashing around in the Thar, he had finally heard the ghostly singers and the distant drums and gongs again, and they had led him to the hidden valley. There he found Smithers, fluent now in the local lingo and busy with all manner of public-works projects in a full-scale attempt to bring the inhabitants of the valley into the nineteenth century overnight.

He was married, Brewster said, to that lovely long-legged native princess who had been teaching him the language.

"Married?" I repeated foolishly, thinking of mournful Helena, the Adjutant's beautiful daughter, faithful to him yet, still waiting hopefully for his return.

"I suppose it was a marriage," said Brewster. "They were man and wife, at any rate, whatever words had been said over them. And seemed very happy together. I spoke to him about returning to his assignment here. As you might suspect, he wasn't eager to do so. I spoke more firmly to him about it." I tried to imagine the diffident Brewster speaking firmly to his strong-willed friend about anything. I couldn't. "I appealed to his sense of duty. I appealed to him as an Englishman. I spoke of the Queen."

"And did he yield?"

"After a while, yes," Brewster said, in a strange tone of voice that made me wonder whether Brewster might have made him yield at gunpoint. I could not bring myself to ask. "But he insisted that we bring his—wife—out of the valley with us. And so we did. And here they are."

He indicated the box, the skull, the bones beneath, the bed of sand.

"Hardly had we passed through the barrier but they began to shrivel and age," he said. "The woman died first. She became a hideous crone in a matter of hours. Then Smithers went."

"But how—how?"

Brewster shrugged. "Time moves at a different rate within the valley. I can't explain it. I don't understand it. The people in there may be living six or eight hundred years ago, or even more. Time is suspended. But when one emerges—well, do you see me? How I look? The suspended years descend on one like an avalanche, once one leaves. I spent a few weeks in that village the first time. I came back here looking ten or twenty years older. This time I was there for some months. Look at me. Smithers had been under the valley's spell for, what, two or three years?"

"And the woman for her entire life."

"Yes. When they came out, he must have been a hundred years old, by the way we reckon time. And she, perhaps a thousand."

How could I believe him? I am an engineer, a builder of railroads and bridges. I give no credence to tales of ghosts and ghouls and invisible spectres whose voices are heard on the desert air, nor do I believe that time runs at different rates in different parts of our world. And yet—yet—the skull, the bones, the withered, trembling old man of not quite thirty-seven who stood before me speaking with Brewster's voice—

I understood now that Brewster had been aware of what going back into that terrible valley to fetch Smithers would do to him. It would rob him of most or all of the remaining years of his life. He had known, but Yule had ordered him to go, and, yes, he had gone. The poor man. The poor doomed man.

To cover my confusion I reached into the box. "And what is this?" I asked, picking up a pinch of something fine and white that I took for desert sand, lying beneath the little heap of bones like a cushion. "A souvenir of the Thar?"

"In a manner of speaking. That's all that remains of her. She crumbled to dust right in front of me. Shriveled and died and went absolutely to dust, all in a moment."

Shuddering, I brushed it free of my fingers, back into the box.

I was silent for a while.

The room was spinning about me. I had spent all my days in a world in which three and three make six, six and six make twelve, but I was no longer sure that I lived in such a world any longer.

Then I said, "Take what's left of Smithers to the chaplain, and see what he wants to do about a burial."

He nodded, the good obedient Brewster of old. "And what shall I do with this?" he asked, pointing to the sandy deposit in the box.

"Scatter it in the road," I said. "Or spill it into the river, whatever you wish. She was Smithers' undoing. We owe her no courtesies."

And then I thought of Helena, sweet, patient Helena. She had never understood the first thing about him, had she? And yet she had loved him. Poor, sweet Helena.

She must be protected now, I thought. The world is very strange, and too harsh, sometimes, and we must protect women like Helena from its mysteries. At least, from such mysteries as this one—not the mystery of that hidden valley, I mean, though that is mysterious enough, but the mysteries of the heart.

I drew a deep breath. "And—with regard to the Adjutant's daughter, Brewster—"

"Yes?

"She will want to know how he died, I suppose. Tell her he died bravely, while in the midst of his greatest adventure in Her Majesty's Service. But you ought not, I think, to tell her very much more than that. Do you understand me? He died bravely. That should suffice, Brewster. That should suffice."

FICTION SILVERBERG
Silverberg, Robert.
The collected stories of Robert Silverberg.
R2001663604 MILTON

ODC

MILTON LIBRARY

Atlanta-Fulton Public Library